The End of Healing

The End of Healing

A NOVEL

Jim Bailey

The Healthy City 2014

THE FINE PRINT

The End of Healing is a work of fiction. The story's main characters, institutions, academic programs, hospitals, and corporations depicted are the solely the product of the author's imagination, completely fictional, and should not be interpreted to portray real individuals and locations. Outside of Dr. Sampson's seminar classroom, real institutions, governmental offices, corporations, and products are used fictitiously and the characters occupying them are wholly imaginary. Any resemblance to actual persons, living or dead, or actual events is entirely coincidental. However, inside Dr. Sampson's seminar, all references to historical events, public figures, institutions, corporations, products, statistics, and scientific studies are factual and either documented in the Health System Seminar Syllabus or Acknowledgements in the appendix of this book or are readily substantiated from public records. All patient medical histories presented are based on, or are composites, of real cases. Except in matters of public record, the names and characteristics of the individuals and places depicted have been changed in order to protect patient confidentiality.

The following trademarks, slogans, and company names are used without permission, and their publication is not authorized by, associated with, or sponsored by any of the trademark owners or companies. The companies named below are those who owned the products listed at the time in which the novel is set, and they are listed in the order of their appearance: Nike, Nike, Inc.; Demerol®, Sanofi-Aventis; Betadine®, Purdue Pharma LP; Silastic®, Dow Corning Corporation; Cecil Textbook of Medicine, Saunders; Ford Escort, Ford Motor Company; Pretty Woman, Touchstone Pictures, The Walt Disney Company; Formica®, Formica Corporation; South Beach Diet®, South Beach Diet Trademark Limited Partnership; Cambridge Diet, Cambridge Diet USA; Versace, Gianni Versace S.p.A.; Viagra®, Pfizer Inc.; Carousel® and Kodachrome, Eastman-Kodak; Pepsi®, PepsiCo; Dr. Pepper®, Dr. Pepper Snapple Group; Budweiser®, Anheuser-Busch InBev N.V.; Ronald McDonald, Happy Meals®, and McDonalds®, McDonald's Corporation; Coke® and CocaCola®, The Coca-Cola Company; Kentucky Fried Chicken (KFC), Yum! Brands; M&M's, Mars, Inc.; Toy Story, Walt Disney Pictures, The Walt Disney Company; Burger King®, Burger King Holdings, Inc.; Oscar Mayer® Weiners, Kraft Foods; Ruffles®, Cheetos®, Fritos®, Doritos®, and Lay's®, Frito-Lay North America; Kool 100, R. J. Reynolds Tobacco Company; Morgan Stanley; U.S. News & World Report, L.P.; Mercedes®, Mercedes-Benz, (a division of DaimlerChrysler AG, now known as Daimler AG); BMW (Bayerische Motoren Werke AG); Ferrari S.p.A.; Marlboro, Phillip Morris USA; Magic 8 Ball, Mattel, Inc.; The Monsanto Company; Nature, Nature Publishing Group; Science, American Association for the Advancement of Science; Journal of Biological Chemistry, American Society for Biochemistry and Molecular Biology; The Atlantic Monthly, Atlantic Media Company; Gore-tex®, W. L. Gore and Associates; Operation®, Hasbro; Goodwill®, Goodwill Industries International, Inc.; Cable News Network (CNN), Turner Broadcasting System, Inc. (a Time Warner company); Meet the Press, NBC (National Broadcasting Company); Associated Press; The Boston Globe; Los Angeles Times, Tribune Company; Igloo cooler, Igloo Products Corporation; American Medical Association (AMA); Mirage®, MGM Resorts International; Ernesto's; Ernesto's Pizza; Amicar®, Xanodyne Pharmaceuticals, Inc.; Blue Cross Blue Shield Association of America; Dow Corning Corporation; Acqua di Selva, Visconti di Modrone; Miata, Mazda Motor Corporation; iPod, Apple, Inc.; Risk, Hasbro; Cigna HealthCare, A Business of Caring®, Cigna Corporation; Wellpoint Health Networks, Inc. (now merged with Anthem and doing business as Wellpoint, Inc.); UnitedHealth Group Incorporated; Aetna, Inc.; Vacutainer, Becton, Dickinson and Company; Boston Art Commission; Brylcreem®, Combe Incorporated; Prudential Financial, Inc.; John Hancock Financial Services, Inc.; Metropolitan Life Insurance Company (MetLife, Inc.); Health Insurance Association of America (renamed America's Health Insurance Plans following its merger with the American Association of Health Plans); Alliance for Managed Competition; National Association of Life Underwriters (renamed National Association of Insurance and Financial Advisers in 1999); Like a good neighbor, State Farm is there®, State Farm Insurance; Gucci, a subsidiary of PPR; Microsoft Excel, Microsoft; Paxil®, GlaxoSmithKline; Ritalin®, Novartis; Gerber®, Novartis, now owned by Nestlé; Remicade®, Centocor, a subsidiary of Johnson & Johnson; Lipitor®, Pfizer; Nexium®, the purple pill®, AstraZeneca; Prilosec®, AstraZeneca; Glucophage®, Bristol-Myers Squibb; Taxotere®, Sanofi-Aventis; Procrit®, Johnson & Johnson; Sandimmune®, Novartis; Xalatan®, Pharmacia Corporation; Gemzar®, Eli Lilly and Company; Camptosar®, Pfizer Inc.; Lupron®, TAP pharmaceuticals; The Price is Right, FremantleMedia, Ltd., subsidiary of the RTL Group; Zoloft®, Pfizer Inc.; Augmentin®, GlaxoSmithKline; Zocor®, Vioxx®, and Cozaar®, Merck & Co.; Celebrex®, Pharmacia Corporation (formed by the merger of Pharmacia & Upjohn with Monsanto Company); Claritin®, Schering-Plough Corporation; Budweiser®, Anheuser-Busch; Miss Universe, Miss Universe Organization; Loeb Classical Library, Harvard University Press; Tenet Healthcare Corporation (previously known as National Medical Enterprises); American Cancer Society; BarleyGreen® Premium, YH International, A Division of Green Foods™; Omniflox®, Abbott Labs; Tambocor™, 3M Pharmaceuticals; Enkaid®, Bristol-Myers Squibb Company; Seldane™, Marion Merrell Dow; Rezulin™, Parke-Davis (a subsidiary of Pfizer); Zyprexa®, Eli Lilly and Company; Plexiglas®, Altuglas International; Xerox®, Xerox Corporation; American Hospital Association; Wal-mart Stores, Inc.; MD Anderson Cancer Center; Prostate Cancer Foundation; American Beverage Association; National Association for the Advancement of Colored People (NAACP); Gino's East; Katherine Dunham Company; F. W. Woolworth Company (renamed Foot Locker, Inc.); American Academy of Family Physicians; Oreo®, Nabisco division of Kraft Foods; General Electric Company (GE)Siemens AG; HealthSouth Corporation; Oracle Corporation; Boeing; Murciélago; Corniche, Rolls Royce; Health Net, Inc.; Columbia/HCA (renamed Hospital Corporation of America); Metro-Goldwyn-Mayer Inc. (MGM); Access Med Plus; Anthem, Inc. (Now merged with Wellpoint Health Networks, Inc. and doing business as Wellpoint, Inc.); Congressional Services Company; Pharmaceutical Research and Manufacturers of America (PhRMA); AARP (formerly known as the American Association of Retired Persons); Humana Inc.; The Humane Society of the United States; PNC Financial Services Group, Inc.; Bank of America Corporation; SunTrust Banks, Inc.; The American Petroleum Institute; Moët & Chandon Champagne Cuvée Dom Pérignon Oenothèque; United Airlines, Inc.; Smith & Wesson; American Disabled for Accessible Public Transportation (ADAPT); Milliman, Inc.; Anthem® Blue Cross Blue Shield; LabCorp, Laboratory Corporation of America; C-SPAN (Cable-Satellite Public Affairs Network); Federation of American Hospitals; Pharmaceutical Care Management Association; JPMorgan Chase & Co.; ExxonMobil Corporation; Sourcewatch, The Center for Media and Democracy; and The Scooter Store®, The Scooter Store, Ltd.

The Healthy City
956 Court Avenue, D222
Memphis, TN 38163-001
Print ISBN: 978-0-9854203-0-7

The Healthy City is an Imprint of The Healthy City, Inc.

Copyright © 2014 The Healthy City, Inc.

Printed and bound in the United States of America.

We at The Healthy City enjoy hearing from readers.
Visit our websites
EndofHealing.com
TheHealthyCity.org

10 9 8 7 6 5 4 3 2 1

Cover design: Bill Oates of Oates Design
Interior design and composition: Peter Bain and Alexa Werling
Interior illustration: Joel Hilgenberger

Sleepers, wake!

Table of Contents

Prologue

I KNOW WHAT IT IS LIKE to be out of place, to be an idealist in a world of pecuniary traitors, to be hated for doing what is right. And so I know something of Dr. Don Newman's story. He starts his journey much as I did, a disappointing protagonist and unlikely hero who finds himself in a dark place where the straight way is lost. He discovers treachery, torture, and killing where he least expects—in the sacred halls of healing—the hospitals, pharmacies, operating rooms, and intensive care units where your generation places its greatest hope and trust. He is ill-equipped to deal with the world he inadvertently uncovers. You can justly call him idealistic, naïve, even foolish.

History does repeat itself. Old temptations present themselves in new and surprising ways. Our best stories ebb and flow through time in tides of glacial speed and periodicity. Dr. Newman's story is an ancient one. It has been told in many tongues and many lands; it is my story and your story. Just as my *Comedy* captured the critical events of our time, displayed the underlying currents for all to see, and turned the tide of history, Dr. Newman's story will reveal the hidden darkness of your time.

Therefore, let me beg your indulgence for our unlikely hero. Travel a little while with this unseasoned young man. Bear with him as he discovers he has stumbled into hostile territory, succumbed to base influences, and benefited from the very corruption he loathes. Our most innocent ones often bear the curse of seeing things as they really are. So it is with young Doctor Newman. He seeks to be a healer in a world where true healing has nearly ended.

With him, perhaps you can find a way out of darkness into paradise. I entreat you to follow him and behold: everything necessary to find the right path through the perils of modern healthcare—the path to true health and healing—is available to Don Newman all along.

Let us go with him and see.

DANTE ALIGHIERI

I

The Dark Ward

In the middle of the journey of our life I came to myself
within a dark wood where the straight way was lost.
DANTE ALIGHIERI, INFERNO I, 1–3

DR. NEWMAN DREADED the task ahead. Like countless others in these so-called halls of healing, Sibyl Bellamy was more victim than patient.

He'd been on the night shift three months earlier—the first time she was brought to the emergency room. He'd admitted her to the hospital and worked her up for the team that would care for her starting the next morning. He'd known at once she had suffered a very big stroke. It didn't take a genius to see that. She couldn't move anything on her right side, her mouth drooped and leaked drool from the right corner, and she couldn't speak or squeeze his fingers. Mucus rattled in her windpipe with every breath and she showed little inclination to cough it up. Her eyes were wide open and filled with fear. Cords of muscle in her good arm strained against the padded leather strap around her wrist.

Her panicked daughter had rushed into the room and launched a battery of questions: "What's going on, Doctor? What's wrong with my mother? Why can't she talk? Can you help her? Will she be okay?"

He took a deep breath before answering. "I'm Dr. Newman. Your mother is very sick. Could you tell me what happened?"

Words erupted in a breathless rush. "I found her this morning in her house on the floor and I don't know how long she was there but she was fine when I saw her yesterday morning—she had gone to the bathroom on herself and she couldn't move so I called the ambulance and they brought her to the emergency room about ten this morning—I've been in the waiting room ever since and no one has told me anything!" Tears filled the wells beneath her eyes and overflowed. "What's wrong with her, Doctor? Was it a stroke?"

The physical exam left no doubt—yes—she'd suffered a large middle cerebral artery stroke. The left half of her brain was dead. She would probably never walk, talk, or eat again. But he was trained never to give a diagnosis until the history was complete and all test results were in.

"Let me ask you a few questions first. Does your mother have high blood pressure or other medical problems?"

"Yes, she takes medicine for high blood pressure. It runs in our family."

"What medicine was she taking?"

"Well, she used to take a water pill, I think."

"Hydrochlorothiazide?"

"Yes, that's it! She took it for years."

He nodded and noted it in the chart. Hydrochlorothiazide prevents strokes better than anything. "Go on," he encouraged.

"Mom stopped taking it when the doctor gave her free samples of a new medicine. Norvasc, I think it was. She didn't like the new medicine because she said it stopped her up but the doctor told her it didn't have any side effects."

"When did she last see her physician?"

"Four months ago. That's when the receptionist said the doctor couldn't keep seeing her since she didn't have insurance anymore. He was nice enough to give her those free samples but she couldn't go ask him for more after that lady told her not to come back and she didn't have the money to fill the prescription. The new drug cost over fifty dollars for a month's supply so she just quit. Her old pill had worked fine and it only cost five dollars."

"She lost her insurance?"

"We are not fancy people, Doctor. My mom has worked every day of her life, mostly two jobs. She's worked right here at the University Hospital as a housekeeper for years. You know they outsourced housekeeping five months ago, right? The new cleaning service company kept her on but dropped her health insurance."

He did know. The hospital had signed a management contract with New American Healthcare in July 2000, right at the beginning of his third and last year of specialty training in internal medicine. Contracting out the housekeeping service was one of the ways New American Healthcare was helping the University Hospital save a little money. Mrs. Bellamy might not have health insurance for a simple doctor's office visit, or a prescription to control her high blood pressure, but now she was so sick no hospital could legally turn her away. She'd be declared disabled, Medicaid would kick in, and the expensive hospital tab would get paid—courtesy of the American taxpayers.

The daughter's body shook with silent, heaving sobs. Dr. Newman put his hand on her shoulder and waited. She took a deep breath to steel herself, shook off his comforting arm, and looked him hard in the eye. "What is wrong with my mother?" she demanded again.

He'd tried to give her the straight scoop. Pulling two molded plastic chairs over alongside Mrs. Bellamy's gurney, he motioned for the daughter to sit down across from him. He reached out, took her hand in both of his, and spoke slowly. "I think your mother has had a very large stroke. I'm sorry to tell you this, but I'm afraid she will never recover no matter what we do. Your mother is dying."

The daughter's face was blank, flat, as if she hadn't comprehended a single word of what he just said. She wasn't ready to process the horrible news. After all, her mother was lying nearby, asleep and breathing on her own.

"There is a slim possibility that dehydration is a contributing factor," he offered. "Perhaps with fluids, feeding, and rehab, your mother might be one of the lucky few to partly recover."

He intended his words to comfort the daughter just enough to tide her over until she was ready to process the grim reality that her mom was essentially gone. Once the words were out, however, it was too late.

Mrs. Bellamy's daughter's eyes lit up and she clapped a hand to her chest. "Oh, Doctor, please, I want you to do everything possible to save my mama!"

Everything possible. The magic words. That was all it took to set the gears of the hospital machine in motion to grind out a whole slew of hopeless interventions and procedures, or—as Sibyl Bellamy would call them if she could speak—torture.

Mrs. Bellamy had fought against every intervention. The GI team hadn't inserted a PEG tube to funnel food directly into her stomach because she would have ripped it out with her good left hand. Instead, they had stuck a feeding tube down her nose, which she could pull out without really hurting herself. As expected, she had pulled the feeding tube out of her nose again and again. Each time, the team had shoved the greased tube back through her nose and down the back of her throat. They had alternated between drugging her up—a medical form of bondage politely termed "chemical restraints"—and tying her left hand to the side of the bed.

Her second week in the hospital, she regurgitated and inhaled some of the blue liquid nutrition formula they pumped through the feeding tube into her stomach. She had nearly drowned in the blue food, which damaged her lungs and resulted in a severe case of pneumonia. She had survived only with the help of powerful antibiotics. After fifteen more days in the hospital, she had been discharged to a nursing home, where they kept her alive with more artificial feeding and hydration. Three more times she had returned to the University Hospital for lung infections caused by breathing in the spit she couldn't swallow, and each time she was discharged on another round of antibiotics. Don had followed her course from afar, glad he was not responsible for her hopeless case.

Until today. It started like every other call day. He slept in until 6 a.m. On his way to the hospital he stopped at Caffe DiMartino for a double cappuccino at 6:25 a.m., as he did each fourth day when he was on call. The coffee bar on the Italian North End near Don's one-room apartment had served the best espresso in Boston since 1932.

The barista looked up and smiled. "Ciao Dottore. Buongiorno! On call today?"

Don smiled back as he leaned on the marble bar, "For the hundredth time, Giulio, call me Don. Yeah, on call. Every fourth night—the worst."

"Your mamma would want me to tell you that you have dark circles under your eyes, Dottore. How 'bout you sit down over by that window, and taste your cappuccino for a change?"

"Not today, Giulio, gotta go," Don said.

"Okay, Dottore, just this time, I will give you the best cappuccino in Boston to go. But you must come back when you are ready to enjoy life."

"I'll do that Giulio. Grazie," he said, completing the charade Giulio always required before he'd allow Don to take his steaming espresso to go. Don grabbed the tall frothy drink and headed out the door.

By 6:45 he was walking into the hospital, and by 6:50 he was finishing his cappuccino as he scanned labs on the hospital computer for the fourteen patients on his service. He figured he could discharge at least three before the onslaught of new patients that evening.

His day was unremarkable—examining patients and writing notes from seven to ten, rounding with the attending and team from ten to twelve, noon conference with a drug company lunch, stabilizing a patient who crashed and had to be transferred to the ICU, dictating three of the five discharge notes for the day, aspirating a swollen joint. Before he knew it, it was already 5:00 p.m. and his team was on call for the night.

At 5:05 his pager went off—he glanced at the number—the emergency room. He wasted no time in getting there. In minutes his long strides brought him face-to-face with the automatic doors before they opened. He had to stop short.

Looking through the glass window across the crowded emergency department, he spotted Sybil Bellamy strapped to a sheet-covered gurney in Exam Room 8. His heart sank. A quick review of her chart revealed the depressing details of the heroic measures the hospital staff had taken to keep her alive. The resident physician's notes from that first admission documented the daughter's insistence they "do everything possible." Apparently, the original care team hadn't been able to get the daughter to hear the hard truth, either.

Now she was back again, her congested lungs cultivating yet another crop of drug-resistant bacteria. Sibyl Bellamy was a spunky woman who might withstand the daily blood draws, intravenous lines, and tube insertions for months before being blessed by a resistant infection that antibiotics couldn't cure. Or maybe one time she would be lucky enough to arrive at the hospital too late to be forced back to this brutal reality. But on this night, Dr. Newman was on call, she was still among the living, and he would do his job.

He was glad he didn't need to take a history. Sibyl Bellamy couldn't speak. As he walked up to her gurney he heard secretions rattling in her throat as she struggled to breathe. Her eyes locked on his.

Dear God! She recognized him. He was sure of it.

Her wide eyes accused him. Her irises disappeared, overmatched by her dilated pupils and the whites of her eyes, and she opened her mouth wide to scream.

AAAAAAAAAA!   AAAAAAAAAA!   AAAAAAAAAA!

He had committed no crime, but her stare and mandrake screams unnerved him as if he had.

Don managed to complete a brief physical without meeting her eyes again. The exam added nothing to what he already knew. The chest x-ray showed her lungs were cloudy where they should have been clear. Aspiration pneumonia again.

He couldn't reach the daughter and suspected the usual—the daughter thought she was doing the right thing keeping her mother on artificial feeding and was angry the greatest hospital in world couldn't cure her. Who wouldn't be angry? People had come to expect the great hospital and its brilliant doctors to bring life from death. And no one, including Dr. Newman, had been honest enough to tell Mrs. Bellamy's daughter the whole, unvarnished truth: the help of the hospital in Sybil Bellamy's case was a joke and no doctor possessed the power to make her well again.

It would have been kinder to tell the daughter everything, keep Mrs. Bellamy clean and comfortable, and allow her to die with dignity. Instead, everyone strung her along, encouraging vain hopes of an impossible recovery as they rushed to accomplish the business of prolonging Sibyl Bellamy's death.

After admitting Sibyl Bellamy and seven more patients, Dr. Newman had finally crawled into the hard twin bed in his windowless call room at one-thirty in the morning. His body ached all over. Having worked up patients nonstop for nineteen hours, all he wanted was a good night's sleep. He was out the instant his head hit the pillow.

AAAAAAAAAA!   AAAAAAAAAA!   AAAAAAAAAA!

Her siren screams set his heart pounding before morphing into the earsplitting screech of his pager. He groped for it on the nightstand, silenced it, and hit the light switch on the wall above the narrow bed. The stark call room materialized in a buzz of artificial light.

He shielded his eyes and squinted at the clock. Three-fifteen. Less than two hours sleep, yet he felt a stab of guilt for indulging in the luxury when a pile of admission paperwork and progress notes from the previous day's parade of new patients awaited his attention. He forced himself upright and dialed the number on the pager.

A nurse picked up before the first ring. "Will you please come see Mrs. Bellamy right away? She's thrashing around so much I had to put her in restraints to keep her from falling out of bed. She lost her IV and I can't get it back in."

After four years of medical school and nearly three years of residency, Dr. Don Newman was annoyed to be woken up in the middle of the night to do medical student scut work. He started to tell the nurse to call his intern, Edward, but the reason she had skipped protocol was obvious. Don was the third-year resident physician in charge of the medicine service for the night. It would not be easy to get the needle back into Mrs. Bellamy's vein, and Edward—who was in the seventh month of first-year training—would end up calling him for help anyway.

He stepped out of bed right into his Nikes, splashed cold water on his face from the sink in the corner, and burst through the door into the hallway of the half-abandoned old hospital. Someone had removed the fluorescent tubes in every other fixture. He ran down the half-lit hall under the stripes of light and dark toward the new hospital, his ears still ringing with the screams of the pager.

AAAAAAAAAA!   AAAAAAAAAA!   AAAAAAAAAA!

He ran like Dr. Joe Gannon, the doctor in blue scrubs he had admired as a boy in television reruns of *Medical Center*. Dr. Gannon always ran and he always arrived just in time to rescue his patient from the brink of death.

Of course, this was the real world. Fewer than one in six CPR recipients survive to leave the hospital, and many of those survivors are pretty messed up. He knew that now. Nonetheless, from old habit he emulated Gannon's heroic dash to the bedside.

He ran into the unbearable bright light of the new hospital, following the painted blue line contrived by some diabolical Daedulus-architect to lure people into the maze. The blue line snaked through a labyrinth of hospital corridors, past countless procedure rooms and operating rooms, down the stairs and past the radiology suites and laboratories, through billing and administration, then past pharmacy and central supply. To anyone who saw him run by, he appeared to be a confident young doctor eager to get to the patient's bedside. Little did they know how he dreaded what he was expected to do to poor Mrs. Bellamy.

He considered the options. There were a couple of ways to get an intravenous line in without patient cooperation. He could give her a painful intramuscular shot of Demerol, but it would be tricky to administer enough to knock her out without impeding her breathing. Or, he could get the nurse to pin her down so he could stick the line into her arm, neck, or groin, while she fought and screamed and stared at him with her damning eyes.

The nurse shot him an exasperated look as he entered the room. "Oh, I thought you'd never get here!" she said. "What do you want to do?"

He went to Mrs. Bellamy's bedside and pulled the covers back. The overpowering stench of diarrhea hit him like a wave. A stained hospital gown was twisted around her midsection. The head and foot of the adjustable hospital bed were elevated, causing a pool of liquid stool to cradle between her thighs. The greenish-brown slime covered her lap and bottom. An IV in the groin was clearly out of the question; it would surely get infected.

"Why don't we clean her up, for starters?" he said in a businesslike voice. He silently cursed the nurse for not having washed her before he got there.

The nurse rolled Mrs. Bellamy over like a dead log and wiped the raw bedsores of her backside with a wet rag. The translucent skin of her pale arms and hands was scarred, swollen, and mottled purple. Her thin skin and mutilated veins wouldn't take another IV. It would have to be the neck.

Damn it! Mrs. Bellamy was only fifty-seven years old. Worst of all, the thinking part of her brain was alive. Her furious stare indicated she was keenly aware of her desperate state.

But she had no control, no choice. She was the hospital's prisoner. She jerked her good hand and struggled against the leather shackle binding her wrist in a vain attempt to reach the tube in her nose. She writhed in the foul sheets as violently as if she were having a seizure, but she did not meet the diagnostic criteria for a seizure. She was fighting. She looked straight at Dr. Newman. Her eyes demanded recognition and begged for mercy.

He hung his head and looked away. He was sure Sibyl Bellamy regretted surviving her stroke three months earlier. She wanted to die but couldn't verbalize it. All she could do was to glare at her doctors and try to pull out the tubes that kept her alive.

"Give her that Demerol, now!" he heard himself shout at the nurse. "Where is that central line kit? Let's hurry up and get this done!"

He was relieved when the narcotic began to kick in and Mrs. Bellamy grew calmer. Gently turning her face away from the side of the bed where he stood, he stretched wide cloth tape from one side of the bed frame to the other, strapping it across her temple to hold her head to the side. He painted her neck with Betadine and covered her head with a large blue paper drape. The blue shroud had a window cut out, leaving only a portion of her stained skin exposed.

For a quiet moment she was just a neck. He numbed the skin with a bee sting of lidocaine, studied the anatomical landmarks to find the right spot, and stabbed her neck with the three-inch needle. She screamed beneath the drape. Dark blood shot from the hub of the hypodermic. He passed a long stiff wire through the needle into the jugular vein and deep into her body.

The pager started screeching again but he couldn't reach under his gown to turn it off. A voice in his head whispered the oath he had taken at the beginning and again at the end of medical school: *and at least I will do no harm*. Bullshit! Harm is my business. How could any good ever come out of what I'm doing here to Sibyl Bellamy?

His bloody gloved fingers worked to thread the Silastic tubing over the wire, through her soft skin, and down into the first chamber of her heart. Sibyl Bellamy began to whimper.

Out of nowhere, water filled his eyes and blurred his vision. What was this? It wasn't like him to become emotional while dealing with a patient, and he bristled with irritation at the sudden unprofessional display. He blinked hard, hoping the nurse didn't notice the single drop that spilled from the corner of his eye and trailed across his cheek and around his mouth to balance on the tip of his chin.

Mrs. Bellamy had once been a beautiful woman. Something about her reminded him of his own mother. Momma was gone now, and he had done nothing to help her, either. As he struggled to suture the line into place, the tear dropped off his chin. It landed on the sterile blue drape and spread into a dark circle over Sibyl Bellamy's heart.

AT EIGHT the next morning he dragged himself to Grand Rounds at the University Hospital auditorium. Dr. Desmond, Medical Director and Chief of Cardiology—renowned for his encyclopedic knowledge as well as his bowtie collection—would not abide any of his residents missing this weekly pompous lecture. Per Desmond's rule, he had donned brown leather loafers, a dress shirt, and a necktie, as scrubs and tennis shoes were not tolerated during normal work hours. Don Newman admired Dr. Desmond, but he wouldn't be caught dead wearing a bowtie.

Don collapsed in a seat near the back next to Sarah Moore, his intern from the previous month. A faint yet familiar scent of jasmine stirred about her, calming his nerves. His eyes met hers in a millisecond of recognition. How did she always manage to look so good, even after a long night in the hospital?

Sarah was a good doctor, too. Her kind voice would have comforted Mrs. Bellamy and eased the pain. Their month working together had been incredibly busy, yet Sarah had handled the pressure far better than most first-years, making another month of hell a little easier for Don to bear...

A deep voice rumbled through the auditorium like an earthquake tremor and commanded Don's attention.

"You are in the trenches! You know the problems in American medicine are serious! Almost one-fifth of Americans have no health insurance and no preventive care, but they still get expensive emergency and hospital care after things go bad. Americans pay a ridiculous tab for these end-stage medical heroics…and nearly a third of our healthcare dollars pay for bureaucratic paperwork."

The speaker slammed his fist on the podium, making everyone jump.

"That's right, we pay middlemen a third—middlemen who make more money if they deny people the basic, preventive healthcare they need most."

The lecturer looked out of place. He wasn't wearing a suit like most Grand Rounds speakers—not even a white coat. Just a blue shirt with sleeves rolled partway up his broad arms, a dark tie, and black horn-rimmed glasses. He inspected the crowd coolly, as if he faced an angry army of Philistines.

Resolute, he rumbled on. "A conscientious doctor has a tough time making his practice economically viable because the system discourages a focus on preventive care—even though most fatal diseases are preventable. The payment system pressures doctors to pack more and more visits into every hour, perform as many surgeries, tests, and treatments as possible, and speed patients out the door. Procedures and hospital stays, whether they're needed or not, generate profits. Doctors and hospitals get paid more for complications. Should it surprise us that waste and serious medical errors are routine? Did you plan on a career in an assembly line that produces so much needless suffering and death?"

Don sat up straight in his chair. Was he hearing this right?

"My question for you today," the speaker said pointedly, "is the same one Rosie Greer put to his crack-addicted friend Richard Pryor: 'What are you going to do?'"

Sarah nudged Don with her elbow and whispered in his ear, "This is exactly what you keep talking about! What are *you* going to do?"

He turned to look at her. Sarah's light brown eyes met his and she smiled, raised her eyebrows, and nodded her head, intimating the question was meant for him.

Don shrugged and looked back to the speaker, trying to appear unfazed. The truth was, he was quite taken aback. In all his years of training, Don had never heard any attending physician talk this way. Doctors were trained—brainwashed, really—to believe they could fix any problem. They might gripe about this and that, but he had never heard anyone condemn the entire premise of the health care system in this way.

The plainspoken words rang true and intensified Don's gnawing sense that he was no Dr. Joe Gannon, that the idyllic medical center where everyone was healed was a television fantasy. At the same time, the speaker's question hinted at the possibility of liberation and planted a fledgling idea in Don's brain: *there might be another path.*

The speaker dimmed the lights and began his slide presentation. He detailed the major causes of premature death and disability in America and the evidence-based treatments most proven to help. He shared concrete data from study after study showing how little money Americans spend on care proven to save lives—and how much we spend on services that do more harm than good. He concluded with the heretical claim that most healthcare spending is misdirected and does little to encourage health.

"But," he said, turning the lights back up, "there is hope. My colleagues and I are working with legislators in Washington, D.C., to reorganize American medicine. I am helping the Senate Health Committee draft revolutionary legislation to reform the way we pay for healthcare. We want to incentivize prevention and patient safety. The proposed Medicare Quality Improvement Act is the first step toward creating a healthcare system that would serve health before profit."

The cold dark pit of the lecture hall faded away. Dr. Newman stood on a high green hilltop under the warm sun amongst the greatest healers of his knowledge and memory. Drs. Gannon, Welby, Kildare, Schweitzer, and Holmes stood beside him, and Sarah was there too, all bathed in golden sunlight. They greeted the arriving people with gentle words and stood together on the summit, healers and healed, caressed by a balmy wind in the full midday sun. Don felt warm, content, at peace with himself…

His head fell back and he snapped it forward with a jerk—back to the lecture hall and the draft of forced hot air from the vent above his head. What was he thinking? The new healthcare system the speaker described was pure fantasy. It was ridiculous to think American medicine was about to be reorganized. What was it Dr. Desmond always said? *The best way to fix healthcare is to work in the trenches and give people the best care you can. You have to learn to work the system.*

Yes, Dr. Desmond was right. During his first two years of residency Don had copied the way Desmond worked the system and admired how he rounded late into the night to make sure his patients got the care they needed. Don could pretty much do it all now: penetrate any vein, artery, or organ in the body with a needle, catheter, or intravenous line, and run a code so systematically he restored circulation of the blood more often than any other resident. He could keep the dead alive—whether they wanted to live or not.

He'd learned to push away the nagging reality that most of the patients he coded never lived to walk from the hospital, that most of the "survivors" were left with severely damaged brains from the lack of oxygen. He couldn't allow himself to become discouraged by that. The important thing for him was to do his job.

His interns and his teachers knew he was good. Dr. Desmond had just offered him a coveted cardiology fellowship position at the University Hospital. Everyone knew it was the best program in the country. Don was thrilled. After that, he could go wherever he wanted. With only a couple more years in training, he would be doing cardiac caths for a cool half million a year.

He pictured himself working in the North Shore Cardiovascular Institute, that cool, mirrored-glass building on Lake Michigan near Loyola University. He had borrowed an obscene amount of money for medical school and residency, so he couldn't afford to do primary care with its long hours and low pay. Why not do a little more training, focus on something simpler than primary care, and earn four or five times as much money?

He contemplated a life of days and nights in the cardiac catheterization lab. Cut the skin over the blood vessels in the groin and insert a big plastic tube right into the pulsating artery. Ram a long, thin, tubular wire through the artery and up the great aorta, the biggest artery in the body. Hope and pray not to knock loose any calcified cholesterol lining the aorta and cause a stroke. Finally, with the help of x-rays that give as much radiation as a year in the sun, twist that wire into the little coronary arteries and squirt in the poisonous dye.

He would be a hot shot in the cath lab. He would control the greatest technology modern medicine has to offer. Of course, occasional strokes and collateral kidney failure were an unfortunate cost of doing business—he knew he would have to accept that—and his authority to decide who needed testing would be limited. Like a trained monkey, he would stab and twist wire again and again, maybe four to ten times a day. Day after day, month after month, year after year...he began to imagine the fright-filled eyes of countless Sibyl Bellamys hidden beneath the great blue drapes...

Polite applause at the lecture's end startled him out of his stupor. His heart pounded, his palms were sweaty, and the ideal health system the speaker had conjured had evaporated like a phantom. Obviously, this guy was one more in a long line of idealistic, ivory tower academics. He sounded good, but Don knew he had to work in the trenches and just do the best job he could for each patient.

He started toward the door, remembering the hospital wards and the giant stack of paperwork awaiting him, but Sarah held his arm.

"Come on," she said, "let's go talk to him. He's a friend of my father. Remember Dad telling us about his training program?"

Sarah's dad was a doctor. He had bought them coffee in the hospital cafeteria one night in the winter when Sarah's parents were visiting from Minnesota, but Don couldn't remember anything they'd talked about.

Sarah steered Don down to meet the speaker before he had time to object. "Hello, Dr. Sampson," she greeted him.

"Well, if it isn't Dr. Sarah Moore! It's good to see you. How are your parents?"

"Oh, they're doing well. You know Dad. He'll never give up his patients. He seems to keep working harder than ever."

The speaker was shorter than he had appeared from the back of the room, but he had a commanding presence, like an aging warrior captain. His arms and legs were thick as tree trunks. His hairline receded beyond the shiny crown of his head, encircling it with a ring of dark gray hair. His deep gray eyes looked from Sarah to Don.

"So, this must be Don Newman." The speaker's deep voice reverberated from his broad chest. "It's a pleasure to finally meet you." He thrust out a thick hand and gave Don a vigorous handshake.

"You know my name?"

"Oh, yes. Sarah has told me of your interests."

"My interests?"

"I'm always on the lookout for kindred spirits. I don't find many among your generation. Guess I'm just a contrarian old doctor, born into a time known as the golden age of medicine." He laughed. "For over twenty-five years I've been telling people who did not want to hear it that modern medicine isn't nearly as good as it's made out to be."

"Don always gives us articles on how dangerous healthcare is and how many people get tests and treatments they don't really need," Sarah informed him.

"You're a third-year resident?"

"Yes, sir."

"And your plans?"

"I'm thinking cardiology."

"After what Sarah has told me, I am surprised to hear that. Why are you planning to labor on the assembly line of an outmoded industry? You must see the writing on the wall. Why don't you consider doing something to help change healthcare in America?"

Don was taken aback by these comments from a perfect stranger. Most people were impressed when he said he was thinking of cardiology. What in the world had Sarah said about him?

Don's eyes wandered to the blackboard behind the podium, where the name DR. GIL SAMPSON was written in large block letters. He hadn't noticed it from his hiding place in the back of the hall.

Oh, crap! This was the Dr. Sampson who authored the famous papers on variations in care for coronary artery disease. The Dr. Sampson that proved whether you got medicine, stents, or bypass surgery depended more on how many cardiologists and heart surgeons there were in your town than it did on which treatment was most likely to help prevent a heart attack. Sampson had made a career of studying why medical care varies so much across the country. His work had helped father the field of health services research in America.

"I just realized—you are Dr. Gil Sampson," Don admitted. "I've read many of your papers and admire your work. Forgive me for not making the connection. I just had a horrible night in the hospital—how can you be a good doctor these days?"

Don was surprised to hear himself revealing his true feelings to this man he hardly knew.

"If you want to be a good doctor, you have to either work outside the system or work to change it. Either way is hard." Dr. Sampson glanced around to make sure no one was listening and lowered his voice. "I'm sure you would make an excellent cardiologist. But you must see that cardiology will only pull you deeper into the current system. The procedural subspecialties like cardiology are flush with cash, and they draw the best and brightest into their ranks. The prestige and hefty paychecks quiet the voices screaming in their heads that much of the work is useless and vain. The champions of healthcare reform will address *real* health care needs and seek to eliminate the copious waste that is especially common in the procedural disciplines."

"I want to be part of the change; I just don't know how," Don replied, looking down. "All I know how to do any more is put in IVs, catheters, and chest tubes. There's no time to think."

"If you are sincere in your desire to be part of the change, you must take another path. Why don't you do a general medicine fellowship and become a health services researcher? There are many training programs you could consider, but the best is the one I run at Florence College, a short distance away in Florence, New Hampshire."

Everyone knew of Florence College. One of the top Ivy League colleges in the country, it had a reputation for free thinking and intellectual rigor.

"I must go now to meet with Dr. Desmond and the faculty," Dr. Sampson said. "Meet me this afternoon. Five o'clock in the Social Medicine annex of the School of Public Health."

It sounded more like a command than an invitation.

"If I can get free from the hospital I'll try to make it," Don heard himself answer.

Dr. Sampson gathered his papers and walked with Sarah up the narrow stairs, out the back doorway, and into the hall outside the auditorium. The audiovisual staff dimmed the lights from front to back as everyone filed out. Don bounded up the stairs two at a time and headed back to the hospital.

2
The Choice

All I am offering you is the truth, nothing more.
MORPHEUS, THE MATRIX

THE PAGER SCREECHED. Don checked the number and returned the call.

"Are you going?" Sarah asked as soon as she picked up the phone.

"Am I going where?" he asked, already knowing the answer.

"You know where I mean. Are you going to talk to him?"

"Well, I have three more notes to write and a spinal tap to do, and I'm still trying to get in touch with Mrs. Bellamy's daughter."

"Excuses, excuses! I think you're afraid to talk to him. Come on, Don, you'll never get another chance like this. Dr. Sampson's program is the best in the country."

"I know, but my attending will kill me if I don't get that tap done."

The attending physician on the University Hospital staff oversaw and got paid for Don's work.

"Forget the tap. Your intern can do it and the chief resident can supervise it. And listen, I could help. I'm done with my work and I know Sibyl Bellamy."

Even though she was a new intern, Sarah was confident and always seemed to know just what to do. Maybe it was because her father was a doctor. Don had had to learn how to put patients at ease, but Sarah just knew.

"Let me call Sibyl's daughter," she offered. "Maybe I can set up a family conference for tomorrow. At this point, that's about as good as you can do."

As a general rule, Don didn't think doctors should use a patient's first name, but Sarah did it without sounding disrespectful or unprofessional. She made it personal and caring.

"I can't ask you to do my work," he protested. "She's my patient and my responsibility."

"First of all, you didn't ask me to do your work. I offered. And what do you mean, she's your patient? She's your intern's patient, which I guess means she has no doctor at all. Where was Sibyl's intern at three o'clock in the morning when you were putting in that line? That was his job."

They both knew the nurses would only call Edward as a last resort. For someone who possessed a far-reaching knowledge of textbook medicine, he didn't seem able to apply his learning for anyone's benefit in a particular situation, especially if it meant physically touching a patient. Edward did too well on tests and rounds for Desmond to fire him, but no one trusted him. The nurses never called him if they had another choice.

"Listen," Sarah continued, "I'll call the family and try to walk Edward through what he needs to do. I'll be managing a team myself in only a couple of months—it'll give me good practice. It won't hurt you to go and at least hear what Dr. Sampson has to say. Whether you're ready to hear it or not, he has the answers you're looking for. You have to go."

Don knew she didn't really need the practice, but Edward sure needed someone's help to become a competent second-year resident, and the thought of avoiding that miserable responsibility, even for a short time, was too tempting to pass up.

"All right," he agreed, "but I don't expect much from it. He's from Florence College, after all. Just another head-in-the-clouds philosopher type. What could he know about caring for sick people?"

"Okay, then. You're going! Don't worry about Sibyl. I'll talk to you later. Bye now."

She hung up.

Don found Edward in the resident's lounge. He was sitting cross-legged on the couch, bent over a massive, blood-red book in his lap. It was his beloved Cecil Textbook of Medicine. Edward bragged he had read it cover to cover—all three thousand pages of it three times. This would be his fourth.

"Edward."

The slump-backed intern didn't respond.

"Edward!"

"Huh?" He glanced up over the tops of his thick-lensed, horn-rimmed glasses and struggled to focus.

"Stick with Sarah, and do what she tells you. I'm going across campus for a meeting. Any problems, anyone calls you to see a patient, and you call Sarah first. Hear me?"

"Yeah, sure, Don. No problem. I got it."

Don was sure he did not. "And don't leave the hospital until I get back. I'll check in with you in an hour or so."

Don traded his white coat for his long black wool one before heading out into the cold. He paused for a second to admire the tall, broad-shouldered figure in the mirror, but instead his eyes zeroed in on a lacy pattern of corridors carved in his left sleeve by a relentless moth.

As he walked though the hospital's historic front lobby, the dark veins of its marble floor seemed to form swirling currents bent on sucking him back into the hospital. He dragged himself against the tide through the entry hall. As he passed the reception window, his eyes caught the old guard's stony stare through the glass.

Despite Don's nearly three years of passing this way, no glimmer of recognition appeared in the guard's sunken eyes. The old man leveled the same cold stare at everyone who walked by. The deeply wrinkled face, three-day gray stubble, uncombed white hair, and long skeletal frame suggested homeless bum rather than hospital guard, but the ever-present wooden nightstick dangling at his side proclaimed the old man's priorities. No one entered the University Hospital without his acquiescence.

Don pushed out through the brass revolving door. It was tarnished except where countless hands had pressed their way in. Cold winter air blasted between the huge stone pillars supporting the hospital's façade and stung his face. He was glad for his old black coat. He figured it would have to last another year or two, or at least until he started to make some real money.

The afternoon was dark. Billowing storm clouds were moving in from the west. Don picked up his pace and cut across the campus quad through soggy brown grass and scattered patches of half-melted snow.

Voices contended for control of his sleep-deprived brain. *Why in the world are you doing this? What could you possibly learn from this guy that you don't already know?* He never should have let Sarah talk him into going to see Dr. Sampson.

He glanced at the threatening sky and considered heading back to the protective crypt of the hospital lobby. It wasn't too late to back out. But then he remembered the dark abyss in Sibyl's wide-open eyes. *Damn! Why can't I shake the feeling she is still watching me?*

Don kept going. Explaining to Sarah why he changed his mind would be too embarrassing. Better to go on, even though it was just a waste of time. After all, he'd already decided to specialize in interventional cardiology. Dr. Desmond had just offered him a position at the best program in the country. He had until the end of the week to decide, but he had already made up his mind. Why in the world would anyone throw away such a great opportunity? Don enjoyed the envious looks of his fellow residents when he passed them in the halls. And with eleven years of education loans to pay off, he deserved to finally make some serious money. *I'm on the cusp of a prestigious fellowship and profitable career. So why do I feel so damn ambivalent and confused?*

A sudden crack of thunder interrupted his reverie of self-recrimination. He looked up to gauge the storm and walked right into a deep puddle, plunging his right foot down past the ankle into thick, brown, sucking muck. He jerked his foot hard and it came out shoeless. *Damn loafers! Shit, how could I be so stupid?* He fished his shoe out of the mud, wiped it off in the grass, and slipped his foot back into it. He laughed out loud—now he had a perfect excuse to chicken out and skip the little chat with Dr. Sampson—and turned back toward the hospital.

That's when he saw it.

An enormous new billboard atop the parking deck loomed over the original part of the historic hospital. Built in the early 1800s, the old hospital had long since been engulfed by an elaborate complex of buildings and enclosed pathways connecting the various parts of the compound. The mishmash of additions dwarfed the original structure and obscured the perfect proportions of its neoclassical architecture.

Two buildings now dominated the University Hospital grounds. The first was a marble-sheathed high rise with five hundred beds. It was built in the 1950s, when money poured into the new scientific tertiary care hospitals. The second building was a gleaming black glass medical tower built in the 1980s, designed to house thousands of examining rooms and several state-of-the-art intensive care units. The University Hospital system had over one thousand beds scattered among its five buildings, making it one of the biggest hospitals in the world.

The gigantic billboard towered over the old heart of the hospital. Wasn't any place free of marketing anymore? Of course, it wasn't as if the hospital was anything beautiful now. The uncoordinated mass of concrete and glass looked like an overgrown industrial mill. But it was the surgeon on the billboard—magnified to the size of a titan—that really galled Don.

The surgeon was clothed in the familiar green operating gown of the hospital. His stance was proud and defensive at the same time: arms crossed over his chest, body turned sideways, face in half profile. Although the smiling faces of his surgical team were uncovered, a surgical mask obscured the surgeon's mouth and nose, revealing only his left eye.

The calculating eye looked oddly familiar. Where had he seen it before? Slowly it dawned on him—it was none other than Dr. Desmond. On a billboard, for crying out loud! There he was, presiding over an unconscious patient, spotless attendants, and a glittering cardiac procedure room full of the latest technology. The message across the bottom was printed in big black letters: YOUR PATH TO HEALTH IS HERE! THE UNIVERSITY HOSPITAL. IT MAY SAVE YOUR LIFE!

Don stood there, paralyzed by Dr. Desmond's monocular gaze. He cringed at the thought of spending his life wearing one of those suffocating masks. But that was interventional cardiology—like Dr. Desmond, he'd spend hours a day hovering over unconscious patients.

His chest tightened. He felt the mask gagging him, choking off his air, muffling his words. Perhaps that was the worst thing about the mask: he loved words, especially when they sprang from his lips at just the right moment to offer a patient comfort. He wanted to talk to his patients, to hear their stories. His best teachers in medical school and residency had shown him how to use words to discover the true reasons for illness and to reassure and heal.

In the cath lab there was no time to question, no time for words. Your job was to wear a mask and thread steel catheters through veins and arteries. He had talked to the cardiology fellows—cath jockeys, they called themselves. They complained—just as Dr. Sampson had warned—that the only available jobs in the Boston area were on heart cath assembly lines. They hardly knew the reason a patient was getting a cath or whether the procedure was even necessary. Their job was simply to cath the people sent their way. Sure, they found consolation in cardiology's prestige and they enjoyed the generous salaries. But was their work satisfying? Was it important for health?

The darkness deepened and a raindrop hit Don's forehead. "Oh, hell, what can it hurt?" he muttered out loud. With refreshed determination, he did another about-face and marched, muddy foot and all, to the Shattuck Social Medicine building on a back corner of campus. He arrived at the small brick building he thought was the Department of Social Medicine. Sure enough, there was a small sign, but the front door appeared to be locked and the front of the building was dark. It started to rain harder.

Don spotted a small gate leading around to the back. A single bare light bulb hung down and illuminated the way to the back door. He ran through the small courtyard, just gaining the protection of the back porch as the rain started to pour. He knocked and glanced at his watch. It was well past five-thirty now, so he was probably too late.

No one answered the door. The sky turned pitch black and the wind blew stronger. Ice-cold rain blew into the porch from the side, and the bulb above his head swung wildly, sending his shadow careening to and fro. Grimacing at the thought of walking back to the hospital with no umbrella or raincoat, he gave the door a gentle shove. It swung open.

"Is anyone here?" he called.

"Don, is that you?" a voice called from down the hall.

"Here I am," he answered.

Dr. Sampson's hulking figure lumbered toward the back door. He looked Don up and down. "You're a mess," he chuckled. "Better take your shoes off. Bernie would not appreciate muddy footprints on his carpet."

"Bernie?"

"Oh, you know, Dr. Bernard Lown of Lown Cardiology Institute. He won the Nobel Peace Prize for his efforts against the proliferation of nuclear arms. He's an old friend of mine, and when I'm in town he lets me use this office. He calls it his thinking office; it's a good place to talk."

Don pulled off his coat, loafers, and the mud-soaked sock. Then, feeling ridiculous wearing just one sock, he pulled off the dry one, too. He stood there dripping and barefoot, wishing he had paid better attention to where he was stepping.

"I'm the only one here?"

"Yes. I'm not one to draw a big crowd. The truth is, I'm not looking for a lot of doctors, only one. A doctor with the desire and ability to communicate to others what a mess the practice of medicine is and how to improve it. My staff says I'm as likely as Diogenes to find an honest doctor willing and strong enough to take this on."

DR. SAMPSON SAT in one of two overstuffed chairs and motioned to Don to take the other. "So, make yourself at home."

Don walked across the soft oriental carpet and sat across from Dr. Sampson. Uncomfortable with the closeness of the two seats and Dr. Sampson's trenchant stare, Don tried to hide his bare feet under his chair and gazed at the wall full of pictures of Dr. Lown conferring with world leaders.

"So, why did you come to meet with me today?" Dr. Sampson sat back as if expecting a long answer.

Don hadn't prepared for an interview. "Well, uh…I wanted to know a little more about your program…tell me, what is it called again?"

"The Florence College Health System Science Program. There is no other fellowship like it. Sure, a few general internal medicine fellowships train doctors to become experts in evidence-based medicine. They study the scientific evidence for what doctors do in everyday practice. As in those programs, our fellows study biostatistics and epidemiology and learn how to conduct and analyze scientific research. Plus, they earn a degree in public health, which is guaranteed to lower a doctor's starting salary." Dr. Sampson chuckled again.

That was the rub. Don's best teachers in medical school and residency had done general medicine fellowships. It was hard enough that during the two years of fellowship training they made hardly anything, but after completing the extra education, they were still stuck with low salaries. Why do that, when two years of cardiology training tripled your starting income?

Don wanted to be one of the best doctors. He wanted to know how to keep people out of the hospital, not just shuttle them through it. He wanted to be a generalist, but how in the hell could he afford it?

"But our program goes further," Dr. Sampson explained. "Our fellows train to become agents for health system change. They study how health systems function and analyze the root problems in American medicine. I am looking for the doctor who wants to take on the status quo. The doctor for whom making money is not the first concern. The doctor who wants the healthcare business focused on the patient—instead of the paperwork. The doctor burning with desire to bring true healing to the American people. Sarah tells me you are that doctor. Is that true?"

"Well, Sarah's opinion of me may be a little inflated. After all, she was my intern."

"And she is a smart woman, whose opinion I would not take so lightly." Dr. Sampson's tone was serious, almost reprimanding.

Don squirmed and tried again to redirect the conversation away from himself. "So, how do you know Sarah?"

"Her father and I were residents together here at University Hospital years ago, in the same class as Charles Desmond, as a matter of fact. I chose research and teaching; John became a cardiologist, one of the best. He's an old-style, non-interventional cardiologist like Bernie. He doesn't cath, at least not anymore, but he can take a patient's history and get to the heart of most problems faster than any doctor I've ever seen. He can determine as much using his stethoscope as others do with an echocardiogram. He practices in his town of Eden Prairie, Minnesota, and everyone in town knows and respects him.

"Unfortunately, there is little demand for cardiologists like him anymore, and you would be hard-pressed to find a cardiology fellowship program where you could learn to use a stethoscope half as well as he does. Most fellows now spend the majority of their time in the cath lab, the echo lab, or reviewing test results. That's what group practices want these days. That's where the money is. Most cardiologists have little time to talk to patients or take an old-fashioned history and physical."

"What exactly do you do in your fellowship training program?"

"Our fellows learn the fundamentals of health system design and how to accomplish health system change in multi-specialty groups, hospitals, government, and insurance companies. The first year involves learning the ugly truth about the American healthcare system, how bad it really is, who controls it and for what purposes. Unless you know what you are up against, you have no chance to make positive changes. You have an idea of how bad modern medicine is, don't you, Dr. Newman?"

Remembering Mrs. Bellamy from the previous night, Don nodded. "But who am I to be a healthcare leader? I'm just a lowly resident doctor. Who would listen to me?"

"You're one of the top resident physicians at one of the top programs in the country. Everyone is going to listen to you. Besides, Sarah tells me you have a way with words. That's an unusual trait among doctors these days. But the important thing is you have an inkling of the truth, an uneasy feeling you can't shake. That is what brought you here."

"But what about cardiology? What will I tell Dr. Desmond? How can I change course this late in the game?"

Don heard himself discussing a drastic change in his life plan as if it were someone else talking. His pulse quickened. Why did this brand-new possibility—which he had never imagined until today—feel inevitable? How could he even think of turning away from a prize cardiology residency? He must be going crazy, or sleep deprivation had clouded his mind. On the other hand, the mere thought of cardiology evoked the suffocating, gagging mask and Sibyl Bellamy's accusing eyes.

Dr. Sampson ignored his discomfort. "Listen, you have a choice. You can go back to the wards, try to forget this conversation, and work for the medical system as it is. Or, you can follow me to the bottom of the rabbit hole. If you come to Florence College, all I can promise you is the truth. No salary guarantee. No fancy car. My program isn't easy, and only time will tell where it will lead you, but you will learn the truth about the healthcare industry and might find yourself in a position to help change things for the better. So, the choice is yours. What are you going to do?"

3

The Gates of Hell

Lasciate ogni speranza, voi ch'entrate.
DANTE ALIGHIERI, INFERNO 3, 9

"COME NOW, Mr. Newman. You, of *all* people, should know what these words mean."

The words were emblazoned over the dark entrance to a black bottomless pit. LASCIATE OGNI SPERANZA, VOI CH'ENTRATE. Panicked, he searched the strange words for clues.

"Well, Dante? What is it, Dante? Don't you know what it means?" Desmond stood guard at the entrance, his starched white coat silhouetted against the dark void behind him. He opened his mouth wide, displaying his canines, and cackled like a hyena. His laughter echoed back from the depths of the dark cavern.

Don racked his brain, desperate for an answer and frantic to pass this final test. Why hadn't he studied this? Was it some Latin phrase for an obscure disease? Something from his pathology class long forgotten? "I, uh, I don't know," he stammered, "what does it mean?"

"You don't know? You, *Dan...te* Newman? You, of all people, should know this!"

Desmond gave a loud whistle. Out from the bowels of the dark pit marched a horde of grinning orderlies in white uniforms. They were coming for him.

"No! Please! Let me try again!"

Desmond smirked and pointed a crooked index finger in his direction. "No, Dante, you failed the test. You will require further instruction. Don't worry, our pleasant staff will teach you all you need to know."

The demonic orderlies swarmed around him. They grasped, pulled, picked, and tore at him from all directions, ripping off his white doctor's coat. To his horror, he was naked underneath.

"You can't wear a white coat now, of course," Desmond gloated as he watched the claws dig into Don's flesh.

Don thrashed and struggled to get free, but there were too many of them. The demons drug him closer and closer to the broad gate and the dark abyss. His bare feet struggled for purchase on the wet stone floor. Inch by inch he lost ground, slipping and sliding across the slippery stone toward the entrance.

"Give up, Dante," Dr. Desmond commanded. "There is no hope for you now!"

DON AWOKE with a violent jerk just as the demons yanked him over the threshold. His sheets were twisted and drenched with sweat.

Two days earlier, he'd driven his old Ford Escort out of Boston for the last time, leaving Dr. Desmond and the University Hospital behind for a fresh start at Florence College. The old hatchback was so packed with stuff he couldn't see a thing in the rear view mirror. Not that he wanted to. He'd crossed the Charles River and headed out of town, not bothering to glance at Boston's skyscrapers in the side mirror. His spirits lifted as he sped toward a new life and a new home—a studio apartment on a quiet street half a mile from campus.

On the first night in his new place he came down with a late summer flu. No surprise. He was exhausted from night after night of sporadic nocturnal awakenings. After finishing his internal medicine residency, he'd increased his moonlighting to seventy hours a week and spent almost every night for two months working in the emergency rooms of Boston. He had no choice. He had to make some serious money before school started.

Having borrowed for college, medical school, and his first year of residency, he owed more than two hundred thousand dollars. That was a ton of money, but a lot of his friends owed more. His college loans had started coming due as soon as he finished medical school. He wasn't allowed to moonlight the first year of residency and his salary was only thirty-two thousand, so he took out another loan to cover the college payments and the high cost of living in Boston. The banks were all too happy to have his business. Doctors are considered a safe bet.

In the reflected light of the street lamps he could just make out the louvered aluminum windows lining the eastern wall of his second floor walkup. With his boxers and t-shirt completely wet, the night wind whistling through the poorly sealed windows chilled him to the core. He had rented the duplex because it was cheap and had big windows, but with the gloomy weather and his confused sleep schedule, he had yet to see much light coming in. And now it was clear the leaky windows were a real liability—it would cost a fortune to heat this place.

At least his fever had broken. He threw back the damp sheets, climbed out of bed, stripped off his wet clothing, and toweled off in front of the bathroom mirror. Checking himself out in the buzzing fluorescent light, he didn't like what he saw. His body looked droopy. He'd played Division III football at Sewanee, a star running back scoring eight touchdowns his senior year. The quads, shoulders, biceps, and washboard abdomen were all still visible, but his muscles had grown soft. He figured his body fat was approaching ten percent—time to get back to the track and the weight room.

In truth, Don was a handsome man with an athletic six-foot-two, one hundred and ninety-pound frame. Dark brown hair curled in soft ringlets that trailed into his sideburns and merged into the two days' growth of dark beard highlighting his strong jaw. His aquiline nose was too broad to be strictly Roman but still gave him a classical aspect. His deep-set eyes were dark chocolate. Despite living under fluorescent light for years, his skin was all golden brown, except for a hint of pink that graced the inner edge of his full lips.

At Sewanee his rugged good looks drew attention. He could have had any number of women but allowed himself only one. Jessica. Their connection was not premeditated—at least not by him—and in retrospect he did not view it as his wisest choice. On their first night together he invited her to his dorm room to watch videos. They ended up watching *Pretty Woman*. The premise was preposterous, but the steamy scenes seduced them all the same. As the movie ended, Jessica looked up at him with her sultry brown eyes and repeated the penultimate line, "So what happened after he climbed up the tower and rescued her?" Don played her knight and didn't look away.

They didn't find much else in common. Only the sex. They fed on it like a drug, alternating between delightful romps in the sack and utter boredom whenever they came up for air. The on again, off again relationship dragged on through most of his junior and senior years and long distance through four years of medical school. After each dramatic break up they made up—just like in the movies—but after the passion cooled there was no real bond or friendship between them. Halfway through his first year of residency they called it quits for good.

Don crawled back under the covers on the dry side of the bed. It had been a long time since a woman had shared it with him. He was terribly lonely, and had been so for a long time, but he wanted more than a series of one-night stands. He wanted warmth, sympathy, someone to drink coffee with in the morning, someone who cared about him like family. Someone who would understand his decision to walk away from a guaranteed, lucrative career to venture into uncharted territory.

THE SAME NIGHTMARE had haunted Don ever since the day—almost four years ago now—he had first met Dr. Charles A. Desmond. Don was a lowly applicant interviewing for an internal medicine residency position in the halls of what everybody said was the greatest hospital in the country. Winning a spot at the University Hospital was a long shot. The program represented the height of prestige and learning, and the competition was fierce.

As the reigning medical director, Dr. Desmond was the lord of that realm. Don picked up his schedule on interview day and was surprised to find he was assigned to Dr. Desmond instead of one of the affiliated physician faculty members. Dr. Desmond was famous—even outside the University Hospital—for his strictness and his photographic memory. He knew every medical fact there was to know and was notorious for tormenting nurses, interns, and residents with obscure questions.

The brochure describing the training program charitably called this approach the Socratic method. During Don's undergraduate education in the classics, he had read many of the *Dialogues* where Plato dutifully recorded Socrates' conversations with his students. Socrates asked lots of questions for sure, but unlike Desmond, he actually seemed interested in the answers. Socrates' questions led students to a better understanding of the truth.

Questions at the University Hospital had a different purpose. They were part of a teaching style that was autocratic rather than Socratic. The interns knew this method well; they called it pimping. The attending physicians and upper-level residents pimped interns on a daily basis. The point was to reveal the intern's complete lack of knowledge and make the pimp look amazingly smart. Dr. Desmond was the acknowledged master of the technique. To avoid complete humiliation, an intern had to anticipate what arcane piece of knowledge Dr. Desmond might seize upon on any given day. Figuring that out was never likely.

Don wondered if Dr. Desmond was really as bad as his reputation indicated. He feared he would soon be put to the test but also felt a little thrill. A good impression on Dr. Desmond would be sure to land him one of the coveted residency spots at the University Hospital.

One of the chief residents guided Don and two other nervous applicants on a hospital tour. The wan, slope-shouldered chief proudly sported a striped bowtie and waxed on about the superiority of the University Hospital.

Don became completely disoriented. Every hall looked alike and the twists and turns became too numerous to count. There was no spool of thread to help him track his way back through the maze, but he didn't think about that. He was going eagerly toward the center of power, where he might gain admission to the most prestigious medical training program in the country. He shivered with anticipation.

After the tour, the chief led them through the maze of hospital hallways to Dr. Desmond's office. He paused long enough in front of Dr. Desmond's office to impress upon Don what a rare privilege it was to land an interview with the real genius behind the training program. The other two applicants looked on with equal measures of envy and relief. The chief led them off to their respective interviews, leaving Don to fend for himself.

He felt important for the few seconds it took to make his way to the secretary's desk, but his morale faded as the tight-lipped woman clicked away at her keyboard with long red fingernails and refused to acknowledge his presence.

"Excuse me," he said.

"Dr. Desmond will be with you shortly," she answered in a curt voice, not bothering to look up from her typing.

There was no place for him to sit in her narrow office. Don's discomfort escalated over the next thirty minutes as he stood in front of her desk, shifting his weight from one foot to the other and gazing at the files lining either side of the room.

The secretary ignored him completely. Apparently, she compensated for her confined workspace by pretending no one else was there. To her, Don Newman was just another naive supplicant coming to grovel at the feet of the great Dr. Charles A. Desmond.

Without warning, the opaque glass door behind her flew open and Dr. Desmond strode through it. He wore a burgundy and blue-striped bowtie and a hard-starched, long white coat. He held an open file folder in his hands. He must have seen Don reach out to shake hands but did not reciprocate or acknowledge the young man's presence in any way. He focused intently on the file for a moment before giving the purse-faced woman a slip of paper and some instructions under his breath. Finally, he turned to face Don.

Dr. Desmond arched his back and leaned forward from the hip to examine his applicant. His left eye stared straight at Don, but his right one pointed off somewhere over Don's left shoulder. The good eye seemed oversized for his face and bulged beyond its socket, as if straining to do the work of the lazy one, too.

Don felt the eye's laser-like focus pierce his forehead from an uncomfortable distance of about fifteen centimeters, which intensified his nervousness. He looked down at the folder and saw his proper name, DANTE NEWMAN, printed on the tab.

"So, Mr...Newman," Dr. Desmond growled, stealing another glance at the folder. "Are you ready to do what it takes to succeed here and become a real doctor?"

Don glanced up. The eye still blazed into his forehead. "Yes, sir," Don heard himself answer. Why did his voice sound so timid?

"Then come into my office. But first, tell me, what does the sign over my door mean?"

Don hadn't noticed the sign and cursed himself for not being more observant during the long wait. *Lasciate ogni speranza, voi ch'entrate.* It looked similar to Latin, but he couldn't decipher it.

"So, what does it mean, Mr. Newman?" Dr. Desmond asked in a strange, anticipatory tone.

This was it. The test! Don felt himself probed and examined by the terrible eye, as if he were a slime-smeared glass slide under a microscope.

"Well? At least you must recognize the language! So, what is it, Mr. Newman?"

"Is it Latin, sir?" he stammered.

"No, it is not Latin, sir." His mocking laughter echoed in the empty room. "Your first name *is* Dante, is it not?"

"I go by Don, sir," he mumbled.

"Surely you, of all people, must recognize this phrase!"

Don scoured his mind for clues as he reread the inscription. The word *speranza* caught some fragment of a memory. "Is it about hope? Hope and healing, maybe?"

Dr. Desmond's condescending laugh was almost sinister. "No, Mr. Newman, this is not about hope. To the contrary, it says, *Give up all hope all ye who enter here.* It is Italian. Since it comes from Dante, I should think you would have recognized it. It was written over the entrance to hell, where Dante went as a visitor. You, of course, would be entering hell to stay."

Hell? What was he talking about? No wonder Dr. Desmond had the reputation he did.

"The rest of the sign over the gate to hell reads: *Through me is the way to the woeful city, through me is the way of eternal pain, through me the way among the lost people.* In your case, Mr. Newman, through *me* is your only way into the University Hospital, and only through *me* will you come to know the plagues that infect this place, the causes of pain and degradation, and the diseased people the rest of the world wants to forget. So you can see why you must abandon every hope to enter here." His disdainful laughter reverberated through the room again. "We don't have time for hope. This is reality. You must make sacrifices to be a real doctor. Come, Don, let's talk about your future."

Don followed him into the office, feeling uneasy as he passed under the ominous words, but still not fully comprehending where he had just arrived. In spite of what he thought was a horrible interview Dr. Desmond offered him a residency position. He couldn't imagine turning it down, but his encounter with Desmond tinged his enthusiasm for working at the University Hospital with a persistent, unavowed dread.

LYING AWAKE in the darkness of his new apartment, Don contemplated the years that had passed since that awful interview. Dr. Desmond had been right— he should have known that phrase. His Italian mother loved Dante Alighieri, the great Italian poet who penned those famous words. *She named me Dante, for God's sake!* She would have been so disappointed he did not recognize the very words she'd read to him as a boy, words every Italian child committed to memory in grade school.

He had forgotten who he was! For seven years he'd surrendered his soul to learn the art of medicine. He knew from the start sacrifice would be necessary but had no idea what that really meant. During training, everyone worked insane hours and lost touch with family and friends in the frantic rush of endless tasks. There was no time to write a friend or attend a family gathering.

Some handled the indoctrination better than others. Edward devoted so much of his life to the study of biomedical science he couldn't make small talk. Others gave so much of themselves to the house of the dead they couldn't find their way back to the world of the living—like his best friend from medical school, Jack.

Jack Jordan was about the only black friend Don had ever made. With his jet-black curls, moustache, goatee, and dark brown skin, *his* heritage was undeniable. Although Don was mixed race—the product of an Italian mother and a black GI—he lived white, he acted white, and all his other friends were white. But Jack was one of those rare people who was blind to race. It simply didn't concern him.

Jack was near the top of his college class. Although he could have gone the easy route and taken over his family's New York jewelry business, he wanted to be a doctor. On the first day of medical school Jack made his intentions clear. "Bringing new life into the world is the greatest privilege a doctor can have," he said. "Women are sacred vessels for that new life, Don, let me tell you. Caring for a woman with child—there's no higher calling!"

Jack loved women, and women of all kinds gravitated towards Jack. He always had one or two on his arm. Jack's ready smile, resonant voice, and radiant eyes attracted everyone. At the end of medical school he landed a top OB/GYN residency at Columbia back in his hometown. He was living his dream, or so he thought.

The weekend before Don moved to New Hampshire he'd visited Jack in New York. They hadn't seen each other since medical school in Chicago and he looked forward to renewing their friendship. Don arrived at Jack's small apartment in Manhattan around ten on Friday night and was shocked to see how much his friend had changed. Jack was at least twenty pounds heavier. Something had sapped the life from his eyes, turned his dark skin sallow, and twisted his face into a near perpetual smirk.

When Don awoke early Saturday morning after a poor night's sleep on Jack's lumpy sofa, Jack had already gone to the hospital. It was supposed to be his short day, and they had plans to visit museums, eat dinner out at a nice restaurant, maybe even catch a show at the old Apollo Theater, where Jack's mother had sung and danced long ago. Don was looking forward to catching up with Jack and enjoying a bit of New York.

Jack called at one o'clock to tell Don he was running late, so Don went on to the Metropolitan Museum of Art alone. Jack said he'd meet Don there but never showed up. At eight that night, Jack met Don back at his apartment with an excuse about two emergency C-sections. That would have been understandable, but Jack didn't seem bothered about missing an entire day romping around the city with his old friend. He was juiced up about his surgery and only wanted to talk about work. It was as if he couldn't think of anything else to talk about.

Since Jack had to go in early the next day, they went to the greasy spoon on the block for a quick bite. Over burgers and beer, he talked nonstop about cases he had seen and procedures and techniques he had mastered over the last three years, without any reference to the women he had operated on.

He leaned over the stainless-trimmed Formica table and lowered his voice, speaking to Don as if he were a co-conspirator. "Shit, Don, I'm working on an unending assembly line of some of the nastiest female genitalia you have ever seen. It's enough to make you swear off sex forever." Jack started to devour his second order of cheese fries and kept talking as he chewed. "You won't believe it, Don, but this young chick I saw in the emergency department today told me she liked anal sex but wasn't sure if she should keep doing it. She said it didn't hurt her, so I said it was probably okay as long as she took care not to get pregnant. Her eyes got really big and she said, 'You can get pregnant from anal sex?' I didn't miss a beat. I told her, 'Sure, where do you think lawyers come from?'"

Jack convulsed with laughter, but Don found his joke pathetic. He missed the old Jack. Three years of brain-crushing residency and sleep deprivation had altered him.

The next morning, Don pulled his Ford Escort out of the parking lot—forty dollars for a weekend spot—feeling sadder than when he arrived. Jack's situation was not so unlike his own, he realized with disgust.

I was on the same path as Jack. The same thing almost happened to me.

DON FELL BACK ASLEEP and his dream started again. He saw the yawning black mouth of the abyss and the dreadful words marking the entrance. Once again his stomach tightened and his knees wobbled. But this time a low voice murmured in his right ear.

"Snap out of it, son." It was Dr. Sampson. "Abandon your fear of sickness and death and follow me."

Don looked to his broad-shouldered guide. Dr. Sampson was grim and unruffled. Don sidled up to him and the demons stepped back. Don and Dr. Sampson passed unmolested through the dark gate.

"This time you are going to look, not to stay," Dr. Sampson explained. "Look and remember your former colleagues: *woeful people who have lost the good of intellect.*"

Far below them, a bevy of white-coated student doctors and residents surrounded Desmond like a flock of honking geese. Desmond's white coat flapped behind him as he darted from room to room and sped down the dark, twisting corridors. The great crowd of devotees followed him, hung on every word, and mimicked every move. At every door he asked questions with answers that couldn't be found in any major textbook. His flagellant followers castigated themselves for not knowing. They whipped their backs with their own stethoscopes, then redoubled their mad scribbling and struggled to record Desmond's meaningless recitation of memorized medical minutiae word for word.

Suffering patients cried out to Desmond and the passing clique from pallets lining the crowded halls. The sick begged for a simple explanation, a word of kindness, a sip of water, or relief from pain. Desmond ignored their pleas as he paraded past and lampooned the bedridden unfortunates, much to the delight of his loyal retinue.

In the midst of that mindless crowd of his former colleagues, Don spotted Jack and called out to him. Jack gave him a guilty glance, but then his brow furrowed, his face twisted with crazed determination, and he renewed his futile chase, shouting out wrong answers to Desmond's esoteric questions with the rest of the flock.

Desmond led his groupies into the University Hospital's famous domed lobby. The round ceiling arched over them like the bell of a stethoscope and the heartbeat of the hospital thumped and echoed through the chamber. With each thump, the dark veins streaking the lobby's marble floor pulsed and sent dark rivulets of fluid streaming into a wide river as black as blood.

The towers of the massive hospital rose above the river's mist. Within the towers, dour doctors slaved over microscopes in basement cubicles, scrutinized shadows in dark radiology suites, restructured natural forms in cavernous operating rooms, drained and analyzed body fluids in tiled laboratories, dissected devitalized flesh in refrigerated morgues, and probed and biopsied the unconscious and brain-dead in monitored ICUs.

Desmond stood on the shore and pointed across the vast river. The wannabes crowded along the river's edge, each clamoring to be the first to cross the dark water, to go to work in the great towers. A white-haired ferryman with a grizzled face stood on the shore, brandishing a long wooden oar and barring the young doctors from passage. His eyes were burning coals that seared into each heart like twin laser beams, eager to ablate any residual compassion they detected within.

The young doctors climbed over pleading wives, crying children, and anxious parents in their determination to climb aboard the ferryman's moldering barge. Those who hesitated or looked back were rebuffed and left behind.

The old bastard swung his huge oar to and fro, beating back the unworthy. In the end, he eliminated about half. He only took those ready to sacrifice all. The worse half—that was the half that was taken. The ones willing to be slaves. Willing and ready to be slaves to the system.

DON WOKE with renewed conviction that he had made the right choice. Now he saw clearly where his old path led. After seven grueling years of giving everything to Desmond's idea of medicine, Don was embarking on a new journey. Here he was in a new apartment in Florence, New Hampshire, of all places! For the first time in a very long time he was excited about his future. Dr. Sampson's health systems seminar would start in a week. This time, Don didn't have the admiring support he had enjoyed when he announced his plans to go to medical school or pursue cardiology. He wasn't sure how he would pay his bills. But he was headed somewhere he needed to go.

Don looked around at his apartment and smiled to himself. All my colleagues think I'm crazy. Well, all except Sarah. And so what if they're right? I might still be in hell, but I am no longer alone.

4

Great Scientists Who Couldn't Cure

The good Master said to me: "Do you not ask what spirits are these you see?
I would have you know that...they did not sin; but though they have merits
it is not enough, for they [are]...without hope."
DANTE ALIGHIERI, INFERNO 4, 31–42

HE NOTICED HER the moment he entered the room. How could he not? Long, lithe legs emerging from a short skirt, bountiful wavy blond hair, that knockout figure—his visual cortex traced and recorded the graceful lines of her toned body.

She assessed him in turn with a steady gaze from her intense green eyes, reminding Don of the direct look a top linebacker gives the running back on the other team just before taking him down. Her direct catlike gaze made him draw an unconscious breath, as if to prepare for the hit. She wore a hint of a smile but her inquisitive look was too direct for a woman, he thought, and those eyes threatened to devour him just like one more piece of new information.

He had to look away. It would be days before he learned to steel himself to meet her stare. For now, Don just said hello to her while daring a second reflexive glimpse, nodded at the guy in the oxford shirt, and joined them at the old square table in the middle of the small classroom.

The little space above Florence College's anatomy theater had been hard to find. Fortunately, Don had set out early. After wandering around the old medical school building for at least ten minutes, he spotted a security guard wearing a dark green uniform and a massive key ring on his belt.

"Excuse me?" Don called.

The guard turned and gave Don an inscrutable look. The whites of his eyes stood out in striking contrast to the blackest face Don had ever seen. Deep valleys of concern separated the broad ridges in his forehead, curved over his heavy brows, and plunged down to join the deep creases lining the downturned corners of his broad mouth.

"Uh...can you tell me where to find the amphitheater? Dr. Sampson's seminar?"

The corners of the guard's mouth flattened in amusement. He motioned for Don to follow and led him through the fire door in the back of the first floor stairwell, down worn brick stairs into cool air suffused with odors of mold and formaldehyde, and through a maze of dank halls lined with dusty display cabinets and deserted classrooms and labs.

"Nowadays, most of the courses are taught in the new anatomy building down the way," the guard explained. "The labs over there are outfitted with the latest video-assisted technology. They haven't figured out what to do with this old building yet."

He opened a door at the end of an empty hall and pointed the way up some steep stairs that led between the rows of wooden seats in the antique amphitheater up to a door in the back wall. Don climbed the steps, opened the door, and was relieved to arrive in time to claim a seat. The table was only big enough for eight people.

The three of them waited in silence for everyone else to arrive. Trying hard to look nonchalant and not stare at the gorgeous woman seated next to him, Don studied his dim reflection in the golden patina of the old table.

The wood was oak but the grain was finer than any he had ever seen. The tree must have been ancient, grown in difficult conditions. The wooden slab was too large to be one piece but the planks were so seamlessly matched the joints were invisible. Students had gathered around this table after dissections and surgical demonstrations for years. Numerous gouges marring its glossy surface had been rubbed smooth by thousands of books and elbows.

"Good morning, everyone," Dr. Sampson greeted the three students as he entered the small room.

He wore a blue polyester shirt with military-style collar, rolled-up sleeves, and a dark tie with no blazer. He deposited a stack of books on the table, pulled an unoccupied chair forward to the fourth side, sat down, and leaned forward on his hairy arms. Belying his age, his arms were as muscled as a football player's.

"Here we meet around this old tabula rasa for the first of our weekly seminars, he said. "Let's begin."

Don glanced at his watch. Wasn't anyone else coming? There were just three people in the class? He had heard the health system science program at Florence College was small and used an Oxford-style tutorial method for graduate students, but this seemed ridiculous. All his other classes in the school of public health had fifteen to twenty people. Why weren't more students from the biostatistics and epidemiology courses here?

"Our seminar is small because our work is intense," Dr. Sampson answered his silent question. "You are here because you are the best of the best in your fields in nursing, medicine, and surgery," he nodded to each student in turn as he recognized their specialties, "and because you want to help change the system. Don't disappoint me."

Don's gut tightened with apprehension.

Dr. Sampson's face softened, allowing the barest hint of a smile. "We will work closely together over the months ahead," he said, "so why don't each of you begin by telling us your name, where you trained, why you are here, and… how about the name of your favorite pet, or your favorite animal?"

Dr. Sampson was famous for getting right down to business, and this caught them all by surprise.

"Okay, Dr. Newman, you first," he ordered.

Don ran his forefinger over the small knot near the bridge of his nose—a childhood injury. "Okay, well, I'm Don Newman. I went to Sewanee—The University of the South—for undergrad and then medical school at the Pritzker School of Medicine at the University of Chicago. I just finished my residency in internal medicine at the University Hospital in Boston. As to why I entered this program, I'm still figuring that out. It seems like the world is conspiring against me to try to lower my starting salary."

Everyone laughed.

"And my favorite pet was a dog," Don concluded, "a Spitz named Steppenwolf. Wolf for short."

"Thank you," Dr. Sampson said. "Ms. Hunt?"

"I was in Boston, too," she said, flashing Don a warm smile. "I'm Frances Hunt. I graduated from Radcliffe College of Harvard, and after that I trained back home in California as an acute care nurse practitioner with a secondary focus in health policy. I am here to learn the business of medicine because I believe that working through the business sector is the best way to really impact health policy in a significant way. I'm going for a combination MBA/MPH degree. Oh, yes, and I have a cat named Cleopatra—a beautiful Bengal with leopard spots."

"That's interesting," said the guy in the oxford shirt. He looked straight at Frances. "I had a cat once, but it didn't have a name."

"Go ahead, Dr. Markum. Tell us about yourself," Dr. Sampson said.

"I'm Bruce Markum." He looked at the others over a bridge he formed with his well-manicured fingers. "I went to Yale, like my father and grandfather, but I majored in biochemistry. I went to Vanderbilt for medical school and stayed there for a residency in general surgery and a fellowship in thoracic. After that I joined the faculty at Duke, where I have been for the past three years. Now I'm moving toward administration or something in health policy. Oh, and I'm with Frances here. I admire cats, especially the big ones that lie under the trees and let the females do the hunting."

Frances gave Bruce the same unwavering Mona Lisa stare-down she had given Don, but Bruce met her gaze, held it, and returned his own wry smile.

"I can see this is going to be an interesting class," Dr. Sampson said.

Don considered Bruce's comment inappropriate but could hardly blame him for flirting with Frances. This woman—with her golden hair cascading down to frame a sun-kissed oval face and sensuous almond-shaped green eyes—was irresistible. Like Helen of Troy, she could probably change the course of history if she wanted to. And she'd made it clear she wanted to.

But what was Bruce doing here? Why would a surgeon—particularly one who had been on the faculty at Duke—sign up for this program? With his impressive credentials he could go almost anywhere and make big money, and with all that expensive private education he probably had big student loans to pay.

"All of you are here because you know there are big problems in American medicine," Dr. Sampson began. "In this seminar we will study where, how, and why money is spent in American healthcare. Is it spent for *health care*, or is it spent on an outmoded *healthcare* machine that is spinning out of control? We will cut through the political rhetoric and discover why healthcare costs so much more here than anywhere else in the world.

"This is how our seminar will work. You got the syllabus from the bookstore, right? Read the assigned readings carefully before each seminar; they will guide us on our journey. In this seminar you must support your opinions with hard evidence. Not all studies are created equal, and it is not easy to distinguish the good from the bad. Determining which studies are trustworthy and which are biased requires discernment. The sources in your syllabus provide the best evidence available. If you want a firm understanding of how American healthcare works, study them. To keep this class focused on how the material relates to the real world, we will begin each seminar with a related case, preferably from your own experience. Your case studies are very important. They will help us examine how health systems affect people's lives. Ms. Hunt, will you present the first case next week? It can be brief, five or ten minutes."

"Sure, Dr. Sampson, I'd be glad to."

"Thank you. Finally, a warning. This year we focus on the worst failings in American healthcare and where our system has gone wrong. Next year we move on to solutions and the healthcare heroes who are trying to set things right. But we start with the evils of the system. We must understand problems before we can fix them.

"*Do not* take this to mean that I think American medicine is all bad, or that all doctors and nurses are villains. To the contrary, healthcare workers today struggle to heal in a dysfunctional system—a system designed to serve causes other than human health. Doctors and patients are both victims of this dysfunctional system. Until we meet the victims, hear their stories, and understand the system's impact on their lives, we can offer them little hope for healing.

"Today, I'll review the history of medicine, but don't get used to me doing most of the talking. Let me emphasize: this seminar will not be like most of your past training experiences. Feel free to express your thoughts and ask any questions that occur to you. But please understand that for this process to be worthwhile, it is critical we have accurate data and facts close at hand. What you learn here depends on your contributions. So, study your readings!"

Sampson paused to appraise each student once more. Just before the pause became truly uncomfortable, he barged ahead with his lecture.

"LET ME BEGIN by telling a story. I'll start at the very beginning. During the first ninety thousand years of human history, people lived in the forest—a wild garden where the greatest dangers to health were injury and childbirth. They walked and ran for miles each day to gather wild vegetables, grains, nuts, and fruits. They tracked and hunted wild animals through the forests and fields and ate their lean meat.

"Because there were no cities then, no clustering of people and domestic animals in tight quarters, the infectious diseases we know today did not exist. Because dietary fat and refined sugars were extremely rare, everyone had very low cholesterol. Hardening of the arteries—which causes strokes, heart attacks, and the majority of premature deaths in the United States today—was unknown. Cancer was far less common in the absence of smoking, obesity, and the toxins found in animal fat and compounds used to cure meats. In this Eden, modern diseases were virtually unknown.

"The first city appeared about ten thousand years ago. In Plato's *Republic*, Socrates hypothesizes the city was born of human need, first and foremost the need for food. Anthropologists and archeologists agree that the first city formed when the forest could no longer provide enough food for the growing population. Agricultural society developed to increase the yields of the land.

"Socrates suggests this first city was healthy in the beginning. It was a small city surrounded by fertile, well-drained lands. There were no palaces; people still lived close to nature. Disease was rare. Healers were holy men and women who focused on wholeness and helped people order themselves properly in relation to the environment. Their main tools were diet, exercise, prayer, meditation, herbal teas, and salves. These ancient physicians of the healthy city saw their role as supporting the life force that heals naturally. With little infectious disease, cardiovascular disease, or cancer, a man who survived childhood might indeed live to be well over one hundred.

"But soon after its genesis, that first healthy city became ill. Socrates says the first city became feverish when people, wanting more than simple subsistence, began to desire luxury. Farming, herding, and division of labor developed as humans learned to coax more from the earth than it naturally provided. Modern scholars agree that sickness began to flourish along with this rise of agricultural society.

"Agriculture and population growth led to the cultivation of flat and swampy lands, which in turn led to the common occurrence of the mud puddle, an unnatural condition in the forest. Mud puddles provided perfect breeding grounds for malaria-carrying mosquitoes. The pattern persists today, making malaria the number one killer in the world. The cereal-heavy diet of the agricultural age made nutritional deficiencies common for the first time and compounded the mortality from many infectious diseases that arose over the ensuing ten thousand years.

"As the hunger for luxuries continued to feed the growth of cities, masters took slaves or servants to meet their ever-expanding appetites. Cities added coliseums, operas, brothels, delicacies, art, and everything else imaginable. Green hills were overgrazed, wars flared over competition for water and farmland, and backs were bent by the toil of carrying rocks to build castles and fortresses for the victors.

"Humans crowded together in cities with chickens, ducks, horses, and pigs, inadvertently cultivating the worst infectious diseases that have ever afflicted mankind. Living with cattle gave humans tuberculosis, small pox, and the other viral poxes; horses spread the common cold and measles, which still kills one million people worldwide every year; cattle, dogs, cats, ducks, chickens, and rats spread bacteria like salmonella and viruses that cause deadly childhood diarrhea, typhoid fever, polio, cholera, and hepatitis; and pigs, ducks, and birds gave us deadly influenza. Human waste in the fields, streets, and water gave us worms, flukes, and other parasites.

"Sex in the city was different than in the forest. With crowding, people had more partners and poor women sold sex to survive. Sexually transmitted diseases followed merchants and traders from city to city and from port to port. Soon after 1492, syphilis arrived from the New World and spread across Europe, as Renaissance palaces celebrated sex and fraternization among humans and animals. Paintings, statues, and stories depicted orgies with half-human centaurs and Satan disguised as a horny goat reveling with party guests. Priests proclaimed that sexual diseases signaled the wrath of God—the rotting nose cartilage caused by syphilis was considered a visible sign of sin.

"Cities became deathtraps. For most of the last five thousand years, cities were cesspools crammed full of humans and animals living together in their own filth. Before the advent of adequate sanitation, excrement was everywhere, providing the perfect culture media for dangerous microorganisms. From the Middle Ages up to the last century, cities continued to grow in population only through immigration from rural areas. The fertility of a city could not keep pace with its death rate. Throughout time, almost every one of these feverish cities has devoured many more people than it created.

"Medicine came to the fore in these urban deathtraps. Sickness doctors appeared—physicians and barber-surgeons. Horrible diseases were thought to require horrible cures: mercury and arsenic for syphilis, cautery for wounds, bleeding for fever. Surgery was only performed in desperate circumstances—as during the wars that invariably accompanied the accumulation of wealth in cities—because almost half the patients died of post-op infections.

"Here in the center of the feverish city I would like to introduce you to medicine's greatest heroes of old." Dr. Sampson looked straight at Don. "The famous writer of *The Divine Comedy*, Dante Alighieri, called them 'the masters of those that know.'"

Dammit! He knows my given name? Don prayed he would keep it to himself.

"A great secret has been hidden from you and all Americans. The secret is this: that the wisest doctors of the last five thousand years saw little hope for healing at the end of the day. Although our most heroic physician-scientists discovered how to diagnose illness, they were unable to cure. Even today, the promise of their science remains largely unfulfilled. The many marvels of modern medical technology still cannot cure most of the ills of the feverish city."

Bruce raised his hand. "Excuse me, Dr. Sampson, I understand the part about the healthy Garden of Eden where our ancestors lived, and I can buy your interpretation of how modern illnesses came on stage in the last ten thousand years because of agriculture and urbanization. But come on. Modern medicine's secret inability to cure? Do you really believe that?"

Don knew Bruce had been a faculty member, but he was taken aback by the tone of the question. Even though Dr. Sampson had encouraged them to participate and ask questions, to Don he sounded disrespectful.

Dr. Sampson appeared unfazed. "I know this is a lot to take in, but bear with me while I delve further into the history of modern medicine. Consider the great teachers, the most brilliant fathers of modern scientific medicine: Hippocrates, Aristotle, Galen, and Ibn Sina. They gave a little light to the feverish city, but study their teachings carefully and you will find them skeptical regarding the potential for their scientific medicine to cure."

Bruce raised his eyebrows but listened while Dr. Sampson continued.

"Now, who do you think was the most influential of these sickness doctors of ancient times?"

"Hippocrates," Bruce responded.

"Indeed. Medical students have read the works of Hippocrates of ancient Greece—and the great Roman physician, Galen—for over two thousand years. Hippocrates and Galen were considered the most authoritative guides to therapy right up through most of the 1800s. Hippocrates—best known for his oath that admonishes physicians to *at least do no harm*—is justly regarded as the father of modern medicine. But remember, the main therapies Hippocrates recommended were bleeding, purging with laxatives, and a nutrient-deficient meat and cereal diet. These treatments were followed for centuries, but we now know they were mostly ineffective and frequently did harm.

"Over time, medical scientists shifted their attention away from therapy to focus on the underlying causes of disease. This shift gave rise to both triumph and hopelessness, because even though the *masters of those that know* advanced the knowledge of cause, they did not discover how to cure. They lacked—and still largely lack today—the science of application. For the last twenty-five centuries growth in medical knowledge has mostly focused on the scientific method and the subjects of anatomy, physiology, and microbiology. Physician-scientists have found it extremely difficult to translate discoveries into effective cures for common diseases. In fact, the greatest discoveries have contributed almost nothing to the ability of doctors to save lives."

What? Twenty-five hundred years and doctors hadn't learned *anything* about how to cure? Don found this unbelievable. He glanced at the other two students to gauge their reactions. Bruce had leaned back in his chair, folded his arms across his chest, and was shaking his head slowly back and forth; Frances had her head down, taking copious notes and indiscriminately devouring each new piece of information.

"Let me explain. Take Aristotle, who pioneered the scientific method and championed science based on careful observation. His anatomical descriptions of animals were fundamental medical school material until the late 1700s. Aristotle apprenticed as a physician in his youth but discovered no medical cures. Ironically, his work was a barrier to investigation in the Middle Ages and Renaissance because scientists honored his work so much no one wanted to challenge it.

"Galen's animal dissections and observations as a war surgeon markedly expanded our knowledge of anatomy but did not add significantly to our ability to cure. The Persian physician Ibn Sina studied Hippocrates, Aristotle, and Galen and markedly expanded on their observations of physiology, pathology, and hygiene. His *Canon of Medicine* and *Book of Healing* were standard medical textbooks at most medieval universities, but even though he took the ability to diagnose disease from signs and symptoms to new heights, he added little to doctors' practical ability to heal the diseases they could now classify.

"The scientific method really took off at the great medical universities of Europe in the 1400s, when scientists rediscovered the works of the great ancient physicians and built upon their foundations. Artists like Leonardo da Vinci and Michelangelo snuck into church crypts to dissect, observe, and understand the structure and function of the human body. The scientists followed their lead.

Vesalius and his colleagues dissected corpses in the famous anatomical theater in Padua, the model for our anatomical theater here at Florence College, where we are sitting right now. Scientists traveled from all over Europe to attend the public dissections at the Paduan theater, where they peered inside bodies and hoped to discover the secrets of health and disease.

"Champions of medical science in Renaissance Italy made discoveries on a near-daily basis. Famous Paduans like Giambatista da Monte and Santorio Sanctorius provided physicians with scientific methods for diagnosing and naming diseases. We remember the names of Paduan scientists like Falloppia, Eustachio, and Bartholin because of the anatomic structures they discovered. Englishman William Harvey visited Padua and demonstrated that blood circulates through the body and is not created in the chambers of the human heart, as Galen and his students had thought. Physicians like Harvey used physiologic experimentation to advance the frontiers of knowledge.

"Fabulous discoveries, all. However, these bright lights of knowledge were surrounded by sickness and suffering. Epidemics and plagues ravaged Europe. The *masters of those that know* brought little light to the dark alleyways tracking through the feverish cities of Europe. They did little to change the common medical practices of their time, which were based on folk traditions and faith healing. They did nothing to significantly alter the treatment methods of bleeding, cupping, and purging. The great medical schools mostly produced professors and scholars, not healers—and few scholars at that—far short of the number needed to serve the population of Europe. So as you can see, most scientific medicine of the last twenty-five centuries has been about advancing knowledge, not health."

Was he kidding? Don was dumbfounded. Every biochemistry and biology course he had ever taken refuted this thinking. The treatment of disease has come a long way since the plagues of old Europe! Dr. Sampson was basically ignoring modern advancements and implying Don's hard labors over the past seven years were a waste. What had he gotten himself into with this program? He couldn't suppress his primal urge to refute Dr. Sampson's heretical interpretation.

"Wait, I have a question," Don interrupted. "What about the discovery of germs in the 1800s that gave us marvelous cures and saved millions of lives?"

"You are right, Dr. Newman, that the discovery of germs led to marvelous gains in knowledge, but until the last sixty years it added little to the ability of physicians to heal. There's a long, long road between discovery and practical application.

"Let's look a little deeper at the discovery of germs. In the early 1600s, while Galileo was examining the distant heavens with a telescopic lens, medical scientists were beginning to use microscopic lenses to look closely at structures within the human body and the infectious agents that contributed to sickness.

Malpighi in Pisa, Italy, discovered capillaries, the missing link in the blood circulatory system Harvey had searched for. By the late 1800s, great microbiologists like Pasteur and Robert Koch were identifying the causative agents of many of the worst infectious diseases.

"These scientists did contribute much to our understanding and to the eventual development of wonderful antibiotics and vaccines. Penicillin, the first commonly used antibiotic, was invented in the 1940s and became readily available in the U.S. in the 1950s. The vaccines for tetanus and pertussis—also known as whooping cough—became readily available in the 1940s, polio in the 1950s, and measles in the 1960s.

"However, all of the major killer infectious diseases—including cholera, typhoid fever, tetanus, whooping cough, and polio—were conquered before these vaccines and antibiotics came on the scene. Vaccines and antibiotics did almost nothing to contribute to the overall decline of infectious diseases in the world. What do you think did diminish these plagues of the last twenty-five hundred years?"

Frances tentatively raised her hand. Dr. Sampson nodded and she said, "Like, clean water?"

"Good Ms. Hunt! Exactly. What else?"

"Public health measures like chlorination, sewage systems, and decreased crowding?"

"Excellent!" he replied. "Improved sanitation—not antibiotics—conquered infectious diseases. The evidence is incontrovertible. Immunizations and medicines had little to do with conquering the vast majority of infectious diseases that tormented mankind through history."

Don held his hand halfway up. "So, you're saying the major benefit of the germ theory was not the development of curative antibiotics or vaccines, but an understanding of the importance of prevention? Things like clean water, latrines, safe sex, and handwashing?"

"Right, Dr. Newman. Even tuberculosis was largely conquered through public health measures by the time TB medications first became available in the 1950s.

"Now, since doctors couldn't cure until the last fifty to seventy-five years, what did they spend their time doing?" Dr. Sampson asked.

"Hold on, now!" Bruce interrupted again. "Maybe medicine doctors couldn't cure before then, but surgeons sure could."

"You have a point, Dr. Markum," Dr. Sampson admitted. "War surgeons learned to drain life-threatening abscesses and amputate limbs hundreds of years ago. They saved many a soldier who otherwise would have died. But the high mortality of major surgery meant you avoided it unless it was the only hope.

Only after routine antiseptic technique and anesthesia became available around 1900 did surgical mortality rates finally fall below fifty percent.

"Medicine, on the other hand, took longer to develop." Dr. Sampson pulled a tattered paperback from his stack of books and opened it at a bookmarked page. "The famous American physician Lewis Thomas makes Dr. Markum's same point. While Thomas was a medical student in the 1930s—before antibiotics—he carried a little book called *Useful Drugs*. Here's what he said about it:

> *I cannot recall any of our instructors ever referring to this volume. Nor do I remember much talk about treating disease at any time in the four years of medical school except by the surgeons...*
>
> *The medicine we were trained to practice was, essentially, Osler's medicine. Our task for the future was to be diagnoses and explanation. Explanation was the real business of medicine...the name of the illness, and...how it was likely to turn out.*

"When I started practicing medicine, I took Thomas's view. That's how we were trained. Diagnosis was the goal because we had less hope of healing than you do today. Now don't worry, Dr. Markum, we will return to surgery later on. For now, let's focus on the medicine doctors. Let me ask again. Since medicine doctors really couldn't cure, at least not until recently, what did they spend their time doing?"

"That's easy," Don answered, "diagnosis and testing. It's still where we spend most of our time."

Bruce laughed. "I'll agree with that! You medicine doctors never do anything except talk and order tests, and it just makes my day to hear one of you admit to it."

Typical surgeon bastard, Don thought.

"Well, admit it we must if we want to join the ranks of the best scientists of our time," Dr. Sampson said. "Dr. Newman and Dr. Markum, you are both correct to recognize medicine's preoccupation with diagnosis and testing rather than treatment. The greatest physician-scientists throughout history have readily acknowledged this insufficiency. Many have even expressed lack of confidence in the benefits of their own profession."

He flipped open another book. "Let me read just a few of their words. Matthew Baillee, who wrote the first great textbook of pathology in 1793 and was physician to King George III, said that despite the huge advances he and others had made in pathology,

I know better perhaps than another man, from my knowledge of anatomy, how to discover disease, but when I have done so, I don't know any better how to cure it.

"Oliver Wendell Holmes, the great Harvard medical professor and leading physician of the mid-1800s, said:

Throw out opium...throw out wine...and the vapors which produce the miracle of anaesthesia, and I firmly believe that if the whole material medica, as now used, could be sunk to the bottom of the sea, it would be all the better for mankind, and all the worse for the fishes, and the best proof of it, [is that] no families take so little medicine as those of doctors.

"Even Sir William Osler, perhaps the greatest bedside diagnostician of all time, admitted about scarlet fever that:

Medicines have little or no control over the duration or course of the disease, which...takes its own time to disappear.

"Osler's great *Principles and Practice of Medicine*, the first modern textbook of medicine, published in 1892, was a testament to medicine's inability to cure. It was, as our Porter reading tells us, *first and foremost a catalogue of disease*. Doctors, unable to cure, focused on diagnosis and classification, a trend that continues to this day. What does this mean for the average patient in the hospital?"

Bruce leaned back in his chair and folded his arms across his chest. "Like I said," he quipped, "I've been around enough internists to know the answer to that one. Testing. Lots of testing. All they do is testing. The rest of the time they spend waiting or talking. I've noticed that they do a lot of talking," he said, stealing a glance at his watch.

"You've hit the nail on the head, Dr. Markum," Dr. Sampson said, ignoring Bruce's supercilious attitude. "In the last one hundred years, more and more people have come to believe doctors and hospitals are the best way to health, and people are willing to pay for good health. Not surprisingly, the testing industry has taken off. About two billion diagnostic tests were done in 1971 in the United States. That number leapt to four and a half billion by 1976, and the numbers have continued to climb exponentially. We are up to over fifteen tests per year for every man, woman, and child in America. Does all this testing make us healthier? I think not. What are the wasteful and adverse effects of this diagnostic approach to medicine?"

"Well, the list goes on and on," Don answered. Useless tests were ordered day after day at the University Hospital—he hardly knew where to start. "For instance, most physicians run tests and cultures on the mucus coughed up by pneumonia patients, even though we no longer need this information to choose the best treatment."

Frances added, "According to the Sox study we read for today, almost all the components of the annual physical exam have little usefulness and often lead to more unnecessary testing."

"That's right," Don smiled at Frances. "Most people know that rectal exams are ineffective for colon cancer screening, but we do them all the time. And we do annual prostate blood tests even though they're unreliable. Thanks to false positive blood test results, one-third of men who get annual screening for ten years end up getting unnecessary biopsies with a large needle through the rectum. We order expensive blood chemistry panels on every visit, even though we have known for years that good history taking—you know, actually *talking* to the patient—is much better at detecting unsuspected disease. I could go on all day."

"I know you could," Dr. Sampson said. "You have seen how discovery-based science has led to discovery-based practice. Doctors often order tests even when the results won't change the treatment. Doctors and patients are fascinated and preoccupied with the rediscovery of disease, even after the cause is well established and the recommended treatment is clear. We neglect to apply best scientific treatments in a systematic, evidence-based manner."

Frances spoke up. "Okay, I get what you mean about the medical profession's inability to heal in the past. But all that has changed, right? Today we have medicines for diabetes, hypertension, cancer, and a hundred other diseases, right? New miracle drugs come along all the time now."

"Yes, Ms. Hunt," Dr. Sampson acknowledged. "In the last hundred years the sickness medicine industry has really taken off. The major event that kick-started it happened in 1910. In fact, this event continues to define medical education today."

"You mean the Flexner Report?" Frances said.

"Right. The Flexner Report radically reformed medical education, first in America and then worldwide. Who knows where it came from?"

Bruce spoke up, "Well, I did my reading. Abraham Flexner wrote it, and the Rockefellers funded it."

"True enough," Dr. Sampson responded, "and one Reverend Frederick T. Gates was a strong force behind them both. Gates was a noted Baptist preacher who advised John D. Rockefeller on how to do good works with his millions. He read Osler's *Principles* so he could better advise Rockefeller how to improve American healthcare. Gates was horrified to discover how few diseases were curable, so he convinced Rockefeller to pour his millions into curative medicine to help bring it up to snuff.

"Together they started the Rockefeller Institute of Medical Research. Rockefeller appointed Simon Flexner as director of laboratories and sponsored the efforts of Simon's brother, Abraham, to reform medical schools. In 1910, Abraham Flexner's famous report demanded that American universities invest in biochemical and laboratory sciences, and the Rockefeller Institute stood ready to help.

"After the Flexner report, medical schools devoted their resources to laboratories and finding cures. They discovered many treatments, but not nearly as many cures as the public has been led to believe. For example, despite billions upon billions of dollars invested in cancer research, cancer death rates have remained remarkably unchanged. Although we have learned to cure a few childhood and adult blood cell cancers using desperate cures that nearly kill people with powerful poisons, most cancers are far easier to prevent than they are to treat.

"Today, most disease and premature death is caused by one of two things. Both are preventable. First, the modern plague of metabolic syndrome caused by overweight and inactivity. Second, the noxious American weed, tobacco. If the great Hippocrates had one hope, it was not in the cures he resorted to in desperation. It was for a simpler life where health came from a wholesome environment and lifestyle, a philosophy he promoted in his most famous work, *Airs, Waters and Places*. His philosophy of healthy living is still the best prescription for health today.

"Diagnosis is no longer the issue. Almost everyone in America has some manifestation of the same deadly metabolic syndrome. We're largely free from the infectious diseases that plagued earlier peoples. Today, we suffer from a modern plague of our own making—a plague of plenty—resulting in obesity, diabetes, and cardiovascular disease.

"A person diagnosed with metabolic syndrome has a choice: either take up exercise and healthy living, or take five to ten pills a day in an attempt to counteract the multiple manifestations of this one disease. Most people choose pills in spite of the fact they're expensive, have side effects, and are less effective than a daily walking program. Our bloated pharmaceutical industry provides a medication for every symptom. Why do doctors prescribe pills they know have little benefit? Why not teach patients that living a balanced life is the best cure?

"Dr. A.E. Hertzler gave a great answer to this in his memoir, *The Horse and Buggy Doctor*, about medical practice at the turn of the last century. His answer still holds true today. He revealed the medical profession's dirty little secret. Here's how he described what he and his colleagues did when they went to see a patient:

Of course, one left some medicine...this was largely...bunk, but someone had to pay...and just plain advice was never productive of revenue unless fortified by a few pills.

"Pills are magic, and people want magic from their doctors. They want hope. Pills have been the only hope modern science has had to offer, but that hope has been a lie!"

Dr. Sampson banged his fist on the table on the word "lie," making all three students jump. He took a deep breath through his nose and let it out in a loud exhale through his mouth.

"This is our topic for the rest of the year. I know you have many questions and frankly, I cannot answer them all. I can only promise that we will explore the depths of the lie, the false promise of modern medicine, and how far it has led us astray. Your readings will guide you, but ultimately you must answer the most important questions for yourselves."

With that startling pronouncement the class was over. Don's brain felt numb from trying to assimilate this barrage of new information that contradicted all his previous training.

As they walked out of the little room above the anatomy theater Bruce said in a loud stage whisper, "Is he a nutcase, or what?"

Don shrugged. He hoped Dr. Sampson hadn't heard Bruce's insult. What Dr. Sampson was saying did sound crazy, but down deep, Don had to admit a lot of it rang true and gave voice to doubts that had besieged him throughout his training.

Bruce Markum, on the other hand, made him uneasy. Don couldn't put his finger on what disturbed him about Bruce. It wasn't just the brash way he challenged Dr. Sampson—it was something more. Of course, Bruce had chosen this program—he deserved some credit for that. Don resolved to give Bruce the benefit of the doubt and not rush to judgment.

Little did Don know then what the coming year would reveal about Bruce Markum.

THAT NIGHT Don returned to his duplex and found a letter in his rusted tin mailbox along with the usual pizza coupons. The letter had no return address, but the neat, flowing, rounded script on the envelope immediately identified the sender as Sarah. He sprinted up the twelve worn steps to his apartment, sat at the kitchen table, carefully broke the seal, and unfolded three neatly penned pages.

Dear Don,

I trust all is going well with you at Florence College. The health system science program suits you and I'm sure that Dr. Sampson will lead you where you need to go.

Let me update you on Sybil Bellamy and my progress as a second-year resident. I didn't think I was ready to take charge of a team of interns and medical students—to stand in your shoes. But you prepared me well. You were the resident who showed me how to think for myself, how to avoid ordering every test available willy-nilly just in case the attending physician asked if his favorite test had been ordered. When I most needed guidance in my intern year, you showed me how to be a true healer. The habits and careful thinking you fostered in me will stick with me throughout my career. I hope I am as good a resident to my interns as you were to me. You showed me how to always follow what was best for the patient. I cannot thank you enough for that.

For Mrs. Bellamy things have not gone so well. You know, the last time she was admitted on your service I made a lot of progress with the daughter and we even sent her back to the nursing home with "do not resuscitate" orders. But she was readmitted in July, not long after you left, and Edward was the resident on call. Can you believe it? They've put Edward in charge of a team. And one of the new interns on his team told me that when Mrs. Bellamy came in a month ago with another pneumonia Edward pointedly asked the daughter: "Do you want us to do everything for your mother? You want us to do everything, don't you?" Of course, every loving family wants everything done for their loved one that will truly help. But as you know, families don't understand that "everything" means <u>everything</u>, whether it will help or not.

Pretty soon Mrs. Sybil was carted off to the ICU, sedated, strapped down, and kept on a breathing machine for three weeks. Somehow she made it off the vent and back to the nursing home, for a little while, anyway. So I'm sorry to say her suffering continues. I wish we could have done more for her.

Thank you again for being my best teacher. Working with you made a tough intern year bearable.

Sincerely, Sarah

Best teacher? Don was flattered but considered himself unworthy of her high praise. With a student like Sarah, no teacher could look bad. Sarah had taught him at least as much as he had taught her, maybe more. Sure, he had imparted medical knowledge and practical skills, but Sarah possessed an innate gift, an instinct for healing. She was a natural healer and that could never be taught. Edward would never have it. Sarah really wanted her patients to get well and if there was a way to make a person whole she would find it. Her steady kindness in the midst of disease, suffering, and death astounded Don.

We were a good team. Don smiled to himself and wondered if Sarah had ever considered him as more than just a friend. The possibility had not occurred to him before. Not that it would have changed anything. They had both been too duty-bound to even think of romance. Relationships between residents and interns were strongly discouraged, and with good reason. You couldn't afford to have your judgment clouded. That's when mistakes happen.

They weren't working together now, but it was too late. They were a hundred miles apart and both of them were working as hard as ever.

5

The Beauty Industry

The hellish storm, never resting,
seizes and drives the spirits before it;
smiting and whirling them about, it torments them...
who subject reason to desire.

DANTE ALIGHIERI, INFERNO 5, 31–39

DR. SAMPSON WALKED into the small seminar room where the students waited around the old table. He took a seat and wasted no time in getting started.

"Today we discuss the beauty industry and how it relates to health and healthcare," he said. "Ms. Hunt, are you ready to begin?"

She certainly looked ready. She wore a gray pinstriped pantsuit tailored to fit her trim figure, and her notes were arrayed before her.

"Yes, Dr. Sampson."

Frances ran an index finger over the crest of one ear, tracing a delicate line through the downy hairs on the side of her neck and curling over her collarbone in a beckoning motion. This practiced gesture from teenage years was now a subconscious nervous habit.

"I hesitated to present this case because it is the story of a friend, but Dr. Sampson said a detailed personal story would be best, so here it is." Francis took a deep breath and launched into her presentation.

"Susie and I grew up together in central California. Everybody liked her. She was fun to be with and a way cool artist. Her notebooks were covered with sketches of models dressed in fabulous clothes, and she wore gorgeous jewelry and handbags she made herself. In junior high we spent a lot of time together—talking about boys, reading teen magazines, and painting our fingernails.

"Like all teenage girls we obsessed about our figures, and in ninth grade we went on the South Beach Diet together. We joked it was named for us, because we hung out at the beach and worked on our tans every chance we got. Susie always had more trouble with her weight than I did. She went back and forth between pizza and Cokes and wanting to go on another diet.

"After ninth grade Susie was zoned to a different high school. We lost touch and didn't see each other for a long time, but one day during senior year I ran into her at the mall. She looked terrible. Her face was puffy and she looked bloated all over. She had definitely put on weight—I felt really bad for her. She was so cute in junior high, even though she was a little plump even then.

"Well, apparently we had gone in really different directions. While I had been getting into vegetarian food, yoga, and aerobics, she had continued her yo-yo dieting. Her breath smelled horrible—it had this funky metallic odor. I was curious so I asked her, 'what diet are you on now? South Beach, I hope?'

"She said, 'No, I'm doing the Cambridge Diet. It's really great. You just buy the powder and mix it with water. Three liquid meals a day and you get all the vitamins and minerals you need. It's so easy and you don't have to cook anything! You can even make slushes with it in the blender—the ice fills you up and doesn't have any calories.'

"I asked her how long she had been on it and she said, 'I've been on it a month and I've already lost ten pounds. But I'm just getting started.'

"I tried to convince her to think about natural food and invited her to take aerobics with me, but she really didn't get it. I think I made her feel bad. We got together a few times after that during college breaks. She kept trying new diets and her weight went up and down. I never knew what she would look like the next time I saw her."

Bruce interrupted. "Do you think she was bulemic?"

"Well, I guess she could have been," Frances said. "Sometimes when she gorged on junk food she would joke about throwing it up, but I never saw or heard her do it.

"Anyway, right after college she met Mr. Right. Chuck was working as a male model, and Susie was finishing her degree in fashion design. They met window-shopping on Rodeo Drive in Beverly Hills. Susie said they saw each other's reflections in the glass storefront of Versace and were both instantly enchanted. He was the man of her dreams, and they got engaged after just three months. She asked me to be in her wedding.

"Susie wanted to look perfect for Chuck, so for her wedding present to him she decided to get liposuction. 'I just want to look perfect for this one day of my life,' she told me. I totally understood and didn't try to talk her out of it. Really, at the time I thought it was no big deal. I wish I had tried to stop her.

"She went to a popular plastic surgeon in Beverly Hills and had the liposuction a few months before the wedding date. The surgeon worked on a bunch of places around her hips, legs, and stomach, and everything went well the morning of the surgery. Chuck drove her home from the outpatient surgery center at noon and Susie crashed on the couch at her apartment.

"Chuck checked on her after work and she seemed fine, but early the next morning he stopped by on his way back to work and found her dead in the bathroom. Apparently, a huge blood clot had formed in her leg, broken off, and blocked the path from her heart to her lungs. She was supposed to wear some kind of support hose on her legs all day and night, but…but she had taken them off." Frances pursed her lips and looked down at the table.

Her obvious sorrow drew Don like a magnet. He imagined reaching out and touching her trembling shoulder to give her comfort.

Frances steeled herself. She tossed her golden tresses over her right shoulder and continued her story.

"I flipped out when I heard. I was screaming and crying. Susie's family was devastated. Her father was a well-known general surgeon, but she did the lipo on an installment plan without telling her parents. Her dad was furious and wanted to sue, but since blood clots are a well-known risk of liposuction and Susie was over twenty-one, the lawyers said there wasn't much of a case. Her mother had a serious nervous breakdown. It was horrible for Chuck, I'm sure, but after the funeral I never saw him again."

Frances took a deep breath. "For me, even though we had been out of touch, she was totally my best friend in junior high. Even if she was a little nutty." Francis laughed and her eyes brimmed with tears. "She was only twenty-three. I should have tried to stop her. I still can't believe she's gone."

Don swallowed hard, feeling a familiar lump in his throat. His mother had died of a blood clot only one year before. He gave Frances an empathetic look.

"Thank you for sharing your story, Ms. Hunt," Dr. Sampson said softly. It's exactly the kind of example we need to discuss. Now, before we move on to consider this case in light of our readings, are there any questions?" Dr. Sampson looked at Bruce and Don.

"Wow, it's got to be pretty unusual for that to happen to someone so young," Bruce said. "How common are blood clots after liposuction?"

"Not very," Frances responded. "It's hard to find data on the side effects of liposuction, but because it rips so much tissue under the skin and that tissue gets into the bloodstream, liposuction encourages your body to make clots. Best estimates are that clots happen in about one percent of liposuction surgeries, and one in a hundred of those clots are fatal or near-fatal."

"But she probably had some other risk factor that would make her more likely to clot," Bruce persisted.

"Well, she was on birth control pills and was a closet smoker," Frances said. "She knew that combination increased her risk of a clot, but she didn't tell the doctor because she was afraid he wouldn't do the surgery." Frances took a deep breath and blinked away tears.

"That must have been awful to lose your friend," Don said. "I'm sorry."

"Thanks." Frances looked at him gratefully.

"I think this is a good point to turn to our reading," Dr. Sampson said. "First, let's consider whether liposuction qualifies as healthcare. Can liposuction contribute to health?"

"Well," said Bruce, "it's not necessary for health, unlike reconstructive surgery after breast cancer or burns. The doctors that do liposuction, nose jobs, and boobs? They're in a different kind of business altogether. I wouldn't even say they are doctors, at least not real doctors. Maybe we should call them 'plastic doctors' because they look like doctors and talk like doctors, but God forbid they ever take care of sick people. They are more concerned with appearance than health."

"Whatever," Frances countered. "Lots of people have plastic surgery that helps them feel attractive and good about themselves. Isn't that important for health?"

"Ms. Hunt, do you have any idea how many Americans have plastic surgery?" Dr. Sampson asked.

"The numbers have skyrocketed. From what I read, American women undergo around eight million cosmetic surgeries every year, and almost one in ten have had some kind of plastic surgery. In Brazil and Australia, almost half the women have breast augmentation."

"I read the number of kids having plastic surgery is growing fastest of all," Don said. "Over three hundred thousand U.S. teenagers had it last year. Some say it builds self-esteem, but I think just the opposite—they buy into all the marketing of sex and perfect bodies and think they aren't worth much unless they look like the people on magazine covers."

"As if you guys had a clue!" Frances fired back. "There is immense pressure on women to look perfect. Surveys show the majority of American women and girls think about their bodies every day, are unhappy with their bodies, and would consider plastic surgery in spite of the dangers. Like Susie."

Frances looked like she was about to cry, but much to Don's relief she held back the tears and kept talking.

"Let me tell you something," she said. "None of you men could possibly know what it's like for a woman to be teased for being fat, or skinny, or flat chested—to be treated as some kind of non-being solely because of your appearance. You have no idea."

For a moment the men were silent, unsure how to respond. Frances's openness that day would set the stage for honesty and openness in all their seminar discussions to come. But this time, only Bruce, like a true southern gentleman, knew how to restart the stalled conversation.

"You know, Frances, you're right," he said. "I think men can never fully understand the pressure women face in our society, just like whites have a hard time understanding what it's like to be black."

And then he blew it.

"You know," he rambled on, "maybe all this pressure women are facing has something to do with the epidemic of obesity. From an evolutionary perspective, a woman's survival depends on her ability to attract a male to protect her and her offspring. Women attract males by looking healthy and fertile," he said, directing a not-so-subtle smile at Frances. "Maybe the fact that so many women are overweight is the real problem. There's a good reason liposuction is the most popular operation for plastic doctors."

What a chauvinist pig! Don had a sudden urge to stand up for Frances. "It's not as simple as that," he countered. "Remember those old Rubens paintings? Back then heavy women were most fertile and big was sexy. I think it has more to do with the image of beauty portrayed by the media. You're right that everyone wants to be attractive to others, but we're barraged by images of thin, buxom women. If there is a culprit here, it's the media."

"Undoubtedly, media messages focusing on physical attractiveness and promoting sex influence children and adults," Dr. Sampson concurred. "I think we can agree these messages promote the appearance of health rather than actual health. Let's enumerate a few more adverse health consequences of pursuing what Naomi Wolf calls *the beauty myth*."

"Teenagers get hit way hard by the obsession to have a perfect body," Frances said. "Anorexia and bulimia affect over one million girls and women in the United States alone. Each year, one hundred and fifty thousand die of anorexia. It seems like these days eating disorders are the norm."

"And the way girls are subsisting on diet drinks is causing an epidemic of weak bones," Don added. "Phosphorous-rich soft drinks replace milk in their diets and leach calcium out of their bones. They will have curved collapsing spines and broken hips in their fifties."

"What about tanning?" Bruce stole a glance at Frances's smooth golden skin. "You know about tanning beds, don't you Frances? I mean, we've all seen women with leathered skin and cancers from sunbathing and tanning salons. Aren't they another example of the dangers of this beauty quest?"

"It's time you men stopped talking about women and looked at yourselves," Frances said. "Ever heard of a woman dying from a Viagra overdose? That's about the same, isn't it? Aren't men foolish when they risk heart attacks and sudden death for erections? And men are the ones totally fascinated with pornography. That leads them into all kinds of unhealthy relationships. It's men that go looking for prostitutes and do most of the spreading of sexual diseases like AIDS. So don't talk to me about tanning salons."

"I would go further than that," Don said, unable to resist the urge to take her side. "Male obsession with pornography leads to violence against women. Men want to possess women the way they possess cars, video games, and TVs. This attitude leads to domestic violence and sexual abuse, which are all about power and control."

"We all like to be in control," Bruce added with a wry smile, "but what you don't realize, Don, is that many women are on the prowl as well—women who would be happy to have you as a personal possession. You better watch out," he laughed.

"I'm talking about violence, Bruce, not courting."

"*Courting*? What generation are you from, Don?" Bruce was really laughing now.

His condescension spurred Don on. "Oh, get real. Everybody knows that America's prosperity has led to this 'me generation.' People don't depend on one another like they used to. We're used to getting what we want and getting it now. We don't lack food, shelter, or clothing. Most of us can get what we need on our own. It really isn't that hard to be financially independent in the land of opportunity, and we carry that independence to relationships too. It's made us selfish."

Frances nodded her head in agreement.

"We started out talking about the beauty industry," Dr. Sampson said, steering them back to the day's topic. "It's interesting to note the first nose job in the western world was done by a Dr. Tagliacozzi in Bologna in 1597 to correct the disfiguring rotting nose cartilage caused by untreated syphilis. Nose reconstruction was going on as early as 600 B.C. in India, where surgeons operated on people who had their noses cut off as punishment for adultery. To make the punishment fit the crime, you see; they were caught sticking their noses into other people's business."

Bruce chuckled.

"People have long sought an elixir for eternal youth, and that search has often gotten them into trouble. In recent years, women became convinced they could extend their youth by overcoming the natural process of menopause. How wonderful to live in an age when a simple pill could eliminate hot flashes and keep skin supple, membranes moist, and hair luxuriant. Unfortunately, like many elixirs of the past, hormone replacement therapy proved deadly for many women because it encouraged blood clots and heart attacks.

"People inject their faces with a paralyzing poison made from the deadly botulism toxin—to get rid of wrinkles. There are parties where doctors inject many people at a time, and many general practitioners offer botox injections in their offices to raise more income. Is this about promoting health? I think not. People all over America are walking around with their faces partly paralyzed, and a few end up with permanent double vision.

"So you can see, the quest for eternal youth often focuses on appearance. Superficial beauty doesn't lead to true health, yet this is where many Americans look for health today. So, what is health? Was anyone able to find a definition in our readings for today?"

They all shook their heads. Don had struggled through the relentless discussions of this in the readings, but the authors never offered firm conclusions on the subject.

Dr. Sampson waited.

Frances spoke up. "What about Katherine Mansfield's last journal entry when she was dying of tuberculosis?"

Dr. Sampson beamed at Frances. "Ms. Hunt, you have just hit on the best definition of health I've ever found. People say you can trust a person's last words. Go ahead, read it for us."

Frances thumbed to the back of her book and read:

> By health, I mean the power to live a full adult, living, breathing life in close contact with what I love—the earth and the wonders thereof—the sea—the sun...I want to be all that I am capable of becoming so that I may be...there's only one phrase that will do—a child of the sun.

"A child of the sun," Dr. Sampson repeated. "Asklepios, the ancient Greek god of healing, was represented as a rooster. The rooster begins every morning with a vocal prayer to the sun. When ancient physicians dedicated their lives to Asklepios, they pledged to promote growth, true life, and health. The ancient Greek name 'physician' means 'growth promoter,' from 'phusis,' the Greek word for growth. A physician stimulates growth toward the light, toward what is good and healthy.

"In light of that definition, is a plastic doctor a physician? Does he stimulate growth toward the sun? Certainly, a plastic surgeon promotes life and growth through reconstructive surgery. But the doctor who focuses on a superficial image of health that will pass away quickly is more aesthetician than physician. It is our task for the weeks ahead to see how far our system goes astray in reaching toward its proper goal."

Class ended and the three students walked out together, Frances in the middle.

"You did a great job today, Frances," Don said. "It must have been hard talking about your friend."

"Thanks, Don," she replied, flashing him a sweet smile. "Yeah, I guess it was."

Something in her expression reminded Don of the come-hither look of his old girlfriend Jessica.

"Yeah, great job, Frances." Bruce leaned closer to her. "You must be wiped out. Let me buy you a drink, and some lunch."

"Okay, uh, I guess so." She glanced at Don.

"Oh yeah, you come too, Don," Bruce added.

"I can't. I have to get ready for my epidemiology presentation in one hour."
Damn. Why did I put that off until the last minute?

Bruce smiled. "Oh, too bad. Frances and I will miss your company."

In spite of his polite words, it was evident from the smug look on his face he was all too happy to have Frances to himself.

Frances looked back and flashed Don an apologetic smile. Her obvious disappointment reassured him that she, for one, would miss his company.

6

Institutionalized Gluttony

*They believe the greatest enemy of all is the man who tells the truth—
namely that until one gives up drinking, stuffing oneself, sex and idleness,
there will be no help for one in drugs, burning or cutting.*

PLATO, REPUBLIC, BOOK IV, 426A

THE THREE STUDENTS sat on the hard wooden seats in the third row of the old anatomy theater. The closely spaced rows of fixed folding chairs in the steep-sided theater had been designed in the early days of the medical school for viewing anatomical dissections, not for comfort. Don's shins jammed into the seatback in front of him and his long legs were nearly bent double.

Dr. Sampson climbed up the steep staircase behind them to the projection room, where they had met around the old table for the first two seminars. He stood in the doorway and spoke in a low and measured voice.

"First, we must remember where we are."

Without warning, he doused the lights in the windowless amphitheater, making it pitch-black like the depths of a cave. His voice rose and rumbled in cold waves through the underground chamber.

"Almost everyone in the world today is completely in the dark," he bellowed in a dramatic bass timbre.

"Oh, please. He's got to be joking," Bruce muttered under his breath.

"People have little idea about the real causes of suffering or where to find true healing. They fill their minds with false shadows of reality. Shows and commercials promote an artfully crafted fantasy world where cheeseburgers, cokes, and chips are natural foods for humans. Where heart attacks occur unexpectedly and mysteriously, due to some unknown genetic aberration. A world where the best hope for these random victims of coronary disease lies in gleaming marble hospitals with heroic doctors and nurses, lifesaving bypass surgery, and emergency angioplasty. Let me show you that dream world."

Dream world? Don knew that world; its promises had drawn him into medicine. He was going to be a new Dr. Joe Gannon. He was going to hold a human heart in his hands and massage it back to life. *Please don't spoil my dream!*

But Dr. Sampson's old Carousel slide projector came to life with a click and a whirr and the disillusionment began. Shadowy black and white images flickering on the wall showed the advertising world's version of America: a family

entranced by a mahogany-veneered television set—*click!*—Independence Day
picnic tables piled high with hamburgers, hot dogs, corn on the cob, potato salad,
pie, cake, brownies, cotton candy. Next, vivid color Kodachromes from television commercials: smiling people in grassy parks drinking Pepsi, Dr. Pepper,
Budweiser—*click!*—seven-year-olds singing and dancing with Ronald McDonald
and hamburger flowers in a magical land of Happy Meals and Coke—*click!*—a
family gathered around the dining room table, admiring a bucket of Kentucky
Fried Chicken—*click!*—delighted boys and girls doling out brightly colored chocolate candies from red and yellow M&M's spokescandy dispensers—*click!*—kids
playing with Woody and Buzz Toy Story action figures while munching Burger
King Kids Club Value Meals—*click!*—a dad presiding over the glowing coals
of a barbeque grill in his suburban back yard, turning lightly charred burgers
and Oscar Mayer Weiners—*click!*—smiling children snacking on Lays, Ruffles,
Cheetos, Fritos, and Doritos—none of them able to stop at one.

Dr. Sampson's voice, soothing now, narrated the slide show, "This is the
world in which we live comfortably, where we mindlessly follow well-traveled
ways to care for our health."

The magic lantern showed magnificent hospitals and surgery centers that
looked like vacation destinations: lush campus of verdant trees, green pastures,
still waters—*click!*—a father jogging along an asphalt trail through the manicured
hospital grounds, thanks to a lifesaving cardiac stent—*click!*—a family, reunited
after Mom's cancer treatment, bicycling down an open lane lined by graceful
trees—*click!*—an energetic senior couple power walking through a green park in
the reassuring shadow of an emergency cardiac care center.

Don found himself reminiscing about childhood picnics in Lincoln Park in
Chicago and walking along the edge of Lake Michigan with his mother while his
father worked in his lab at Loyola. Momma used to remind him about the time
he first saw the North Shore Cardiovascular Institute on one of those walks. The
building sat on a generous parcel of prime real estate, where a narrow strip of
sand separated neatly trimmed grass from the endless water of the lake. Three-
year-old Don was fascinated by the lake's reflection in the beautiful mirrored
glass building. As they admired the building from a hundred yards down the
beach, a well-tanned man in a white lab coat walked out the front doors.

"Is that my dad?" he'd asked.

"No dear," she'd replied, "that is a doctor."

Sampson's next images glorified that physician-savior: a well-dressed woman
smiling in gratitude at her handsome physician as they stroll together through a
marble hospital lobby just one day after her minimally invasive surgery for gallbladder disease—*click!*—a doctor standing before a modern temple of healing,
wearing a long white coat and an enigmatic smile and staring into the camera
lens, a silent Sphinx promising eternal youth.

Dr. Sampson switched the light back on. "Wake up!" he shouted.

Don turned around and squinted at Sampson's looming figure in the back of the room, shielding his eyes with his hand as he readjusted to the blinding light.

"That world is not real! That lifestyle doesn't lead to happiness! Watching cartoons lulls people into believing they are happy and healthy, when in fact they are sick and shackled to a prison floor. You have chosen another way. Come, look behind the curtain. Follow me!"

Don's stiff knees cracked as he stood up from the tiny seat. The three climbed the stairs and followed Dr. Sampson through the small door in the back of the theater and into the seminar room. A collection of photos was spread out on the old wooden table.

"Look for yourselves—the truth," Dr. Sampson announced. "Real pictures don't lie. Look carefully and compare the black and white photo of Times Square in 1895 and in 2000. What has changed?"

The buildings in Times Square were mostly unaltered, but the billboards had multiplied and grown to gigantic proportions. In the modern photo, whole sides of buildings featured the fantasy worlds of Coke and McDonalds, writ large on the world's most expensive advertising space. But the most interesting difference between the two photos was the crowd.

In the 1895 photo, people looked like sticks; almost every person was straight and thin. In stark contrast, most people in the 2000 photograph looked globular. To put it bluntly, they were fat. In the foreground of the recent photo was a mother with two boys of about ten and twelve. Layers of fat spilled over her waistband like thick folds of saltwater taffy. She appeared to weigh about four hundred pounds and the boys nearly two hundred apiece. One of the boys was eating a big hot dog and the other was holding what appeared to be a large deep-fried, sugar-glazed donut.

"The truth is plain to see," Dr. Sampson said. "In 1895 only three people in one hundred were overweight, and fewer than one in one hundred was obese or diabetic. Most people couldn't afford donuts and hot dogs and they spent their days doing hard, physical work. Today, over seventy people in one hundred have thick layers of fat because they sit all day and feed on high-calorie foods and sweet drinks. Is it any wonder that one in three Americans is obese and twice as likely to die an early death as someone of normal weight?

"Diabetes rates doubled over eleven times between 1895 and 2000. A disease that was almost unheard of now afflicts over one in ten people. Fewer than five cases in a hundred are type 1, the type caused by autoantibodies in children. More than ninety-five in a hundred are type 2, the adult type caused by overweight and obesity. People want to believe type 2 diabetes is not their fault, that some mysterious genetic aberration or faulty metabolism causes it. But the old country doctors were right when they nicknamed it 'sugar' or 'sweet' blood. It's simply what happens to blood sugar when people consume more calories than they burn.

"In ancient times the Catholic church called it gluttony. Gluttony was associated with greed and hoarding and was considered a diseased mode of life, a willful sin against God. Calories were not so readily available in those days, so a person required an unusual degree of wealth to afford a life of leisure and an overabundant supply of food. Modern Americans, on the other hand, have no problem finding salt, sugar, and fat-laden food. In fact, these things are nearly impossible to avoid—even sandwich bread is loaded with salt and corn syrup. In many low-income neighborhoods, processed foods are all you can find.

"Unfortunately, consuming salt, sugar, and fat intensifies, rather than satisfies, the natural human cravings for these once-rare commodities. People want more and more. These refined food products cater to our instinctual cravings and feed the primitive brain within all of us. Even the artificial sweeteners that give diet drinks their intense sweetness feed these cravings and stimulate people to eat more.

"The round fleshiness you see in these pictures marks these victims for suffering and early death. See the woman in this picture? Her name is Bess Aldrich. We interviewed her and her boys and she gave us permission to use their names.

"Bess is thirty-eight years old but looks over fifty. Her father died of a heart attack at forty-eight. Her mother is only sixty but lives in a nursing home, completely paralyzed by a stroke. Imagine the life of this young woman. She takes four medicines for diabetes, three for high blood pressure, and two to lower her cholesterol, plus daily medicines for constipation, acid reflux, depression, and chronic pain. Her legs stay swollen and ache all the time because of varicose veins and arthritis in her knees. She has to sleep sitting up because her weight makes it difficult for her to breathe lying down.

"Her twelve-year-old son, Tommy, has type 2 diabetes, a condition virtually unknown in children a few years ago but common in kids in the United States today. Tommy told us he hates taking insulin shots and hates checking his sugar even more, but he can't seem to get his sugar down no matter how little he eats. He says exercise is impossible because his knees hurt too much to walk.

"Jared, the ten-year-old, admitted he cries himself to sleep many nights because kids at school tease him for being fat. Sometimes he wets his bed. He is ashamed of his body—he feels like it belongs to someone else—and he's tried to lose weight again and again. He likes girls but believes no girl will ever want to be more than a friend because he is so fat.

"You know where this road leads. Given her disease burden at age thirty-eight, Bess's life expectancy is about fifty-four. Given their morbid obesity, her sons will be lucky to see fifty. Worst of all, they will all suffer physical and financial pain before they die, and spend a lot of time in clinics and hospitals being probed, treated, cut, medicated, and stuck with needles.

"Tragically, diabetes is mostly preventable. More than nine times out of ten it's caused by lifestyle choices—eating too much and exercising too little. People become obese by consuming more calories than their bodies burn. Like the Black Death of the Dark Ages, this modern plague of plenty is killing nearly half of the population. People just don't notice the killing because it happens so slowly."

Don knew Dr. Sampson was right. *It's so obvious!* People sit around TVs and eat siloed corn, like hogs in feedlots fattening themselves for the slaughter! Don had seen the stone gate to the now defunct Union Stockyards of Chicago, the entrance to the four hundred seventy-five acres of holding pens and slaughterhouses that made Chicago the "hog butcher of the world." In its heyday, some thirty thousand herders, butchers, and glue makers passed in and out every day under the eyes of the stone steer's head decorating the stone arch. Through the years, billions of cows and pigs passed through as well, but none left alive.

Sister Mary Connelly made everyone in his eleventh grade AP English class read Upton Sinclair's book *The Jungle*, about how animals spent their final days in the endless pens, mired and wallowing in a sea of toxic excrement. When the wind was right, the smell permeated the entire city—Chicagoans called it the smell of money.

Dr. Sampson took a deep breath and let it out in a long sigh. "Our diagnostic approach emphasizes ferreting out the myriad medical problems stemming from this overindulgent lifestyle and giving each problem a separate name. You know the diseases this lifestyle causes, don't you, Dr. Newman?"

"Yes, well, you said diabetes," Don answered, "and overweight causes high blood pressure and high cholesterol. High blood pressure and high sugar cause most of the heart attacks, strokes, hardening of the arteries, kidney failure, and gout in America. And erection problems and failure of the ovaries, too."

"Right! We doctors talk as if all these diseases—diabetes, hypertension, coronary disease, vascular disease, kidney disease, gout, and erectile dysfunction—were unrelated. What is the name of the one disease that leads to all these others?"

"Metabolic syndrome," Don answered.

"Exactly! What we once thought were separate conditions are actually part of one metabolic state caused by excess calories. People say it's beyond their control because of a slow metabolism. That's bunk. Metabolism is mostly controlled by habits. Metabolism responds to the type and amount of food you eat, whether you engage in regular, vigorous exercise, and whether you take the stairs or the elevator. Now, let's ascertain how common this abnormal metabolic state is."

Dr. Sampson turned to Bruce, the biochemistry wiz. "Dr. Markum, what is the natural cholesterol level for the human species?"

"Average cholesterol in the U.S. population is two hundred."

"Yes, two hundred is the average cholesterol in the United States and other rich countries, but is this level natural?"

Bruce raised his eyebrows. "What do you mean by natural? That is not a medical term I'm familiar with," he said with a trace of sarcasm.

"Natural is an older term, from the classical works in philosophy, theology, and natural sciences. Aristotle and Aquinas used the term. You're familiar with evolutionary biology, Dr. Markum?"

"Of course."

"As you know, evolutionary biologists examine how creatures adapt to their environments over hundreds of thousands of years. Sugar, fat, and salt are extremely scarce in the natural environment. Humans evolved to crave those things because they had to seek them avidly—running, hunting, and gathering food every day—to survive. Long periods might pass when they were unavailable, so the human body is designed to need little, crave their taste, and conserve them well.

"Once humans moved away from the sea, salt was most easily found in the blood of animals. Meat was also one of the best fat sources and a great food for early humans because it had more calories than other available foods. Today, fat calories and salt are ubiquitous and readily available without physical activity, but our craving for them persists.

"As every biochemist knows, cholesterol is made from the fat and sugar we take in. The more calories we consume and do not burn in exercise, the higher our cholesterol. So, Dr. Markum, what do you think the average cholesterol level is for the primitive native people living in the wilds of Papua, New Guinea? They live as our ancestors did—they gather fruits, vegetables, and nuts, and hunt wild game."

Bruce thought a moment. "Oh, maybe one hundred twenty?" he guessed.

"Not quite," Dr. Sampson replied. "Try fifty."

"I have to admit, I didn't know a person's cholesterol could go that low, much less that it might be healthy."

"Study the literature. Among primitive people eating a natural diet of vegetables and lean meat, total cholesterol averages between fifty and seventy. Total cholesterol for all other primates eating a natural diet ranges from thirty to seventy. Humans and other primates with these low cholesterol levels almost never have high blood pressure, diabetes, coronary disease, heart attacks, strokes, hardening of the arteries, or loss of sexual function."

"There's another thing," Don added. "The cardiologists say high cholesterol causes inflammation in the blood vessels. The excess calories and fat in the blood stream cause blood to clot and tissues to swell."

"True enough." Bruce pressed his fingertips together and looked at Dr. Sampson and the other students over the bridge formed by his immaculate fingers. "The metabolic syndrome causes a total body inflammatory state that contributes to many diseases. And let's say I buy your idea about natural cholesterol, Dr. Sampson. But aren't you oversimplifying things? What about the effects of homocysteine, apolipoprotein-B, and C-reactive protein? They're huge risk factors for coronary disease."

"Dr. Markum, hundreds of serum proteins have been proposed as *the cause* of cardiovascular disease. Every biochemist has his favorite. But the truth is, all those fancy proteins in the blood you talked about are just markers of the metabolic syndrome, and no one is solely responsible for all its harmful manifestations." Dr. Sampson said.

"Well, elevated homocysteine levels increase risk of heart attack by at least ten to fifteen percent."

"Right. But on a primitive diet, elevated homocysteine levels are almost unknown, all the other compounds you mentioned drop to very low, natural levels, and risk of cardiovascular disease decreases to almost nothing."

Bruce dropped his hands and sat back in his chair.

"Your readings show the metabolic syndrome is connected to other diseases, including Alzheimer's, dementia, asthma, and arthritis. About one-third of cancer is caused by obesity. Obesity is an epidemic in our country—perhaps the worst epidemic we have ever seen, given all the premature death and disability it causes. The flu has never killed so many people.

"I ask you, why don't we declare this plague a national emergency? Why do our National Institutes of Health still focus on the old infectious agents—the ancient plagues that have killed hardly anyone since the Dark Ages?

"The deadliest agents of modern times are served three times a day at drive through restaurants and on American dinner tables: fat, sugar, and salt in doses poisonous to humans. Along with tobacco and lack of exercise, these poisons are far more deadly than most environmental toxins to which modern humans are routinely exposed. And they are everywhere! Like the fleas that carried the plague in ancient times, the vectors for obesity are overlooked *because* they are everywhere. Even the expert scientists at the NIH ignore them. Why?

"Contemplate this question in the weeks ahead: why do we ignore the worst plague of our time? Consider the money interests behind the sales of fat, sugar, salt, inactivity, and tobacco. What businesses profit when Americans sit down and fatten up? Should they bear some responsibility for the suffering they cause?

"Before our next seminar, think about how we should advise our patients. Should we prescribe them up to fifteen pills a day to combat the many horrible manifestations of this plague of plenty? Or should we encourage them to live a lifestyle of daily exercise and simple food that restores them to the natural metabolic state for which the human body is designed?"

Dr. Sampson took off, leaving Frances, Bruce, and Don to gather their books and walk out together. They made their way from the projection room down the steep steps and into the long quiet hall. Their footsteps echoed through the empty old building.

"Have either of you found a good place to study?" Frances asked. "Cleopatra wants my attention every second and my little apartment is making me stir-crazy."

"I've requisitioned a table in The Down Under, that coffee shop across the quad," said Bruce. "You're welcome to join me there." The Down Under was in the basement underneath the classrooms and laboratories of the medical school and was a favorite place to hang out between classes for students and faculty alike.

Frances laughed. "No way! I've been there. No windows and nothing but old smoke-stained brick walls to look at. That would be worse than my apartment."

"Well, I could tell you what to do with the damn cat," Bruce said with a smirk.

Don decided to put off the run he had planned to take after class. Trailing Frances seemed much more attractive. "How about the old library?" he suggested. "It has great windows. Why don't we check it out?"

"Sounds awesome," Frances replied. "Maybe it would be a good place to get some work done. I already have a big project due for my intro economics class."

The three arrived at the end of the long hall.

"You two have fun," Bruce said as he opened the outside door. "I'll be where the coffee is strong. I have to go to the computer lab later to run my stats program for our biostatistics class—maybe I'll see you there." He took off.

"Computer lab?" Frances snorted. "He sure is behind the times. Hasn't he ever heard of the internet?"

Don smiled at Frances, glad he had not revealed his own plans to visit the computer lab later that night. Mostly he was pleased to be strolling across campus with one of the best-looking women he had ever seen. They walked to the old library and crossed under the high arch framing the front door.

Don looked up. The beamed ceiling of the main reading room was at least forty feet above the floor. Tall windows capped by semicircular arches rose up two stories, interrupting the lines of walnut bookcases surrounding the room on both levels. The shelves were filled with old leather-bound books. He wanted to stop right there and camp at one of the great oak tables with the brass lamps.

Frances was hunting for something else. "Come on," she said. "Way too old-fashioned, and we can't talk here. Besides, we need the internet."

She motioned for Don to follow her. They meandered through the library and found a private study room on the second floor of the new annex. The wall surrounding the door was all glass, and the opposite wall was lined with windows overlooking the quad.

"This is perfect!" Frances exclaimed. "And check this out." She grabbed a laptop out of her backpack, uncoiled a cable and plugged it into an outlet. Pretty soon she was cruising the library website and catalogue. "The Florence College library is one of the few in the country to have an OC192 optical fiber connection hardwired into the T-3 internet backbone in New York. It can transmit data at 9.6 gigabits per second. Look…wow, this is way fast. Check out these streaming videos on this internet connection!"

What was she talking about? How did she know all this technical stuff? Don admired the graceful aluminum case of her laptop and decided not to pull out the beat-up old PC he'd bought secondhand at the end of medical school. Don admired Frances's casing as well—a fitted green blouse and tight jeans that accentuated every curve. He was entranced.

Frances had work on her mind. "Check this out!" she said. "I can totally access the datasets in the computer lab for our biostat homework."

So began their habit of studying together in the library, often for long hours. When it came to schoolwork, Frances was in overdrive. She was hungry for everything Florence College had to offer.

Don, on the other hand, was hungry for Frances.

7

The Waste Land

Here I saw far more people than elsewhere, both on the one side
and the other...shouting: "Why hoard?" and "Why squander?"

DANTE ALIGHIERI, INFERNO 7, 25–26

FRANCES, BRUCE, AND DON SAT scattered in the front two rows of the old basement anatomy theater. Mute, numb, and heartsick, Don tried to process the previous day's nightmare. Had we reached the bottom, the deepest and darkest place imaginable? Don hoped so, but many people feared it was only the beginning of more terror to come. He felt the ceiling pressing down on him, as if all the weight of the smoldering rubble rested on his chest.

The towers! The towers were gone—both of them! Unbelievable. The twin giants of the New York City skyline—the World Trade Center towers that housed the greatest financial power center in the world—had tumbled down. In a matter of hours.

Don had been drinking coffee in The Down Under, one eye on the morning news and the other on his seminar reading, when the television showed the first plane slamming into the side of the South Tower. He assumed the pilot had veered off course or had mechanical problems—a terrible freak accident—and went back to his reading.

Just after nine o'clock, a student in the coffee shop screamed, "Oh, my God!" The panic in her voice caused Don to look at the screen just as a second jet slammed into the North Tower. Boiling orange flames exploded from all four sides of several floors. Glittering glass and metal showered the streets below, and billowing black smoke poured out of the jagged, gaping holes in the gleaming towers.

Everything changed in that moment. The concern in the room turned to palpable fear and everyone was now riveted to the news. Some were crying; others were desperately dialing their cell phones. Word came that classes for the rest of the day were cancelled.

Bruce was at his usual table in the back, punching numbers into his cell phone and cursing when he got no answer. Bruce knew three people who worked in the South Tower at Morgan Stanley and had no idea if they were alive or dead.

Frances sat across from him, her cheeks streaked with tears. She cradled her phone with both hands to her ear, reassuring a friend whose father had just missed a meeting in the Windows on the World restaurant at the top of the North Tower. His plane had landed in New York an hour late; he was in a taxi heading for the trade center when the first plane hit.

Don wondered about Jack. Columbia's College of Physicians and Surgeons was in upper Manhattan far from ground zero, so there was probably little chance he would be in harm's way.

The newscast reported a third airliner had hit the Pentagon. Video showed flames leaping from the ruined rampart of the bastion of our national defense. By the time they reported a fourth plane was missing, everyone in the Down Under was terrified. What next? How many planes had been hijacked? What new horror would befall our nation next?

The South Tower crumbled first, just before ten o'clock. The giant building collapsed in slow motion. It started with a barely noticeable shudder and a slight sagging that warped the skyscraper's straight lines. The people up on the roof hoping in vain for a helicopter rescue must have felt the steel beams give up beneath them as the floors began to collapse, accelerating to a machine gun staccato. Puffs of smoke shot out from between the floors with each percussion, and gray-brown clouds of dust began to rise and swell. The interminable fall ended with a huge belch as the floors slammed to the ground. The building exhaled its last breath—a thick, rolling cloud of dust and debris that advanced from the heap and engulfed everything in its path.

The fall of the North Tower thirty minutes later was predictable and right on time. In spite of that, a steady stream of fearless firemen filed into the building right up to the very end.

The news anchor estimated more than five thousand people were trapped inside those towers, and a wave of claustrophobia crashed over Don. The Down Under no longer felt safe; he had to get outside fast. He left his books, shot up the stairs, and took off at a full sprint. He didn't slow down until he reached the outskirts of Florence, a mile or so away from the buildings of campus and downtown. When he finally stopped running, his shirt and khakis were soaked with sweat, and his pulse pounded in his ears.

The world was eerily quiet. The blue sky was empty, free of clouds and planes. It was an ideal day to spend outside but that didn't seem right. Unable to erase the horrifying images from his mind's eye, he walked back to his apartment and turned on the television to find out what was happening.

Don didn't plan to watch for long, but soon he was glued to the set. He watched the surreal scenes over and over: bodies raining down onto the courtyard between the towers, the collapsing towers burying workers and rescuers beneath concrete tonnage. He wondered whether the people on the roof were alive and aware as they rode the collapsing building to the ground. He watched the advancing dust tsunami overtake the people running away and the survivors emerging zombie-like from the darkness.

Don wanted to stop watching, but he couldn't look away. He searched the faces in the crowds flowing over Brooklyn Bridge. The refugees, some of them ash-covered, walked out of their wasted cityscape and the spreading brown fog and didn't look back. But Don sat, still as a pillar of salt, and stared at the burning city late into the night.

DR. SAMPSON ENTERED the room and stood at the podium. He didn't speak for a minute or two.

"I think it will be a long time before we fully understand what happened yesterday," he finally said in a quiet voice.

In the next breath, he abruptly changed his tone, like a battle-worn soldier who recognizes the only way home is to return to the front. "Now, let's move on. There is much material to cover and our best course is to move ahead."

"Is that all you can say, *move ahead?*" Bruce barked. "The Twin Towers are on the ground, the Pentagon has a gaping hole in it, our country is under attack, and you just say *move ahead?*"

Dr. Sampson did not reply.

"Good God!" Bruce erupted, "I thought you were supposed to be a champion for the downtrodden, but all we do here is talk. Can't we *do* something?"

Dr. Sampson stiffened. "What would you have us do, Dr. Markum?"

"Half the doctors in the hospital are on their way to New York to help out, and what are *we* doing?"

"There aren't many wounded, so there is little we can do there. Sometimes the best thing to do is talk."

Bruce rolled his eyes in disgust. "Talk? That's all we'll ever do here. At least the president is doing something—he's preparing to declare war on our enemies who did this."

Dr. Sampson's face darkened. "And what do you know of war, Dr. Markum?" he thundered.

Don held his breath. He had heard Dr. Sampson was a platoon leader in Vietnam.

Bruce held up his hands in a gesture of surrender.

Dr. Sampson had a point. Don had finally gotten an email back from Jack. All of Columbia University Medical Center had been mobilized to assist with the disaster. Jack and a bunch of his colleagues got permission to go to Saint Vincent's Hospital near ground zero to assist. They took the 1 line to the new last stop at 14th Street Station and walked down Seventh Avenue to St. Vincent's.

Seventh Avenue was closed to traffic so the ambulances could get through, and hundreds of empty gurneys covered with white cotton sheets lined the street, awaiting the incoming wounded. But no one came.

There was nothing to do; it appeared no one trapped in the buildings had survived.

After a long awkward silence Dr. Sampson continued as if nothing had happened. "Let's begin with a few pictures."

Dr. Sampson went up to the projection room, and soon the room went pitch black, like Don's windowless call room. The three students waited while Dr. Sampson struggled with the equipment. Finally, the old projector came to life with a whirr, a click, and a clunk as the first slide dropped into place.

Familiar images appeared on the screen again. Good-looking, confident, white-coated doctors posed in front of lavish new medical clinics with fresh asphalt parking lots and sculpted landscapes. Don pressed the small knot on the bridge of his nose between his thumb and forefinger as he watched the pleasant scenes. He knew Dr. Sampson was gearing up to reveal the dark side. Don stole a glance at Bruce, who appeared to be fuming.

Dr. Sampson's voice resonated in the cavernous hall. "These are lovely places to get healthcare, aren't they? These pictures were taken in an average city." In the reflected light from the projector, Dr. Sampson made his way down the steps to the podium next to the screen. "I won't name this town, but it looks pretty much like your hometown and every other city we analyzed in the United States; you'll find the same patterns almost everywhere. Some of these clinics were rated America's best in *U.S. News and World Report* and other publications, and they have the most popular doctors in town.

"Let's look at the *best clinics* and the *best doctors* in this city, according to people we interviewed there." Using the clicker on the podium, Dr. Sampson advanced to a slide depicting two tall, gleaming buildings faced with black glass, stainless steel and marble...side by side, like the Twin Towers.

"This is one of the most popular and highest-rated clinics in town. Its doctors do what doctors in all the most popular clinics do; they see a lot of patients. This clinic has thirty doctors, who—with the help of numerous personnel—process around fifteen hundred patients a day. That's fifty patients per doctor.

"If you're lucky enough to actually see the doctor during your appointment, you can bet he will be supervising a procedure or will have his hand on the doorknob. The average face-to-face time is less than ten minutes per patient."

The next slide showed a large room filled with floor-to-ceiling shelves, all jammed with colorful boxes of medication samples.

"The *best clinics* have drug sample rooms; the largest clinics have several. Doctors dole out free samples of the latest miracle drugs, which have been personally delivered by pharmaceutical representatives."

Dr. Sampson clicked through dazzling images of sparkling laboratories, radiology suites, procedure rooms, and personnel in perfectly starched long white coats.

"These clinics all provide onsite testing and procedures. Look at this beautiful facility. It has a full-service laboratory to handle virtually any test you might want. There's a huge radiology suite with MRI, CT scans, and nuclear imaging facilities. They even have a cardiac cath lab where you can get your coronary arteries squirted with dye, dilated, and stented at your first complaint of chest pain."

Don knew Dr. Sampson was showcasing this high-tech clinic just to shatter their illusions about it. But what an incredible place to work! It was exactly the kind of clinic he had envisioned practicing in as a cardiologist—an ideal world where the most respected physicians practice, where a doctor controls all the variables and performs miracles, has every test at his fingertips, where he is master of the universe. Don pressed his thumb and first finger hard against the knot on the bridge of his nose. He wished Dr. Sampson would just go ahead and get it over with.

"This clinic has ten other procedure rooms," Dr. Sampson continued. "You can get your colonoscopy, video imaging colonoscopy, upper GI endoscopy, bronchoscopy of your airways, cardiac stress testing, and numerous other procedures—frequently all on the same day. Six radiologists and twelve radiology suites offer PET scanning, ultrasounds, echocardiograms, total body CT and MRI, and coronary calcium scanning."

The next picture was of a newspaper ad for a total body MRI. *Get your whole body scanned now. Catch cancer early. Save your life.*

"Many people visit the clinic just to get these new procedures and sophisticated imaging studies," Dr. Sampson said, bringing up the lights a bit. "The advertisements promise wonderful health benefits, but let's take a closer look.

"First, let's consider the doctors. Who are they? The staff list reveals more than two-thirds of the doctors are *proceduralists*— high-paid subspecialists that perform or supervise procedures—the radiologists, cardiologists, gastroenterologists, and surgeons. The rest are *funnelers* or *rounders*. Funnelers are trained, paid, and controlled by the proceduralists to refer or 'funnel' clinic patients into the procedure rooms. Rounders do the same thing on the hospital side. They're attending physicians who happen to request consults from their own practice group's proceduralists on every case they see.

"Of course, this often leads to confusion in the hospital about goals of care and who is in charge, but everything in the hospital—as in the clinic—is set up to do procedures quickly and efficiently. Why is that? Does anyone know?"

No one answered.

"This is important and I don't want you to forget it. You must remember this one thing." Dr. Sampson turned the lights up and raised his voice almost to a bellow. "If you want to understand the truth about American healthcare, follow the money! *Fol-low the mon-ey!*"

He paused a moment for effect, took a deep breath, and asked in a calmer tone, "So ask yourselves, why is the *best clinic*, with the *best doctors*, oriented around making procedures readily and rapidly available?"

"Because that's what insurance companies pay the most for," Don answered. In residency he'd figured out early on that a quick steroid injection was the financial equivalent of an hour-long history and physical. Getting to the root cause of a patient's illness or counseling about healthy habits didn't pay. "I did an outpatient orthopedics rotation at one of the best orthopedic clinics in Boston," he explained. "I knew from playing football about exercises for knee pain; our trainer had us do them all the time. Strengthening the thigh muscle that supports the knee works better than shots, but at this clinic almost every patient got a steroid injection. My attending physician could do one in under a minute. We seldom spent time teaching knee exercises. Also, every patient on every visit got a full set of x-rays before they saw a doctor, whether they needed x-rays or not."

"Were they concerned about the long-term effects of steroids?" Dr. Sampson asked.

"I asked my attending whether he worried about the well-known effects of steroids—bone loss, muscle weakening, occasional tendon rupture—and he just shrugged and said, 'Yeah, but patients like it, it seems to help them, and they aren't going to do the exercises anyway. Besides, I get paid more for injections than I do for wasting my time trying to convince people to exercise every day.'"

"Are steroids even effective for arthritis of the knee, Dr. Newman?"

"No, I guess not."

"You had better guess not, Dr. Newman, because it's your job to think like a scientist, not like an automaton of the healthcare machine. Study the data. Steroids for common knee arthritis are little better than placebo, yet tens of thousands of people get them every day in America. And for what?" he prompted.

"For the money," the students chimed in.

"Yes, for the money, at least in part. Because of the way we pay for healthcare, doctors feel intense pressure to do things a certain way. Many truly believe steroid injections for common arthritis of the knee are beneficial. Of course, it is easy to overlook the scientific studies when injections are standard practice in your community and insurance companies reimburse so handsomely for them.

"Now, many patients do feel better after a steroid injection because faith—what we believe and trust will work—plays an enormous role in medicine. Placebos work. Studies show that for conditions like common arthritis there's a thirty percent reduction in pain just from placebo.

"Placebos work better when delivered in an impressive way. A pill works better if it has side effects, medicines tend to have stronger effects if delivered in red capsules rather than blue, and medicines delivered with needles or surgical treatments have the greatest placebo effects of all. A steroid injection is helpful, but a placebo injection with water or saline is equally effective and far less dangerous."

Dr. Sampson advanced the slides and stopped on a photo of a parking lot full of Mercedes, BMW sports cars, and other fine luxury cars. There was even a Ferrari.

"The *best clinics* in your city are doing extremely well for themselves, aren't they? Here's the doctors' parking lot at the *best clinic*. Even the funnelers and rounders have Beamers. You should see their houses and boats. There are great perks if you focus your practice on lucrative procedures."

"So is it a bad thing for doctors to be well paid?" Bruce erupted again. "After what we go through? We deserve everything we get."

"Of course doctors should be reasonably paid. And doctors go through more training than any other profession."

"If you didn't pay doctors more, nobody would go through the grueling years of study and training," Don said, "and the quality of healthcare would really decline."

"Doctors, like everyone else, need to be paid for their work, and a high level of training and education should be compensated," Dr. Sampson agreed. "However, the current payment system too often causes quality to fall by the wayside. This may look like the *best clinic*, with its beautiful buildings and pretty grounds. But a clinic set up to maximize reimbursements doesn't necessarily provide the best care. This particular clinic has terrible quality statistics. Small clinics that provide basic primary care without the smorgasbord of tests and procedures frequently do a better job than fancy places in providing the care people need.

"Let's turn to the published scientific evidence regarding the performance of these so-called *best clinics*. Ms. Hunt, I asked you to focus on the two papers on fast physicians and clinics. Report."

"Well," Frances replied, "the studies are pretty clear. Doctors who see more patients per day have less time to listen, take proper care of common diseases like diabetes, and do the simple things proven to prevent strokes and heart attacks and save lives. The fastest doctors are more likely to prescribe more drugs to get people out the door."

"Exactly." Dr. Sampson nodded. "What's more, orienting a practice around delivering a procedure to as many people as fast as possible means people get procedures they don't need, and some procedures are very risky. A doctor should only recommend a procedure likely to benefit a patient. Problem is, insurers pay for procedures regardless of whether they are medically indicated or even appropriate.

"What does this lead to? Consider the common procedures for coronary artery disease. Dr. Newman, report what the evidence shows."

"Um…well, we know bypass surgery can save your life *if* you have severe coronary disease involving either the left main coronary artery or all three major branches. But the studies you gave us show that a lot of bypass surgery patients don't have either of these conditions. Their chests are split open and ribs pried apart for this brutal surgery when only one or two of the lesser coronary arteries are narrowed—and heart surgery and stents do nothing to reduce deaths or heart attacks in these cases. It's unbelievable, really. Every day, people get bypasses and stents for mild coronary artery disease, even though medicines, healthy eating, and physical activity save more lives for this group."

"That's right," Dr. Sampson added, "ten to thirty percent of coronary bypass procedures in the United States are of questionable benefit or clearly inappropriate. Dr. Markum, report. What about the data on cardiac caths?"

"Our readings say that over fifteen percent of coronary angiography or 'cath' procedures—where they thread a steel catheter through the leg into the small arteries feeding the heart to take pictures of those arteries—are done without good reason. And angioplasty and stenting where they use a balloon to dilate and then insert tiny metal mesh tubes into blocked arteries during coronary angiography—they're even worse. Looks to me like these procedures are done more often for the benefit of the cardiologist than the patient.

"Wait a minute," Don interrupted. "Angioplasty and stents save lives when performed at the beginning of a heart attack. Because of this miraculous therapy and other modern miracle treatments like aspirin and blood pressure medicines, people seldom die from heart attacks nowadays if they make it to the hospital in time."

"Sure, Don," Bruce replied, "but the fact is most angioplasties and stents aren't done to treat heart attacks but to treat chest pain, a situation for which they have never been shown to save lives. For chest pain, medicines are more effective and less dangerous."

"Good summary, Dr. Markum," Dr. Sampson said, before Don could argue further. "Today I want to share a story, to help bring these numbers to life. It's about my neighbor—let's call him Frank. Frank had chest pressure off and on for months, usually after a big meal. After one particularly bad episode his wife convinced him to get it checked out, so he went to the *best clinic* in town. The funneler there neglected to take a complete history—which would have indicated classic indigestion—and made no attempt to determine if the pain would respond to antacids. Instead, the minute he heard the words 'chest pressure,' he conjured the specter of deadly coronary disease that might lead to a fatal heart attack at any second. Frank was whisked off to the catheterization lab before he could ask questions or talk to his wife. He was awed by the impressive display of medical technology and terrified at the threat of a looming heart attack.

"Like most Americans, Frank had some fatty deposit and calcification in one of his coronary arteries, so the doctors dilated that artery with a balloon. Thank God, it didn't burst. They placed two metal mesh stents in his artery and put him on dangerous blood thinners to keep it open. When Frank came out of the balloon angioplasty and stenting procedure, guess what they told him? 'You're lucky we discovered this just in time! You could have died from a heart attack if we hadn't caught it.' Frank was relieved and grateful and told everyone how the wonderful doctors at the *best clinic* saved his life.

"Of course, Frank continued to have chest pressure after big meals or whenever he ate late at night. He discovered that taking antacid gave him immediate relief, but he came to see me at the Florence College Health Clinic just to make sure everything was okay.

"I checked him over, reviewed his records, and reassured him. I explained his chest pain never had anything to do with his heart—that his stents were unnecessary and put him at greater risk of heart attack in the future. He didn't want to hear it. No one wants to learn his greatest risk of death was because of his mistreatment in the *best clinic*. No doubt he was worse off—physically and financially—but I didn't persist; the damage was done.

"Frank is not alone. Hundreds of thousands of people in the United States think they were saved by risky procedures that in fact they never needed. They were harmed and they have no idea, but they are the lucky ones. They survived.

"The doctors mean well; they convince themselves they are saving lives. What if they do nothing and someone dies? Better to do a procedure just in case. It would be easier to forgive the funnelers, rounders, and proceduralists if what they did was simply worthless, but procedures can be very dangerous. Can you report on the dangers of cardiac catheterizations, Ms. Hunt?"

Frances glanced at her notes. "Absolutely. Caths can cause strokes, heart attacks, and even death. Yet every year twenty percent of the 1.4 million Americans who get one—that's some three hundred thousand Americans—don't need it. As many as half of the 1.2 million coronary artery stent and balloon angioplasty procedures like your neighbor had are unnecessary. About a fifth of coronary artery bypass surgeries are unnecessary, which means one hundred thousand bypass patients every year have their breastbones split open, ribs pried apart, hearts cooled, and brains damaged without real hope of benefit. One or two percent don't survive the surgery. All this from physicians who swear to do no harm!"

"Your numbers are accurate, Ms. Hunt. In the past year, more people were killed in this country by unnecessary bypass surgery than in yesterday's attacks.

These casualties have occurred for years and years and persist because almost no one recognizes the deaths as avoidable. The killing in healthcare is well hidden—even from the doctors.

"Proceduralists are confident performing techniques they spent years perfecting. If you need a procedure, that's a very good thing. But the system discourages them from questioning whether a procedure ought to be done in the first place. You know the saying. *To a man with a hammer, everything looks like a nail.*"

Don's eyes turned inward to the secret icon cradled deep in his heart. A tall, tanned, broad-shouldered figure in a freshly starched, pure white coat, stethoscope coiled in his right front pocket—like Dr. Gannon and the tall doctor reflected in a mirrored glass building on the shores of Lake Michigan.

Boooooom! The looking glass exploded—glittering daggers showered down around him, each shard a fragment of his old future. Dr. Virgil Sampson stood behind the window frame, holding the cudgel that shattered it.

"...many recent studies show high rates of unnecessary procedures are not limited to a few practices or isolated geographic areas," Dr. Sampson was saying. "To the contrary, high rates of unnecessary procedures are the *norm* throughout the country. Unnecessary procedure rates range from ten to forty percent in almost every community and for every common procedure studied. When doctors are operating—whether cutting fat deposits out of narrowed arteries, removing a uterus, performing endoscopy, or whatever—between ten and forty percent of the time they are doing something the patient does not need.

"Despite clear scientific evidence that certain procedures offer little or no benefit, insurance companies continue to shell out the money. Dr. Nelda Wray in Houston just completed a study on arthritic knee pain showing surgery with a scope is no better than sham surgery, where the surgeon just makes a little cut on the knee and pretends to do surgery. Arthroscopic knee surgery has never been proven to help except in very special cases, yet surgeons perform over ten thousand arthroscopic surgeries for knee pain in the United States every week."

Shit—I had that surgery in college! Don rubbed his knees and felt through his pants for the scars. His knees hurt a lot those first two years on the football team, and the team doctor recommended he have the surgery between sophomore and junior years. It took him months to recover. Was it just the strength training and rehab that helped him get better? Did he have the surgery for nothing?

"Okay, Dr. Markum, the Cochrane systematic review of spinal injections of steroids for back pain. Report."

"Sorry, didn't get to that one."

"Dr. Newman?"

"Yes, sir. That's the same story. Several randomized trials—the best type of scientific study to compare treatments—proved that spinal injections of steroids for chronic back pain have little or no benefit. Still, hundreds of thousands of Americans receive them each year in pain clinics, even though people who get steroids are no better six weeks later than those who get placebo. And the steroids cause bones, muscles, and tendons to break down, so these clinics are doing real harm. It would be safer if they just used empty needles."

"Who should we blame for all these useless procedures?" Dr. Sampson asked. "The patients who demand them? The doctors? Or is it the way we pay for healthcare? Doesn't the pay tempt every doctor and nurse to enter a lucrative, procedurally-oriented subspecialty practice?"

The pay had certainly tempted Don. Thoughts of a successful North Shore cardiology practice had tantalized him since medical school. All doctors are driven to succeed, or they wouldn't go to medical school in the first place. Besides, he was raised in a family where hard work and good behavior were rewarded. He had always assumed procedural specialists had to be smarter—had to be doing more valuable work. Otherwise, why would they be paid so much more? With only a year or two of additional training, Don could have easily doubled, tripled, or even quadrupled his starting income.

"Who wouldn't want to join a high-income practice, have everything you want, plus be one of the most respected practitioners in town?" Dr. Sampson asked. "It's appealing, isn't it? We're talking about a very old temptation to which almost anyone can succumb, and doctors are not immune: to go where the money is."

"So isn't it just greedy doctors who are killing people with unnecessary procedures?" Don blurted out.

"Come on, Don!" Bruce said. "Get real for a minute. Most doctors doing these procedures are following the standard of care in their communities. Look, they have a procedure. They're good at it. People come to them expecting it and they may get sued if they don't do it."

Dr. Sampson nodded in agreement. "Dr. Markum is right. Labeling this as plain greed is too simple. Though there is greed in the system, most doctors don't do procedures just for the money. So why do we do twice as many procedures in America as anywhere else in the world? Three reasons.

"First, proceduralists here have incredible technology at their disposal and the insurance company pays for using it—regardless of need. Typically, a technical procedure is only beneficial in selected cases, but it's paid for in all cases where the doctor wants to try it. The payment system encourages doctors to experiment. Besides, you only get paid if you *do* something.

"Second, proceduralists are trained more to perform procedures than to study the reasons for doing them. Keeping up with the medical literature is very difficult. They believe they are practicing great medicine as long as they are adept at their procedures.

"Third, patients expect procedural specialists to do all they can. If they fail to act and something goes wrong, they risk malpractice. Therefore they act. It's less likely they'll face blame for doing too much, because most patients don't know when a procedure is not indicated.

"Most people can't resist going where the money is. Healthcare providers are no different. Cardiac procedures are the most lucrative, so people figure they must be the most valuable and important."

"Wait a minute," Don interrupted, "you can call these doctors funnelers and proceduralists if you want to, but surely most are doing the best they can to provide good care. They must have studied evidence-based medicine and epidemiology, and I'm sure they have regular journal clubs to review the evidence from recent papers. They're bound to at least do that!"

Bruce laughed out loud. "What planet have you been living on? Practicing doctors participating in weekly journal clubs to review the latest evidence? Like maybe one in a thousand. You really are naïve if you think doctors in the *best clinics* take time to study epidemiology."

Bruce's look of utter incredulity made Don want to hide under the table, and he was relieved when Dr. Sampson carried on without a pause.

"I have one more thing to show you. The procedure-oriented practice that characterizes the *best clinic* in most American cities is inextricably linked to waste. In other words, doing lots of procedures squanders a tremendous amount of healthcare resources. Not only do you often get substandard healthcare in the *best clinic,* but you pay a lot more for it. Waste is more common in some cities than others and I can show you exactly where it occurs most. Let's go to the projection room."

According to Dr. Sampson, the whole medical payment system was upside-down. Doctors' pay was not just unrelated to the benefit provided; it was often inversely associated with benefit. In other words, the more money you made, the less good you were doing. Don wanted to believe Dr. Sampson was exaggerating the extent of the problem, but the studies strongly suggested he was not.

Don stood up, swayed on his stiff legs, and scaled the steep stairs out of the pit behind Dr. Sampson, Bruce, and Frances. They gathered on one side of the table in the projection room.

"Look at this map," Dr. Sampson said as he rolled out a large United States map on the table. Each state was divided into regions and each region was colored one of five shades, ranging from light ginger to blood red.

"This is from a Medicare atlas produced each year by some colleagues of mine. It tracks variations in use and costs of healthcare and shows the cities where healthcare costs are the highest for people of similar age and health status. This makes it pretty clear, doesn't it? Ms. Hunt, in which cities does healthcare cost the most?"

"Well," she said, "there are lots of little red areas throughout the country, but the biggest are in Florida, especially around Miami, scattered areas in the South, and in the Northeast around New York and Boston."

"Right," Dr. Sampson said, "those are the places where people use the most healthcare services. So, if healthcare makes people healthier, you would expect people starting out with similar health status in these places to end up better off, wouldn't you? Wouldn't you expect people in these areas to live longer, or to at least get more recommended care?"

"Totally, I would surely think so," Frances replied.

"So let's see what people get for all this extra spending on healthcare. Compare low-spending Minneapolis to Miami. The differences are huge. Our Medicare program spends more than twice as much per person per year in Miami. Instead of the thirty-seven hundred dollars per person we spend in Minneapolis, we spend seventy-eight hundred per year in Miami. And for that extra forty-one hundred dollars per person, what do you think the *best clinics* of Miami provide?"

Frances paused, "Well, until today, I would have said people get more recommended tests, they're healthier, and they live longer."

"That is what you'd think, but we discovered people starting out with the same health status in high-spending cities are *less* likely to get the most important recommended healthcare. So what do they get? More visits to funnelers, rounders, proceduralists, and consultants, more days in the hospital, and more unnecessary care in the ICU in their last days of life. Despite the extra doctor visits, people in high-spending regions are much less likely to get critical preventive care like flu and pneumonia vaccinations and pap smears. Worst of all, their mortality rates are two to five percent *higher*. They're actually *more* likely to die. It seems with more doctors involved, preventive care is forgotten and things more often go wrong."

Frances gasped. "That's totally unbelievable—crazy—to pay so much more and to get so much less. How can that be?"

"I believe it," Don said. "With many doctors involved, each one feels less responsibility. Each doctor figures some other doctor has taken care of it. They aren't paid based on whether the patients get recommended care, and they have little incentive to take on responsibility to do the most important work, which is typically reimbursed at the lowest rates."

"I think you are beginning to catch on," Sampson said. "Remember the phrase?"

This time they answered in unison, "Follow the money!"

"Before we close, let's think about this backward situation. Why is it that *the best clinics*—the ones that seem to run so efficiently—waste the most resources?"

No one answered.

"Greed and waste are two sides of the same coin; they go hand-in-hand in healthcare," Dr. Sampson continued. "Remember the beautiful *best clinics* we saw earlier? People with health insurance, or just lots of money, love the *best clinics* in town for their high-tech marvels. They love tests. They think more tests, x-rays, procedures, drug samples, and blood draws equals better care,"

"Are you saying there are no best clinics?" Bruce asked.

"No, not at all. There are definitely true best clinics out there. But being the best requires more than proficiency with procedures. It requires the good judgment to do procedures only for the right reasons. The truly best clinics aren't flashy, they are unlikely to call attention to themselves, and they usually aren't widely known as the *best clinics* in town."

"I get it," Frances said. "Most people think the *best clinics* are the practices where it's easy to get procedures. But the practices where it is easiest to get procedures are the ones most dedicated to profit."

"Right," Dr. Sampson said. "And they are prodigal with other people's healthcare resources. They waste money on costly gadgets and machines more likely to harm than help us. Some procedures offer only minor benefits at best, but to get a return on investment, the *best clinics* use them on everybody they can, including patients who don't need them. As a result, they end up causing more harm than good, because there are risks in procedures that involve radiation, needles, and biopsies. So, who is to blame for this waste?"

"That's easy," Bruce laughed, "the lawyers."

The students laughed, breaking the tension for a minute.

"Maybe the lawyers are partly at fault," Don added, "but what about the doctors, clinics, and administrators that shift their attention from people to profits without even realizing it?"

"Don, don't you get it?" Bruce said. "It's not all about money-grubbing physicians. The doctors are victims, too. General surgeons who trained for years to do it all, from gall bladder surgery to lung transplants, get stuck doing hemorrhoids and the occasional appendectomy..."

Don's right hand quivered. He pushed his palm against the table so no one would notice and looked down at his reflection in the glossy patina of the old table. Bruce had a point. Primary care doctors spend years learning to provide comprehensive care, only to get employed by procedure mills that require them to practice as robots and run patients through as quickly as possible. With no time to get to know their patients, they're supposed to find satisfaction through the financial rewards a fast-paced funneler practice brings.

"...the problem is the payment system," Bruce was saying, "and the old-fashioned notion of physicians as some sort of high priests. We trust physicians to always do the right thing, but the truth is they do what they get paid for. You can't blame them. It's insane to expect them to work against their own interests.

Sure, some go too far—doctors who blindly follow the toxic payment system may even do bad things. But the system gives doctors no incentive to do better—that's the real problem."

"The big mistake is putting doctors up on a pedestal in the first place," Frances said. "We pretend doctors are different from other professionals, that they have a higher calling, when nurses can do most of the procedures doctors do just as well or better. Maybe this idea that know-it-all doctors are so superior is what keeps us from questioning them and figuring out what we need to do to make healthcare better."

"How can you blame it all on medicine's high ideals?" Don asked. "Real doctors in the trenches don't think about money when they're caring for patients. If you want to blame someone, blame the administrators. After all, they're the ones running the show these days, not physicians."

"Should we allow doctors and administrators to control our healthcare choices and how we spend our healthcare dollars?" Dr. Sampson asked. "Perhaps we should start by looking at ourselves."

Bruce squirmed in his seat. He appeared uncharacteristically self-conscious. Frances, on the other hand, seemed pleased, as if all her deepest suspicions were confirmed. She was nodding her head and scribbling away in her notebook.

All of it left Don with a sick feeling in the pit of his stomach. He had spent the last seven years learning to be a cog in this perverted system.

"That's enough for today," Dr. Sampson announced. "For next week's seminar, I've decided we should meet for lunch on the mountain at the Sentinel Bar and Grill. It's on me. Do you all know the Sentinel?"

All three nodded. Everyone knew about the Sentinel. Among the students and faculty of Florence College, it was the favorite off-campus place to hang out.

"We'll meet in the back room. See you then."

Bruce and Frances left the room, but Don lagged behind as Dr. Sampson finished rolling his map.

"Dr. Sampson?"

"Yes, Dr. Newman?"

"Are you saying that much of our healthcare amounts to torture?"

"Yes, Don, I guess I am…and I know a thing or two about torture," Dr. Sampson said gravely. "One doesn't expect to find it in the world of modern medicine. Of course, it's different from torture in war, because the perpetrators aren't aware of what they are doing and victims haven't a clue. But people need to see the horror. They need to know what really goes on in our hallowed halls of healing."

Don left the seminar feeling despondent. It was so hard to see the right path in this screwed-up system. If there even was one. If he hadn't come to Florence College it would have been easy just to look the other way, work within the system as it is, and hope not to be a victim. But now it was too late. He had seen the hell in healthcare up close. The images seared in his mind were far worse than the drawings in his mother's copy of the *Inferno* that horrified him as a child. He couldn't just go back to work with blinders on and forget what he'd seen.

Don's dreams of a career as a cardiologist working on the North Shore had turned to nightmares of cogwheel doctors, tortured visitors, and glass towers crashing down around him in a holocaust of black fire and smoke. Images of America's best clinics fused in his mind with the ruined towers of New York, the damaged Pentagon, the smoking crater in Pennsylvania.

A smoldering wasteland lay before him. He saw no future in medicine.

8

The Arrogant Physician

How many above there now account themselves great kings
who shall lie here like swine in the mire
leaving of themselves horrible dispraises!
DANTE ALIGHIERI, INFERNO 8, 49–51

DON HURRIED BACK to The Down Under as soon as epidemiology class ended. As he stumbled down the stained brick stairs his mouth dried up and the low ceiling pressed down on his chest. His panic, trembling hands, and sweaty palms went unnoticed; all eyes were riveted on the large screen on the far wall. Don took two deep breaths and joined the quiet underground crowd gathered around the television to watch the nation's president, who was speaking from the pulpit in Washington's hallowed Cathedral:

> *Just three days removed from these events, Americans do not yet have*
> *the distance of history. But our responsibility to history is already clear: to*
> *answer these attacks and rid the world of evil. War has been waged against*
> *us by stealth and deceit and murder.*

A war? Was it war, or the work of a few fanatic criminals? Don stood unrecognized among the unfamiliar undergrads, listened to the entire sermon, and left The Down Under more disconsolate than when he arrived. He wasn't sure why.

That night, lying sleepless in his dark apartment, a montage of Tuesday's horror ran over and over through Don's mind: planes plowing headlong into the iconic skyscrapers, formidable glass and steel buildings exploding in flames, masses of innocents racing down endless dark stairs and choking on acrid fumes, workers plummeting to the pavement from the towers' shattered sides, the twin giants collapsing and crushing scores of trapped workers and fearless firemen, frenzied fugitives fleeing the roiling cloud of bone and ash, billowing plumes of black smoke drifting over Manhattan, shell-shocked survivors streaming across the Brooklyn bridge on foot staring straight ahead, their signature skyline marred by a smoldering hole where its proud focal point had stood—majestic and intact and full of people—that very morning.

These images tangled in Don's exhausted brain with memories of the clinics and hospitals where he had worked—sleek modern medical laboratories harboring a surprising amount of secret destruction. They aren't all bad; most doctors, nurses, and administrators work hard to help patients. But the healthcare machine harms people. For every miraculous cure, there's lots of collateral damage.

"Every system is perfectly designed to produce exactly what it produces," Dr. Sampson had said.

That made sense. Businesses are designed to make money. But to make money in healthcare, the *best clinics* emphasize speedy tests over careful history taking. Unnecessary operations and procedures are inevitable byproducts, and people suffer torture, maiming, and impoverishment as a result.

The estimated death toll had risen to fifty-five hundred. Nothing else on the news. We must never let it happen again, they said. But where was the outrage over people killed by unnecessary cardiac procedures? More than fifty-five hundred die in cath labs every year, and they were just a few of those in the mass grave of medicine's secret victims!

America's esteemed medical establishments have morphed into multiheaded hydras—insatiable monsters luring patients, doctors, and healthcare workers inside their huge glass and marble pantheons to devour them—and they must keep up a steady stream of lucrative procedures to feed the ravenous beasts inside.

But it's all hidden. *Nobody knows!* Why can't everyone see that the so called *best clinics* are just castles built on sand? What happens when the sands shift and the foundations crack? When the gleaming façades of glass and marble fall away to reveal the monstrosities inside?

Don't let me be on the inside when that happens! I can't just take my place in a heart cath production line; that's not why I became a doctor. I can't slave away for an industry that uses people for its own selfish ends, no matter how much money I might make. But what can I do instead?

Don's eyes were open now, but he was lost in the labyrinth and had no idea how to get out. Bit by bit, he had been pulled into a place he never planned to go. He stared at his apartment's dark louvered windows and felt the cold air seeping through the cracks around their aluminum frames.

How in the hell did I end up here?

DON'S MOTHER, RACHELE, loved her family with her whole heart, and she considered the whole world her family. She came from the old country and took to heart the ancient duty to cook and care for all those who came into her sphere, including homeless people in their Old Town neighborhood on the Near

North Side of Chicago. If they were sane, sober, and sanitary—those were her rules—she would invite them over for supper. Despite her imperfect English she could assess prospects for those three essential characteristics very quickly and never made a mistake. Almost every week she brought home someone who needed a home, a family, and a home-cooked meal.

She served in the old Italian way, one course at a time. Sitting in silence awaiting the antipasto, the person was always wary. But when the tiny plates of warm crostini or bruschetta arrived and Rachele's gentle questions began, an unintended smile invariably formed somewhere deep inside the hardened stranger. Then came the first course of pasta or soup, followed by a small meat course, vegetables cooked to perfection, green salad, and fresh fruit for dessert. The warm food and unexpected hospitality pulled a distant man's voice forth from out of his hard crust. By the end of the third course he'd be regaling the Newmans with his life stories and all of the passages that had led to his current sad state.

Don's father always complained when Rachele announced the impending arrival of another homeless dinner guest. Jacob remained apart and silent during these visits, but Don was fascinated. Even as a toddler he would fix his dark eyes on the strangers and listen to every word from these unshaven men who came to Chicago from all over the country. Through these stories around the dinner table Don's mother schooled him in sympathy, and he was an excellent student.

Don emulated Rachele's friendliness toward her neighbors and practiced caring for others. He learned to reveal little about himself and turn the conversation to the other person. Asking questions and figuring out what motivated and disheartened people was like a game. He was proud when older people remarked to his mother they enjoyed talking with him. His mother would always say, "That is my Dante. He is gifted with a healing tongue."

Three signposts in Don's early life pointed to his calling to become a healer. The first involved Lábano Innocenti, his wrinkled old Italian grandfather, Nonno. Lábano had moved into the walkup apartment on the third floor of their townhouse after his wife—the nonna Don never met—died suddenly of pneumonia. Don remembered climbing the tall steps up to Nonno's apartment and his confusion when he found Nonno crying, "Il mio caro tesoro" and "mia culpa" in agony over the loss of his partner of over fifty years. Don had never seen a grown man cry like a baby. Weren't nonnos always happy? The toddler put his hand on Nonno's back just the way his mother did for him when he was sad, and although his nonno cried even harder, a smile of gratitude signaled to the young boy that his effort to comfort was received.

One day when Don had just turned three, his mother watched from their front steps as Don walked four doors down the street to the convenience store to buy Marlboro cigarettes from the well-prepared clerk. When Don returned with the cigarettes Nonno rubbed his head, kissed him twice on both cheeks with his sandpaper stubble, and thanked the boy for bringing "la mia medicina." Don's mission as a doctor was born. After that he wanted to go to the convenience store every day to repeat the ritual.

A few months later, Rachele found her father still in his bed at ten o'clock, clutching his chest and gasping for air. The paramedics carried an empty stretcher through the house up to the third floor and returned with a pale, pasty, empty facsimile of Don's nonno, passing by the living room and out the front door. Nonno Lábano was already dead.

Don was furious. He kicked his tower of alphabetized building blocks across the living room floor so hard that one hit the television screen with a loud clink. He pummeled the couch pillows with his fists and screamed, "No-no-no-no-no!" His father wrapped his arms tightly around the boy and squeezed him while he kicked and screamed louder. Only when Don noticed the tears streaming down his mother's face did his tantrum stop. Later, Jacob told his son that Nonno had died from cigarettes, but Don's mother said it was a broken heart, and Don believed her.

The second sign of Don's destiny came when he was nine. He and his mother had taken their usual daily walk to Harlin's corner store for the makings of lunch and supper. While his mother was inside, Don waited outside the store and watched the people go by.

A dark-skinned black man sat on the curb with his head in his hands, an empty pint bottle of something labeled Red Rose at his feet. Alongside him was a clear plastic bag knotted to the end of a galvanized metal pole where a fishing net once had been attached. The bag bulged with faded shirts, a stained coat, single socks, and a half-spilled bag of potato chips. As Don watched, the man lifted his head and talked first to one hand and then the other.

"They ain't no way I'm goin' with that. She don't know nothin'. I'd be liable…"

He didn't meet at least two of his mother's criteria, but all the same Don sat down on the curb a safe distance away to listen to the conversation the man was having with his hands.

The man turned his head toward the young visitor and stared past the boy through cloudy white corneas. His face was as black as the Magic 8 Ball Don's mother had denied him for Christmas and seemed every bit as likely to hold secret answers. A ridged scar ran across the bridge of his nose from the brow of one unseeing eye to the cheek below the other. He grabbed a beaten-up, child-sized guitar leaning against the curb and began to play.

> Tranein' up to Chicago—git drunk as I could be.
> Tranein' up to Chicago—git drunk as I could be.

Prayed to dead up dere, take my soul, I don' care.
Wooooooooooo!   Wooooooooooo!   Wooooooooooo!
Tranein' in on Chicago—ridein' on a dead line.
Wooooooooooo!   Wooooooooooo!   Wooooooooooo!
Tranein' in on Chicago—ridein' on a dead line.
Don't no body know me—dere the dead dey feel jes fine.
Tranein' up to Chicago babe—darkness fallin' on me.
Tranein' up to Chicago—darkness fallin' on me.
Rumblin' deep in my soul—Lawd, it's a comin' fo me.

The man let the last chord ring into silence and for a long time neither of them said a word.

The little boy broke the silence with his mother's words. "Sounds like you've had a mighty hard time…what brought you here?"

The man touched the empty bottle of Red Rose beside him. "That drink's what done brought me here. Made me so I can't live with nobody else. Nobody'll have me. Not even my Mama. Hate to tell it to a boy like you, but I guess there's no one else to tell. Chasin' that Red Rose right there, that's what's brought me here and just 'bout killed me least eight times. Cat's only got nine, y'know."

"So, where do you want to go now?"

"Might as well 'mit to you—where I really wanna go is home to Memphis. Chicago—this ain't my place. This was just a hole I ran into where my people wouldn't see me. I wadn't worth seein'. But my people, my mama, she in Memphis, and she sick, too. Mightn't be there long…"

Seeming to forget the boy, he crooned,

Guess I mus be leavin' now—Red Rose yo bloom is gone
Guess I mus be leavin' now—Red Rose yo bloom is gone.
Time I mus be movin' on—Red Rose yo day is done.

Don's mother pulled her two-wheeled grocery cart out the front door of Harlin's corner store and spotted her son on the curb alongside an unkempt man playing a guitar. Her eyes moved from the grizzled man to the empty bottle in the gutter beside him.

"Come on, Dante, it's time to go home."

Don hopped up from the curb, but a black hand shot out fast as lightning, took Rachele's hand, and held it tight.

"Excuse me, Ma'am. Forgive me, Ma'am, but you need to know, you got yourself a fine boy. That boy showed me. He showed me what I needed to see. He a natural born healer, sho nuff, and you need to know it."

The old man let go of Rachele's hand and turned his unseeing eyes back toward the street. He lifted up his guitar again and sang:

I'm a no count broken man, I done the best I could.
I'm a no count broken man, I done the best I could.
Maybe now I been broken, I be leavin' here fo good.

They never saw him around Old Town again, but Rachele Newman never forgot that day and the prophecy of the blind man from Memphis.

The third sign had to do with Mrs. Rossetti. On Don's block in Old Town there were no other children his age—just a few self-absorbed working people and the old ones. Don only knew the old neighbors: Mr. Thompson in 42, Mrs. Clay in 58, and his favorite, Mrs. Rossetti, a widow who lived on the next block in a second floor apartment. Like Don's mother, she came from the old country, the city of Naples, and had worked most of her life alongside her husband in Rossetti's Grocery six blocks away.

When Don was ten, his mother asked him to go by Mrs. Rossetti's apartment every day after school to check on her. His main job was to make sure she took her medicines properly. Don liked the responsibility of counting her pills each day and was proud when Mrs. Rossetti called him "mio piccolo dottore," or "my little doctor."

On Saturdays the two of them had a special ritual. Mrs. Rossetti would make cannoli—deep fried homemade pasta tubes filled with sweetened ricotta cheese and chocolate. Don would sprint all the way to her house, pretending he was Dr. Gannon on his way to an emergency. He bounded over cracked sidewalk slabs uplifted and tilted by the roots of half-dead elm and ash trees and always arrived right on time.

Mrs. Rosetti would open her door and the sweet warm air of her apartment would rush out and envelop Don in the aromas of chocolate, pastry, and peanut oil. Mrs. Rossetti would pinch his cheeks to assess their thickness and disappear into the kitchen while Don waited in the living room on the threadbare floral fabric of her overstuffed couch. In minutes, Mrs. Rossetti would waddle from the kitchen on her bowed legs, swaying from side to side on account of her knotted knees, and place a large tray of warm cannoli on the coffee table. The two of them would gorge themselves on cannoli while watching reruns of their favorite show, *Medical Center*.

Dr. Gannon, the hero of the show, was a heart surgeon who spent most of his time sitting on the edge of his patients' beds listening patiently and counseling them about life and death choices. On occasion, he'd have to strike a patient's chest with the full force of his fist to get their heart beating again and wheel their gurney into the OR himself for emergency surgery. With all his heart, Don wanted to be like Dr. Gannon, a tall, self-assured, white knight always ready to come to the rescue.

Don counted Mrs. Rossetti's pills for three years. During that time her memory worsened, the cannoli became inedible, and her kitchen grew dangerous. Don found her one Saturday morning on her kitchen floor covered with flour, tears streaming down her face. A pot of burning oil right above her head was filling the room with smoke.

"Dottore!" she cried, "what happened to my cannoli?"

Don was no longer little, no longer pretending. He knew what to do. He called his mother, who saw to it Mrs. Rossetti moved to a good nursing home. They continued to visit her there until she died, when Don was in tenth grade, and Don was the last person she recognized.

Don's memories of Nonno, the blind man from Memphis, and Mrs. Rossetti—along with his infatuation with Dr. Joe Gannon—prefigured his life's purpose and pointed him toward a career in medicine. Everything in his young mind aligned and confirmed this mission. But the greatest influence of all on the young Don Newman was his mother, Rachele.

Rachele Innocenti Newman knew what it was to be an outsider. Though she lived in the States for half her life she never completely assimilated. When she first arrived in Chicago in the 1960s, the xenophobia, prejudice, and hatred were intense. To the Anglo-Saxon Protestant majority she was just another wop. Wop meant "dude" in the Neapolitan dialect, but the Anglo majority used the word to curse all Italians—not just the poor, uneducated immigrants from southern Italy. Though the Innocentis came from northern Italy and were educated and reasonably well off, when his mother conducted business in the grocery store or post office in accented English she heard the ugly whispers of "wop" just the same.

Rachele was from Vicenza, a small town near Verona, but her family roots were in Tuscany. Family tradition claimed Dante Alighieri, writer of the poem *The Divine Comedy*, as an ancestor. Don's mother had told him of a famous vintner, Count Alighieri of Verona, who traced a direct paternal line to the ancient poet. His line inherited the rich vineyards and estates Italian nobles gave to Dante in the 1300s. The Innocentis' ancestry, on the other hand, was legendary, unproven, and unaccompanied by wealth or titles. Don's mother and her parents never met the famous count. Still, the Innocentis of Vicenza embraced the connection to Dante Alighieri. Lábano Innocenti even named his bookstore Libreria Alighieri.

Jacob Newman was an outsider in Chicago as well—a Southerner from New Orleans. He met Rachele while stationed at the Army base in Vicenza, where he ran the hospital laboratory. They met in the Innocenti's bookstore, where she worked. He knew almost immediately he wanted to marry her, but she and her family would put him off for almost fifteen years. When his army stint ended,

Jacob Newman departed Vicenza alone, attended college and graduate school on the GI bill, and worked for nearly seven years in Monsanto's labs in St. Louis as a chemist. Finally, after he landed a job as a chemistry professor at Loyola, he won Rachele's hand and brought her to Chicago.

Don's mother was thirty-eight years old and had lived in Chicago nearly six years before she became pregnant. Don did not come into the world easily. Like the ancient Greek physician-hero Asklepios, he was cut out of his mother's womb. Unlike Asklepios' mother, Rachele survived the ordeal, but her doctor warned her not to get pregnant again, and Don remained an only child. This must have been a huge blow to Rachele but she never complained, at least not in Don's hearing. She was worlds away from her parents, grandparents, and home country and she was lonely. She lavished all her attention on Don and he adored her.

Rachele named him Dante in honor of Dante Alighieri. No other name would do. As a little boy, Don's real name filled him with pride, but once he started school he came to despise it. It brought problems, like when he was late to his first day of school at St. Patrick's Elementary. The assistant principal escorted him to class and opened the door to the classroom. Twenty-one heads turned to examine him, every single one with pearly white skin and sandy, blond, or red hair. Only the occasional freckle matched Don's darker skin.

"Dante—that's such an interesting name," the teacher remarked. "Where does it come from?"

His first name always triggered questions, but even his English-sounding last name stood out amongst the Irish Catholic names like O'Shaghnessy, Glendon, MacMurray, Reilly, and O'Shay. As the teacher tried to match his name and heritage with his skin color, her questions led with invariable progression to: "You said your mother is Italian originally? And your father, is he from Chicago? No? New Orleans? How did they meet?"

Don hated it. When his parents came for a basketball game or school play, Don hated how everyone stared at them, examined them, and interrogated him about their background. The other parents were in a different circle, from a different part of the neighborhood, and his parents' conversations with them were always awkward. Over time the name Dante came to represent everything that was awkward in his life.

In fourth grade one boy called it a nigger name. Don fought him for that, and even though the other boy was older and bigger, they both left the fight bloody. Don suffered two black eyes and a broken nose, which was left with a slight but permanent tilt to the left and a tiny knot near the bridge. The other boy had it worse. Don had caught him by surprise and hit him under the chin with such force it smashed his teeth together, broke off one front incisor, and made his gums bleed. The bigger boy pulled the broken tooth piece from his mouth and stared at it with disbelief before hauling off and smashing Don's patrician nose.

Both in the principal's office and at home, Don refused to tell what had provoked his outburst. The older boy had no intention of revealing his bigoted comment and so, as the instigator, Don took all the blame. Only his mother's intervention prevented his expulsion. He got off with fifty hours of community service. Each day after school he scrubbed graffiti from the school's old brick walls using bitter orange-smelling solvent, only to see the names, signs, and gang designations repainted within days. The older boy went unpunished.

Don's mother didn't understand his reticence. Her son's silence about the reasons for the fight tormented her. Had the boy abused him in some way?

Don reassured her, "No, nothing like that," but otherwise refused to answer. He was sure Momma would never understand. However, his father's sympathetic look told Don somehow his father knew exactly what had happened. The two of them shared a silent understanding neither ever felt inclined to voice out loud.

Not only did Don refuse to tell the reason for his unaccountable rage, he also refused to have his nose straightened. The knot reminded him of the reasons for his anger and cemented his determination to leave the school of the Irish. When Don asked to change schools his parents agreed, and in fifth grade he moved to a new Catholic school across town called Saint Sebastian. This time Don made sure from day one everyone knew his name was Don, and it had been Don ever since.

Coach Fry from St. Sebastian's upper school noticed Don's size, speed, and broad shoulders the first month. He told Don he looked like a football player and in sixth grade encouraged him to run every day. That spring, Coach suggested he add weights. The strategy worked—Don played first-string running back through middle and high school. And once he was a star running back, people stopped asking uncomfortable questions when they saw his parents sitting in the bleachers.

Don went with his mother to St. Roch's Catholic Church in Old Town every Sunday. One Sunday, Father Tom led a particularly good catechesis class for the fifth graders on the story of St. Roch. St. Roch was a French medical student in the 1300s who dropped out of school, gave his worldly goods to the poor, and went on a pilgrimage to Italy to help plague victims. Though St. Roch contracted the plague himself, he miraculously survived and continued to comfort and heal the sick and dying all across Italy.

Father Tom's story filled Don with a fervor to serve others. After catechesis he sneaked into the sanctuary before the service to pray. Don knelt in the second row, where he could see past the wooden Jesus nailed on the cross to the painting of St. Roch behind. Don studied St. Roch's draining wound—the ruptured bubo from the plague—on his right inner thigh. St. Roch looked straight at Don and pointed to the deep ulcer in his thigh as if it were very important.

The young boy wondered…why did Jesus have to be wounded? Why did St. Roch have to get sick? He listened for an answer but didn't hear one. St. Roch smiled in peace as he looked into Don's eyes and pointed to the wound. Don prayed to Jesus and then to St. Roch. Make me a healer, but please protect me from nails and deep sores! Let me be a doctor so I can heal and help others, too. Heal Nonno's broken heart in heaven, help the blind man from Memphis, wherever he is, save Mrs. Rossetti, and let me be just like Dr. Joe Gannon.

Of course, when young Don left the church to join his mother in the parish hall he promptly forgot everything he had asked for, but at some deep, subconscious level his yearning was not forgotten.

Don's father only attended St. Roch's on Easter and Christmas. He spent Sunday mornings in his study reading articles from *Science, Nature,* and the *Journal of Biological Chemistry.* In time Don began to find church as tedious as his father did, especially since St. Sebastian's School required chapel attendance every day. In eighth grade Don began to complain he'd been in church all week, but he continued to go to St. Roch's until eleventh grade, when he stopped going. His mother worked to banish the wounded look from her eye, but he still felt a little guilty every Sunday morning.

That same year he declared his plan to go to medical school. He wanted to be a heart surgeon like Dr. Joe Gannon.

"Bravo, Dante!" his mother told him. "You will make a very good doctor."

She relished telling everyone who would listen how her son was going to become a doctor. From then on it was unthinkable to turn back or change course. The die was cast.

He wanted to go away for college and chose Sewanee, the University of the South, where he could study both biology and literature. He wanted to read the greatest literary works of European civilization and get a top-notch premedical education. Secretly, he thought spending time in the South might help him understand and connect with his father in a way that had eluded him most of his young life. Of course, Sewanee was nearly as white as St. Patrick's Elementary, and though Don would never admit it, he wanted a white introduction to the South. Sewanee was perfect and a football scholarship sealed the deal. Even his father was glad for him.

In the first couple of years he completed the basic premedical requirements, courses involving long hours of tedious memorization of formulas and facts. After that he followed the advice of his college counselor and majored in the classics. She said choosing something besides straight biology and chemistry would improve his chances for medical school. It was just what he wanted to hear.

He spent many happy hours lounging under the great oaks atop the Cumberland Plateau and reading the best books ever written. He recorded his loftiest thoughts in his journal and doodled his daydreams in its margins. His literary mother had raised him on Dante, Cervantes, and the Bible. At Sewanee he built upon this foundation, searching the ways of the human heart through stories of people that went astray or ran true, from the classics of ancient Greece and Rome to Dostoyevsky.

The physician and novelist Oliver Wendell Holmes, Sr., was a favorite because he led both an active and a contemplative life. He visited the sick. He was among the first American physicians to admit that physicians who didn't wash their hands caused most childbirth fever, and that bloodletting didn't work. He helped his friend Henry Wadsworth Longfellow translate *The Divine Comedy* into English. He helped start *The Atlantic Monthly*. Dr. Holmes was the kind of physician Don wanted to be, and in his senior thesis he also tied the medical and literary together. His thesis centered on another Holmes—Sherlock Holmes— and the way he demonstrated that taking a thorough history was the key to making an accurate diagnosis.

Medical school was a rude awakening. The first two years were all biological structures and chemical pathways, with no stories or human lives to tie them to. All his skills in ferreting out causes and purposes were to little avail, because many of the dry facts memorized and regurgitated on tests were unrelated to one another. He studied hard and struggled to make sense of the disjointed information. Although he was back in Chicago, he rarely saw his mother. That was part of the cost, a personal hardship he had to endure for the greater purpose of serving others as a physician.

Somehow, Don survived those first two years of basic sciences and in the third year entered the clinical training phase. This was a completely different endeavor—applying scientific knowledge to real patients—and his talents emerged. He became skilled at treating heart failure with diuretics, and angina with aspirin and blood pressure medicines. But Don excelled most in getting stories from his patients and using these stories to diagnose illness. Despite mediocre grades in the basic sciences, in his clinical years he received all A's.

In his fourth year, Don asked to do his required surgical subspecialty rotation at the prestigious cardiac surgery unit at the University of Chicago Medical Center. At this point he still aspired to be a cardiothoracic surgeon like Dr. Gannon. He was good with his hands, had done well on his general surgery rotation, and had taken care to inform the surgeons he might choose a surgical career. It was the habit of medical students to leave a flattering impression with the attending physicians in each specialty rotation—the egos of their doctor-teachers required every good student to recognize the teacher's chosen field as the best—but in this case Don was sincere.

His request was accepted. To Don's dismay, he was assigned to work with Dr. Agamemnon Barkley, a world-famous heart surgeon who claimed to have implanted the first mechanical heart. Barkley only took a few medical students each year on his service. Everyone feared him. He intimidated patients, students, residents, and faculty alike, but his technical competence was unparalleled. Barkley had become famous and achieved his many firsts—including the first quintuple coronary artery bypass, the first mechanical heart transplant, and the first external heart pump use—by putting experimental techniques into practice before anyone else. Patients were guinea pigs on which to practice his bold techniques. He was willing and able to operate on the most complicated cases: bypassing impossibly clogged arteries, repairing completely ruined valves, resecting useless and damaged portions of bulging hearts to help them pump again.

Competing cardiac centers complained that he stole many of the ideas for which he was given credit, but at the University of Chicago he was considered an innovative pioneer who scrutinized international cardiovascular surgery experience and emulated the most promising new techniques. He would visit other campuses, track their newest discoveries, put them into practice, and publish his experience far before others dared to take such steps. As chairman of the department of surgery, Barkley had nearly limitless power and a fleet of fellows who, if they disobeyed him, would find themselves fired and unable to find a job anywhere in the country. He and his chief fellow made this threat crystal clear every opportunity they got.

The day before his rotation started, Don called the cardiovascular surgery fellow assigned to the service to introduce himself, just as Joe Gannon would have done.

"Yeah, it's about time you called," he replied, "and you better get to know your patients before tomorrow. You'll be expected to have them all prepped and ready for surgery and if they're not ready it will be your head, not mine. Oh yeah, and the post-ops, especially the long-termers, you take care of them, too, and keep their family members away from Barkley. He does not want to hear about them, and believe me you don't want him to hear about them. If something goes wrong with them it will be both of our heads." The fellow rattled off the names of the patients Don was supposed to pre-round on before morning rounds. There were thirty-four.

"Are all those *my* patients?" Don asked. He was used to splitting the responsibilities for a smaller service among several residents and medical students.

"Yeah, they're your patients. What did you expect? Barkley likes volume. Besides, he operates on cases no other surgeon will touch. Fourteen of those are pre-ops, seven are routine post-ops, and thirteen are long-termers. Remember, Barkley does not want to hear about the long-termers. And he has me busy in the OR and running up to check on the pre-ops and down again to crack ribs in the OR from six a.m. until nine p.m., so don't expect any help from me. You're on call every third night. Your first night is tomorrow, so make sure you come prepared. If I were you, I'd check out your patients tonight, and you should get started on the pre-ops no later than three a.m. Oh, and change Mr. Jacob's dressings. You should do that every day. He's a long-termer. Anyway, if you screw up, it's your butt. Good luck getting a residency spot. Everyone knows Barkley, and nobody, and I mean nobody, wants to be on his bad side, including me. So listen, don't make me look bad." He hung up before Don could ask any more questions.

Shit! What had he gotten himself into? He was just a medical student. If he screwed up Barkley would ruin his career and probably enjoy making it impossible for him to find a good residency position anywhere.

Don was bone-tired from a month's rotation in the ICU and had been looking forward to one night off to have a beer and sleep eight hours. Instead, after finishing his off-service notes on his ICU patients at six that night, he dragged himself over to the cardiac surgery suites to begin another harrowing month. He walked through the huge reception area packed with frightened family members waiting for news of loved ones. He entered his new code in the keypad by the secured doors. The doors swung open with a swoosh and Don entered the inner chambers.

Some of the best-looking and longest-limbed young nurses he had ever seen scurried around, attending to their tasks. The nurses eyed him with skepticism. Like him, they worked in perpetual fear of incurring an attending surgeon's wrath for some overlooked detail. For them, Don was just one in a long line of burdensome, inexperienced coworkers.

For the next five and a half hours, he went through his list and checked on vitals and fluids, often guessing what to do based on his experience from previous rotations in medicine, surgery, and the ICU. He paid particular attention to the frightened pre-ops—the patients about to have surgery. He didn't spend time allaying their fears; he had no time to spare. Don brushed aside questions as he checked off the pre-op testing and preparation requirements. The immediate post-ops looked relatively stable, as best he could tell. None of the long-termers seemed in danger of imminent death except for Mr. Jacobs, the last patient on his list.

Mr. Jacobs was fifty-three years old. Smoking and diabetes had given him severe coronary artery disease. Despite two coronary artery bypass surgeries, hardening of the arteries had recurred and blocked the bypass grafts. At that point, no one but Barkley would operate. Post-op complications were common when you opened a chest the third time—assuming the patient survived the surgery—but Barkley pooh-poohed concerns about scar tissue and poor wound healing and dazzled the Jacobs family with his apparent ability to perform miracles no other doctor could.

The chart indicated the surgery had been hard; it lasted eight hours despite Barkley's usual speed. Afterward, Barkley called Mr. Jacob's wife to announce his amazing success in attaching two new grafts—one made of experimental Gore-tex and the other from the one remaining major superficial vein in Mr. Jacob's leg. Barkley bragged to all his colleagues the surgery was a great success.

Except it wasn't. Two days after surgery Mr. Jacobs' huge chest wound began to dehisce, or separate. It refused to heal. Infection invaded his sternum and didn't respond to antibiotics. All the wound debridements—operations to cut away infected, pus-laden, rotting tissue—had failed. The surgical residents put him on total intravenous nutrition to provide the building blocks necessary to heal his devastated body, but despite this the wound came completely apart. The intravenous nutrition sent his blood sugar higher, which in turn made the infection move more rapidly into his bloodstream, and the infection made his sugar go higher yet. No one expected him to live. Yet he refused to die, as if to spite Barkley, who liked his patients to thrive or at least to die on someone else's watch.

Mr. Jacobs went back to surgery at least eight more times, but Barkley was not present for those operations. No one liked to deal with Barkley's failures, least of all Barkley. He had washed his hands of the case once he learned of the intractable infection. He made it clear he did not handle wound complications; his job was the delicate surgery of the heart. Mr. Jacobs was left to the supervision of other surgeons in the department, primarily the chief cardiovascular surgery fellow, who had assigned the case to Don.

Despite having read of his horrible condition in the chart, Don was completely unprepared for what he found. Approaching Mr. Jacob's door at the end of the hallway, he smelled the unmistakable rancid odor of anaerobic bacteria that flourish in deep pockets of pus. Although the room was designed for patients with active tuberculosis and had a system to suck all germs into an external ventilation system, the stench was overwhelming. Don forced himself to the bedside.

At first glance, Mr. Jacobs looked like a normal, middle-aged man. He had long sideburns, closely trimmed wavy light brown hair, and the shadow of a beard from missing a morning shave. But his cheeks were red and glistening. Sweat trickled from his brow, collected in the deep sockets below his wide-open eyes, and streamed around his nose, over his jaw, and down his neck. His face and body twitched uncontrollably, and his sheets were soaked with sweat. "You're new ... it's bad. It's bad. Look for yourself. You'll see."

It was obvious he had sepsis. His flushed cheeks, fever, and rapid pulse indicated the infection had spread into the bloodstream again, despite almost three months of antibiotics. Don went to find the nurse and asked her to bring supplies for changing Mr. Jacobs' dressings.

The nurse paled a bit and rolled her eyes. As the most junior nurse on the floor, she was assigned Barkley's worst failures. She left and returned a few minutes later with a rolling cart containing a two-foot pile of gauze dressings.

"What's all that for?" Don asked.

"You haven't done this before, have you?" she said, pulling back the sheet.

Don lifted the first dressing and almost fainted from the smell, despite his mask. He began to pull the wadded pus- and blood-soaked gauze from the open chest wound. This was no easy task; there were yards of the mephitic gauze packed in and around the infected crevices inside his chest. Don couldn't wait to finish his task, but if he went too fast Mr. Jacobs whimpered, grimaced, or even cried out in pain.

"Can we give him morphine?" Don asked after twenty excruciating minutes.

"He's already getting boatloads. We can't give him too much at once or his blood pressure drops."

"Can't we give him some anyway?" Don begged.

The nurse sighed and administered the extra "as needed" dose allowed by his orders. It didn't appear to make any difference.

Sweat formed on Don's brow as he pulled out more dripping gauze. Like a kid playing the game *Operation*, Don painstakingly avoided touching the exquisitely tender raw skin edges. He did not want to hear a scream—the real-life buzzer announcing his failure. As he got to the lower wadding, Don felt Mr. Jacobs' pulsing aorta and laboring heart beating against his hand.

My God! His chest was open to the backbone and Don saw the stomach and esophagus through the split diaphragm. Yellow-stained wadding filled half a large trashcan. He packed new gauze back in, added a fourth antibiotic, upped the IV fluids, and prayed Mr. Jacobs would make it through the night.

It didn't take Don long to realize he didn't want to be a cardiothoracic surgeon. Cardiothoracic fellows and attendings lived in the OR and spent their time cutting on unconscious patients. Heart surgery was nothing like what he had imagined. The first time Don assisted in the operating room he was astounded by the amount of blood. Suction catheters slurped up the bright red blood, which then flowed through the suction tubing, filled the canisters, and was siphoned back into large veins to replace the loss. Blood squirted from uncontrolled bleeders and splattered on the floor. It filled the OR with an odor of rusty iron and gave Barkley cause to shriek at the fellows about the mess.

Don's job was to help hold the ribs apart. He hated it, especially feeling the sternum pop after the little buzz saw had mostly separated it into two halves. He cringed when he heard the ribs crack. He detested hearing Barkley shout to pull them ever farther apart to get "exposure." He came to dread putting on a stifling surgical mask, knowing the surgery might last three or four hours, but he learned to suppress the panic and sensation of suffocation that met him whenever he put on the mask.

Dr. Barkley, on the other hand, seemed most at home in the OR. Tall and wiry, his wrinkled face and white hair covered in surgeon's garb, his back bent like a vulture's, he oversaw the entire operating field from on high. His flaming bright blue eyes displayed intense pleasure as he wielded his scalpel and flayed open the skin and muscle of his latest prey.

Don's main realm was the floor, where he labored twelve to eighteen hours every day. He prepped the pre-ops and checked on the post-ops from three to five-thirty in the morning. Then came rounding—or going through the patient list—with the cardiovascular surgery fellow from five-thirty to six. He finished up missed pre-op details for the rest of the morning and greased the way for the early post-ops. In the early afternoon he took care of post-ops and discharges and tried to keep the long-termers alive, or at least tried to keep Barkley from learning about their worsening status. Pre-ops for the next day occupied the late afternoon. He rounded with Dr. Barkley on his alleged successes whenever Dr. Barkley wanted, usually from six-thirty to eight at night. As long as patients lived three months past surgery, Barkley could include them in one of his publications as having survived. And that was what Barkley cared about.

By some miracle, Mr. Jacobs survived the month. He lived for the two hours each evening his wife was allowed to visit, and Don always made sure his dressing change was done by then.

Mrs. Jacobs called Don into the room one of the last nights of his rotation. "We both want to thank you for all you have done," she told him. "We know there is no hope, but thank you for acting as though things were going to be okay."

Don didn't know what to say. He had felt guilty for keeping up the appearance of helping when they all knew it wasn't for Mr. Jacobs. It was for Dr. Barkley.

As if reading his thoughts, Mrs. Jacobs turned to Don and spoke softly so her husband could not hear. "I guess we really shouldn't be doing all of this. I mean, he has suffered through so much pain and indignity. Sometimes I think I just can't take it anymore, to see him like this. But it is all for the best, I'm sure."

Don nodded. What else could he do? Barkley might be a butcher, but Don was just a lowly medical student. There was nothing he could say, or so he thought.

The last night of rounds with Barkley began late. The old surgeon lumbered down the hall toward Don at nearly eight that night. A long reflex hammer handle tottered in the pocket of his white coat like a metronome. Don wondered why he carried it; he had never seen Dr. Barkley use it.

With an uncanny sense of timing, Dr. Barkley asked about Mr. Jacobs' condition for the very first time. "So, Jacobs is still alive at three months, am I right?" His wrinkled face contorted itself into a wry grin.

"Yes, sir." It had been exactly three months to the day.

"Well, that was certainly a success! That makes seventeen out of twenty of my third-time redo bypasses that have made it. That's the best of anyone in the country and will look good in print. Good work, Newman."

Good work? The words rang hollow in Don's ears. He had followed orders and worked incredibly hard that month, but he left the cardiac center late that night with a terrible ache in the pit of his stomach. Still, when the time came to get recommendation letters for residency program applications, Don knew he had to ask Dr. Barkley. His prestige and the weight it carried could help him land one of the most coveted residency spots in the country—it was one of the reasons Don had stuck out the month.

Don sent Dr. Barkley's office his resume and a cover letter highlighting his rotation in cardiovascular surgery but announcing his intention to go into internal medicine and cardiology after that. This meant Don planned to go into cardiac medicine, not surgery. He hoped Dr. Barkley would not be offended and would write him a strong letter of support.

They met two weeks later in Dr. Barkley's walnut-paneled office. Barkley motioned for Don to sit in a leather chair twice his size and assessed him with his customary contempt. He reminded Don he was a member and faculty advisor for the prestigious medical fraternity Alpha Omega Alpha. Membership required nearly straight A's through the preclinical years of medical school. Given that Don's college background was in the liberal arts and not biochemistry, this requirement had been impossible for him to achieve, and Dr. Barkley expressed disappointment not to see Don in these ranks.

Don explained he was interested in a residency at the University Hospital.

Dr. Barkley laughed. Not just a chuckle, but a loud belly laugh. "You'll never get in there!" He laughed again. "Look, you did a great job keeping our long-termers alive on your rotation here, but you're not AOA and you don't have publications. Don't get your hopes up. You'll never get into the University Hospital. You're not that good."

His words burned like a brand, sealing Don's future course. Dr. Barkley had thrown down the gauntlet; Don had to apply. Barkley must have written a strong letter on his behalf after all, because to Don's surprise and great satisfaction, he got in. Once accepted, he felt compelled to go. His mother was so proud.

Don couldn't wait to visit his medical school faculty advisor to tell her the good news. Dr. Terri Reese ran the teaching practice at Pritzker, where resident physicians took care of their own patients under her supervision. Whenever Don visited her clinic he found her moving from exam room to exam room, greeting patients and their families like old friends, gently touching places of pain and offering words of encouragement. She encouraged resident physicians to go into primary care, and taught both patients and physicians the best ways to heal.

He couldn't wait to tell her he was going to the University Hospital in Boston, one of the best programs in the country. He expected she would be thrilled for him.

"I'm thinking maybe I'll go into cardiology." Don shrugged, as if to indicate it wasn't an important decision and could easily be undone.

Dr. Reese became serious, her face darkened, and though she looked toward him, her eyes were focused somewhere past him, somewhere far away. Just like the blind man from Memphis.

"Don, it is hard to follow your ideals if you are chained by debt," she said. "The residents there make less money, your expenses will be very high in Boston, and you'll pay for that prestige for the rest of your life."

Don couldn't believe what he was hearing. She should be glad and excited for him! It was the chance of a lifetime; all his colleagues were jealous. Besides, Dr. Reese had always said you should strive for excellence over material concerns.

"You made this decision based on what others see in the world, but you must discern your own gifts and find your own path. Don, you are not meant for cardiology. Remember this. Now it will be difficult for you to do the primary care for which you are so gifted and strongly inclined. Your path will be long and hard. God bless you. I hope you'll find your way to peace."

He was stunned and hurt. If he had been wiser he would have stopped right then and asked her why. Why wasn't he meant for cardiology? What did she know? But he wasn't that wise. It would take him years to understand what she saw so clearly. He didn't even have the heart to call her to say goodbye after that. Little did he know then how horrible their next conversation would be.

So, in the summer of 1998 Don packed up the old hatchback his parents gave him for graduation and moved away again. There was little time for visiting before he left. His mother was proud but sad he was leaving Chicago. His father questioned the career value of going to Boston but was dazzled by the prestige of the University Hospital. They all believed the sacrifice would be worth it, but his trials at the University Hospital would prove far worse than he could have ever guessed.

Before he knew it he had put in two years of endless work punctuated by rare, sleep-filled vacations. His mother called right before Thanksgiving in his third year. "Come home for Thanksgiving, Dante," she pleaded. "I want to be with you, to cook for you, and celebrate together. You have accomplished so much. And we have so much to be thankful for."

"Momma, you know I'm not scheduled to come home until Christmas. I can't just leave in the middle of a rotation. It'll have to wait another month; we'll celebrate then."

"I want you home now." There was a long pause before she dropped the bombshell. "I have breast cancer."

Before he could respond she was comforting him. "But don't worry, I'm seeing your friend Dr. Reese, and she's getting me in to see the best doctors."

Don knew she was putting on a positive spin for his benefit, but as she shared the details of her diagnosis and plans for treatment he was reassured. It sounded like she was getting all the recommended care. No one was a better doctor than Dr. Reese. Don ignored the twinge of unease in his gut. He told himself he'd be home soon enough and she was in good hands.

"Don't worry, Mom. Average survival with newly diagnosed breast cancer is fourteen years. Most people who get it die of something else. With your health and good cooking, this won't slow you down a bit. I'll be home at Christmas and we can talk more about it then."

Dr. Reese called Don one week after Thanksgiving and revealed the crucial detail his mother had left out: her tissue diagnosis. She had inflammatory breast cancer, a rare type known to be the worst kind of breast cancer. It was usually rapidly progressive, metastatic, and deadly. "You know this is very serious," Dr. Reese said. "You should come home as soon as you can."

Later on he realized he should have asked more questions, taken a better history, called her oncologist right away. He should have gone home immediately. But Christmas was just around the corner, only three weeks away. He would make up for it then. He still thought they would have plenty of time.

His mother put on a brave front. She didn't complain about the nausea and vomiting from the chemotherapy, nor when her thick beautiful brown hair began to fall out in clumps. When she finally told her doctors about the pain in her back, they discovered the cancer had spread into the bones of her back, legs, and pelvis. On the phone she sounded bright, cheery, and healthy, unlike so many patients who complained bitterly of their tribulations. Don hoped she would respond to chemotherapy, as most patients with breast cancer do, and that the cancer would temporarily leave her bones and give them more time.

One week before Christmas Don's father called. His mother had been admitted to the hospital with a blood clot in her leg. This time Don began to make arrangements to go home immediately, and eight hours later he was frantically packing his bag to run to the airport when Dr. Reese called. The blood clot had broken loose and blocked the path of blood from her heart to her lungs—a massive pulmonary embolism. She was gone.

The pain came in waves.

"There's something you need to know," Dr. Reese told him. "The blood thinner we ordered in the emergency room still hadn't been started by the nurse on the floor when your mother died six hours later. She was covered up with cancer, Don, and you know how that can predispose to clotting. Even if we'd started the blood thinner immediately, the clot probably would have broken free anyway. But there was a chance it might have given you more time with her. I'm so sorry, Don. I know how much your mother meant to you."

He mumbled "thank you" and dropped the phone in its cradle.

It can't be! Momma's young and alive; she can't be dead! People get sick and die all the time, but not Momma. Oh my God! This can't be happening.

He replayed everything Dr. Reese had said, and his initial disbelief turned to fury. She should have gotten the blood thinner in minutes. Six hours? *Six fucking hours without getting the one thing that could have saved her life? My own mother received substandard care! What fucking shit. Those fucking assholes! They killed my mother. Why couldn't they have just done their fucking job?*

But deep down, Don knew his mother's care wasn't out of the ordinary. Who was he kidding? What use was there in being angry? Don knew what Dr. Reese said was true—his mother would have died soon no matter what had been done. And he knew long delays before getting lifesaving medicines are the norm. The doctor's written order is just the first step. A clerk has to receive the order and fax it to the pharmacy. If the pharmacist can read it, the pharmacy processes the paperwork and prepares, labels, and sends the medicine to the floor. The nursing staff finds the medicine, reviews the orders, starts an IV, and hangs and infuses the medicine. Even in the University Hospital it often takes six to eight hours before people get the medicine they need most. And sometimes he was the one who caused the delay—the one who forgot to write down a critical order in time to help someone who was deathly ill. Don knew that. His anger turned to despair.

I should have gone home sooner. She asked me to come. I should have listened to her. Instead, I had all the answers. I didn't listen. I was the arrogant doctor. I'm trained to get full and complete histories on every patient, but didn't bother to learn hers. My own mother! She deserved better.

His father insisted on having an open casket for visitation at the funeral home the night before the service at Saint Roch's. She would have never wanted it. Don refused to go see her body before the small crowd of curious visitors descended. He didn't greet any of those who came to give their condolences. He was afraid to face her or anyone else, and he waited until everyone was gone to sneak a look.

When his father went to talk with the funeral director about arrangements for the service and burial, he darted into the parlor where her body was laid out. But it wasn't her. Just a cheap wax copy with fake hair and a painted face—a mask of orangey makeup she never would have worn. That wasn't his mother. His mother would have been horrified.

He would never see her again. His colleagues would have cursed him if he had taken time off to visit when she was alive, but it was easy now that she was dead. *That* his fellow residents could understand. That was excusable—to go bury someone who was already gone.

NOW HE COULD SEE what Dr. Reese had seen all along: cardiology was not for him. Chasing the prestige of the University Hospital was a huge mistake. He could have stayed at the University of Chicago for residency, saved tens of thousands of dollars, received fine training, and been there for his mother. Instead he was chained by debt and couldn't afford to go back to primary care, and Dr. Sampson had shredded any desire Don had for success in the clinical towers of high-tech medicine.

Why did he have to ruin it for me? What was to be gained by seeing the hell underneath the surface?

Don had no idea what else to do or where else to go. He had ventured into the depths of healthcare hell and was about to pay for it, in more ways than he could possibly know.

9

The Marble Hospital

THE FERRYMAN PLUNGED his long oars into the foul river, propelling the travelers through dense fog in the dark night. Black waves grabbed the oars like tar and threatened to swallow their small vessel. Acrid mist rose from the churning currents. With each stroke they lurched ever deeper into the gloom. Where were they going?

A massive bulwark emerged from the murky vapor. Don could just make out the shape of a great tower, an impregnable fortress. It might secure hoards of riches, or prisoners, but the glint of granite walls sheathed with vertical bands of iron banished any thought of plunder or escape. A second tower of gleaming black glass materialized alongside the first. They drew closer and the two towers loomed high above their little boat. His stomach grew queasy with dread. Were people locked inside?

Surrounding the towers was a sprawling complex of heaped-up buildings, parapets, and ramparts that appeared to have been thrown together in a hasty, haphazard manner. Smog surrounded the dismal city. No tree or trail softened its iron perimeter. It struck him—this was the University Hospital. He gaped in fascination and fear as the towers grew taller above him, piercing the polluted mantle overhead and reaching out of sight.

The boatman turned his wrinkled face toward Don and yelled, "There's the entrance, you piece of shit. Now get out!"

The ferryman's flaming blue eyes disarmed his passenger. Don felt a wave of panic.

"But I'm warning you…" he cackled, "they'll never let you in there. You're not AOA. You're not good enough!"

Don leapt to the shore, eager to get away from him. Dr. Sampson stepped out of the barge after Don and stood a moment between him and the ferryman. Don cowered behind Dr. Sampson and fought the urge to cling to him like a frightened child. With a stern glance at Don, Dr. Sampson turned and strode toward the tower entrance, leaving the bitter old boatman behind. Don took a deep breath, squared his shoulders, and followed close on Sampson's heels.

They came to a pair of enormous iron doors. Over the top of the doors, carved deeply into the stone archway, was the phrase *Work Makes You Free*. "These words have always been inscribed here," Dr. Sampson explained. "It's the false promise tyrants make to those whose lives are consigned to endless work. This is the entrance to the feverish city of sickness and death. This citadel guards sickness and hell; life and nature are forgotten here."

Dr. Sampson stepped up to the information desk next to the massive doors.

The clerk behind the thick glass shuffled papers, looked at her computer screen, and pecked her keyboard with two fingers. She looked up and scowled. "Do you have an appointment?"

"We are visiting doctors and we are here to tour the hospital," Dr. Sampson replied.

"*You* are visiting doctors?" She looked them up and down, then turned back to her monitor and ignored them.

"Madam, I would like to speak with your supervisor."

"I'm sure my supervisor would be delighted to help you," she spat. She strutted over to a covey of nurses, doctors, and office workers standing around a coffee pot and chortled with them at an inside joke. After what seemed an eternity she returned to her desk and resumed typing.

Dr. Sampson roared, "Excuse me, Madam! Please let us in!"

"Oh, you're still here. And what is your business?"

"We are here to see the University Hospital, as I told you."

"Oh, I'm sorry, but I'm afraid that is quite impossible." More bellicose laughter rang out from the halls behind the desk. "You see," she smirked, indicating the clock behind her, "visiting hours have just ended."

"We are not here to visit a patient. We are physicians and we intend to tour the hospital."

"Do you have hospital privileges here?"

"No, as I told you, we are visiting physicians and we are expected. Let me speak to Dr. Desmond!"

More snickering erupted from the back hall.

"As I said before, that is quite impossible. Dr. Desmond is really quite busy and I'm sure he cannot speak with you now. Perhaps one of the chief residents can help." She picked up the phone and began to dial. "Or maybe I should call security." She eyed them with suspicion.

"No, I'm sure the chief resident can clear this up." Dr. Sampson turned to Don. "Do not be surprised by their insolence," he reassured him. "Everyone here is just following orders. They all must answer to the administrator. Of course, some take great delight in flaunting their little positions of power."

A hunch-backed chief resident appeared behind the desk. He had the unhealthy pallor of one who never sees the sun, and his thick glasses magnified the dark circles under his sunken eye sockets.

"So you are Sampson," the chief resident said, looking at Don's mentor with contempt. "Dr. Desmond has told me about you," he snarled. "Don't practice medicine anymore, do you?"

"I know my way around a loud-mouth lackey like you," Dr. Sampson thundered. "You and Dr. Desmond cannot hide your work from us. You cannot keep us out. Tell Dr. Desmond we are here and open the doors, *now!*"

"Who's this young fresh one you've brought with you, old man? He might make a good patient for us, or maybe he'd like to help us with a few experiments. Leave him here with me and go on."

"He is not for you; you'll not have him!"

"Oh, but I think he will like it here. If he does well in the experiments, maybe we'll let him operate on someone." He leered at Don. "You would like that, wouldn't you? Any medical student would give his right testicle just to work here for a day. We can get a few gomers for you to take care of all by yourself."

Gomer was an ugly term referring to the sick people who spent months slowly dying in the hospital. Don had heard it, he'd even used it, but hearing the chief resident utter this derogatory epithet disgusted him now.

The massive automatic doors screeched and rumbled open in response to an unseen command. A fiendish laugh echoed out of the halls, followed by screams of agony and despair. A familiar, nauseating smell wafted from the doorway and Don recognized it as the sickly sweet concoction of disinfectant blended with feces, urine, and blood.

Dr. Desmond blocked the entrance. His face was half turned away, his bulging left eye emitting a menacing glare. His feet were planted more than shoulder width apart and his arms were folded across his chest. "I see you have brought me a plaything, Sampson," he said. "We'll see if something can be made out of this lump of dirt. He could be used, perhaps, but since he has been corrupted by you he probably never will be much good. He certainly won't make a real doctor."

"You must let us see the hospital. You are not allowed to keep us out!" Dr. Sampson insisted.

"No, old man, you must leave. Leave the young one to us; we'll take care of him. Now leave him here and get out!"

"I will not leave him in your hands!" Dr. Sampson bellowed, stepping forward in front of Don.

"This is not your domain, Sampson, I'm in charge here." He stepped back and the doors rumbled shut with a loud clank.

"What do we do now?" Don asked.

Dr. Sampson sighed. "We wait for help," he replied. "This place will fall, like Sodom and Gomorrah. It holds the seeds of its own destruction. The only question is when and how."

Don opened his mouth to speak but the words would not come out. What about the people inside? Will they all die? Surely they are not all to blame. What about the sick? They are prisoners. Who can blame them? And what about the workers doing their best to heal? Surely there must be at least five or ten who are good. They cannot all be bad!

A godawful shriek sounded again and again from the uppermost rampart, high above the gate, filled with wrath and fury, warning them away.

AAAAAAAAAA!   AAAAAAAAAA!   AAAAAAAAAA!

Surely it was not Mrs. Bellamy calling from a room in the tower? Surely she would not be here. Shaking from fear he began to look up, but in that moment Dr. Sampson clapped his hands over Don's eyes.

"No!" he yelled. "Do not look at her now. There are certain things you are not yet ready to see."

The earth began to shake and a violent wind buffeted them and the hospital walls. The iron doors obstructing the portal broke open with a loud crack and crashed to the sides.

A grim Dr. Reese, her dark brown hair now shot with silver, appeared beside them. Her dingy white coat trailed behind her like a faded light gray veil and she held a stethoscope ready in her hand. "Come with me," she said." She strode through the great doors and Dr. Sampson and Don followed close behind.

The three entered, determined to examine the condition of the poor souls held within the hospital prison. They passed through a vast waiting room packed full of grieving families. No one was there to comfort them. Dr. Reese led them through a doorway at the far end of the waiting room into an immense, high-ceilinged open ward. The center aisle was lined by hundreds of bedridden inmates. They strained against the chains and leather straps tethering them to the wrought iron bedsteads.

An emaciated man with stick arms and legs, sunken eyes, and a brown-spotted, shiny white scalp was strapped to one of the iron beds. It was Mr. Brady, Don's first ICU patient in the University Hospital. He looked toward Don in desperation while an officious orderly stuck a needle deep into his arm. Another poked a clear plastic tube down his throat, connected antique accordion bellows to the protruding end, and forced air into his over-expanded chest until it seemed ready to explode.

They passed through another door at the end of the ward. The mingled smells of sweat, vomit, urine, stool, and pus struck them as they crossed the threshold. Don choked down the bitterness rising in his throat and followed his two guides into an endless corridor marked at regular intervals on both sides by open passageways. Each passage led to a dank windowless cell with a sickbed.

A whimper came from a room to the right. A man with long sandy brown sideburns, his face covered in sweat—Mr. Jacobs—screamed in agony as Edward, Don's old intern, reached carelessly into the open seam running from his chest to his abdomen. Edward pulled out little bloody bits of liver, like the buzzard pecking away at the chained Prometheus. He examined each piece through his thick horned rimmed glasses as if he might find some answer he needed for an upcoming exam.

"Edward? What the hell are you doing?" Don yelled. Edward didn't look up. He didn't even seem to hear his former supervising resident. He just continued to stare with fascination at each piece of liver he extracted, ignoring Mr. Jacob's moans and pleading.

In another cell, a husky charge nurse hovering over the bed of an emaciated elderly man threatened, "You shouldn't have complained about your nurse last night. She'll be here again tonight. So you damn well better behave." The man shrank from his tormenter, trying to disappear underneath his paper-thin sheet. The charge nurse ripped the sheet away and yelled, "I smell your pee, old man. You won't be wetting your bed again on my watch! You will get a bladder catheter now, whether you like it or not!"

Across the hall, folds of white flesh spilled like saltwater taffy over the sides of a bed. Mrs. Aldrich groaned and tried without success to roll from side to side. Her head and massive legs—swollen to the size of tree trunks—were elevated so high her huge body was trapped against itself in the crevice formed by her hospital bed. Her chin and the flowing flesh of her jowls was jammed against her chest, and she struggled to breathe. Cracked, crusted sores penetrated the thickened bark of her legs, and sap seeped from the open ulcers where the bark had peeled away. Her two obese boys, Tommy and Jared, waddled around her, calling out, "Help! Please help! Can't somebody help our mother?"

From thinly veiled procedure rooms came the sound of cracking bones and tearing flesh intermixed with the wailing and sobbing of the wounded. From one room Don heard the buzz of a rotating saw severing a breastbone and a surgeon's scream: "Get me more exposure, damn you!" The hall reverberated with screams for mercy and angry curses of ill-equipped personnel. There was no anesthesia.

In another room Don saw Mrs. Pinckney, his patient in Boston's Robert Richardson Cancer Center, emaciated and unconscious. IV tubing carried fluorescent yellow fluid into her veins, while blood trickled from her eyes, nose, and every skin puncture and soaked her sheets in expanding round circles of red. The hematology fellow stood by her bed, bored and bemused, holding one test tube at a time down below the bed to collect the blood dripping from the sheet. He carefully placed the test tubes one by one in a felt-lined container.

Don called to him, "Help her!" But the fellow went on gathering samples for his experiment as if he hadn't heard a word that Don had said. Don yelled, "Please, help her!" But, once again, he was unheard or ignored. It was as if he and Mrs. Pinckney were not even there.

Don wanted to run into the rooms and push the devil doctors and nurses away, but found his legs unable to move from the prescribed path down the hallway. He could not act to change anything. It was all out of his control.

Dr. Reese looked back at him and said, "This is your nightmare, Dante. This is what you have seen. There is nothing you can do, but remember."

At the end of the long hallway they arrived at a dark wood paneled door. In the center of the door was a bronze doorknocker—a delicate lady's hand holding a round piece of fruit—he knew it well. It was the hand of Mary from his family's townhouse in Chicago. His Italian grandparents had given the knocker to his parents as a wedding gift.

"Don, I must leave you now," Dr. Reese said. "This door is for you alone. You can find your own way—if you follow your heart. I warn you, it gets worse from here. But there is no going back now."

Don reached out a trembling hand, pushed open the heavy wooden door without knocking, and went inside. She sat still on her hospital bed, waiting for him. A mask of orangey makeup covered her face. His mother had never worn makeup. She had never needed to; her smooth, olive-skinned complexion had been perfect. The dark brunette funeral wig sat above the woman's thin face like an oversized cartoon crown. The bouffant hair was a shade darker than natural and was not sewn with the fine threads of gray his mother said she had earned through the long years of waiting for Don's father.

"Hello, son," she said. Her warm brown eyes shone through the lurid mask, peering over the horizons formed by her still high cheekbones.

Momma! It was her!

"I am so glad you are here," she said with a slight smile. "This is where I needed you on my last day in the world. I tried to wait for you."

Don rushed to her bed to hold her. He tried to wrap his arms around her but his arms met with nothing but air.

Lines of care creased her painted forehead.

Two more times he tried to embrace her before giving up in despair.

"Listen to me, Dante. I know you are angry. You see what is bad here, but do not forget what is good. Even the nurses who failed to start my blood thinner on time were kind. They were so distraught when I died. I forgave them and I forgive you. Now you must forgive yourself. Only then can you help the others. We are all dead here, but you still live. Go through the depths of this place and remember it well. Remember those you have seen in this prison, as if you were in prison with them. Remember those who are being tortured here, as if you were being tortured. Remember these victims of hunger, fear, injustice, and oppression. Their pain will become your strength, so you can find a better way, Dante, a way of life. Open the doors and windows of the hospitals and free the prisoners. Free the living from the trappings of death. Release them all."

10

False Teachers

I saw on every hand a great plain full of pain and cruel torment…
graves…on every side…All their lids stood open and such dire lamentations
issued from them as plainly came from people wretched and suffering.
And I said: 'Master, who are these people buried within these chests
whose groans of pain we hear?'

DANTE ALIGHIERI, INFERNO 9, 109–126

AN IMMOVEABLE ACHE to embrace her was all that lingered. In the dim glow of the streetlight shining through his apartment windows, Don could just make out the shape of the oversized, leather-bound volume on top of his beaten-up bureau from Goodwill. The old copy of *La Divina Commedia*, once displayed in the front window of his grandfather's bookstore in Vicenza, had been one of his mother's prize possessions. Now she was gone and it belonged to him.

Don couldn't go back to sleep. Memories of countless days and nights in the hospital deluged his mind and mixed with the currents of his dream. He had worked so hard to become a doctor. He had been so eager to begin his internal medicine residency, to enter the hallowed halls of the most famous hospital in Boston, to work at the epicenter of modern healthcare. He got in. He was in thick. What he had found there had terrified him, but he didn't know what else to do. Hospital work was all he really knew.

The black heart of the University Hospital was the intensive care unit, or ICU, and the undisputed ruler of the ICU was Dr. Reginald Baker Faris. If Dr. Desmond was King Minos, Dr. Faris was the Minotaur. As Director of Intensive Care Services, Dr. Faris supervised the medical intensive care Unit (MICU), the cardiac care unit (CCU), and the pulmonary care unit (commonly referred to as the chronic vent unit) all under his control. The fellows doing subspecialty training in pulmonary and critical care under Dr. Faris were considered by all to be the crème de la crème, the ones who held the power to bring life from death.

The MICU and CCU occupied an entire floor of the biggest and newest of the University Hospital's two towers. Steel-clad sky bridges reached out like tentacles from each side of the ICU floor, connecting to radiology on one side and the doctor's office building on the other. Staff joked they could bring anyone to the ICU in minutes from anywhere in the medical center, if only they could find their way through the maze.

The dazzling ICUs were filled with millions of dollars' worth of the latest equipment. Each bedridden captive was tethered to a sophisticated computer by information-hungry probes inserted into every natural orifice, oxygen sensors taped to the skin, and pressure sensors attached to newly-created portals into major veins and arteries. All these gizmos relayed data to the monitors, where every physiologic parameter scrolled across the screen in real time. The goal was to keep the heart rate, respirations, and blood pressure within normal limits at all times. Physicians and families felt safer when every pulse, breath, and movement was monitored. Every tool of technology worked to keep a body function going—even when the patient had no chance of meaningful recovery, and whether he would have wanted it or not.

Don had been exhilarated to begin his first day of critical care training at the University Hospital. Three interns were assigned to the ICU for the month—one for each of the three units. Don arrived early in hopes of getting a little guidance from the critical care fellow who would be his lifeline in the ICU. The other two interns apparently had the same idea and were already waiting by the impressive array of video display terminals at the nurse's station when Don arrived.

The fellow was late. All they could do was wait, watch the nurses, and admire the amazing view across the city. A cacophony of beeps, bells, and buzzers called from every room, but no one was talking. Don wondered which of the immobilized and speechless bodies would be assigned to his care.

The fellow finally arrived, coffee in hand, a mere five minutes before the time assigned for rounds. "You're the new interns?" he inquired.

They nodded.

"Follow me."

They struggled to keep up with him as he sped through the ICU, raced onto the elevator, and pressed the up button.

"Dr. Faris is doing an urgent bronch," he explained as the elevator doors closed. "You know, using his ever-ready lighted scope to check out the bronchial tubes of some poor devil in the chronic vent unit who started bleeding from his right lung during the night. The pulmonary hemorrhage was probably caused by a necrotizing pneumonia—an infection that causes a portion of the lung to rot—but we must make sure. He said to meet him up there."

"Any advice to get us started for the month?" Don asked the question with real interest, given this was only his third month as a resident and he was still intensely afraid of taking responsibility for critically ill patients.

All three interns leaned toward the fellow to hear his response.

"Yeah," he said, "start praying you aren't assigned to the chronic vent unit. At least the poor suckers in the other units have half a chance to make it out of here."

The elevator doors opened on an entirely different scene. The chronic vent unit, only one floor above the frenetic MICU, was quiet. Too quiet. There was no reception desk; a buzzer let them through the automatic doors. No visitors sat in the small dusty waiting room. Medical assistants and nurse's aides moved in slow motion from room to room, staring straight ahead like zombies.

They passed the nursing station, where a lone nurse sat before the terminals monitoring vital signs. Down the hallway, all the doors and curtains on the row of glass-fronted cubicles were open, giving the place the appearance of a forgotten mausoleum in an ancient, looted necropolis. The rooms were silent as tombs, except for the rhythmic swoosh of forced air from the ventilators that gave bodies the semblance of life. Unlike the patients in the bustling ICU, the people on this floor appeared to have been forgotten.

They walked into one of the open cubicles and found Dr. Faris standing erect over an elevated bed. The scope in the doctor's hand penetrated the patient's mouth through a wide plastic ring that held the jaws wide open. Dr. Faris held himself well away from the bloody mucus that was splattered across the man's sunken cheeks, barrel chest, and white sheets, but was unfazed by the desperate gagging and rattling gasps for air.

The gagging sounds stimulated Don's own gag reflex. He looked around for a trash can in case he needed to throw up. He took two deep breaths and gritted his teeth.

Like the fellow, Faris skipped introductions. "Where did *you* train?" he asked, looking straight at Don.

"University of Chicago, Pritzker School of Medicine, sir," Don replied, swallowing back the bile in his throat.

"Has anything good ever come from Chicago? Make yourself useful and suction this bloody crap blocking my view."

Eager to obey, Don took another deep breath, grabbed the respiratory suction catheter, and shoved it down through the tracheostomy as best he could. The tracheostomy was a hole cut through the old man's neck and plugged with a short plastic tube that penetrated into his windpipe. It made chronic ventilation and "pulmonary toilet" easier. Don finished suctioning and began to watch the monitor.

Dr. Faris confirmed the diffuse bleeding the fellow had already identified on the x-ray of the infected lung. He took samples, withdrew the scope, and—much to Don's relief—the patient stopped gagging. The low oxygen alarm ceased its incessant beeps and the ghostly white skin grew pink as forced air from the ventilator perfused the body again. The man's arms were little more than loose skin over bone, his eyes were sunken, and a few brown tufts of hair ringed his shiny white- and brown-spotted scalp.

Dr. Faris ripped off his bloody gloves and turned to the medical assistant. "Every hour, run the suction catheter through the tracheostomy deep into that lung and suction as much crap out as you can. And you, Dr..." he looked at Don's nametag, "...Newman, this is your patient. See that you keep all the parameters in line."

That was how Don met Mr. Brady and learned he was the unfortunate intern assigned to the chronic vent unit and its living dead. Most patients there could not be restored to life, but neither were they allowed to die. Half were unconscious or minimally conscious.

Day after day, in room after room, Don forced rarified air in and out of them and pressed his stethoscope against their ribbed chests to listen to the crackling of their scarred fibrotic lungs. It sounded like the rhythmic popping of wood in a fire fed by oxygen, accelerated with each squeeze of the bellows. The ancients thought of air as life force, soul, or psyche. What would they think of doctors forcing air into these half-dead bodies?

Every day the three interns spent three or four hours rounding with Dr. Faris through the MICU, the CCU, and finally the chronic vent unit. They moved from bed to bed or—in the case of Don's unit, deathbed to deathbed—and discussed each patient's case. The rest of the time Don tried to practice medicine in his usual fashion, caring for the people assigned to him.

On the afternoon of his second day, Dr. Faris accosted him while he was dialing the phone. "What are you doing, Dr. Newman?"

"I'm trying to reach Mr. Brady's family."

"You need to focus on your job, Dr. Newman. Nursing and social work can contact the family. Your job is to make sure every physiologic parameter is correct. Forget about living wills, family conferences, and all that rot. That is the referring physician's job. We can't be responsible for his failure to do it. If people come here we keep them alive. That is what we do."

Faris was masterful at that—at keeping a body technically alive—beyond reason, will, or expectation. He knew how to calculate the exact combination of rate, tidal volume, and air pressure, and how to adjust the ventilators to maximally oxygenate without rupturing the stiff lungs. His skill commonly added twenty, thirty, forty, fifty, or even one hundred agonizing and expensive days to the end of life. About thirty percent of his patients had terminal conditions, and he gave those patients a few extra months of suffering at an unbelievable cost.

The chronic vent unit was the worst. It was located in the hospital, but unlike the other intensive care units, it was run by a for-profit company called VentaCorp. An inter-hospital transfer was required to admit a patient. Dr. Faris, as the medical director of the chronic vent unit, placed a resident physician there during the months he supervised the ICUs but left most of the day-to-day management to VentaCorp staff.

The company's business was to maintain those unable to speak or move. They slowly weaned those few who might be salvaged and prepared a few more for life on a home ventilator. They taught families how to suction copious sputum, adjust vent settings, manage feeding tubes, and prevent bedsores. Homes became little hospitals supplied by VentaCorp and loved ones found themselves working around the clock as unpaid caregivers, nurses, and respiratory therapists. Most of the patients were either unaware or resigned to life on a vent.

Mr. Brady was different. Every time he awoke from his heavy sedation the ventilator went crazy. Dr. Faris kept adjusting the dials on the vent, infuriated that he could not get Mr. Brady to succumb and let the ventilator breathe for him. Dr. Faris insisted that for every patient there was a vent setting on which the patient would breathe comfortably, but Mr. Brady seemed to cast doubt on this maxim.

In general, Don found ICU medicine simpler than outpatient medicine. Most patients were sedated and on a ventilator, so there was no history-taking to do. Besides, with a breathing tube in your windpipe, talking is not an option. Everyone cooperated fully with his physical exam and he could—no, he was *required* to—know every physiologic number. That often meant putting another IV into a pulsing artery or even into the heart itself to get heart or lung pressures. All he really needed was a strong stomach and the ability to record data: ins and outs, pressures, and lab values. It was like working in a laboratory or in veterinary medicine. He didn't have to worry about what the patients might actually want. Few of them could talk, express their needs, or thank him for his services.

In Mr. Brady's room, however, Don felt ill at ease. Although he knew all his numbers, Mr. Brady's case remained a mystery. He reviewed the chart carefully and began to put the history together.

Mr. Brady had been on the ventilator almost three months, but no one had tried to communicate with him to find out what was on his mind. He was found at home after a neighbor heard strange noises coming from the house and called the police. The police broke down the door, discovered Mr. Brady on the floor, and called the paramedics. He was delirious and his oxygen levels were so low his skin was blue. Suspecting he was psychotic, they restrained him and tied him down.

Mr. Brady fought. He repeatedly ripped off the oxygen mask they forced on his face. When his oxygen levels did not correct, the emergency room doctors intubated him, and because he struggled and resisted, his vocal cords were damaged, leaving him unable to speak. His right hand was paralyzed by a stroke; no one knew when that had occurred. When not overly sedated or in restraints, he made squiggly movements with his left hand. Don brought him pen and paper, but his scribbling was illegible.

He had lost one lung to cancer two years earlier. His good lung left him with little pulmonary reserve, and the severe pneumonia for which he was admitted to the ICU this time had almost killed him. He received several weeks of antibiotics and ventilator support and barely survived. He'd spent most of the last three months with his arms strapped down so he wouldn't pull out his endotracheal tube and IV lines. The previous month's team of doctors had obtained permission from Mr. Brady's estranged son to do a tracheostomy when it became clear he couldn't come off the ventilator any time soon, and the surgeons cut the hole in his throat, as they did for all the chronic vents.

In one of Don's daily reports, he suggested they contact the community hospital where Mr. Brady had the cancer surgery to see if they could find his regular doctor or old medical records.

Dr. Faris ridiculed this proposal. Community physicians and hospitals were incompetent, he claimed. How could they do anything to help once a patient reached the University Hospital?

One afternoon, Don removed the restraints and helped Mr. Brady write with his left hand. It trembled terribly, and he took fifteen minutes to write his message. His focus was intense, as if his very life depended on it. He finished, looked back to Don, and nodded.

On the paper he had written, "NO NO NO NO NO." It was very messy and barely legible, but the message was clear.

Later that day, Don showed Dr. Faris the note. "Maybe Mr. Brady is fighting the vent because he doesn't want to be on it?" he suggested.

"Don't show me that scribbling crap and tell me it means something," Dr. Faris snapped. "There must be some physiologic problem you've overlooked. Get back to your job, Dr. Newman."

By the end of the month, Mr. Brady appeared more resigned and more alert. He had stopped reaching for his tracheostomy or the ventilator tubing connected to it, so Don started to release him from his restraints more often.

One day, while listening to a lecture on ventilator management in the adjacent tower, Don got a call from a panicked nurse.

"Mr. Brady has yanked his trach and his oxygen levels are dropping fast!"

Don bolted from the lecture hall and ran all the way to the bedside, all the while unsure of what he'd do when he got there. By the time he reached the room, he had pretty much made up his mind to tube him again. Then he saw Mr. Brady face-to-face.

He was resting. The usual furrows and ridges lining his forehead were absent, his expression calm and pacific. His complexion was dusky and the blood oxygen monitor beeped loudly, but he wasn't struggling. For the first time since Don had met him, he appeared to be at peace.

The nurse and respiratory therapist looked at Dr. Newman for instructions. His resolve was gone. He didn't know what to do.

Dr. Faris stormed in. "What the hell is going on here? Get me a tube!"

"Sir, he doesn't want the breathing tube," Don said.

"How in the hell could he possibly know what he wants?" Faris shouted. "Either tube him now or I will, *Dr.* Newman. Right before I throw your ass out of this program!"

Don tubed him.

Near the end of the month, Mr. Brady was fitted with a speaking valve. His vocal cords had recovered enough to allow him to talk through the tracheostomy using a microphone. His first words in the buzzing mechanical monotone were clear.

"Take me off this machine," he croaked. "I told you all last time I never wanted to be on it again. Why are you doing this to me?"

Don broke the news to Dr. Faris on rounds that afternoon as they walked into Mr. Brady's room.

"Very well, take him off," he snarled. Dr. Faris turned on his heel and marched out of the room as if he had already forgotten Mr. Brady. "Now, let's move on and go talk about someone who actually wants good medical care."

Mr. Brady died quickly when they took him off the vent. The fellow stuck around for a bit and tried to cheer Don up.

"Listen, Don," he said, "remember how much better care is now. These chronic vent patients would have lived in iron lungs in the past if they lived at all. Hell, in the 1950s, paralyzed polio victims who couldn't breathe on their own were imprisoned in the iron boxes for life. You've heard what Dr. Faris taught us. Over ten thousand people live on vents in the United States alone, and these days one in ten chronic lungers actually lives to get off the vent, at least for a while. You have got to feel good about that, don't you?"

Despite this pep talk, Don noticed the fellow didn't like to spend time on the chronic vent unit, either. Despite extraordinary efforts and expenditures, most of the patients had permanently damaged lungs that would only get worse. Don had read the studies. They would never get off their vents. A third or more of the conscious patients would eventually ask to be taken off their breathing machines, even if it meant dying sooner. Most of them would never make it home. The doctors who worked the unit knew it and the scientific literature confirmed it. Patients died there more often than in the ICU, but because they died slowly, it was easier to pretend outcomes were good.

Dr. Faris almost never sent young people to the VentaCorp unit, even when they had hopeless lung disease. Instead, for the sake of parents and appearances, he maintained them in the ICU, well beyond the time when reasonable hope had disappeared. The chronic vent unit was for those without connections outside the hospital, those without an involved family member to advocate for them, those whose brains had been too damaged—by drugs, alcohol, gunshots, dementia, or strokes—to speak for themselves.

On the third day of his residency and his rotation in the ICU, an eighteen-year-old girl named Emily was admitted with a life-threatening case of viral pneumonia. The next day during rounds, Dr. Faris berated Mike, Don's fellow intern, who had been taking care of her.

"How can we have any chance of extubating her if we don't test her readiness every day? Don't you know you put her at greater risk of secondary pneumonia by keeping her doped up and not elevating the head of her bed? While she's sleeping, all that mucus just collects in her lungs. She's a setup for worse pneumonia if she has a tube in her throat and can't cough."

Sure enough, that is exactly what happened. Emily got a secondary bacterial pneumonia, a bad one. It spread rapidly from one lobe of her already fragile lungs to involve her entire chest. She developed ARDS, Acute Respiratory Distress Syndrome, caused by diffuse damage to her lungs. It's the same thing that happens to soldiers who almost bleed to death on the battlefield.

Don worried how Mike would handle this tragic mistake, especially since Emily had had a good chance of full recovery.

They had almost been ready to remove Emily's breathing tube when she worsened. Mike and Don hovered around her bed. She looked like Sleeping Beauty, her long dark hair spread over her pillow. They desperately wanted her to wake up. Emily was too young to get a diffuse lung injury like this. It could leave her crippled for life, assuming she survived.

"How did you manage to explain to her parents about the mistake?" Don asked Mike.

"What mistake?" Mike's brow furrowed in confusion.

"You know, not elevating her head and giving her a break from sedation to see if she could come off the vent."

"Oh, that." Mike replied. "That's not exactly a mistake, is it? People forget to do those things all the time. That's just usual care. It's not really anything I need to explain."

Don stared at him.

"Hey, don't worry about me, buddy. I'm a professional. I'm not going to get all emotional and let this stuff get to me."

At first, Don was stunned to see his fellow intern imitating the callous attitude of Dr. Faris. But Mike had taken to sporting his stethoscope as a necklace in the cafeteria, just like Dr. Faris. And he'd heard Mike mimicking Dr. Faris' superior air of authority when he taught the team's medical students.

"Hey, are you all right?" Mike asked. "Listen, don't get too attached to the patients, Don. Be careful! That kind of thinking will cloud your judgment."

They didn't talk much after that, and Don was able to forget about the incident until the end of the month. They had just finished rounds and were standing with Dr. Faris at the ICU nurse's station, just across the hall from Emily's bed.

She was "on autopilot" now, according to Mike and the fellow. That meant she was a chronic vent, with a trach and daily suctioning instructions and little hope of being weaned. She might live a year or two—might even get off the vent for a day or a month or, with a miracle, a year or more—but her chance at complete recovery was gone.

The nurse manager for the ICU came up to the group. She was a nurse who really knew her stuff.

"Could I have a moment of your time, Dr. Faris?" she said.

"Certainly," he replied with a condescending, paternal air.

"Many of the nursing staff and I recently returned from a conference on improving survival in the ICU, and we learned that death rates in the ICU go up to near fifty percent when people on the ventilator get a new pneumonia."

"Correct, Miss Nelson. You are talking about ventilator-associated pneumonia. That is why we work so hard to prevent pneumonias in our patients on the ventilator."

"Well, I know this is something you care about. At the meeting, they presented several studies showing a new way to prevent these pneumonias. It's called a 'ventilator bundle,' and it consists of four crucial things: elevating the head of the bed, giving daily sedation vacations to see if people are ready to wean, strong antacids to prevent reflux of bacteria in the lungs, and medicating to prevent blood clots. If you provide the bundle to every patient in the ICU, you can markedly decrease pneumonias and even cut death rates. Also…"

Dr. Faris interrupted. "Are you suggesting, Miss Nelson, that we should practice *cookbook* medicine here?"

"No," she replied, "of course not. But…"

"But you just said you thought we ought to have standing orders here for your 'vent bundle.'"

"Yes, but I meant…" she paused, confused by his response.

"Do you really think a nurse can adequately consider all the factors involved in making the decision whether or not to use these potentially dangerous treatments?"

"No, not at all," she replied, "but if—"

"Miss Nelson. Stop and think before you make such a suggestion again. This is the problem with modern medicine. Everyone thinks good medical care can be provided by following a cookbook. Then what would you need doctors for? Why not just use a computer, Miss Nelson? Do you know how many people bleed to death because of inappropriate use of blood thinners to prevent blood clots that never happen? Do you know how many drugs can interact with those simple antacids that you want to order willy-nilly? These modern practice guide-lines make me sick. Every patient is different, and if you give a one-size-fits-all nursing approach, then you nurses will end up killing people, and the blood won't be on my hands, damn it."

He turned his back on the embarrassed nurse and addressed his doctor students. "Everywhere in healthcare these days you will find administrators with a fraction of your education telling you how to practice medicine. All they preach is cookbooks, practice guidelines, and standardization. It's a mark of mediocrity. If you want to provide mediocre care and be a mediocre doctor, then go right ahead. Treat all patients alike. But if you believe in individualized patient care, stand up for medicine. Don't allow them to make us into short-order cooks."

Mike was nodding his head vigorously in approval.

Don's eyes were trained on the room across the hall behind Dr. Faris, where Emily's parents and younger sister were gathered around her deathbed.

11

The Plan of Healthcare Hell

If you are going through hell, keep going.
WINSTON CHURCHILL

THE SCREEN DOOR of the Sentinel Bar and Grill slammed behind Don as he walked across the creaky wooden floor toward the ancient bar.

A dark-eyed woman polishing glasses behind the counter looked up. "You're here for Dr. Sampson's class? You're a little early—no one's here yet. Why don't you make yourself at home?" She indicated a barstool with a sideways nod of her head and smiled. "Guess you won't be having a beer."

"No, I guess not." Don claimed a stool and looked up at the television in the corner of the bar.

Eight days since the 9–11 attacks, CNN news cameras were stationed just yards away from the ruins of building five of the World Trade Center at St. Paul's Chapel, where people gathered to look for lost family and friends. Footage from days earlier showed the sanctuary filled with ash and soot and the grave-yard littered with remnants of desks, paper, office supplies, and God knows what else. Scattered branches and a shattered trunk were all that remained of a huge sycamore tree that stood between the twin towers and St. Paul's and saved the historic church from complete destruction.

St. Paul's Chapel was Manhattan's oldest public building in continuous use. George Washington and Alexander Hamilton worshipped there in the early days of the republic, when New York was the nation's capitol. Now, it was a shrine brimming with pictures and memorials for the dead and missing—an oasis in the financial district's desert of heartbreak and horror.

Firemen, relief workers, and those searching for loved ones wandered in for counseling, food, and rest. Rescuers with ash-marked foreheads and tear-streaked faces slept on mattresses in the aisles, prayed with priests, and wept with counselors. Massage therapists and chiropractors soothed overburdened muscles and backs. One of Bruce's friends who had worked at Morgan Stanley was spending his days there. His other two friends were dead.

The repurposed sanctuary at St. Paul's was the closest thing to a hospital tending the injured that Don had seen on the news. He tried to imagine Bruce going to New York to help. There was no surgery to be done; for him it would all seem a waste of time.

The barmaid gave Don the remote control and indicated with a wave of her hand it was okay to change the channel.

NBC was showing excerpts from an interview with Dick Cheney on *Meet the Press.* The vice president was methodically explaining the White House strategy to fight the al Qaeda terrorists responsible for the attack. He spoke, as he always did, in a grave monotone that implied absolute infallibility:

> *We also have to work, through, sort of the dark side, if you will. We've got to spend time in the shadows in the intelligence world. A lot of what needs to be done here will have to be done quietly, without any discussion, using sources and methods that are available to our intelligence agencies, if we're going to be successful. That's the world these folks operate in, and so it's going to be vital for us to use any means at our disposal, basically, to achieve our objective.*

Don imagined infiltrating his nightmare hospital, unseen and unsuspected, to liberate the prisoners within. *I'd have to fit in. I'd have to look and act just like one of those demon doctors to accomplish that.* He shuddered.

Dr. Sampson strode into the bar. He wore a black M-65 military field jacket and carried a bunch of newspapers under his arm.

"Hello, Judith, Don."

"Hello, Dr. Sampson," she answered, "your room is ready upstairs."

"Thank you, Judith. Two more are coming. Send them right up, will you?"

Don followed Dr. Sampson around the empty tables and chairs, past the back windows, and up the side stairs next to the kitchen. They walked down a hallway past some offices on the left and entered the single door on the right.

The Sentinel Bar and Grill was built as an inn in 1947 and was a popular destination in its day, drawing vacationers from Boston and beyond. This back room was a closed-in sleeping porch that cantilevered out over the rocky cliff at the highest point of Sentinel Mountain. The mountain bordered the edge of town, giving the place a commanding view of Florence.

Before Don could admire the scenery, Frances came in. Dr. Sampson signaled them to join him at a square table on one side of the small room. The table was vaguely reminiscent of their seminar table in the projection room, but it was smaller, darker, and stained by the rings and spills of thousands of late-night symposiums.

"Welcome to the Sentinel," Dr. Sampson said.

Frances flashed Don her perfect smile.

"Hi," he said, smiling back at her. "What a view!"

"You can certainly see a lot from up here, can't you?" Dr. Sampson replied.

The door creaked and Don turned around to look.

Bruce pulled off his sunglasses as he came through the door. He looked directly at Frances. "Wow. What a view!"

"Whatever," Frances replied, rolling her eyes.

"Have a seat, Dr. Markum. I'm glad you're all here today," Dr. Sampson began. "Before lunch, I want to outline our course for the upcoming year. But first, did any of you see the paper today?" He passed them each a copy of *The Florence Herald*. "Go on, take time to skim through it."

Across the top of the front page was a headline in large bold letters.

Could 9–11 Have Been Prevented?
Evidence of Planned Attack Available 3 Months Ago

The article—assembled from Associated Press reports from *The Boston Globe*, *Los Angeles Times*, and several European newspapers—featured a timeline of facts available to the FBI three months prior to the attacks. Gathered together in linear progression, they made an attack on the World Trade Towers seem certain.

The FBI had received more than the usual number of credible threats. Some of them suggested an imminent attack on a major building or monument, possibly using a commercial plane. The FBI was also aware that some Saudi Arabian immigrants were taking pilot training in Florida and asking questions about jet fuel capacity. And over the previous six months, recorded conversations of two cells of known bin Laden associates—one in Los Angeles and one in Germany—had indicated an upcoming large hit on an American target using airplanes.

"That's terrible," Bruce said.

"Well, they say hindsight is twenty-twenty," Dr. Sampson responded.

"Who could have predicted that the World Trade Towers would be attacked with passenger planes?" Frances asked.

"Only someone very informed and very alert, that's certain. Someone with a healthy fear of the real possibility of a major attack. Someone who knew the World Trade Center was bombed in 1993 and understood it was still a desirable target. Someone with all the critical facts and the ability to sort through the clutter of a million false leads."

They sat silently for a few minutes and read the tragic details of the article.

"It's hard to think about this logically while we are still reeling from what we've seen on television all week," Dr. Sampson said. "However, you can see that the chances of gathering exactly the right information, finding a pattern, and organizing an effective response to avert this disaster were low, but not impossible. Given the right information in the right hands at the right time, someone could have predicted it."

"Yes," Don replied, "I think you're right. It says the frontline junior FBI agent in Florida repeatedly tried to warn the agency about the internationals taking pilot training in Florida but couldn't get anyone's attention."

"Did you hear the president's first move after the attacks was to allocate nine hundred million dollars to the CIA?" Bruce asked. "It looks like he's determined to fix this intelligence blunder."

"Just as he should," Dr. Sampson answered.

Don's mind raced. Why did the president invest in foreign intelligence instead of domestic—didn't the FBI handle domestic threats? Were our biggest problems coming from the inside or the outside? Was the vice president talking about CIA agents when he said we needed to work on *the dark side...in the shadows of the intelligence world*? Was the hijacking and bombing a federal crime or an act of war? If it was war, then what country had declared it?

"Effective organizations gather the precise cluster of data that can help predict the future and relay that critical information from the front lines to those who can act on it," Dr. Sampson explained. "Information and communication. That is the business of both prophets and entrepreneurs, and it is our healthcare business for the rest of the semester. Your study here is important. Many people will depend on the intelligence work you do here and your ability to communicate it. Remember, many more lives are at stake in healthcare than we lost in the towers and the Pentagon."

Bruce pressed his fingers together and gave Dr. Sampson a skeptical look across the bridge formed by his hands. "Oh, come on. Aren't you exaggerating? I mean, I know what it means to have lives at stake in the operating room, but lives at stake here? Forgive me, but we're in an ivory tower here at Florence College, quite removed from the noble act of saving lives."

"Wait a minute," Frances said, leaning toward Bruce. "Our reading for next week from the Institute of Medicine report, *To Err is Human*, says that one hundred and twenty thousand patients die because of medical mistakes each year. *Mistakes*. That's the equivalent of a jumbo jet crashing every day! Think how devastating the attacks were, and then imagine the equivalent of a huge planeload of people dying every day—and no one mentions it."

"That's exactly what I'm talking about, Ms. Hunt," Dr. Sampson said, "and those numbers on deaths from medical errors don't include those who die outside the hospital or from lack of healthcare. Nor do they account for pain and suffering from unnecessary operations and procedures. Considering the numbers of casualties, what happens every day in healthcare is like war. To win this war, we must understand the true objectives of those working to keep the healthcare system as it is and convince—or force—them to accept change.

"To defeat bin Laden we have to get in his head and understand the real reasons for his actions. We need to know what his next move will be even before he does. Why is bin Laden so angry? What could drive him to hate America so much? Was the killing of mothers, fathers, and children his main goal?" Dr. Sampson ignored their looks of shock and answered the question himself. "No, of course not. His main objective was to diminish the wealth and power of the United States by destroying a colossal icon of American dominance. The victims were innocent bystanders, weren't they? Like the representative they quoted from the State Department said: "Bin Laden is like a puritan on crack...He is someone convinced that the U.S. is a source of evil, which you must destroy to eradicate that evil."

"I think I get what you're saying," Frances said. "In a way, what happened in New York is like what happens every day in hospitals all over the country. Harm is a byproduct of the healthcare industry. From the medical director to the floor nurse, everyone is just following orders because that's how the system works. They intend to do the right thing, and convince themselves they are doing the right thing, even though the system is organized in a way that makes deadly mistakes routine."

"This is insane!" Bruce shouted. "How dare you compare what terrorists have done to what good doctors and nurses do in healthcare? Bin Laden wanted to kill all those innocent people!"

"True enough, Dr. Markum," Dr. Sampson nodded. "That is a fundamental difference. But as Ms. Hunt pointed out, the effects of terrorism and business as usual in healthcare are not that dissimilar. For the most part, doctors and nurses are like the workers in the Twin Towers—like your friends that worked for Morgan Stanley. The workers in the financial industry did not set out to make bin Laden angry. They went about their work and tried to do a good job for their banks and their shareholders. But the financial success of American banks made them some international enemies.

"Concentrated wealth breeds jealousy. Castles and fortresses filled with loot have long been targets for plunder. Bin Laden hates America's wealth and power. He can't have that power and wealth, so he's determined to destroy it. The workers in the financial industry represent the institutions he hates most, and they are legitimate targets in bin Laden's crazed mind.

"Are the towers of American healthcare really so different from the banks? The healthcare industry sucks up more money than the financial industry does each year—more than enough to safeguard against mistakes. But the status quo is lucrative. Just like workers in finance, workers in healthcare must consider the interests of their companies. They do not set out to harm others. They are just going about their work, trying to do a good job for the hospitals, clinics, and insurance companies that employ them."

Dr. Sampson's voice began a slow crescendo.

"But when a husband realizes that his beloved wife died because their insurance company canceled their policy in the middle of her chemotherapy treatments and refused to pay for potentially life-saving breast cancer surgery? When he realizes that administrators at his insurance company were paid extra to cut off people like her who worked for small companies whose business they could afford to lose? When he realizes their years of health insurance policy payments went for caviar and five-hundred-dollar-a-bottle champagne for executives who got fat bonuses to reject claims and prevent payouts? What is he to think? Isn't he likely to wonder why they let his wife die? Don't you think he will be angry, too?"

The volume of Dr. Sampson's voice continued to escalate. He leaned forward and gripped the edge of the table until his knuckles turned bony white.

"And when a father realizes his one-year-old daughter died from a minor skin infection—because a hospital pharmacist carelessly stored adult heparin right next to pediatric heparin, and because the pharmaceutical company packaged adult and pediatric heparin in exactly the same type of vial, and because a hurried pharmacist grabbed the wrong heparin vial; and because the exhausted nurse working double overtime for an understaffed hospital didn't double-check and gave the most beautiful little girl in the world a heparin dose that was one thousand times too high—don't you think he might have a right to be a little angry?"

Dr. Sampson's voice had reached shouting pitch; his bellow of rage blasted through the dead room. Not one of the three students moved a muscle. Dr. Sampson took a deep breath and continued in a commanding but less bellicose tone.

"We must act now on our best intelligence to save people from harm. We know what happens if we don't intervene. By not anticipating bin Laden's fury, over two thousand people were killed. In healthcare, over two thousand Americans are killed *every week*! That is real cause for fury. Medical mistakes kill more people than car wrecks. The deaths may be accidental, but they are preventable! When they happen week after week, year after year, how can we continue to absolve ourselves of responsibility? This is one war worth our fight. Intelligence and communication are the keys to winning.

"You have joined the battle to save American lives. That is what this course is all about. Think of this year as your basic training. I will make you competent intelligence officers so you can lead the fight and be good generals in this war. But don't get in too much of a hurry to fight. Run off in the fever of the good cause without your body armor and rifle, and you'll just get yourself killed.

"This first year, you will learn who the enemy is and what you are fighting for and against. In the second year, you will gain the tools necessary to be effective intelligence officers. Because many health system changes require government action, you will spend two weeks each semester at American University in

Washington studying health policy. This fall, we will study bureaucrats and the implementation of laws, and in the spring, we'll look at the political process and rulemaking.

"The seminar syllabus takes us from bad to worse in the world of health-care. In our first four classes, we started with the world at large and considered the mistakes people make in the pursuit of health and healthcare: scientists seduced by knowledge and erudition, people pursuing a full life through unnatural health habits and superficial beauty. We saw how well-meaning doctors in the *best clinics*, when they unconsciously focus on wealth instead of health, can cause extraordinary waste of lives and money."

Dr. Sampson stood, sending his chair clattering across the wooden floor behind him. "Come over here," he said, walking to the window. "Look at this." He indicated the valley below with a grand sweep of his arm. "See all the medical buildings? Over the next several weeks, we will be touring the world of the hospital—the premier mall of medical errors—where you will see a surprising level of violence."

They stood alongside Sampson and gazed out at the valley from their mountainside vantage point. Florence's two largest building complexes were hospitals. They flanked the town on two sides and, along with Sentinel Mountain, dominated the little town. On their left was the New American Healthcare hospital, where most of the private doctors in town admitted locals. Don had already lined up a moonlighting job at New American starting the following week. On the right was a giant complex of white buildings that made up the Florence Medical Center. It served the entire region as a referral hospital.

"Tell me the truth, Dr. Markum," Dr. Sampson said, "knowing how dysfunctional our current health system is, would you really want to be in charge of all this? Would any of you really want to control the health system as it is today?"

Bruce shook his head but appeared unconvinced.

Dr. Sampson grabbed Don's arm. "And what about you, Dr. Newman? Do you really want to give yourself over to cardiology and work in that system as it is now? Or do you want to fight for what is right and take an active role in the re-creation of American healthcare?"

Dr. Sampson didn't wait for a response. He looked over the valley and prophesied the end of the healthcare industry as they knew it. "As you can see—even here in this small rural American town—medicine is a major industry. And you can be assured," he thundered, "it will fail."

Dr. Sampson led them back to their seats at the table.

"We spend one and a half trillion dollars per year in America on pills, procedures, and bedpans," he continued. "This level of spending is unsustainable. Most of this spending occurs in the large temples to modern medicine: our hospitals. They host a world of medical errors, brutality, and violence against people who go there for help. Granted, most healthcare violence stems from the broken system, not evildoers. As Dr. Markum pointed out, the people who work in the system do not intend this violence to occur, but the factory has poor management and poor quality control, and its leaders have forgotten the intended product.

"After medical errors, we will study the healthcare industry, a world of money, power, and deception. We will uncover the secrets of the medical industrial complex that governs healthcare today. We will investigate deception in the most profitable areas of healthcare: pharmaceuticals, malpractice, procedures, images and tests, hospitals, insurance, and health plans. We will go to our nation's capitol to observe how federal bureaucrats, lobbyists, and lawmakers impact health and healthcare in the United States, and you will see how the wheels turn for health and illness in the halls of political power. By the end of this year, we will finish our survey of the current health system and the industries that dominate it. Then, and only then, will we be able to see our way forward."

Bruce seemed agitated, but just as he opened his mouth to speak, Judith came in with a large tray of glasses, plates, pita bread, dip, and a pitcher of lemonade.

"Do you have sweet tea?" Bruce asked.

"Sure...we can do that." She turned to Dr. Sampson with an admiring smile. "You can have this upper room as long as you want today. We don't usually get a huge lunch crowd on Wednesday."

"Thanks," he answered. "Judith, I'd like you to meet Don, Bruce, and Frances. Everyone, this is Judith Salameh. Her family owns the Sentinel, and they sure know how to cook."

Judith smiled again and put the bread and the bowl on the table.

"This is baba ganoush. It's made with eggplant and spices—I hope you like it." She headed back down to the kitchen.

"Lunch is on me," Dr. Sampson said, passing around the bread. "Let's eat."

Judith returned with a small pitcher and filled Bruce's empty tumbler with golden brown liquid. Ice cubes clinked in the glass and a fragrance of wilting roses filled the air.

Bruce took a sip. "This is not what we would call sweet tea in Charleston, but it sure is good."

"Rosewater and pine nuts," Judith said. "It's Lebanese."

Judith left and returned a few minutes later with a large salad and a platter of lamb and rice. She hovered a moment near the table to make sure they were satisfied, then addressed Dr. Sampson.

"So you have a new crew, Dr. Sampson."

He nodded.

"I sure hope they can help you change things for the better."

"Yes, I think they will help, Judith. And I know you'll take care of them when they come up here to visit."

"You know I will, Dr. Sampson." She smiled at them, her dark brown eyes lighting up her bronze face.

Bruce directed an overfamiliar smile back at her, as if her warm welcome was meant only for him.

She ignored him and turned back to Dr. Sampson. "You have done so much to help us; it's the least I can do."

"Thank you, Judith," he replied. "Everything is delicious."

"Thank you. Mom's in the kitchen today and she'll be pleased to hear it."

As Judith headed out the door, Frances turned to Dr. Sampson and asked the question they had all wondered about. "Dr. Sampson, could you tell us about why you went into medicine and how you ended up at Florence College?"

"Surely we can find something more important and interesting to discuss."

"No, please, Dr. Sampson," she said, "you know all about us; now tell us about your background."

"Yes, please do," added Bruce. "It would be very interesting to learn how you ended up here doing health services research."

"WELL, IF I MUST. Let's see, my path here really began when I was ten years old. I was raised in a small town near Pittsburgh called Youngstown, Ohio, also known as Steel City, USA. At that time, America was building skyscrapers all over the country and the steel industry, much like the healthcare industry now, was going strong.

"Youngstown was a rough, blue-collar town, and my father did not tolerate any slack. If I stepped out of line, I could count on a whipping I would remember the next day. Nothing was as important to my father as education. He said there were two keys to survival in the world: intelligence and treating other people with respect. He also said two things went hand-in-hand: knowing and minding your business.

"My grandfather worked in the Pennsylvania coalmines and died of black lung at age fifty-six. Before he died, he told my father to get out of the mines and go to the steel mills, which he thought were cleaner. My father followed his advice and worked hard, long hours at Youngstown Sheet and Tube. He put in twelve-hour shifts at least five days a week, feeding furnaces in blazing heat and breathing noxious fumes. The work was tough, but he was in Germany in World War II and said nothing in a steel mill could be worse than what he had seen in towns like Dresden, Dachau, and Berlin. He saved every penny so that I—his only son—could get an education. Starting at age thirteen, I worked every summer cleaning up the yard for the steel mill. Dad made sure I stayed far away from the furnaces.

"Dad always said the mill was a jungle, a hell of a job. Everyone depended on each other. If someone in the factory didn't do his job right or didn't look out for you, it could be fatal. Everyone at the mill respected my father because they knew they could count on him. He served as Grand Master for the Youngstown Masonic Lodge year after year."

Sampson paused and looked out pensively over the city below.

"But how did you decide on a career in medicine?" Frances prompted.

"One day, when I was twelve, Dad came home in a far graver mood than usual. Unfortunately, that was the same day I had to tell him that because I played baseball when I should have been studying, I made a D on my final science exam. I fully expected a beating, but he just looked at me. He looked incredibly tired. Usually he kept his troubles to himself, but this time he decided to share something with me.

"There had been a terrible accident at the mill. A catwalk broke over a big cauldron of molten steel and two men fell in. They screamed for a few seconds before they slipped under and disappeared. Dad was right there when it happened and saw the agony in their faces, but there was nothing anyone could do. A third man fell on the side of the cauldron. He shattered his ribs and one arm, and the other arm went in the molten steel.

"'We need to go to the hospital to see him,' my Dad told me. He said the man might live, but the chance of saving his burned arm or using either of his arms again was pretty small. So I went to the hospital with my father, feeling proud he was treating me like a man, but scared to death of what we would encounter there.

"The hospital, unlike the mill, was clean and quiet. We walked down the long, empty hall—I remember how our footsteps echoed so loudly. At the man's door, a nurse stopped us and said I would have to wait outside. My father told me to wait there, and he knocked softly and opened the door. I heard him say, 'My son is here and he needs to come in with me. Is that okay?'

"The nurse protested. She said they were in the middle of changing the dressing, but a deep voice said, 'Of course. Bring that boy in here if he needs to see.'

"We entered the room. A tall, elderly doctor and an obviously distraught woman—the injured man's wife—glanced our way. Both appeared to know my father because they parted, yielding the way between them to the bedside. Dad moved directly to the head of the bed and pulled me alongside.

"The man's eyes were glazed but he brightened a little upon the sound of my father's steady voice. The nurse had removed the man's dressing and there was little left of his arm but red, charred meat. Only bony stubs remained where his fingers had been. His breathing was labored and he looked to my father as if searching for hope, for assurance he was going to make it.

"Dad looked to the doctor, who shook his head.

"My father turned back to the man and said, 'Peace John, rest now, let your body rest.' The man seemed to relax a bit and started to breathe easier.

"I watched the liquid drip through the IV, drop by drop.

"The doctor turned to the nurse and said, 'You can give him three drops of morphine each hour, and give him five right now.'

"The doctor and nurse finished dressing the ruined arm with salve and gauze while the man slept. My father comforted the woman who would soon be a widow as she sobbed on his shoulder.

"When we left, the old doctor followed us into the hall. Dad introduced me to Dr. Owing and he shook my hand. I still remember what he looked like—he had bushy white eyebrows and fine smile wrinkles in the corners of his eyes. His grip was firm but the old skin of his hand felt like soft leather.

"'Son, I see you have a strong stomach and a caring heart,' he said. 'Perhaps some day you will be the doctor, after I'm gone.'

"Later my father explained that Dr. Owing was a fellow Masonic lodge member. There was a time when the lodge paid him two dollars per member to be available whenever needed. But then the state medical society promised to exclude and discredit any doctors who persisted in what they deemed unprofessional contracting. Dr. Owing stopped taking the fee but continued to treat lodge members whenever he was called. He would go to a sick person's home, regardless of whether or not he was paid. Like my father, he was a working man. He put in long, hard hours helping other people in their times of greatest need.

"My father did not drive straight home from the hospital that night. Instead, he drove to the lookout point on the mountain where we could see over the city center, much like where we are now. He turned off the motor and we sat for a long time looking at the flames leaping from the steel mill stacks.

"The valley was covered with dark clouds of ash and sulfur. It looked like hell with the lid off. At that time, most of America was still agrarian; farming was the main industry. Not in our town. Youngstown was completely given over to the steel industry, and the steel barons were making tons of money. Huge mountains of slag, the waste product of steel production, stood next to each of the flaming cookers.

"I felt ashamed. Our lives were built on destruction and pollution of the earth. And yet, it was hard to imagine it any other way.

"Dad said, 'You know why I want you to study. I don't want you to work here. I don't want you to work in the hellhole of the mill. It's no life, not for anybody. And I don't want you to die here. So far, I've been lucky, and I plan to stay lucky. We are survivors, so don't you worry about me.'

"He told me the steel industry would soon die because the war was over and the iron and stone towers had mostly been built. Steel production would decline and they wouldn't need our aging mills with their soon-to-be outmoded production methods. 'No one believes the mills will close and that they will lose their high-paying jobs,' he told me. 'They think this will go on forever but it won't. Somehow, we'll have to rebuild the city after all the plants close and the jobs dry up. You deserve a better life. Get an education and pick a different industry where you'll always have a job. All I want is for you to have the chance to live in a healthier city than this, to have space for a little yard and a tree you can sit under.'

"I decided right then and there I would be a doctor like Dr. Owing and look out for the little guy like my father had...So that's it. Back to work. Too much reflection can paralyze you. Dr. Markum, bring us a case on medical errors next week, will you?"

Bruce nodded.

"Okay, then. See you all next week."

Dr. Sampson was gone before they could ask any more questions. He left without telling them a word about getting married in college, his infant daughter's death, or Vietnam. He never would. He would never speak openly of the private things that informed everything he did.

Bruce gave Frances and Don a knowing glance. "That old man is as full of rage as Osama bin Laden."

"I wonder why?" Frances answered.

"I don't know," he said. "But I'm going to find out."

Bruce and Frances left. Don lingered a moment to take in the view one more time.

Judith came in to clear off the table. "I can tell you like him," she said, "and that makes you a friend of mine. I'm glad to meet you, Don."

"Good to meet you, too," he said. Don shook her hand, feeling its strength and the callus of her palm.

"You know," she added, "I've seen your friend Bruce up here a few times already, except usually it's for power lunches and drinking. Seems like he's always meeting up with someone important."

Don laughed. "Really? Sounds like he's having a lot more fun than I am."

"Maybe..." she replied, but her eyes held an earnest look that Don remembered long afterward.

LATE THAT NIGHT DON returned to his apartment with a plan to record his thoughts on Dr. Sampson's bizarre remarks while his memory was fresh. He grabbed a new composition book from his backpack, sat down at his small kitchen table, and stared at the first blank page for fifteen minutes. Frustrated, he glanced around at his spartan studio apartment until his eyes settled on the large book atop his bureau at the far end of the room.

The antique copy of *The Divine Comedy,* a special facsimile edition from 1821, had been a wedding gift to his parents and was one of his mother's prized possessions. Don's father had given it to him as soon as they got home from the funeral.

"You know what this meant to your mother," he had said. "It was her connection to the old world, her homeland. She always wanted you to have it."

He pushed the heavy book into Don's chest. "Take it," he urged. Don tried to push it away, pretending not to want it. Water began to spill from his father's eyes across the dark umber cover, and he hadn't been able to stand that. He took it then and wiped the tears away.

Don did want the book, with all his heart. When Don was little, his mother had told him stories about its pictures, and he had studied the macabre illustrations with morbid fascination. The image of devils driving pitchforks into the burning flesh of corrupt politicians that dared to rise out of the boiling tar gave him nightmares. After that, his mother forbade him to look at the great book without her supervision. She seldom let him see the scenes from the *Inferno* and instead steered him to the reassuring pictures of *Purgatorio* and *Paradiso.*

Since her death, Don hadn't opened the old book—the memories it evoked had been too painful. But now he was ready. He went to the bureau to retrieve the leather-bound folio and hauled it back to the kitchen table with nostalgic anticipation.

The lustrous leather binding, oiled by hundreds of hands, pressed into his hands as if wanting to fall open again to reveal its secrets. The cover was embossed with grotesque, half-human, half-animal figures interlaced with colorful geometric patterns. The spine read simply: *Commedia, Dante,* but the cover gave the full title, *La Divina Commedia di Dante Alighieri,* and in smaller letters, *Illustrata da Botticelli.* Don regretted never having learned Italian. His mother always wanted to teach him, but he was too impatient.

The color plates were wondrously illuminated and produced by one of the best printers in Europe. Much of the book was filled with line drawings few people had ever seen. Unlike Albrecht Durer's famous drawings of *The Divine Comedy,* these older illustrations from the late 1400's by the Italian Sandro Botticelli were not well known. Although Botticelli's scandalous paintings of naked nymphs and goddesses and his sacred paintings of Mary and the Christ child were among the best-recognized masterpieces of the Renaissance, his drawings of the *Inferno*—of burning heretics and dancing devils in the city of Dis—had largely been forgotten.

The first plate was Botticelli's map showing a diagram of Dante's *Inferno.* Don studied the levels of hell from top to bottom: nine circles of suffering, each one gradually increasing in wickedness as Dante and Virgil spiral down the tornado-shaped cone toward the greatest evil imaginable.

Hadn't Dr. Sampson said something about the course moving from bad to worse in the world of healthcare? An absurd thought occurred to Don: what if Botticelli's diagram could be used to illustrate the faults of American healthcare? What would be the worst part, down at the bottom of the funnel? How would Dr. Sampson draw a diagram of American healthcare?

Follow the money. Dr. Sampson said where fraud was the greatest, the most money was made. Was there really an inverse relationship between money and healthcare benefit? It seemed impossibly backwards.

Don began to meticulously copy Botticelli's image of Dante's hell on the final two pages of his composition book. He marveled at how well the different aspects of healthcare seemed to fit into the hierarchy of Dante's sins. The parapets of the City of Dis in Dante's hell separated the sins of indulgence—those addressed by primary care—from the sins of violence occurring in the lower levels—those that mainly occur in the hospital. The parallels between their planned journey through American healthcare and Dante's journey through hell long ago astounded him.

Don decided to estimate the money spent and lives saved in each area of healthcare covered by the seminar. He resolved to redouble his efforts in epidemiology class. He'd need to learn some healthcare economics from Frances to make the best possible estimates. He reviewed his notes from the first three sessions and wrote down his initial estimates for the first three levels in the pages of his journal. But Don decided to wait until he had finalized his numbers before transcribing them into his Dantean diagram of healthcare hell on the last pages of his journal.

Maybe Bruce was right. Maybe we need to take the war to our enemies, get in their heads like Dr. Sampson said, go underground. Don trembled at the thought. *But then, how will they distinguish us from the terrorists?*

12

Medical Violence

...the boiling stream...deepens its bed til it comes again to the place
where tyranny must groan. There Divine Justice stings
[the tyrants who were]...a scourge on the earth.
DANTE ALIGHIERI, INFERNO 12, 128–134

BRUCE APPEARED RELAXED and self-assured as he prepared to present his case. He wore starched khakis and a blue gingham button-down oxford shirt so finely woven it glistened under the fluorescent lights. A burnished leather belt perfectly matched his tasseled brown loafers. Bruce exuded confidence and authority. Of course, that was how Bruce always looked.

"I'm going to be very honest with you," Bruce began. "Looking at the details of these medical errors has been hard for me. You all know I'm a surgeon, and a fair number of errors occur on the surgical side—I might as well admit that right up front. And there were plenty of bad cases in our readings to choose from. One of the most notorious cases was Andy Warhol, the famous artist who died after routine gallbladder surgery, supposedly because of careless post-operative monitoring. If you've seen Warhol's art, that may not have been the greatest loss."

Bruce looked at the other students with a wry smile.

"When the comedian Dana Carvey had a coronary artery bypass on the wrong arteries, that was no joke. One of my personal favorites is the woman who kept setting off the metal detector at the airport. The handheld wand detector indicated metal in her abdomen. Airport security diagnosed a stomachache that had persisted since the woman's abdominal surgery three months before; it turned out a foot-long retractor used during the operation to hold her wound open was left inside by mistake."

Frances clapped her hand over her mouth.

Bruce grinned. "Yes, there are some incredible clowns out there doing surgery—docs who trained at the worst hospitals. Surgeons leave sponges or instruments inside people once every ten thousand surgeries. That doesn't sound like many, but given twenty-five million surgeries in the United States every year, sponges or instruments are left in over two thousand people."

Bruce's jaw tightened, deepening the fine lines of his face and forehead. He pressed together his fingertips before his chiseled face and appraised the others over the steeple formed by his well-manicured nails and trimmed cuticles.

"The case I chose to present today is the case of Mr. Willie King. Mr. King was a fifty-one-year-old African-American man who lived in Tampa, Florida, with his three children. He suffered from the modern plague of diabetes, or 'sweet blood.' He had taken insulin for years but still had difficulty keeping his blood sugar in the normal range.

"This unnatural metabolic state slowly clogged Mr. King's arteries and damaged the nerves in his feet. He got a blister on his right foot and didn't feel it. The blister burst, and the rubbing of his shoe on his insensate foot caused the sore to ulcerate. Because of the clogged arteries to his feet, it didn't heal. The ulcer deepened, and the bacteria on his skin found their way down to the bone. By the time he made it to the doctor, he had a deep bone infection and gangrene. Amputation was about the only option.

"As you guys probably know, this happens all the time. Thanks to uncontrolled diabetes and hardening of the arteries, we surgeons amputate the feet or legs of about seventy thousand diabetics every year. Anyway, Mr. King agreed to have his right leg amputated. He checked into the hospital and the brilliant clerk in admissions—who probably had a high school education at best—mistyped into the computer that Mr. King was to have a *left* leg amputation."

"Dr. Markum," Dr. Sampson broke in gently, "just report the facts of the case, and we can talk about the reasons things went wrong later."

Bruce resumed, his voice betraying a trace of irritation at the interruption. "Now, there was a sharp nurse on the floor," he said, winking at Frances, "who saw the mistake on her printed paperwork and called the operating room nurse, who in turn corrected the OR copy of the computer printout by hand. Of course, they were unable to access and correct the computer record, so the computer still indicated he was to have his *left* leg amputated.

"Another OR nurse went up to see Mr. King right before he was brought down to surgery, and he actually joked with her, 'You know which one it is, don't ya? I don't want to wake up and find the wrong one gone!' Unfortunately, that is exactly what happened.

"Copies of the master schedule indicating Mr. King was to have his left leg removed were posted all over the hospital. When the surgeon arrived that morning, he reviewed the posted copy. Apparently, no one in the OR noticed the correction on the surgical clipboard, and the sharp floor nurse who had caught the mistake wasn't there. The surgeon and his team scrubbed and prepped and— without double-checking the OR clipboard—cut off the left leg instead of the right one.

"Just before they finished slicing through the bone, the scrub nurse found the correction and alerted the surgeon, but it was too late to reattach the leg. With Mr. King's hardening of the arteries, a partially amputated and reattached leg would never heal, so they finished off his good leg and a few months later cut off the bad one, too. Mr. King was left without any legs, wheelchair-bound for life. It's hard to use artificial limbs when both legs are gone."

There was a long pause after Bruce finished his presentation.

"Excellent job presenting this terrible story," Dr. Sampson said. "Now let's sew it up. Dr. Markum, tell us where you think things went wrong."

"It's fairly obvious, isn't it? The clerk was inept and should lose her job for this. That doesn't excuse the surgeon, who was also grossly incompetent. He should have reviewed the OR chart, seen the patient right before surgery, and looked at both his legs. That's standard practice. He was probably too lazy to get up in the morning. Really, this guy—whoever he is—ought to be run out of town."

"But is it always possible to review the chart again right before surgery?" Don asked. "After you guys scrub in, isn't it hard to break scrub to look at the chart, since you are in sterile gowns and masks?"

"Yes, it's hard, but the good surgeons do it."

"They do it most of the time, but not always, right?" Dr. Sampson pressed him. "Dr. Markum, haven't there been times when you've been too busy to look at the chart before an operation, and you trusted what a posted schedule or a nurse or colleague told you?"

"Sure, I guess. I mean, you've got to trust your colleagues and the information you are given, or it's impossible to get any work done."

"What was the source of the information Mr. King's surgeon trusted that he shouldn't have?"

"Well, that is the secondary problem—the damn computer system. Once something is in there, it replicates itself like bacteria, and it's impossible to get rid of it."

"How many of you have experienced problems where computers or charts had incorrect information that, if left unquestioned, would have put your patient's life at serious risk?"

Don, Frances, and Bruce all raised their hands.

"Virtually every healthcare provider in America has seen information errors put lives in serious danger. It happens every day. Healthcare is one of the most complex industries in the world, and the possibility of errors increases exponentially with every new diagnostic test and treatment. However, our information systems have not kept pace with those of other industries. The healthcare industry has been one of the slowest to computerize and use simple automated approaches to detect and prevent mistakes."

"You can't let the surgeon completely off the hook," Bruce argued. "He's responsible. He's the one who is going to get sued, and he should. This guy screwed up. He probably was one of those lousy surgeons who jam-packs his schedule full of surgeries and doesn't bother to take a clear history on each patient. Don't blame it all on a faulty information system."

"You are right, we must hold doctors accountable," Dr. Sampson said. "Given the level of complexity in healthcare today, more details must be checked than ever before. Doctors who take less time with a patient before and after surgery are bound to skimp on details and make more mistakes. The data shows that faster doctors generally make more mistakes. The truly incompetent physicians should be identified early and removed from practice. However, you presented no hard evidence Mr. King's doctor was incompetent or rushed through the surgery. For all we know, this surgeon followed the routine practice for the area and generally has good results. Couldn't this have happened to anyone?"

"I can't believe you are actually defending this surgeon," Bruce said. "He cut off the wrong leg! No matter what the information system did, you can't forgive him for that. What he did was inexcusable."

"Think carefully, Dr. Markum. You said earlier that you also have trusted the information received from colleagues and paperwork. Was it really inexcusable? Do we really want to put most of the blame for this on the doctor?"

Frances spoke up. "As disorganized as our system is, and as pressured as doctors and nurses are for time, I think this could happen to anyone."

"Dr. Markum," Dr. Sampson said in a soft rumbling voice, "have you ever had an experience like this, where a truly stupid error was made?"

"Not that I remember."

"You taught at Duke, right? One of the best surgical hospitals in the world?"

"That's right." Bruce beamed, enjoying the compliment to his prestigious medical center.

"Were you there when the famous liver transplant went wrong?"

The color drained from Bruce's face. His hands fell, wrists crossing and covering his gut. The question had clearly caught him off-guard, and he didn't answer at first. He drew a deep breath and expressed it with a hiss, like a deflating balloon. As his lungs contracted, his chin fell to his chest.

"Jesica Santillan. Yes, I know a lot about it," he finally admitted.

"Can you tell us what happened?" Dr. Sampson continued. "It would really help us to know the details, because if such a terrible error can happen at one of the best hospitals in the world, it can happen anywhere."

"I have tried to put that day out of my mind," Bruce said. "I was involved, but I sure wish I hadn't been. Jesica Santillan's family brought her to Duke from Mexico to try to save her life. She had a very bad heart condition called restrictive cardiomyopathy. By the time she reached Duke, it had ruined her lungs, so she was unlikely to live more than a few years. Her only chance was a total heart-lung transplant. Her family didn't have that kind of money, so they started asking for help. A prominent philanthropist heard about her on the local news and took an interest in her case. He started a charity, raised a half million dollars, and we got her on the transplant list."

"How did you get involved?" Don asked.

"I'm a thoracic surgeon," he answered with mild annoyance. "I had been on the faculty two years and occasionally assisted on transplants. The Santillan case was a big deal for Duke. Everybody knew about it from the papers, and everybody wanted to scrub in on the famous case that would boost Duke's reputation for saving lives. Incidentally, the guy footing the bill was a family friend, so I knew about the case from the very beginning. When I got the call in the middle of the night to come to the OR because a matching heart and lungs were on their way, I bolted for the door. Now I wish I'd never heard of the case."

"What happened?" Dr. Sampson asked.

"When a transplant is found, everyone goes into overdrive because organs only last about six hours after harvest. Organs should never be harvested until a match is confirmed, but somehow they jumped the gun and flew them in without confirming a blood type match. It's unbelievable really, because that's the most important thing to match. We had a ten-member transplant team, and we all assumed the match was correct—the organs shouldn't have been there otherwise."

"Didn't someone confirm the blood type match when the new organs arrived?" Dr. Sampson inquired.

Bruce crossed his arms over his solar plexus and bent forward at the waist. "You really have no idea how fast all this goes. Just before the new organs arrive, we crack the chest, remove the old heart and lungs, and get the patient on the pump, ready, so the new organs spend as little time as possible without oxygen. We don't waste any time.

"Anyway, the surgery was textbook. It took five hours. Dr. Jaggers, the lead surgeon, did everything perfectly. And then, just after we finished putting in the new heart and lungs and the new heart was beginning to pump, we got an urgent message from our immunology lab that the blood types were mismatched. We looked at the Igloo cooler, and it was right there on the side in large letters: 'Blood Type A'. The lead nurse broke scrub and flipped through the chart to find Jesica's blood type. She was type O. She had a deadly blood type mismatch, and it was too late to go back.

"We still tried to save her. For two days, we desperately gave her anti-rejection drugs and tried to get another set of organs, but there was no way. Rejection started right after surgery. Her blood pressure kept dropping as her heart weakened, her lungs filled up with inflammation, and we couldn't oxygenate her. She didn't have a chance."

"Let me get this straight," Don said. "With medicine, Jesica Santillan could have lived another four or five years with her bad heart, but you cut it out and replaced it with a healthy heart that was fatal to her but could have saved another person?"

"Yeah," Bruce mumbled. He bent further forward over his crossed arms and stared down at the table, as if trying to read an encrypted message inscribed in its glossy surface.

"How old was she?" Frances asked.

"Seventeen."

Frances gasped.

Dr. Sampson stared straight across the table at Bruce. "What should we learn from this case, Dr. Markum?"

"Well, for Dr. Jagger, it just about ruined his career," Bruce answered. "Yeah, he is still at Duke, but..."

"Was he incompetent? Should he be barred from practice?"

"Dr. Jagger was one of the best surgeons I have ever seen. I think he has been punished enough. It should never have happened." Bruce shook his head as if to clear it from the oppressive thoughts.

Dr. Sampson was unrelenting, "Could anything have been done to prevent it?"

Everyone was silent.

"Come on," Dr. Sampson urged, "What dangerous industries can you think of where mistakes rarely occur?"

"Like, the airline industry?" Frances asked.

"Exactly! What made you think of the airlines, Ms. Hunt?"

"Well," she said, "my dad—my biological dad I mean—was an airline pilot. I just remember him talking about all the safeguards and standard routines they used. He said too many lives were at stake to make stupid mistakes. Lots of lives are at stake in healthcare, too, only it sounds like we make stupid errors all the time."

"I'm afraid you are right," Dr. Sampson said. "Though flying could easily be very dangerous, airlines almost never make mistakes. Your chance of dying on your next commercial airline flight is about one in fifty million. On average, you would have to fly nonstop for four hundred and thirty-eight years before you would be in a fatal crash. The risk of fatal accidents in cars is around one in two million every time you drive. But what about your risk of death from a preventable medical error?"

"Let's see," Frances said, "The Institute of Medicine—the IOM—agrees there are around one hundred thousand deaths from preventable medical errors in the U.S. hospitals every year. Combine that with the thirty-four million hospital admissions a year, and that gives you a risk of death...of around one in three hundred thirty-six every time you go in the hospital."

Did she just calculate that in her head?

"One in three hundred and thirty-six die from mistakes?" Bruce said. "Are you kidding?"

"Unfortunately, Ms. Hunt's calculation is right on the money," Dr. Sampson said. "The IOM is made up of America's foremost medical scientists, and their figures can be trusted. But your instincts are right to question this data. Who remembers where they got their data on medical errors?"

"Lucian Leape, right?" Don answered. "The Harvard Medical Practice Study?"

"Right. Dr. Leape, a pediatric surgeon, was brave enough to expose the epidemic of deadly healthcare mistakes in 1991. No one wanted to hear about it. The facts are difficult to accept, but we run a dangerous industry. It's time we acknowledged the truth. Dr. Leape and his colleagues were the first to show what many studies have confirmed since: healthcare routinely causes great harm. In the past, our mistakes were hidden, but for the sake of our patients we must bring our mistakes to light. How many are killed, like Jesica Santillan? How many are maimed, like Willie King?"

Frances answered, "Like we talked about last week—a jumbo jet's worth are killed by preventable mistakes every day, just in U.S. hospitals. Many more people die from preventable mistakes in hospitals than from breast cancer or car accidents."

"Does anyone know the old name for illness or injury caused by doctors?"

"Iatrogenic," Don said, "after the ancient Greek word for physician, 'iatros.' I always heard iatrogenic illness was common, and God knows, I've seen my share of it, but these numbers are mind boggling."

"And that's just the mistakes," Frances added. "Barbara Starfield's article points out that mistakes only account for about half of the iatrogenic deaths caused by doctors. Her data shows that another eighty thousand are killed by hospital-acquired infections, a hundred and six thousand by adverse drug reactions and overdoses, and twelve thousand by unnecessary surgery, for a total of around a quarter of a million iatrogenic deaths per year. And that doesn't include the tens of thousands of deadly medical errors and other iatrogenic deaths that occur outside the hospital."

"Affirmative," Dr. Sampson said. "Deaths like Jesica Santillan's are routine. Experts estimate three million Americans and one hundred million people worldwide were killed or maimed by dangerous and ineffectual health systems over the last decade. This body count does not include the suffering of those mutilated by successful but unnecessary procedures. Hospitals, doctors, and nurses often try to cover up these deaths and injuries because they are ashamed. But, like you, everyone knows someone who was harmed, mistreated, or killed by mistake.

"If this were a war, one hundred million dead and wounded over the past ten years would make it the war with the most casualties ever, and everyone would be outraged. In our medical system, casualties are less obvious. Horrors are hidden by trusted professionals in white coats and shrouded underneath fancy covers, behind drapes, and in secret ICUs and nursing homes few people visit. Huge business interests mesmerize people with slick commercials. Few know how bad it is. Those who have an idea try not to think about it because they think it can't be changed."

"Aren't these errors a lot less common here than in other countries?" Bruce asked.

"Most people think so, Dr. Markum. Error rates may be even higher in the developing world. For example, unsafe injections account for over one percent of the mortality in developing countries, where they spread AIDS by reusing dirty needles. In developed countries, however, the ubiquity of technology, specialists, and hospital beds leads to even more mistakes. In Australia, one in six hospital patients suffers from a serious mistake unrelated to the condition for which he or she was admitted. For every two people killed by avoidable mistakes, five are left with permanent disabilities, like Mr. King. When many specialists are involved and it is unclear who is in charge, more errors occur."

"So most errors in the U.S. happen in the hospital?" Frances asked.

"No question," Don answered, "but similar things happen in clinics—providers get confused about who is in charge, hand-offs from primary doctors to specialists get mixed up, no one follows up on a test result, or there's no system to check for dangerous drug combinations."

Dr. Sampson nodded. "Neglecting to provide basic recommended preventive care is an error, too. If Mr. King had received proper diabetes care, the nerve damage that led to his amputation could have been prevented. Good outpatient diabetic care could help us avoid forty thousand amputations every year. Think of the lives we could save if everyone with diabetes got recommended care in the first place and avoided the hospital altogether. The marble-lined lobbies of our hospitals make us believe they are safe and secure. But nowhere in America is more dangerous…"

Don's nightmare of the University Hospital commencement ceremony came flooding back: Desmond ushering the bright young doctors into the great domed lobby, Barkley tapping the worthiest ones to work in the midst of death and destruction, the chosen ones crossing the river that flowed from the veins in the marble floor to the dark towers guarding the entrance to the labyrinth.

The dream's warning made sense to him now. The majestic lobby was a menacing reminder of the underworld beneath the polished stone of the hospital—the underworld Don had come to Florence College to escape. But for some reason Don didn't understand, Dr. Sampson kept dragging them back down. Something bad awaited them behind the façade—some Minotaur lurking in the shadows. Venture in too far and the beast would rise up in a violent rage.

Don felt an overwhelming urge to run, to get out, to go far away. He scanned the bare walls of the basement seminar room in vain. There was nowhere to go.

"…Most of the conditions treated in hospitals can be treated more safely at home, so why do we treat them in the hospital?" Dr. Sampson asked, oblivious to Don's turmoil.

"We've been looking at the Medicare atlas data in my health econ class," Frances said. "The data shows the main factor determining whether you get hospitalized or not isn't how sick you are. It's the number of hospital beds in your community. Doctors and administrators like to fill empty beds; it's called supply-induced demand."

"Wait a minute," Bruce interrupted. "It's not hospital administrators that create demand for hospital beds. Consumers do. They feel safe there. It's consumers that want to be treated in the hospital when they get sick."

"No, you're wrong, Bruce," Frances replied. "Sure, consumers buy hospital marketing. But hospitals build the beds to create the demand, not to help their community. Do you know what happens to a city's death rate when their hospitals close?"

"What are you talking about?" Bruce answered. "That never happens."

"Guess you missed that reading Bruce," Don said. "It's happened lots of times. Our reading was about what happened in Los Angeles County when doctors stopped providing elective surgery and other non-essential hospital care there when malpractice premiums went up. To everyone's surprise, county death rates went down! The same pattern has been seen in other countries too—when doctors go on strike or hospitals close death rates usually go down."

"And we've chosen the hospital as our main place to provide humanitarian assistance to the sick," Dr. Sampson added. "So are hospitals really the best places to provide charity care?"

Don spoke up. "No. Definitely not. Nearly twenty percent of Americans have no health insurance and typically avoid the doctor until they're desperate. By that time, it is far too late to prevent disease, and they end up needing emergency, hospital, and nursing home care for strokes and heart attacks that simple outpatient treatments could have easily prevented. And the rest of us have to pay for this expensive, last minute, dangerous hospital care."

"So if hospitals are so bad, why does everyone want to go there when they get sick?" Bruce asked.

"Fifty years ago," Dr. Sampson said, "most people with means preferred to get care at home when they got sick. But something has changed. These days, hospital CEOs are used to controlling healthcare delivery and resources. They know the hospital world. They are not comfortable with home visits or ceding control to the patient or his family, and they want to fill their beds. After all, insurance pays."

"And hospital doctors are accustomed to sick patients waiting in their beds to be seen at the doctor's convenience," Frances said. "Patients don't question it because they think physicians are gods. Are hospitals really what's best for the sick, or is it all about doctors wanting control?"

"Wow. That's too psychological for me," Bruce said with a nervous laugh. "Can we get back to the details? What do we do to make hospitals safer? Some of us have to work there, and certain patients need hospitalization."

"Of course," Dr. Sampson replied. "How can we make hospitals safer? Most mistakes are not a doctor problem; no doctor wants them to occur. Mistakes are an industrial problem, or—as *To Err is Human*, the famous Institute of Medicine report, puts it—a systems problem. Perhaps we should return to Ms. Hunt's example of the airline industry. Ms. Hunt, why are airplanes so much safer than hospitals?"

"Well, they use checklists—the pilots and the control towers do—before every takeoff and landing. Dad said it's almost impossible to make a mistake because everyone double-checks everything. It's totally different than the Jesica Santillan case. No one is in a mad rush."

"Exactly. Simple industrial techniques like checklists can markedly reduce mistakes in the hospital. Standardized pre-op and post-op checklists for each type of procedure, along with a process for independent double-checks, can prevent surgical mistakes. Dr. Markum, do you think a checklist system could have prevented Jesica Santillan's death?"

"Yes, I guess it could have," Bruce confessed. "We all just assumed the proper blood type match had been done."

"You'll be glad to know that technical complications like surgical and procedural injuries, including wrong site surgery, are not the most common type of deadly medical mistake. How do you think the greatest number of patients are killed and hurt?"

Bruce looked relieved—even glad. He pointed a finger straight at Don and smirked. "Medicines. We surgeons cut, but we don't poison."

"Drug complications and errors do occur more often than you'd think," Don replied, ignoring his taunt. "With all the prescriptions people take, it's no surprise some get the wrong drug, the wrong dose, the wrong combination of drugs, or a drug reaction. Sometimes the pharmacist can't even read the writing on the prescriptions and has to make an educated guess."

"The only difference between medicine and poison is the dose," Dr. Sampson said, "and system errors abound when it comes to dispensing medicine. Consider John Cavolocci, age fifty-five, who was hospitalized for a colonoscopy and resection of a very large polyp. When the nurse began to administer an enema prep, he screamed in pain and begged her to stop. She reassured him everything was fine and did not stop. Three days later, Mr. Cavolocci died of a ruptured colon because two bottles were confused—he got an enema of formaldehyde by mistake.

"Blaming the nurse in this case would do no good. Remember, medication errors are not purposeful. They are industrial problems created by standard business routines. In this case, the enema and formaldehyde bottles were stored right next to each other, were the same size and color, and the formaldehyde was unlabeled. Inefficiency causes serious bodily harm and wastes a lot of money. In Australia, eighty thousand people are hospitalized each year for medication errors, costing Australia three hundred fifty million dollars annually. The number of patients hospitalized for medication errors in the United States is much higher and likely costs us billions."

Don jotted down the figures in his notes. Billions of dollars just for drug mistakes—had he heard that right?

"Now, what's the number two cause of deadly mistakes in the hospital?"

"Infections, I would guess," said Frances. "Nurses and doctors forgetting to wash their hands between patients. Not following standard protocols, like whenever an IV line is inserted or a procedure is done in the patient's room, everything is sterile. Hospitals harbor extremely dangerous germs; they're on everyone and everything."

"Frances is right," Don added. "Probably half the IVs we put in get infected at some point, and sick people almost always get serious pneumonia if they're in the hospital long enough."

"Hospitals have always been dangerous," Dr. Sampson said. "The hospital poorhouses of the eighteenth century were quite deadly. In some, over half the patients died from infections due to unsanitary conditions, and wound infections occurred in more than half of surgery patients. It's much better now, but there's lots of room for improvement. For example, a dose of antibiotics right before abdominal surgery markedly reduces the risk of serious post-operative infection, but in most hospitals only half the patients get it at the right time. This is not a knowledge problem—we know the right thing to do. It is a delivery problem, an industrial problem. What are the other common types of errors in hospitals? Ms. Hunt?"

"Let's see—well, misdiagnosis, patient falls, burns, pressure ulcers…and injuries caused by restraints. We know how to prevent these injuries too; we just aren't doing it. Hospitals can cut deaths in half by sending a rapid response team of nurses to the bedside of any patient whose condition worsens or whose vital signs go beyond certain boundaries. Of course, doctors concerned about control refuse to allow rapid response teams in many hospitals."

Dr. Sampson nodded. "We must stop the routine and unnecessary violence in our industry. To that end, there is a nationwide coalition of healthcare workers and health services researchers working with the Agency of Health Research and Quality to launch a war on errors. You may have the opportunity to work on this legislation…"

From far down in the trenches, Don heard a clarion call to arms, and a drumbeat rallied him, called him up, urged him to crawl over the mounds of bodies of the heaped-up dead to fight for a better way. *Maybe this is something I can do!* He could begin by tallying the casualties caused by each part of the healthcare system in his diagram of healthcare hell in order to see where the most lives could be saved.

"…To bring safety to the level of the airline industry, our war must start in the hospitals," Dr. Sampson was saying. "What actions can we take now to eliminate these errors?"

"Making sure every hospital has a good computer system would be an awesome start," Frances said. "Computerized physician order entry—CPOE—can drastically reduce medication mistakes, especially those related to illegible handwriting or drug interactions. Good data systems also check for drug interactions and allergies automatically. The best health information systems have clear procedures and lines of accountability so the right information is available at the right place and the right time."

"Wait a minute—building the kind of information systems you're talking about would require huge upfront investments," Bruce pointed out.

"True," Dr. Sampson said. "It may take spending on the magnitude of a great war to attack this problem, but in the long run it will save money. Complications are expensive."

"It seems to me we should encourage doctors to admit mistakes," Frances added, "so we can take the industrial steps needed to prevent them from happening again."

"Good, Ms. Hunt. Studies show that doctors who admit and reveal their mistakes are much safer than those who claim never to have made an error."

"Doctors and hospitals will have to give up some control," said Don. "Like that article about physician autonomy and power said, doctors will have to embrace protocols and industrial methods. And I think they'll do it, once they see the good it will do for them and their patients."

Bruce guffawed. "Are you kidding? You think the American Medical Association will cede any of its power? And doctors and hospitals? They've invested too much money in the status quo. Besides, doctors don't like systems;

doctors want to be in charge." He turned to Dr. Sampson. "With all due respect, I wouldn't expect to win your war, at least not any time soon."

"I expect you are right, Dr. Markum, yet it still needs to be fought. No one said the job of reforming health systems would be easy. Well, that is enough for today. Our readings for next week focus on unhelpful cancer treatments. Dr. Newman, you will present the case, right?"

"Yes, sir."

"Very good. Between now and then, think about the obstacles Dr. Markum has raised and what we can do to overcome them. Class dismissed."

Don grabbed his books and followed Dr. Sampson, who had rocketed out of the classroom and down the hall. Dr. Sampson glanced over his shoulder and took note of Don racing to catch up.

"Yes, Dr. Newman, what is it?"

"Well, Dr. Sampson, excuse me for asking, but what do you really think? Will the healthcare industry ever give up any of its power?"

"What do you mean by the healthcare industry, Dr. Newman?"

"Well, uh, you know, the real power brokers in American health care: health plans, hospitals, doctors, and drug companies. Is there any chance of real reform?"

"Only if there is light, Don, enough light that people in all those sectors are ashamed to even look at themselves."

"If we're the ones shining the light, won't the power brokers be angry?"

"Oh, yes, I'm afraid they will, Don. I'm afraid they will."

13

High-Tech Suicide

We set out through a wood which was not marked by any path.
No green leaves, but of dusky hue; no smooth boughs, but knotted and warped;
no fruits were there, but poisonous thorns.
DANTE ALIGHIERI, INFERNO 13, 2–6

"THIS CASE OCCURRED near the end of my residency," Don began. "Oh, did everyone get the paper I added to the syllabus—the *New England Journal* one about bone marrow transplant for breast cancer?"

Frances, Bruce, and Dr. Sampson nodded.

"I suspect that article will contribute to our discussion a little later," Dr. Sampson said, "but present your case first, Dr. Newman."

"All right, so here goes. One of the supposed privileges of residency training at Boston's University Hospital is that in your last year, you spend a month at the world-famous Robert Richardson Cancer Center, fondly known as the "Rob Rich" for short. I drew the month of April and was looking forward to it, in spite of its reputation for being a very tough rotation.

"I arrived for my first day at the main Salem campus north of Boston on April Fool's Day about six-thirty in the morning. If you know the Rob Rich, this will come as no surprise, but it's like entering the Mirage in Las Vegas. Blue-green glass and chrome cover the entire outside of the building, and a fake forest of sculpted trees surround the complex. There's a valet at the entrance, a glassed-in atrium at least eight stories tall, and a glass elevator, which I took to the ninth floor.

"A nurse buzzed me into the bone marrow transplant unit—we called it BMT for short—and directed me to the clean room. I put on some blue disposable scrubs and stood at the nurse's station waiting for the blood and cancer fellow in charge of the BMT service to show up. The nurses all had to gown, glove, and mask before they could enter any of the isolation or chemotherapy rooms.

"The blood fellow rushed in at ten past seven, all out of breath. He had a big calculator sticking out of his front pocket and an overstuffed briefcase. 'Sorry I'm late,' he told me, 'I had a lab experiment to check on first thing this morning. I have a cell culture of human T cells—immune cells—that could be used to produce antibodies to fight cancer. Do you want to come see them?'

"I was confused. 'Don't we need to see the patients before rounding with our attending?' I asked him.

"'Sure, we can look up labs on everyone, but we don't need to *see* them all,' he said. 'Our attending this month is Dr. Meyer. He pioneered many of the cell culture techniques I'm using, so he'll be really interested in my lab work. And he gives the best teaching sessions in the world on using monoclonal antibodies in experimental cancer treatment protocols. He's the world's expert, you know. All attending physicians in the Rob Rich—even Dr. Meyer—have to take a month running the BMT unit, whether they like it or not.'

"'How many patients do we have?' I asked.

"'Six in the prep rooms getting chemotherapy, and twenty in the isolation rooms, where we put patients once their blood counts drop.'

"As you know, chemotherapy destroys the bone marrow that produces all blood cells: the white cells that fight infection, the red cells that carry oxygen, and the platelets that prevent bleeding. After four or five days of this poisonous treatment, all the blood counts plummet to dangerous levels. The trick is to keep the patient alive until the new bone marrow takes hold and begins producing new cells. That means prophylactic antibiotics to prevent infection, red blood cell transfusions to treat anemia, and platelet transfusions to prevent bleeding. Usually it takes about three or four weeks before the blood counts come up enough to allow the patient to leave the hospital.

"'You take half the charts and I'll take half, and we'll write the notes before attending rounds,' the fellow said. He showed me how to write notes using only the labs, vitals, and nurses' records.

"I realized we were not going to see the patients before rounding with our attending. Instead, we finished the notes and went to the fellow's research lab to get a cup of coffee and look at his human T cells.

"We met Dr. Meyer for rounds at ten o'clock. At first, I was nervous he might ask me a question about one of our patients, but all he did was lecture for over an hour on experimental cancer treatment techniques and how they were using antibodies made in the Rob Rich labs to attack cancer cells. The blood fellow devoured every word. Finally, the fellow gave him a five-minute update on the labs and vitals of our twenty-six patients.

"It dawned on me we weren't going to visit the patients during attending rounds, either. As you know, it's called 'rounds' because you're supposed to go *around* with the attending physician to see patients. We didn't personally see any patients—even the sick ones. After the update, we went to a drug company-sponsored lunch, where the salespeople discussed new chemotherapy drugs and we ate pizza from Ernesto's in the North End. After lunch, Dr. Meyer and the fellow headed down to their labs, and the blood fellow invited me to come.

"'Don't I need to visit the patients?' I asked.

"'Oh, you should go in and take a peek at the patients every day or so, I guess,' he said, 'but the nurses are really good and the patients are on protocols anyway.' Then he leaned over close to me and whispered, 'What I do a lot of the time is to look through the window and wave. You can tell from their lab values what is really happening, and the nurses will tell you if there's a complication. You know it's not good to go in the isolation rooms too often; you risk communicating infection. Even the patients know that.'

"I didn't know what to think. In my prior training, we had always examined every hospitalized patient every day. But this was supposed to be one of the top cancer centers in the world, so I figured they knew best.

"In his lab, the fellow pulled pink agar-filled Petri dishes of live cultures from a cell incubator and waved them under my nose. 'This media is made from calf's blood,' he said; 'it works well as long as it's not contaminated. I'm trying to fuse these T cells with HeLa cells—you know, those immortal cells harvested from a woman who died of cervical cancer at Hopkins in 1951?'

"I was getting panicked about not seeing our real-life patients, but he wouldn't let me go. After an hour and a half studying test tubes, sera, reagents, automated cell counters, and his liquid nitrogen-cooled cytostorage container, it was obvious he was trying to recruit me to help with his lab experiments for the rest of the month. I made a lame excuse about needing to prepare for boards and got out of there.

"Bone marrow transplant patients are among the sickest patients in the hospital. Cancer has invaded their entire bodies, and on top of that, they get near-lethal doses of dangerous chemotherapy agents that indiscriminately kill any growing cell in the body—cancer or not. BMT units take people who are walking around and feeling relatively well and make them so sick they want to die. After a month of pain and suffering, they're pulled back from the brink of death. If it's not too late.

"When it came to diagnosing and treating the routine, life-threatening complications that were part and parcel of almost every bone marrow transplant, I was it. The blood fellow and Dr. Meyer were lab rats who spent their time devising new treatments based on theory, not clinical experience. Dr. Meyer resented time away from his lab, and why shouldn't he? His promotion and tenure depended on research, not patient care. When it came to caring for real people in the unit, Meyer and the fellow were oblivious and incompetent.

"So here I was, in one of the very best blood marrow transplant units in the country, and the care of these extremely ill individuals—most of whom were paying over half a million dollars for their treatment—was left to me, a mere third-year resident with almost no experience caring for chemotherapy complications.

"I got back to the unit at three that afternoon, and a burly, middle-aged guy with a full head of dark red, wavy hair stepped right in front of me and blocked my way. He looked like a thug, but it turned out he was the head nurse, David.

He must have seen the baffled look on my face because he gave me a knowing smile and quipped, 'Is it a laboratory, or is it a hospital? Hard to tell, isn't it?' He tilted back his head and let out a deep belly laugh. 'Looks like things are in our hands this month, but don't worry. I'll let you know what you need to do. Here, this is the most important thing you need to know.'

"I was so relieved. David handed me a journal article that questioned the benefit of isolation rooms and demonstrated that good hand washing prevents the spread of infection in BMT units. 'These people do need you,' David said. 'Come on, time for us to get to work.'

"So, that's how I finally started seeing patients. Mrs. Pinckney was day fourteen in an isolation room after having her own bone marrow infused, and it was eighteen days since she had entered one of the prep rooms to get high-dose chemo for metastatic breast cancer."

Don realized he had gotten a little carried away with setting the scene and half-expected Dr. Sampson to interrupt his long-winded presentation, but Dr. Sampson, Frances, and Bruce all seemed interested.

"I donned a new gown, gloves, and mask for about the tenth time that day—you have to change for each patient—and went into Mrs. Pinckney's room. She was fifty-one years old, a college professor, and had very aggressive breast cancer. Three years after mastectomy, radiation, and starting hormonal treatment, the cancer had reappeared in her liver, leg bones, and in the lymph nodes around her aorta—the huge artery from the heart.

"I could tell she had been a beautiful woman. Her high cheekbones and the delicate way she extended her hand to greet me suggested past elegance. But her body was devastated. She was deathly pale, the whites of her eyes were tinged with yellow, and black circles ringed her eyes. Her skin hung loosely on her bones; she was as emaciated as a concentration camp victim.

She looked at me that first time with a remnant of hope. She mustered a smile and said, 'You have nice eyes. Are you my doctor? Do you work with Dr. Mirak?'

"'Well, Dr. Meyer is the attending this month, but we are following Dr. Mirak's protocol,' I told her.

"'Dr. Mirak said this was my best chance at a cure,' she said. 'He said the bone marrow might cure me, that even though the odds were not good it was my best chance. When is he coming to see me?' She stared at me with a blank expression and looked around the room, like she was searching for Dr. Mirak.

"I told her I didn't know, but that I would come see her every day. She complained of the usual chemotherapy side effects like memory loss and a sore mouth. The nausea and relentless vomiting had stopped, but she still had watery diarrhea, and her bottom was painfully raw. Tiny spots of bleeding appeared in the skin of her legs because of her very low platelet count.

"'How long do I have to be in here?' she asked. 'I feel like I've lost everything. My children and husband can hardly come because the visiting hours are when they are at work. When will I start getting better?'

"She was desperate for answers. I gave her what few I could, but things were not looking good. Her new bone marrow showed little evidence of taking hold, and her platelets—the cells that kept her from bleeding to death—remained dangerously low despite daily transfusions. Her body was using up platelets and red blood cells as fast as we could pump them in.

"The reason for her low blood count didn't take too long to sort out. Sitting there on the side of her bed, I noticed the smell of blood mixed with stool. The stool in her bedpan was black, a sure sign of stress gastritis—bleeding from the stomach—a common occurrence in blood marrow transplants. I started a powerful intravenous antacid medicine.

"David called her husband and told him the prognosis was not good. He advised Mr. Pinckney to take off from work to visit her each day and to tell their grown children to do the same.

"I was on call the night of April fourteenth. Things were slow, so I had a little extra time to spend with Mrs. Pinckney. It was looking bad. Two days earlier, I'd been called to her room because her legs and abdomen had swelled up, making her look pregnant. This was the result of another dreaded complication— blood clots blocking the main veins through the liver. On top of that, her new bone marrow had not begun to grow and produce the blood cells she needed to survive. She had a 'graft failure,' which occurs in about ten percent of blood marrow transplants.

"Unfortunately, a second transplant using her own marrow was not an option. None of her marrow was left. Dr. Mirak had told her the BMT was an emergency, and that they couldn't waste time harvesting more bone marrow blood cells from her bloodstream. Anyway, the lab rats discussed whether another bone marrow donor could be found. Her husband and children had bone marrow samples sucked out of their pelvic bones. We waited for the results and hoped a suitable match would be found before it was too late.

"The nurse called me to Mrs. Pinckney's room around eleven that night. Blood was oozing from her IV sites, and she was asking for me. I ordered an immediate transfusion of more platelets to help stop the bleeding and sat down beside her bed. The bed sheets were spotted with blood from the IV in her hand and the extra IV we put in her groin after the 'permanent' chemo catheter under her collarbone clotted. Her belly was swollen to three times its normal size. Her legs were like logs, too heavy for her to move. In spite of all that, she had that clarity of mind that often comes with the last burst of energy before death. Her sunken eyes sparkled and burned with purpose.

"'Dr. Newman,' she said, 'I need to confess to you what I have done. I need you to know, I made a mistake. Coming here was suicide.'

"I shook my head and began to argue, but she stopped me.

"'Please, let me finish,'" she said. "This is suicide. I knew the odds were terrible, despite Dr. Mirak's encouragement, and I knew from the beginning I would die here. I knew it in my heart, and I came anyway. I could have been at home with my family and seen my grandchildren again. I could have lived for months and died peacefully at home. But it's too late for all that now. I know the chemo has made me dumb; don't look at me that way. I know it makes you stupid by damaging your brain. I've read about it.'

"I tried to put a positive spin on things. I told her Dr. Mirak's new way of doing BMT in breast cancer could be the newest breakthrough, that she was getting the very best type of BMT therapy available for her kind of cancer.

"'Dr. Newman, I'm not that naïve,' she told me. 'I've read the studies. There's no increase in survival with BMT treatment. Standard low-dose chemotherapy would have been much easier. I just wanted so much to live.' She started to cry. 'Instead I chose this horrible death in a depressing laboratory where my family can barely visit me. I don't know why I did it. It was crazy to come here. I felt like I was being invaded by the cancer and I wanted more than anything to kill it. I let them stab me a hundred times in the back of my pelvis with that huge biopsy needle. They sucked out my good marrow with that huge syringe. They sucked out my life. I was willing to take the highest doses of chemo imaginable to kill the cancer, but I've ended up killing myself. Please...tell my family...I'm so sorry.'

"I made sure the platelets were hanging and then went to the call room across the street to get some rest. I fell asleep a little after midnight but woke up suddenly at three in the morning with this strong urge to check on Mrs. Pinckney. I ran from my call room all the way through the tiled tunnel under the street to the basement of the Rob Rich and up the back steps, three at a time. I charged through the staff entrance to the BMT unit on the ninth floor.

"I saw at once her isolation was broken—the night nurse was dashing into the room with four bags of blood products clutched to her chest. 'I'm sorry, Dr. Newman,' the nurse said, 'she's dying and there's nothing we can do. I didn't want to wake you for this.'

"The fellow was standing beside the blood-soaked bed. Blood oozed from IV sites and puncture wounds in her neck and from her groin, where he had succeeded in inserting yet another IV. A bloody central intravenous line kit was spread across the foot of her bed.

"'What are you doing here?' I yelled.

"He smirked at me. 'You think I enjoy being here at four in the morning doing this?'

"'There's a standing order to call the blood fellow when a patient has life-threatening bleeding we can't stop,' the nurse explained.

"'And I implement Dr. Mirak's experimental study protocol for bleeding, using multiple transfusions of crossmatch compatible platelets, Amicar, intravenous immunoglobulin, and clotting factors,' the fellow added, glancing at the unconscious Mrs. Pinckney, 'not that it will do her much good.'

"'You can't do this!' I said. I pointed to the rivulets of blood running from her saturated sheets and dripping onto the floor. 'She did not consent to this!'

"'Yes, she did!' he snarled at me. 'She signed the universal consent form for approved studies on admission. And you are out of line, Dr. Newman. You've gotten emotionally involved. Keep your professional distance and stick to your job. And by the way, she is bleeding to death because you failed to diagnose a severe bloodstream fungal infection. You know fungal infections can cause the clotting system to go wild and use up all the natural factors in the blood that make it clot—didn't you see the positive fungal cultures from her blood this morning?'

"'I thought those were just contaminants,' I said, 'and besides, she was already on high oral doses of antifungal medication.' I tried to defend myself, but to be honest, I felt sick to my stomach.

"'Obviously that was not enough,' he said.

"Once before, I'd taken care of a man who'd jumped from the Mystic River Bridge in Boston. He was barely alive after twenty minutes in the freezing water. Every cell in his body was irreparably damaged, and the oxygen deprivation set his entire clotting system on fire in a last ditch attempt to repair the damage. Just like him, Mrs. Pinckney was oozing blood from her eyes, nose, and gums. Her clotting system had exhausted itself.

"I stood there and watched her life slowly ebb away. A tangled web of intravenous lines penetrated her arms, legs, and trunk in multiple places. As fast as the lines poured blood products in, the IV wounds leaked the vital red blood out. Red and purple bruises covered her thin skin. For an hour, I watched blood flowing in and blood pouring out, until finally she died in the pool of blood.

"The fellow called the family and told them she was dead. I guess I should have done it, but I just sat at the nurses' station. I sat there for the longest time, even watched the orderlies wheel her body away to the basement morgue. Housekeeping came, cleaned her room, and left. I still didn't move; I figured by the time I walked all the way back to my call room, I would just have to turn around and come back to the unit again anyway.

The night nurse offered me the bed in Mrs. Pinckney's room. 'I know this is a little weird,' she said, 'but you need some sleep. It's unoccupied, has clean sheets, and no one will care if you sleep there an hour or two.'

So I did. I hung my white coat on the door hook and lay down on top of the clean sheets, on the same bed where Mrs. Pinckney had died an hour before. The scent of bleach evaporating up from the floor was comforting. I was so bone-tired, I was sound asleep within minutes."

EVERYONE WAS QUIET for a few moments after Don's story. Don was embarrassed. What in the world had possessed him to share the part about sleeping on Mrs. Pinckney's deathbed?

Dr. Sampson broke the silence. "That was a good story for us to consider, hard as it was to hear. Does anyone have any questions?"

No one answered.

"Well, I have one," Dr. Sampson said. "Dr. Newman, why do you think Mrs. Pinckney said her choice was like suicide?"

"Well, I didn't understand at first," Don replied, "but then I read the scientific literature she had read about bone marrow transplant for metastatic breast cancer."

"Can you briefly review the research?"

"Sure. The bottom line is that when Mrs. Pinckney had her transplant, it had already been demonstrated and published in *The New England Journal of Medicine* that bone marrow transplant with high-dose chemotherapy did not improve survival for women with metastatic breast cancer. If anything, those women died faster than the group receiving conventional lower-dose chemo. In both groups, only about a third were alive three years later."

"Then why did they do it?" Frances burst out. "How could they do that to her?"

"That's what I wondered," Don said, "so I did some background research. Some preliminary studies in the late 1980s indicated bone marrow transplants might work for metastatic breast cancer. People with advanced breast cancer were desperate for hope, and doctors were desperate to cure, so together they took the insurance companies to court and forced them to cover this experimental therapy. Problem was, those early studies did not compare bone marrow transplant to the standard low-dose chemotherapy available at that time. The insurance companies had to pay for an exceedingly expensive, highly dangerous, and scientifically unproven treatment.

"In 1995, a famous cancer researcher named Dr. Bezwoda released study results claiming high cure rates and bolstering support for bone marrow transplants in metastatic breast cancer, but in 1999 and 2000, several studies came out—like the one I sent you—proving they don't work. Dr. Bezwoda's work was investigated, and he confessed to falsifying his research. He said he believed in the therapy and wanted the recognition that came from being the first to recognize its benefits."

"And Mrs. Pinckney had her bone marrow transplant after 2000?" Frances asked.

"Yes, she did," Don replied. "I guess that's why she called it suicide—she had read the studies. Many doctors still use bone marrow transplant for breast cancer, hoping little adjustments in the chemotherapy protocol may yield better results.

"Do you think that's possible?"

"Probably not, but here's the thing: Dr. Mirak did not have her on any approved study protocol, so he couldn't scientifically evaluate or prove anything. Believe it or not, there were over five thousand bone marrow transplants for breast cancer every year through the late 1990s, and the vast majority had no approved study protocol. They used people as guinea pigs—did experimental and painful treatments that cost over half a million dollars each—but couldn't publish results to confirm or contradict those preliminary studies. Even now, hundreds—maybe thousands—are done every year without proof they work better than the old-fashioned, low-dose chemotherapy."

"Let me sum up," Dr. Sampson said. "Bone marrow transplant for advanced breast cancer is a common therapy people often choose despite the lack of evidence for its benefit. As you see it, Dr. Newman, doctors offer—and patients eagerly accept—this radical therapy based on false and desperate hope?"

"Right."

"Then the task for the rest of today is to consider whether this is an isolated occurrence, or if there are other examples of common therapies that diminish life without reasonable hope of benefit. Let's take cancer treatment in general. Dr. Markum, how are we doing in the war on cancer? Can you summarize the two studies on cancer death rates from *The New England Journal of Medicine?*"

"Well, I must admit I was shocked to see that despite our substantial investment in cancer treatments, cancer death rates overall have steadily risen in the United States from the 1930s until now. From the 1950s through the early 1990s, the number of cancer deaths continued to rise, despite a period of astronomical government investments to cure cancer. Forty years of heavily funded cancer research—centered on treatment with powerful poisons—have utterly failed to cure cancer. It looks like there could be a little downturn or flattening of the rate of cancer deaths over the last five years, but we have not come close to winning the war on cancer."

"But isn't cancer treatment working real miracles for children?" Frances asked.

"Qualified miracles," Bruce replied. "Death rates for childhood cancers have decreased by about half since the 1970s. That's a great success. But childhood cancer is relatively rare. In the United States, only seventeen hundred children died of cancer in 1993, while well over half a million adults died of cancer that year. And don't forget, many kids who survive are crippled for life by radiation and chemotherapy. They have to cope with heart problems, kidney failure, deafness, or even brain damage and developmental problems. Meanwhile, we haven't seen much improvement in most adult cancers. Despite all the hoopla about new cancer therapies, the majority of cancer patients don't live longer with fancy treatments."

"Wait a minute," Don interrupted, "aren't people living with cancer for much longer these days?"

"Not really," Bruce said. "Remember epidemiology class? People are diagnosed with cancer much earlier than they were three or four decades ago, so they *seem* to live longer when they really don't. After urologists started aggressively marketing the test for prostate cancer twenty-five years ago, rates of prostate cancer diagnoses doubled—not because more men got prostate cancer but because it was diagnosed earlier. Prostate cancer testing has had absolutely no effect on overall death rates from prostate cancer, once they adjust for age. Why? Because we don't have very effective treatments for it.

"Through the 1930s, 40s, and 50s, doctors were excellent diagnosticians—probably as good at diagnosing cause of death as they are now—so increases in cancer death rates can't be explained away by saying it's just due to more cancers getting diagnosed. Even accounting for the fact that people are living longer nowadays, a greater percentage of people are dying from cancer today than they were fifty years ago."

"What has caused the increase in cancer deaths in the United States, Dr. Markum?" Dr. Sampson asked.

"Unhealthy behaviors. Smoking, number one, diet and obesity rates, number two. Smoking causes a third of those five hundred thousand cancer deaths each year—not only lung cancer, but also mouth, throat, esophageal, stomach, colon, rectal, bladder, and kidney cancer. For the majority of the smoking cancers, chemotherapy and surgery are mostly palliative, meaning treatment may make the patient more comfortable but is not likely to appreciably lengthen life.

"Overweight, obesity, and poor diet cause another third of cancers, in part by elevating the levels of hormones made from fat. That's how excess weight leads to breast and prostate cancer. In addition, fat carries cancer-causing toxins, so the high-fat foods that cause obesity also cause colon cancer. Having multiple sex partners greatly increases the risk of cervical cancer. Heavy alcohol use leads to breast, throat, esophageal and liver cancer. Overall, bad health habits cause more than two-thirds of cancers."

"Bruce is right. The vast majority of cancers are caused by self-destructive behavior," Don added. As soon as he said it, a wave of guilt crashed over him. No one deserved to be blamed for getting cancer.

"I guess you could say that," Bruce answered. "The screening tests we make a big deal about will never turn the tide of cancer caused by poor health habits. Of the main cancer *screening* strategies we have, only pap smears for cervical cancer and screening for colon cancer definitely improve survival. Breast cancer screening probably does, but the studies aren't definitive. For the vast majority of cancers, chemotherapy provides very little help."

"What is cancer chemotherapy good for, anyway?" asked Frances.

Don answered this one. "Well, sometimes it gives people a few more months. It can definitely prolong life or even cure a few relatively uncommon cancers, like Hodgkin's lymphoma. But for the vast majority of common cancers, oncologists make a big deal about ten percent improvements in short-term mortality rates. It's possible that some of these minor improvements are simply due to the placebo effect, because people who believe they will live longer usually do. Some people choose chemotherapy for cancers for which it has never been shown to offer real benefit. Patients and families want to do everything possible, and they have unwarranted faith in the power of modern medicine to cure, but chemotherapy is not nearly as effective as people like to think. Most of the time it is not a cure."

"Let me get this straight," Frances said. "People hear about the rare chemotherapy cures for uncommon cancers. When they get common cancers for which chemotherapy is not so effective, they expect the same cure. Crazy!"

"As they say," Bruce said, "hope springs eternal."

"What things are proven to substantially lower cancer death rates?" Dr. Sampson asked.

Bruce smiled, "Surgery, of course, at least for lung cancer and a few others, if you catch it early enough to cut it out. But we don't catch most cancers that early."

"Like Bruce said, screening works well for cervical and colon cancer," Don added, "but for most cancers we don't have good screening tests. Even mammography is not nearly as good as people think. The only thing proven to substantially lower cancer death rates is prevention. Stopping smoking tops the list, and improving eating habits and decreasing overweight and obesity would be next."

"How much are we investing in these proven preventive approaches in the war on cancer?"

"Hardly anything, from what I can tell," Bruce said. "Most of our cancer research is focused on treatment—mostly with poisons. We have taken this approach for forty years without much success."

"So," Dr. Sampson summed up, "Dr. Newman's story reminds us that some want to believe in a cancer cure so much they ruin the end of their lives for a chance to beat the cancer, even when no real chance exists. And doctors oblige them. Are there other examples of people throwing their lives away by choosing the false cures of modern medicine? Ms. Hunt?"

"Going to the ICU for a very advanced chronic illness," Frances said, "seems like suicide. In the United States, as many as one in four people die in the ICU, and many of them are terminal. I mean, if you knew you were going to die, why would you want to die in the hospital on machines instead of at home with your family?"

"Most people who die in the hospital get cardiopulmonary resuscitation— you know, CPR," Don added. "That means in the last moments of life, doctors and nurses rush in, pound on the chest hard enough to crack ribs, shove a tube down the windpipe, and chase the family out of the room in a fit of panic. This is routine practice, despite the fact that only about one or two in ten of those who get CPR survive long enough to leave the hospital, and only one in twenty live for a year. Doing this to people who will die soon anyway is insane."

"It's abusive," said Frances.

"When I think of medical suicide," Bruce said, "I think of all the prescription drug addicts. They dope themselves up on whatever they can get their hands on. I've seen two or three die from mixing prescription drugs. And some people don't want to get well. All they want is for the doctor to certify they're disabled and can't work. They spend their time and energy trying to be sick."

Don nodded, picturing the hoards of drug and disability seekers he had seen every single week of residency in his primary care clinic. "What about the people addicted to surgery?" he said. "Some people want surgery for every problem, whether it's likely to help or not. Like men in their 70s or 80s that get prostate cancer surgery and risk impotence and leaking urine, even though there's no good evidence it will prolong their lives. Or the people that have repeated back surgeries for chronic pain, even though surgery works no better than simple exercise. Or those who get cardiac catheterizations for vague chest pain, in spite of the high risk of mini-stroke. There are so many cases where people throw away their lives. We shouldn't let them do it."

"Ah, but we do," Dr. Sampson said. "Sometimes we even encourage them, as Mrs. Pinckney's doctor did. Or we let people undergo dangerous ineffective treatments because we don't have better answers. This isn't anything new. Consider George Washington. Our first president died after his doctors bled him again and again and again to treat a throat infection. They knew bleeding worked for some things, so they tried it for everything."

"And the doctor always gets paid, right?" Bruce added, "whether he saves or kills. People are so naïve. They pay insurance companies a bundle to tell them what they can and can't have. Providers get paid millions for completely unproven treatments. What if mechanics could do that? They'd go wild: order any parts they wanted, do any repairs they wanted, and—however things worked out—they'd still get paid."

"Excellent discussion everyone. Let's stop there for today," Dr. Sampson concluded.

Don stood up on his stiff legs, looked to Dr. Sampson, and turned up his palms in a gesture of contrition. "I'm sorry I took so long on that case today."

"You obviously cared about her," Dr. Sampson replied. "That is the kind of story we need here. I want stories that matter to someone. But don't beat yourself up over Mrs. Pinckney's death. You didn't kill her. She said it herself—she made her own choice. You were competent and did your job under very difficult circumstances."

Don shrugged, his shoulders sagged, and he didn't say anything. He felt too drained to reply.

Dr. Sampson left the projection room and Bruce, who had been eavesdropping, walked by Don on his way out and whispered, "Wuss."

Frances was still there. Don looked at her. Her beautiful blond hair cascaded in waves across her shoulders and her brilliant green eyes searched his with concern.

"Mrs. Pinckney's case was about something else for you, wasn't it, Don?"

That's all it took. His eyes filled with tears. "My mother," he choked. "She died of breast cancer last fall. And I couldn't...I didn't help her."

Until this moment, Don had held his grief in check. He thought he had dealt with his mother's death. Everything was under control. He was just fine. But Frances's empathy was the key that opened the floodgates. To his complete surprise and embarrassment, he began to cry. He put his head in his hands and tried to compose himself, but once he started, he couldn't stop.

Frances put her arms around him and pulled his head onto her shoulder. She stroked his hair. "I know just how you feel," she crooned.

Don's body racked with sobs. He buried his face in her thick mane, and it cushioned his face like a soft silk pillow. She seemed in no hurry to pull away.

As his torrent of tears receded, Don felt electricity building between them. He could not help but notice her sweet-smelling hair and the sensation of her firm breasts pressed against his chest. His hands rested on her supple back where her toned lats met the swell of her strong gluteus muscles, and he felt her hips gently pressing against his own.

His tears dried in salty streaks and pulled the skin of his face tight. He didn't know what to say and he felt an urge to get out of the classroom. Looking around, he rubbed his face on his sleeve and mumbled, "Maybe we better go."

She just smiled and held him closer.

"Look," Don said, "Why don't we go get some lunch?"

"That would be awesome." She beamed at him. "Let's go."

Frances linked her arm with his and they walked through the door together.

He was thrilled. This beautiful and intelligent woman was eager for his company! Don looked at her and she smiled in her captivating way. They moved down the hall, their heels tapping in unison on the old linoleum.

As they exited the back door onto the quad, a knotted and gnarled gray-white branch scraped Don's arm. He looked down and saw the contorted limbs of a leafless bush sticking out at right angles like giant thorns. He reached out and broke off a small piece as he passed, thinking it dead. It broke halfway with a snap; he had to rip a long shred of bark to get it off. Twirling the twig in his hand, he felt the wet sap within. He looked to Frances and started to ask her what it was.

But then he remembered. Frances was from California and wouldn't know. Not like Sarah. Sarah would have known. She knew her trees—bushes and flowers too—living things of all kinds.

There had been something in her look at him that day at Walden—something now lost and out of reach. Yes, Sarah might have wanted to be something more than just a friend.

14

Health Care Assassins

Beware of the false prophets, who come to you in sheep's clothing,
but inwardly are ravenous wolves. You will know them by their fruits.
MATTHEW 7:15–16

DON WALKED DOWN a cobbled path through the wooded campus to class.
Red and yellow leaves hung dying on the huge oaks and maples that dotted the
campus, biding time before their final descent to the umber autumn earth. In
the middle of a quad surrounded by stately oak trees, Don paused to look at the
college's famous omphalos.

The finely carved gray stone had been placed at the center of campus in
1801. Omphalos means umbilicus; this stone navel marked the newly founded
Florence College as the intellectual center of the universe. Regarded then as one
of the most prestigious institutions in the new world, Florence College still liked
to think it was at the center of things, a fact Don was not aware of yet but would
discover in the months to come.

He was aware, however, of the symbolic importance of an omphalos. Four
centuries earlier when Galileo dared to suggest the earth revolves around the
sun instead of the other way around, the Catholic Church tried him for her-
esy and sentenced him to life imprisonment. Philip Henry Gosse was upset by
Darwin's rejection of the church's man-centered universe and came up with the
famous "Omphalos hypothesis" to reconcile his literal view of the creation story
with the natural world. Gosse decided God gave Adam a navel to make him look
like he was born of a woman and created canyons, fossils, and light from distant
stars to make the universe *appear* old.

The omphalos was shaped like an old beehive made from an upside-down
woven basket. A black iron fence with a locked gate surrounded the alien rock.
It was added in the 1960s at the college president's command, presumably to
protect the ancient artifact from vandalism.

Don idly wondered if the old omphalos was misappropriated property, like
the Greek artifacts in the British Museum. Perhaps one of the college's early
fraternity brothers on his grand tour of Europe had stolen it for fun, as if it were
just one of those decorative pineapples sitting on the front steps of a rival house.
Or maybe it was the long-lost omphalos from Delphi, the famous stone marking
the navel of the universe for the ancient Greeks. People traveled to Delphi to

consult the Oracle, a priestess who channeled Apollo's prophetic messages from the underworld. The idea was appealing: a fortune-teller that knew the gods, saw the future, and advised a person what to do.

I could use something like that, Don thought. He bent over to take a closer look at the marker in front of the fence—a granite slab buried in the ground, its surface level with the earth. A small bronze plaque was riveted into the stone.

> *Nam Sibyllam quidem Cumis ego ipse oculis meis vidi in ampulla*
> *pendere, et cum illi pueri dicerent: Σίβυλλα τί θέλεις; respondebat illa:*
> *ἀποθανεῖν θέλω*
>
> PETRONIUS, *Satyricon*

It took Don a long time to decipher it, but he had studied Latin through most of his six years of Catholic parochial school and had gone on to study even more Latin and a little Ancient Greek in college. It read:

> *The Sibyl of Cumae I saw with my own eyes hanging in a jar, and*
> *when the boys said to her: 'Sibyl what do you want?' she responded: 'I want*
> *to die.'*

The plaque implied this omphalos wasn't dedicated to the Delphic Oracle but to a different prophetess—the one who guided Aeneas through the underworld. For Don, however, the name Sibyl conjured the woman whose tortured eyes still haunted him. He could feel her presence, see her wild-eyed, demanding stare…

He shook the absurd musings from his brain and headed for seminar. His mind flittered from thought to thought, searching for a saner subject.

What would come of his relationship with Frances? They were studying together every day in the glass-walled conference room on the second floor annex of the library, and most days they shared lunch there over their books.

One day, however, they had joined Bruce for lunch in the Down Under, where—as Frances put it—Bruce liked to hold court, drink coffee, and scope the coeds. Walking down the worn brick steps for only the second time since September 11, Don felt a split second of panic, as if the low-beamed ceiling was caving in on him, but they joined Bruce at his regular table in the back, and he soon had both of them laughing. Bruce's presence always made everyday banter easier.

Don realized he and Frances tended to be too serious together. They struggled to find conversation topics outside their school assignments. Don was still self-conscious about losing his composure and unleashing his bottled-up grief in front of her. Why had he bared his deepest feelings to Frances?

With Sarah, it would have been easier, less embarrassing. But Sarah was not here; she was in Boston and fully occupied with doctoring. She had no time for a long-distance boyfriend. Frances was comforting, beautiful, and sensual. Besides, Frances was here in Florence. *Frances is ready for me here and now.*

Dr. Sampson, Bruce, and Frances were already in the classroom when Don arrived. Frances flashed a secret smile at Don. To him, her expression suggested smug satisfaction. The memory of his breakdown in this same classroom one week earlier intensified all his feelings of nakedness before her. She knew his secret sorrow, his hidden vulnerability.

Dr. Sampson glanced up at Don with a look of impatience, as if he could read his hidden thoughts and disapproved of his preoccupation.

"Let's get started," he said in his typical gruff voice. "As you know, today we will discuss the destructive effects of legalized monopolies in healthcare. Are you ready, Ms. Hunt?"

"Yes," she answered, "and with your permission, Dr. Sampson, I may take a little longer than Don."

He nodded.

She flipped her blond locks over her right shoulder and began her presentation in an assertive, professional tone.

"Allopathic physicians—doctors who specialize in using medicines—were very effective around the turn of the century at excluding others from competition. Even before their medicines were effective at treating much of anything, they had established a near-exclusive monopoly, having convinced most of the public only they could heal. They used notorious examples of charlatans to build public sentiment against all rival practitioners, good and bad. Through rumor and innuendo, they expanded their influence and took control of the healthcare kingdom. They found ways to exclude or destroy other healers that might interfere with their dominant position.

"Doctors worked through the American Medical Association, or AMA, to secure a monopoly for allopathic medical doctors. The AMA successfully lobbied for laws giving doctors exclusive rights to prescribe medications, perform surgery, and practice medicine. Soon after the 1910 Flexner report, doctors took advantage of public desire for more scientific medicine and pushed through laws that secured a virtual monopoly for physicians and surgeons.

"My story begins in the small town of Thebes, California, where I grew up. In 1946, an English nurse-midwife named Ann Tighe moved to Thebes with her husband, a young American soldier returning home after the war. She had received impeccable training on the Nightingale wards at St. Thomas Hospital in London, which is where they met.

"She was assigned to the operating theater at St. Thomas. Her confidence, nimble fingers, and comprehensive knowledge of anatomy gained notice right away. Soon, she was closing wounds for all the surgeries she assisted—with an expertise surpassing that of many surgeons. Within a year, she was performing surgery under close supervision, and eventually with only a supervising surgeon nearby. She assisted or performed thousands of surgeries during the war years.

"Nurse Tighe's real passion was obstetrics. She loved bringing life into the world. Doctors were in short supply in wartime and had little time for birthing babies. After graduation from nursing school, she was left to manage most deliveries in her district of London on her own. In 1944, she personally delivered 1,129 babies. Thanks to her extensive practical experience and a voracious study of every obstetrics book she could get her hands on, she honed her intuition of when a baby was in distress or when a mother was bleeding and needed assistance.

"All of her deliveries occurred at home, unless there were complications. Her results were as good or better than those achieved in some modern hospitals today. She kept meticulous records. Of those 1129 deliveries, only 101 required forceps, which she used both in the home and in the hospital. She transferred eighty-eight high-risk women to the hospital for delivery. Only thirty-three of those required C-sections, many of which she did herself with minimal assistance. Only twenty of her newborns died, and only five were born with problems that may have resulted from difficult delivery. Her results were so good, she was asked in 1945 to oversee eight other midwives in one of the largest districts in London. Her midwives were beloved by the people of London for their tireless, dedicated, and effective work.

"In Thebes, she naturally wanted to continue her practice. There were no obstetricians in town, and the one general practitioner there, Dr. David Oakley, was elderly and glad for her help. Dr. Oakley and Nurse Tighe worked out an arrangement. He served as supervising physician, as the law required, but was almost never physically present at her deliveries. She transferred her most complicated cases to the Sacramento University Hospital, a little more than an hour away. The local general surgeon was impressed with her work and assisted her with the rare emergency C-section that could not be transferred to Sacramento in time.

"Nurse Tighe practiced in this way for over ten years and delivered an entire generation of children in Thebes. Many owed their lives to her gentle hands and experience in childbirth emergencies. Her C-section rate was around five percent, and her complication rate was lower than that of any obstetrician in the surrounding counties.

"In the mid-to-late 1950s, some of the obstetricians in the small towns nearby began to resent that their would-be patients chose her instead of them. The supply of doctors was increasing, and they felt threatened by the competition. They worried other midwives might move into the area and take their business. One or two of the area obstetricians mentioned their concerns to colleagues on the State Medical Board.

"A young obstetrician named Dr. Capon moved to Thebes in 1956 and was very eager for business. He was trained in newer, more aggressive obstetrical approaches and believed they would prevent complications and result in the best outcomes for women and babies. Nurse Tighe sought to embrace Dr. Capon as a colleague and made the mistake of sharing with him her meticulous statistics.

"First of all, he thought her numbers were impossible. No one—particularly not a nurse—had results that good. Second, he was extremely perturbed by her low C-section rate and decided it could only be maintained by outdated and risky methods. Third, he saw an extraordinary amount of business there for the taking.

"Dr. Capon went on the attack, accused Nurse Tighe of fabricating her statistics, and the volume of anonymous complaints to the Medical Board markedly increased. Dr. Capon convinced the town elders to expand the surgical facilities at the local hospital, and one year later he was proudly trumpeting a C-section rate of twenty percent. One in five of his patients had their bellies cut open under general anesthesia and their babies ripped from their wombs. Although Dr. Capon was a competent surgeon according to the standards of the day, some of these women had serious complications.

"That first year, three women had life-threatening infections after surgery, including one with pus draining from a deep abdominal abscess and one with a recto-vaginal fistula, which allows feces to pass through the vagina. One woman bled to death immediately following surgery. Several babies suffered brain damage after getting excessive anesthesia from the mother's bloodstream and failing to breathe on their own. These were normal obstetrical surgery complications for the time, but word got around, and half the expectant mothers in Thebes continued to choose Nurse Tighe as the safer, more conservative option, despite vicious propaganda spread by Dr. Capon to the contrary.

"My parents moved to Thebes as newlyweds in 1958. My father was an airline pilot based in Sacramento, and my mother an early feminist. Even before the women's movement took off, she believed there was nothing a man could do a woman couldn't do as well or better, so when she became pregnant with my oldest brother the choice of Nurse Tighe was obvious.

"Nurse Tighe visited my mother at home each month to monitor her progress, and the two became best friends. She taught Mom what to expect and how to breathe and relax through the pains. When the time came, my Mom was unafraid of natural childbirth. Nurse Tighe came to the house as soon as my mother established regular contractions, and my oldest brother James was born—at home and with little to-do—after six and a half hours of labor.

"By the time my mother was pregnant with my brother Samuel two years later, things had gotten difficult for Nurse Tighe. Dr. Oakley was eighty-five, he'd had a small stroke, and was unable to practice. There was a family doctor willing to act as her supervising physician, but he demanded she deliver in the hospital, where he could personally supervise, and for this he wanted half her collections. She objected, but he said, 'Take it or leave it. You're high risk, and I'm not going to chance getting sued without something to show for it.'

"Complaints—some anonymous and others from local doctors Dr. Capon had influenced—continued to flow into the state medical board about her lack of credentials. Dr. Capon finally convinced the local medical society to launch a formal complaint to the board citing Nurse Tighe as a threat to the health of women throughout the region. The board launched an investigation, although none of her patients had ever complained and she had never been sued, as Dr. Capon had. The investigation relied almost exclusively on testimony from local physicians and resulted in the decision to prohibit Nurse Tighe from further practice in California, under threat of substantial fines if she didn't comply immediately.

"When Mom called for help with her second birth, Nurse Tighe explained her predicament. Because of the controversy surrounding her, not one local surgeon would provide backup for her C-sections. She couldn't take on new patients and saw little way out of the situation other than to quit practice. Well, my mother was not about to stand by and allow this to happen! In the end, Nurse Tighe agreed to advise her as a friend, and Mom vowed to assist her in fighting the state medical board.

"On the day of the hearing in Sacramento, Nurse Tighe and my mother were prepared, but the six so-called impartial jurors were all male physicians. One was an obstetrician friend of Dr. Capon's, and two more were surgeons.

"Nurse Tighe presented her case well. She presented detailed evidence of her substantial training and the meticulous statistics documenting her actual performance over the previous ten years. The aged Dr. Oakley and my mother each testified on her behalf, and when the opposing attorney accused her of falsifying the statistics, they were ready. They presented what should have been the crowning blow.

"A county health department official presented statistics demonstrating not only that everything Nurse Tighe said was true, but that she had far fewer complications than any doctor in the county. Since obstetricians had come to practice in the county, C-section rates had climbed over two hundred percent, complications of pregnancy had tripled, childbirth fever had gone up, deaths of mothers in childbirth had doubled, and infant mortality had increased. Furthermore, he concluded none of these increases were related to the women and children Nurse Tighe had seen.

"After that strong performance, their attorney looked chagrined, and my mother and Nurse Tighe were very pleased with the way the hearing had gone. Their optimism faded as the board continued to deliberate throughout the afternoon. Finally, at almost five o'clock, they were called back in.

"The chairman of the board was Dr. Samuel Green, an elderly but respected internal medicine physician from Sacramento. With a look of resignation, he stood up and directly addressed Nurse Tighe. My mother requested and saved the transcript of the hearing. Let me read what Dr. Green said:

> Nurse Tighe, it is with honor and respect that I address you today, because I cannot help but recognize your expertise in matters of childbirth and care of the mother and newborn child. However, as you yourself admitted, your training is not typical of that usually found in the United States, and current law does not grant full practice privileges to nurse-midwives, no matter how competent they may be. The law requires that you work under the supervision and guidance of a duly licensed physician, whether you need such supervision or not.
>
> I must admit that given your substantial qualifications and demonstrated competence, I was prepared to investigate whether we might waive this requirement in your case. I suspect that such an exception with the board's agreement might have withstood the legal challenges of the medical society. But the board was unwilling to take such courageous, and I would say just, action. They have not granted you such an exception.
>
> Therefore, I must inform you that you cannot practice in the State of California without the direct supervision of a duly licensed physician, who may dictate the terms of said supervision. That is the law we are sworn to enforce, as my colleagues here have repeatedly reminded me. The law prohibits you from practicing in the State of California until you have secured an agreement with a licensed physician to supervise and take full responsibility for all of your work. Furthermore, until such supervision is secured, you are subject to all previously stated fines and sanctions, should you continue to practice. Following this hearing, on the first day of any such unsupervised practice, you will be fined three thousand dollars, lose your license for one year, and may be subject to imprisonment. These are the requirements of the law.
>
> Nurse Tighe, I hope you will take some consolation in the fact that this board has completely cleared you of all malpractice charges. The record will show that your practice has been exemplary and your outcomes unparalleled in your community. It is my opinion that should you discontinue your practice in Thebes, it will be to that community's great loss. You should also know that because of the serious concerns raised in this hearing about the

quality of obstetric care in Thebes, I have asked for a follow-up investigation of the care provided by the obstetricians there. Lastly, let me express my own personal regret over the outcome of this hearing. It is my sincere hope that the law that prohibits you from practicing in the State of California be reconsidered. Thank you, Nurse Tighe—for your time, your service, and for the opportunity to meet you here today. It has been an honor.

"The consequences of that day were profound. Soon after the hearing, the board asked for Dr. Green's resignation and replaced him with Dr. Capon's obstetrician friend. Not surprisingly, nothing came of the investigation of Dr. Capon; the board determined the case lacked merit and discontinued the investigation. Nurse Tighe closed her practice and moved with her husband back to England, where she could practice and be appreciated.

"My second brother, Sam, was born without the assistance of Nurse Tighe. Mom refused to let Dr. Capon have anything to do with it. She wanted to have the baby at home, but no one was willing to assist her. She went to a large hospital in Sacramento instead, armed with detailed knowledge of the benefits of natural childbirth and having prepared her doctor for what she wanted. 'No drugs, period,' she told him at every visit. In reply, he always said, 'But Dianna, everyone uses anesthesia and painkillers these days. Do you really want to go through all the pain of childbirth again?'

"When her contractions began, my Dad was flying overseas, so a friend drove her to the hospital. The friend was directed to the waiting room and had to remain there for the duration. In the early 1960s, they were in no position to argue; doctors were in charge.

"The nurses in the prep room pushed pain medications. She refused. She claimed she didn't have pain—only some cramps—but they insisted childbirth is always painful. Unlike Nurse Tighe, whose calming presence reduced fear and pain, the nurses and doctors at Sacramento General promoted maternal helplessness and heroic medical interventions; they told her everything that might go wrong and require anesthesia or C-section.

"The doctor said, 'Look, you don't want to go into the delivery room and be the only one awake, do you?' Mom told him, 'I *will* be awake when my son is born and don't you dare give me anything.' From then on they left her alone.

"Mom knew lots of babies were delivered at Sacramento General, but when they wheeled her gurney into the delivery room, she was unprepared for what she saw: a dozen women—each one spread-eagled on an examining table with her feet in stirrups—lined up around the perimeter of the room. Except for a few covered by sheets, most every woman had her knees spread and her shaved pudenda exposed. All were unconscious or close to it—those with open eyes had the glazed look of the dead. Mom watched the nurses and doctors go from gurney to gurney, inserting gloved hands into open vaginas. Someone tried to put something over my mother's face and she screamed, 'No, no!'—thinking it was ether to drug her to sleep.

"The doctor said, 'Relax Dianna, it is only oxygen for the baby.'

"That's my story. Samuel was born with little help from the hospital. He was fine, but my mother was so upset about the experience and what happened to Nurse Tighe, she waited fifteen years before having me."

"I wasn't too far off when I figured you were an only child," Bruce quipped.

Dr. Sampson cleared his throat. "Thank you, Ms. Hunt. This case gives us an excellent opportunity to talk about healthcare monopolies. For most of recorded history, midwives—not doctors—have assisted with the vast majority of deliveries. Doctors have only gained a monopoly over obstetrical care in a few industrialized countries—and only in the last fifty years. Do you think obstetrical care has improved overall in the United States in the last fifty years?"

"You better believe it has," Bruce answered. "According to the readings you gave us, maternal death rates from childbirth fever have dropped from fifteen percent to fewer than one in a thousand, and death rates for newborns have dropped even more."

"What has led to these improvements?" Dr. Sampson asked. "Is it because of the things obstetricians do? Or have similar improvements occurred in countries that use home births and nurse-midwives?"

"As far as I can tell," Don said, "it has little to do with doctors providing obstetrical care. Childbirth fever and maternal death rates dropped because of sterile techniques. Most of the decrease in neonatal death rates occurred before doctors had a monopoly."

Frances nodded. "In the mid 1800s, a Hungarian doctor named Semmelweiss noticed that over ten percent of women delivered by doctors at his teaching hospital in Vienna died from childbirth fever, but women delivered by midwives in the same hospital died less than four percent of the time. The reason? The doctors didn't wash their hands. They would go straight from dissecting infected corpses of young women who had just died from childbirth fever to the maternity ward, where they examined women in labor with their bare hands. Semmelweiss introduced routine handwashing in 1846 and reduced childbirth fever deaths to around one percent. The doctors of the time ridiculed him and challenged the integrity of his data. It took almost a century for doctors to get on board with simple handwashing and improve their childbirth fever and maternal death rates enough to match those of the midwives."

"So, what has changed as a result of the recent monopoly of allopathic medical doctors in obstetrics care?" Dr. Sampson asked.

"It's rather obvious, isn't it?" Frances answered. "C-section rates. They've made natural birth into a surgical procedure—a bloody operation where the belly and womb are sliced open to get the baby out. In the 1940s, over eighty percent of births occurred at home. C-sections were a last resort, only about one in eight hundred deliveries. Today most births occur in hospitals, and the average C-section rate is almost one in four deliveries. In some hospitals, the C-section rate exceeds forty percent! Home births are proven as safe as hospital births for low-risk mothers. In England, where many births still occur at home, the complication rates are lower than in the United States."

"Sure, but C-sections save a lot of babies and mothers, don't they?" Bruce said.

"A *few* lives are saved by C-sections," Frances snapped, "but not many. Most are done for convenience, not for the health of the mother or baby."

"Please be precise, Ms. Hunt," Dr. Sampson said. "What percentage of C-sections are medically necessary?"

"The World Health Organization says no country is justified in having a C-section rate greater than ten or fifteen percent. Many countries with the lowest death rates for mothers and newborns have rates well under ten percent. However, in the United States nearly one in four babies is delivered by C-section, meaning that almost half a million American women a year get C-sections they don't need."

"They wouldn't be doing all these C-sections if women didn't want them," Bruce said. "As for home births, what woman in her right mind would want that? Anesthesia and spinal blocks have made childbirth painless, and isn't that what women want, a painless birth?"

Don found himself wanting to side with Frances. "A painless birth might be what some women want," he said, "but they should know the risks. A spinal block relaxes the pelvic floor muscles and makes it more difficult for a woman to push when it's time. More deliveries fail to progress, and that leads to more C-sections. And spinals cause other problems: low blood pressure, medication reactions, a need for IV hormones to force the uterus to contract, and fetal distress."

Frances could barely contain her fire. "The monopoly physicians have on obstetrical care is all about control, isn't it? Women forced by doctors—mostly male doctors—to go to hospitals to have babies, as if childbirth is some kind of disease! They're pressured to go pain-free, so they get paralyzed and lose even more control. Then some of them get C-sections they don't even need and they have to pay big money for being cut wide open just to have a baby."

"I think the current system does medicalize childbirth and take control away from women," Don said. "Doctors and nurses push spinal blocks and pain-killers by encouraging fear of pain. They push women to agree to all kinds of procedures by encouraging fear of complications. The amount of coordinated coercion that occurs in maternity units is really amazing."

"One more thing," Frances added. "Guess which hospitals have the highest C-section rates? The for-profit hospitals with fancy private rooms have average rates of thirty percent. Not-for-profit, university, and public hospitals have average rates of fifteen percent, and guess what? Babies and moms do as well or better there than in for-profit hospitals. It makes you wonder about the real reasons behind C-sections in American hospitals."

Bruce looked like he was about to protest, but Dr. Sampson changed the subject. "Let's expand beyond obstetrical care and discuss how allopathic medical doctors gained a monopoly in the United States and most other developed nations. As you know from basic American history, the colonies sought independence in order to get free of England's control. The United States was founded on the principle of liberty. The founding fathers wanted each citizen to have the freedom to work in his chosen profession and be free from England's burdensome system of guilds, licenses, and taxes.

"America's founders wanted these freedoms in the healing arts as well. Dr. Benjamin Rush, who served as a physician in the Continental Army and signed the Declaration of Independence, wrote that *To restrict the practice of medicine to only one class of men would constitute the Bastille of medicine.* Government placed little if any restrictions on healthcare providers for the first century and a half; anyone could become a doctor or open a clinic, hospital, or medical school.

"Early Americans could choose from a large variety of healers and healing methods, including osteopaths, homeopaths, and herbalists. Competition kept prices down, improved access to care, and encouraged innovation. No class of healers was given a legal advantage over any other. On the downside, there were many quacks and charlatans, but the healers that helped people the most were generally the most successful. None of them—even the well-trained doctors— made a lot of money. Following the rise of the scientific method, allopathic physicians—the drug and bleeding doctors—underwent more education than any other type of healer, and they wanted to be compensated for it. So, Ms. Hunt, what did the allopaths do about it?"

"They formed a union in 1847 called the American Medical Association, and began a long-term campaign to outlaw competition, reduce the supply of physicians, and raise prices. They did this with clean consciences. In fact, they were quite self-righteous about it—saying their goal was to improve the quality of healthcare in America. For a long time, their efforts to restrict practice to *one class of men* were unsuccessful, but a world-shaking event finally made their hopes a reality."

"The Flexner report," Bruce interjected.

"Exactly. Abraham Flexner and the AMA began collaborating in 1910 to survey medical schools. Their report branded the majority of schools in the healing arts as substandard. Then the AMA and the Carnegie and Rockefeller

Foundations used the Flexner report to convince Congress to close substandard schools, create licensing requirements for doctors and hospitals, and begin subsidizing research-oriented allopathic medical schools. While this may have been great for allopathic medical science, it is not clear it improved public health, and opponents of the law argued it circumvented freedoms promised in the Constitution."

"You're right, Ms. Hunt," Dr. Sampson said. "And despite lack of public demand for licensing laws, the AMA's heavy lobbying was successful. The allopathic medical monopoly was buttressed by over 120 new state and federal licensing laws between 1910 and 1920, and a *Bastille of medicine*, the very thing Dr. Rush had warned of, was created. So, what happened to the medical schools, Dr. Newman?"

"By 1940, the number of medical schools was cut by half: all the schools that admitted women and almost all the schools that accepted blacks were closed."

Frances added, "And state medical boards—composed of allopathic physicians—persecuted and even imprisoned those who practiced without a license. The practice of medicine became completely controlled by *one class of men*. In other words, *men* made laws that gave *women's* care over into the hands of *men!*"

Dr. Sampson nodded. "In our modern healthcare system, allopathic doctors—male and female—are entitled and empowered by law. Their medicine is generally more scientific and evidence-based than that of other practitioners, but the current allopathic medical establishment often resists innovative changes, particularly if those changes might threaten its monopoly with real competition."

"The allopaths always clothe their efforts to maintain their monopoly in the guise of maintaining quality," Frances said. "But they seldom demonstrate that they can do things any better than anyone else."

"Frances is right," Don said. "The subspecialty organizations are the worst. They are always battling for exclusive rights to perform this or that lucrative procedure. Organizations like the AMA expend a lot of effort wrestling for control that could be better spent promoting health."

"What else would you expect them to do?" Bruce asked, his skepticism apparent.

"How about advocating for their patients' best interests and promoting health?" Frances said. "Would that be too much to ask?"

"That is for you to decide," Dr. Sampson said. "Some advocate doing away with licensing laws altogether and allowing the various professions to certify themselves. Doctors, nurses, naturopaths, and chiropractors would still be subject to liability if they harmed someone by practicing outside their sphere of expertise, and health plans could choose who to include in their provider panels based on public demand and cost."

Frances said, "If a nurse-run clinic thinks it can do as well or better than a physician-run clinic, the law shouldn't prevent that. Public or private health plans should monitor care using standard quality measures and pay for results instead of titles. Then nurses could share some of the fruits doctors have monopolized. As it is now, we're often treated like slaves—forced to do the doctor's bidding, keep our mouths shut, and make a fraction of the income."

"Gosh, I kind of like it that way." Bruce winked at her.

"Of course you would," Frances fired back, "you're a member of the allopath elite. Let's face it. This is all about money. For years, you doctors"—she pointed a polished red fingernail like a laser at each man in turn—"have been getting almost all of it, and I for one am tired of it. As if nurses don't work every bit as hard or harder than you doctors, but we don't make even half as much. We actually take care of our patients—listen to them, calm their fears, empty their bedpans, wipe up vomit, change bloody dressings—and meanwhile, you doctors just breeze in and pontificate about diseases and diagnoses. It's totally bogus. You forget the patient's health is the goal. You've constructed this intricate system of control, and you rationalize it in your self-serving little minds in order to justify huge salaries."

"Whoa, missie!" Bruce chuckled. "I think we hit on a nerve, Don," he said, turning and winking at Don.

Don squirmed in his chair and looked away, hoping to convey to Frances he was nothing like Bruce Markum and did not share his attitude on this matter in any way.

"Look Frances," Bruce said more gently, "of course doctors make more money—they have more training and bear the responsibility."

"And not all of us get paid so much," Don added. This was something he knew about. "Some primary care physicians work over eighty hours a week but make less than nurse anesthetists working under forty."

"You're missing the point, Don," Bruce said. "The point is doctors should get paid for their training and skills. Nurse practitioners shouldn't be allowed to prescribe medicine or operate without direct physician supervision. They simply don't have the training. Our clinical training lasts more than twice as long. Nurses often miss the subtle variations in the presentation of a disease, and that can be the difference in life or death."

"You are both missing the point, you thick-headed Neanderthals," Frances said. "Nurses should get paid—like Dr. Sampson said—for hard work and results, not for training and titles. I should have the choice to work a hundred hours a week if I want to and the opportunity to make as much money as you do for it. I don't need anyone to tell me what I can or can't do, particularly not the doctor cartel!"

Dr. Sampson paused for a moment and said, "I think it is worth giving some thought to Ms. Hunt's story and what she has said. Have doctors been set up like kings, entitled by law? Are they acting as a sort of healthcare mafia, controlling all the business and always getting a cut? Consider also, are there bigger fish siphoning off the public's health care dollars?"

Frances smiled. She glanced at Bruce and then Don, obviously feeling vindicated by Dr. Sampson's remarks.

"Okay, that is it for today. For our next seminar, Dr. Markum, I believe you are on?"

"Yes, sir."

"Very good, I'll see you next week." Dr. Sampson gathered his things and left the room, with Bruce following close on his heels.

Don turned to Frances. "You were heated up today," he said.

"I guess I'm just passionate about equal opportunity. Women so often get the short end of the stick."

"Yeah, I guess you're right."

"The woman is always right," Frances teased. "Listen, I'll see you later, Don. I've got to get ready for my next class. After preparing that case, I'm a little behind on everything else." She flashed Don her winning smile and left him alone again.

TWO DAYS LATER Don reported to Florence New American Hospital to begin the first of two fourteen-hour shifts for the weekend—one Friday and one Saturday. Both shifts ran from six in the evening until eight the next morning. Not much chance of seeing Frances this weekend. Unlike Bruce, Don had to work to pay his bills.

Friday evenings were always crowded with people who for one reason or another didn't get in to see their doctors during the week. As soon as he got to the call room to ditch his stuff, he got the first page. It was the ER. Don sat on the firm twin bed and picked up the phone on the nightstand to call the number.

A woman answered. "Dr. Newman? This is Mary Simpson—the charge nurse in the ER? The attending physician down here asked me to call you with an admission."

Don grabbed an index card and pen from his breast pocket so he could jot down the basic information. "Okay, go ahead."

"Mrs. Shaw is a seventy-six-year-old female with crampy left lower quadrant abdominal pain for three days. Her pain got really bad this afternoon, but her doctor's office was closed. Dr. Mallock checked a urinalysis and says she has a urinary tract infection with probable urosepsis."

Her matter of fact tone and clear presentation of the case instantly gained Don's trust. He detected a hint of doubt in her voice.

"Does she have fever?"

"No fever. She does have a slightly elevated white blood cell count, but that's it."

An elevated white blood cell count by itself meant nothing. Any type of stress, even a cold, could cause it, yet inexperienced interns often assume it means infection.

He asked the critical question. "Does she have a left shift?"

A left shift   an increase in the percentage of young white blood cells in the bloodstream—portends a serious blood infection or sepsis. Patients who do not exhibit fever, low blood pressure, or other signs of serious bloodstream infection such as a left shift can be safely treated at home.

"No," she reported, "no left shift, no fever, and her blood pressure's fine— just a few white cells in her urine."

She said nothing more, leaving it up to him to make his own conclusions. Don could tell Nurse Simpson was skeptical. He imagined her frustration—to know the diagnosis better than the doctor and still have to defer to his more "expert" judgment.

"I'll be down in a minute."

Don hung up the phone. *Shit!* It was bad enough to be on call on a Friday night. But having to work all night processing bogus admissions was absolute torture.

He walked into exam room five, slid the glass door closed behind him to shut out the emergency room clamor, and turned to introduce himself.

Mrs. Shaw, a woman with bright eyes and curly gray hair, greeted him with a puzzled stare. Bright yellow liquid antibiotics were pouring from a plastic bag on a pole through thin plastic tubing and into a vein in the soft skin of her inner arm. "Dr. Newman, what's happening? I came in here with a little stomachache. I thought I was just constipated, but they tell me I have a serious infection."

"Let's see. Can I ask you a just a few more questions?"

They reviewed her history and he pressed on her stomach. Within a few minutes Mrs. Shaw had convinced him her diagnosis—not the doctor's—was correct; constipation was the cause of her pain. She hadn't had a bowel movement in five days.

Don checked the urinalysis results. Just as he thought—only a few white cells. Why had they even ordered the test? No burning on urination, no upper back pain from the kidneys, no fever. Urosepsis patients often exhibit all three symptoms, but she had none, and urinalysis testing isn't recommended for most asymptomatic patients.

Nonetheless, in almost every emergency room in the country, every woman with abdominal pain gets a urinalysis. False positive results are common; it's almost impossible to get a clean-catch urine sample, so most specimens contain a few white blood cells, like Mrs. Shaw's. It doesn't necessarily mean infection. It could just be the sample was contaminated because the woman didn't clean herself perfectly, or didn't collect a mid-stream sample, or didn't hold her labial folds apart when she peed into the cup. Women are seldom instructed on the proper technique; they're simply told to pee in the cup. Every night, people in emergency rooms all over the country are admitted and shot up with powerful antibiotics, when a decent history-taking and exam would allow most of them to go home.

"What about my CT scan?" Mrs. Shaw asked. "What did it show?"

Don had difficulty hiding his surprise. A CT scan, too? Four hundred chest x-rays worth of radiation for a constipated woman who didn't even look sick?

"Uh, well, let me check on that," Don said. "Don't worry. I'm sure it will turn out all right. I'll be right back."

He went out to the nurse's station and pulled up the radiology results on the computer. *Just as I thought.* She was FOS, all right—full of shit.

Don spotted a nurse in a white, short-sleeved tunic and polyester pants striding down the hall, taking rightward glances into each patient room as she passed. That had to be the nurse who had called.

"Nurse Simpson?" Don asked.

The nurse turned and approached the desk on cushioned white shoes. Her light brown hair was streaked with gray. She looked to be about fifty-five.

"You must be Dr. Newman. You can call me Mary."

"Thank you, Mary. Listen, it looks to me like Mrs. Shaw is just constipated. She doesn't need antibiotics. She just needs an enema and then she can go home."

Mary gave Don an understanding glance and looked both ways to make sure no one was nearby. "I wouldn't tell that to the attending unless you are looking for a fight," she whispered. "The ER is busy as hell, and he doesn't appreciate advice. Besides, the hospital likes to keep the beds full, and we have half a floor available. Once the decision has been made to admit, there is almost no turning back."

"Who decides to admit?"

"The admitting physician. In this case that's Dr. Mallock, the attending physician in the ER, who also happens to be the chief of staff. I wouldn't challenge him unless it is a case of life or death. You must pick your battles. Best thing you can do for poor old Mrs. Shaw tonight is to make sure she doesn't come to any real harm."

"Well, I guess it wouldn't hurt to watch her overnight." Don sighed and cursed under his breath.

Ridiculous! Mallock was too senior to make such a rookie diagnostic mistake. Don felt as if he were working for some kind of healthcare mafia—bent on making money off unsuspecting patients.

"By the way, Dr. Newman, there's another admission for you in room number three. This one I think is a real pneumonia, though not a bad one. This is a crazy place, but every once in a while you get to help someone."

She dashed off down the hall to see her next patient.

Don liked Mary Simpson. She was a diligent and competent nurse, as he imagined Frances must be. He was glad she was there. Dr. Mallock, on the other hand, sounded like a real bastard.

Don scribbled out an admission note he hoped would make clear to the doctor taking over in the morning Mrs. Shaw could go straight home. He figured it would work, but his conversation with Mary had left him unsettled. He hated to be dominated by a senior physician he had never even met.

Don knew Mallock's type. Same ilk as Desmond. Don remembered, word-for-word, what Desmond had said when he broke the news he was postponing his cardiology fellowship to do the health system science fellowship with Dr. Sampson.

"Dr. Newman, you're making a big mistake." His cold and certain tone brooked no doubt. "Do it, and you'll never work here again."

Don didn't comprehend at first. "Dr. Sampson said I could do cardiology after my fellowship with him, maybe even pursue a career doing healthcare research in cardiology."

Dr. Desmond had answered with veiled contempt, "He did, did he? Don't you see? He'll ruin you. You'll end up like him. Not good for anything practical. Mark my words: leave the University Hospital now, and you'll never practice here again."

Don second-guessed his decision once again—he was beginning to think he *had* made a big mistake—but Sarah convinced him to talk to her father, Dr. John Moore. He was an old classmate of Dr. Desmond and a cardiologist who practiced in Eden Prairie, Minnesota, where Sarah grew up. Sarah's parents came to Boston to visit and they all went out to lunch together.

Don told Sarah's dad about Dr. Desmond's threat.

"Desmond likes to think he is king of the universe, but he is not," Dr. Moore laughed. "At worst, Desmond is a minor capo."

Don found it strange he used that word. If Desmond was a minor capo, he wondered, who was the godfather?

"You know, we physicians in America used to work for our communities in a more direct way," Dr. Moore said. "We accepted what people could afford to pay—sometimes that was a chicken or a fish or some other thing. Heck, I still have patients that bring me a pie or some homegrown tomatoes on occasion. But now, we've worked ourselves into a situation where strangers—faceless middle-men from the government and insurance companies—guarantee our payment.

"First, associations like Blue Cross started guaranteeing payment. Then Medicare did it, and suddenly country doctors like me were getting paid good money for treating the poor—people for whom we had never expected payment before. Before Medicare, we just expected to have to provide some charity care, but now, with nearly everyone on Medicare, Medicaid, or private insurance, doc-tors expect generous payment for everyone. Somewhere along the way we doc-tors lost our calling and got caught up in the lure of all that guaranteed money.

"Yep, Desmond is a little fish. The academics always like to think they are in charge, but the real healthcare powers are deeper in the money trail."

He came around to Don's question.

"Virgil Sampson is a good man. You know, he postponed medical school at Penn and volunteered to go to Vietnam at a time when most premeds were ready to cut off a finger to get a deferment, if getting accepted into medical school didn't work. The word is that in Vietnam, his platoon went deeper into the jungle and lost fewer men than any other. Yep, he's intense; that comes from living behind enemy lines.

"In residency we were all in awe of him. He got in trouble once or twice for chewing out other doctors who gave lackadaisical care. But he handled emergen-cies and ran codes better than anyone. You can count on him to be a good team leader. I'm sure his fellowship would be excellent. The only question is whether it's right for you, and only you can answer that. Follow your heart and you'll know what to do."

Well, Don had followed his heart then, and he would do it now. *To hell with hospital hierarchy!* Maybe I can't send Mrs. Shaw home tonight, but damned if I'll give her a dangerous intravenous drug she doesn't even need!

Don wrote an order to discontinue Mrs. Shaw's antibiotics and administer an enema instead, then set off to see his next patient.

15

The Ambulance Chasers

*...among the bitter sorbs it is not natural
the sweet fig should come to fruit.*
DANTE ALIGHIERI, INFERNO 15, 65–66

"I HAVE TO ADMIT I was shocked last week," Bruce began, "when Frances demonstrated high rates of C-sections do little to improve outcomes for women and children. Since then, I've been thinking about what's driving the numbers up. It's defensive medicine. The problem isn't doctors trying to control women's lives; it's not some feminist issue. It's about avoiding malpractice."

Frances looked at Bruce with unabashed skepticism, but he didn't give her a chance to interrupt.

"So let's return to the average town—Dr. Sampson's healthcare wasteland— to show you how ambulance chasers operate. They are the ones causing the most waste in healthcare. This is a real case involving a medical school classmate of mine, but it could have happened anywhere. In fact, this story is repeated all over America, week in and week out. It will show how these opportunistic trial lawyers are responsible for the greatest problems in healthcare today.

"A couple months ago, I was at my ten-year medical school reunion, and I heard about how our classmate, Jim Kerner, had just gotten screwed—uh, sued—in his first year of practice. I took particular note of it because Jim was the last one you'd expect to get sued. If it could happen to him so soon after finishing an excellent, surgery-oriented OB residency, it could happen to anyone, even to me. It was my job as the outgoing class president to keep up with everyone's news, so I decided to find out all I could about his case.

"Jim Kerner was the perfect doctor, the one every woman wanted, the kind doctors recommend for their wives and mothers. He was a smart and skilled physician, but that was true for all of us—we hadn't gotten into medical school by slacking off. But what was special about Jim was his total dedication to his patients. He actually *wanted* his patients to understand their options and participate in their own healthcare decisions, and he went overboard for them. Somehow, he reminds me a little of you, Don. I mean, he was a really nice guy, the opposite of the old-style, paternalistic physician like Dr. Capo—or whatever his name was—you told us about last week, Frances."

"Capon," she corrected him.

"Right. If anything, Jim Kerner was maternal," Bruce continued. "He spent hours talking to mothers, nurturing them, preparing them for childbirth, and answering all their questions. Anyway, late on the night of our reunion, I spotted Jim sitting alone at the hotel bar. He looked haggard and despondent—as if he had aged twenty years instead of ten. Even though we weren't exactly close friends, I sidled up to him and offered to buy him a drink. I said something like, 'I heard you had a tough year,' and, to my surprise, he seemed eager to tell me about it.

"'I expected you sooner,' he told me. 'The politician. You're a mover and shaker, so naturally you want to know what happened. Maybe some good can come out of it—my year from hell. You know I'm a good doctor, right? That's all I ever wanted to be, you know. Well, this year I got sued by someone I knew, after I did the very best I possibly could to help her.'

"Jim told me the whole story and I've written it down in his words, best I could remember them. Here goes."

"EVELYN MERTENS was a modern woman who wanted everything: a career that's interesting but not too grueling, a beautiful house, a doting husband, and perfect children. She was an investment banker; she worked her way up to vice president and waited until the perfect time to have children. Or so she thought; age thirty-eight is not perfect biologically, and it took her two years to get pregnant.

"I counseled her about the increased risk of complications—like birth defects—because of her age and overweight, but she said that only happens to other people. I did all the recommended prenatal testing. I encouraged her to enroll in childbirth classes because she claimed she wanted a natural childbirth.

"However, Evelyn soon made it clear she didn't expect childbirth to involve any pain. She said, 'With those pain blocks, you don't feel anything, right?' I explained that with spinal anesthesia, labor had to establish itself—likely with some discomfort—before we could safely administer a block, and she said—as if to inform me of what I should already know—'Oh, but you or the anesthesiologist can give me something to take care of that!'

"You know I worked hard to bring her back to reality, right? I had several counseling sessions with her and documented everything. I explained how narcotics and spinal anesthesia could make it more likely she would fail to progress in her labor, but she was undeterred.

"'Let's not worry about that,' she said on our last visit before the anticipated delivery date. 'Everything will be perfect, I know. I have great confidence in you. You're the best OB in town; everyone says so.'

"As is often the case in real life, everything was not perfect. Three days later, her water broke and she came to the hospital. With the help of the anesthesiologist, I was able to get her the narcotics and the spinal block she demanded, all in fairly short order. This had the effect she desired, and she sat there, comfortable and in charge, like she was overseeing her boardroom.

"The pain management also had the side effect I feared. After five hours of labor, she showed very little evidence of progression, and from then on almost everything went wrong. Contractions went from strong, natural, and regular, to weak, irregular, and non-productive. The external monitor we use to measure contractions and fetal heartbeat was not working well, and I had to plead with her more than fifteen minutes before she let me place an electronic monitor under the skin of her baby's scalp. She kept insisting she was going natural and that was the last intervention she would allow.

"By that point, I was completely frustrated. Given her insistence on a pain-free childbirth, I had no idea what she meant by 'natural.' It wasn't long before I found out.

"Something about the fetal heart beat tracings from the scalp monitor caught my attention. The heartbeat patterns did not meet any of the textbook criteria requiring a C-section, but there were minor irregularities that worried me. After more than six hours of non-productive labor, she was not progressing at all. I began to get that gut feeling this baby needed to be delivered immediately. And after a few thousand deliveries, I trust that feeling.

"I told Evelyn and her husband straight out, 'I am beginning to get very worried about the health of your baby, and your labor is not progressing. I would like to do a C-section now.'

"Well, Evelyn Mertens was used to being in charge, and she had liked the way I encouraged her to think carefully and make her own decisions. She was clearly the one that made the decisions in her family; her husband never said a word. He just turned to her. I remember exactly what she said.

"'Dr. Kerner, I've gotten this far without a C-section, and I am *not* going to have one now!'

"I started to argue, but she cut me off, saying, 'This is ridiculous, we talked about all of this long ago. I am not going to have a C-section!'

"Now, I don't do unnecessary C-sections. My rate was the lowest in the hospital; my complication rate was low as anyone's. But I sure wanted to do one then. I replied calmly that in my professional opinion, her baby was in serious danger and might even suffer brain damage if we didn't intervene.

"She got really angry and yelled, 'You listen to me! I'll have no more talk of C-sections. Everything is going just fine, I'm not in pain, and I'm sure the baby is fine. I chose you to be my doctor because your C-section rate is the lowest. I have no intention of being cut open and ending up with some grotesque scar.

We agreed this would be natural and you are not to say one more word about C-sections, or I'll ask for another doctor.'

"I told her I would ask another colleague to come right away to give a second opinion. I had the anesthesiologist back off on the spinal a bit, so by the time my colleague arrived, the contractions were more regular, the fetal heart tone abnormalities had completely resolved, and despite her complaints about the pain, she was finally progressing well and preparing to deliver.

"My colleague agreed with all my findings, though he was less worried than I had been, since the minor abnormalities had completely resolved. We agreed it was better to go ahead with a vaginal birth, and Evelyn gave birth to a beautiful baby boy after nine hours of labor. Michael, she named him. The Apgar scores—which assess a newborn's vigor—were on the low end of normal, suggesting he was basically healthy.

"However, something about the boy worried me. He didn't seem quite right. His reflexes were a little slow, his muscle tone was weak, he was less responsive than normal, he didn't suck hard on the nipple, and he hardly moved one side of his body. My exam suggested he was neurologically impaired. Usually it takes a few months before we're certain, but I was already pretty sure Michael had cerebral palsy.

"The next day I broke the news to Evelyn and her husband. I said the cause was unknown—it could have been something during pregnancy or fetal hypoxia caused by prolonged labor.

"At first they didn't believe me. Then they got angry. Evelyn was particularly bitter. 'You think this is all our fault, don't you?' she said.

"That's a normal grief reaction, so I tried to reassure them. 'No, and assigning blame won't help anyone, especially Michael. No one knows what causes cerebral palsy most of the time. It's likely his developmental problems started well before childbirth, maybe even in the first or second trimester. It's impossible to tell. The good news is that with love and attention, he may develop into a completely normal and healthy young man. You should focus your attention on him because he needs you.'

"I counseled them about the things for which they needed to be particularly alert, including the possibility of seizures. I gave them information to read about cerebral palsy and promised to come to their home personally in one week to counsel them more about how to proceed. I arranged for a visiting nurse to make sure Michael got adequate nutrition.

"That was the last I saw of the Mertens until the trial. I did call a week after the birth to arrange a visit.

"Mrs. Mertens answered the phone and said in a tearful voice, 'I think you had better not come.'

"I pressed her for a reason.

"'The baby...it had a seizure!'

"Her husband got on the phone and said, 'You leave my wife alone! You've harassed her enough!'

"I was stunned. 'Please,' I begged, 'let me come by to speak with you and your wife to help you get through this difficult time.'

"He said, 'You've done quite enough, don't you think?' and he slammed the phone down.

"I was tormented for months. I found out later what had happened. Three days after they got home from the hospital, a lawyer called to express his sympathies. Someone in the hospital must have tipped him off. Obviously, he encouraged them to look for a scapegoat they could blame to avoid blaming themselves.

"The lawyer's first goal was to sever all contact between us, to build suspicion and cut the bond between physician and patient. Before Michael had his first seizure, they were already primed to go to another hospital. Michael never came back to our hospital, even though we had all his records and could have served him best.

"I got my summons six months ago. Of course, my insurance company wanted to settle. They usually lose cases like mine. But I hadn't done anything wrong! I couldn't do it.

"I never met the Mertens' lawyer—Bill Slaughter of Simmons and Fine—until we went to court. One of his underling associates had handled the pretrial questioning, which was awful enough, but I was totally unprepared for what happened in the courtroom. He was vicious. He treated me with suspicion and disgust, as if I had done something horrible. And, of course, he brought in a well-paid expert who claimed the fetal heart tracings "clearly indicated" severe fetal distress, and who testified for a big fee it was "clearly malpractice not to do an immediate C-section" in that situation.

"There were lots of detailed pictures, test results, head scans, and seizure studies showing 'how terribly Michael had been damaged.' They portrayed him as a victim of poor medical care who would never recover and would need full-time residential care for life. It was clear the lawyers and their hired doctors had encouraged the Mertens to think for months only about how hopeless things were for their son.

"The Mertens bought this tragic vision hook, line, and sinker. They branded their son as a hopeless case. They put all their energy and resources into documenting his sickness instead of helping Michael maximize his potential through physical, sensory, language, and cognitive therapy. Their smug lawyer sat there gloating over the sick relationship he had cultivated between the Mertens and their son.

"The worst of all was when I testified. You know I had to testify, don't you, Bruce? You understand why I had to testify, don't you? They were killing the truth, and killing all hope for healing that boy and his family. They had decided the most important thing was to have someone to blame, and when I took the stand, they all stared at me with real hatred.

"The cross examination was almost unbearable. Bruce, for almost forty-five minutes I was crucified up there. They accused me of lying and falsifying the records to make myself look good. They even claimed I had advised against a C-section! It was all I could do to sit there and take it without losing my composure.

"At the end of the trial, the jury read their verdict. Negligent. They found me negligent, Bruce, and I did nothing wrong. A jury of ordinary people—not medical professionals–decided it was malpractice, and awarded the Mertens every last dollar of the two million they asked for. Double what my malpractice insurance covered! I put my head down on the table and cried right there in the courtroom while they all celebrated their victory.

"As we were leaving the courtroom, I followed after Evelyn Mertens and called, 'Evelyn! Evelyn!'

"She turned halfway toward me, but would not look at me.

"'Why did you do this to me?' I cried out.

"She looked pained but didn't answer.

"'Did I ever mislead or harm you in any way?'

"'No, but my baby, my baby, my baby,' she wailed.

"Then her attorney swooped in, gave me that fierce look of disgust and hatred, and whisked her away.

"I realized the verdict would not lessen her pain. Whatever she got after the lawyer took his cut would never compensate for her loss. To win the money, she threw away hope and invested in tragedy instead."

"NOW JIM RESTRICTS his practice to gynecology, where he is less likely to get sued," Bruce said. "So that's it: the best obstetrician I've ever known doesn't deliver babies.

"Unfortunately, this happens a lot. The law firm Simmons and Fine does more medical malpractice plaintiff work than any firm in Jim's state. They have a finely tuned system for chasing ambulances and suing doctors. They have twenty-four lawyers—eight partners and sixteen associates—and almost a hundred other employees, including a ten-person marketing department for TV and radio direct-to-consumer advertising. The commercials make it seem noble and profitable to sue people. They have offices and billboards directly across the street from each major hospital in town, so many people assume they're a legitimate part of the local healthcare system. They have a 1-800 number and a well-staffed center to screen calls for payout potential.

"It's unethical for attorneys to directly solicit individuals, but unscrupulous lawyers use others to do the dirty work: telemarketers obtain police accident reports and make follow-up phone calls to people involved, and hospital employees—particularly in the neonatal units, intensive care units, and birth centers—work ostensibly as consultants but get paid to provide information about cases where something went wrong. These moles befriend patients and call them at home to show sympathy, gently suggest physician incompetence, and refer them to 'an attorney they can trust.' Jim told me there was an investigation of several suspected employee moles in their childbirth center, but they were never able to prove anything."

"Isn't it illegal for nurses or staff to reveal confidential patient information?" Don asked.

Bruce laughed. "Of course it's illegal. But some hospital staffers resent doctors and think they're doing the right thing to help. A nurse or ward clerk can simply guide a patient to a malpractice attorney, without revealing the patient's name to the attorney's office. It is very hard to prove a person in the hospital is an informant.

"With OB cases, all that's required to interest a lawyer is a bad outcome. My friend in the malpractice insurance defense industry tells me if a baby dies or is impaired in any way, the case is virtually indefensible—no matter how good the doctor was. The jury will sympathize with the distraught family and will award them money because they feel sorry for them. They think it won't hurt the doctor because he's rich and has insurance."

"Okay—excellent case, Dr. Markum," Dr. Sampson said. "Any questions?"

"I'm wondering about the data on cerebral palsy, fetal heart monitoring, and C-sections," Don said. "Are you really sure doctors aren't at fault in some of these cases? Can't they do something to prevent cerebral palsy?"

"Look at the New England Journal of Medicine article I passed out," Bruce answered. "The research is pretty clear. Nobody knows for sure what causes cerebral palsy, and brain damage can occur in any trimester. All we know is babies with certain unusual heartbeat patterns have increased risk, and babies with very high or low heart rates do better if delivered by C-section. Problem is, if we did a C-section on every baby with any abnormalities on the heart tracing, most women would end up getting one. But like Frances said last week, for most pregnancies C-sections do more harm than good. When the C-section rate skyrocketed in the eighties after fetal heart monitoring became routine, the percentage of babies born with cerebral palsy actually increased. Who knows why? Maybe C-sections themselves can cause transient fetal hypoxia."

"So Bruce, what do you think is the right rate for C-sections?" Frances asked.

Bruce smiled. "It all depends on where you live, he said. "In some parts of Brazil, more than two-thirds of deliveries are by C-section, and wealthier, low-risk women are most likely to get them. In Ireland, where C-sections are viewed as a last resort, C-section rates are typically lower than the fifteen percent that the World Health Organization recommends."

Sampson asked, "What should women in America be looking for, Dr. Markum?"

"Well, C-sections are a pretty big deal. I mean, it's major surgery. Women who get C-sections die five times more often than other women. They are more likely to get life-threatening blood clots and post-op infections. Scarring and adhesions can lead to follow-up surgeries. So, unnecessary C-sections aren't a good thing for women. But think of it from a doctor's point of view: why let women deliver naturally when you are more likely to get sued, you're paid substantially less money, and it might take hours to stick with a woman through labor?"

"So," Don said, "it isn't just about defensive medicine, is it, Bruce? Many are done for the doctor's convenience. Think about it. Teaching hospitals, group practices, and hospitals with OB coverage around the clock have much lower C-section rates because there's always a doctor in-house to deliver a baby, no matter what the hour. That's not true at many of the private hospitals, and the rates are much higher. Everyone knows what happens to C-section rates when doctors want to get home during the holidays, right?"

"Sure," Bruce said, "but either way, it's to the doctor's advantage to do a C-section. Otherwise, it's impossible to determine if the baby is getting damaged somehow. It's natural for doctors to want to stay in control. They know the argument in court will be the doctor *could* have done more and failed to do so."

"That may be the natural impulse for the doctor," Frances said, "but it isn't necessarily good for the mother or baby. You said women are more likely to die from a C-section; wouldn't a doctor get sued for that?"

"You would think so," Bruce replied. "I guess it's harder to show malpractice if the doctor *does* something, even if things don't turn out well. If he refrains from doing something, it looks like he didn't do his job, even if it was the right call."

"Sort of the opposite of 'do no harm,' don't you think?" said Frances.

"Good point," Dr. Sampson said. "Now let's discuss the real scope of the malpractice problem. How many medical malpractice cases are there in the typical city you described?"

"A lot!" Bruce said. "Best I can tell, ambulance chasers file about four hundred cases per year in each of the seventy-five biggest cities in the country. That's about thirty thousand malpractice cases a year. Most settle, but in each city about fifteen a year go to trial for really big money."

"What kind of money are we talking about?"

"Well, of the four hundred cases filed in each city, about half settle for an average payment of almost one hundred and fifty thousand dollars—that's almost thirty million per city. Of the fifteen that go to trial they win about five, and they each get somewhere between four hundred thousand and one million dollars. So, we are talking about a thirty-five million dollar business per year in the typical city, about four billion nationwide."

Bruce interlaced his fingers and leaned back in his chair, cradling the back of his head in his hands and wearing a self-congratulatory smile. He clearly was quite pleased with himself, having proved his case. He twisted his face toward Frances and addressed her in a decisive tone, as if giving a closing argument to the jury.

"So you see, Frances, it's not fair to expect doctors to assume liability for nurse midwives or home births. They simply can't afford it."

"Who asked them to?" she said, not missing a beat. "You doctors used the law to take away nurses' legal responsibility for their own practices, and we would love the opportunity to take it back!"

"But doctors need to ensure high quality care..."

"Hold it," Dr. Sampson interrupted, "that was our conversation last week. Today we focus on the malpractice system. As Dr. Markum showed us, medical malpractice is not a benign business. What percentage of doctors get sued? Dr. Newman?"

"Each year, around one in four practicing physicians gets sued, and most physicians get sued at least once in their careers."

"Let's think about whether all these lawsuits actually help victims of medical errors. Ms. Hunt, can you tell us what percentage of serious medical errors lead to lawsuits being filed?"

"This totally surprised me," Frances answered. "According to the Harvard Medical Practice Study in New York and the Utah and Colorado malpractice study, most adverse events in hospitals aren't caused by negligence. Of those that are, fewer than one in thirty result in a malpractice claim filing, and only about half of those result in a payout. On the other hand, three out of four malpractice claims filed don't involve any negligence and in over half the cases there is no injury caused by the doctor or medical system. It's unbelievable how poorly our malpractice system works. It fails to help people that are harmed and rewards people who aren't."

"Good summary, Ms. Hunt," Dr. Sampson said. "Now, what..."

"Doctors like Jim Kerner are the victims here," Bruce interrupted. "He got sued and wasn't negligent, and this happens around three quarters of the time? That means most malpractice lawsuits are frivolous. The ambulance chasers win big money by ruining the careers of good doctors!"

"Yes, Dr. Markum, your case clearly reveals the flaws in our current approach to malpractice. The laws, legal system, and punitive approach to medical errors encourage disability, frivolous lawsuits, and ambulance chasing, all of which punish innocent doctors and harm patients. This is a good point to remember the two major goals of our malpractice system. What are they?"

"First," Don answered, "to reduce errors, and second, to compensate victims of mistakes that occur despite our best efforts to prevent them."

"Is the malpractice system helping to reduce errors?"

"No, I don't think so. The data shows little relationship between the number of malpractice suits and quality improvements. I haven't seen any evidence that the current legal system improves the quality of American healthcare."

"Oh, I wouldn't go that far," Frances said. "Like, what about the anesthesiologists? Twenty years ago, they undertook a huge campaign to reduce anesthesia accidents. Working with nurse anesthetists," she intoned, looking directly at Bruce, "they introduced standard procedures and reduced anesthesia deaths from one in five thousand to one in two hundred thousand. As a result, malpractice premiums for anesthesiologists have seriously dropped over the last twenty years."

"But it's not clear the threat of malpractice was the main thing that encouraged anesthesiogists to improve safety," Don argued. "As I see it, incentives have to be consistent and rational to be effective, but current malpractice incentives are sporadic and irrational."

"Yeah," said Bruce, "care is not improved by the threat of lawsuits. Good docs feel pressured to practice unnecessary and dangerous defensive medicine and spend lots of time documenting everything. That time should be devoted to patient care. Defending yourself takes time, too. Jim Kerner spent over two hundred hours—almost a month of his practice year—reviewing records and going to meetings in preparation for his trial."

"What about compensating victims of medical malpractice?" Dr. Sampson asked. "How well do we do that?"

"Not well at all," said Frances. "That part is clear. Fewer than one in a hundred victims receives compensation for a real medical error, and a large percentage of the award goes to the attorneys."

"Yeah, for their yachts in the Bahamas," added Bruce.

"Ideally, the system should restrain overall expenditures by reducing the number of errors and minimizing their costs," Dr. Sampson said. "For example, reducing hospital infections not only improves outcomes for patients, but also reduces expenses related to long hospitalizations and disability."

"That's why we need tort reform," Bruce argued, "to cap the ridiculous liability insurance costs that cripple doctors and hospitals."

"Solutions will be our subject next year, but let's briefly consider Dr. Markum's suggestion. Caps on damages would reduce overhead but might also reduce the incentive to prevent errors and decrease the minimal compensation to victims. Is that the right thing to do?"

"Probably," Don said. "Thanks to high malpractice premiums, many doctors have just called it quits, and access to doctors is already a problem. Many rural areas have no practicing OBs, so women must travel across several counties to give birth."

"That's right," Bruce said. "Most people agree it's these damn ambulance chasers driving up healthcare costs. Experts say tort reform would reduce costs five to ten percent!"

"What people agree, Dr. Markum? What experts?" Dr. Sampson challenged him. "I know that is the rhetoric we hear. But there are no studies showing that tort reform reduces overall healthcare costs, and I predict there won't be in the future. Anyone want to venture a guess as to why malpractice reform is unlikely to reduce costs?"

Frances spoke up. "It's like you said, Dr. Sampson. *Follow the money*. Like Bruce said, ambulance chasers rake in about four billion a year nationwide. That sounds like a lot, but it's only three thousandths of our 1.4 trillion dollar annual healthcare costs. So, malpractice reform may be good for doctors, but it won't do much to decrease overall healthcare costs."

Bruce pursed his lips in frustration. "You are forgetting about defensive medicine. That's how malpractice really runs up costs."

"What do you mean by defensive medicine, exactly?" Frances asked.

"That's when a doctor starts making medical decisions based on self-protection rather than what the patient needs," Don answered. "Docs do it all the time where there is little or no potential harm to the patient but great potential for a lawsuit."

"It's basically just CYA—cover your ass," added Bruce.

"Come on," Frances said. "Haven't you guys been studying any health economics? People, including doctors, respond predictably to strong economic incentives. Doctors may claim that they order lots of tests and procedures simply to cover themselves, but they get huge fee-for-service monetary incentives for those procedures. These direct financial incentives to do tests are far stronger than the weak theoretical incentives related to avoiding the extremely rare event of a lawsuit. So, decreasing the relatively weak incentives to CYA through malpractice caps is unlikely to do anything to change physician behavior.

"Either way, do we really want our docs to make healthcare decisions for us based on what is good for them?" Frances asked. "Like, what's that all about?"

"That's precisely what we will talk about next year," Dr. Sampson said. "A good malpractice system should encourage good care and we want our doctors to be encouraged—and paid—to do what is right for our health.

"Now, let's follow the money a little further and talk about the plaintiff attorneys making the really big bucks."

"You mean the product liability lawyers?" Bruce asked.

"Exactly," Dr. Sampson answered. "They will help us think about a very important question related to the case you presented, Dr. Markum. To what extent does our legal system serve the truth?"

"Oh, that's why you included the article on breast implants and lupus."

"Right," Dr. Sampson said. "Breast implants were the subject of one of the most famous—and expensive—product liability cases ever. Product liability cases raise the cost of many important medical advances, including drugs, devices, and appliances like artificial hips.

"Dow Corning, manufacturer of the most popular silicone breast implant, was sued in a class action lawsuit by one million women. Some of the plaintiffs suffered from deep tissue diseases like lupus and scleroderma that can cause arthritis, inflammation, and scarring throughout the body; all claimed some type of connective tissue pain. The lawsuit alleged Dow implants had caused these problems, and the plaintiffs won more than one and a half billion dollars. Now, the central question in the case was a scientific one: did the implants *cause* the diseases of these unfortunate women?"

"I remember this case pretty well," Don said. "The *New England Journal* article you gave us was the best scientific evidence on the subject at the time of the trial and remains so today. The study showed women with silicone implants were no more likely than other women to get lupus or other connective tissue diseases."

"But many of the silicone implants ruptured, causing women to get really horrible scarring." Frances said.

"Yes," said Bruce, "I saw one of those women in my practice. It didn't happen often with those implants, but it did happen on occasion. However, rupture and scarring were well-known complications, and every woman who got the implants was informed and consented to those risks before surgery. That wasn't what the case was about."

"So," Dr. Sampson asked, "in this case, did the adversarial legal process promote discovery of the truth?"

"No," Don said, "because this excellent scientific study was given the same weight as other so-called expert testimony in the case, and for the right price, you can find an expert willing to testify to just about anything. Juries of regular people must judge their credibility and sort through complicated, conflicting evidence. If scientific panels judged the scientific issues in medical malpractice and product liability cases, courts might help to reveal the truth. As it is now, scientific truth counts for little or is disallowed."

"What happened as a result of the trial?" Dr. Sampson asked. "Did it reduce errors or the likelihood of future harm?"

"Quite the opposite," Bruce said. "A good company was almost destroyed by a false claim. What happened to Dow Corning was just like what happened to Jim Kerner. The system didn't serve the truth at all. Instead, shareholders were harmed and lost value because of a lie."

Frances added, "Well, silicone implants are gone, so you could say that women are now protected from a potentially dangerous product. On the other hand, some women still try to get the old silicone implants and say they are the best. For them, the false claims led to the loss of a valuable product on marketplace."

"Were real victims compensated here?" Dr. Sampson asked.

"You have to feel sorry for the women with deep tissue diseases," Bruce answered, "but blaming the implants and ignoring the best scientific evidence is an outrage. Americans seem to think that nothing bad can happen without it being someone's fault."

"In summary," Dr. Sampson said, "the Jim Kerner and Dow Corning cases show that our current legal system does not always serve the truth and sometimes does violence against it. Although people tend to think otherwise, it appears unlikely ambulance chasers are the biggest contributors to unnecessary health care costs.

"Next week, we'll examine how government regulation contributes to the waste of healthcare resources. Some people blame government for all our problems, and undoubtedly there is much blame to assign there, but you will find there are bigger fish to fry."

Dr. Sampson gathered his notes and left in a blur, as usual. His steps barely made a sound as he slipped out the door and down the linoleum hall.

Frances looked at Don with her beautiful doe eyes. "Maybe we should go out to eat or something this weekend?"

"Sure," Don replied, "Friday night might be good."

Don turned to Bruce, aware he was listening while he gathered his papers. "What about you, Bruce? You want to join us?"

"No, you two go ahead," he answered. "I've got a little traveling to do this weekend."

"Where are you going, the Riviera?" Frances quipped.

Bruce grinned. "I wish! No, just Richmond for a little family business and then some fundraising event in D.C. Nothing too interesting."

Frances and Don exchanged amused glances.

"So, what is your family business, anyway?" Don asked.

Bruce grinned again as he headed for the door. "Oh, nothing much, just a typical middleman moneymaking business," he said, grinning at some private joke. "So give me a rain check if you don't mind."

16

Unnatural Law Makers

Stop thou, who by thy dress seem to be one from our degenerate city.
DANTE ALIGHIERI, INFERNO 16, 8–9

DON TOSSED the tattered New Hampshire guidebook onto his kitchen table. He picked up the internet phone he had bought to make free long distance calls on his high-speed connection. He considered calling his father but found himself dialing Frances instead.

"Hello?"

"Hey, Frances, it's Don. Listen, my afternoon class got cancelled, so I thought I'd check out a trail or two in the White Mountains this afternoon. Want to go?"

"Oh, I'm sorry, Don. I'm totally booked. My epidemiology study group meets today, and I have an appointment with my econ professor. I'm not much of a hiker, anyway. But why don't we go to the Sentinel Bar and Grill for supper? I could meet you there; that way you won't have to backtrack."

"That would be all right, I guess. Sure you don't mind driving up there?"

"No, that's fine. I'll just meet you at the Sentinel at six-thirty."

"Casual?"

"Yeah, definitely casual. Got to go. See you then."

"Okay, see you at six-thirty. Bye."

Don hung up the phone and looked out the window at the dreary sky. He was disappointed to go alone, but eager to seize this rare opportunity to tramp through the forest. The last time Don had been in the woods was with Sarah—it was the only occasion they ever spent time together outside the hospital. She had jumped at the chance to go hiking around Walden Pond near Boston...

It was in early spring, not long before Don left for Florence, and the sun was shining for what seemed like the first time that year. He pulled in front of Sarah's apartment outside of Cambridge before eight.

Sarah's sandy brown hair danced across her shoulders as she ran down the steps of her duplex with a knapsack stuffed with their picnic lunch. She jumped into his rusty Ford Escort hatchback before he had a chance to open the door. Sarah was as relaxed in faded blue jeans and an old Minnesota Golden Gophers sweatshirt as she was in her starched white coat and stethoscope, and she didn't seem to notice the cracks in the dashboard or the torn upholstery as she tucked one leg beneath her and turned to greet Don with a warm smile.

They walked together in the crisp morning air along Walden Pond's pebbled shore and meandered through the open woods. She told him the names of birds and pointed out the maples and willows just beginning to bud. Don tried to commit the names of the various trees to memory.

"How do you know all this stuff?" Don asked.

She laughed. "Remember, I grew up in Eden Prairie—in Minnesota. My parents were bird watchers."

They climbed up to the grassy meadow on top of Emerson's Cliff and looked down on the still lake in the valley below. The hilltop was alive and magical. Sunlight shone through the translucent green cloaks of hundreds of yellow crocuses erupting all over the rise.

Sarah pulled an old blanket out of her knapsack, spread it on the grass, and arranged an epicurian feast: whole grain bread, smoked salmon, aged Jarlsberg cheese, Greek olives, roasted almonds, dried figs and apricots, and dark chocolate. She opened a bottle of wine and poured deep red Cabernet into real wineglasses.

The wine's fruit perfume wafted up and joined with the rich aroma of the damp earth and sweet honey saffron scent of the budding crocuses. Sunshine illuminated Sarah's hair in a halo of light and crowned her, like Botticelli's Flora, the queen of spring. Her hazel eyes reflected the golden light and sparked green fuses that drove flowers up through fertile soil all over her hillside meadow throne.

Sarah's eyes met Don's and the corners of her lips turned up in a gentle smile that lightened his heart.

"This has been a tough year for you, Don," she said. "I can't imagine how hard it must have been losing your mom, and you've had some difficult decisions to make. I know you feel unsure, but deep in your heart, you know Dr. Sampson's program is right for you. You want to see the big picture, make things right, and Florence College will give you a chance to do that. It won't be easy—cardiology with Desmond would be easier, at least at first—but something would always be missing. You need to do this. So go to Florence College, Don. Train with Dr. Sampson. I don't think you'll be sorry."

Sarah knew Don's heart, and in that moment he'd known she was right. But that day had faded and was gone like a fleeting dream...

Don picked up the newspaper from his kitchen table and read the main headline: SENATE OFFICES CLOSED, ANTHRAX FOUND. Letters containing deadly anthrax bacteria had been delivered to the offices of Democratic Senators Leahy and Daschle, exposing thirty people; five were deathly ill. The article quoted Director of Homeland Security, Tom Ridge, speaking at a press briefing about the deaths of two postal workers who handled the mail:

We are still undergoing final tests to determine absolutely that these two deaths were related to anthrax exposure...I think the President said it quite clearly that we are waging this war. There's one war, but there are two fronts. There is a battlefield outside this country and there is a war and a battlefield inside this country.

Were these anthrax attacks connected to September 11? Was this all part of an organized attack against the country?

Don threw on a sweatshirt. He stuffed his fleece, rain jacket, a bottle of water, two energy bars, and an apple in his backpack. Remembering his date with Frances, he ran to the bathroom and grabbed the Acqua di Selva cologne his mother had given him when he graduated from medical school. He picked up the guidebook and his keys and headed out the door. He tossed the backpack into his old hatchback and headed out of town toward Daniel Creek.

The guidebook described the Daniel Creek area as a low, narrow valley famous for its deep and wide crystal-clear stream and magnificent maple, beech, birch, ash, and hemlock trees. Don couldn't wait to see the famous fall leaves coloring the mountains. He imagined them floating down and covering the trail, like a red and gold carpet rolled out just for him—a king in the great open woods.

Don's idyllic fantasy of a perfect day in the country would prove to be short lived. The "picturesque back road" leading east from Florence had been straightened for the first two miles and was now a gauntlet of strip malls, gas stations, and fast food joints. Don was forced to stop at every traffic light. The smell of cooking grease mingled with foul whiffs of gas and burnt oil from an old truck just ahead and penetrated his car. The road began to wind through what he had imagined would be his private sylvan domain, but grids of identical houses had supplanted the guidebook's fields and forests.

Don pulled into the Daniel Creek Recreational Area after an hour of driving. To his dismay, the great trees were almost bare. The unseasonable cold of an early fall had caused the leaves to drop early, and the few remaining were brown and shriveled. So much for the glorious autumn colors of New Hampshire; leaf season had come and gone while he was busy juggling classes, studying, and moonlighting.

The book said the Daniel Creek trail was an old railroad bed restored in the 1960s as a walking path that hugged the walls of a gorgeous rocky chasm and crossed the creek back and forth on the railroad's old timber trestles. Don found the trailhead and dashed up the trail. At the first trestle, his heart sank.

The water of Daniel Creek was ruddy brown. The creek was nearly one hundred feet wide and lined by rocky cliffs, suggesting a depth of at least half that distance, but it was filled in with clay and sand. Soda cans and chip bags lay half-submerged in the muck. Rusty rivulets of muddy water capped with foam cut the sandbars of the creek and streaked them with orange and red iron ore. It looked like Phlegethon, the underworld's boiling river of blood.

The guidebook said the creek was full of rainbow and brook trout, but no fish could live in this. How on earth had this scenic river—one of the most beautiful places in New Hampshire, according to the guidebook—been transformed into a scene from hell?

Don climbed up to a rocky outcropping above the chasm to survey the ruined scene, choked down an energy bar, and headed upstream to look for the source of the sand and gravel. He crossed three more trestles over the next three miles. At the third trestle, he found a way down to the silted-up creek and walked right out into the middle by stepping from sandbar to sandbar.

A glance at his watch revealed it was already three o'clock. There was still a two-hour walk back to the car, plus the long drive to the Sentinel Bar and Grill, and he did not want to be late. He imagined Frances waiting impatiently at the bar, a queen on her throne, rebuffing the hapless guys who dared to hit on her.

Don turned around and started back toward the creek bank, but one wrong step sunk his left boot down in muck to the top of the laces. Cold water drenched his sock. He struggled back up to the trail and paced back toward the car, his left foot squishing with every step. By the time he reached the black asphalt of the parking lot, his wet sock had rubbed a painful blister on his heel. Why hadn't he brought some moleskin? He took off his boots, beat them free of mud as best he could, and put them back on.

Don gassed his car out of the parking lot, still hoping to see some remnant of the ancient forest on the back roads to Sentinel Mountain. He turned onto the road leading up the ridge above Daniel Creek and tried to imagine what could be silting up the river. One hundred yards up the ridge, he found out.

Where great trees had once stood—the birch, larch, and maple described in the guidebook—only withered stumps remained. They stretched as far as the eye could see, like gravestones in an endless desert bearing silent witness to the demise of an entire forest. The rich topsoil accumulated over five million years was gone, too. With no trees to hold the earth in place the rain had simply swept the soil, sand, and gravel down furrowed gullies and into the river. Gone, in a single generation.

The narrow road followed along the ridge above the creek for several miles. Don passed culvert after culvert, dirt road after dirt road, and a fine residue rose from the dusty tracks and coated his white car in grime. He spotted a lonely clump of straggly trees on a steep slope, pulled off where one of the rutted logging roads met the blacktop, and got out of his car to look around.

The sun had not made an appearance on this downcast day, but the western sky glowed orange and red, coloring the dense wisps of clouds above the horizon. Against that backdrop, three gray men stood around a colossal logging truck in a hilltop parking lot about seventy-five yards up the road. The truck had the name *Leviathan Logging* lettered on the side and held six giant tree trunks wrapped in iron chains.

The men eyed Don with suspicion. They gathered their tools and kicked up puffs of dust with each step as they trudged back to their own dust-covered cars. The logging truck pulled off and made its way down to the blacktop, belching black smoke into the red sky. The sunset colors had intensified, as if the heavens were raining down flames of fire on the scorched desert to wither every living thing.

Don got back in his car and glanced over at the dog-eared book on the passenger seat. He flipped it open to read the copyright date inside the front cover. 1982. A lot of help it had turned out to be! He grabbed up the old guidebook and flung it out the window into a dusty culvert.

Don drove higher up the backside of Sentinel Mountain. The sky grew dark, and soon his path was lit only by the blacktop's white lines. At times, it was impossible to tell whether he was going uphill or down. The drive seemed to take forever. His mouth was dry and parched from dust and grit, and his water was long gone.

How stupid! Even a Cub Scout knows one quart of water is not enough for a full day on the trail.

At last, Don rounded a bend in the road and spotted the familiar Sentinel Bar and Grill. The gentle crunch of fine gravel under the tires was music to his ears. He pulled into the far corner of the parking lot beneath the branches of a grand hemlock, finger-combed his untamed curls in the rearview mirror, and splashed a drop or two of the Acqua di Selva on his neck to blunt the sweat of the trail.

Don got out of the car, stretched his legs, and gazed up at the majestic hemlocks. His spirits rose at the sight of those few standing soldiers—surviving aboriginal denizens of the deep New Hampshire forest. Someone must have treasured these great hemlocks, appreciated them for something other than their net worth in board feet. The high branches almost covered the parking lot with an evergreen canopy, and one low branch caressed the dusty hood of his car. They seemed to welcome him; he felt he was among friends there in the dark. He inhaled deeply, savoring the rich, earthy smell as he crunched across the parking lot to the entrance of the Sentinel.

Judith looked up at the familiar sound of the creaking door. "Hey, Don. Looks like you could use something to drink!"

"You could say that again," Don answered. "For starters, I'll take a whole pitcher of water."

"You got it."

The place was mostly empty, but it was only six o'clock. Judith stood behind the scarred and burnished antique wooden bar, site of countless late-night watering hole conversations. She was wearing low-rise jeans and a blue, thermal underwear top that emphasized her lithe torso and long, black hair. She filled a pitcher and reached across with her steady and strong right arm to pour Don a tall glass.

"So, where've you been today?"

"Hiking and exploring the backside of Sentinel Mountain."

"I see," she said. "Judging from the look of your boot, I imagine you hiked down to Daniel Creek?"

"Yes, if you want to call it a creek. What in the hell happened to it? It was supposed to be beautiful there."

"It used to be," she said with a resigned shrug. "My grandfather, Solomon Salameh, came here as a young man in the twenties and thought he'd found paradise. The White Mountains here in New Hampshire reminded him of his homeland of Lebanon. Did you know the name Lebanon means 'white ones?' People think it's because the mountains are snowy in winter and white from the calcium-rich rocks in summer."

"I didn't know that."

"Anyway, when he found this hilltop overlooking Florence, he tracked down the owner, George Henry Townsend, and offered to buy it. Mr. Townsend was from an old New Hampshire family that owned most of the land around Florence. His family had been farmers here forever, and he couldn't understand why anyone would want to buy a hilltop with a small road that was impassable in winter and hillsides too steep for farming or cutting timber.

"When my grandfather revealed his plans to build a restaurant and inn for tourists, Mr. Townsend told him it was a harebrained idea but sold him the land anyway. I think he was curious to see if my grandfather could make it. He said he admired my grandfather's spirit and thought there was an outside chance—with growing wealth and the advent of the motorcar—the crazy idea just might work.

"It took all the money he had to buy the land and build the original restaurant. My grandmother joined him and began to cook her famous meals, and pretty soon people were driving up from all over Grafton County to eat her kibbeh, barbeque lamb, and cabbage rolls. By the 1950s, the parking lot was lover's lane. Young people would park up here and—*ahem*—take in the view of the town, as they say." Judith smiled and winked.

Judith refilled Don's water glass and continued on a more serious note.

"Grandfather loved this place. He used to say he was the king of a new Lebanon, one that had not been pillaged. He roamed, hunted, and fished all over this mountain. I'm glad he didn't live to see it ruined." Judith shook her head slowly back and forth. "If only we could have stopped the clear cutting."

"How did that happen?" Don asked.

"Well, old man Townsend and my grandfather understood and liked each other. For decades my family fished and hunted and hiked the Townsend woods on the east side of Sentinel Mountain, and it was Grandfather who convinced Townsend to deed the Daniel Creek Preserve to the town of Florence.

"By that time, Townsend's son, Richard, was an ambitious developer, and he was hot to outdo his father's accumulation of wealth. Richard hated the Daniel Creek Preserve idea because the area was perfect for upscale homes and logging. He tried to convince his father not to donate the land and accused him of giving away his inheritance. But old man Townsend wasn't swayed.

"After the old man died about seven years ago, Richard sold all the surrounding land to a Canadian timber company. By the time we found out, it was a done deal. Not that there was much we could have done anyway. We couldn't afford to buy it, and with so much National Forest land in the next county, the state didn't see any need to buy the land for recreation."

"I thought New Hampshire was full of tree-huggers. Doesn't the law prevent clear-cutting here?"

"You would think so. But get this: the timber company was paid by the U.S. government to cut it all down and send it to chip mills in Canada. The money came from 'hazardous fuels reduction funds,' supposedly to prevent forest fires. Anyway, it was private land—multiple town meetings couldn't stop it. Now they're talking about some sort of new 'healthy forest initiative.' I'm afraid the backside of Sentinel may be the poster child for what's in store for the rest of the country."

The heavy wooden front door swung open with a groan. Frances made her grand entrance like an Egyptian queen. The few subjects in the bar turned their heads in unison to marvel at her figure, which was showcased by tight designer jeans, high-heeled black boots, low-cut crimson blouse, and those thick golden locks tumbling over her shoulders. Her keen eyes sized up the entire rustic scene and registered a glimmer of disappointment not to see more admirers.

"Hey, Frances!" Don called as she approached.

"Hi, Don. How was your hike?" she asked, glancing down briefly at his muddy boots.

"Don't ask," he replied, shaking his head.

Frances ordered a glass of chardonnay, Don ordered a beer, and they moved to a table.

Distracted by her cleavage, Don found it difficult to think of what to say to Frances. They had studied together a lot, but he didn't know much about her. He did remember she had spent time in Boston.

"How was Radcliffe?" he asked. "Did you like Boston?"

"Oh, it wasn't quite San Francisco—you know I got my nurse practitioner training at UCSF. But I loved Boston, especially Cambridge and the Charles River...in the summer, that is."

They both laughed.

"So Don, what was it really like being at the University Hospital? It must have been incredible to work in the top hospital in the country."

What could he say? If he told the truth—*Yeah, it totally sucked*—it would just lead to more questions.

"Yeah, it was interesting, all right."

"So remind me, where did you grow up...and where did you get your beautiful skin and dark hair?"

"Chicago. My Mom was Italian. What about you? With your looks, you must have spent a lifetime fighting off boys."

"Actually, I was a late bloomer. I didn't get noticed until college. But you've already heard my story in class. Tell me about your hike."

Don recapped his pitiful afternoon at Daniel Creek and Frances feigned interest. Judith came over with the drinks and took their dinner order.

"I can't believe how slow it is tonight," Don said. "What's the deal?"

"Don't you know?" Frances answered before Judith could reply. "It's Florence College homecoming and the big hockey game is tonight. Everyone is there."

"Football on ice doesn't sound like much fun to me," Don said. "Dodging linebackers is hard enough on grass."

Both women gave him a blank stare. *Obviously not football fans.*

Frances eyed Judith's outdoorsy clothing with a hint of disdain, but Judith seemed oblivious.

"So Judith," Don said, "tell the rest of the story about your family. What about your grandfather—what happened to him?"

"Oh, that's a long story—it involves Dr. Sampson and a hell of a lot of New Hampshire politics. I don't think you want to hear it."

That piqued Frances's interest. "Oh, yes we do!" she chimed in. "Totally! Come sit down and tell us all about it. Give us all the juicy details." Frances leaned forward, eager for the chance to hear some good gossip.

Judith looked around at the mostly empty bar. "Okay, but first I need to get your food order back to the kitchen." She darted off, and a minute later returned and sat down at their table.

"You know," she began, "in New Hampshire we have town meetings, where citizens discuss important issues face-to-face. In the past, the meetings gave regular people the chance to debate and solve problems with common sense. But we've gotten too modern for that.

"One of those laws killed my grandfather and almost took everything our family had. When my grandfather needed nursing home care he moved to the Franklin Care Home, a family-run, eight-bedroom home in the valley. My grandmother had lived there the last two years of her life, and he visited her there every day. He felt safe and at home there.

"One day, the health inspector came with bad news. The state legislature had passed a law requiring the health department to crack down on unlicensed nursing homes, and his office had received an anonymous complaint about the Franklin home. According to the law, the home was operating illegally because it was not licensed. He ordered them to get licensed immediately or close. Otherwise, they'd be subject to high fines or even criminal penalties.

"Of course, the code was designed for large, for-profit nursing homes. The Franklins had fire alarms and wall-mounted fire extinguishers in every room, but they did not have the required sprinklers. A sprinkler system was thirty thousand dollars, more than they could afford.

"Dr. Sampson helped them apply for a low-cost loan, but before they could close on it, a county building official showed up and informed them of a complaint—anonymous, of course—that the home wasn't zoned for business. He said they'd have to send a rezoning request through the Board of Zoning and Adjustments. He pointed out this might take months or even years, and it would be difficult to succeed, since the neighbors would have to agree to let furniture stores and other businesses in as well.

"Dr. Sampson called an emergency town meeting. More than a hundred citizens came, and not one wanted family care homes done away with. Next, there was a public hearing attended by dozens of citizens, health officials, and industry representatives. Even Richard Townsend came—and he tends to be a recluse.

"At the hearing there were lots of promises and reassurances, but later, our state legislator told us it just wasn't practical to keep the Franklin home open. Of course, we knew he had been meeting with the nursing home executives. No doubt they had promised large contributions to his campaign. You know how the game works.

"We never found out who was making the anonymous calls, but it was probably someone in the local nursing home industry. Everyone who had ever been to the Franklin home loved it. They never had an unhappy resident or family member because they treated residents like family and took great care of everyone.

"Anyway, when they closed the Franklin home, finding a licensed nursing home bed for my grandfather was nearly impossible. Lots of other people from care homes needed beds at the same time. Grandfather was forced to take a bed at Canaan Manor Nursing Home thirty minutes away—there was nothing closer.

"My grandfather was ninety-one when he was forced out of his home. He cried like a baby the day we took him to the new place. He kept saying, 'Where are you taking me? Please don't take me there. Please, I don't want to go. I don't want to go.'"

"That's terrible!" said Frances.

"It was terrible. Dr. Sampson told me the federal government was monitoring nursing homes in order to assure the public of high-quality care. But if you ask me, it wasn't working. Canaan Manor reeked of pee because the residents were wearing urine-soaked diapers. Patients were drugged up, they got bedsores, and they all were depressed. Who wouldn't be depressed, treated like a slab of meat in a place where people go to be stored until they die? But, thank God, they *did* have sprinklers.

"Dr. Sampson was as torn up about it as we were. He went every week to the nursing home and chatted up the nurses to make sure they gave Grandfather personal attention. But Grandfather was never the same. He started to die as soon as he got there. He shouldn't have been dishonored that way. No one should, but that's how America treats its elders nowadays."

Frances and Don absorbed the story in the silence of the nearly empty bar.

"Listen, let me get your food," Judith said. "It should be about ready."

Judith went to the kitchen and returned a few minutes later with fresh salads of parsley, mint, and lemon-soaked cracked wheat, and tender kebobs with lamb and vegetables on saffron rice.

"I hope you like it," she said. "These are my grandmother's recipes."

Judith went back to the bar to pour beer for some guys who had just arrived. They were all wearing Florence College sweatshirts so she changed the channel on the TV to the hockey game.

For a while Don and Frances ate in silence, savoring the Lebanese flavors.

"Listen," Frances finally said, "I think Judith's story would be perfect for seminar this week. Let's ask Sampson if we can present it."

"Good idea. Maybe we'll learn a little more about Sampson with this one as well. He's still a bit of a mystery."

"Yeah," she laughed, "I get the feeling there is more to him than meets the eye."

Don figured she was joking about Dr. Sampson's short stature.

"Seriously, I would love to know what makes him tick," she added.

Judith returned to clear the plates. "Hey, by the way, what's going on with your classmate, Bruce?"

"What do you mean?" Don replied.

"Do you have a crush on him?" Frances teased.

"Are you kidding?" she said to Frances. "I think you can tell he's not exactly my type. No, I'm just wondering if his family has a connection with the school or something."

"I don't know," Don replied, "why do you ask?"

"Because," Judith glanced around to make sure no one was listening, "the other day, Bruce was in here with three other suits—nice suits, you know—the tailored kind that fit like a second skin? Anyway, I recognized one of them. It was Hugh Lender, the president of the college."

"Really? The college president?" said Don. "What could that have been about?"

"Could you hear what they talked about?" Frances asked.

"Not really. Someone from Lender's office called ahead and reserved the private room. They were in there for over an hour, but they'd stop talking when I came in the room."

"Who else was there?" Don asked.

"Well, the two other suits seemed to be in charge. I think one of them was one of those slick drug salesmen, but a high-level one. He was a lean, dignified man with gray hair, a good physique, and perfect white teeth. Anyway, when I was pouring water, I did hear Bruce ask about contributions from 'the big three.' The drug salesman guy laughed and said, 'Oh, we can deliver. That's what big pharma is all about.' The other suit also had that CEO demeanor—like he was used to being in charge. Lender seemed very interested in his opinion. He looked like an older version of Bruce; I'm thinking it was his father."

"Wow, I wish I could have been a fly on the wall," Frances said.

"Frances, you know we don't allow any flies in here," Judith teased.

They all laughed.

"Judith, with your powers of observation, you would have made an excellent doctor," said Don.

"Well, thanks, Don. I knew…well, I just had a gut feeling that they were up to no good."

"Ah, don't worry, Judith," Don said. "Bruce is all bluster. He may have some important friends, but I wouldn't make too much of his hobnobbing."

The hollow sound of his voice communicated all too well what Don really thought, and he could tell by Judith's raised eyebrows she wasn't buying it either.

Just as Judith was clearing the plates away, Frances spotted an old jukebox in the back corner of the bar. She sauntered over and peered into the glass case to scan the titles of the old vinyl 45s. In a few minutes, she called out to Don to come over and pick his favorite.

He picked *Soul Man*, a song he remembered hearing on Saturdays in his Chicago brownstone. Don pressed in a dime and the rhythms of Sam and Dave began.

"Ooh, I love that song! Let's dance!" Frances grabbed Don's hand and pulled him to a clear space.

Don tried. God knows he did. But he felt so awkward dancing in front of Judith in the almost empty bar. Besides, he wasn't nearly drunk enough to dance. Despite Frances's alluring movements, he was relieved when the song ended and they decided to call it a night. He paid for dinner, and they walked out to the parking lot.

Frances walked up to a sleek, bright red sports car. She turned and leaned against the curve of its glossy driver's side door.

"Is that yours?" Don asked.

"Graduation present from my Dad. Isn't she beautiful?" Frances twisted around to admire the black leather interior, her tight jeans pressing against the new Mazda Miata. Her red blouse matched the car.

"Beautiful." Don's eyes were trained on Frances now.

Frances turned to face Don and flipped her gold locks over her shoulder. Wisps of golden hair softly brushed his cheek. "What's that smell?" she said, wrinkling her nose. "What *is* that—your *grandfather's* cologne?" she teased, sliding her hands around his waist.

He didn't know what to say. Did fragrances go out of style, like clothes?

"Come here, Soul Man," Frances cooed.

She took him gently by the ears and pulled him toward her, looking straight into his eyes. Her body drew Don like gravity. His hands slipped slowly down the curve of her lower back. He was falling, spiraling downward in her orbit, and was both thrilled and terrified. Her polished fingernails danced through his dark brown ringlets, starting at his temples and moving around to the nape of his neck. She laced her fingers behind his head and pulled him down to kiss her. As their tongues met, Don's trepidation vanished. How long it had been since a woman had kissed him like this! Don felt an old, familiar tightening, a tug deep in his gut.

Frances pulled away, laughed, and hopped into her car. She rolled down the window and gave him a mischievous smile. "I sure hate to drive home alone," she said. "Too bad we're in two cars. Anyway…great being with you, Soul Man. We should do it again soon—maybe next time, we'll uncover the cryptic brain of Dr. Sampson." Before Don could reply, she started the car with a vroom and backed out of her parking spot.

Don stood there and watched her drive away, trying to make sense of what had just happened. Her sudden departure had reopened a yawning gulf in his heart. Could he love Frances? Did he love Frances? Would Momma approve? But Momma was gone. He wasn't a boy, but a grown man, for crying out loud!

Don jumped into his car, intending to chase her back down Sentinel Mountain, but by the time he pulled out of the parking lot, she was gone. He raced down the mountain in his old Escort, hoping to catch a glimpse of her taillights.

As Don descended the steep, curving road toward Florence, his sense of unease returned, and the excitement of kissing Frances dissipated. She might be hot, but what kind of girlfriend would she be? Why had she acted like such a tease? Was she just playing with him? Come to think of it, she hadn't even bothered to thank him for paying the dinner tab. She probably had no idea how strapped for cash he was. Yeah, she had probably done him a favor to break it off and leave in a hurry. Otherwise, he would have gone as far and as fast as she would let him. And then what?

Back at his apartment, Don heard an intermittent beeping sound. At first he thought it was his pager, but the location of the sound drew his eyes to the answering machine's flashing message light. He walked over and pushed the button to retrieve the message.

"Hey Dante, it's Sarah."

Don's heart skipped a beat at the sound of her voice.

"Just checking in to see how things are in the wilds of New Hampshire." There was a pause, as if she were going to say something more, but the message ended with a click.

Don was instantly awash with guilt. But why? He had never had any kind of real relationship with Sarah outside of work. They had never even kissed. She was in Boston caring for boatloads of sick patients as a second year resident and didn't have time for him. And yet, he felt as embarrassed as if she had caught him kissing Frances there on the mountain in the middle of the night. It was ridiculous—he was a free man—but he couldn't shake the feeling.

THE FOLLOWING WEEK Frances and Don met in the annex of the library to prepare their presentation of Judith's nursing home story. Don entered the glass room and Frances, wired to her computer with a pair of earbuds, looked up at him with her big green eyes and broke into a big smile.

She pulled the plugs from her ears. "I have something for you—look!" She held out a white and chrome box about the size of a deck of cards.

"What is that?"

"Don't you know? It's called an *iPod*. Just released yesterday—it's a digital music player you can carry in your pocket. A friend got me a special deal, so I got you one, too. It's totally cool; you will love it!"

Frances took Don's iPod out of the box, plugged a wire into it, and pushed small white earpieces into his ears. "Listen!" she said.

Don expected music, but instead he heard someone speaking in a booming voice.

"Is that Dr. Sampson?" he asked.

"I downloaded his lectures from the Florence College server. They're all there."

"Wow!" Don was speechless. No woman had ever given him such an extraordinary gift.

"It holds one thousand songs," she added. "Here, listen to this."

She tapped the buttons, and within seconds he was rocking to *Soul Man*.

"That's our song, Soul Man," she crooned.

Don's mind reeled at the implications. He knew he should probably refuse the gift, but he couldn't bring himself to do it. He didn't want to hurt Frances's feelings. Besides, he liked this new toy too much.

"LET ME TELL YOU what the hearing was like," Dr. Sampson said after Don and Frances finished telling the story of Judith's grandfather. "It was nothing like an old-fashioned town meeting with impartial moderators and citizen debate. We testified by turns, and no discussion was allowed.

"The state public health officer—whose inspectors would be responsible for cracking down on "illegal" homes—testified first. He said, 'Look, no one in the health department wants to see these unlicensed facilities closed down. We just want them to get licensed.' He expressed frustration that time spent bringing places like Franklin Family Care Home into compliance would take time away from looking at licensed facilities.

"The nursing home industry representatives looked smug at this testimony; the regulation would be a big win for them. It would eliminate a major source of competition, and as a bonus, their licensed homes would have less supervision while the inspectors were busy putting the competition out of business.

"When it was my turn, I argued people should be allowed to decide for themselves, especially since the Franklin home, like most private homes, didn't take state or federal money. Solomon Salameh was paying out of his own pocket, and his family knew the nursing home owners and safety features. Why should private homes be subject to the same licensing requirements as the large nursing homes funded through Medicaid and Medicare?

"I brought out what I thought was our ace in the hole—a quality report. I handed out copies of it and made my argument. Here's what I said: 'I reviewed data on over one hundred individuals in the past year who came to the Florence College Medical Center from licensed nursing homes in the tri-county region. They arrived overmedicated, with bedsores, and near death because of poor nursing home care. During the same period, not one person came in so mistreated from an unlicensed care home. Show me one person who has been harmed by unlicensed homes in this region!'

"The head of the New Hampshire Association for Nursing Homes spoke next. He ignored my challenge and the evidence and defended the benefits of the licensing law as if he were on the public's side. I suppose he had convinced himself he was. The nursing home industry had worked long and hard to get the law on their side, and he wasn't about to back down.

"'Without regulation,' he argued, 'the geriatric population is at increased risk of injury and death. We just want a competitive marketplace so the consumer can choose the style of nursing home they want. But these illegal facilities have to follow the letter of the law like everyone else. Under our law, it's a Class C felony to operate an unlicensed assisted living facility, and violators will get what the law requires: one to ten years in prison and fines from five to one hundred thousand dollars.'

"The president of the American Nursing Home Association, who had traveled all the way from Washington, D.C., for the hearing, chimed in, saying, 'Lack of staffing for enforcement and lack of demand for enforcement by the public are just excuses to skirt the law. I don't care what your data shows, Mr. Sampson, all nursing homes must follow the law. Unlicensed homes are illegal in New Hampshire. As far as I am concerned, they're all operated by crooks and take advantage of our most vulnerable citizens. It's up to our industry to protect people like Mr. Solomon from unscrupulous entrepreneurs like Mrs. Franklin.'

"After that, everyone in the room was silent, too shocked to speak. These guys were deadly serious. We never found out what the anonymous complaints alleged, so we could not rebut them. The hearing was more or less a sham because the law had already passed. Our state legislator repeated the same script when we talked to him, saying that the nursing home industry just had the best interests of our elders at heart. He had clearly been learning his lines from the lobbyists at some of the better restaurants around the state Capitol.

"The bottom line was that my old friend Solomon was dragged out of a home he loved and forced to live out his remaining days in a hellhole—all to help out some carpetbagger nursing home company's bottom line."

"Wow! Strong language, even for you, Dr. Sampson," Bruce said. "But for once we agree. The problem is big government. Federal control always leads to impersonal, heavy-handed government and unnatural budgets."

"Was this case about federal control, Dr. Markum?" Dr. Sampson asked. "This was a state law issue, as it played out in one large county."

Bruce ignored the question. "People want everything to be a right. We can't afford that! Look at what special rights for the disabled have cost us, for example. As our reading pointed out, the cost of making every bathroom, bus, and public building wheelchair accessible—regardless of whether anyone in a wheelchair is even around to use them—has exceeded one hundred billion dollars. A hundred billion dollars! For half that price, we could provide a free apartment and a personal car and driver to every person in a wheelchair. Look, everyone agrees helping the handicapped is a good thing. But giving a special class of people an entitlement to equal everything? It just makes no sense for the federal government to mandate what every city and town must do and pay for."

"Bruce has a point," Don said. "As it is now, two-thirds of Americans are in some protected class: race, gender, age, disability, or sexual orientation. They can sue at the drop of a hat. There are too many laws, and the only winners are the lawyers and those who find a way—like the nursing home executives—to use the law to their own advantage."

Dr. Sampson sighed and flipped through his papers. "Perhaps you are right. Let me close with Socrates' words from *The Republic*—they emphasize that very point:

> When licentiousness and illness multiply in a city, aren't many courts
> and hospitals opened,…Will you be able to produce a greater sign of bad
> and base education in a city than its needing eminent doctors and judges…

"So, next time we'll talk about all forms of insurance: for-profit, not-for-profit, and national health insurance. This is perhaps the most important seminar of the year, and your grades for the semester will reflect your performance accordingly. We will meet in the anatomy theater next door. You have your assignments."

Frances, Bruce, and Don walked together over to The Down Under, talking along the way about their presentations for the following week. Bruce kept up a flirtatious repartee with Frances on the way across the quad.

As they made their way down the dank brick steps of the coffee shop, Don once again had an illogical urge to bolt, but he resisted the impulse and followed the others to Bruce's spot near the back. The table was covered with Bruce's books and papers, an open declaration of ownership to anyone who might dare to sit there.

Bruce pushed his books to the side, they sat down, and he took charge. He ordered three coffees—without bothering to ask Frances and Don if they wanted one—and pulled out the papers they had to present at their next seminar. "I'll present the chapter on the history of health insurance," he said. "Frances, what about you?"

"I'll take the World Health Organization report on health system performance."

"That leaves me with the paper on administrative costs in the U.S. and Canada," Don said.

They divided up the major industrialized countries as if they were starting a game of Risk, the object of which was to rule the world.

"Speaking of Canada," Bruce said, "let me have it. I'll make sure we learn the truth about how socialized medicine really works."

"Then I want Europe," Don said. "I'll focus on France and Germany."

"I'll take the Far East," said Frances. "I've always been interested in how those countries organize their economies. Maybe I'll center on Japan or Taiwan."

In a matter of minutes they had divvied up the richest countries in the world.

Bruce looked pleased. "Very good," he proclaimed. "And now, let the games begin!"

Insurance Salesmen

Lo, he that infects all the world!...His face was the face of a just man,
so gracious was his outward aspect, and all the rest was a serpent's trunk.
DANTE ALIGHIERI, INFERNO 17, 3, 10–12

DON WANDERED through the basement of the basic sciences building on his way to seminar. He hadn't come this way since that first day when the campus guard led him through the maze of underground halls to the old anatomy theater. Sickly sweet formaldehyde fumes wafted up from the cracks beneath the laboratory doors, as if an evil scientist's secret garden of poisonous flowers was emanating strange and deadly perfumes inside.

The hallway outside the anatomy labs was lined with glass-front cabinets, all of them jammed with jars containing embalmed body parts of all shapes and sizes. Everything in the underground hall was labeled and catalogued by a scientific mind. Human babies and animals at various stages of development— from embryos to newborns—were arranged in neat rows. A coiled diamond-back rattlesnake as fat as Don's arm stared from one jar, forever poised to strike. From another jar, the four doll eyes of a two-headed baby followed him down the hall. Don passed rank upon rank of diseased, disfigured, misshapen, and malformed hands, legs, heads, and hearts, suspended for eternity in the foul fluid: malformed kidneys, a nodular liver, a tortuous aorta with a huge ruptured bulge in the center of the arch, a foot with seven toes, a cancerous, football-sized growth with hair and teeth.

Death was pickled, preserved, and cherished here. Don was struck by the immaculate order of the collection. It was in stark contrast to the scattered body parts in the rubble of the Twin Towers. Underneath the smoldering ruins of the trade center were 2,752 people, including 341 firefighters and 70 other emergency workers who rushed into the burning buildings to save others. Soon, their remains would be hauled along with the rubble on a barge to the Fresh Kills Landfill on Staten Island, where the debris would be sorted, searched for parts and personal effects, and buried in a mass grave.

Don had seen death up close for the first time when he uncovered his assigned cadaver in an anatomy lab on his first day of medical school. In those early days, he thought dissecting a dead human and deciphering its complexities would make him a better healer. He tolerated the stench of formaldehyde, the sickly perfume of death that permeated his skin, clothes, and books and followed him home. For months after the class was over, he found bits of human fat pressed between the pages of his anatomy atlas, where they'd landed during long sessions over his split and flayed cadaver.

Don was expected to dissect, examine, and study the cadaver without emotion or concern for the person who had once inhabited it. His teachers referred to that cool attitude as professionalism. They said doctors must never allow sentiment to impair medical judgment and gave him a white coat at the beginning of his third year to reinforce this mindset. He learned to express empathy from a safe distance and cultivated the demeanor that would protect him from the blood and gore that followed.

Don's footsteps reverberated down the tiled passageway. He imagined the echoes rousing the rows of devitalized remains and waking the diabolical scientist in charge of this underground lair. Would it be Dr. Jekyll or Mr. Hyde? Cool, controlled, and reasoned? Or wild-eyed, disheveled, and erratic?

Real and imagined demon doctors swirled through Don's brain with the toxic fumes—Mengele, Frankenstein, Faust, Rappaccini—all of them cool, rational, and scientific on the outside. But within every one of these Dr. Jekylls was a Mr. Hyde: a hidden, secret, and unnatural passion that drove them and overrode their reason. Don had been surprised at the video of Bin Laden from his underground hideout. He talked like a doctor: professional and detached, with logical aims. But hidden beneath the practiced veneer was a heart bent on power and control.

Most horror movie scientists were surgeons. Now that Don thought about it, they were surgeons who reminded him of Bruce. They wanted to play God—to reconstruct dismembered limbs in new configurations never seen before in nature and bring new life into the world. And their inhuman obsessions gave birth to monsters.

Don had been trained to view surgeons with skepticism. Surgeons are bent on power—they want to overcome nature and bring the dead back to life. And patients like it. They want to have someone else take control, to fix them with electricity and paddles, scalpels and sutures, even mechanical hearts. For their mastery of these implements, the surgeons gain prestige, income, and authority.

And what do we internists get? The surgeons call us "fleas." The last living creatures to leave a dead dog.

Don rounded the corner of the basement hall, entered the oldest part of the building, and walked into the anatomy theater. He took a seat in the raised front row under the flickering fluorescent lights and waited, idly wondering who among them might reveal himself to be a mad scientist at heart. Bruce? Bruce was a typical surgeon all right, yet Don found himself liking Bruce at times. Dr.

Sampson, on the other hand, was gruff, preoccupied, and moody. Of course, that doesn't make you a mad scientist. *Maybe it's me—I'm the one thinking about all these preserved remains coming back to life!*

Don squirmed on the hard wooden seat and contemplated what medical school must have been like a hundred years ago, with the theater full of students watching an expert physician-anatomist dissect a corpse on a table in the middle of the room. In those days before formaldehyde, an overwhelming smell of putrefaction would hit the front row like a wave when the abdominal cavity was opened.

Don heard Frances's quick steps echoing in the hall outside. She entered the theater, smiled at him, and took a seat nearby. Bruce wandered in seconds later, gave a cursory nod to each of them, and sat on the other side of Frances. They all waited in silence, preoccupied with their upcoming presentations.

Dr. Sampson came in five minutes after the hour and marched straight up the steps to the projection room.

"Since it is Halloween, or All Saints Eve," his voice boomed from above, "I thought it appropriate to meet here in the place where scientists cut apart so many bodies looking for the truth."

That sounded like something a mad scientist might say.

"They wanted to discover the life, the soul, the source of vitality. Of course, all they ended up with was a bunch of cut-up bodies. Today we will look for the lost heart of insurance. Once again, we must begin by remembering where we are."

"Oh, great," groaned Bruce under his breath. Here we go again."

Dr. Sampson doused the lights and the room went pitch-black.

"Insurance...what is it? Where can we find it?" Dr. Sampson's deep voice resounded. "Let's see what we can learn from the advertising campaigns of the five biggest private health insurers in the world."

Whirr—*click*—the Carousel projector flashed an image on the large screen of a beautiful tree branching up into the sky.

"This is Cigna HealthCare," said Dr. Sampson. "The third largest, with revenues last year of 20 billion, income of 987 million, and 43,000 employees."

Click—A mother, father, and two children walk hand-in-hand across a park's green grass in the shelter of towering oaks. Intoning in a trustworthy advertising voice, Dr. Sampson read from their annual report, "Cigna Healthare...This beautiful tree they call the Tree of Life is their corporate logo, and their corporate slogan is 'A Business of Caring.'"

"Next, Wellpoint Health Networks."

Click—a baby with clear blue eyes twinkling and first big smile—*click*—a colorful cartoon titled *The Wellpoint Way*. A meticulous tailor attends to a dapper man in an elegant black pinstriped suit. The caption: *Wellpoint tailors products to meet customer needs.*

"Annual revenues 9.2 billion, profit 342 million, 14,000 employees, and over 7.9 million insured. Like its competitors, Wellpoint offers hundreds of insurance plan options to its member employers"—*click*—*Health Insurance 101*—*click*—three men of vastly different sizes all wear the same size black pinstriped suit; the tall man's pant legs hemmed too short, the short man's hemmed too long, and the fat man's pants bursting at the seams. *One size does not fit all.*

"But Wellpoint goes a step further..."—*click*—a cartoon Mom, Dad, Daughter, Son, and Dog all want something different. "...Wellpoint's *FamilyElect* solution lets each family member choose a different health plan"—*click*—a lemonade stand offers four different kinds of lemonade—*click*—*Wellpoint promises to preserve people's right to choose...*

"Next is UnitedHealth Group," Dr. Sampson continued, "the second largest insurer. Revenues 21 billion, profit 705 million, nearly 50,000 employees, and 8.4 million insured"—*click*—a young father smiles in relief while his attentive wife and three children all gaze at him with affection. "This is Sam. Suddenly sickened by a rare hereditary blood disease, only the help of UnitedHealth got him the lifesaving treatment he desperately needed, just in time. UnitedHealth offered hope and protection in this family's darkest moment."

Click—"Finally, we turn to Aetna, the nation's largest health insurer, a company with annual revenues of 27 billion and market value over 43 billion. This ad just came out" *click* the Statue of Liberty, framed by the World Trade Towers, holding her flaming torch aloft in the dark blue sky at dusk. Dr. Sampson spoke in a solemn voice. "Aetna calls us to remember September 11, 2001, to remember the victims, and their families. Their 'Culture of Caring' has led their employees to reach out and assist people in need in times of war, disaster, and tragedy. Aetna has protected families against vagaries of fortune since 1853."

Dr. Sampson left the beautiful image of the towers on the screen for a long time. The majestic pillars framed Lady Liberty in the beautiful evening light. They stared at her for a long time in the quiet dark, all of them wishing the same thing: that they could go back in time, back before that terrible day of destruction changed their world forever.

He broke the silence gently. "These insurance companies have become our caregivers. We have come to depend on their providence as medical innovators, teachers, and healthcare leaders. And, in times of plague and disaster, these companies have become our trusted saviors."

Dr. Sampson turned on the lights and came back down to the podium.

"Okay, you've seen the commercials. So what is the reality? Dr. Markum, you may begin by relating some of the history of the insurance industry in America."

Bruce squinted around the room to make sure everyone was watching. "Let me tell you, the guys...and gals"—Bruce winked at Frances—"running these businesses have got it all figured out. They do very well for themselves. The corporate income figures Dr. Sampson just quoted don't include the salaries of executives and staff. The CEOs all make somewhere between three and ten million a year just in salary, plus they have stock options often worth ten times that. Of course, none of those amounts are included in the company profits; they're just a normal cost of doing business." Bruce smiled.

"The Starr reading pretty much lays it out. Insurance evolved in a natural way. We humans have always tried to protect ourselves from catastrophe. Just as squirrels put away nuts for winter, our hunter-gatherer ancestors saved for predictable hungry periods. But for farmers hungry times were less predictable. They could lose an entire crop for the season. When people moved away from small farms, families became dependent on one wage earner, and making their financial security even more precarious. People were ripe for plucking by insurance salesmen.

"In Europe, fraternal orders—like our Elks or Masons, and trade associations—like our unions, had served as voluntary health associations for years. Members pledged to help one another with medical costs if someone got sick or injured. Poor workers in Europe had been pooling their resources to protect themselves from health catastrophes for centuries before national health insurance came on the scene. When compulsory sickness insurance programs started throughout Europe, they built on this model. National health insurance started in Germany in 1883, Austria in 1888, Hungary in 1891, Norway in 1909, Serbia in 1910, Britain in 1911, Russia in 1912, the Netherlands in 1913, and Italy in 1978. Other European countries, like Sweden in 1891, Denmark in 1892, Switzerland in 1912, and France in 1945, simply subsidized the mutual benefit societies and voluntary funds of the established trade associations.

"In the United States, on the other hand, voluntary health associations were much less developed in the later part of the industrial revolution, so entrepreneurs stepped to the fore. Let me tell you, these guys were shrewd businessmen, and they took the factory workers for a ride. They started with death benefits. After 1850, several insurance companies, including Prudential and Metropolitan Life, built a good business selling funeral insurance. When the War Between the States started, business boomed. Even though over 600,000 young men were killed in the field, income from monthly premiums far exceeded the payouts.

"In the late 1800s, private insurance companies added limited disability benefits for accidents and sickness and hired armies of insurance salesmen to infiltrate the factories of America. They had astronomical administrative costs, but the take was enormous. Organization men visited workers every payday to collect premiums. Millions of workers paid ten to twenty-five cents a week, and only thirty to forty percent of the collections went back to the workers in benefits.

"Americans were so afraid of being buried in pauper graves they spent some 183 million dollars in 1911—mostly to Prudential and Metropolitan Life—for coffin insurance paid out at death. The amount paid in premiums equaled the amount Germany spent on its entire national health insurance system in the same year for a population nearly the same size as that of the United States. The insurance companies made a mint, and Prudential ultimately sold its healthcare business to Aetna, making Aetna the biggest private health insurer in the world.

"Then the Blues were born. Blue Cross got started by hospitals that wanted to make sure they got their bills paid, and Blue Shield was started by physicians for the same reason. They made themselves not-for-profit so they could get public approval, then poured money into operations and their own salaries. Right after World War II, these new insurers took advantage of wage freezes, strong patriotic feelings, and the middle class quest for postwar security, and business took off like a rocket. The employers liked it because they controlled the health care benefit and could use it to keep workers locked into jobs. The insurers liked it because they got their money up front, deducted right out of people's paychecks. From the 1950s forward, the insurance salesmen, for-profit and non-profit alike, have taken charge, and their companies have made tons of money.

"Over the last hundred years, idealists have whined that American workers were getting ripped off, paying astronomical premiums without getting the health benefits people of other countries enjoyed. But the idealists didn't have any money. Three times they mounted major efforts to overthrow the private insurance companies. But they never had a snowball's chance in hell.

"The first attempt was by Teddy Roosevelt and the progressives in 1912. Their model insurance bill had strong initial support from big business because it promised to foster prevention and a healthier workforce, but insurance industry executives launched an aggressive lobbying effort against the national plan through an influential business organization called the National Civic Federation. The beginning of World War I provided the perfect advertising angle: they denounced supporters of compulsory health insurance and death benefits as Bolsheviks and Communists. They defeated the bill and their lucrative business was preserved.

"The second attempt was near the end of the depression in the late 1930s, when FDR and many of his allied legislators considered adding health insurance to the proposed Social Security program as part of the New Deal. Medical costs were rising, and people were demanding access to the new capabilities medicine offered. National polls at the time showed three out of four Americans wanted the government to help people pay for medical care, and most Americans preferred extending Social Security. However, organized medicine didn't want third parties intervening, controlling, or profiting from their medical industry. Roosevelt realized the AMA and state medical societies would not allow a government 'third party' to control the market, the plan was ditched, and the insurance companies continued building their domination of the industry.

"The third attempt was in the late 1940s, when Truman proposed expanding Social Security and adopting a universal health insurance system. His reform-minded supporters spent thirty-six thousand dollars in 1950 to promote the plan. Meanwhile, the AMA aligned with private insurers and spent two and a quarter million on a 'national education campaign.' Their insurance industry sponsors contributed two million apiece to put five-page ads in all 10,333 U.S. newspapers denouncing the national health insurance supporters as enemies of free enterprise. They successfully capitalized on cold war fears of communism and reversed public support overnight."

"Wait," Frances interrupted, "wasn't health insurance conceived from the beginning as a way to help the poor?"

"You are such an idealist, Frances. People conceive all sorts of things. But it takes businessmen to get them done. That is, *if* you can pay."

Frances opened her mouth but was too shocked to reply, and Bruce kept going.

"Nixon actually got us closest to universal insurance coverage in 1974 by taking a business approach. After Ted Kennedy made a feeble attempt to cut out all the insurers by extending Medicare to all, Nixon outmaneuvered him by proposing to expand employer-based, private insurance coverage to everyone instead. His Comprehensive Health Insurance Act would have passed if the Watergate scandal hadn't taken him down. At least Nixon was living in reality, I say. Let's face it: the insurance companies will only allow health insurance reform to pass if it will benefit them.

"The rest is history. Yeah, the liberals did get Medicare and Medicaid through after Kennedy was shot, but thank goodness we stopped it there. Of course, Hillary's plan never stood a chance, either. Harry and Louise saw to that."

"Harry and Louise?" Don asked.

"You know," Frances piped in, "that couple on the commercial that denounced the Clinton plan and turned public support against it."

"Yes," Dr. Sampson said, "we'll get to that in a minute. Thank you, Dr. Markum, for summarizing the history of insurance." He turned to Don. "Okay, Dr. Newman, give us a quick synopsis of the research from my friends at Harvard on the real costs of health insurance in the United States and Canada."

Don was ready. He had spent two hours the previous night at his kitchen table, calculating the money spent on health insurance and the lives it saved. The data on costs were easy—they came right out of the Harvard study. But estimating the lives saved by health insurance had proven much harder. He knew uninsured people got much less lifesaving preventive care. But how could he come up with a number?

He found a paper in Dr. Sampson's syllabus showing people without insurance were twenty-five percent more likely to die. It was simple multiplication: the expected number of deaths in the people uninsured times twenty-five percent. That meant twenty thousand Americans lost their lives each year because they didn't have health insurance! Don entered the numbers of the dead and dollars spent in his diagram of healthcare hell in the back of his journal.

He paced across his apartment, grabbed his mother's old edition of *La Divina Commedia* from the bureau, and lugged it to the kitchen table. He flipped it open and gazed at Botticelli's drawings of Geryon, the chimeric monster with the face of a just man and the body of a snake. It wore the same slight smile Don had given Mr. Eldrich.

Don had met Mr. Eldrich in the clinic his intern year. Mr. Eldrich had been hospitalized for severe ascites; fluid leaking from swollen veins inside his abdomen had made his belly swell like a watermelon. Blood couldn't pass through his liver because of scarring from hepatitis C contracted thirty years earlier from a blood transfusion after a car wreck.

Mr. Eldrich was a brilliant artist. His paintings of "nature alive"—spiritual creatures living in the trees, rocks, and lakes of Massachusetts—hung in the best houses of Boston. One of his works hung in the National Gallery. Mr. Eldrich dreamed of completing a series of twenty-four earth spirits commissioned by the Boston Art Commission. He showed Don his design drawings one afternoon in clinic. They were to be his magnum opus and Don found them breathtaking.

But Mr. Eldrich would never make it without a liver transplant. He was a perfect candidate, so Don sent him to GI clinic for a liver transplant evaluation. Mr. Eldrich had four appointments there, but all the reports Don got back focused on palliative medical therapy for end-stage liver disease. Don finally called to learn the results of their evaluation. He still remembered the GI fellow's words: "Stop wasting our time, Dr. Newman. Mr. Eldrich can't get a liver transplant. He doesn't have insurance."

Don saw Mr. Eldrich for two more years. At each visit, Don increased diuretics to higher doses to reduce swelling, but the fluid kept reaccumulating. Mr. Eldrich's abdomen protruded more and more, until he waddled like a woman with a full term pregnancy, and finally he couldn't walk at all. For the first half of the last year, Don performed a weekly paracentesis to drain the fluid in a desperate attempt to reduce the swelling and make him more comfortable. Each week, Don stared at the Caput Medusa—the network of bulging snake-like veins visible on his protuberant abdomen. Don became a little colder each visit, embracing a professional demeanor so he could keep moving, perform his routine quickly. He even managed a frozen smile as he inserted a large needle into

Mr. Eldrich's swollen belly and pulled off several large glass Vacutainer bottles of clear, straw-colored fluid. After some twenty paracenteses, Mr. Eldrich began to leak the clear yellow fluid continuously from the needle track. In his last months, his starving body broke down his muscles to replace the protein dripping out through the hole Don had made in his side.

Don tried to smile at Mr. Eldrich and hold out some hope he might obtain insurance and get the transplant he needed. He told him the drainage of fluid might buy him enough time to finish his work. Don smiled at Mr. Eldrich right up until he lapsed into a coma and never woke up. So Don knew what it was like to smile with the face of a just man, while deep inside he felt like a snake. Had Mr. Eldrich been an insured or wealthy man, things would have been very different.

Alongside the number of American dead from lack of insurance, Don doodled Geryon with the face of an insurance salesman. Of course, this was a story Don would never tell in seminar. Far easier to hide behind scientific studies, impassive and unmoved, under the cloak of professionalism. As Don sat before his mother's *Divina Commedia*, viewing Geryon descending into the realm of fraud, the tension between fiction and non-fiction was unbearable. Between the one and the many—the story and the science—he chose the easier path. In Dr. Sampson's seminar he would stick to the data—the cold numbers no one could criticize. He would retreat into the language of science, back under the cover of the white coat.

"Well, the bottom line on the real costs of health insurance in the U.S. is pretty clear," he said. "The U.S. spends a much bigger percentage of its health-care dollar on administration and bureaucracy than Canada. The Harvard researchers figured out the cost of insurance company overhead and profits in both countries. They added what it costs providers to bill all the different insurers in both places: the cost of processing bills and insurance paperwork in hospitals, nursing homes, and clinics. They discovered healthcare administration in the United States cost 294 billion dollars in 1999. That's one thousand dollars per person in the U.S., compared to only three hundred dollars per person in Canada the same year. Over thirty percent of American healthcare dollars go for middlemen, billing and administration, compared to seventeen percent in Canada."

"Wait a minute," Frances interrupted. "You're saying Americans pay thirty cents on the dollar to have a middleman who makes more profit if he can prevent them from getting needed care?"

"I guess you could say it that way," Don replied.

"Well, I wouldn't," Bruce said. "That's ridiculous. Look, Canadians are always coming here for healthcare. If things are so good in Canada, why are all their doctors and patients coming here?"

"Good question, Dr. Markum," Dr. Sampson said. "Let's come back to it a little later, when we discuss the national health insurance programs of other industrialized nations. For now, let's stick to the question at hand: why are administrative bureaucracy costs so much higher in the United States?"

"It seems obvious to me," Don said. "We have more than fifteen hundred insurers in the United States, including over one thousand commercial carriers, over seventy BlueCross BlueShield plans, and five hundred or more HMOs. Each of these fifteen hundred plans has different forms, different rules for billing, different procedures for approving referrals and tests, and different drug formularies. It's difficult and expensive for physicians and hospitals to keep up with all the paperwork, and the proliferation of bureaucracy harms every patient. Did you read that Seattle study in our syllabus? They interviewed twenty-two hundred typical patients with depression and found seven hundred fifty different insurance plans, all with varying coverage, copayments, deductibles, and billing procedures. Do Americans tolerate this degree of inefficiency in any other industry?"

Bruce started to respond, but Frances beat him to the punch. "What gets me," she said, "is the insurance industry has managed to avoid any obligation to insure people with preexisting illnesses. People who need health care the most can't join or change plans. Insurance companies pay actuaries to ferret out the 'bad risks'—the ten percent of people that incur some seventy percent of medical expenses. On average, they spend ten percent of premium revenues on actuarial analysis to avoid bad risks. Add that to spending on other administrative overhead and profit, and investor owned BlueCross plans spend over twenty-five percent of revenues on overhead, commercial carriers spend about twenty percent, and not-for-profit Blues plans spend about sixteen percent. Our public insurance programs—Medicare and Medicaid—only spend about three percent on overhead, and they don't disqualify anyone for pre-existing conditions."

"Now look," Bruce said, clearly frustrated, "the great thing about a free market is consumers can buy what they want."

"Are you kidding?" Frances retorted. "When people are forced into whatever plan their employer offers? Why shouldn't people be free to choose any plan? Do they really want to pay thirty cents on the dollar for so many hassles and so little choice? And you can't even opt out of this crazy bureaucratic system. Since insurance is regulated at the state level, people don't even have the choice to cross state lines for care, and national plans can't standardize their plans and increase efficiency. Do people even know what they're paying for? These insurance salesmen intermediaries are just 'second-handers.' They don't produce anything; they just pass things along and take a cut. I'll tell you what's ridiculous, Bruce. What's ridiculous is for these middlemen to get between people and their health providers. They're completely non-productive, like parasites…"

Don envisioned armies of 1950s-era insurance salesmen rising up out of the ground like the living dead. They had short Brylcreem-slicked hair, and the skin of their faces hung like thin fabric masks draped over their bones. Each head looked almost normal on the outside, but en masse, their similitude was horrific, as if their bodies had been snatched and taken over. They moved in unison as one terrible monster, their reconstituted bodies controlled by some insidious underground consciousness. The organization men looked at Don and nodded in unison, mesmerizing him with their perfect smiles. "Trust me," they seemed to say, "I'll have it for you when you need it." The multi-headed monster had more resources than Pluto, the underworld god of wealth—limitless, subterranean hoards of gold and silver. No one could destroy the hydra because for every head you managed to sever, two more grew in its place.

"…Even small hospitals often have more administrators than nurses," Frances was saying. "Since 1970, with the growth of managed care, the number of healthcare administrators has increased twenty times—that's two thousand percent—while the number of doctors and nurses has not even doubled. The worst fears of doctors have been realized. Not only do third parties take a big cut of medical profits, they have taken full control! Can't we imagine a way to budget our own health care dollars? Why should we pay strangers to tell us what doctors and treatments we're allowed to have?"

"Okay, Ms. Hunt," Dr. Sampson said, "go ahead and summarize the 2000 World Health Report on health system performance."

"Well," Frances began, "in this report, the WHO rated health systems according to a uniform set of criteria. Recognizing some health systems perform better than others—even given similar levels of healthcare spending—they measured differences in expenditures, out-of-pocket expenses, death and disability rates, efficiency, quality of care, access to needed care, waiting times, and other measures of responsiveness to the critical health needs of the population. How do you think the United States rated?" Frances asked, glancing at Bruce and Don.

"In the top five, for sure," Don answered.

"Come on," Bruce rolled his eyes. "Surely we ranked number one. We have the best health system in the world!"

"We ranked number one, all right," Frances replied, "but only in health-care spending! Out of 192 member states, we were number *thirty-seven* in overall system performance, and *seventy-two* on level of health. The bottom line is the United States spends almost twice as much per person as any other country in the world, yet roughly one fifth of us are uninsured.

"Here we are, the richest country in the world. We spend the most on healthcare, but we're the only industrialized country without universal health insurance coverage for our citizens. We do a poor job of delivering critical preventive and primary care services, so it shouldn't surprise anyone we do a poor job of producing health. Our infant mortality and premature death rates for adults from preventable diseases are higher than most other industrialized countries. I can only conclude that improving health is not the goal of the system. No, the U.S. healthcare system is designed to make money."

"Let's discuss the national health insurance programs of the other industrialized countries," Dr. Sampson said. "Who will begin?"

"I'll start," Bruce offered. "I think it's time we dispelled some of this nonsense about the evils of private insurers. I can imagine no better cure for fear of private insurers than a brief examination of the public insurance programs in the rest of the world. My country is Canada.

"Canada began its path to socialized medicine in Saskatchewan in 1944, when that province legislated universal hospital insurance. They started with five fancy founding principles and a bunch of naïve idealists who claimed health care must be universal, portable, comprehensive, accessible, and publicly administered. By 1971 the entire Canadian health care system was socialized, and all Canadians were guaranteed access to essential medical services. Of course, there's the rub. Do you really want the government telling you what's essential?

"Since then, Canadians have come to the United States in droves to get good health care. Sure, their health care costs are low—because they provide so little of it! The entire country has fewer MRI scanners than Dade County, Florida, and the average wait time for an MRI is over twelve weeks. God forbid you need an elective hip or knee replacement in Canada. The average wait time between the initial doctor visit and surgery is over four months. People suffer for months or even years to get needed procedures. That's what drives thousands of Canadians to come across the border.

"And it's not just the patients. Doctors have come from Canada by the thousands to practice in the United States. Did you know private practice is essentially illegal in Canada? Yes, the doctors are mostly self-employed and own their practices, but no one is allowed to pay them except the government; it's illegal for doctors to receive payment directly from patients. Even doctors who opt out of accepting public insurance must charge patients the same rates mandated by the public insurance fee schedule.

"Listen to what a Canadian thoracic surgeon told me. He saw a fifty-five-year-old man who needed a triple bypass for severe coronary artery disease. Because the man experienced chest pain only with exercise, his case was deemed non-emergent. In the U.S., he would have had surgery the next day, but the Canadian government hospital where the surgeon worked had a waiting list for heart surgery, and the man was put at the bottom of the list. They scheduled the surgery three months later, but one day before the surgery, it was postponed for three more months because of an emergency case. Two weeks before the new surgery date, he had a fatal heart attack. Saved their thrifty system a big chunk of change, didn't it, Frances? This is a true story. Canadians are more likely to die of heart attacks than Americans, probably because they're less likely to get lifesaving cardiac procedures in Canada.

"Canadians pay for their inefficient system through ridiculously high taxes. And there is no opting out. A Canadian can't pay for health care another way in Canada, or he's liable to get arrested. He cannot pay for prompt service—that's considered a bribe and can result in both patient and doctor going to jail. By suppressing private health care completely, Canada has removed all incentives for excellence and ended up with mediocre health care for all. All doctors are paid equally—no matter what services they provide or how much demand there is for them. Having a private health care market could help make the public system honest, but in Canada there isn't any private choice."

Dr. Sampson nodded his head, "Dr. Markum is right. Canada is the only place in the world where the private system is illegal. There is no alternative to the public system. Any questions?"

"Sure," Don said, "I've got one. What are income taxes like in Canada?"

Bruce hesitated. "Well, I can't say exactly, but I think over forty percent for most citizens."

Dr. Sampson answered, "Actually, federal income tax in Canada ranges from fifteen to twenty-nine percent, similar to the United States. Provincial tax rates range from four to eighteen percent, depending on the province and the taxpayer's income. The higher total tax rate of forty percent only applies to people with income above one hundred thousand dollars or so."

"Let me get this right," Don said. "Canadians only pay slightly more in taxes than we do, and most of their health care is covered?"

"Correct," said Dr. Sampson. "They have a single-payer insurance system, as does every high-income, industrialized country in the world except the United States. In Canada, the single payer is the government, and everyone is expected to pay his or her share."

"Well," Bruce replied, "*some* people pay a lot more than their share, and that discourages investment and innovation in the whole economy. Let's face it, Canada's system is just socialized medicine."

"Not exactly," said Frances. "In my health economics class, we learned that true socialized medicine is when the whole system is owned and operated by the government, like our Veterans Administration system. Single-payer insurance is simply social insurance, like our Medicare and Medicaid, and is typically coupled with a private delivery system. Most doctors favor a single-payer system because it would simplify paperwork and significantly lower administrative costs. Single-payer insurance could even be administered by a private or not-for-profit company like BlueCross BlueShield, if everyone could agree on which company."

"Yeah, right!" said Bruce. "One company, no competition. That's a sure for-mula to bring down costs."

"Think about it," Frances replied, "do we really benefit from competition among health insurance companies? The single-payer system is really just about the paperwork, not the care itself, and it would streamline the billing, reduce the bureaucracy, and markedly lower costs."

"Come on! What about choice?" Bruce shot back.

"But people can choose any doctor or hospital they want in Canada, right?" Don asked.

"In theory," Bruce said. "But they have a hell of a time getting an appoint-ment in Canada. For the really expert doctors, you could wait months or even years."

"But what about the most essential health care, the care that is most likely to save your life," Don persisted. "You know, primary care?"

"Getting primary care is no problem," Bruce admitted. "But if you need something important, really life-saving, you may find yourself at the end of a very long line."

"I'm not sure that's really true," Frances said. "Sure, sometimes things go wrong, like your example, Bruce. But that happens here, too. And you've seen the surveys. On average, Canadians are no more likely to complain of waiting for urgent surgery than Americans. Waiting is generally only a problem for elec-tive surgery like hips and knees, so some Canadians do come here to get those faster. But the survey data is pretty clear. Overall, Canadians are slightly more satisfied than Americans with their system and the healthcare they receive. Their quality and error rates compare favorably as well."

"But they don't have a choice," Bruce countered. "Who wants the govern-ment telling them what to do?"

"No one," Frances answered. "But in our system you don't have much choice, either. Usually your employer chooses a health plan for you or limits you to two or three options. Often, the doctor you want is not on your plan, or your employer switches your health plan and you can no longer see the doctor you've had for years. Every other industrialized nation in the world spends half as much on administration as we do, yet people can choose their doctors."

"But what about the case I presented?" Bruce said. "From what I hear, Canadians are killed all the time while waiting in the queue."

"Killed all the time? That's an overstatement," Dr. Sampson said. "However, Dr. Markum, you are correct that cost containment the Canadian way can result in serious queues that can be dangerous."

"Shouldn't we look at overall patient outcomes instead of isolated anec-dotes?" Frances asked, looking pointedly at Bruce. "Look, even with queues, people live about five years longer in Canada than in the United States, and their infant mortality rates are less than half of ours."

"That's because everyone in Canada is thin, white, and educated," Bruce replied. "I've studied my epidemiology too, Frances. Blacks and Hispanics in the U.S. are less educated, poorer, and genetically more inclined to cardiovascular disease and diabetes. They're the ones that drive our death rates up."

Don's face flushed with anger. Sure, there were racial disparities. But blaming blacks for America's ill health was racist bullshit.

"People in Canada live longer despite their health care system, not because of it!" insisted Bruce.

"Let's move on to the next country," Dr. Sampson interrupted. "Who's next?"

"That's me," Don said. He struggled to collect his thoughts. "I took the European countries. According to the WHO report, France has the number one health care system in the world. Americans living in France say it's far better than the U.S. system. Numerous surveys indicate patient satisfaction in France and Germany is much higher than in the U. S.

"So why do people in France like their health care system so much? Benefits. Hospital care, ambulatory care, and prescription drugs are all publicly financed and universally covered. And the systems in France, Germany, and Italy all emphasize primary care. People choose their doctors and hospitals. France has more doctors and more hospital beds per capita than does the United States. The bigger supply of doctors and hospitals means more competition among providers, and this encourages quality. A lousy service provider risks going out of business.

"Primary care providers generally work in group practices with after-hours care. If you get sick at night, you call the practice and get a home visit. That's right, a doctor will come examine you in your home, draw blood if necessary, and send you to the hospital if you are really sick. And it's all covered; you never even get a bill.

"France, Germany, and Italy all cover spa treatments, thermal baths, and massages through their national health insurance systems. The spa services are supervised by special arthritis and skin doctors. In Germany, for example, arthritis patients can go to a spa for three weeks a year and have it all covered by national health insurance. To Americans it sounds frivolous, but spa treatments offer lots of health benefits at low cost and low risk. For lower back pain, spas work as well as drugs and surgery and cost far less.

"How do they afford it? Effective primary and preventive care reduces the use of hospitals, emergency rooms, and procedures. They save millions, and people get better care. But studies show if you truly need emergency care, you are just as likely to get it in Europe as in the United States. Death rates and use of invasive lifesaving procedures for heart attack patients are similar in Europe and the United States, but because of the emphasis on healthy living and prevention, a French person is only a third as likely to die of a heart attack as an American.

"Drug costs are much lower in Europe because the governments negotiate with drug companies on price. The drug companies still make a profit, but out-of-pocket costs for patients are much lower. In contrast, the United States government is virtually prohibited from group purchasing of pharmaceuticals.

"France, Germany and Italy all allow private doctors, surgeons, and hospitals. They avoid the queue by having a generous supply of physicians and allowing them to opt out of the public system and charge whatever they like. If patients can't get what they want from the public system, they can pay out-of-pocket for private care, but generally, people like the public system. National health insurance doesn't pay for everything, but it pays for the things people need most, and basic services are covered for everyone. French, German and Italian patients can choose any provider they want, even after they get sick. They won't lose coverage if they get sick or change employers, or go bankrupt because of medical bills. It's no surprise that people in Europe like their health care."

Frances added, "I can see why the World Health Organization ranked the U.S. number thirty-seven."

"This all sounds very nice," Bruce said, "but would you really want to be a doctor or surgeon in any of these health systems? Doesn't the oversupply of physicians drive down doctors' salaries? And doesn't this end up giving you dumb physicians?"

"What these countries have found," Don answered, "is they don't have to pay doctors ridiculous amounts to attract the best students to medicine. Doctors make a decent living and enjoy prestige without the administrative hassles. They spend more time with patients, less time worrying about paperwork, and have a higher degree of career satisfaction."

"Primary care doctors, you mean," Bruce said with disgust. "Anybody can do what they do. Let me tell you, none of the top surgeons or specialists I've met want to practice in Europe. They make far less money and innovation is stifled. The really exceptional doctors all want to practice in the United States."

Don felt the blood rise into his face again. "What the hell are you talking about? Primary care doctors have to have the broadest knowledge of all and deal with the most complex..."

Dr. Sampson cut him off. "You two can argue about who the best doctors are later. Today we are discussing insurance. We're moving on. Frances, report on your countries."

Frances flipped her blond curls over her shoulder and tapped a red fingernail on the table three times, bringing Bruce and Don to attention. "Okay, so I chose Japan and Taiwan. The WHO ranks Japan number eight in the world.

Japan's system is characterized by compulsory insurance and price fixing; they've had universal insurance since 1973. They cover all corporate employees through Employee Health Insurance and the elderly, students, and everyone else through National Health Insurance. Like Germany, there are hundreds of different sickness plans depending on your employer or region, but all of them must cover the same services and use the same fee schedule.

"The sickness plans are prohibited from making a profit. If they don't spend all of the premiums they collect in a year, they roll the money over to the next year and may even cut premiums. Even though administrative overhead is very low, the sickness plans still compete with one another—like our BlueCross BlueShield plans compete with for-profit plans. Even if there is technically no profit, health plans still want to stay in business.

"Insurance in Japan covers massage, acupuncture, thermal baths, and other ancient healing methods. Patients choose the doctors or hospitals they want, but a government committee sets the prices. From what I've learned of economics, you'd think fixed prices would prohibit innovation and new technology, but this hasn't happened in Japan. I think it's because the Japanese love technology and have kept demand high even where profit is low. For example, Japan has twice as many MRI units per person as the U.S., even though the Japanese government has cut prices for MRI scans again and again. An MRI scan costing twelve hundred dollars in the U.S. is only about one hundred dollars in Japan. Doctors and hospitals keep buying MRI scanners because patients demand the latest technology.

"Surveys show the Japanese people generally like their health care more than we do in the U.S., but there are some problems. As you'd expect in a system where everything is covered, people complain about long waiting times and rushed service. Payment in Japan is mostly fee-for-service, and with low prices, that means care is often delivered in an assembly line fashion and lacks personal attention. So that's Japan: compulsory insurance, fixed prices, traditional oriental healing, and assembly line, high-tech care.

"Taiwan, on the other hand, is worth considering because it is the latest industrialized country to launch a universal national health insurance program. In the early 1990s, Taiwan's health system was in worse shape than ours today. Costs were soaring and nearly half of Taiwan's citizens were uninsured. Experts studied health systems around the world and totally redesigned Taiwan's health care by adopting the best characteristics from different systems.

"In 1995, Taiwan went from a market-based system to universal coverage nearly overnight by making their national health insurance program compulsory for everyone. By the next year, ninety-six percent of citizens were enrolled. It's a single payer system; a government agency pays all the bills. The insurance premiums are paid partly by individuals, partly by employers, and twenty-five percent is paid by the government through taxes to subsidize the premiums of those who cannot afford to pay.

"Taiwan's program is basically Medicare for all. The program seems to be designed with all the right incentives. Most preventive care is free, co-payments for primary care are low, and inpatient care is subject to a ten percent co-payment. They limit total out-of-pocket costs to ten percent of the average annual income in Taiwan. They avoid queues by using copayments to discourage over-utilization. Waiting times did not increase following the implementation of the national plan. In fact, you can usually see a doctor the same day in Taiwan, even on Saturdays and evenings.

"Taiwan's system is very efficient. Everyone in Taiwan gets a smart card so a doctor can access a patient's electronic health record instantly anywhere in the country. That improves patient care, eliminates duplication of tests, and saves money. The smart card allows providers to bill for services electronically and automatically at the time of service. As a result, Taiwan has the lowest administrative costs in the world, like two percent. Remember, we pay thirty percent for our hundreds of insurance companies and the hassles that go along with them.

"Taiwanese patients have free choice of doctors and hospitals, which encourages competition on service and quality. But Taiwan decided that choice of insurance companies wasn't worth the high overhead. Private insurance companies can still sell supplemental health insurance policies that cover things like private rooms in the hospital or other uncovered costs. But all basic health care costs are covered.

"The world watched to see if Taiwan's health care costs would escalate with expanded access to care. It's amazing—overall, health care costs went down after the national program was started and since then have more or less remained stable. So, that's it. Taiwan's program has reduced administrative costs to two percent and provides essential health care to everyone at very low cost. It's hard to see what's not to like."

Don nodded his head in agreement. National health insurance was a no-brainer.

"Right, Frances, it is hard to see what's not to like," Bruce seethed, "unless, maybe, you don't want to be a communist. Being forced to provide services through the government is a recipe for disaster. This socialist system screws the docs. They get no choice. Taiwan just looks like a dressed-up Canadian system to me. Count me out. I didn't go through four years of pre-med, four years of medical school, and eight years of surgical residency and fellowship to work for the damn government!"

"Well, Bruce, you could always build a lucrative private practice doing boob jobs," Frances retorted.

"Wait a minute," Don said, "Taiwan's system would be great for primary care. Automatic electronic billing right there at the visit? I could forget about billing and focus on the patient? Internal medicine docs would love this! Every primary care office could let go the two or three employees who deal fulltime with all the stupid insurance paperwork and overhead would go way down. It might even make primary care profitable."

"Would you really give up your freedom and liberty to practice the way you want for a little convenience?" Bruce blasted.

"Freedom and liberty? What planet do you practice on?" Don shot back. "I don't have the freedom to treat my patients the way I want now. The insurance companies are the ones who decide what treatments and medications my patients get—not me, not my patients. The only ones with freedom and liberty are the insurance companies."

"Good points, Dr. Newman." Dr. Sampson said softly. "Dr. Markum is also correct that universal national health insurance involves tradeoffs. All health systems have problems. Just because an insurance program is public doesn't make it free of graft, fraud, or the pursuit of money. We will learn more about the pitfalls of government-run health care when we go to Washington next semester.

"The Clinton plan was America's fourth major push for universal coverage. Does anyone remember the famous couple that led the opposition to defeat it?"

"Harry and Louise," Frances said.

"That's right. A fictional couple in a commercial funded by the Health Insurance Association of America. And who funds the HIAA?"

"The insurance companies," Don answered.

"Exactly. What was so compelling about the commercial that it turned the tide of American history?" Dr. Sampson asked.

"Well, they designed the ad to scare people," Frances said. "And boy did it ever work. Harry and Louise sit at a kitchen table agonizing over a huge pile of bills. Both of them look dejected, like they are afraid of losing their home. Louise sighs, holds up a bill for her husband to see, and says that their insurance had always paid their healthcare bills before...before the government stepped in. Harry tabulates figures and finally wads up his paper in disgust. Then comes their famous line: Harry begins, 'If they choose,' and Louise ends, 'we lose.'"

"The message is clear," Dr. Sampson said. "Government can only make things worse."

Bruce's head bobbed vigorously. Frances resumed her usual furious note taking. Don couldn't figure out what she would be writing down at this point. What was she doing—taking dictation word for word?

"To summarize," Dr. Sampson said, "taking care of the sick was once a moral duty. Our health insurance system grew out of a need for people in a community to help one another. But somewhere along the way this industry forgot its purpose, and today our system is built on greed. Insurance salesmen still promise to care with slogans like *State Farm is there,* but their corporations' attention is trained on your money."

"And hospitals have transformed from places of rest and recovery into places that hold patients captive for profit," Frances added.

Don's mind wandered back to the captive specimens in the anatomy hallway...the embalmed foot with seven toes twitched, then jerked, like a part from *The Frozen Dead,* electrically revitalized by its Nazi doctor-scientist re-creator. The two-headed baby turned its heads to look straight at him. The bottled body parts all came back to life—thrashing, rocking their jars, until they fell from the shelves and smashed on the floor below. Misshapen hands, malformed kidneys, hearts, livers, and aortas—all freed from their prison jars—slithered across the linoleum floors through shattered glass, desperate to organize. Their angry spirits assembled and plotted vengeance on the grave robber anatomists who drew and quartered their decomposing corpses in crypts and morgues. Partially reconstructed parts came out of the dank catacombs from hundreds of side passages into the main corridor, knitting themselves together in grotesque configurations along the way...

Don shook his head and looked over at Bruce. Was Bruce was on a personal quest for power and control? Wouldn't he be pissed off to know Don was imagining surgeons as mad scientists!

"Let's finish up here," Dr. Sampson said. "For our next seminar, I want you to conduct a research project on pharmaceutical company marketing here in Florence. I want your best estimates of what they spend here on free meals and other incentives for physicians. No seminar next week, so you have two weeks to complete your research, and you will present your results at our next meeting. Class dismissed."

Dr. Sampson headed up to the projection room.

"So," Frances said, "how about we three do this project together?"

"Sounds good to me," Don answered.

"To research drug company marketing, I'm afraid we'll have to go to some nice restaurants," Bruce said, winking at Frances. "I suggest we go have a drink in every restaurant there's a drug company-sponsored dinner."

"Awesome!" said Frances. "We should do it Thursday. Every Thursday is D-day, or Drug day, when the drug pushers have the best dinner meetings for doctors. It's not the only day they have dinners, but it's the biggest one."

"And the fanciest of all is at Chez Henri downtown," said Bruce, "so why don't we meet there Thursday night at six-thirty? We can take a cab to the others from there."

"Good idea," Frances said. "But what about all the drug company lunches at the medical school?"

"Right. Let's count them all." Bruce seemed genuinely excited for once. "I bet we can track down more over- and under-the-table gifts than you can imagine. Here's what we do. Let's start by divvying up the medical school departments. Don, you'll have the biggest job, the department of medicine. Check with all the divisions, including cardiology, GI, rheumatology, endocrine and the lot. Oh, and do psychiatry as well. Make a spreadsheet, and find out every breakfast and lunch conference they have this week. Find out how many people usually attend, and estimate the cost per head."

"Frances," Bruce went on like a general barking orders, "you take the nurse practitioner program, family practice, and the pharmacy school. If you can't get the info you need on the phone, go see them in person." His eyes traveled up her long legs to her firm breasts. "You can get them to tell you whatever you want to know, I am sure of that."

Frances was busy scribbling down Bruce's instructions, but hearing this last comment, she rolled her eyes.

"I'll take surgery," he continued without missing a beat. "You know they are more interested in fancy devices than drugs, so I'll have to ferret that out. And I'll do pediatrics. Hey, I like this business of following the money." Bruce checked his watch and grabbed his books. "See you two later!" he said as he blazed out of the room.

Where was he going in such a hurry? Don was pretty sure he didn't have another class at that hour.

"I have to meet with my epidemiology study group," Frances said wistfully. "You know we've got a big-deal test coming up. I'll see you later, Don."

Don was glad they were gone. He wanted to ask Dr. Sampson for advice. The more ugliness they uncovered about modern medicine, the less sure he was of his identity as a doctor. Dr. Sampson's class was eroding his confidence in the knowledge he had struggled to accumulate in medical school and residency, and the Health System Science Fellowship was giving him tenuous new connections to his profession at best.

What will I do with this stuff? Don felt like the bodiless woman in *The Frozen Dead,* her decapitated but still-alive head linked by wires to alien arms and legs by her fiendish scientist captor. Like her, Don had not yet learned how to make use of his new synapses.

Don gathered his things and went up the stairs to the projection room, where Dr. Sampson was taking his slide carousel off the projector and putting it into his briefcase. He tapped on the open door, and Dr. Sampson turned his grim visage in Don's direction. Don shivered involuntarily in anticipation of his disapproval. Outside of class, Dr. Sampson was often preoccupied and quiet, as if he carried some great burden, and today was no exception.

"What is it, Dr. Newman?" he said in a gruff voice.

"I, uh, wondered if maybe, uh, we could, I could, talk to you a bit about my next steps, you know, my career and everything. I guess I'm feeling a little lost." Don braced himself for the response.

Dr. Sampson walked toward the door and motioned with a nod of his head for Don to follow him. "Come with me, let's go for a little walk." Dr. Sampson threw on his old black windproof field jacket and headed out the door of the projection room.

Don worked to keep pace with his purposeful strides. He followed right behind him out the classroom door, down the basement hallway, past the rows of jars of dismembered creatures, out the back door, and toward the front entrance on the eastern side of campus. They crossed the quad at the geometric center of campus, where the old omphalos rested like a giant upside-down acorn dropped by one of the college's great oaks. They passed through the stand of trees and approached the tall rock wall that encircled the campus.

Don had never walked this way—the car entrances were on the north and south sides of campus, and his apartment was near the south entrance—so they were nearly upon the gate before Don spotted it. Centered in front of the quad, its towering limestone slabs stood on end and flanked the narrowest passageway he had ever seen. It was capped with a huge stone slab carved with what appeared to be horns, or a crescent moon pointed upwards.

"This was called the Horn Gate," Dr. Sampson said. "Now most people call it the Narrow Gate. The founder of Florence College brought it over from Greece in the early 1800s, along with the omphalos, and reassembled it here to remind our scholars the path to knowledge is not easy. In the old days, students marched in through this gate in a special ceremony on their first day, and back through to the outside at graduation. In the 1940s, the college president decided the tradition was too old-fashioned. He bricked up the gate and broadened the north and south entrances for automobiles. The very night after it was bricked up," Dr. Sampson laughed, "the students tore the bricks out again, and it's been open ever since. But the tradition was lost."

It looked impossible to pass through the narrow passageway. By the time Don squeezed through the crack between the limestone slabs sideways and emerged on the other side, Dr. Sampson was several steps ahead. Don jogged up alongside him and waited for him to say something more. He didn't.

As they walked down Main Street and into the old downtown, Don took the opportunity to study Dr. Sampson. Despite the solid gray ring of hair around his balding head, his broad shoulders and thick arms suggested strength that belied his late middle age. He looked to neither side, yet seemed intensely aware of his surroundings.

The world noticed his presence as well. As they passed the shops of Main Street, several shopkeepers and passers-by waved or called out to him, and he responded to each with an almost imperceptible nod. A young woman came out of the supermarket, struggling to carry six plastic bags of groceries and with young children in tow. Her three-year-old son bolted for the street. Dr. Sampson reached down with his massive arm and without breaking his stride gently corralled the child back toward his mother.

"Thank you, Dr. Sampson," the beleaguered mother said with a grateful smile.

They turned the corner and headed toward the outskirts of town, passing the barbershop, an old-fashioned small bank, and a liquor store. A grizzled man with a long, gray ponytail and a shuffling gait came out of the liquor store clutching a brown paper bag. He eyed Dr. Sampson and moved back toward the door as if to hide, but then thought better of it.

"Hello, Dr. Sampson," he said meekly. He bowed, as if on encountering a king. "You know, I tried to do better."

"I know, Joshua," Dr. Sampson said gently. "Keep your appointment in clinic next week. We'll talk then."

"Yes, Dr. Sampson," he replied, nodding his head again and again. "I'll be there, don't you worry."

They passed the old Florence Police Station. Its granite walls were bleached white, and a pair of white globe lights marked POLICE framed the doorway. By now they were almost at the edge of the old downtown.

Don had no idea where Dr. Sampson was leading him. His curiosity was intense. *Where are we going? Is he going to answer my questions?* Don didn't dare ask out loud.

The last storefront on the block was the Grafton County Cemetery Preservation Society and Bookstore. The front door was unlocked. Dr. Sampson pushed the door open with his left shoulder and walked inside, and Don followed close behind. A clang of bells on the backside of the door announced their entrance.

Don looked around. The front room was filled with new books about colonial history and slavery in the Americas. A map on the wall was covered with pins marking the graveyards of New Hampshire. A small sign—*Used Books*—pointed through an open doorway behind the counter to the next room, where stacks of old books lined the shelves. Through the same doorway came a white-haired woman with a broad smile and honey-brown skin.

"Yes, yes, you're here!" The woman greeted them warmly with an accent Don couldn't place. "Well, Virgil," she said, "It has been a long time. Too long, I think, old friend."

"Yes, Julia, I'm here to see what you've found, digging under the earth all these months. Are you still teaching the freshmen at Florence College the real history of New England?"

"Oh yes, of course," she replied. "As long as they'll let me. You do know how much I like uncovering those things that polite and proper people don't like to see! Tell me, who is this young man you've brought with you today?"

"Dr. Don Newman, one of my new students. Dr. Newman, I'd like you to meet Dr. Julia Chambers, Florence resident archeologist extraordinaire."

She squeezed Don's outstretched hand in both of hers, and with a surprising grip, pulled him closer and looked him straight in the eye. He had the uncomfortable sensation she was examining the connections deep in his brain, probing his soul.

"Nice to meet you, Dr. Chambers."

"Likewise. Please, call me Julia," she said, still holding his hand.

"Julia, why don't you tell Dr. Newman here a little about what you do?" Dr. Sampson said.

She released Don's hand and turned her attention back to Dr. Sampson. "No, no, no, first you must tell me what you've been doing in your free-thinking classroom. Fomenting rebellion again, are you, Virgil?"

Dr. Sampson gave her an enigmatic smile.

"Today we were talking about how the American public is getting used by the insurance industry and doesn't even know it," Don offered.

"Ah," she said with a twinkle in her eye, "I know something about that. My late husband and I, we certainly had our experiences with insurance plans."

Don was already entranced with this delightful woman and her elegant accent, and her comment piqued his curiosity even further.

"What happened?" he asked, looking to Sampson for approval.

"Go ahead, Julia," Dr. Sampson said. "We're not in any hurry."

Julia leaned forward and rested her elbows on the counter, which was strewn with maps and brochures from historical sites and graveyard tours. She took a deep breath.

"Well, I grew up in England, but with periodic stints in Jamaica, where my father worked with the British Consulate. I never felt quite at home in either place, so when it was time for University, I decided to come to America. I ended up here at Florence College. I met my dear late husband here, and after we graduated we both went to graduate school at Oxford's Institute of Archaeology. After Oxford, we secured positions at the University of Bristol in England and worked there most of our careers. Given our common interest in archaeology and anthropology, we took several long sabbaticals, which we spent excavating old Roman villas in Italy. I specialized in the living quarters of servants and slaves.

"Since my husband was from New Hampshire, we came to visit his family every summer. We loved it here and made it our home after we retired. So, you see, I experienced four health insurance systems: the United States, Italy, Jamaica, and England."

"How did your experience here compare with the others?" Don asked.

Julia glanced Dr. Sampson's way, and after seeing his nod, she pressed ahead with her tale.

"Well, our experience with healthcare in America was very good, but it was extraordinarily expensive. It flabbergasts me that you Americans tolerate such inefficiency in your healthcare system. You pay an arm and a leg to go-between insurance salespeople who add absolutely nothing to your care.

"Anyway, in England it was all covered by our taxes, so we were rather shocked at how much we had to pay every month in the U.S. At Dr. Sampson's recommendation, we signed up with an HMO. We always knew who our doctor was, someone was always there to see us if we needed help, and we always got our preventive care.

"Now my favorite health system was in Italy. Since we were members of the European Community, they took care of us just like we were Italian citizens. Even though everything else in Italy was extraordinarily bureaucratic, healthcare was not, at least for patients. We never had to wait.

"I remember the first winter we spent there, ten years ago. Henry took a bad fall skiing in the Italian Alps, and we asked the owner of the pensione where we should have his knee evaluated. She asked whether we preferred a private or a public doctor, so we asked which was better. She explained the private doctor in town would see him right away, and it would probably cost about thirty dollars for x-rays and evaluation, or we could drive to the public hospital in the next town and be seen in the emergency room for free. I asked her again which place offered better care, and she said, very matter-of-factly, 'Neither is better. They are the same, only the private doctor is right here, and for the public hospital you must go to the next town about twenty minutes down the road.'

"We decided to drive to the public hospital. In the emergency room we were surprised to see no clerks about. A nurse pointed us to a hallway where people sat in chairs and waited to be seen. I asked, in the best Italian I could muster, where the clerk was so I could sign in. Another patient told me, 'Oh, don't worry, the doctor will sign you in.'

"After a minute or two, the doctor poked his head out of one of the exam rooms, saw my husband, and asked him what his problem was. Henry told him it was his knee, and the doctor said, 'It shouldn't be more than thirty minutes.' Well, indeed, in thirty minutes, it came Henry's turn and we went into the examination room.

"The doctor himself asked for my husband's name, passport number, and our address, and then he began to examine my husband's knee. I asked the doctor if he needed more information, and he said, 'No, that will be fine, and since you are a European citizen, the government should cover it, but if there is anything due, you will get a bill in the mail.' Thank goodness, Henry's knee was fine; it was only strained. We were in and out of there in less than an hour and a half, even though the hall was filled with several others, most of them also skiing mishaps.

"In England, when Henry was diagnosed with prostate cancer at age fifty-nine, we felt privileged to have private as well as the national public insurance. I was suspicious of the public system and insisted Henry go to a private hospital in the north of England. It had the finest reputation, and both of us expected his care there would be far better. But let me tell you, despite their reputation and the high bills we paid, my God, they almost killed him! The room had fine linens and pretty curtains, and the meals were incredible, but Henry wasn't able to enjoy them.

"After his surgery, Henry just didn't look right. As soon as he woke up, he complained of severe pain. At first I thought he was having normal post-operative pain, but he looked ghastly. His face was as pale as his sheets. That night his pain got worse and worse. I asked the nurse to get the doctor, but she told me there was no doctor in house at night, like there would be at a teaching hospital. The nurse reassured me Henry was fine and a doctor would be by to see him in the morning.

"Well, in the morning, another nurse was on, and she informed me Henry's doctor was in surgery and wouldn't be there until the afternoon. Meanwhile, Henry's heart was racing and he was writhing in pain. All they did was give him more morphine. By the time the doctor finally came at three in the afternoon, Henry's blood count had plummeted and he was in shock. The doctor was clearly worried, and seeing that, I was frantic. They gave poor Henry transfusions in both arms and he came around, but after that I never wanted to go to the private hospital again.

"So, that's my story. It astounds me how much you Americans pay to insurance middlemen. Do you really need such an overseer? The hospitals have more people handling insurance paperwork than they do treating patients."

"I guess it astounds me, too," Don replied. "Until this year, I had no idea how little American patients get for their money."

"We Americans are caught in a system few understand," Dr. Sampson said. "We are virtually slaves to a system perpetuated by tyrants who love the dark and want the dark to persist because they profit from it so. This is what our young Dr. Newman is beginning to see. So, Julia, speaking of slaves, tell Don about the work you do here."

"Yes, yes, the Cemetery Preservation Society. After Henry died, I was at a loss of what to do with the rest of my life. Then one day, I read in the local paper about construction workers who made a shocking discovery when they dug up a major section of road right here in front of this office. They found coffins! That very afternoon the mayor called me for help, and it didn't take long for my students and me to find a map from 1695 identifying the site as the Negro Burial Ground.

"Now, people in New Hampshire don't take very well to the discovery of slavery in their own backyards. In fact, most people in New Hampshire will tell you slavery never existed here. But, as any good historian knows, in early colonial times there were well over five hundred slaves in New Hampshire and over one hundred here in Grafton County. Of course, after colonial times the town expanded, land near town became more valuable, and everyone conveniently forgot about the existence of the burial ground. It was paved over, and houses were built nearby.

"Well, the city council wanted to take out all the coffins and put them in the graveyard across town with the white people. But I was not about to stand by and let them do that. 'No, you leave those coffins right where they are!' I told them. People need to know there were slaves in our town, just like in the South, and our forebears literally covered them up. This must not be hidden; it must be held up for all of New Hampshire to see. So, I found a purpose for the end of my life: to show this cemetery to all those I can and uncover what's been covered up."

"Would you show Don the graves?" Dr. Sampson asked.

"Come with me," Julia ordered, pulling keys from her pocket.

They all walked outside into the blustery air and over to a historical society sign near the curb. Under the sign was a large sidewalk grate like the ones that ventilate subways in big cities. It seemed out of place on the small town sidewalk. Julia bent over, unlocked the grate, and pulled it back with a loud screech of un-oiled metal, revealing stone steps going deep down into darkness. She handed a flashlight to Dr. Sampson.

"Virgil, you know the way. You show him. Those steps are getting a bit steep for me."

Don looked down into the dark, yawning pit and imagined the dry bones of the dead re-hinging themselves, pushing up from under the earth, pushing up through the sidewalk, coming toward them. What a surreal Halloween this was turning out to be! He hung close behind Sampson as they descended the steep stone stairs into the dark, into the underworld realm of the dead slaves. All he could see was the glow from the flashlight outlining Sampson's broad shoulders. He put his hand on the damp stone wall to steady himself, counted twelve steps down from the level of the street, and waited for his eyes to adjust to the dim light.

There—hidden beneath the street and shops of Florence—was a narrow chamber with brick-lined walls. Three elegant bronze plaques commemorated the slaves whose unidentified bodies were presumed to rest here. All 114 names of slaves her students found in old church, city hall, and *Florence Herald* records had been listed. The slaves had names like Pompeii, Caesar, and Augustus. Most of them lacked surnames, but the three that did drew his eye. They were all named Townsend: James, Sarah, and Clay.

So, the Florence town fathers had profited from slavery. They oversaw the economic system that used slaves, buried them, and built over their bodies. Their wealth and security had depended on slavery then, and everything the Townsends owned now derived from it.

The American insurance industry was built on that same desire for security. Insurance companies made huge profits from burial policies sold to soldiers during the Civil War and to northern factory workers afterward. Insurance was the foundation of America's healthcare system, and it was the new overseer. Insurance controls hospitals, doctors, and drugs, and organizes healthcare so that every life, breath, and death reaps profit. For fear of hospital bills that could bankrupt almost anyone, we had all become its slaves.

Was I any different? Don remembered his student loans and felt a familiar pang in the pit of his stomach. One hundred and fifty grand. *I'm a slave, too; the system owns me.* He had to work in the system, like it or not. Otherwise, how would he ever pay it all back?

Dr. Sampson broke the preternatural silence with an eerily prescient piece of advice. "Remember, Don, you don't have to remain a slave to the system. But before you can find freedom, you must know you're a slave."

18

The Drug Pushers

For all their treatment, they accomplish nothing more than to make
their illnesses more complicated and bigger, always hoping
that if someone would just recommend a drug, they will be, thanks to it, healthy.
PLATO, THE REPUBLIC, BOOK IV, 426A

THEY MET JUST INSIDE the front door of Chez Henri, the most expensive French restaurant in town. The thin-mustached maître d' eyed the students with suspicion. He surveyed each one from head to toe, his eyes lingering on the shoes. His faint smile at Bruce's fine-checked houndstooth blazer and shiny, tasseled, cordovan loafers waned when he saw Don's corduroy jacket and scuffed-up brown oxfords, but waxed large as he took in Frances's gray pantsuit, low-cut silk blouse, and high-heeled pumps.

"Good evening," Bruce said to the maître d'. "We would like to sit at the bar for appetizers and drinks."

"Of course. And how many will be in your party this evening?"

"Just the three of us."

The maître d' frowned and hesitated for a split second, then waved his arm toward the bar in a mimed gesture of hospitality.

"Excuse me, sir, could you help us out?" Don said.

Bruce shot him a warning glance, but it was too late.

"We are from the medical school, and we're doing a class research project on the scope of pharmaceutical company-sponsored meetings."

The maître d' bristled. "Excuse me, sir," he mimicked, "the business of our customers always remains their business at Chez Henri. I cannot assist you." He turned on his heel and marched away.

Bruce scowled. "Thanks a lot, wise guy. You blew our cover. For someone who trained at the University Hospital, you have a lot to learn."

They went in and sat at the bar. The bartender made his way over, and Bruce ordered three martinis, not bothering to ask Frances and Don what they wanted.

"So how did everyone's work go at the medical school?" Bruce asked. "What did you find out?"

From his breast pocket, Don pulled out the graph paper on which he had scribbled his estimated figures, unfolded it, and slapped it on the bar.

"Don, please don't be so obvious," Bruce scolded. "Are you completely determined to screw this up?" He shook his head in disgust.

Don tried to ignore the insult, but his cheeks burned.

Bruce laughed. "Of course, you may need that paper later, Don, to keep track of where we've been. It may become a little difficult to remember." He nodded his head at the collection of liquor bottles behind the bar. "Anyway, tell us what you found out."

"I'll do that." Don looked Bruce straight in the eye. "The bottom line is the drug companies invest a lot of money at the medical school. Here's what they did just last week."

Don picked up his paper and rattled off the numbers. "Internal medicine had six drug company lunches for some three hundred medical students, residents, fellows, and faculty members at about ten dollars a head—roughly three thousand dollars. There were four breakfast journal clubs totaling about a thousand. The grand rounds speaker received seven thousand plus travel costs from the drug company sponsor. Psychiatry had a nice lunch with their grand rounds lecture for about one hundred fifty people at ten bucks a head—that's another fifteen hundred, not counting all the paraphernalia they gave out. Neurology only had fifty-five at their noon conference, but they ate well, with cheesecake for dessert. Also, neurology and psychiatry had two breakfast journal clubs or pre-clinic conferences apiece, all of them with some version of drug company donuts. In addition, drug reps bring weekly lunches to three clinic sites. I figure these extra psych and neuro conferences add up to about another fifteen hundred bucks a week. So, the total for the medical subspecialties, psychiatry, and neurology is about...let me see..."

"Over fourteen thousand dollars a week," Frances said.

"Yeah, that's right," Don said. "How did you figure that out so fast?"

"I'm good with numbers. What can I say?" She smiled. "Look, why don't both of you email me your figures, and I'll prepare an Excel spreadsheet, run the totals by category, and project annual expenditure estimates for our presentation."

This offer caught Bruce and Don by surprise. Both doctors smiled at Frances and nodded their heads, trying once again to reconcile this California blond bombshell—a nurse, no less—with the uncomfortable notion she might prove smarter than either of them.

Bruce quickly recovered his bossy attitude. "So Frances, tell us what you found out at nursing, pharmacy, and family practice."

"Well, I haven't gotten to family practice yet, but there is more going on at the college of nursing than I thought. At the nurse practitioner research rounds, they had a speaker for Paxil who told me she makes over ten thousand dollars for giving five talks in three days. The drug reps were good-looking men, and they passed out some adorable stuffed animals as we left the auditorium."

"Stuffed animals? Are you kidding me?" Bruce laughed.

"Stuffed animals, no joke. The pharmacy school was even richer. They have three different drug company noon conferences each week, and about thirty pharmacy students and faculty attend each one. Plus, I counted fifteen different weekend events for November on their bulletin board. One pharmacy student said he got two leftover tickets to see the Rolling Stones!"

"So what about you, Bruce—what did you find in surgery and pediatrics?" Don asked.

"Oh, you know, much the same. There's a big push in pediatrics to make sure children get screened for ADHD, because now they can treat it with Ritalin. And the surgeons? Well, Don, you should know by now, the surgeons don't have any conflicts of interest."

Don was growing tired of Bruce's smug self-assurance, so he excused himself and took a scouting trip to the well-appointed bathroom. When he got back to the bar, Frances and Bruce were leaning toward each other, engaged in lively conversation.

Don was glad to have a reason to interrupt. "Hey, guys, there are two large private rooms back there with some sort of sponsored dinners," Don announced. "Each one has a slide projector and screen set up, and there are about twenty people in each."

"Good start," Bruce replied, "but let me handle it from here."

The bartender brought the martinis and set them on the bar.

Bruce took a long gulp from his chilled glass. "Yes, excellent," he said, turning to the bartender, "and I do know my martinis. So, tell me, what companies are here tonight?" Bruce slid a fifty across the bar. "For the martinis. Please keep the change."

The bartender looked around to make sure the maître d' was out of view. "Not sure exactly. We have something going on here almost every night. Tonight the arthritis doctors are with one drug company in our biggest private dining room, and the hospital pharmacy directors are with another drug company in the other."

"Thanks." Bruce flashed his winning smile. "Actually, we're doctors, too. We're doing a little work with Florence College."

"Welcome to Chez Henri," the bartender replied. "Let me know if I can help you any further."

The bartender left and Bruce laughed, "That's how it's done, Don. Stick with me and I'll show you how to get along."

Yeah, you'd like nothing better than to show me how to get along—with Frances. Bruce was shamelessly flirting with Frances and taking every opportunity to make Don look like an idiot, but Don couldn't think of anything to say that wouldn't make it worse.

Bruce was also keeping an eye on the entrance to the larger private dining room. He spotted a well-dressed doctor heading for the bathroom and jumped up and followed him in. Two minutes later, they walked out of the restroom together and headed into the private dining room, laughing all the way like a couple of old friends.

Five minutes after that, Bruce returned to the bar with a wine glass in one hand and a black folder in the other.

"So, what have you got?" Frances's green eyes sparkled with excitement.

"A 1988 Bordeaux, Chateau Margaux, a very good year," he said, grinning with obvious satisfaction.

"Not the wine, silly, the folder!"

"Oh, that," he said, looking at the folder in his hand as if noticing it for the first time. "That was Dr. Robison, a rheumatologist here in Florence. We started talking at the urinal about pharmaceutical golf trips, and I mentioned something about how much surgical device makers pay us to use their equipment, and he said, 'You think that's something—you should see what you can make on Remicade.' By the time we left the bathroom, he had invited me to come with him to taste the Margaux."

Bruce was a smooth operator, all right. Don wondered whether he could have pulled it off.

Bruce opened the folder. "Here's the scoop. Remicade is the latest arthritis drug from Johnson & Johnson's subsidiary, Centocor. It's used to treat rheumatoid arthritis, a pretty common disease, but has to be delivered intravenously in a doctor's office for a couple of hours every month or so. It costs about twenty thousand dollars a year per patient."

Don gave a low whistle.

"Medicare reimburses the doctor the average wholesale price for the drug. The trick is, the company often provides the drug for substantially less than the wholesale price, and the doctor simply pockets the profit. Between his administration fee and the drug company payment, a rheumatologist can net several thousand dollars a year per patient. Dr. Robison said he knows of centers infusing Remicade and similar drugs virtually around the clock, and their doctors make upwards of a million a year."

"Isn't that illegal?" Frances asked.

"Frances, at occasions like this we never ask impolite questions." Bruce grinned and handed Frances the folder.

Frances flipped through the pages. "Oh my gosh! Here's a worksheet to calculate estimated revenue per patient. This is totally unbelievable!"

"You know," Don said, "rheumatoid arthritis isn't always easy to diagnose. But since patients like to have a diagnosis for their aches and pains, and no one has to verify the doctor's diagnosis, some rheumatologists seem to find rheumatoid arthritis in every patient they see."

"No wonder, with a financial incentive like that," added Frances.

"There were a bunch of notorious Boston of rheumatologists who treated nearly every patient they saw with incredibly expensive drugs that suppress the immune system," Don said. "Some people even die from taking them."

"Wow," Frances said, but her eyes were scanning the restaurant. She stood up. "Okay, Bruce, you did pretty well, but watch this."

Bruce and Don stared. Her tailored outfit emphasized her perfect figure and firm breasts. A drop pearl necklace dangled over the deep V of her cleavage and with her spiked heels, her legs looked like they would never end. She was professional and sexy at the same time. She could be a top-selling drug rep.

Frances made a slow, sultry walk to the bathroom. On the way she managed to bump into a man in an elegant, tailored suit and make it look accidental. "Oh, excuse me, sir, I didn't look where I was going," Frances said. "Of course, if I had seen *you* I would have come this way *way* sooner, I'm sure."

Frances returned about ten minutes later looking very pleased with herself. "I got the scoop on the other meeting," she reported. "Merck is hosting a five-course wine-tasting dinner with local insurance company and hospital pharmacy directors. They are talking about the economic benefits of Merck formulary options. The director of Aetna's pharmacy program was more than happy to tell me about it."

The maître d' stalked over to the bar, his face beet-red and his hands curled up into fists at his sides. "I am going to have to ask you to leave," he said, glaring at Frances. "At Chez Henri we do not allow ladies of the evening to market their wares to our customers."

Frances gaped at the maître d' and slowly shook her head back and forth. Bruce opened his mouth to speak but started laughing so hard he couldn't make himself understood.

The maître d' repeated through clenched teeth, "I must ask you to leave."

Don stood up. "I have never heard anything so ridiculous in my life! We are all students at…"

"Whatever you are, I will not have you accosting my customers." He stood in front of Frances, feet planted and hands on hips, and leveled his menacing stare at her.

Bruce regained his composure and stood up. "We'll leave, don't worry. We're happy to take our business elsewhere." He looked at Don and Frances, raised his wine glass high like the haughty young Athenian general, Alcibiades, and compelled them to drink. "Bottoms up!" he ordered.

Frances and Don obeyed. They downed the remainder of their drinks and followed Bruce straight out the door. As soon as they were outside, Bruce burst into laughter again.

"Shut up, Bruce," said Frances testily. "My God, he thought I was a hooker!"

"Sorry, Frances, " Bruce said, oblivious to her embarrassment, "but you have to admit..."

Don elbowed him hard in the ribs and cut him off. "We have work to do. Let's go; we can walk to the next three restaurants."

Next on their list was The Crab Shack. This time, Bruce announced to the hostess they were there for the drug company dinner, and she escorted them to a huge steak and lobster feast for primary care doctors in one of the back rooms. This feast was on Pfizer and featured Lipitor for cholesterol and Norvasc for hypertension.

Poor Sibyl Bellamy...her downfall came when the free samples of Norvasc ran out and she couldn't afford the prescription. Don looked around at the crowd of gorging carnivores. A steak and lobster party—no wonder the drug was so damn expensive!

Bruce led the way through the open door. Don spotted the two drug representatives at once. One was female and one male, but they were similar enough to be twins. Both sported the requisite drug rep look: perfect smiles, white teeth, tailored suits, and the best haircuts and manicures in the room. The reps spotted the three newcomers at the same time and made their way over through the press of doctors.

Bruce grinned and shook their hands. "We're from the medical school and we heard about the meeting. I'm Bruce, and this is Don, and Frances."

"Hello and welcome! I'm Mike, and this is Susan. We both got our graduate degrees from Florence College as well. Make yourselves at home," he said, as if he had expected them all along. "We're glad you're here."

Mike and Susan greeted each one of them with eye contact and a firm handshake, and their warm smiles were genuine. They gestured toward the cluster of doctors at the open bar and urged them to get a drink. Frances got a glass of chardonnay, Don and Bruce got beer, and they meandered over to the appetizer table and grazed on fried shrimp, fried crab claws, and fried cheese dipped in a sweet red sauce.

Don found himself standing next to a portly doctor with a red face and thinning hair. The man was gobbling down appetizers as if he might never see food again. Don introduced himself and tried to make small talk. "So, what do you think about this Lipitor stuff?" he asked.

"What's not to like?" the doctor replied between bites. "Just take a little Lipitor and you can eat all the steak and lobster you like!" He laughed heartily, exposing a mouthful of partially chewed food.

Susan glided to Don's other side on her tall heels. He glanced sideways, his eyes moving up her lissome legs past her tailored skirt and blouse to meet her cheerful blue eyes and pleasant smile.

"Did you know that Pfizer is developing a combination with both Norvasc and Lipitor in one pill?" she asked. "Since almost everyone with high blood pressure has high cholesterol too, lots of your patients will be able to use it. It will make things so much easier for doctors and patients."

Easier? Did a fancy brand-name drug make things easier for Sibyl Bellamy? How could doctors prescribe expensive brand-name drugs in good conscience when reliable, affordable, generic alternatives were available?

But Don didn't say any of this out loud. Instead he said, "Maybe so," and swallowed his remaining words with a big swig of beer.

When everyone started sitting down for dinner, Bruce told Frances and Don it was time to make a getaway. On their way out, Bruce stopped to apologize to the reps, saying they had studying to do and had to leave early.

Mike and Susan looked terribly disappointed, as if the students were abandoning their dearest old friends, but Susan brightened and explained they had ordered way too much food, and wouldn't the students please take some home with them?

Bruce politely declined, and they passed by the piles of take-out boxes on the hall table outside the banquet room. Only Frances looked back longingly at the platters of lobster and steak left behind.

"Now, follow me," Don said. He marched down the back hall toward the other banquet room, where he had noticed doctors entering earlier. The door was closed, but Don tilted his head to indicate they were going inside. He opened the door just enough to pass through and then led the way.

A lecture was in progress. In the dim light, Don could see several of the doctors in the room resting their eyes. In other words, sleeping. Two female drug reps in the back of the room looked at the trio curiously.

Exuding the easy confidence born of alcohol, Don walked over and whispered quietly to one of them. "We're doctors from Florence College. Someone told us about this meeting and said we should come."

One of the reps, a handsome redhead with a seamlessly smooth complexion, beamed at Don with recognition. She nodded her head in welcome and winked at her colleague. The three stood against the back wall and watched the remainder of the presentation.

"So, there you have it," the speaker concluded. "Nexium has proven efficacy in short-term healing of erosive esophagitis. Nexium has proven symptom control for people with severe gastroesophageal reflux disease. Safety and tolerability of Nexium are similar to Prilosec. Nexium is the latest advance in the powerful new class of antacid proton pump inhibitors. As you can see, Nexium is now the drug of choice for bad reflux disease. Now, are there any questions about Nexium?"

The audience was composed of gastroenterologists—doctors who spend their days inserting scopes up rectums and down throats. They asked the expected questions. Which patients benefit from Nexium? What is the pharmacologic mechanism of action? What about potential interactions with other drugs?

Not one of them asked the question that Frances whispered in Don's ear: "Isn't the esomeprazole in Nexium like totally identical in biochemical structure to the omeprazole they market as Prilosec? The one that's going generic later this year?"

"Exactly," Don whispered back, "it is a stereoisomer—a mirror image—of the exact same drug. Nexium acts on the same receptor and has the same biologic action. That tiny change in chemical structure does nothing to affect the way it works; it just buys AstraZeneca another seven years of patent time."

"So this whole conference is to market an old pill in a fancy new purple coating?

Don nodded. "Yes, and the fancy new pill will cost a lot more than the generic version of Prilosec."

"Amazing." Frances shook her head and made a little clucking sound.

None of the doctors asked about the difference between the two drugs. They suspected, but they didn't really want to know. It was better to go along and humor the nice rep. After all, the company had studies and FDA approval, so who were they to question? Besides, this was a nice party, and they were guests; it was not their place to bring up doubts. And they could always read up on it later...

The meeting began to break up. A waitress appeared with three glasses of red wine. Bruce took one, raised it, and nodded to the blonde drug rep. "To the purple pill!"

"To the purple pill," they all repeated.

Guests cruised the goody table on the way out. It was loaded with free stuff, all of it emblazoned with the company slogan: *Nexium, the purple pill.* "Wow, I love these purple polo shirts!" exclaimed one doctor. "And they're well made, too." He held one up to check the size.

"Oh, these shirts are way cool," Frances said.

"Look, but don't touch." Bruce commanded. "You can get plenty of that junk later, but we can't go to the other drug meetings carrying a bunch of loot. Now, bottoms up! We're on to the next drug party."

They polished off their wine as they moved toward the door, making their way through a herd of spirited doctors sporting purple hats, purple pens, purple mugs, and well-made purple polo shirts.

The next stop was George's, where Bristol-Myers Squibb was hosting a steak and beer bash for the diabetes doctors. A famous diabetes doctor from Harvard was speaking about Glucophage, the new diabetes drug. Bruce, Don, and Frances watched from the back. A number of residents and fellows were in attendance with their university mentors. The guests ate thick fudge cheesecake, sipped George's famous sweet brown ale on tap, and seemed too sedated by the free beer to take in much of what the speaker was saying. Bruce made sure Don and Frances tasted the beer as well, and once again, they finished their drinks on his command.

At Emmanuele's, another fancy French restaurant, they found a party for urologists. Bruce marched right in to talk it up with the urologic surgeons and drug reps inside the private dining room.

Frances and Don took a detour to the bar. Frances looked over her shoulder to make sure Bruce was out of earshot and asked for water, and Don followed her lead. As the bartender passed them tall glasses of ice water, Don noticed his ink-stained fingers. He wore a tuxedo shirt and black bowtie, horn-rimmed glasses, and long brown hair tucked behind his ears.

"You're in graduate school, aren't you?" Don asked.

The bartender nodded. "Sociology. A guy's got to find some way to pay the bills. So, why aren't you two celebrating tonight?"

Frances leaned over the bar, displaying her generous cleavage. "We're doing a little research project—sociology of a sort. We're trying to stay sober enough to finish collecting our primary data. Do you think you could help us?"

The bartender was eager to tell everything he knew. He said Emmanuele's typically had about eight drug company events a week, most of them marketing high-cost medications like cancer drugs. He showed off his collection of pens from the various companies. Each pen advertised the company's latest drug on the market: Sanofi-Aventis' Taxotere for breast cancer; Johnson & Johnson's Procrit for low blood count in kidney failure; Novartis' Sandimmune for suppressing the immune system in transplant patients; Pharmacia's Xalatan for glaucoma; Lilly's Gemzar for all kinds of cancer.

"Last night was the big oncology meeting," he whispered, tucking his hair behind his ears. "You should have been here then." He leaned forward and pulled a lovely blue pen from his pocket. "One of the docs was at the bar after the party and gave me this one. Camptosar. He said this drug is like gold. It costs about ten grand a year for folks with advanced colon cancer. It doubles survival time from one to two years, he said. Apparently, the cancer docs get a cut of the drug sale and a juicy administration fee. No wonder they want to go all out, even when people are eaten up with cancer. Those cancer docs are serious, man."

Bruce came to the bar wearing a big grin. The bartender went to the other end of the bar to fill an order for a waitress, and Don and Frances turned to hear what Bruce had found out.

"Let me tell you," Bruce said, "TAP pharmaceuticals is going all out with this Lupron stuff. They want a shot of it delivered to every guy with advanced prostate cancer in the country, so they are offering a cash upfront administration fee of two percent per patient to every urologist in the country that agrees to prescribe it. In addition, they get big-screen TVs and a whole bunch of other prizes for consulting. All the urologists in there are really excited. I thought I had stumbled into a shooting of *The Price is Right*."

"I think I'm going to be sick," Don said.

Bruce laughed, "No, not yet. We have some more places to explore. And you have to follow the protocol. No more cheating and drinking water. Tonight we have to get thoroughly drugged."

Frances stood up and teetered on her heels. "I think I already am," she said. "Hey, did you see that sign in the front? Let's go fix it." She took off for the front of the restaurant.

Don gave Bruce a palms-up, quizzical look. Bruce shrugged his shoulders in reply and they followed after Frances.

They found her rummaging around behind the hostess' podium. She emerged with a dry erase marker, and with a gleam in her eye, she sashayed over to a large whiteboard sign directing doctors to the TAP Pharmaceuticals meeting. She wiped the slate clean with the heel of her hand, drew an arrow, and wrote,

Hey Docs: Get Looped with Lupron!

She turned the sign so it could only be read by people entering the restaurant and bolted out the front door. Bruce and Don followed close behind, fighting to suppress the chortles that grew into howls of laughter once they were outside.

Bruce addressed a pimpled valet in khakis and a polo shirt. "Lieutenant, requisition us a chariot, or some other suitable transportation befitting our station."

The teenager looked at the three adults like they were crazy, but called a cab just the same. They piled into it and went to three more restaurants, following leads for pharmaceutical meetings as they went along.

Pfizer had a meeting for psychiatrists and pediatricians on the depression drug Zoloft at Angelina's Italian Bistro. GlaxoSmithKline featured antibiotic resistance and Augmentin at Kaspar's Fish House. Merck's meeting on coronary disease at The Butcher's Block Steak House touted three drugs: Zocor, Vioxx, and Cozaar.

Bruce continued to insist they take advantage of the free drinks everywhere they went. Don poured some of his into plants when Bruce wasn't looking and encouraged Frances to do the same, but by the time they got to the Merck event they were all sloshed. They were walking past the bar at The Butcher's Block when Bruce ran into a man he knew. Bruce looked flustered for a split second but quickly regained his composure.

"Hello, Mr. Pan," he said. "What in the world brings you here?"

"Well, if it isn't Bruce Markum!" A lean, graying man wearing an impeccably tailored suit greeted him with a big smile, showing off a perfect set of straight, white teeth. "I'm Frank Pan of BioLexa Pharmaceuticals," he said, turning to Don and Frances, "and more importantly, a friend of the family." He clapped a hand on Bruce's shoulder.

Don and Frances introduced themselves and shook hands.

"You all seem to be enjoying the evening," Mr. Pan commented. His eyes lingered on Frances's low neckline. "You're in good company, Bruce. I hope you're here to learn about our latest compounds."

"Actually, we just finished up a little research project for school and now we're out to relax a little."

"It would appear you are out to relax a lot." Mr. Pan grinned. "Our dinner is over now, but let me buy a round. What are you drinking?"

"Martinis," Bruce answered without hesitation.

Frances looked at Don behind Bruce's back and mouthed, "No way!"

"Bartender!" Mr. Pan called, "Four dry Bombay Sapphire martinis, up, one olive. Put it on my tab." He turned back to face Bruce.

"So, what brings you to Florence?" Bruce asked.

"Oh, you know, just checking in with our field reps. BioLexa is hosting a big alumni conference for the college in the spring, and I want to make sure everything is in place."

"What do you do for BioLexa?" Frances asked.

"Whatever they ask." Mr. Pan laughed and the three joined in. His good humor was contagious.

"Mr. Pan is president of consumer affairs for BioLexa," Bruce explained. Turning to Mr. Pan, he added, "We're honored to have you here in Florence."

"Oh, the honor is all mine, I assure you."

They sat at a table in the bar and Mr. Pan quizzed Bruce, Frances, and Don about the health system science program. The drinks arrived and he led them in the familiar doctors' toast: "To better living through chemistry."

"To better living through chemistry!" they all chimed in, lifting their chilled martini glasses high to clink together.

Don, who was feeling rather uninhibited by this time, asked Mr. Pan, "So, tell me about these talks companies like BioLexa give around the country—how much do you pay university doctors to speak?"

Mr. Pan feigned dismay at this forward question. "Well, Don, certainly we pay them what they're worth. It all depends on their expertise and position. Of course, our rates are competitive and we look for thought leaders who can influence their colleagues to adopt best practice."

"You mean...to use your drugs," Don blurted out.

"Don, don't be rude," Frances said. "Mr. Pan just bought us drinks."

"We believe our drugs are an important component of best practice," Mr. Pan replied. He continued to grin, but his eyes held a steely glint. "You must be considering a career in academic medicine yourself."

"You'll have to excuse Don here," Bruce laughed. "There's one in every crowd who can't hold his liquor."

Fuck you, Bruce. Don came close to saying the words out loud.

"Well, I must be off." Mr. Pan stood to leave. "Watch out for your friend," he said to Frances and Bruce, nodding his head in Don's direction. He walked out the door, leaving his full martini on the table.

"Wow, a president for BioLexa," Frances said. "And you know him, Bruce? Gosh, did you see his suit?"

"Hey, Don," Bruce said, "why didn't you keep your tongue in your mouth for a change?"

"You're one to talk. I'm the most sober one here."

"We'll see about that," Bruce laughed. "Okay crew, bottoms up!"

Bruce drained his glass, but Don and Frances took little sips and managed to leave their unfinished drinks on the table without Bruce taking notice this time.

They headed for The Local, a popular Florence College hangout and the only sports bar in town. Above the front door hung a lighted sign with plastic letters:

CELEBRATE HOMECOMING

FC HOCKEY ON NOW!

UPSTAIRS CLOSED FOR PRIVATE PARTY

WELCOME PHARMACIA

"Ooh, I have an idea!" Frances squealed. "Put me on your shoulders, Don!"

Before Don could protest, she had kicked off her heels, grabbed his arm, and climbed up on the wooden railing alongside the door. Don decided it was wiser to comply than argue while she teetered on the rail. Frances swung one leg and then the other over his shoulders. As she situated herself around his neck and squeezed his ears with her firm thighs, Don swayed from side to side on the porch, fighting to maintain his equilibrium under her shifting weight and the effects of the alcohol.

By this time, Bruce was laughing so hard he could barely stand.

"Quick, Don, get me over to the sign!" Frances begged.

Don inched to the left until he stood beneath the illuminated letter board.

"I can't reach it," she wailed.

"I'll fix that," said Bruce. He grabbed some wooden coke crates from the corner of the porch, stacked them two by two, and spanned the space with a wide board he found propped against the wall. "There, Don, stand on that."

Bruce pushed up on Frances's bottom while Don held his shoulder and stepped up on the board.

"Hurry up, before someone sees you!" said Bruce.

Frances clamped Don's ears harder and lunged for the letters, throwing him off balance and almost toppling them both off the precarious perch. "Oh my God! Grab my knees, my knees! Hold them up!" she screamed.

Bruce gave her rear another intimate push, but Frances was oblivious. Focused on reaching the top row of letters, she squirmed higher and higher up until, with a satisfied grunt, she was sitting right on top of Don's head.

Oh my god, I'm going back into the womb.

Frances was in a frenzy. She rearranged the letters and threw down unwanted characters, her whole body jiggling with laughter. "Oh shit, I need that N. Bruce, get me that N!"

Bruce rustled through the letters scattered on the ground around the porch. "I got it! I got the N!"

"Give it to me now, Bruce!"

"I thought you'd never ask, baby," Bruce quipped right back.

That was all it took to send all three of them into hysterics. Frances managed to communicate she was finished and ready to get down. Don stepped backwards off the plank, lost his balance, and they toppled over onto the porch. Don and Frances were laughing so hard they couldn't get up, and seeing that, Bruce fell to his knees and rolled on the ground alongside them, whooping and holding his side.

Don caught his breath and looked up through tear-blurred eyes at Frances's handiwork, written up there in lights for everyone to see. He read it aloud:

CELEBRATE!

ONLY PLEASURE

NO PAIN

GET HOSED AT PHARMA PARTY

That brought on another spell of uncontrollable laughter. For several minutes they sat there, watching the passing cars slow down to look at the sign and catching their breath between bouts of howling laughter. It took ten minutes before they finally recovered their composure, brushed themselves off, and went inside.

The Local was old and grungy. The long wooden bar sported tall, colorful beer taps, and there were big-screen TVs in every room. This was Don's kind of place; it reminded him of the neighborhood bar near his family's townhouse in Old Town Chicago. The bar was packed with fans watching a hockey game.

Bruce asked the hostess where to find the medical meeting. She pointed them toward the back stairs, where another sign proclaimed,

CELEBRATE THE GAME!
FLORENCE COLLEGE MEDICAL SCHOOL WELCOME!

At the top of the stairs, another cute and congenial drug rep, a tall blond dressed in Florence College black and white, welcomed them and gave them Pharmacia company trinkets: Celebrex pens, hats, and balloons.

"Game's on, and drinks are on the house!" an amiable redhead rep shouted over the crowd's hoots and hollers. "Florence just got ahead!"

Everyone in the place was riveted on the hockey game, so the three had no trouble finding an empty table away from the television screen. Frances and Don collapsed in the chairs. Bruce disappeared and returned a few minutes later with three pints of golden ale, sitting down a little too close to Frances, in Don's opinion.

Don had lost count of how many drinks they had consumed after so many restaurants and drug dinners, but Bruce still managed to carry on a coherent conversation. "You know," he said, "this no pain thing is catching on. The pain drugs are the most popular of all; there are millions of people living on them. We're a nation of addicts. Did you know that three hundred thousand pounds of legal narcotics are dispensed in this country every year?"

"Here's to better living through drugs," Don said, raising his glass.

"To no pain!" Frances added.

"No pain!" They clinked their glasses once again.

Bruce scooted his chair even closer to Frances and whispered something in her ear, eliciting a peal of giggles. Then he brushed a hand against the side of her breast while reaching for his beer.

At first, Don thought it was accidental, but when Bruce put his hand on her thigh, he decided it was not.

Frances responded by giggling and arching her back. That was even worse. Was she actually falling for it?

Bruce looked over at Don to make sure he had noticed.

Arrogant asshole. Bruce was showing off, seducing Frances right before his eyes. The nerve! Well, he would put a stop to it.

Don stood up. "It's time to go home. Come on, Frances."

"Oh, come on, Don," she said, "we're having such a time…a fun time, I mean." Frances glanced at Bruce.

"No, it's time to go," Don insisted.

Dejected, Frances acquiesced. "Okay," she said in a singsong voice. She stood up and stretched her arms over her head, showing her deep cleavage and tight belly to best advantage. "Anyway, I'm tired, Bruce, I caaan't go t'nother druggie party. I'm sorry. I'm like sup-er tip-sy."

"I'll walk you home," Don said. "It's not far from my place."

"Sure," Frances said.

"All right, you weenies. If you're leaving, then I'm leaving," said Bruce.

"No, that's really not necessary." Don said.

"Well, then," Bruce said, "If this is our last stop, then my last order is…bottoms up!"

Frances took her glass and poured it into Bruce's glass. Several ounces spilled over the rim onto the table. "Oops! Bottoms up for you, Bruce."

Don left his mostly full glass on the table. "Good night, Bruce," he said. "Sure you can get home all right?"

"Oh, yeah." Bruce looked around at all the fresh young medical students; at least half were female. "I'm sure I can find someone to take me home." He picked up the overflowing glass and moved into the crowd.

"See ya, Bruce!" Frances said a little sadly, pressing up against Don.

Don walked Frances back to her apartment. She held tightly to his arm and stumbled along, weaving on her spiked heels and leaning close against him at every step, Despite her drunkenness, Frances could tell Don was pissed off.

"Oh c'mon, Don. Loosen up! Why are you so serious? Like, you are sooo jealous."

"I can't believe you were playing along with Bruce's sleazy antics."

"We were just joking around. Having a little fun. You're silly to be sooo jealous. After all, you're the sole soul man bringing me home. Get it? S-O-L-E and S-O-U-L?"

At her apartment, Frances fumbled with the key but managed to open the door. In one fluid motion she grabbed Don's hand, pulled him inside, and slammed the door shut. She grabbed the back of his head and kissed him hard. Cleopatra appeared out of nowhere and began encircling Don's legs in a figure eight, rubbing her body against his ankles and purring loudly.

Fire rose in Don's loins and melted his anger away as Frances's tongue explored his. She ran her fingers through his tight, dark curls. He wrapped his left arm around her hips to pull her closer and inched his other hand up to her left breast. His thumb fingered her erect nipple through the flimsy cloth of her camisole and she moaned softly.

Through the fog of alcohol and lust, Don felt a vague but nagging awareness that something felt wrong. He continued to kiss Frances, but his hand moved into automatic doctor mode and began to execute a clinical breast exam. Her breast was too full, too hard. She had a hard mass, like his mother probably had. But why? She was young. It took him a moment to clear his head and figure it out. Of course. Implants. Her breasts were fake.

"Ooh, nice work. Who did your boobs?"

Frances twisted out of his arms, swung her right hand around, and slapped him hard across the face. Cleopatra scurried for cover underneath the couch. "How could you?" Frances cried. "You are a total bastard! Get out!"

Don's left ear rung and his face burned with the print of her hand. Before he knew what had happened, Frances had shoved him outside and slammed the door in his face.

Dammit! What was that about? Don found himself out in the cold, aching and frustrated, like someone had slipped him a reverse Viagra. He pounded on the door. "Frances, let me in! I didn't mean anything. I'm sorry, Frances."

Don peered into the entryway, hoping Frances would return. She was nowhere in sight. He knocked again. Cleopatra padded over and stretched up on her hind legs and pressed her paws against the lowest pane in the sidelight next to the door. The spotted Bengal cat met his gaze with its unflinching, light green eyes and stared at him with scorn.

Frances never answered and Don was getting cold. It occurred to him the neighbors might call the police. He gave up, stumbled down the steps, and headed down the dark sidewalk for his apartment.

The next morning, Don felt like hell. He had a pounding headache, churning stomach, and his dry tongue was stuck to the roof of his mouth, which harbored the bitter taste of an unripe persimmon. He wondered how Frances must be feeling.

Don glanced at the clock. He would have to scramble to pull himself together before biostatistics class. He stumbled into the kitchen to make some dark espresso and noticed the red light on the phone blinking. He pressed the message button.

"Hi, Dante, this is Sarah. Just checking in. You must be working too hard. Talk to you later."

Once again, Don felt embarrassed upon hearing Sarah's voice. It was ridiculous, of course—he knew she had no idea what he had been up to—but he felt he had been caught. *I would hate for her to see me now.*

Don didn't call Sarah back then or even later that weekend. In fact, he put her call completely out of his mind. Sarah wouldn't reach him for months.

THE NEXT WEEK they met in the projection room to give their report. Don arrived late and went straight to his seat. He avoided eye contact with Frances and prayed she had been too drunk to remember what had happened at the end of their barhopping spree.

"I'm looking forward to hearing the results of your research on pharmaceutical company marketing to physicians," Dr. Sampson said. "Who wants to go first?"

"Frances," Bruce said. "Actually, we all worked together, but she's the one that put the numbers together."

"The floor is yours, Frances."

"Okay, so here are my totals. In a typical week at the Florence College School of Medicine, pharmaceutical companies sponsor events to the tune of about twenty-nine thousand dollars. The department of medicine, including subspecialties, gets the most—around ten thousand when you add up lunches, conferences, speaker fees, gifts, and paraphernalia."

Frances's brilliant green eyes flickered Don's way but did not meet his; Don was keeping his eyes trained on the hollow at the base of her throat.

"Psychiatry gets about twenty-five hundred a week, neurology one thousand, family practice thirty-five hundred. Nursing came in at fifty-six hundred, but they had an unusual week with a highly paid speaker, so we estimated an average of two thousand. Pharmacy gets three thousand a week, but where they really make out is through drug company-funded research by their faculty and lucrative consulting gigs on nights and weekends. Pediatrics with its subspecialties receives four thousand a week. Surgery is three thousand. Of course, they are more into devices than drugs. That all adds up to almost thirty thousand a week. Assuming a few weeks off for holidays, a million and a half a year. We're an average-sized campus, and with 146 medical schools in the United States, that's 220 million dollars a year.

"Of course, these school events are just the tip of the iceberg. We have to add the teaching hospitals where doctors, nurses, and pharmacists get hands-on training. Florence has three teaching hospitals, two of which are affiliated with the medical school. There are about twelve hundred teaching hospitals in the country, and most run specialty training programs without a medical school affiliation. Based on our experience and conversations with colleagues, we estimated the roughly four hundred largest teaching hospitals have about two-thirds as much drug company-sponsored education as the medical schools, or about one million apiece a year. That's like four hundred million a year. We figured the eight hundred smaller teaching hospitals get a little less, about seven hundred fifty thousand a year each, or all together, about six hundred million a year. So the total for pharmaceutical-sponsored education on medical school and teaching hospital campuses comes to 1.2 billion a year!"

Over a billion a year! Don was astounded. He glanced over to gauge Dr. Sampson's reaction; he appeared unsurprised.

"Now for the fun part. Off-campus parties."

Don felt a little wave of panic, as if the ignoble details of their research outing were about to be revealed.

"In the ten Florence restaurants we visited Thursday night—the most popular night for pharmaceutical meetings—drug companies put on twelve so-called educational events. We estimated each dinner averages three thousand dollars, including honorariums for speakers, gifts, and consulting fees. Florence has about two hundred restaurants. We went to ten. We figured five others had big drug parties Thursday night, so fifteen parties at three thousand a pop comes to forty-five thousand dollars, just for Thursday night! There are half as many parties on the other weeknights, usually less fancy, so we estimated fifty thousand for those. Weekend events get more elaborate and often include travel and consulting fees for the docs that participate. We guessed there were about ten of these per weekend involving Florence doctors, pharmacists, and nurses, totaling about fifty thousand a week. Of course, we didn't include the salaries for reps and marketing teams, just the party costs."

Except for an occasional glance at Dr. Sampson, Frances's eyes stayed fixed on Bruce. *Dammit! Does she remember everything? Is she attracted to that pretentious son of a bitch?* Don was jealous.

"So that's almost a hundred and fifty thousand dollars a week, times forty-eight weeks a year, allowing for holidays. That's seven million a year just in Florence! With over four hundred practicing doctors here, that's fifteen thousand in gifts and entertainment per Florence physician per year. Remember, drug reps are swarming in every other city as well. There are roughly six hundred thousand practicing medical doctors in the United States, so at fifteen thousand per doctor, the total for off-campus pharmaceutical-sponsored education in the U.S. comes to…"

Bruce grinned at Don. "Drum roll, please!"

"…around nine billion dollars a year, bringing our grand total for on- and off-campus drug company education to over 10.2 billion bucks a year!"

In stark contrast to Bruce's glee at the announcement of the final tally, Dr. Sampson was somber. Don dreaded the dour summary he knew was coming.

"Very good analysis, Ms. Hunt," Dr. Sampson said. "Your figures are amazingly accurate. You have the instinct of a true businessperson and have seen straight to the source where money changes hands."

Frances was unable to hide her pleasure at his compliment. "Nothing an Excel spreadsheet and a few imbedded formulas couldn't handle," she replied.

"In the year 2000," he continued, "there were over three hundred thousand drug company-sponsored meetings at fancy restaurants and hotels and even more at medical schools, professional meetings, hospitals, and clinics. Doctors love these perks. Last year, they accepted about half the invitations they received, and they admit the cash honoraria make a big difference in the decision to attend."

"Including drug rep salaries, drug companies spent some fifteen billion dollars on marketing in 2000, eighty-five percent of it directed at physicians. That's close to twenty-five thousand per doctor. The amount spent on these enticements goes up exponentially every year. In fact, the drug companies spend much more money on 'educating' physicians and other health workers than do universities and state and federal governments all combined."

Don wished he could just take his share in cash instead of steak and purple T-shirts.

"Countless studies show drug company-sponsored education overstates drug benefits and minimizes risks and side effects. Of course it does; it's advertising! Doctors insist they are not swayed. Do you think this is true?"

"Yes!" Don blurted out, feeling compelled to defend his profession. "Most physicians are not sucked in by this stuff. Yeah, there are a few bad apples, but most aren't influenced by dinners and trinkets."

"Good grief, Don!" Bruce said. "Do you still not get it? Do you really think drug companies would spend billions of dollars to curry favor if it didn't work?"

"Bruce is totally right," Frances agreed.

Frances was looking directly at Don now. Was there a hint of hostility in her expression, or was he just paranoid?

"You read the article about antibiotics, didn't you, Don?" Bruce continued. "When doctors attend a nice dinner promoting an antibiotic, lots of them start prescribing it. They are so eager to try it, about half the time they use it for an infection for which it's not even recommended! Don't be naïve. The big spenders sell the most drugs."

They were right, of course. Don had read the article; he knew better. Why had he spouted off like that?

Dr. Sampson censured him further. "Research indicates Ms. Hunt and Dr. Markum are right. The industry hired seventy-five thousand drug reps in 2000 because they do influence doctors. The gang with the most pushers wins the territory. And here is something you may not know: the companies know exactly how much each doctor is influenced. Like most salesmen, drug reps receive big sales bonuses. Drug companies purchase electronic prescribing data from pharmacies to determine *who* prescribes *what* in a given geographic area. The reps can see the statistics for individual doctors, and they work hard to reward the doctors who prescribe their drugs."

Yes, Frances was glaring at Don! Her expression communicated her opinion: he did not have a clue. Out of the corner of his eye, Don could see Bruce looking back and forth from him to Frances, taking it all in and clearly enjoying himself. Don felt sick to his stomach.

"They design their enticements in just the right way to buy doctors' allegiance," Dr. Sampson continued. "Every physician is influenced. Perhaps most disturbing," Dr. Sampson looked at Don, "is that so few doctors realize how thoroughly they are manipulated. Conscientious doctors review the main scientific studies demonstrating the effectiveness of a new drug, often unaware that many of these studies are designed and paid for by a drug company.

"Furthermore, drug companies frequently pay for speakers at medical conferences and liberally subsidize the expenses of attendees. My academic colleagues who speak at these conferences ought to be guardians of the truth, but many of them—wittingly or not—promote biased research funded by drug companies. Even articles in prestigious medical journals are often ghostwritten by drug company editors who fill the articles with key advertising messages. Drug company marketing experts invent new diseases—like premenstrual dysphoric disorder—to justify new and expensive drug treatments, and the doctors who take credit for naming these new syndromes are praised and paid richly for it.

"Physicians believe the medical conference speakers and journal articles are unbiased. Some are. But much of the education and research trumpeted in these forums is nothing more than dressed-up commercials. Studies show that attending drug company-sponsored continuing medical education leads to worse prescribing practices. I ask you: should professional education make you worse at your job?"

"I guess it wouldn't be so bad if no one got hurt," said Frances," but according to the papers we read, these drug company events result in over-prescribing of the most expensive and least tested drugs. This ultimately results in the killing of innocent people."

"Wait a minute!" said Bruce, "don't you think the word 'killing' is a bit harsh? I mean, they overstate the numbers of people killed by new drugs for drama, don't you think?"

"Not a bit," Don jumped in, eager to reclaim his dignity. "Throughout the 1980s, one hundred thousand Americans were killed every year by heart rhythm drugs that did—as drug company studies showed—make electrocardiogram readings look better. Problem was, they also caused fatal heart rhythms that caused people to drop dead. Throughout the 1990s, doctors switched hypertensive patients from diuretics proven to save lives to newer medicines that equally lowered blood pressure but had not been proved to save lives. When the comparative studies finally came out, we discovered the old, inexpensive, time-tested ones were more effective at saving lives and preventing strokes. Yet, doctors still use the expensive new ones today."

"Perhaps 'killing' is *not* too strong a word for the thousands of accidental deaths caused by new and experimental drugs every year in America," Dr. Sampson said. "Now, before we break, let's look at direct marketing to consumers, a fairly new thing in America, at least for prescription drugs. Doctors used to think it was unseemly, even unethical. Direct-to-consumer prescription drug marketing is illegal in almost every other industrialized country in the world, but in America now it's the norm. Let's look at one or two commercials. Go have a seat in the amphitheater while I start the projector."

As soon as they sat down in the old wooden seats, the room went pitch black.

"Here we go," Dr. Sampson called out.

A glowing light held by gigantic hands appeared on a screen of dark purple. The hands, representing drug maker AstraZeneca, opened like the hands of God, and pills of healing golden light showered out into the purple world. Nexium contained the power of healing. The purple pill could restore life itself—or so the commercial implied.

Don was no longer impressed by the beautiful images. Had he wasted the last seven years of his life in medical school? He thought back to the hundreds of drug lunches and lectures he'd attended, believing he was getting good information. Messages coupled with pleasant scenes and delicious little rewards, repeated again and again until you believed them. Propaganda.

But what could he do now? He was chained by debt to this damn pill-pushing business. The die had been cast when he entered the high-prestige, low-pay residency at the University Hospital. With his debt load, there was no way out but forward. Of course, he knew a couple of doctors who had quit. One of them had gone to work for a drug company. There was always that.

The scene changed to sunlit fields of multicolored flowers under skies of bright blue. It looked like paradise, a land of plenty with great meadows, natural and productive only of beauty.

Dr. Sampson called out, "This commercial helped turn Claritin into a gold mine, producing over two billion dollars a year in profits."

The bucolic scene was interrupted for a second by a terrible sneeze, but soothing music restored the abundant, natural life now possible with Claritin.

"Last of all, look at this one." Dr. Sampson flashed up an antique magazine ad for Coca-Cola. It promised to cure exhaustion, ease the tired brain, and soothe rattled nerves. "Coca-Cola was one of the most popular cocaine liquors. It was available in bottles and at pharmacy soda fountains throughout the country up until Prohibition.

Dr. Sampson flicked the lights back on as the commercial ended, and this time Don found the blinding fluorescent glare came as a relief.

"Let's talk about Nexium first," Dr. Sampson said. "It came out in the United States this year with an unprecedented blaze of direct-to-consumer advertising. In fact, the advertising budget for Nexium this year is greater than that of Budweiser or CocaCola. Like Claritin, Nexium is mostly advertised during commercial breaks during the evening news—some of the most expensive ad time there is—because that's when middle-aged and older people are most likely to be watching. It is expected to do over five hundred million in sales this year and well over a billion by next year. So, it must offer unprecedented health benefits, right, Dr. Newman?"

Don could hardly wait to release the bile burning his throat. "This one I know well. Nexium is a 'me-too' drug and has got to be one of the biggest drug scams ever. AstraZeneca took their hugely profitable drug, Prilosec—which was making some five billion a year but about to go off patent—and made a stereoisomer of the compound to create their 'Nex' antacid. The new compound is formulated as a mirror image—different enough to get AstraZeneca a new patent, but for all practical purposes, Nexium is functionally identical to the old Prilosec. It works exactly the same way, has the same action on the same acid-producing receptor in the stomach, and it's even the same strength. The only real difference is packaging and cost. The purple pill really seems to catch people's imaginations; they come to clinic begging for it and swearing it works better than their old Prilosec.

"Of course, they were really cagy about how they staged the research studies and marketed the purple pill. Their studies compared a double dose of the new compound to a single dose of the old version. They claimed Nexium was better and stronger and won FDA approval. It's ridiculous! Elderly people with little extra income to spend were completely suckered in. Instead of paying forty dollars a month for the old version that had gone generic, they pay a hundred or more a month for the latest and greatest NEX thing. Of course, they might do fine with a simple antacid, or less caffeine, or avoiding eating too much or too late. But who will tell them that? There's no money in it!"

Bruce laughed. "Hey, Don, why don't you tell us how you really feel?"

"Let's move on to Claritin, said Dr. Sampson. "As you know, Claritin is basically an antihistamine, marketed and sold at high price for its single amazing property."

"No sedation," Bruce chimed in.

"Right," Sampson responded, "It doesn't usually make you sleepy. And given that Americans spent over two and a half billion dollars on it last year, it must be extraordinarily effective, right?"

Frances ventured, "One would think so."

"Yes, one would think so," Dr. Sampson agreed, "but Claritin is only about ten percent better than placebo. Placebo pills improve allergy symptoms by about thirty percent on average; Claritin improves allergy symptoms by about forty percent. That means only about one in ten people get real relief from Claritin. The other nine might as well take a sugar pill. The FDA suggested they quadruple the dose to forty milligrams instead of ten milligrams, since the drug is much more effective at the higher dose. But at the higher dose it would be sedating, just like all the older antihistamines. So instead, Pfizer invested a few hundred million on a marketing blitz and convinced millions of patients and doctors they couldn't live without Claritin."

How many hundreds of times had Don prescribed Claritin to an allergy sufferer? Was it because his patients had asked for it by name? Or had he been hoodwinked by clever marketing? A deep discomfort and revulsion came over him, like his nausea the morning after the drug party binge.

Frances summarized, "So you are saying the most profitable drug company used to be the one with the best drug, but now it is the company with the best marketing."

"Exactly!" Dr. Sampson replied. "Furthermore, drug companies have little federal oversight. They can make almost any claims they want; many claims on television are false. There is essentially no enforcement of the FDA requirements for drug advertisers to tell the truth. They reap huge rewards through slick commercials. The more exaggerated the claims, the greater the profits.

We are the only industrialized country, other than New Zealand, where direct-to-consumer drug ads are legal. Since drug ads became legal in 1996, drug use, drug prices, and drug company profits have soared. Most of the world still uses the old-fashioned approach of trusting doctors to diagnose and prescribe medications."

"Wait a minute," Bruce said, "aren't most of the problems you're describing a consequence of the short patent time on new drugs? Everybody knows costly drug research frequently doesn't pay off, because the patents run out before the company recoups the investment. A strong pharmaceutical industry is critical for the American economy, so maybe selling a little harmless Claritin isn't all that bad."

"Well," Dr. Sampson said, "that was Schering-Plough's argument when they lobbied Congress to create a patent review board to consider extending their drug patent on Claritin. But just in case the lobbying strategy didn't pay off, Schering-Plough pulled a NEX-ium and prepared the newly patented clari-NEX for release. Clari-NEX was in essence just Claritin in the active form it takes once it is digested and absorbed by the body, but since it was technically a new drug, they got a completely new patent.

"By the way, Schering-Plough gave a million dollars to Surgeon General C. Everett Koop's foundation around the time Dr. Koop gave his support to their patent extension proposal. Senator John Ashcroft got fifty thousand dollars and Senator Orrin Hatch got over three times that in drug company money about the time they announced their support. But let's be clear: support for patent extension was a bipartisan affair. Democratic Senator Robert Torricelli accepted a fifty thousand dollar Senate campaign contribution from Schering-Plough the day before he introduced a patent extension bill."

"Dr. Sampson," Bruce interrupted, "I'm sorry, but isn't this beside the point? All these donations are just business as usual. All they show is the drug industry wanted the patent extension badly. That doesn't mean that they shouldn't be allowed to extend their patents in creative ways to protect their legitimate business interests. Pharmaceutical development is risky business. The drug companies should at least have fair opportunity to profit from some of the drugs they spend years working on."

"Good points, Dr. Markum," Sampson said. "Please don't get me wrong. The pharmaceutical industry has brought Americans many life saving medications and vaccines. Many pharmaceutical company scientists contribute excellent research that enhances our entire approach to treating common diseases. Of course pharmaceutical companies should have *fair opportunity.* But right now many experts think they have greater opportunity than any other major industry in America.

"Let's look at the facts. Is developing new drugs economically risky in today's economy? Drug industry profits have averaged close to twenty percent each year over the last decade. That's about three times the profits of all other Fortune 500 companies. Does that sound to you like a high-risk industry where the profit margin is so narrow it forces companies out of business? The patent time on drugs is twenty years, and drug companies get special tax protections allowing them to pay less in taxes than any other major industry."

"And look who funds most drug company research," Don added. "Let me tell you, it's not the drug companies. The National Institutes of Health pays for the vast majority of drug research with our tax dollars, even though almost all the patents based on that research go to the drug companies. Where else does the federal government spend billions building the product lines of a few for-profit firms? Profits are almost guaranteed by the government, whether a product is effective or not."

Bruce chuckled and said, "Well, I guess they do have it pretty good."

Dr. Sampson began to put away his papers. "I hope you have begun to see how the drug salesmen operate. This is why many people see a Medicare drug benefit as extremely risky for the health of the American people and our economy. A ridiculous idea is running through Congress of an expansive, federally funded pharmaceutical benefit for the elderly. In reality, it is a thinly veiled welfare benefit for the drug companies. Given the way drug salesmen are allowed to operate, do you think this would improve health? God help us if a Medicare drug benefit passes. Then the evening news will really be ablaze with drug commercials."

FRANCES WAITED until Bruce and Dr. Sampson had left. She gave Don a bashful smile. "Hey Don...ummm...I've been a little worried about the other night. I remember the purple pill party at the Crab Shack and all those purple shirts, and the Butcher's Block and meeting that vice president from BioLexa. But what happened after we left there? I can't remember much of anything after that. Like, I didn't do anything stupid, did I?"

"We went to The Local. That was our last stop. Remember how you changed the sign out front?"

"Oh, yeah," she replied.

Don wasn't sure she remembered because she didn't laugh. "But you brought me home after that, didn't you? We, uh, we didn't...?"

Don shook his head.

She looked relieved at first, and then angry. She clearly had just recalled something more. "Good!" she spat.

Before he could say another word she stomped out, her skirt bouncing side to side in time with her furious steps.

19

Procedures for Profit

Ah, Simon Magus, and you his wretched followers, who, rapacious,
prostitute for gold and silver, the things of God which should be
the brides of righteousness.

DANTE ALIGHIERI, INFERNO 19, 1–4

THE WEATHER WAS TOO COLD all week to run outside, and Don only
made it to the gym once to lift weights. He dialed Frances several times to apologize, but her cellphone always went straight to voicemail. She didn't show at
their library hideout, either.

On Friday Don got a sandwich at the Down Under, hoping to catch her
there. Frances was nowhere in sight, but Bruce was sitting at his usual table, surrounded by piles of books and papers.

Don walked over and made an attempt at pleasant banter.

"Hey, Bruce, are you ready for another drug trip tonight? Shall we try a
repeat performance?"

Bruce was distracted. "Oh, um, yeah, sure Don, one of these days."

Don leaned over to look at the title of the book Bruce was reading: *The
Lobotomist*. "What the heck are you reading that for?"

Bruce glanced at his watch, slammed the book shut, and began to gather
his things. "Oh, you know, the Sampson seminar. Somehow the old man has got
me a little edgy," he said. "It's my turn to present and the topic is 'Procedures for
Profit.' Hell, I'm a surgeon. You know how he reamed me last time I presented.
Anyway, I'm meeting with him a second time to pick his brain about the case
I'm working on. Gotta go." He bolted and disappeared in a flash up the worn
brick stairs.

Don didn't see him or Frances again until the next seminar.

Bruce was waiting in the projection room when Don arrived. He appeared
composed, relaxed, and attentive, and he smiled as Don walked in and sat to his
left. Frances, on the other hand, barely acknowledged Don when she came in.
She sat down across the table and busied herself with her books and papers.

Well, at least now I know she's alive.

Bruce looked from Frances to Don, winked at Don and said, "So, do you
two want to hear a joke?"

"Sure," Don nodded.

Frances raised her eyebrows and looked over at Bruce.

He smiled. "You'll like this one, Frances. Okay, so there was this extremely rich dirty old man, and he was judging the Miss Universe contest. At the end he went up to the winner, who—of course—was a blonde bombshell like Frances."

Bruce flashed Frances a charming smile, which she returned.

"After congratulating her and introducing himself, the old billionaire told her, 'I want to make you an offer. I'll give you three million dollars, and in return all I ask is for you to spend one night with me in the bedroom of my mansion.' Miss Universe blushed, smiled, and agreed to his offer, and he replied, 'Then how about doing it for seventy-five dollars?' She immediately slapped him across the face. 'What do you think I am?' And he said, 'Oh, we've already determined that. I just want to find out your best price.'"

They all laughed.

"Remember, Don, everyone is driven by profit. The only difference between people is their price." Bruce turned to Frances and winked. "Right Frances?"

She laughed again. "Sure, Bruce."

Dr. Sampson arrived, threw his black military parka on a chair in the corner, and sat down opposite Bruce. His tie was loosened and the lines that marked his forehead seemed softer than usual. He gingerly pulled out a small, artichoke-green, cloth-bound book from his briefcase and placed it on the table. Don couldn't read the faded gold lettering on its broken binding but recognized the book as a Loeb Classic, like those he had studied in college. Loeb Classics featured the original Greek and the English translation on facing pages.

"From time immemorial," Dr. Sampson's rich, resonant voice rang out, "healers have had deep connections to the spirit world, and people have considered them holy men and women. In ancient Greek, Christian, Eastern, and Native American traditions, healers were saviors and sources of providence.

"A thousand years before Christ, the Greeks revered the physician-hero and demigod Asklepios above all other ancient healers. Rich and poor alike came to his temples to seek healing. The worship of Asklepios spread throughout the civilized world and continued until the Roman Empire became officially Christian. Asklepios was so similar to Jesus he remained a competitor for the loyalty of the sick and suffering almost until the Middle Ages. Asklepios' staff with the winding serpent is still used today to symbolize the mysterious healing powers of physicians. Healers, like all humans, face temptations that sometimes lead them astray, and this was said to have happened with the mythical Asklepios."

Dr. Sampson opened the old book and gently turned the crinkling, near-translucent pages to a leaf he had marked. He surveyed the pages before him as if viewing a sacred relic. The musty smell of ancient libraries emanated from its pages.

"Around 350 B.C., the poet Pindar told how Asklepios was led astray by one of the greatest temptations healers face:

> And those whosoever came suffering from the sores of nature, or with their limbs wounded either by gray bronze or by far-hurled stone, or with bodies wasting away with summer's heat or winter's cold, he loosed and delivered divers of them from divers pains, tending some of them with kindly incantations, giving to others a soothing potion, or, haply, swathing their limbs with simples, or restoring others by the knife.
>
> But alas! even the lore of leechcraft is enthralled by the love of gain; even he was seduced, by a splendid fee of gold displayed upon the palm, to bring back from death one who was already its lawful prey.

"Greed is a very old temptation for physicians. In ancient times, the gods did not look kindly on physicians selling their skills for profit."

Dr. Sampson wore the hint of an inward smile as he looked to Bruce. "Now Dr. Markum will tell us how and where surgeons have faced this temptation in modern times. Dr. Markum?"

Bruce leaned forward, more engaged than Don had ever seen him in seminar. He nodded to Dr. Sampson.

"Thank you, Dr. Sampson," Bruce began. "Hippocrates said, *He who wishes to be a surgeon should go to war.* In ancient times, a surgeon was thought to be worth many men because of his ability to repair the wounds of war. The famous physician and surgeon Galen, whose textbooks on medical science and anatomy were considered the prime authority from the time of Imperial Rome up through the nineteenth century, learned his surgical skills in wartime.

"People didn't go to the Asklepeions just for illnesses; they went for surgery. Galen claimed he was healed at an Asklepieon by a surgeon-priest who drained his abscess while he slept. In those days, surgery was very risky and horribly painful, so people would only undergo it as a last resort. Before the broad acceptance of antiseptic technique in the twentieth century, surgical infections were common and often fatal. Surgical death rates were fifty percent or more all the way up until the last century, mainly due to infection.

"Three major innovations in the nineteenth and twentieth centuries put surgery far ahead of medicine." Bruce paused, regaining his usual cockiness with a sidewise glance of superiority in Don's direction. "Morphine, antiseptic technique, and ether. With ether, anatomical theaters like ours here at Florence College became surgical theaters. Living people were cut open by famous professors eager to show off their latest surgical techniques. Right, Dr. Sampson?"

Dr. Sampson smiled.

"I'm sure you've been to the Ether Dome in Boston, haven't you, Don?"

Don nodded. Dr. Desmond had lectured all the new interns there in the first week of residency. He'd stood on the very spot where famous Boston medical men, using ether for anesthesia, had performed what Bostonians claimed was the first painless surgery in America (why admit an innovative Georgia surgeon had already been using ether for over four years? Everything happened first in Boston). The pure white marble statue of Apollo stood behind Desmond, staring out at the eager University Hospital interns crammed into the Ether Dome's narrow seats. Back then he'd believed everything Dr. Desmond said.

"In the twentieth century," Bruce continued, "great surgeons arose in many fields. I want to tell the story of one who almost received a Nobel Prize for his contributions to the field of psychosurgery: Walter Freeman.

"Walter Freeman was not a popular boy. He was a nerd who never had close friends and didn't feel close to his parents. A real loner. His mother called him *the cat that walks by himself*. She complained he was aloof and distant from everyone around him, including her.

"The only person Freeman admired was his grandfather, W.W. Keen, a famous neurosurgeon who was among the first to embrace the antiseptic techniques of the British surgeon Joseph Lister. Listerine is named for him. Anyway, Keen became one of the most prominent surgeons in America, and Walter wanted that kind of fame for himself.

"Walter entered Yale in 1912 at the age of sixteen. He wasn't invited to join a fraternity. He never had a girlfriend. He failed to make it on the wrestling squad or the swim team and was kicked off the school newspaper shortly after joining its staff when he spilled the entire alphabetized file of subscribers. Freeman was a complete social outcast but was desperate for attention.

"In medical school he discovered he had a talent for solitary work in the lab. He immersed himself in neuroanatomy and neuropathology and decided to become a neurologist. As an intern he neglected his living patients in order to perform more autopsies and brain dissections in the lab. His first medical job was as an assistant pathologist dissecting the dead. Giving scientific presentations on the diseased brain gave him the attention he craved.

"Freeman's grandfather helped him get a job as the senior medical officer in charge of laboratories at St. Elizabeth's Government Hospital for the Insane in Washington, D.C. That set the course for the rest of his life. Freeman arrived at St. Elizabeth's in 1924, near the end of the period between 1900 and 1930 when American mental institutions grew by leaps and bounds. St. Elizabeth's housed almost five thousand hopeless cases. There was nothing doctors of the time could do for them, and that was just fine with Dr. Freeman.

"He went to work applying his knowledge of anatomy and diseases of the brain. The lab at St. Elizabeth's started doing more autopsies of the brain than ever before, and students from Georgetown began attending. When Dr.

Freeman was asked to lecture at George Washington University, he cultivated his appearance to command attention. His trimmed goatee, round wire-rimmed glasses, cane, and authoritative air were soon well known on campus.

"Students loved it when Freeman brought real patients and dissected brains to class, so he invited second-year medical students to observe his Saturday autopsies at the asylum. He enjoyed holding up bloody, freshly harvested organs for all to see. One of his favorite tricks was to sketch a coronal section of the two halves of the brain on the blackboard with both hands at the same time. This practiced routine always generated applause. His career as a showman had begun.

"To win the respect of the scientific world, however, he needed to come up with a plan to advance science. Besides, he had grown tired of the untidiness and vacant stares of the insane at St. Elizabeth's. Vast masses of mentally ill were warehoused in huge asylums all across the country. Dr. Freeman wondered if these sad souls with no hope of cure might provide his opportunity for innovation. He moved full-time to George Washington University to look for his chance.

"In 1935 he met the Portuguese neurologist, Egas Moniz, and was among the first Americans to take note of Moniz's new brain surgery: cutting cores in the frontal lobes to cure mental illness. Freeman was fascinated. The simple psychosurgery severed the connections between the centers of higher thought and emotion in the brain. Moniz thought it would cure crippling anxiety and depression and bring an insane patient back into productive life.

"Well, no one was better prepared to introduce psychosurgery in America than Freeman. He saw his chance for fame and began at once to perfect the procedure. He renamed it *lobotomy* and found a neurosurgeon partner named James Watts. Freeman wasn't a surgeon but often acted as lead surgeon in the operating room with Watts. They did their first lobotomy on a housewife in 1936.

"The newspapers dubbed it *Surgery of the Soul*. The early procedures of Freeman and Watts mostly confirmed this impression; their surgery radically changed personalities and seemed particularly effective for people with disabling depression and anxiety. In those early days, Freeman helped people for whom there were no other options. Difficult schizophrenics became calmer and easier to control. Patients who had been incapacitated by grief and anxiety for years returned to normal life in the community.

"By 1940, the pair had completed some eighty lobotomies in the operating room. Of these, a third showed real improvement, a third stayed about the same, but a third got worse, suffering apathy, confusion, paralysis, urinary incontinence, or seizures. About two percent died—usually from immediate complications like brain hemorrhage or seizures that couldn't be stopped—but many families of patients with severe mental illness thought a chance of improvement was worth the risk.

"Eventually, Freeman's big ego got him into trouble. He craved the attention his new procedure brought him and became more and more willing to do it for those for whom the possible benefits did not outweigh the substantial risks. This led to some pretty spectacular failures. The failures were generally hidden away from public view. Like Rosemary Kennedy.

"In 1941, Joseph Kennedy sought Freeman out to help with his rebellious twenty-three-year-old daughter. Rosemary was quiet and beautiful as a child. She was considered mentally slower than her eight siblings. She was headstrong, and when she entered puberty she became impulsive, moody, and volatile. Her father sent her to a convent school in Washington, D.C., where she threw temper tantrums and snuck out at night to meet men. Kennedy had heard about lobotomy as a possible cure for Rosemary's mood swings and uncontrollable behavior. A Boston physician had refused to recommend the procedure, but Freeman and Watts diagnosed Rosemary with agitated depression and agreed to operate.

"Freeman questioned Rosemary while Watts cut into her brain until she became incoherent. The surgery had tragic consequences. For months, Rosemary was unable to walk, and she never regained the ability to speak a full sentence. She has spent her entire adult life hidden away in a rest home wearing diapers, staring at a wall for hours, and babbling unintelligibly.

"In spite of failed cases like this, Walter Freeman continued to promote and perform lobotomies. Some fifty thousand lobotomies were done between 1935 and 1960, and Freeman was the prophet who popularized them. During the early 1940s, as war occupied the world, Freeman developed a simpler procedure that could be done in a doctor's office. He would sever the critical connections in the brain by tapping an ice pick through the soft bone of the orbit of the eye while the patient was awake. Freeman did the first transorbital lobotomy in his office in 1946, and from that point on, he was the leading practitioner and advocate of what became known as the *ice pick* or *jiffy* lobotomy.

"The technique had spread across America by 1949. Freeman traveled coast to coast every summer, visiting the biggest insane asylums of America and lecturing doctors on its benefits. At the end of each lecture, he demonstrated his jiffy lobotomy technique on preselected patients right there in the auditorium. In 1952, Freeman did two hundred twenty-eight lobotomies in a two-week period in West Virginia asylums, operating on twenty-five women in a single day. Ever the showoff, he liked to perform two-handed lobotomies, hammering ice picks into the spaces above both of a patient's eyes at once.

"Dr. Freeman would never get rich doing psychosurgeries, but he was gaining the fame he so desperately wanted. As his career moved forward, he was increasingly eager for a bigger reward. Freeman nominated his mentor Dr. Moniz for the Nobel Prize, and when Moniz won it in 1949, Freeman was devastated not to be asked to share in the prize.

"He felt powerful when his advice was sought and when his ice pick broke through the bone. But in his lust for prestige and power he became an advocate for the procedure instead of the patient. He lost his ability to discern whether the procedure would be appropriate for a particular patient. He even did lobotomies for things like headaches and postpartum depression.

"Neurosurgeons were outraged. He wasn't even a surgeon and here he was going all over the country gouging people's brains with an ice pick. James Watts left him around 1950, and the hospital where Freeman practiced refused him access to the operating room once they realized he was performing his ice pick procedures alone, without a surgeon present, and without anesthesia or even a sterile field. Freeman had no patience for these details. He was carving up brains with an ice pick without even being able to see what he was doing. It was insane."

"Now Dr. Markum," Dr. Sampson said, "as you know, neurosurgeons in gloves and gowns did the same operation in expensive operating rooms all across the country and charged more than five times as much as Freeman. They condemned him for his unsophisticated approach, but their outcomes were no better."

"That's true," Bruce admitted. "In fact, the neurosurgeons typically had worse outcomes. Their patients had more seizures, paralysis, incontinence, and deaths, because they removed more of the brain. Since their procedure required opening the skull in the operating room, they also had more infections.

"At least the surgeons recognized their surgery was experimental, and at least they did it in operating rooms, where they could control the situation if things went wrong. Freeman did lobotomies in his office without any surgical backup. Even the Nuremberg code that came out right after the war—at the same time Freeman was experimenting—prohibited experimental surgery without full consent and full surgical backup. Freeman flouted all of that. The consents he obtained from the mental hospitals were superficial. And he encouraged asylum psychiatrists to do his procedure on their own. I think he wanted to be recognized as the one who emptied the asylums, and wanted it so badly he ignored the promising drug therapies for schizophrenia and depression coming out at the time.

"When Thorazine was introduced in 1954, Freeman's world began to fall apart. Thorazine was the first highly effective drug for psychotic patients. Doctors began to accept the new antipsychotic drugs and electroshock treatments for depression as better therapies.

"Before long, his beloved procedure was deemed obsolete, and people began questioning the ethics of operating on normal brain tissue with an ice pick. But Walter Freeman refused to let go. He failed to see or believe in the change. He moved to Santa Clara, California, and pressed ahead with his ice pick lobotomies in a new private office.

"This is where the story really gets interesting. I decided to investigate how far Dr. Freeman went astray at the end of his career. I tried to track down some of the people who worked at Agnews State Hospital, the large mental hospital in Santa Clara. I figured they could help me learn the fate of some of Dr. Freeman's patients there, and after a bit of sleuthing, I found a man who had been at the hospital and knew about Dr. Freeman's work firsthand. He made me promise not to reveal his name, but let's just say he was very credible. Here's the story he told me about one of the patients at Agnews in the late 1960s. I'll call the patient Johnny Doe.

"When Johnny was a boy, he loved to climb trees and play baseball, and he hated to wash up, take baths, or clean his room. His mother died when he was very young. Though he missed her terribly, his early childhood was otherwise normal. Living alone with his father fostered an independent spirit in the boy. But then his father remarried, and the boy was convinced his new stepmother hated him. No matter how he tried to please her, she was never satisfied, and she took him to doctor after doctor to see if they could fix her energetic stepson. After several doctors determined Johnny was just a normal twelve-year-old boy she took him to Dr. Freeman in 1960. This time she was prepared, having learned some of the psychiatric lingo and buzz words guaranteed to get the doctor's attention.

"The stepmother could barely contain her excitement. She had heard how the wonderful Dr. Freeman could change an unhealthy personality, and she made her case carefully. She showed Dr. Freeman detailed records of all Johnny's abuses, disruptive behavior, and emotional problems. She told Dr. Freeman he was her only hope. After two more office visits and a brief discussion between Dr. Freeman and the sheepish father, Freeman agreed that little Johnny manifested the exact sort of personality disturbances that early surgery could cure for life. He assured the parents it was as easy as getting a tooth pulled. He advised them to tell their son nothing, as it would only upset him.

"According to Dr. Freeman's own written description, here is what he did to little Johnny. He placed electroshock pads on Johnny's temples, while reassuring the frightened young boy. He administered the shock and watched Johnny's entire body stiffen and convulse. To keep the patient 'adaptable' and sedated, he gave a second convulsive dose of electricity about one to two minutes after the first convulsion had subsided. In the post-convulsive phase of electro-shock, while the boy was still dazed, he proceeded with the lobotomy.

"He placed a towel over little Johnny's nose and mouth to prevent contamination by saliva and nasal secretions. He pinched Johnny's upper eyelid between thumb and finger, bringing it away from the eyeball. He picked up his transorbital leucotome. Here's how Freeman described this tool: *a steel shaft twelve centimeters long and four millimeters in diameter, tapering for the last six centimeters to a rather fine point with a slight bevel. Its handle was seven centimeters long and eight millimeters in diameter, and…the shaft is graduated in centimeters, a double line being marked at seven centimeters, which is the most frequently used point.* This fancy 'leucotome' was the ice pick.

"Freeman introduced the point of the ice pick into the conjunctival sac in the corner of the eye. He moved it around against the roof of the orbit until it reached the soft bone at the top of the orbital vault. Bringing the ice pick parallel to the bony ridge of Johnny's nose, he tapped the base of the ice pick lightly with a hammer to drive it through the thin bone of the orbital plate. When it reached a depth of four centimeters, he pushed the handle of the ice pick laterally as far as the margins of the orbit permitted in order *to sever the fi bres in the lower portion of the thalamofrontal radiation.* He pulled the ice pick back to a midline position and gently drove it to a depth of seven centimeters, carefully keeping it in the plane of the bony ridge to avoid lacerating arteries in the fissures of the medial or the lateral frontal lobes.

"At this point, Dr. Freeman paused to take pictures from the lateral and medial views to show his ice pick was exactly in the right place—that is, jammed through Johnny's eye into the seat of his soul. Then he made expert sweeps of fifteen to twenty degrees laterally and medially with the probe, turning the handle of the ice pick in tight circles like an egg mixer to scramble the neural connections in the frontal lobes of Johnny's brain. Finally, he rapidly withdrew the ice pick and had his nurse apply moderate pressure over the eyelid for several minutes to prevent excessive bleeding into the orbit. While his nurse held pressure, he tapped a second ice pick into the other side of Johnny's brain and scrambled it in the same manner."

Bruce finished his cold anatomical description and looked around to observe the effect it had had on his listeners. Don was used to gruesome descriptions from medical school, but Frances was not. Her eyes brimmed with tears. It disgusted Don the way Bruce seemed to enjoy manipulating her emotions.

"In fifteen minutes it was all over," Bruce continued. "Except for two black eyes, Johnny looked pretty much like a normal boy with a crew cut asleep on the operating table. But he would never be the same. Johnny no longer defied his stepmother. He felt confused and empty, like he had woken up from an unpleasant dream he couldn't remember. He knew something was missing, but he wasn't sure what. It was as if everything he loved had slipped away during his sleep. He couldn't play baseball, calculate batting averages for his favorite players on the San Francisco Giants, or read comic books.

"When Johnny found out two weeks later what had happened to him, he felt betrayed and violated. How could his father let them shove needles into his brain? Depressed and suicidal, he bounced from one mental institution to the next, spending most of his life at Agnews State Hospital and various schools for the developmentally challenged. He struggled with depression, hopelessness, and anxiety for much of his life.

"Freeman performed his last lobotomy in 1967 on Helen Mortensen, a woman who'd had two lobotomies before. She died of a brain hemorrhage as a result of the operation, and he was finally banned from operating at his California hospital. He spent the rest of his career following up on his old patients and trying to document all the good he had done.

"The story of Walter Freeman illustrates two things. First, not all people are driven by money. There are many kinds of profit, and everyone has their price. Few prizes are more tempting, especially for teachers"—Bruce glanced over at Dr. Sampson—"than the fame and adulation of others. Second, we humans like to think we are better than other animals, and we are proud of our tools. While Freeman was doing ice pick lobotomies in the 1950s, surgeons were doing routine tonsillectomies and radiologists were zapping nearly every child they saw with swollen tonsils. Whenever humans master a new tool they want to try it on everything. And those who are most adept convince themselves their tool is good for everything, particularly when they are paid well for using it."

Don interrupted. "Bruce, everything you talked about is ancient history."

"Oh, no it's not," Frances argued. "We've just substituted modern torture methods for the old ones. For instance, electroconvulsive therapy is still used today. It's not easy to find out how often ECT is done in the United States because the government doesn't want to bring attention to the fact it's still done and they pay for it, but about one hundred thousand people get shocked every year. ECT wouldn't have gone anywhere if it weren't profitable for psychiatrists. It surged when Medicare started paying for it in the '60s at a thousand bucks a pop. Shock treatment works for some people when all else has failed, but there are huge variations in rates. In some areas of the country it's never done, and in other places psychiatrists use it a lot."

"That's my point," Don said. "We need to be talking about the doctors doing procedures for profit today. As long as psychiatrists have a major financial incentive to use shock treatment, we have to be concerned about the temptation to convince or coerce people to do it. Look, you can't have people making big money off a procedure when they are the ones to deciding if people need it. A monkey can be taught to use a tool. The important thing is knowing when to use it and when not to."

"Come on, Don," said Bruce, "you internists just want to control all the decisions and collect all the fees."

"I don't know," Frances said. "Maybe Don is right about the danger of paying providers for expensive services when they are the ones determining the need for them. Look at the case we read. National Medical Enterprises was fined 379 million dollars on criminal charges that its psychiatric hospitals paid for referrals and kept patients incarcerated until their insurance ran out. They were imprisoning people against their will, but only those with good insurance. They were almost closed down, but reorganized as Tenet Healthcare Corporation after raising over three billion dollars in junk bond and bank financing. Now they're one of the biggest for-profit hospital chains in the country."

"The same thing is going on in ICUs and hospitals all over the country right now!" Don blurted out. "Every day, patients and their families are coerced or even forced to stay in the ICU or to submit to procedures they don't understand and probably don't even need."

"As we discussed," Dr. Sampson explained, "this is a natural consequence of our supply-driven system in healthcare. If you set fixed prices and guarantee payment, providers will push the services that pay the most."

"Could it be that both patients and doctors unconsciously view the higher-paid procedures as the best ones?" Frances asked. "Maybe it's not just profit-seeking, but that everyone thinks it must be better care because it's more expensive."

"I agree with Frances," Bruce said. "Doctors aren't just after money; they convince themselves they are providing the best care. They can always find a study that justifies their practice. If it's lucrative, it's easy to convince yourself it's the best thing."

Don remembered his own temptation to subspecialize, to follow the lure of prestige and money. When did the entire public buy into the idea that procedures are the easiest way to health? After his first heart attack and bypass surgery, Bob Larkin, an old family friend, told Don he would rather just have another bypass than take up healthy eating and exercise. How easily people could be convinced to have their bodies cut open by a confident surgeon!

"Remember those procedure mills we talked about?" Don asked. "Working in a place like that, it's easy to forget the reasons for what you're doing. Everyone follows orders to keep the system moving. Without realizing it, surgeons can cross the line and start operating for profit. They fight over who should be allowed to do every new procedure that comes out—like toddlers fighting over a new toy. Right now, the radiologists and cardiologists are arguing about who should get paid for interpreting the new coronary calcium scans. We don't even know yet if these scans have any practical application but—if there is money to be made—each specialty group fights for control, even though high school students could be trained to interpret them.

"Cardiologists are some of the worst, precisely because their procedures are so profitable. A cardiologist takes a person who is scared because of a little chest pain, and—even though the doctor *knows* that plain old *aspirin* is the best-proven treatment to save his life—convinces the patient he needs a cardiac catheterization immediately, and that he may also need an artery opened with a stent to prevent an imminent fatal heart attack. We know that opening arteries when someone isn't having a heart attack has never been proven to save anyone's life. Some cardiologists feed their patients to cardiac surgeon cronies who operate on people for mild coronary disease, even though they *know* bypass has never been shown to be any better than daily aspirin for people with mild disease. The worst thing is that these cardiologists and surgeons *know* better."

Bruce smirked. "Oh, come on, Don. What if they do nothing and the guy dies?" He smiled at Frances, who returned his gaze benignly. "You know they'll get blamed for it. People want aggressive surgery. I mean, look at mastectomy versus lumpectomy for breast cancer. Even though we doctors know they both are just as effective for most breast cancer, look how many women still want to get their whole breast whacked off."

"You really don't get it, do you?" Don said. "Let's make this real! Let's talk about where the procedure mills are operating now. What about these for-profit hospital chains? New American Healthcare is probably the worst of all, or should I say the best—at making money, that is."

Dr. Sampson shot Don a warning glance, but Don was too fired up to recognize it.

"Did you hear about their little hospital near Chicago that was churning out cardiac bypass surgeries at a rate so high the FBI raided the hospital and the offices of their cardiac surgeons? These guys operated on nearly everyone they saw. Their own charts showed they operated on hundreds of people a year who didn't need the surgery. People who had completely normal hearts! Of course, both the hospital and the surgeons had to pay a big fine, but they slipped out of the criminal charges. No one lost a license and no one is going to jail. The fines were just written off as a business expense."

Dr. Sampson's eyes darkened and narrowed. Don, naively assuming this was due to indignation with the unethical behavior Don was describing, pressed on, oblivious to his professor's silent command: *Be quiet, you fool!*

"Listen, everyone knows for-profit hospitals provide lower quality care than not-for-profits. Studies show people are even more likely to die if they go to for-profit hospitals…"

As Don continued his tirade, Bruce squirmed like a suspect under an interrogation spotlight. Beads of sweat formed on his forehead. He opened his mouth three times like a goldfish gasping for oxygen but never spoke. Don was enjoying the effect he was having on Bruce after Bruce had taunted him so many times.

"That's what happens when healthcare becomes a business and money is put ahead of health. We put rank profiteers like New American Healthcare Corporation in charge…"

Dr. Sampson cut Don off. "That's quite enough. I did not plan to get into that today. We need to move on."

"But New American Healthcare is the poster child for the problems in American medicine today…"

"I said move on, Dr. Newman."

The projection room plunged into sudden silence. Despite the mechanical whirr of the ventilation system, the mildewed air was stifling and the space across the huge oak table unbearably close. Frances shot Don an angry look. Bruce's jaw was clenched and his eyes had regained a steely calm that radiated cold fury at Don. For his part, Don had no idea what chord he had struck or why he seemed to be the sudden object of everyone's anger.

"Certainly," Dr. Sampson said, "higher costs at for-profit hospitals are caused in part by the higher volume of unnecessary procedures there. But without a doubt, some for-profit hospitals have substantially higher quality than comparable not-for-profits."

He gave a nod to Bruce and turned to Don. "Dr. Newman, remember that epidemiology and statistics reveal *general* trends. You cannot judge a book by its cover. Whether hospitals are for-profit or not-for-profit, we must expect them all to care for the sick and provide quality care. Otherwise, we will see more doctors, nurses, and hospitals replacing the single snake on the staff, the ancient sign of healing, for the double snake of Hermes, the symbol of trading and commerce."

Dr. Sampson shot Don one last disapproving look as he left the classroom.

As soon as Dr. Sampson and Bruce had left, Frances attacked.

"Oh my God, Don, you are a total idiot! What were you thinking? Bruce Markum? As in, the Markum family that owns New American Healthcare?"

Holy shit! Don's jaw dropped and he stood there, speechless, absorbing this information. *No wonder everyone was trying to get me to shut up!* Bruce's family owns the New American Healthcare Corporation. They run half the procedure mill hospitals in the country—the biggest for-profit healthcare business in America.

"How in the hell could you not know that?" Frances ranted. "Everybody knows who Bruce Markum is. And let me tell you, he and his family deserve a little respect."

What could he say? She was right. He should have known. He should have been aware of who Bruce was and the enormity of what he had at stake.

20

Snake Oil Salesmen

Each seemed to be strangely twisted…Perhaps some time by stroke of palsy
a man has been thus twisted right round…because he would see
too far ahead he looks behind and makes his way backwards.

DANTE ALIGHIERI, INFERNO 20, 11–39

GOLDEN-HAIRED FRANCES sat at the seminar table, composed and mantic, her concentration focused on some object beyond the others in the room. She was like a great cat—lithe, tense, ready to attack, but seemingly unaware Don was watching her.

He feared she would turn her eyes on him. At some deeper, subconscious level, he feared if he fell under the spell of her emerald green eyes she would consume him.

Frances drew in a deep breath and began her presentation.

"Like Dr. Sampson said, most of the history of medicine has focused on natural cures, faith healing, and herbal remedies, and there's a long history of charlatans. In the Middle Ages, doctors could do little to help plague victims. The few treatments they had were totally ineffective, but they wore thick cloaks and large-beaked masks in an attempt to impress patients and protect themselves. Maybe that's what branded them as quacks—they looked like ducks in those silly costumes.

"The most dangerous of the charlatans abandoned simple and gentle herbal remedies for more drastic ones. Bloodletting, for example, has a long and horrible history spanning from before the time of Hippocrates to Dr. Benjamin Rush, the physician famous for signing the Declaration of Independence and for his spirited advocacy of bleeding. As Dr. Sampson mentioned before, well-intentioned doctors who followed Rush's approach likely killed George Washington at Mount Vernon by draining a third of his blood to treat a throat infection.

"Charlatans have caused great harm to many people, but their teachings often hold a grain of truth. Almost every drug and treatment is good for something. Bleeding is good treatment for heart failure. Leaches are good for blood clots. Sometimes the most unconventional practitioners have paved the way for valuable therapies.

"The earliest snake oil salesmen probably came to the United States with the Chinese builders of the Transcontinental Railroad. Snake oil made from the fat of Chinese water snakes has long been used in the East for arthritis pain; they rub it directly on the skin over the joints. The oil is very high in the same inflammation-reducing omega-3 fatty acids from fish that doctors recommend for high cholesterol. Real Chinese water snake oil really works, and you can still buy it in most traditional Chinese pharmacies.

"But for every person selling real snake oil in the Wild West, there were five impersonators pretending to have real snake oil or selling patent medicines with no real active ingredients. For example, Richard Stoughton's Elixer, the first known patent medicine in England in 1712, contained serpentary, a root shaped like a snake. Lots of early patent medicines claimed to contain snake oil when they did not. Snake oil became synonymous with hoax, and worthless 'miracle cures' became known as snake oil.

"Despite its bad reputation, snake oil found a solid market in the United States throughout the nineteenth and early twentieth centuries. Clark Stanley, a cowboy known as the Rattlesnake King, entertained huge crowds at the World's Columbian Exposition in Chicago in 1893. He killed rattlesnakes, made Snake Oil Liniment from 'an old Pueblo Indian recipe,' and sold it for fifty cents a bottle. The authorities seized and tested a shipment of it in 1917 and found it was mostly mineral oil.

"The snake oil peddler became a stock character in many of the Western movies of the twentieth century. In 1936, W.C. Fields played a frontier snake oil salesman in My Little Chickadee, one of the earliest Western movies. In the real world, a traveling salesman with fake medical credentials hyped up his product with the help of an accomplice, a shill planted in the crowd who would claim to be healed on contact with the miraculous stuff.

"These tricky marketing techniques are still used today, but with far more sophistication. As an example, I want to tell you about a so-called snake oil salesman and the death of a classic American anti-hero: Steve McQueen.

"I was four years old when he died—I remember it because my mother cried. She was a total Steve McQueen fan and thought he was the perfect man, tough and cool on the outside but ready to wager his life for a woman or child in danger. His character always put his life on the line—in The Sand Pebbles, for a young Chinese woman being sold into prostitution; with Yul Brynner in The Magnificent Seven, for poor villagers in Mexico; and as the underdog bounty hunter, Josh Randall, in Wanted—Dead or Alive. In all of these films he played the American archetype of an independent man standing against the establishment for what he thought was right.

"He was a rebel in life, too, and nobody's fool. He died at age forty-nine, and the papers said he'd been scammed by a snake oil salesman. Mom never believed that because he was the biggest scam artist of them all. McQueen himself said if he hadn't become an actor he would have been a criminal.

"Steve McQueen's father was a barnstorming stunt pilot who abandoned his family when Steve was only six months old. Steve's uncle was the only father he ever knew, but he was forced to leave his uncle's farm at age eight to live with his mother and the first of several lousy stepfathers. The last one tried to beat Steve into submission but failed to break his spirit. Steve threatened to kill the man if he laid a hand on him again, and for that he spent nearly two years in a prison reform school for juvenile delinquents.

"He got out at age sixteen and struck out on his own. In his first year on the road he crewed on a Greek tanker to the West Indies and worked as a towel boy in a Texas brothel, an oilfield grunt on the rigs, and a lumberjack topping Canada's tallest trees. He worked as a carny and scammed both carnival goers and his boss by selling cheap pen and pencil sets for more than his boss expected and pocketing the difference. During a three-year stint in the Marines, he was promoted and then busted back to private seven times. He spent forty days in the brig on bread and water for going AWOL to see a girlfriend. Finally, he ended up in New York City, where he lived from hand to mouth any way he could. He made his best money returning items he stole and slipped in his bag after entering a store.

"Steve McQueen was a natural actor. After all, he had conned his way around the world. When a girlfriend first introduced him to acting, he figured he had found the greatest scam of all. He made movie after movie and lived hard—racing cars and motorcycles, chasing women, smoking cigarettes, drinking heavily, and doing drugs—until his marriage and family came apart. He took a real nosedive in his forties, gaining weight and smoking and drinking more and more. His decline picked up speed when Charles Manson's gang killed his friends Jay Sebring and Sharon Tate on a night he was planning to go to their house.

"In 1978, he developed a chronic cough, and in late 1979, the doctors finally diagnosed it as mesothelioma. This cancer of the lining of his right lung, caused by years of inhaling asbestos from racecars and smoke from cigarettes, had invaded his abdomen. There was little the doctors could do. He tried chemotherapy and radiation to slow the tumor down, but they were little help. In the summer of 1980 he was gasping for breath just from walking across the room and was told he had only a few weeks to live.

"He decided to go to Mexico to see Dr. William D. Kelley, a notorious dentist whose license had been suspended in Texas. Basically, Kelley was a fellow rebel. He worked with some doctors that offered a promising new but untested therapy made from apricot pits: Laetrile. The American Cancer Society had singled out Kelley and publicly condemned him because of his unorthodox practice. Though he gave no promises of a miracle cure, Kelley suggested that his program of metabolic therapy—including fresh food, megadoses of vitamins, and coffee enemas—would boost McQueen's own immune system so it could fight off the cancer. Many of Kelley's patients claimed this regimen had saved their lives.

"So, like his way cool character in *The Magnificent Seven*, Steve McQueen went to a little town across the Mexican border, only this time to save himself. He knew a cure was unlikely, but figured Kelley's metabolic therapy might offer him a chance. At first it seemed to work—at Plaza Santa Maria near Rosarita Beach, Mexico, he gained weight and his tumors began to shrink.

"He lived for months beyond the weeks his American doctors had predicted, but eventually got stir-crazy in the isolated health spa and headed back to his Santa Paula ranch in California—against the advice of his Mexican physicians and Dr. Kelley. They went to the ranch to check on him a couple of weeks later and found him drinking beer and smoking like a chimney. He soon took a turn for the worse. The mass in his abdomen blocked his kidneys and required surgery. He died the day after his operation, and the media played him as a desperate fool who was taken in by unscientific charlatans.

"But here's the thing: McQueen went to Mexico with his eyes totally wide open. He knew the metabolic therapy only offered a slim chance at best, but he preferred to take his chances with a caring healer who dared to go against the medical establishment and try something new. Besides, he had already exhausted the mainstream treatments. His conventional doctors had given up. Kelley's approach involved boosting the immune system with good nutrition and clean living. He figured at least it couldn't do him any harm. And it was thought at the time Laetrile might eventually prove to be a potent cure.

"Unfortunately, Steve McQueen was wrong about the Laetrile. Two years after his death, a study in *The New England Journal of Medicine* showed Laetrile did nothing for people with terminal cancer. Even though the one hundred seventy-eight people in the study were in good general condition when they began Laetrile, within eighteen months almost all had died. Laetrile contained cyanide, like many of the old-time syphilis remedies. Many people treated with Laetrile suffered from nausea, vomiting, and liver damage from cyanide poisoning before they died, and they died at least as fast as people who weren't treated. So, instead of helping anyone, the apricot pit extract made people worse.

"The medical establishment painted Steve McQueen as a gullible mark of scam artists, but for many cancer victims, he was a total hero who dared to question the medical establishment and pursue an unorthodox but natural treatment. He didn't buy establishment predictions of his imminent death; he chose a sliver of hope. He knew there wasn't much chance, but it was better than no chance at all. McQueen died, as he had lived, on his own terms.

"If Steve McQueen was suckered by anyone it was by the cigarette industry. He completely bought the tough guy, Marlboro man image. He'd stand in front of his racecar, dangling a cigarette from his mouth to show everyone how tough and independent he was, but all the while the cigarettes leached away his life. That's what my mom said: the cigarettes killed Steve McQueen.

"One day not long after he died, I was in my stepdad's pharmacy in Thebes. My stepdad explained he helped people like a doctor, but his job was to sell medicines and teach people how to use them. I remember pointing to the rows of vitamin bottles and tall racks of brightly colored cigarette packages and asking my stepfather why he sold poison cigarettes. He laughed and said, 'We only sell what people are stupid enough to buy.' I wondered how my stepdad could do that. What was he, a healer or a killer? Now I know he was a little bit of each. He was a salesman. He sold what he could sell, whether it helped them or not.

"That's my story. I'm sure there are still snake oil salesmen around, but remember, every once in a while they may be selling the real thing. And in uncertain circumstances, almost everyone would rather take a chance on something new than try nothing at all."

"Come on, Frances," Don said. "Snake oil salesmen like Dr. Kelley feed people false hopes and pretend they know what they are doing when they don't. The world is full of these charlatans. Look at Dr. Lorraine Day, for example. She pushes vitamins, natural food, God, and BarleyGreen Premium powder to reverse cancer by *rebuilding the immune system*. She's getting rich off it. If that's not snake oil, I don't know what is."

"At least no one is getting harmed by it! And who knows, the natural food and exercise she pushes probably do help fight cancer. The Eisenberg paper says one in three Americans turns to alternative treatments every year—things like human touch, natural diets, self-help and meditation—things they are not getting from allopathic doctors."

"Frances is right," Bruce agreed, "Dr. Day is relatively harmless." If someone chose her powder instead of a proven treatment, that would be bad. But she markets her products to those with terminal cancer and as additional therapy for people with treatable cancer. What's the harm in that?"

Don's mother had been terminal, without hope of a cure. Could Dr. Day's nutritional therapies have bought her a little time, a little hope, a little comfort? A few extra weeks would have given them Christmas together last year.

"But some snake oil treatments really are harmful," Bruce continued. "In Mexico, some providers put people with incurable cancers into hypoglycemic comas with overdoses of insulin. Hell, that's a completely bogus treatment for cancer and likely to kill people if they're not careful. I don't think these 'metabolic' and nutritional therapies typically do any major harm but there are tons of examples where serious harm is done by *legal* drugs. Can I share a related story about a patient I saw as a medical student in Nashville?" Bruce looked to Dr. Sampson for approval.

Dr. Sampson nodded.

"Mrs. H was a healthy woman, age fifty-five. She went to her regular doctor for a checkup and got a routine urinalysis. The doctor diagnosed a urinary tract infection and gave her samples of Omniflox, Abbott Labs' newest antibiotic for UTIs at the time. She felt fine but figured the doctor knew best, so she took it. Five minutes after the first dose, she began to feel chilled. After ten minutes she was shaking, feeling weak and light-headed, and her entire back was killing her. Within fifteen minutes she fainted and fell to the floor.

"I saw her in the ER. At first, she was conscious and able to tell her story. She said she ached all over, felt horrible, and thought she was coming down with a bad case of the flu. While we waited for the blood work, her gums started to bleed and her blood pressure began to drop, as if she had an overwhelming infection. Pretty soon she was delirious and incoherent. When her labs came back, we saw her blood count had plummeted to less than half of what it had been in her doctor's office, and her clotting cells had dropped to almost nothing.

"I was just a medical student, but I knew what this was. She had disseminated intravascular coagulation—a strange new molecule in her blood had set her coagulation system on fire, consuming nearly all her clotting cells and cofactors and causing her blood cells to burst. Of course, all this destruction of normal blood cells is deadly to kidneys. Sure enough, within a day, she was on dialysis. Most people who get this bleed to death since they can't clot, but somehow we kept her alive. She was bleeding from around her eyes, stomach, and rectum, and it was touch and go while she was on the ICU ventilator for two weeks. She made it out of the hospital and got off dialysis but required months of rehab and was left with permanent kidney damage.

"All this happened because she had a reaction to the Omniflox. She was unlucky enough to be one of the first people to try this new drug. New drugs are typically only tested on a few hundred or maybe a couple thousand people before approval. Problem is, a deadly side effect might only occur once in ten thousand people. That's one thing if you only give the drug to a few people with a very serious condition, but a drug marketed to millions might result in thousands of people killed. Maybe we should worry less about snake oil and more about drugs rubberstamped by the FDA and given out like candy by internal medicine doctors."

Bruce tossed his head in Don's direction and winked at Frances, who beamed a smile back at him.

Don ignored Bruce's barb and launched into an analysis of the doctor's misdeeds. "There are several things wrong with what this doctor did, if you can even call him a doctor. He was more of a snake oil salesman. First, Mrs. H probably didn't have a urinary tract infection. Routine urinalysis isn't very accurate, yet he relied on it to prescribe risky antibiotics. Second, antibiotics have never been shown to benefit women who have minor, asymptomatic urinary tract infections. Third, if she *had* needed an antibiotic, he should have prescribed a simple, old-fashioned one with well-known side effects. Instead, the doctor went to his drug closet, pulled out a sample he probably knew little-to-nothing about, and told Mrs. H that she needed it. She nearly died because of a drug she didn't need in the first place."

Dr. Sampson cleared his throat. "True. Some of the most dangerous therapies are the newer ones, and many drug disasters involve legal drugs that lacked adequate testing. What have been the biggest killer drugs of the past? Ms. Hunt?"

"Well, mercury for starters," Frances answered. "As far as we know, mercury was first used in medicine in the third century B.C., during the time of Qin Shi Huang, the first emperor of China. In death, the emperor was guarded by eight thousand terracotta soldiers in his great mausoleum, but in life his real soldiers were unable to protect him from court doctors who thought mercury pills would give him eternal life. Instead, the mercury drove him insane and cut his life short.

"You'd think doctors would have given up on mercury. But from the late fifteenth through the nineteenth centuries, they prescribed it for syphilis. Even though doctors of that time knew mercury could make you mad as the hatters who used it to make felt, they theorized that terrible diseases like syphilis required terrible cures.

"Arsenic was heralded as the new magic bullet for syphilis in 1910. As we all know now, arsenic—a heavy metal like mercury—is very toxic. It causes stomach pain, vomiting, cramps, convulsions, confusion, and even death. Strangely enough, both mercury and arsenic do seem to suppress the spiral-shaped bacteria that cause syphilis. So, they may have helped a few patients, but most scholars suspect they killed hundreds of thousands of syphilis sufferers.

"But drug poisonings did not stop with heavy metals, did they, Ms. Hunt?" Dr. Sampson asked.

"No, they didn't. In 1938, over one hundred children and adults died after taking an elixir of sulfanilamide containing antifreeze. This incident led to the establishment of the Food and Drug Administration, which required companies to prove every drug was both safe and effective before it was released. This was supposed to prevent such a tragedy from ever happening again."

"Did it work?"

"No. The next major drug tragedy was thalidomide. It was the newest thing in 1956. It was prescribed worldwide until 1961 to pregnant women, to treat morning sickness and aid sleep. Thalidomide was inadequately tested for safety, and as a result, over ten thousand babies were born with flippers for arms or feet."

"Of course, this led to the passage of even stronger drug safety legislation," Dr. Sampson said. "Did the drug tragedies end, Dr. Newman?"

"It seem like they're just getting worse," Don replied. "Just look at the antiarrhythmic drugs. Heart antiarrhythmics like Tambocor and Enkaid were heavily marketed starting about 1985, and doctors prescribed them to anyone with an occasional flutter in the chest or any abnormality on the EKG. Doctors loved these drugs because they stopped the irregular beats that frequently appear on the EKGs of average adults. They had no idea they might be deadly.

"When the Cardiac Arrhythmia Suppression Trial came out, everyone was surprised to learn the drugs killed far more people than they helped. Experts estimate at least fifty thousand people per year died from these drugs between 1985 and 1995."

"That's a half a million killed in the United States alone!" Frances said.

"Right," Dr. Sampson said. "Many more than died in the whole Vietnam War. But the public barely noticed."

"Then came calcium channel blockers for high blood pressure," Don continued. "They were prescribed like candy in the late 1970s and '80s. They were FDA approved only for anginal chest pain, but marketed for high blood pressure. Thanks to a brilliant ad campaign, every doctor in America got the message that calcium channel blockers were far better and had fewer side effects than other blood pressure medicines. Few questioned whether this was true. Common wisdom was since the blood pressure medicines were newer they must be better. By the time it finally came out in the mid-'90s that calcium channel blockers prevent fewer strokes and heart attacks than the older medicines and have just as many side effects, they had become the most popular drugs in the world for hypertension. And, believe it or not, they remain popular today. Experts estimate their use has resulted in over fifty thousand extra strokes and heart attacks in the U.S. every year, and has cost over a billion a year more than the tried-and-true treatment for hypertension."

"What about Seldane, the allergy drug?" Frances said. "Merrell Dow marketed it as a non-sedating antihistamine. But unlike most antihistamines, it interacted with a lot of other drugs. The FDA warned in 1990 that taking Seldane with certain other drugs could cause potentially fatal irregular heart rhythms, but it took them until 1997 to get it off the market. This was only a couple of years before the patent expired, so the company lost little of its profits, but experts estimate that hundreds of children and adults died from adverse reactions."

"And just last year, the diabetes drug Rezulin was withdrawn," Dr. Sampson noted. "Parke-Davis began marketing it in 1997. Rezulin lowers blood sugar pretty well, but no better than older diabetes drugs. Parke-Davis knew from the beginning it could sometimes hurt the liver but marketed and sold it anyway. It was finally withdrawn last year, but only after being linked to nearly four hundred deaths from liver failure."

"C'mon, Dr. Sampson," Bruce said. "Are you suggesting all new drugs are bad and all old drugs are good?"

"No, Dr. Markum," Dr. Sampson replied, "just that new drugs need to be carefully tested before they are widely embraced."

"That will never work," Bruce argued. "Drug companies have to get their money out quickly to make a profit. If they can't make a profit, there's no incentive to develop new drugs and treatments."

"That's true," Dr. Sampson replied. "But when companies market drugs for untested and inappropriate uses, they can cause injury and death to thousands. They marshal their drug salesmen in the field, just as the insurance companies use their salesmen. Do you know who the best salesmen for the drug companies are?"

"That's easy," Bruce replied, "the doctors. Mostly the primary care doctors," he smirked and nodded in Don's direction. "You guys all have your big drug closets. Usually the biggest room in a primary care clinic."

"You're right, Dr. Markum," Dr. Sampson said. In this case, the drug companies work just like Amway. The doctor salesmen get smiles from their patients and favors from their drug company reps every time they pass out free samples, whether they pass them out for the right reasons or not. Dr. Newman, wouldn't you agree?"

"Unfortunately, it is a problem," Don admitted. "For instance, right now Eli Lilly is marketing Zyprexa—a powerful drug for schizophrenia and bipolar disorder—to primary care doctors all over the country, for patients who don't have either condition. They suggest doctors try it for anxiety, depression, even attention deficit disorder. Zyprexa has never been tested for these problems, yet the company encourages doctors to experiment with it on their patients. It has never been compared directly to older medications for schizophrenia and bipolar disorder, and we know far less about its side effects. All we know for sure is it costs much more, and patients are thrilled to get free samples of what they think is the latest and greatest thing."

"This is exactly what I'm talking about!" said Frances. "Doctors in our traditional, paternalistic medical establishment are the real problem. They brand energetic kids as ADHD, moody teenagers as bipolar, and prescribe drugs to make them easier to control. They drug up nearly a fifth of children in America these days for so-called behavioral problems. Most of these kids don't have anything wrong with them. They just need to get some exercise, make new friends, or go have some fun. Some might need counseling. Instead, they're getting drugged up on powerful stuff that changes their brains and personalities!"

"HRT is another one that is overprescribed," Don added.

"Hormone replacement therapy?" Frances scoffed, "talk about chauvinistic doctors playing God. Doctors have wanted to control women for years. They think they can manipulate the normal female cycle—that has been working just fine, thank you, for thousands of years—and not cause any serious health effects! Their little hormone regimen probably causes thousands of breast cancers and heart attacks every year. I think that's why like half of Americans have turned to alternative medicines. They're sick of taking dangerous chemicals."

"Oh, I don't know about that," Bruce said, "seems to me like lots of women like having their hormones manipulated. Ever heard of birth control pills? They have four times the hormone dose of HRT and four times the danger. But women don't seem to complain about those."

"Well, that's different!"

"How so?"

Frances fought to maintain her poise. "For many women, there's really not much alternative."

"Certainly," said Dr. Sampson, "for every drug, whether herbal or traditional, patients must weigh its risks and benefits. Unfortunately, we don't know the risks and benefits if a drug hasn't been properly tested. Every pharmacy has shelves full of herbal remedies that are probably ineffective. Some are harmless but others are not. Even simple herbal teas can contain potent and perilous drugs.

"For instance, a Chicago woman recently suffered complete liver failure from taking capsules of chapparal, an evergreen desert shrub. Chapparal leaves have long been used for medicinal teas in traditional American Indian remedies, so chapparal teas and supplements are marketed as healthful antioxidants. She would have died if she hadn't gotten a liver transplant.

"Many powerful pills—like digoxin, a heart pill that comes from the plant foxglove, and quinine, a malaria drug from cinchona bark—are available in herbal formulations. However, these are not regulated, and the strength of a dose can vary tenfold, increasing the likelihood of a dangerous overdose."

"What about the FDA?" Don asked. "Doesn't it monitor herbal drugs?"

Dr. Sampson laughed. "Even the herbal drug business has lobbyists. Congress exempted homeopathic remedies from FDA regulation in 1938. Under pressure from the multi-billion dollar dietary supplement business, they exempted dietary supplements in 1994. These products can't be promoted for preventing or treating disease, but the industry manages to make it very clear how they supposedly promote health. Problem is, the benefits are unproven and the harms unknown. Herbal medicines don't have to contain the dose or even the substance listed on the label.

"Still, as Ms. Hunt said, mainstream experimental therapies harm many more people. Desperate patients will grasp for almost any treatment at all. People with advanced cancer enroll in trials of unproven chemotherapy drugs that cut their lives even shorter, and they typically believe their odds of cure with the experimental drugs are fifty-fifty, when researchers only expect a five percent improvement in six-month survival. In other words, for every twenty people made sick by chemotherapy in their last days, only one will live a few months longer. People want so much to believe in a cure, they exaggerate the likelihood of benefit."

"But isn't that what the placebo effect is all about?" said Bruce. "If you convince people they'll get better, they often do. I mean, isn't that what happened to Steve McQueen?"

"You are right. The placebo effect is very powerful. Let's talk about placebos. How strong are they?"

"Very," Don said. "Studies show people get thirty to forty percent benefit from placebos for almost any condition: anginal chest pain, arthritis, stomach ulcers, allergies, depression, anxiety. There are even studies suggesting similar survival benefits in cancer."

Don's voice broke when he spoke the word *cancer*. He cleared his throat and continued.

"So that means the placebo effects of many chemotherapy drugs may be stronger than their biochemical effects. Furthermore, placebo effect is strongest for drugs with stronger side effects, such as sedation. If a person feels an effect—any effect—he believes the drug is doing something and is more likely to feel better. As Montaigne noted in 1572, 'there are men on whom the mere sight of medicine is operative.' Did you know the same antiperspirant works better if it has a blue top rather than a red top? Placebo effect is a large part of the pharmaceutical marketing business."

Bruce jumped in. "And drugs have stronger placebo effects when they are delivered with needles. I wonder if that's how acupuncture works. Think about it: if you get a thirty percent benefit from placebo alone, and needles make people think the treatment is even stronger, a needle may be the best placebo of all."

"At least they're not getting a hazardous drug with acupuncture," Frances said.

"Well, by that token," Don added, "what about surgery? Talk about placebo effect! You said pretend surgery works as well for most knee pain as real surgery, and we saw the study that proves it. What about bypass surgery for chest pain? We know people have less chest pain and live longer after bypass, even if their bypass grafts get blocked. Maybe some of the benefit of bypass is just *thinking* your life was saved. That alone may make you live longer."

Dr. Sampson nodded, "We really don't know, of course. Sham bypass surgery—splitting the chest open without doing the bypass—has never been tested. But it is hard to imagine a potentially more powerful placebo."

Bruce looked at Dr. Sampson as if he were crazy, but Dr. Sampson ignored him and kept talking.

"The point is, regardless of whether it's bypass surgery, acupuncture, light therapy, magnets, or chemotherapy, we cannot ignore the placebo effect. The mind is powerful. Gurus can slow their heart rates to almost nothing. Through biofeedback training, ordinary people can learn to control the dilation of blood vessels, change the temperature of a hand or finger, or suppress bleeding. With hypnosis, people can get rid of warts.

"The placebo can be used for good or ill. The worst charlatans sell poisons and convince people they're beneficial. Other treatments are harmless but have no benefit beyond placebo effect. Perhaps the highest use of the placebo effect is encouraging faith in the healing powers of time, nature, nutrition, and the body's own healing power."

Frances nodded her head in agreement.

"Consumers should go in, like Steve McQueen, with their eyes open. We should demand randomized clinical trials for all drugs, both patent meds and herbals. And we need trials that assess both intermediate outcomes—like blood pressure or blood sugar—and the impact on long-term health. We should consider whether a hazardous treatment offers some benefit beyond placebo effect, and if so, whether it warrants the risks. We need to monitor the safety of approved drugs for uncommon but serious side effects and remove unsafe drugs from the marketplace.

"What are you trying to do, Dr. Sampson?" Bruce said, "Take away people's last hopes?"

"No, Dr. Markum. For every disease and condition there is hope. I just want to take away false hopes. When physicians and faith healers ignore the limits of their knowledge, they set themselves up as diviners and prophet-prognosticators. They err through incompetence and by creating false hopes. No one needs false hopes.

"That's it for today. I won't see you until after the winter break. Keep your eyes open on your field trip next week and learn all you can about how these issues are addressed in Washington."

They all stood up to leave. As soon as Dr. Sampson was out of earshot, Bruce motioned Frances and Don over with a knowing tilt of his head. "I think the old man is out of touch," he said. "Hell, we spend all our time talking about stuff that happened twenty or thirty years ago. I want to learn about healthcare today!"

Don wanted to protest. Understanding history is important for wisdom; those who ignore history are doomed to repeat it! But he said nothing...maybe Bruce had a point. Don's old doubts came rushing back. Had he made a mistake coming to Florence College? But it was too late. What could he do about it now?

Don walked over to the program office to check his mailbox. As he flipped through a stack of the usual campus notices and medical magazines plastered with drug advertising, he noticed Dr. Sampson's secretary, Bettye, watching him out of the corner of her eye. He found it a bit odd and didn't pay much attention to her newfound curiosity until he came across an envelope stamped CONFIDENTIAL. The return address read: OFFICE OF THE PRESIDENT, FLORENCE COLLEGE.

His hand quivered as he opened the ominous envelope. What in the world could this be about? He pulled out the paper and unfolded it.

The message was terse and to the point. *Please contact this office to schedule a meeting with the President at your earliest convenience.*

Bettye asked, "Interesting news?"

"Oh, uh, nothing really," he stammered, remembering the marking of the letter as confidential, "just a notice about a meeting. See you later, Bettye."

Don turned and headed out the door. He felt guilty about his evasiveness and frustrated that he had no idea why he'd be summoned by the president. Did Frances and Bruce get similar letters? Given the marking of the envelope, he wasn't at liberty to ask them.

What could the president of Florence College possibly want with me?

21

Swindler Bureaucrats

There 'no' is made 'ay' for cash.
DANTE ALIGHIERI, INFERNO 21, 42

DON SLUMPED against the passenger side window in the back seat of the Florence College van and drifted in and out of sleep. Bruce drove, and Frances sat in the front passenger seat with a road map spread out in her lap.

Two nights earlier, the first snow of the year had blanketed everything on campus in a chilling cover of pristine white. Farther south down I-95, the snow had slid off the branches of the barren trees, and brown sludge lined a path of thick gray slurry where tires met asphalt. As they drew closer to D.C., the road sludge diminished and finally disappeared, and the roadside patches of snow shrank ever smaller until all were dissolved into the brown, soggy earth.

The squeaky windshield wipers beat time as they swiped away the salt and sand sprayed up by eighteen-wheelers. Bruce cranked up the radio, and it crackled with a static-laced AC/DC song, *Highway to Hell.*

Don gave up on sleep and moved to the middle seat. Bruce and Frances were having a lively conversation about investing. Bruce knew so much about major American corporations, Don wondered whether some of his comments revealed inside information.

Outside the van, roadside trash, graffiti, and empty lots welcomed them to the capitol's northern ghettos. Next came slums and boarded businesses that gradually gave way to brownstone townhouses. Despite the depressing scenery and winter gloom, Don was filled with anticipation. Washington is where things happen! He looked forward to spending the next two weeks studying government's role in healthcare.

They arrived on the American University campus at dusk. Don carried his bags to his assigned dorm room. His heart sank. Cold floor, cinder block walls, and twin bed. Still, American University was the product of George Washington's vision for a national university to educate America's finest young scholars for a life of public service. Over a century passed after Washington's death before his dream became a reality. Would health reform take a century, too? Was there a role for Don to play in changing things, and if so, what?

That night in bed, he tried to picture his role in the society that President Washington had foreseen, but he was too distracted by his present circumstances: the mattress was hard, the synthetic sheets like sandpaper, and the bed impossibly short. He positioned his body at an angle, but his head still bumped the headboard and his feet jammed against the footboard. So far, American University seemed to offer just one more uncomfortable bed in an endless series of lousy call rooms.

Next morning before daylight, the students were on the road again, headed to their first session with a Washington expert. They drove outside the beltway to one of the out-of-the-way places where laws inked in the halls of Congress were implemented. The object of this trip was to view the cogs and gears of bureaucratic machinery up close. They were about to venture inside the health-care machine that sets the pay rules for vendors servicing America's two behemoth national health insurance programs, Medicare and Medicaid.

The van was quiet. Don took advantage of the silence to mentally replay his strange meeting with the president of Florence College two days earlier. He ran through the meeting in his mind again and again, as if replaying the tape of a crime scene to look for clues...

In the reception area outside President Lender's office, Don sank into the cushions of an elegant damask couch, surrounded by the desks and cubicles of the president's staff. He thumbed through a glossy periodical and wished someone would offer him a glass of water. No one did. The officious secretaries ignored him and scurried around answering phones and filing papers in carefully arranged banks of files.

Don tried to appear nonchalant, but his heart was beating fast and his sweaty hands were leaving wet smears on the magazine cover. *Why am I here?* Was he in trouble? For what? He hadn't done anything. Of course, he remembered what had happened the other time he was sent to the principal's office—he was the one who got punished even though he hadn't started the fight.

Five minutes after the appointed time, President Lender's petite assistant appeared. "The president will see you now," she announced in a self-important tone.

Don struggled to escape the couch's low, doughy cushions and followed the assistant to a pair of oak-paneled doors at the end of the room. She opened the doors and stated simply, "Dr. Don Newman."

President Lender came around from behind his massive burnished mahogany desk and strode forward to greet him. "Ah, Don!" he said with feigned recognition, shaking his hand firmly. The deep and measured gaze of his piercing gray eyes seemed calculated to assure Don of his deep concern for Don's welfare. "I've heard so much about you!"

"Yes, uh, it's nice to see you," Don stammered.

What has he heard about me? Don couldn't imagine.

President Lender indicated a glossy mahogany conference table to his left. "Let's sit and talk."

Don was dumbfounded by President Lender's familiarity, but did his best to act nonchalant. He sat in one of the heavily carved and upholstered armchairs next to the president's throne-like one at the head of what had to be an eighteen-foot table.

"Can I get you something to drink?" President Lender offered.

"Uh, water. Yes, water would be nice."

While President Lender filled a glass with ice and bottled water at a hidden bar cloistered in the corner, Don gazed in wonder at the elegance of his conclave.

Great windows filled two sides of the gargantuan corner office, offering a bird's eye view of the quad through the bare limbs of the trees. One wall of the office was lined floor-to-ceiling with built-in mahogany bookcases and cabinets. Between the windows to the left, built-in display cases housed a few new leather-bound books with gold leaf lettering; the rest were filled with trophies, picture frames, engraved silver plates, and fine vases. The few parts of the walls not filled with cabinets, bookcases, or windows were sheathed with mahogany paneling with exquisite architectural detailing: geometric designs, cornices, and egg and dart trim.

President Lender's light gray suit fit his lean frame like a glove. His eyes matched the suit's fabric. The whites of his eyes and his crisp white collar stood out in stark contrast to his bronzed face. Close-trimmed, light gray hair crowned his head like a skullcap. Don couldn't begin to guess his age. In one sense, the president seemed very old—both his demeanor and the thin, brown, spotted skin of his wiry hands suggested as much—but his high forehead was free of wrinkles.

"So," President Lender began, "going from Chicago and Boston to here must have been quite a change."

Don nodded. "It's beautiful here, though." He smiled and attempted to suppress his memory of the treeless, eroding hillsides on the back of Sentinel Mountain.

"Florence probably reminds you of those beautiful mountains in Sewanee, although I bet you prefer the weather in the Tennessee mountains."

"Well, yes, sir, I do, especially this time of year."

President Lender's knowledge of Don's background and preferences was disarming. Don did miss the weather, but it was strange to hear the president say that. Generally, people from the northeast couldn't conceive that someone might actually prefer the sweltering heat of the south.

The president sat down in his throne-chair and placed the glass of water on a silver coaster in front of Don. "How are things going in your program, Don?"

he inquired, with apparent genuine interest. "We want to make sure you are getting the education you need."

"Well, there's a lot to learn, and sometimes there just isn't enough time in the day, but I have to say the program has really opened my eyes," Don answered.

"Uh-*huh*," President Lender said. He moved his great chair as close to Don's as the table leg would allow and leaned forward. "I suppose you are wondering why I summoned you here."

Don nodded. "Yes, sir."

"First, you have to understand, Don, that here at Florence College we take our health system science program very seriously. Why, we're renowned throughout the country! There is no other program quite like ours. We attract some of America's most elite students and train them to become the future leaders of American healthcare. Really, you are one of a select few, and therefore in a very special position."

Lender lowered his voice and his expression became hard, like stone. "For you, your fellow students, and for America's future, the program must be conducted properly. We want your inside perspective, Don, on how we're doing: what you have seen, what you have heard, what your experience has been."

Don had no idea what President Lender was getting at. He was just relieved he wasn't in trouble. "How can I help?" he asked. "What do you need to know?"

"Well, I'd like to ask you a few questions."

"Okay." Don nodded.

There was an awkward silence as President Lender paused to formulate his first question. He seemed reluctant to proceed, but when he finally spoke, his voice was strong and authoritative. "In his seminar, does Dr. Sampson emphasize unethical behavior in American healthcare corporations? You know, cases of companies sacrificing health for profit?"

"Well, yes, we have been studying some of the ethical breaches large healthcare companies make…"

"Does he show bias against large healthcare companies?"

"Well…not bias exactly. I don't think so."

"I need you to be specific, Don. What about pharmaceutical companies? Has he focused on what they are doing wrong?"

"Well…yes. We covered problems with direct-to-consumer advertising and the way drug companies bribe doctors."

"Has Dr. Sampson emphasized any of the many things healthcare companies are doing to improve healthcare and save lives in America?"

"No, not yet…he explained we are going to do that in the second year."

"In the second year? Do you mean to tell me he ignores the good things large healthcare companies are doing for health care until the second year?"

"Just in the seminar. It's designed to move from the problems in healthcare to the solutions."

"Just in the seminar?" he mimicked. "Why, that is the centerpiece of the program! Does he really not review any articles or emphasize any positive aspects of the healthcare corporations that have made the American healthcare system what it is today?"

Don felt sweat gathering on his forehead. He was caught off guard by the sudden battery of questions and fought to maintain his composure. "No, I guess not...not yet. But, like I said, he said we'll study that next year."

President Lender forged ahead with his cross-examination. "What about doctors and organized medicine? Has he emphasized any of the positive and important contributions they have made to healthcare in America?"

"Well, not exactly...but we reviewed the history of medical science."

"Did he emphasize the lifesaving medical breakthroughs of our greatest medical and surgical heroes? Great scientists like the vaccine developer, Jonas Salk?"

"Not really. I guess we talked more about how medical science in those areas fell short," Don admitted with increasing embarrassment.

"Fell short? You talked about how Jonas Salk fell short?"

"Well, not Salk specifically, sir..."

"Unbelievable," he said. "Okay, then, what about insurance companies? Has he spoken at all about the benefits they have brought to American consumers?"

"No, sir."

"Has he contrasted the American healthcare system with the socialized insurance programs of other countries?"

"Yes, sir."

"Stop calling me sir," he reprimanded.

"Yes, s...okay." Don winced. He had almost said it again! His father had taught him always to use "sir" and "ma'am" with elders. His years at Sewanee— where these formalities were customary and accepted—had reinforced the habit.

"So, how does the U.S. healthcare system fare in Dr. Sampson's comparison?"

"Well, it is not his comparison. We read original research articles and weigh the evidence ourselves."

"Don. Who chooses the articles for the seminar?"

"Dr. Sampson, mostly, but we're encouraged to bring articles, too."

"And what do Dr. Sampson's articles say about our system, compared with the systems of other countries?"

"Well, basically that our system is more expensive and less efficient," Don admitted.

President Lender shook his head. "Outrageous! Does the man care nothing for the innovation and lifesaving cures we bring to the entire world? Don, think about it. Dr. Sampson leads the foremost health systems program in the world, our country has the best and most envied healthcare system in the world, and he has nothing good to say about it? Does that sound right to you?" He fell silent and gazed off into the distance.

Was Dr. Sampson's approach wrong? Was his perspective biased and old-fashioned? That's what Bruce thought. Don hated to admit or even contemplate the possibility Bruce might be right.

Don broke the silence, "Is there some sort of problem, sir?"

Lender grimaced.

"Oh, excuse me. I mean, why are you asking me these questions?"

"I'll be frank." He leaned in closer and spoke in a hushed voice, as if his words were too secret to be uttered openly in the large empty office. "Some very serious concerns have been raised about Dr. Sampson and his curriculum." He glanced at the office doors. "There are serious allegations that I am not at liberty to share with you. And you must keep this conversation—even what we have discussed so far—completely confidential."

Don nodded again. He wanted to jump up and bolt through the oak-paneled doors.

Lender assumed the voice of a kind grandfather. "Don, I am not asking you these questions to lead you to doubt the integrity of your teacher, but I do need your perspective so I can do what is right for the college. Please forgive my asking this question. I know it will sound unseemly, but it must be asked. To your knowledge, has Dr. Sampson used his privileged position to take advantage of any of our female students?"

This question took Don completely by surprise. "No, no, sir...I mean, no, I don't think so."

"Think carefully. Dr. Sampson frequently mentors students in his private office. That provides a tempting opportunity. Are you sure you have not witnessed anything suspicious in his behavior toward any of the female scholars?"

Don thought of Frances. The night before her presentation on the beauty industry, he had walked past Dr. Sampson's office after supper and heard them behind the closed door. Don remembered it because he had wanted to be alone with Frances himself at that moment. He had been jealous! But Dr. Sampson... surely he couldn't...it was preposterous!

"I can't say that I have seen anything suspicious that way," Don replied, putting on his best poker face.

Lender's probing eyes appraised Don carefully. He raised his eyebrows but didn't press the issue. "Well, thank you for your time, Don. I must go now to my next meeting. I may call on you again. I want your eyes and ears. Keep me informed about anything irregular. If you have something you think I should know, please call my secretary. I appreciate your doing this for the college."

Don didn't dare voice the obvious question. *Doing what?*

President Lender stood. "That will be all for now."

Don stood up and took two steps from the table.

Lender stepped in front of him, blocking his way. "Remember, Don," he said ominously, "this entire conversation is strictly confidential. You will keep everything I have said to yourself. This is only between you and me. Understand?" he said. His steely eyes bored into Don's skull.

"Yes s…" he caught himself.

Lender's voice snapped back to the friendly tone. "I do want to talk with you more about your education. You remind me of myself at your stage. Come back when I am less occupied, and we'll talk again. There are things you must understand if you are going to be a successful agent of healthcare change."

A successful agent of healthcare change. That was Dr. Sampson's phrase. Where had Lender heard it? How much did he know about Don and what went on in seminar, and who had told him? Don felt baffled, confused, and exposed. He sensed Lender was pleased with the effect his interrogation had produced, but he had no idea why. Maybe he simply enjoyed mentoring graduate students, but if so, he had a creepy way of doing it.

President Lender guided Don to the heavy oak doors, ushered him through with a pat on the shoulder, and closed the doors with a heavy thud.

Don didn't know what to think. President Lender had thrown everything into doubt. Was Dr. Sampson leading his students astray? Did he have a hidden life of depravation? Was he secretly chasing Frances? He had certainly looked at her with admiration. Was something else going on?

Don was jolted out of his pensive brooding when Bruce hit the brakes at the dead end of Security Boulevard in Baltimore and swung a hard right. A large sign bearing the HHS seal—an abstract sketch of an eagle with profiles of human faces for wings—marked the entrance gate. The eagle appeared to be flying out of the government complex.

The guard at the gate eyed the van with suspicion, but spotting the Florence College insignia on the side, he waved the students through. The parking lot was enormous. Bruce drove past rows and rows of boxy and drab economy cars and screeched into a vacant spot at the far end of the lot.

Don, Frances, and Bruce walked across the rain-wet, monotonous plain of asphalt toward an awkward group of Plexiglas and concrete office buildings. A large rectangular bunker in the middle was flanked by two shorter, boxlike structures. Ugly metal grillwork protected the windows. Based on the size of the parking lot, Don figured these squat and fat buildings must be jam-packed with squat and fat bureaucrats as well.

They headed to the building on the left and entered through a pair of smoky glass doors. Frances and Bruce marched across the small, undecorated lobby as if they owned the place.

Don tagged close behind. He envied their easy confidence. *Has Dr. Sampson used his privileged position to take advantage of any of our female students?* Not likely, in Don's opinion. Frances was not the type to be taken advantage of, and besides, he didn't think Dr. Sampson would do that sort of thing.

A uniformed security guard at the reception desk was ranting on the phone about the bad refereeing in some basketball game. He pointed to the sign-in roster and the students duly recorded their names, the time, and which office they were to visit.

"Hang on a minute, would you?" The guard banged the phone receiver down on his desk and looked up to take stock of the three visitors. Much to Don's irritation, he took extra time to ogle Frances up and down. The guard called on the office intercom for an escort, then picked up the receiver and resumed his tirade.

Bruce only had time to look at his watch once before the elevator doors opened and a bright-eyed soldier in a khaki uniform stepped out.

"You must be Dr. Sampson's students," the soldier said. "I'm Captain Frank Stead. Glad you're here. Any students of Dr. Sampson are friends of ours. I'm here to take you to Mr. Yeoman." He turned around and motioned them into the elevator.

As Captain Stead held the elevator door for them, he noticed their curious stares at his uniform. "I'm an officer with the Public Health Service," he explained. "Two years ago, I requested the Commissioned Corp to assign me to HHS to work with Fred Yeoman, so here I am."

Dr. Sampson's friend, Fred Yeoman, was the bureau chief. He had risen to the top not by appointment but through the ranks of the bureaucracy simply by doing a good job. Dr. Sampson said he was famous for his attention to detail.

"You're lucky to meet Mr. Yeoman. He is incredibly efficient. It's amazing he's survived here as long as he has. Sometimes it seems like we're alone here in making the bureau do what it's supposed to do. The majority of people push paper from one desk to the next. Mr. Yeoman is different—he gets things done."

The elevator doors opened on a vast, low-ceilinged room on the third floor. The whole space was divided by fabric-covered partitions Don could barely see over. The students followed the straight-backed captain as he weaved through this maze of cluttered cubicles—the workstations of dozens of minions. Not one person looked up to see who was passing by. The four snaked through the cubicles and Xerox rooms and made their way down a long corridor, finally arriving at a door marked *Mr. Fred Yeoman, Bureau Director.*

Don looked back and could not see the elevators, nor could he tell what path they had taken through the labyrinth of cubicles.

Mr. Yeoman's secretary sat at a small desk just outside his office door.

"Hello, Nancy, here they are," said Captain Stead. He turned to the students and added, "I'll be leaving you here."

"Go right in," Nancy nodded to the door with a smile, "he's expecting you."

Mr. Yeoman was busy typing at his desk. Except for a large computer monitor, the sizeable desk was covered with orderly stacks of paper and manila files. Three chairs faced the right side of the desk. "Just a minute…take a seat…I'll be right with you," Mr. Yeoman said without looking up. They sat down to wait.

Don studied Mr. Yeoman's profile. He was a portly man. His hair was nearly pure white. The skin of his face and hands was also white, but his cheeks bore the palest color, like that of a rose seen through snowy alabaster. Don wondered if he was an albino.

Mr. Yeoman continued his furious typing for thirty seconds and hit the print key. The letter came off the printer into his waiting left hand while his right hand pulled a black pen from the multitude of pens in the plastic guard lining his shirt pocket. He signed and folded the letter, stuffed it into an envelope, affixed an address label, and dropped it in his outbox. He wasted no movement in this perfectly executed, graceful choreography.

He turned toward his visitors and announced, "If you want to be a paper pusher, at least do it well. That means you never touch any piece of paper twice." He smiled broadly and his pale blue eyes peered at them from behind dark-rimmed glasses. The lenses were so thick, his eyes were magnified to at least twice normal size.

"Now, what have we here? Three students of Dr. Sampson getting ready to save the world, I hope. I'm Fred Yeoman. And you must be the one named for the great Italian poet?" he asked, looking at Don.

"Don Newman, sir." Don stood up and leaned over to shake Mr. Yeoman's hand. *How did he know that?* Don hoped Mr. Yeoman would leave it at that.

"…and you must be Frances Hunt"—he glanced down at a paper on his desk—"and you Bruce Markum. As you know, I'm an FOS, or friend of Sampson." He grinned. "There are a few of us here in Washington. Of course, there are many who lean the other way. Anyway, I took his short course at Florence College in 1987 and we have stayed in touch ever since."

Mr. Yeoman launched into a description of the Centers for Medicare & Medicaid Services, or CMS for short. "All bureaucrats are part of the executive branch. Our job is to implement the laws, to get things done. Here at CMS we take pride in being lean and efficient. At 400 billion a year, our budget is second only to the Department of Defense, yet we only have about ten thousand employees. That's less than a tenth of the number they have. We have fewer employees by far than any of the major private insurance companies, but we serve many more people. Say what you want about government bureaucracy," he chuckled, "but in Medicare the money pays for real services, not just bureau-crat salaries…"

While he was talking, Don examined Mr. Yeoman further. Large pink jowls folded over to form flaps over his thick neck. He was at least partly albino, Don decided; the skin showed little evidence of melanin. In the corner behind his desk, Don spotted a small refrigerator and microwave. Don was willing to bet Mr. Yeoman ate lunch in his office and never left the building when the sun was shining.

"Like I was saying, working for CMS used to be a real source of pride, especially back in the days when we were called the Health Care Financing Administration, or HCFA for short. It was real simple. We helped people finance their health care, and we figured at some point we would do it for all Americans because we did it very well. Our overhead is still only three percent, while all the other insurance companies run between ten and thirty-five percent. Not only were we small in comparison with the size of our budget, but we had the most career bureaucrats, and believe it or not, that is a good thing."

He looked right at Bruce, perhaps having noted Bruce's skeptical smile.

"But over the last fifteen years, we have been infiltrated by political appoin-tees and openers. What are openers, you ask? Short-termers who use the position to find higher-paying jobs. Sometimes they even start their work for potential corporate employers while working here."

"Isn't that illegal?" Don asked.

"Of course it is illegal, and just plain wrong. Most of the time, these brown-nosers are smart enough not to accept money from companies while they work here, but they're eager to please their pet corporations for the promise of future favors. They want to show potential employers they are worthy of trust. Of course, this means they are not worthy of the trust of their current employers, the American public."

Frances interrupted, "Why are companies so eager to curry the favor of CMS employees?"

"C'mon Frances," Bruce interjected, "isn't it obvious? CMS sets the rules for spending the government's money on health care. You heard him. They spent some 400 billion dollars last year, and it goes up every year. You better believe healthcare businesses care about CMS rules for spending government dollars. A change of one little word in a rule can cost a company millions of dollars—or make them rich."

Mr. Yeoman eyed Bruce with interest. "You seem to know a lot about how things work here. What's your last name again?"

Bruce shot Mr. Yeoman a steely look. "Markum."

Mr. Yeoman continued without missing a beat, "Oh, yes. Well, Mr. Markum, you have put it quite clearly. Simply put, healthcare companies care a great deal about what we do here, and they are willing to pay for inside information or influence. You would not believe some of the ridiculous things government employees have been caught doing in the last ten years."

Mr. Yeoman laughed out loud, dispersing the room's accumulated tension. His belly shook so hard it threatened to pop the buttons from his polyester shirt and the students couldn't help chuckling along with him.

"Let me give you a few fine examples. Of course, I'll change the names to better portray the guilty. First, Mr. A. K. Nosenbaum, right down the hall here, works in technology assessment for new medical devices. He always manages to find his way into the Redskins' skyboxes at FedEx Field. No one is quite sure how he does it, but we know he's very chummy with corporate leaders for some major medical device manufacturers…and he has over thirty thousand device manufacturers to choose from. His day job is to meet with these corporate leaders to discuss their concerns regarding proposed payment rulings for their devices. Yes, someone is always quite happy to provide a box seat for Mr. Nosenbaum and his family and friends."

Mr. Yeoman held up two fingers. "Roland Graff. He works in the White House Office of Management and Budget and approves our large contracts with Medicare subcontractors. Anyway, we had a large contract to award for nursing homes oversight. And *someone* in the White House had a girlfriend in the nursing home business. The word came down through Mr. Graff that her company looked qualified to get the contract. As they say: *a word to the wise is sufficient.*"

Mr. Yeoman continued recounting the characters in CMS's bureaucratic burlesque, ticking off pseudonyms one after another. Don pictured this comical cast of government swindlers as the slapstick troop of demons depicted in the old copy of *The Divine Comedy* his mother left him. The winged devils in Botticelli's drawings of hell were more corrupt than those they tormented. Their barbed hooks and pikes skewered the pecuniary pen pushers of Dante's day every time they dared raise themselves out of the boiling tar.

"The Bagman. The White House appointed him as bureau chief in the nineties. He came from a fancy job in the private sector and was never happy with his reduced salary and tiny office. It was his job to talk to legislators on behalf of CMS and explain the agency view. Instead, he campaigned day and night to promote the private Medicare+Choice programs that pay HMOs to sign up enrollees for their own special versions of Medicare. He acted like a lobbyist, repeating the mantra that private HMOs would do a much better job with the Medicare money.

"Those of us in the agency knew better: not only do Medicare HMOs cost more, but they provide our sickest enrollees fewer basic services. We couldn't figure out why The Bagman spent so much time trying to put CMS out of business. When Medicare+Choice passed as part of the Balanced Budget Act of 1997, everything became clear. He landed a plush position on K Street with HIAA, the Health Insurance Association of America. His reward for a job well done. Nowadays, he comes here to visit his old friends and push Medicare Advantage programs, the new version of privatized Medicare.

"Next is The Obfuscator. He works for the HHS secretary and adulterates payment rules at the point of issue by secretly submarining the secretary's best ideas for saving taxpayers money and improving care. How? By making the rules ambiguous enough so the hospitals and doctors that buy his lunches and lobby his office can bill for dangerous experimental treatments and get away with it. Instead of writing clear rules and securing the best deals for beneficiaries, he helps his corporate friends get paid for cheap, substandard products. Sad thing is, The Obfuscator believes he is doing the right thing by getting CMS out of the way of the companies that make America great.

"Then there's Jimmy Bribe, a supervisor in one of our regional Program Safeguard Contractor, or PSC offices. In 1999, CMS awarded contracts to twelve PSCs as part of ongoing fraud and abuse prevention through its Medicare Integrity Program. Anyway, Jimmy's analysts gave him data showing the major hospital system in their region had markedly increased the number of angioplasties and cardiac caths billed to Medicare every year from 1998 - 2001. Jimmy already knew this hospital system was advertising its 'latest cardiovascular techniques,' and he had seen HHS audit data from the Office of the Inspector General, or OIG, showing it used unapproved stents and did unapproved atherectomies—cutting out narrowings in coronary arteries instead of widening them.

"Medicare does not pay for these procedures and devices because they are unproven, right? We don't even know if they are safe, much less whether they help save lives. Anyway, Jimmy Bribe knew this regional hospital system would owe the federal government millions if he alerted the OIG. So, ever the efficient bureaucrat, Jimmy snuck around the hospital and confirmed their cardiologists were doing experimental procedures and then squirting a little dye just to make it look like a simple diagnostic procedure they could bill for. Since he knew the administrators at the hospital quite well through his work for the government, he gave them a little visit after hours.

"He offered to retire from his government job and come work for them as a consultant to help 'improve their operations.' We're not sure how much he's made since he retired three years ago, but we do know he bought a new beach house, a sports car, and a condo on the Mediterranean. Lots of retiring CMS executives feel entitled to go out and make some money after doing thirty years of God's work for low pay. Mr. Bribe's consulting may not be precisely illegal, but it stinks of corruption—we are pretty sure he got paid well above the market rate."

"Doctors and hospitals bend the rules for coding claims all the time," Don offered. "Everyone looks the other way. In my surgery elective in urology as a medical student, we did a cosmetic circumcision on a ten-year-old boy because his parents wanted him to look like the other boys. My resident told me to write in the chart that the boy's foreskin wouldn't pull back so Medicaid would cover it. I guess that was falsifying the patient's record, but I went along."

"Oh come on, Don," Bruce scoffed, "everyone knows Medicare and Medicaid billing rules are ridiculous. You have to read about twenty volumes of regulations to even guess what they are. We doctors have to get paid for our work somehow."

"Under the False Claims Act, billing for uncovered services is illegal," Mr. Yeoman clarified, "and can even land a doctor or hospital executive in jail. Sure, there are forces trying to weaken our payment rules. Lots of doctors and health-care companies would like us to pay for everything. The American Hospital Association and the American Medical Association have made weakening the False Claims Act a top priority. They're spending millions lobbying on Capitol Hill to raise the burden of proof required under the False Claims Act. If that happens, we'll find it nearly impossible to prosecute a provider for swindling.

"Given the incredible salary difference between a bureaucrat and a lobbyist or trade association representative, corruption is inevitable. Top agency execu-tives making less than one hundred and fifty thousand dollars a year rub elbows with rich corporate executives and their lobbyists who make a half million to a million dollars or more. Our bureaucrats rule on issues often worth hundreds of millions to those companies. Is it any surprise government servants leave for the private sector?

"So, then..." Mr. Yeoman looked from Bruce to Frances to Don. "Who do you think CMS should serve?"

"The people, of course," Don replied, "the people served by Medicare and Medicaid."

"And what should be the overarching purpose at CMS?"

"Well," Don replied, "that's pretty straightforward, as far as I can tell. High value health care is what we should want to buy for ourselves. Isn't it just getting the best deal you can for the program beneficiaries?"

"Right! I couldn't come up with a better mission statement myself. That is why we try to keep public and private interests separate, for the people of America. Citizens should be able to trust the government to spend their money wisely, as they themselves would want to spend it. But nowadays, too many bureaucrats bargain on using their public position for private gain."

"What about the Food and Drug Administration?" Don asked. "With all the money at stake in getting a drug approved, the pressure on the FDA scientists who review drug safety must be tough."

"You better believe it. In recent years, top FDA administrators have been under intense pressure to approve drugs quickly and keep them on the market. A recent internal government survey showed two-thirds of FDA scientists lack confidence that their agency adequately monitors the safety of prescription drugs, and one in five say they've been pressured to approve drugs despite safety concerns."

"Why would they do that?" asked Frances.

"Drug companies pushed through the FDA Modernization Act in 1997. It allows companies to *pay* the FDA to complete drug reviews at super speed. Many say the FDA has changed its primary purpose from protecting the public to rushing drugs to market—they even amended their mission statement to include a goal about helping to speed innovations.

"An FDA scientist who raises an alarm about a potential danger of a new drug is more likely to be punished than praised. Ask Dr. David Graham. He's one of the best career scientists at the FDA, but he did his job a little too well. He broke ranks with the bureaucratic devils instead of following orders and keeping quiet. After the FDA approved the blockbuster drugs Vioxx and Celebrex, he raised concerns that they may cause heart attacks and for that he was formally admonished, bullied, and intimidated. If he keeps his job the rest of this year, I will be surprised.

"Drug approvals aren't the only problem at the FDA. Over the past five years, citation letters for false advertising have drastically decreased. The FDA allows outrageous claims on television. Drug companies can tell outright lies about their newest drugs with virtually no consequence. At most, drug companies get a little slap on the wrist, well after the drug ad has been aired to millions of people.

"And that's not all. FDA scientific review committees used to be composed of impartial scientists. Now they are stacked with industry representatives and scientists whose research is bought with generous drug company funding. The public used to demand the separation of public and private interests; this is the opposite. Industry reps claim to put the people's interests first, but if the companies only pay for their approval, how can we expect impartiality?"

Bruce countered, "Wait a minute. All these bureaucrats you're talking about are just petty thieves at most. Small-timers. With good management from the top," he said with a derisive look at Mr. Yeoman, "heads would roll and they would clean house of that kind of riff-raff."

"Ah, but there is rub," Mr. Yeoman replied. "The corruption comes from the top. In general, the employees who make the least money work the hardest to get the best deal for the beneficiaries. You see, those at the top are the ones in a position to take advantage of the most lucrative business opportunities."

Mr. Yeoman glanced at his watch. "Let me tell you one more thing, and I must trust you to keep it to yourself." He gave each student a measured gaze through the thick lenses of his glasses and lowered his voice. "For any federal agency, just as in private sector corporations, the worst problems start at the top," he said, nodding to Bruce. "Let me tell you about the current top bureaucrat at CMS, my boss, Victoria Thrash."

Bruce braced himself to speak but changed his mind, crossed his arms, sat back in his chair, and eyed Mr. Yeoman with suspicion. Mr. Yeoman didn't seem to notice.

"The frightening thing about Director Thrash is she doesn't believe government has any role in healthcare at all. Her strength comes from the fact that Congress and our president and his cabinet all agree with her. From Thrash's perspective, health services are the same as any other goods and services. It's not about health. It's about the marketplace. Ms. Thrash does not want the government to compete with the private sector unless it is always impossible for government to win. Remember, this is the woman in charge of the government bureau with the largest pool of citizens' healthcare dollars."

Mr. Yeoman's change in tone chilled Don to the core.

"Thrash gives marching orders to people like The Bagman and The Obfuscator who work to make profit flow from the public healthcare system and want government healthcare administration to look bad. When Director Thrash first arrived, she called me into her office. I'll never forget what she said about Medicare and her own agency: 'I hate this stupid system. I'd blow the whole goddamned thing up if I could, but I'm stuck with it.'

"She would prefer that the government buy private insurance for everyone on Medicare and get out of the insurance business altogether. Perhaps private insurance companies could do certain things better for Americans, but that issue should be taken to the American public and addressed by legislation. Instead, Ms. Thrash undermines the law as it is written in order to benefit her pet companies. She does every thing she can to move operations over to the private sector.

"Her current preoccupation is promoting a Medicare drug benefit. She spends all her time meeting with pharmaceutical executives. My guess is she'll try to help them push through a very expensive pharmaceutical entitlement. She'll hide the real numbers about its cost. Once she's gotten it passed, she'll leave government and take a lucrative job as a lobbyist for the healthcare industry. Mark my words.

"Thrash tried to get me to work for her corporate sweethearts. She asked my bureau to draft a rule establishing a special high payment rate for a new drug-impregnated coronary stent that hasn't even been approved by the FDA! CMS has never set a payment rate for a product before FDA approval. Her friends at the medical device company convinced her this innovation is so good it must be sped to market, so she and her FDA accomplices are doing all they can to rush these experimental stents through the approval process. They are forcing us career bureaucrats to make a major exception to the usual rulemaking process. These drug-impregnated stents are experimental. Sure, they may be good. But we may find out in a couple of years they cause more heart attacks than they prevent.

"Makes one wonder whether the best interest of the beneficiaries is Director Thrash's first priority, doesn't it? Most previous CMS administrators have been career bureaucrats, but Thrash was appointed by the hospitals. She worked as a hospital lobbyist at the National Alliance of American Hospitals for eight years before coming to CMS. Now she is in a position to give the hospitals, big Pharma, and the insurance companies what they want. Question is whether that's in the best interest of the American people."

Bruce moved to the edge of his seat. "Look," he exclaimed, "most of the time the private sector does a hell of a lot better than government bureaucrats..."

Fred Yeoman looked straight at Bruce Markum. His face turned from pink to rosy red. "Listen, you know Director Thrash loves her hospitals. You know her main goal is to keep big money flowing into their ever-bigger marble mausoleums. You studied the Medicare atlas data from Dr. Sampson's seminar. You know hospitals are among the least important contributors to health. You know for most illnesses, hospitalization contributes nothing to reducing mortality. It is just more convenient to the doctors...and of course, the hospital industry."

Don wondered if Mr. Yeoman might be saying a little more than he had intended.

Frances seemed to sense this too. "Don't honest career bureaucrats face some danger standing up against these powerful interests?"

Don imagined Dante's Malebranche, the pack of devils called 'Evil-claws,' grinding their teeth, eager to tear Mr. Yeoman apart.

"Of course, we can always lose our jobs."

"It sounds like things are totally tense these days in CMS," Frances added.

"Well, it could be worse. I could work at the FDA."

Mr. Yeoman laughed heartily. Frances and Don laughed with him, but Bruce's jaw remained clenched and his lips bloodless.

"Here at CMS, we have been threatened many times and under several administrations just for following the rules," Mr. Yeoman explained. "Career bureaucrats are supposed to implement what the law requires. But upper-level administrators face all kinds of pressure from the executive branch to change the way the law is implemented. Implementation: that is where things can get pretty dicey."

Their conversation was interrupted by a knock at the door and Nancy stuck in her head. "Captain Stead is here to escort your students out. You have another meeting in five minutes."

Bruce wasted no time getting out of Mr. Yeoman's office. He stood up without a word and walked out the door to join Captain Stead. Frances and Don thanked Mr. Yeoman, who led them to the door with the parting admonition, "Listen to Sampson."

Captain Stead led them back through the labyrinth of cubicles and down the elevator to the lobby. Bruce shot out through the front doors and stormed across the parking lot. When Frances and Don reached the van, Bruce was already in the driver's seat with the engine running. As soon as they got in, he slammed the vehicle into gear and lurched across the lot and out onto the road.

"So what's eating you, Bruce?" Don asked as gently as he could. "You look steamed."

"I am steamed," he replied. "What a fucking waste of time."

"What do you mean?" Frances asked.

"That bureaucratic son of a bitch! What the hell does he know about Victoria Thrash? Vicky Thrash happens to be a friend of my family. She has eaten dinner with my family at our house. Let me tell you, Vicky Thrash is no cheap, flea-bitten, run-of-the-mill bureaucrat. She knows how the healthcare business operates and she eats two-bit bureaucrats like Fred Yeoman for lunch. It's career bureaucrats like Yeoman that stand in the way of real progress by obsessing over every one of their one million ridiculous little regulations. Everyone knows these fucking regulations are killing American business! We'd be a hell of a lot better off if nit-picking bureaucrats would just loosen up, and that's all Vicky is trying to do.

"Of course she thinks private companies could do a better job than the government in providing high quality healthcare to seniors at a low price. What's wrong with that? I mean, we have antitrust legislation so no healthcare company can get a really huge market share; that is, none except Medicare. With Medicare in the game, run by the government with fixed prices, we'll never have real competition in the marketplace. And competition on price and quality is what will improve both quality and price for consumers. Hell, Medicare only covers fifty-three percent of seniors' healthcare costs, so they are still stuck with huge bills, and because Medicare administration is so *lean*," he said sarcastically, "they overlook billions of dollars of overbilling every year that private insurers would never miss.

"Like power wheelchairs. Medicare will pay for about a hundred thousand of them this year at five thousand bucks a pop. An entitlement for people who need help getting around Wal-Mart. That's half a billon dollars a year for wheelchairs alone. Problem is, a lot of the suppliers collect the money from Medicare but never deliver the goods. Many are fictitious companies with no office and no inventory. Medicare doesn't even know where the money is going. Well you better believe BlueCross and Cigna know where their money goes. But not Yeoman. He'd rather everybody get mediocre Medicare than pay one dime to a good money manager."

Don and Frances had never seen Bruce cut loose like this before.

"We'd be a hell of a lot better off if all those blind sheep bureaucrats were rounded up in a stock car and sent to the slaughterhouse—along with all their stupid rule books!"

"That's a terrible thing to say, Bruce," Frances said. "I don't care whether you agree with Mr. Yeoman or not, that kind of language is uncalled for. That was *way* over the line."

"Sorry, Frances." Bruce fell silent but continued to drive the van hard. He screeched back through Baltimore's endless suburbs and raced down the grimy streets of northern D.C. The three remained quiet all the way back to the protective pillared façades of American University.

Don sat in the back of the van in private turmoil. His conflicting thoughts wrestled like inner demons fighting for control of his mind and heart. In two minutes, Bruce had cast a cloud of doubt on everything Mr. Yeoman had said. Could government ever be part of the answer? Bruce and Mr. Yeoman were both angry about corruption in government, but which one really knew best how to change it? Could people like Mr. Yeoman make a difference in government for good, or were they just part of the problem?

And what about Dr. Sampson? Dr. Sampson's teaching always seemed to ring true. His ideas might be counterculture, but they squared with Don's own experience. But what if Lender was right and Dr. Sampson was misleading them all? Don needed hard answers. Who could he talk to?

Not Frances. She had been pissed at him ever since their drunken drug party tour, and besides, she was taking Bruce's side on everything these days, the way she used to take Don's. It was as if her argument with Don had become a reflex. No way she was going to help him figure things out. And Bruce was too cocky and one-sided to be much help. Don already knew what he thought, anyway.

He could no longer talk to Dr. Sampson—Lender had made that clear. And he wasn't sure he could trust President Lender, either. Sampson had brought him down the rabbit hole, just as he'd promised. Don was seeing the hell in modern medicine up close. But now, who would help him find his way out?

22

National Institutes of Sickness

I have seen before now horsemen move camp, and open the attack, and make
their muster, and at times go off in flight...and I have seen the movements
of raiding-parties...and never yet have I seen horsemen move
at so strange a bugle...
DANTE ALIGHIERI, INFERNO 22, 1–15

DON SHIVERED in the cold night air and listened with growing apprehension to the rumbling of forty approaching hooves. He could just make out an old cobbled roadway in the darkness. He sensed others were with him. Where was Dr. Sampson? Could they find a place to hide before the soldiers came to tear them apart?

They cowered in the shadow of a stone wall along a narrow roadway. At the top of the hill was a locked ivory gate, portal to a walled city with massive, looming towers. Laughter interspersed with screams and shattering wood as the marauders stormed into homes along the roadway leading up to the city. The terrifying commotion moved closer; they flattened themselves against the wall.

Don was paralyzed by indecision. Should he make a futile, heroic attempt to defend his home and family, or run for his life? Where could he run? He was trapped between the locked gate and the advancing army. The thundering of horse hooves and hobnail boots of the marching brigands grew louder. In the red light of the torches, Don caught glimpses of the sweaty faces of the victors as they dragged their spoils from the broken doors of desecrated townhomes.

Soldiers took what they wanted. One dragged a squealing pig by its tied back legs, the poor creature's soft front hooves scraping across the stones. Fat mercenary generals on stout horses inspected loot and managed the plunder. Like tax collectors making their rounds, they confiscated the best of the spoils and made sure they weren't cheated.

The soldiers were looking for him. He held his breath and tried to hold himself as still as the stone at his back.

The hooded commander sat atop his huge black horse in the middle of the road and scanned the scene with his wary, calculating eyes. He spotted Don's group and pointed them out to the demon soldiers. The demons turned their fiery eyes on Don and the other terrified fugitives, opened their mouths wide, and sent peals of hollow laughter echoing down the road.

The leader threw his head back and laughed. His black hood fell back and revealed a familiar, perfect set of white-capped teeth.

The commander was Bruce.

DON AWOKE with a jerk, relieved to find himself slumped in his dorm room chair. Trying to shake off the vivid nightmare, he got up, stumbled through the books and notes scattered around the chair, and flopped down on the hard twin bed. The bedside clock read three a.m. They had an early start the next day, and he hadn't finished listening to Dr. Sampson's preparatory lecture for their visit to the National Institutes of Health.

He reached over to the nightstand and grabbed the iPod Frances had given him. He and Frances might be over now, but the iPod was a keeper. She had showed him how to connect and download lectures from the Florence College site. Don popped in the earbuds, clicked on the NIH lecture, and closed his eyes. Sampson's deep voice calmed his mind.

"The NIH grew from the Marine Hospital Service, which was established in 1798 to provide care for seamen. The Marine hospitals, like the lazarettos of medieval Europe's port cities, protected populations from the introduction of plagues and epidemics. Sick sailors were quarantined there to stem the spread of small pox, cholera, and yellow fever—diseases ravaging the United States at the time.

"In the 1870s the Marine Hospital Service obtained military authority and organized the hospitals under a surgeon general. Congress formalized the Commissioned Corps in 1889 to enforce the health injunctions of this emerging public health service.

"In 1887 the Marine Hospital Service set up its Hygienic Laboratory on Staten Island, where they created vaccines and studied the bacterial causes of infectious diseases. The service gradually expanded its public health responsibilities and in 1912 became the Public Health Service. The Hygienic Laboratory moved to Washington, D.C., and in 1930 was renamed the National Institute of Health.

"Infectious diseases became less prevalent by the end of World War II, and with the addition of new institutes to target emerging chronic illnesses like cancer and heart disease, they amended the name to the National *Institutes* of Health. Each of the institutes focused on laboratory research, reflecting the common presumption that more detailed biomedical understanding would lead to great cures for humankind.

"Many public health experts today think the conventional laboratory—an isolated room with a sterile, controlled environment—is largely outmoded, and the place to conduct studies is in the community. These scholars believe the original objective—of caring for sick travelers and protecting the home population from major infectious diseases—has mostly been achieved in the United States. However, even though the vast majority of premature death and disease today results from unhealthy behaviors and social conditions, the NIH continues to focus on laboratory and hospital research. Is the NIH stuck in the past? If so, how can it reorganize to discover and promote the key ingredients for health?"

BRUCE DROVE the van down Wisconsin Avenue toward the NIH campus. "Wake up, pilgrims!" he announced in a lively, tour guide voice. "Coming up on your left, you will see the renowned National Institutes of Health. The NIH Bethesda campus contains three hundred and fifty acres of prime real estate, about seventy-five buildings, over twenty-five hundred laboratories and six thousand scientists. This is where the best science in the world is conducted."

Fighting off drowsiness, Don sat up and looked around. A tall, black iron fence surrounded the campus. Banners hanging from light poles outside the fence bore the NIH emblem and the words, *Medicine for the Public*.

Don found the motto curious. Shouldn't it be *Health for the Public*? After all, the name *Bethesda* comes from the healing baths at the Sheep Gate of Jerusalem. In his high school bible class at St. Sebastian's, Sister Mary Connelly said Bethesda was where Jesus asked the paralytic to get up and walk, to participate in the cure, make some effort. "Hadn't Elisha required the great general Naaman to wash in the river Jordan seven times to cure his leprosy?" She said.

Gray concrete towers rose high above the bare trees on the right side of Wisconsin Avenue. A sign at the crest of the hill identified the complex as the Naval Medical Center. Bruce turned left into the entrance of the National Institutes for Health. Large red stop signs halted them at the gate, where a stern-looking guard scrutinized the van and eyeballed each of them through its smeary windows.

Bruce was unfazed. He rolled down the window and a rush of cold air swept through the van. "We have an appointment in the office of the director," he said.

The guard waved them toward a lane to the right, and Bruce pulled behind the line of cars that snaked into a wide, drive-through hangar covered with corrugated sheet metal. One by one, the cars drove forward for processing. When it was their turn, Bruce moved up and turned off the engine, as three large signs in front of the building directed.

A guard came over and thrust his hand through the window. "IDs."

They handed over their driver's licenses and he took them away. Another guard swiped the window frame and door handles of the car with a cotton pad on a stick. She seemed to be testing the dust on the car for something. Were they looking for bomb residue? Here? Who in the world would want to bomb the NIH?

The first guard came back and told Bruce to pull under the overhang. The vaulted hanger's ribbed frame formed a pointed seam in the top center, like the ridge a child makes with her knuckles when she recites the nursery rhyme, "here is the church, and here's the steeple, open the doors, and see all the people."

Bruce pulled in. A soldier holding an AK-47 held up his hand and directed them to stop in the center of the building. The soldier ordered them out of the car and told them to empty their pockets and walk one by one through a metal detector. Another opened the van door and searched through their things.

Don turned to one of the younger guards. "So, what are they guarding here?" he asked. "Is this really such a terrorism target?"

The guard was incredulous. "Don't you know? The country's biggest bio-terrorism labs are here. The viruses and bacteria they got in there could destroy the world if they got loose. And you're asking me whether the NIH is a target?"

The first guard returned with their IDs and visitor badges. "Your badges must be visible on your person at all times while you are here," he admonished.

The students got back in the van. Bruce drove toward Building 1 and parked in a space marked for visitors. They bailed out and climbed the right side of a grand double staircase leading up to the front door.

Carved in tall letters in the massive limestone lintel above the door was the name, NATIONAL INSTITUTES OF HEALTH. Dr. Sampson's warning from the recorded lecture was forgotten. Don was thrilled to see the Mecca of medical science—the one place in Washington truly dedicated to the knowledge and pursuit of health.

Masterful oil paintings of the NIH founding fathers decorated the spacious lobby. The students studied the portraits of Dr. Joseph Kinyoun, who founded the Hygienic Laboratory in 1887, and directors dating back to the early 1900s, when the institute was formed. They passed silently in front of the paintings of Drs. Rosenau, McCoy, Dyer, Sebrell. A small plaque alongside a large bust of Dr. James Shannon, for whom the building was named, explained he presided over the "golden years" of NIH expansion in the 1950s and 1960s.

"So, where are all the women?" Frances quipped.

"Here's one," Bruce called from the corner near the stairs.

Frances and Don walked across the thick linoleum floor, which gleamed with the rich patina of thousands of coats of wax. Sure enough, in the darkest corner of the lobby was a photo of Dr. Ida Bengstom, who worked in the lab in 1916.

Next to the director's office was a photograph of Dr. Harold E. Varmus, the brilliant cancer doctor. As NIH director in the early 1990s, Varmus worked hard to double the already enormous investments in Nixon's war on cancer.

A woman poked her head out of the director's office. "You must be the students." Not waiting for an answer, she came out and led them to a small waiting room across the hall. "Wait here," she ordered. "Someone will be with you in a moment."

The little room looked like an old-fashioned doctor's office. There were old magazines and molded plastic chairs from the sixties. The three sat down in the uncomfortable seats to wait.

After what seemed like hours, a balding, middle-aged man wearing a gray suit burst in. His face was flushed, and a drop of sweat trickled from each sideburn. "Ah, Dr. Markum, I've heard so much about you," he said, struggling to catch his breath.

Don felt a twinge of irritation. Did everyone know Bruce?

"I'm the associate director over operations. The director is out. I mean, we don't have a director, not right now. And the deputy director is out. But we've got some great visits set up for you."

The man didn't offer his name or ask for theirs. He handed Bruce a paper list of appointments and a map. "Keep your ID badges visible at all times, and call the office of the director if you get lost."

Bruce, Don, and Frances walked across campus, following the signs to Building 31. They entered the fifties era, bleached white building.

Bruce paused to study the assignment sheet and turned to the others. "Okay," he said, "here's where we split up." He looked at the paper again. "Don, you're going to the Office of Behavioral Health and Social Science Research, Room C501. That's C-wing, fifth floor." He pointed to the obvious sign. "Frances, you're headed to the Institute of Nursing Research, B-wing, B505. I'm going to the National Heart, Lung, and Blood Institute in the A-wing. We'll meet back on the front steps at noon. Don't be late!"

Don headed down the white hallway alone, imagining himself an important NIH researcher. *The highest achievement of an academic doctor!* The lab-coated scientists he encountered in the long halls appeared thoughtful, confident, and purposeful. He was sure they were all deeply occupied with important things and certain in the knowledge their work was of utmost importance. *Perhaps this is where I belong!*

The sign on the door of C501 read, Dr. BEVERLY THOMAS, OFFICE OF BEHAVIORAL AND SOCIAL SCIENCES RESEARCH.

"Dr. Sampson recommends you highly," Dr. Thomas said, once Don had settled into a chair in her office. "He says I should speak candidly with you." Her clear, dark eyes burrowed beneath the surface of Don's. She quietly scrutinized him, like a voodoo priestess peering into his soul and reading his path.

Her skin was chocolate brown, and her southern accent reminded him of his New Orleans grandmother, Reba. But her eyes evoked Mrs. Bellamy's. What did he see there? Fear? Determination? The look of someone who has seen into the darkness and returned? Don squirmed under her penetrating gaze.

At last she spoke, breaking the uncomfortable spell of silence. "I'll do that, Don Newman. I'll be open with you. I'll do that for Dr. Sampson." She stood up and closed the door behind him. "But you must be very careful about what you share with the others. I came here five years ago from the CDC in Atlanta and am still viewed as a bit of an outsider. There are many who would not appreciate my views."

After that short introduction, she launched into a forty-five minute lecture.

"So, you're here to learn about the problems in the NIH? Well, the NIH's most fundamental problem is its obstinate focus on an outdated, disease-oriented research model instead of one devoted to improving health. To understand what the NIH really cares about, you have to follow the money. Just look at what the NIH funds. Billions go to investigate drug effects on esoteric biochemical pathways for illnesses whose causes are already well known. Old illnesses unlikely to be cured—but easily prevented. That's the big problem. Billions of dollars devoted to sickness and almost nothing for health.

"Even though prevention is proven, we spend little money on prevention research. Little for prevention, little for quality, little to determine how to implement the care we know to be most effective. The science of application is paramount. Knowledge is worthless if you never figure out how to apply it in the real world. Most of our scientists hide out in dungeon laboratories, and their work does little good for anyone who doesn't happen to live in a dungeon. The majority of NIH funding goes for making little tweaks to sickness care, not for prevention or quality improvement research.

"The Agency for Health Research and Quality, the NIH sister organization, is a perfect example. You know AHRQ, right? Pronounced 'ark', like Noah's boat?"

Don nodded.

"Well then, you know AHRQ is known as 'the NASA of the quality movement.' It does essential work but gets only sixty million per year. The NIH gets twenty-seven billion. Imagine! For every five hundred dollars we spend in the dungeon labs, only one dollar goes for AHRQ research on how to safely and efficiently deliver the care we *already know* to be effective. We spend a trillion and a half per year on healthcare in the United States, so for every twenty-five thousand dollars on drugs, tests, doctors, and hospitals, we devote one measly dollar to patient safety research. If that doesn't shock you, let me break it down in a more personal way. Think about your own mother."

Don's chest tightened.

"If she's an average U.S. citizen," Dr. Thomas continued, "in one year we would spend roughly forty-two hundred dollars on her healthcare, seventy-five dollars on diagnosis and treatment research related to diseases she might get, but only seventeen cents on research to make her care safer and more effective. Is that what you would really want for your mother?"

It had never occurred to Don that the research priorities of his country were partly to blame for what had happened to his mother. Bitterness welled up in his throat.

"Nowhere is our misspending worse than with cancer. As you know from Dr. Sampson's seminar, we have spent over fifty billion dollars in the war on cancer, but we've had no real improvements in survival. Most research has focused on giving people poisons once they already have cancer, but chemotherapy has hardly done a thing to help. For instance, in spite of all the media attention given to breast and prostate cancer treatments, their death rates have not changed much over the past fifty years. If anything, they have slightly increased. You've studied this in epidemiology. If we're diagnosing so many breast cancers so much earlier, why aren't death rates dropping?"

Don replied without hesitation. "Lead-time bias. It's one of the first things we learned in epidemiology. Most people with breast cancer today seem to live longer because they are diagnosed earlier. Just because they live longer from the time of diagnosis doesn't necessarily mean our treatments are more effective. Some people are helped, but the results have not been nearly so dramatic as the public thinks."

"Right," she concurred. "The real improvements in mortality for certain cancers are mostly related to prevention: decreases in smoking have led to decreased deaths from lung cancer, and increases in early screening have reduced deaths for cervical and colon cancer. Most cancers could be prevented, but the science and work of implementing preventive interventions on a broad scale is undeveloped and unfunded."

Most cancers could be prevented. Maybe Momma's could have been. But most of the popular talk was about curing, not preventing, cancer.

"Here's the great secret. We know how to virtually eliminate early deaths from cancer. Prevention. We pretend not to know because we want to conquer cancer with our medicines. Have you heard the old story about a religious man caught in a flood? He waits for a miraculous rescue, and as the water rises he climbs to the roof of his house. A helicopter comes to rescue him, then a motorboat, and finally a canoe. He sends them all away because he is certain God will save him. The man drowns because he refuses to accept the obvious help right before his eyes.

"Take lung cancer, the number one cancer killer in America and worldwide. Lung cancer research is funded by the National Heart, Lung, and Blood Institute and the National Cancer Institute. We already know how lung cancer could be largely eliminated, right? Get people to stop smoking. Yet the NHLBI only spends ten percent of its lung research budget studying the policy measures and preventive interventions most likely to keep people from smoking, and it spends most of those preventive dollars to study how to help addicted people quit—something very difficult to do. Meanwhile, Big Tobacco invests millions enticing vulnerable prospects and hooking new addicts, and the U.S. government still subsidizes tobacco growers.

"We need real prevention research—studies of the best local measures in our towns and cities to keep people from starting to smoke in the first place. If we really cared about health, prevention research on lung cancer would get ninety percent of the money instead of the other way around."

"So where does most lung cancer money go?" asked Don.

"It makes me furious to think about it! About half goes to study variations on existing treatments, using slightly different combinations of chemotherapy drugs and radiation. And then there is screening research. People hope that if we can just catch lung cancer early enough, we may be able to treat it better. Generally, I'm in favor of screening research. Screening works for cervical cancer and colon cancer, but not all screening makes sense.

"We've known for years you can't catch lung cancer early enough with chest x-rays, so now the NIH is funding research to see if annual CT scans of the chest can do better. The problem with this is one of classic epidemiology, a science the NIH too often seems to ignore. Smoking causes almost all lung cancer, but a smoker's chance of getting lung cancer in any single year is very low—less than one in a thousand. That means you would have to screen a thousand people every year for a decade to detect ten with lung cancer, even if CTs caught every case.

"CT scans expose people to a lot of radiation and would probably end up causing more cancers than they detected. Furthermore, if you see something suspicious on a CT scan, you have to biopsy it to determine if it is cancer, and lung biopsies are risky. So, you can see this high-tech approach for lung cancer is pretty hopeless, not to mention ridiculously expensive.

"The focus on fancy technology, big money, and nearly hopeless sickness medicine is perverse and pervasive. Look at the famous cancer research center, MD Anderson, for example. They get tons of NIH funding, but not one person there gets NIH funding to help prevent people from smoking in the first place! Instead, their dozens of NIH-funded researchers spend time squabbling over the holy grail of a possible genetic cure for cancer, or debating the relative merits of alternative chemotherapy regimens that prolong life by a few miserable months.

"So, there you have it. Fundamental epidemiology receives little funding or attention. Of course, the public has no clue about basic epidemiological facts. Cancer is a great example. People believe their lives are being miraculously saved by the gruesome cancer therapies they undergo. They have no idea of the real truth.

"In New York, where I attended university, there was a wealthy man who underwent prostate cancer surgery at age fifty-five. As a result of the surgery, he couldn't get an erection and had to wear a diaper because he leaked urine—these are common complications of prostate surgery—but he was overjoyed because he believed the surgeon had saved his life. In gratitude, he gave over five million dollars to the Prostate Cancer Foundation to fund more research on treatments for advanced prostate cancer.

"It is true, as far as I know, that five years later this man's cancer has not come back. But he is ignorant of a proven epidemiological fact: 99.9 percent of those with prostate cancer don't die from it in the five years after diagnosis—whether they get surgery or not. Only about one man in fifteen who has prostate cancer surgery lives longer because of it, and it takes around fifteen years for this benefit to show up. At the same time, at least a third of the men who have the surgery end up with sexual dysfunction or urinary incontinence, and these problems start immediately.

"Similarly, the expected five-year survival rate is eighty-nine percent for breast cancer, and most older women with breast cancer die from other causes. Women with breast cancer think their lives are saved by surgery, chemotherapy, and radiation, but the epidemiological truth is that women usually live a long time with breast cancer—whether they get gruesome therapies or not.

Many of our so-called cures for more aggressive cancers only prolong life a little bit, often only two or three months. And the cost is often high—chemotherapy diminishes quality of life and can cause cognitive impairment—chemo brain—that can last for years. A patient might want chemotherapy to buy time, but should make an informed decision based on how much time it's likely to buy, and at what cost.

"Then there's the human genome project, widely touted out as the way to individualize cures. As you know, most human genes are identical from person to person. Less than one tenth of one percent of our genes vary from person to person, and yet over three billion dollars have been devoted to this tiny difference, as if those particular genes would explain why some people get diseases and others don't. Sure, some people are slightly more susceptible to obesity and diabetes than others, but we all are susceptible, and the best cures for the diabetes epidemic are behavioral and environmental.

"Our bodies are made to work outdoors, exercise vigorously every day, and live on natural food: mostly vegetables, nuts, and fruits. We can't get around that. People actually think we'll invent a magic potion to change their genes so they can eat all they want and stay glued to the couch! If we really want to stop diabetes and most other diseases of the modern world, we should fund research to improve our environment and support healthy living. For the government to devote three billion dollars to the human genome project is ridiculous. It's interesting, but has little to do with promoting health."

Dr. Thomas took a brief pause in her tirade. Don looked around her office and spotted the book *Biohazard* on her shelf, the one they had been required to read for this session.

"What do you think about our country's new investments in bioterrorism research?" he asked, remembering the elaborate security measures at the gate.

"Don't get me started! Don, in your years as a doctor, you've probably seen ten thousand people in the hospital or clinic. How many of them had the plague?"

"None," he replied. "Nobody I know of has ever seen a case."

"On the other hand, what percent suffered from some aspect of the metabolic syndrome of pre-diabetes and hypertension that leads to most heart attacks and strokes and causes a third or more cases of cancer?"

"Oh, I would say at least eighty percent."

"Which should we spend more money on? The plagues of the Middle Ages or the plague of obesity affecting the majority of Americans right now? We are spending almost nothing on obesity, the major plague of *our* time. Almost nothing! We have no national strategy to address this epidemic. Less than seven percent of NIH spending goes to fund research on obesity and diabetes. The government looks the other way and ignores a serious modern killer plague while lavishing resources on cancer research.

"Why do you think the government has ignored the obesity epidemic?" Don asked.

Dr. Thomas dropped a report onto the desk in front of him. "Here are the edits the United States government recently demanded in the World Health Organization report on obesity. The U.S. focused on denying the report's claims that obesity is linked to fast food and soft drinks. These revisions came from a very high level in the administration—not from the scientific reviewer assigned to the case.

"We suspect soft drink and fast food lobbyists, led by the American Beverage Association, fed these edits to the administration. Basically, they claimed there was inadequate research to prove that fast food consumption leads to obesity. Well, of course there isn't enough research to prove it—because the government refuses to fund it! The main reason we don't have proof of the environmental

factors contributing to obesity and diabetes is the NIH itself refuses to adequately support it!

"What about bioterrorism research? It is well funded, in spite of the fact
that committing an act of bioterrorism is a lot more difficult than using a bomb
and not nearly as effective. No one has done any better using plague as a weapon
than the Tartar marauder Janibeg, who in 1346 catapulted plague victims over
the city walls of Caffa to infect the Genoese inhabiting the city. And let me tell
you, that was a lot of trouble.

"Today, the most likely way of spreading deadly diseases like plague and
smallpox is from the biocontainment labs themselves. There have been many
hundreds of terrible accidents in and around the hot labs governments run.
Remember Marburg, Germany, in 1967? Lab personnel playing around with a
hemorrhagic virus from the deep jungles of Africa accidentally infected thirty-
one people. Seven died. The new bioterrorism research initiatives at the NIH
paradoxically increase the risk of loosing more lethal germs on the world."

"That explains all the security around here," Don said.

"Yes. You know, one of the biggest bioterrorist attacks of all time just
occurred with anthrax. It killed five people—the fifth died a little more than a
month ago. It's rumored that the particular strain of anthrax used could only
have come from the Army lab in Fort Detrick, Maryland. In any case, the source
was domestic—not from a terrorist country but from here! The FBI is confident
it was someone connected with the U.S. biodefense program, but the American
public has no clue. It would seem our government prefers people to suspect it
came from Iraq."

"But don't lots of countries have biological weapons programs?"

"No. Only a few. The thing is, these programs threaten the countries that run
them more than they do their enemies. Look at the Soviet Union. Dr. Ustinov,
the leader of the famous Vector Institute, was killed by the same Marburg virus
when it accidentally got loose in his lab."

"What about Svedlovsk?" Don asked. He'd read over sixty people were
killed there in 1979 because Soviet workers at a secret weapons-grade anthrax
production facility forgot to replace an exhaust filter. If the wind had been in a
different direction that day, the death rate would have been far higher.

"Thank God, no country today has a bioweapons program as aggressive
as the Soviet Union's was," she replied. "These days, the most likely place for
foreign bioterrorists to train is in U.S. labs, where they're planning to double the
number of labs approved to handle the world's deadliest infectious agents to
over four hundred. No one wants the American public to know it, but accidents
happen. Stuff turns up missing in these labs all the time.

Don raised his eyebrows.

"I know, hard to believe, right? But true. Our government plans to spend over five hundred million dollars in the next few years on regional biohazard labs. Add that to the three billion they budgeted for biodefense through the CDC and the Department of Homeland Security. The administration just devoted another one and a half billion to the NIAID—the National Institute of Allergy and Infectious Disease—for bioterrorism research. In addition, the U.S. Army Chemical and Biological Defense Command at Fort Detrick has its own set of high-cost biohazard research facilities, and their lab that handles the deadliest agents like the Ebola virus is right across the street from us at the Naval Medical Center. They have an entire elite Army regiment guarding it. And you should see the security at the CDC in Atlanta. They're one of the two official repositories for the smallpox virus, a killer disease that has been completely eradicated in people. It only exists in the lab.

Dr. Thomas pointed toward the window. "See right out there? That's the newest addition, Building 33."

Don looked at the gleaming brick and glass building outside her window.

"That's their latest state-of-the-art biocontainment facility. Building 33 is a level-3 facility, made of specially hardened concrete that's more difficult to blow up. They handle SARS, drug-resistant TB, tularemia, and even avian flu there. But the real excitement is in the BSL-4 lab in Building 41A. Germs assigned to biosafety level 4, the highest level of security, include most of the hemorrhagic fever viruses like Ebola, Lassa, and Marburg, and the worst encephalitis viruses, like Hanzalova."

No wonder the NIH was like a prison under lock-down. It was a real-life Jurassic Park, a zoo for extinct infectious killers. The barricades weren't just there to keep terrorists out, but to keep the perils in!

"Ever since September 11th, everyone here is in a rush to do something," Dr. Thomas complained. "The NIH is throwing money at biological weapons research, and university researchers follow the funding. Troops of microbiologists, biochemists, even physiologists, are bellying up to the trough. And who do you think wants to study these deadly germs? The same ones who wanted to collect tarantulas, poisonous snakes, and black widow spiders as children. People fascinated with death, not life. If they want to study those things, fine. But should we trust them with our lives and security? Should the government spend the bulk of its medical research budget on them? Unfortunately, as the number of research labs and personnel handling lethal germs explodes, safety, security, and oversight become more difficult.

"Tell me," Don interrupted, "what about corruption? Is that a big problem at the NIH?"

"To be honest, most researchers here at the NIH are above board. There are a few notorious exceptions, like Trey Sunderland at NIMH, the National

Institutes of Mental Health. He got over half a million dollars in 'honoraria' from Pfizer while collaborating with Pfizer on behalf of the government to lead an Alzheimer's study. He endorsed the company's drugs at national meetings without revealing his financial connection with Pfizer to the NIH or to his colleagues at the national meetings. Thank goodness, government researchers as brazen as Sunderland are few and far between.

"But the university researchers we fund? That's another matter. Some researchers care more about winning NIH grant money than any possible benefit their research might have for humans. Some will even steal or falsify data to get the money. Unfortunately, researchers skilled in getting money are beloved by universities these days. They hire them as mercenaries and let them do almost anything, so long as they keep bringing in the money. I've even heard of schools covering up sexual abuse and rapes of graduate students in their efforts to avoid losing the research dollars well-funded perpetrators bring in. Also, university researchers that take additional money from private industry are less likely to share the results of their NIH-funded research with others. The private companies end up getting the benefit of their NIH research.

"Those are the outrageous examples, but most corruption at the NIH is more insidious. Don, you know the NIH supports the development of the most influential practice guidelines in the world, right?"

Don nodded.

"Biased selection of members for scientific review panels or consensus guideline panels can corrupt all the science they oversee, fund, and interpret. The panels determine what science to fund and what guidelines doctors follow. In the past, these panels were the realm of the scientists and generally free of politics and industrial conflicts of interest. But things are changing. If a company can influence the guidelines to favor their drugs, they stand to gain millions, right?

"Let me give you a few examples. The 2001 NIH cholesterol guidelines promise to triple the number of Americans on expensive cholesterol-lowering drugs. Did you know the guidelines were adopted by a panel in which five members—over a third of the panel—had major financial ties to companies that stood to gain billions?

"In another case, a Public Health Service panel in 2000 put out an aggressive government message urging smokers to use nicotine replacement drugs and other medicines to help them quit, not bothering to mention that most people who quit successfully do it cold turkey. Is it any coincidence the chair of the panel and at least half the panel members had direct financial ties to the companies making the nicotine replacement products they touted?

"Look at what happened to AHRQ. AHRQ was a respected source for clinical guidelines, but Congress forced them to stop publishing them after the orthopedic surgeons objected. The AHRQ guidelines summarized the strong evidence that most people with acute back pain do better without surgery. The spinal surgeons donated huge amounts to their congressmen and lobbied to shut the agency down, and they nearly succeeded. This kind of politicizing of NIH, AHRQ, and HHS committees and panels results in less research based on science and more commercials posing as science."

By this point in Dr. Thomas' discourse, Don was thoroughly depressed. So little of the work of the National Institutes of Health was pro-health. None of the institutes focused on the whole body or on how to promote health and prevent disease. The brick buildings and biohazard labs he had admired were like plague homes marked for quarantine, isolation, and study—houses for the worship of disease and death. In fact, each institute was named for a disease or diseased organ and focused on the body cut up, corrupt, and decaying.

Lost in his gloomy thoughts, Don missed most of the rest of what Dr. Thomas said, and when he finally looked at his watch it was ten minutes past noon. He was late! He thanked her, excused himself, and ran out the door and down the hall.

Bruce and Frances weren't waiting on the front steps of Building 1. Don found them inside, talking with the administrator.

"So, Dr. Newman, after your visit today, which institute do you plan to work in?" the administrator asked.

"Well, I guess I'd like to do health services research to improve healthcare quality."

He looked disappointed. "Oh, I see. You could always try to get funding from AHRQ, but there's not a whole lot of money there."

Bruce laughed. "AHRQ? Ha! The majority party has cut that budget to the quick and would love to shut it down. Remember, it's all about money, Don. They don't want researchers to document how bad the healthcare in America is. That would be bad for business."

The students said their goodbyes to the administrator and walked toward the exit.

"Yeah," Bruce whispered, "by the time you finish your little Sampson wannabe training there won't be much left of AHRQ."

Bruce was probably right. Dr. Sampson had lured him onto a path to academic disaster. Health services research almost never gets funded. He'd end up like Dr. Thomas, with little funding or respect. How ironic that her fierce loyalty to the cause of human health made her odds for survival at the NIH poor. Did Dr. Sampson expect him to follow her on this hard path? A career in academic healthcare quality research looked even worse than cardiology. NIH might be the marker of research success, but to get funding he'd have to venerate sickness and death.

On their way out, Don noticed a large bronze plaque near the entrance of Building Number 1.

THIS INSTITUTE IS DEDICATED TO MATTERS
PERTAINING TO THE PUBLIC HEALTH

Like hell! Maybe that was once true. But now the NIH was serving other masters.

A few minutes later, they passed the famous NIH Clinical Center, the monolithic research hospital where people go for cutting edge, experimental cures. A nurse pushed a frail man in a wheelchair up the sidewalk. The man looked up into the bleak midwinter sky. His hair was gone and he wore a hospital gown and white support hose. The nurse wore a yellow gown and mask typical of a bone marrow transplant unit.

What hopeless last-ditch chemotherapy treatment was that poor man getting?

LATE THAT NIGHT in his American University dorm room, Don estimated the money spent on government bureaucracy and NIH research. The totals were growing. He estimated the number of lives saved by each, using the best epidemiological methods he could muster. He had to admit a few lives were likely saved by the new devices and motorized scooters promoted by industry-connected bureaucrats, and a few lives were prolonged by the latest chemotherapy regimens developed at the NIH. *But at what cost?* He totaled the dollars saved and spent and added them to his version of Botticelli's hell, then lay down on the hard, crinkly, plasticized mattress and fell into a turbulent sleep.

23

White Coat Hypocrites

There below we found a painted people who were going round with very slow steps,
weeping and looking weary and overcome. They had cloaks with cowls
down over their eyes…so gilded outside that they were dazzling,
but within all lead…O toilsome mantle for eternity!
DANTE ALIGHIERI, INFERNO 23, 58–67

IT WAS HARD to be with his father in Chicago over the Christmas holiday. Really hard. Jacob Newman was utterly lost without his Rachele. He tried to put on a brave face, but underneath the mask was nothing but anguish and sorrow. Several times he asked Don how things were going, but didn't listen to the answers. He didn't seem to hear much of anything Don said.

At their makeshift Christmas Eve dinner, they sat in silence across from one another at the dining room table. No tablecloth graced the table, and his mother's centerpiece of handmade nativity figurines was missing. No scents of cinnamon, marzipan, or panettone wafted from the kitchen. There was no Luciano Pavarotti singing "Oh Holy Night," no sparkling wine to celebrate the coming of Babbo Natale, their Father Christmas. Dinner came from Rossetti's Grocery, where Don was now a stranger. They ate warmed-over bean soup, pungent pecorino cheese and crackers, imported panettone, and store-bought cannelloni, cold and stale and nothing like Mrs. Rossetti's.

As Jacob opened the colorful box and removed the cellophane from the panettone, Don eagerly anticipated the eruption of marsala, cinnamon, and citron that always accompanied the cutting of his mother's warm sweetbread. But when his father cut the cake nothing happened. No steam, no vapor, no incense rose around them. Jacob stared at the foreign panettone in front of him, knife in hand, as if waiting for a miracle. He held the knife far too long, pointing it at Don across the table.

Jacob's gaunt face hung over their Christmas Eve repast like a grinning skull. He struggled to maintain the habitual grin he had long used to insulate himself from the world. To Don, his grin looked like risus sardonicus, the involuntary smile of tetanus as the muscles spasm and force the face into a joker's grin before death.

Don felt completely powerless to help him. He knew his father had no hope for the future and wanted to die. Was his own future any brighter?

Don rubbed his left knee beneath the table. Don's knees always ached when he sat a long time in one place, especially the left one. He had only been sitting for a few minutes, but he felt fidgety. He couldn't wait to escape his father's presence. He wanted to run away down the street from this house and never return.

There was something else. Don felt guilty. He imagined what his father must be thinking as they sat across from each other in silence: *My son is a doctor, for God's sake! I'm only a chemist. He should have done something to help her. He should have helped his mother. He should have helped save my Rachele!* Of course, his father would never say those things out loud, but his eyes accused Don with every glance.

Don and his father had talked little since his mother had died. The two of them had never been good at conversation with one another. Momma had been the mediator; she always did most of the talking. Though they weren't comfortable talking directly about her, no one else shared their common sorrow, so in a perverse way they each longed for—and despised—the other's presence.

Don spent much of his Christmas break in the arched gothic halls of the University of Chicago library, even though it took an hour to get there from the house. Don told his father he was researching national health policy, but the truth was he couldn't stand to be at home alone with his father all day. He had never really liked his father. Deep down, he thought his father wasn't worthy of Rachele Innocenti.

Jacob Meriweather Newman was born and raised in New Orleans, the second son of a compounding chemist and pharmacist. He came from an old New Orleans family. His people had always lived just back of the French Quarter, in Tremé, a world apart from the rest of the United States. Creole descendants of French and Spanish settlers lived and worked there among free blacks long before Uptown New Orleans was developed.

Though Creoles usually didn't marry blacks, longstanding interracial relationships were common, and many children were born of these unions. Don's father was black, though he would never admit it. He considered himself French Creole, but he was what they used to call a Creole of color. Since his skin was a shade darker than a paper grocery sack, he wouldn't have been able to pass through the doors of New Orleans' finer Creole social clubs in the '40s.

Jacob Newman's family was proud of their heritage. Their earliest known ancestor was known as Kahimbe Torneau. Family tradition held he was an African healer with a gift for languages. He arrived in New Orleans with the first French settlers around 1717 as a slave from Senegal. From Senegal, he brought knowledge of the herbs, poisons, gris-gris charms, and amulets that gave the sick new strength and power. From the Native Americans in Louisiana, he learned the local medicinal herbs and their uses.

The family claimed Torneau was the legendary Negro physician who taught the famous historian Le Page du Pratz to cure the distemper of yaws. He presumably helped du Pratz write his *Histoire de la Louisiane,* a book Meriwether Lewis took as a guide some seventy years later on his famous expedition of the American West in the early 1800s.

In the bayous of Louisiana, Torneau found entire forests of sassafras trees for treatment of syphilis, ginseng root for cough syrup, sarsaparilla for root beer and impotence, and St. John's wort for depression. He learned to combine herbal remedies with voodoo healing rituals, customizing his blends depending on the needs of individual clients. Even whites called on him in times of sickness, which were frequent in the "mal-aria," the bad air, of New Orleans. The fetid, stagnant waters and swamp gases of the bayou seemed to carry sickness to almost everyone. Yellow fever, malaria, and dysentery killed almost a third of the first sixty-seven hundred French immigrants shortly after they arrived. The survivors were thankful for whatever had seemed to help.

Torneau saved the life of one well-born French child from the blackwater fever. He sat vigil by her bed, without apparent fear of the deadly contagion, and gave her sips of willow bark tea for fever and sweet gum sap for diarrhea. She survived, and her grateful father bought the black slave healer and freed him. That was the family legend that had come down through the generations, and as far back as anyone could remember, Don's father's family had been free blacks. They had long been well educated and worked in pharmacies and with folk medicines.

On her rare visits to Chicago, Don's paternal grandmother, Reba, told him bedtime stories about his ancestors. Don loved to lounge in her lap in her favorite living room rocker, resting his young head against her soft pendulous breasts, staring up at her smooth, golden brown face and twinkling eyes, listening to her recount the family tales.

Reba loved to tell the story of their first white ancestor, Guillaume Bonhomme. He was a free-thinking Frenchman who believed in the revolutionary slogan, *Liberté, égalité, fraternité,* the ideals that fanned the French Revolution and infected Benjamin Franklin, Thomas Jefferson, and the young nation with the idea of equality. The French did not hold as much prejudice against dark-skinned people as the English. For the cosmopolitan inhabitants of the French Quarter, it was a matter of pride to treat blacks with respect, to contribute to their education, and to free slaves when they had a chance.

Of course, the proper New Orleans society in which he lived only carried these ideals so far. Bonhomme met Don's great-great-great grandmother at a quadroon ball, where white men could dance with women of color and contract with their mothers for visiting privileges, typically in return for housing and support. The two fell in love at first sight.

Their son, Don's great-great-grandfather, was considered a bastard, and Bonhomme's family never acknowledged the relation. After all, Louisiana's *Code Noir*, established in 1724, prohibited free blacks from marrying whites. But Bonhomme never married anyone else, and he sent his son to the best schools available to persons of color. Meanwhile, the boy's black family taught him everything there was to know about pharmaceuticals. Don's great-great-grandfather took the black family name Torneau, and with it, he carried on the family's work with cures and potions.

In 1803, with the Louisiana Purchase, the Americans took control of New Orleans, and they did not take kindly to the idea of free blacks. In virtually every American colony outside Louisiana, it was illegal for blacks to prescribe medicines or treat the sick, for fear slaves would poison their masters. According to the Virginia slave act of 1748: *If any slave, 'free negro or mulatto', shall prepare, exhibit or administer any medicine whatsoever [except upon order of the master], he or she so offending shall be adjudged guilty of a felony, and suffer death without benefit of clergy.* Laws in South Carolina, Georgia, and other southern states prohibited Negroes from using *any poisonous Root, Plant, Herb, or other sort of poison whatever,* and made it illegal for whites to employ any Negro—slave or free—in any shop where medicines were kept.

Naturally, these laws and attitudes were of great concern to the Torneaus, since medicines were their livelihood. In their efforts to assimilate to the new order, the Torneaus changed their name to Newman. That wasn't enough to appease the whites, however. Business lagged amidst rumors the Newman pharmacists practiced voodoo and witchcraft, and they were forced to give up their independent pharmacy.

Don's great-great-grandfather went to work compounding remedies for one of the oldest pharmacies in town. Louis Dufilho had opened his Pharmacie Française on Chartres Street in the heart of the French Quarter in 1823. People would consult Mr. Dufilho, or Don's great-great-grandfather when Mr. Dufilho was out, before they would go to see a licensed physician. Dufilho's pharmacy had porcelain urns filled with medicinal herbs, roots, and fungi from all over the world, even leeches imported from Europe. In those days leeches were sold as a remedy for all sorts of infections.

Some people said Dufilho's pharmacy discretely concocted and sold herbal potions using the old recipes for those who didn't want to be seen associating with voodoo healers. It was rumored if the price was right, you could get special cures devised by the renowned voodoo queen, Marie Laveau. But these were likely only rumors. Dufilho's shop was the first pharmacy to be licensed in the United States because of its reputation for scientific competence.

By 1830 the number of free blacks in New Orleans had grown to almost twelve thousand, and the Newmans were able to reestablish their own pharmacy in the early 1840s. Like Dufilho, the Newman men prided themselves on their ability to compound medicines supported by scientific evidence in the best French and English medical journals. They refused to sell voodoo cures, even though there was substantial demand in the frequent periods of pestilence in New Orleans. The family had never produced a licensed physician, but when someone was seriously ill and the traditional doctors offered little hope, it was not uncommon for the Newman men to be called out late at night to do what they could to heal.

The family enjoyed relative freedom in New Orleans for one hundred and fifty years, until the Civil War began. At first the Newmans sided with the South, but once New Orleans was captured, they quietly sided with the North. Like many free blacks of New Orleans in that period, they refused to take a stand for civil rights for all blacks because it was bad for business. The Newmans and others like them had no problem with slavery, so long as free blacks remained free. Free blacks didn't have much in common with the uneducated, less civilized slaves. Besides, many of their friends owned slaves. From the Newman family's perspective, certain people were suited for slavery.

However, the Newmans were quick to take advantage of the new business opportunities emancipation offered. They didn't protest when the Jim Crow laws throughout the South mandated separate facilities for blacks—they just made sure their pharmacy became the pharmacy of choice for all the black residents of New Orleans. They built one of the most successful pharmacies in town by selling their compounded elixirs, liniments, and herbal cures from their home and door-to-door. Business really took off in the 1930s when Jacob's father, Isaac Newman, advertised they were the first black-only pharmacy in New Orleans.

Isaac Newman had two sons, Ethan in 1930, and Don's father, Jacob, born in 1932. Ethan grew bigger and stronger; Jacob was the studious one. When Jacob was just reaching puberty, Ethan took it upon himself to toughen his brother up, giving him regular drubbings "to make a man out of him." One day he gave thirteen-year-old Jacob a bloody nose and earned a fierce tongue-lashing from his mother. At that point, Ethan gave up and mostly ignored his younger brother.

Ethan joined the high school football team and hunted and fished in the bayous with his friends every chance he got. Jacob was a loner. He got top grades but had few close friends. Of course, both boys spent most afternoons and weekends working in the pharmacy. It was understood they would attend college and then return to work in the family business. The family could only send one son to college at a time, so the plan was for Ethan to attend college first, while Jacob helped run the pharmacy and waited his turn. Jacob, however, had other plans.

In 1948, Isaac opened a second pharmacy on Carrollton near the end of the trolley line, and he made it clear it was a critical time for the family business. Jacob liked compounding chemicals and elixirs in the back, but his father usually did that. The help Isaac really wanted was someone to man the cash register and deliver drugs to shut-ins. In other words, he needed a people person, and Jacob Newman was not a people person; he preferred figures and formulas. Ethan, on the other hand, was great at the cash register and knew all the customers by name. He was, without a doubt, his father's favorite.

Jacob quietly and determinedly pursued his studies and bided his time. He knew his father would never send him to college before his older brother, but he'd heard about the GI bill, and at age sixteen he started talking to an Army recruiter. In 1949 he turned seventeen, passed the GED, and signed up with the Army. He confided in no one except his mother, Reba, who encouraged him to follow his heart. He waited until the day before his scheduled leave to tell his father.

All Isaac could say was, "Why couldn't you have just waited for your brother?" That was it. He didn't say goodbye. He simply turned his face away.

Ethan was livid. "Why, you no-good son of a bitch," he said. "Yeah, get the hell out of here and leave me to watch over these two-bit drugstores, but don't you ever come back, 'cause if you do I'll kill you."

Jacob took him at his word. He never went back to New Orleans and never talked to his brother or his father again. He wrote them a couple of letters—when he returned to the States and when he got married—but was rebuffed with silence. He stayed in touch with family news through his mother, but despite Reba's best efforts, she was unable to make peace.

Isaac died ten years after Jacob left New Orleans, before Don was born. Jacob did not attend his father's funeral. Ethan never went to college, but he thrived in the pharmacy business. By the 1960s, success in the pharmacy business was all about sales, Ethan's strength. The times for compounding were gone and Ethan was glad. By the 1970's, he had grown the family business into a chain of six pharmacies.

Jacob's early years in the Army went by in a blur. After basic training at Fort Benning, Georgia, he signed up to be a medic and was transferred to Fort Sam Houston in San Antonio for training. His first posting was at the U.S. Army Health Center in Vicenza, Italy. He thought it would be temporary, but the captain in charge of laboratory services soon discovered Jacob's talent with chemicals and drugs and put him to work in the lab. When the expected transfer orders came, the captain cited an extraordinary need for Private Newman, and Jacob spent his entire tour in Vicenza rather than Korea, which he didn't mind at all.

The rest of the story Don knew by heart. His mother had told him of their first meeting and romance hundreds of times, and the portents and themes of their story were emblazoned in his memory.

One day, while walking down a narrow cobblestone side street in Vicenza, Jacob came across a small bookstore called Libreria Alighieri. A large, leather-bound volume in the window lay open to reveal a vivid illustration that reminded him of a painting in the St. Louis Cathedral, where as a child, Jacob used to sneak inside to gawk at the elaborate interior. A gilded scene above the altar depicted Saint Louis, the King of France, attended by a long line of eager followers and announcing the Seventh Crusade. The antique volume in the bookstore window showed a similar stream of devotees or priests in dazzling orange robes, walking and hunched over, as if bent under the weight of some terrible burden.

Jacob became lost in the scene for several minutes, finally looking up when he sensed someone was watching him. There in the bookstore window was a dark-haired beauty, studying him with a curiosity that matched his own. Her pale skin and gray eyes were luminescent and drew him like a moth to the light. She held his gaze a little longer than was proper, or at least that was his impression. He was entranced. He had never seen a young woman so beautiful. She abruptly disappeared behind the rows of bookshelves.

In that very moment, Jacob decided to learn Italian. Over the next year, he returned to the Libreria Alighieri every chance he got, and slowly he pieced together that the beautiful young woman was Rachele Innocenti, the sixteen-year-old daughter of the storeowner. Rachele was as intelligent as she was beautiful, and he became thoroughly smitten. She knew all the stories of ancient literature as if they were the stories of her own family, and she was eager to practice the English she was studying in school. Likewise, he seized every opportunity to ask her questions, under the pretext of practicing his Italian.

Jacob was wise enough not to betray his strong attraction to her. After all, he was a black man, and even in post-war Italy, few families would welcome him as a companion for their daughter. For a full year, he never broached the formal decorum of merchant and client, and he practiced Italian like a fiend. He began to attend mass again, something he had seldom done since his childhood. Each Sunday he took the bus into town and climbed up the one hundred ninety-two steps to the Church of the Madonna of Monte Berico, where the Innocentis attended. He sat in the back and never spoke to Rachele, but he made sure the family noticed his presence. Afterward, he'd stand alone in front of the basilica, look out over the city below to the Dolomites rising majestically in the distance, and imagine a future with Rachele.

In the Libreria Alighieri, their hushed conversations between the stacks grew more serious. Both Rachele's English and Jacob's Italian became passable. Jacob learned how to time his visits to the bookstore when Rachele was working alone. He remained extremely careful, however; when her parents came in he focused his attention on the books. Usually, he would buy whatever volume he was holding and leave.

After a year of increasingly delicious moments of real conversation in the bookstore, Jacob mustered enough nerve to invite Rachele to join him for the passeggiata, the ritual stroll through the town center. It was a big step. Everyone in town was outside for the passeggiata each evening, strolling down the streets, chatting, and greeting each other. Everyone would see them together, and this was sure to provoke gossip. Despite the risk, she agreed to ask her parents, who in turn invited him over to their apartment on Sunday afternoon.

When the day finally arrived, Jacob's nervousness nearly overcame him. His knees wobbled on his way up the two flights of stairs to the Innocentis' apartment above the bookstore. His hand shook as he grasped the doorknocker and gave it three taps.

Rachele's father answered and invited him into the living room. He sat on the couch and indicated for Jacob to sit in the upholstered chair across from him. The whole family gathered round. Rachele's mother sat silently with her hands tightly clasped in her lap, Rachele sat beside her mother and glanced nervously back and forth at her parents, and her sister and three brothers sat in silence and gave the black man curious stares.

Signore Innocenti grilled Jacob about his background for what seemed like hours, and Jacob responded to each question in his best Italian. He explained he was French Creole and recited his polished presentation of his distinguished family history, carefully omitting the obvious—that he was black. He parlayed his minor position at the U.S. Army Health Center into a task worthy of a general.

Rachele's nervous parents were skeptical of their daughter's acquaintance and his intentions. Would he prove like Othello—the dark skinned Moor general from nearby Venice—and their daughter end up like Desdemona? But the American private's determination impressed them. After thirty minutes of conversation, Lábano, Rachele's papa, decided to tell a story.

When American tanks rumbled into Vicenza at the end of the war, Lábano was a young boy. The American liberators were greeted as heroes, as saviors, and everyone was ecstatic. Lábano had never witnessed such happy exuberance in his short life. He was sitting on his father's shoulders in the piazza, surrounded by the cheering crowd, when a black soldier popped his head out of the hatch of an American tank. He was the first black man Lábano had ever seen. The soldier reached down and gave him a stick of gum.

As Lábano told the story tears welled up in his eyes. The ice was broken. The Innocentis permitted their daughter to go on the passeggiata with Jacob provided they take Rachele's littlest brother along, and that evening Jacob bought the little boy the first of many gelati.

Not long after, Jacob bought a motor scooter, and soon he and Rachele were taking unchaperoned picnics in the countryside together on Sunday afternoons. It was a glorious year they would remember as the best in their lives. Before Jacob knew it, his two-year tour had come to an end.

He didn't reenlist; he knew this was his chance to get the education he had always wanted through the GI bill. He asked Papa Lábano for Rachele's hand; he wanted her to join him in America.

Lábano laughed at first, and then replied in rapid angry Italian, "Voi due siete troppo giovane!" Lábano said the two were much too young, the relationship was completely unrealistic, and to come back when he had a real future to offer her, not an imagined one.

Jacob tried to convince Rachele to elope, but she refused. There were tears, grief, and Jacob's repeated promises to return—"tornerò!" He left Vicenza in despair, hopeless of ever gaining Rachele's hand.

Don had heard the legend of his parents' marriage many times—how his father earned his degree and returned seven years later to be refused by Lábano again, how Lábano finally agreed to their mixed marriage after another seven years, when they were thirty-four and thirty-two. But his parents had kept the rest of the story from Don, and he had no idea what his father had been up to in those fourteen intervening years.

Over the Christmas holiday, the townhouse was disturbingly quiet. Even Wolf was gone. His beautiful, white longhaired Spitz had died shortly after he left for medical school. He had been too busy to notice then, but he sure missed him now.

One day, Don offered to stay home and help with cleaning, organizing, and preparing some of his mother's old things for donation while his father went to the grocery store and pharmacy. He started in his parents' closet.

Everything of his mother's was untouched. Her favorite dresses still hung in a row. Her fine Italian leather shoes were lined up side by side. Sweaters and fine wool and silk scarves were all neatly stacked on shelves. Standing there alone, he caught a whiff of her jasmine perfume and buried his face in her sweaters and wept.

Don realized he was not ready to pack and donate her clothes, so he moved on to the library. His mother had always dealt with the household business, and the paper had really piled up. Don sorted through the stacks of bills and junk mail, tidied the desktop, then started on the drawers. That's where he discovered the five-inch stack of old letters.

The letters were in the very back of the bottom left desk drawer, neatly bundled and tied with cotton twine. The postmark on the uppermost envelope, "Decatur, Georgia," piqued Don's interest. There was no return address. Don glanced out the front bay windows through the leafless limbs of the elms lining the street below, confirmed his father's car was not there, and began to untie the cord that bound the mysterious time capsule. It took him a long time to loosen the knots.

He thumbed through the pile. Every letter was addressed in the same hand, and they were ordered by the postmark dates, which ran from 1956 to September 1966. The oldest were from Decatur, but the ones on the lower half of the stack came mostly from Atlanta, with a few from places like Raleigh, New York, and Washington, D.C. The final postmark date Don recognized as the day of his parents' marriage.

Don's hands shook as he opened the first letter and unfolded the brittle paper inside. The letter's corners were grimy and bent.

> Dear Jack,
>
> I am pretty well settled in with Grandma Mae here in Decatur. Of course she won't let me leave the house, at all. She wants to make it so that none of her neighbors even know that I'm here. Despite the blazing heat this fall she has all the shutters closed and when people call she pretends she's ill. Even with all the fans running in the house, by mid-day the tin roof makes it like a pressure cooker in here. You can imagine how overheated I'm getting.
>
> Grandma Mae is very old-fashioned as you know, and being stuck here is driving me crazy. Only after reaching my limit and blowing my temper a time or two, I've discovered Grandma has a temper to best mine; something I never knew about her. The other day when I threatened to leave, she yelled at me, "Girl, you have frazzled my last nerve, and if you don't go back to your room right now and shut your mouth, I'm liable to throw you out and not let you back in." That set me back a bit. Of course I could go back to New York and stay with my mother and her new husband. But that would be worse. At least here I have my own room and I don't have to face my mother.
>
> I never expected to be imprisoned in some southern country shack in a place with such primitive customs. I guess it serves me right, and will help me understand the mind of the Southern Black if I ever get to do that PhD research in sociology. But right now Spelman College and the idea of graduate school seem awfully far away.
>
> Send me news about how things are at Spelman and Morehouse. Have you ever been back to hear Dr. King preach? You really should go hear him again. He is up-and-coming, and with his Harvard education people say he may be the one who could help to lead a real civil rights movement.
>
> How is your PhD work coming? I'm sure you will do well. You are where you need to be right now as I am. My answer to your question on

graduation day is still no. If you really think about it, you know it's not what you want most. And that is not good enough for me.

Nights are the worst here. The katydids are so loud that I feel like I'm in some far off African jungle and I can't even hear myself think. I miss you so much. I miss having you with me. Please come soon. Grandma says that if you park on the street down by the Presbyterian Church and take the back way following the path I showed you from the dirt road that you can visit on Saturday afternoon between 3 and 5. Who knows? One time she might even let you stay for dinner.

Don't worry. I'm feeling fine. It's moving a lot. I think it's a boy. Grandma nods her head when I say that and looks at me strangely. She is absolutely convinced that I've gone crazy and threatens to tell my mother all the time. But don't worry. No one will ever know it's your child. He will be our secret. But please come soon. I need you near me.

Yours now and always,
Love, Leah

Don ransacked the oak shelves of the library and found a Spelman volume from 1954 tucked amidst the four years of Morehouse yearbooks. If they had graduated together, 1954 would have been their sophomore year. He rifled through the pages to the second-years and there she was. Leah Chattam. Wearing an afro, skin black as coal. Don shot through the rest of the pages and found another picture of her with the Spelman track team. She stood facing the camera straight on—confident, tall, athletic, hands on strong hips. She wore the cornrows and dangling fine braids only children wore in those days. The caption indicated she ran sprints, and Don could tell by her muscled frame and the records listed on the bottom of the page she ran them well.

Don poured through the rest of the stack, totally engrossed. One of the last envelopes included a photograph. Like the letters, its edges were dingy and worn. On the bottom the name Judah was written. The picture was of a boy about nine years old, with chocolate brown skin and black, short, kinky hair.

He looks more like my father than I do! Damn it! How could he not have told me I have a half-brother?

Sensing movement, Don glanced up from the letters lying in his lap and saw his father standing at the library door, stricken and pale as a black man could be. All the blood had drained from his face.

"How could you hide this from me?" Don heard himself scream. "I have a fuckin' brother?"

"I, uh, meant to tell you...sometime," he mumbled.

"A brother! And you never told me? How could you not tell me?"

Don slapped the letters down on the desk and bolted, grabbed his coat from its hook in the foyer, and slammed the front door so hard the hand of Mary doorknocker lifted its fistful of fruit and rapped it down behind him. He flew down the sidewalk, rounded the corner, turned south, and sprinted full out down Wells Street, hands clenched in tight fists, arms pumping, and street shoes slapping the concrete.

How could his father have done it? Kept Don's own brother a secret! Their family's life was built on a lie! *I'm not an only child, or even a firstborn!*

He raced through Old Town, his unbuttoned wool coat flapping in his wake, oblivious to the cold and traffic, blind to the cars swerving and screeching to either side, past Gino's East, unconscious of the swirling scents of its baking crusts, and under the metal framework of the elevated train, deaf to the thundering 'L' as it rumbled over his head.

Only the sound of half-melted, refrozen snow crunching under his feet as he crossed the Chicago River bridge jolted Don back to consciousness. But he wasn't ready to return home. He turned and walked toward the lakeshore. The bitter wind whistled between the skyscrapers across the frozen concrete, asphalt, and steel of the deserted city. Despite the bitter cold, Don didn't go inside anywhere. He walked on into the gathering darkness, and only returned to his ash and elm-lined street late that night. Hoping his father would be asleep, he opened the door and crept in as quietly as he could.

His father was awake. Don found him at his desk in the library, reading the letters.

"Don," he said, "for twenty-five years I didn't read these letters. I didn't look at them. I promised your mother."

"But what about *him*? Damn it, Dad...what about *him*?"

Jacob Newman shook his head. His jovial mask was gone now, his agony on full display. He tried to speak, but no words would come. He buried his face in his hands and began to sob.

Don had never seen his father cry. He looked so helpless, like a baby. Don waited in agony.

After several unbearable minutes of anguished weeping, Jacob finally regained control. He took out a handkerchief and wiped his face.

"I should have told you long ago, Don. Sit down. It's a long story."

"WHEN I WAS TWENTY I got accepted to Morehouse College, the black men's college in Atlanta—you know colleges were segregated in 1952. I was on the GI bill and wanted to study chemistry, and Morehouse had a strong chemistry department.

"I loved your mother. You know I loved your mother. But at that time, I thought I had lost her. On my first day at Morehouse, I was walking through registration and this woman's voice caught my attention. She stood at a registration desk, oblivious to the growing line of men behind her. She was virtually the only woman there—taking advantage of a little-known opportunity allowing Spelman women to cross-register at Morehouse.

"So there she was, demanding in a loud voice the class of her choice, despite the fact it was not open to freshman. The class registrars looked frantic and upset, but she was cool and collected. I couldn't take my eyes off her. She got in that class. I knew one thing from the start; this woman was not from below the Mason-Dixon line. I had never seen a woman like her anywhere.

"I soon found out her name was Leah and she grew up in Harlem. Her father was a newspaperman and aspiring novelist, and her mother danced with the famous Katherine Dunham Company. Their small apartment in Harlem was a hangout for writers, artists, and black intellectuals, so she heard many late-night discussions about the plight of blacks in America. Her parents fought a lot, usually over money. Her father wanted to quit his job and write something important, which he finally did after the couple separated in Leah's high school years. He moved to Chicago to pursue his dream, and Leah and her mother moved to the Bedford-Stuyvesant neighborhood in Brooklyn because they could no longer afford to live in Harlem.

"Leah felt out of place in Brooklyn and grew tired of her own tumultuous relationship with her mother. She decided to go to Spelman College in Atlanta. It was near Decatur, Georgia, where her mother grew up and her Grandma Mae still lived. Her mother said Leah wouldn't be able to handle the racism and prejudice in the South after living in New York, but the fact that her mother hated the idea made it all the more attractive. Leah wrote to her Grandma, who was eager to have her grandaughter come South, and Leah got a generous scholarship at Spelman.

"She left New York on the Continental Bus. When they crossed the Mason-Dixon line at the Maryland border, she heard for the first time in her life those awful words, 'You people, move to the back of the bus.' The driver's words filled her with anger. Little did she know her struggles had just begun.

"Leah was unlike me on every count: direct, aggressive, politically involved. She served as president of the NAACP student branch at Spelman. She personally met Dr. King when he preached at his father's Ebenezer Church after his graduation from Morehouse, and she was leading student meetings on civil rights at Spelman in 1953, two years before Rosa Parks refused to give up her seat on that Montgomery bus. She was the first woman at Spelman to wear an afro. It was her political statement—she had seen poets and intellectuals in Harlem sporting afros to reclaim their African heritage. In Atlanta her kinky hair really turned heads, since all well-to-do blacks there had straightened their hair since the Civil War.

"With Leah it was passion one day, a breakup the next, and a passionate make-up the day after that. Our big breakup happened when she got pregnant her senior year. Leah realized I still loved your mother—in spite of the fact Leah carried our child—and she was furious. Looking back on it now I think she got pregnant on purpose. My father had warned me to watch out for aggressive women who use men like that. Leah was an aggressive woman, Don, and let me tell you, she usually got what she wanted, and she wanted me.

"Leah was over five months pregnant at graduation. Nobody knew—she was tall and slim and the gown hid it. The baby was born at her Grandma Mae's house in Decatur with the help of a discreet midwife. Leah named him Judah. Grandma Mae made Leah tell people she was married to a soldier overseas, and eventually she started telling people the marriage just hadn't worked out.

"Leah refused to get an abortion, refused to give up her young son for adoption, even refused marriage. Yeah, I offered. Maybe it was partly because of her parents' terrible relationship, but she also knew my heart wasn't in it. I was still in love with your mother. Thank God, Leah was too proud and stubborn to enter a marriage of obligation.

"Leah's grandmother wanted her to suffer the consequences of what she had done. Leah had already delayed graduate school, and soon after the baby was born, Grandma Mae forced her to work in Decatur as a waitress in a white café. Leah hated every minute of it. She couldn't stand the subservient role, especially when customers made racist remarks.

"She worked there two years. Meanwhile, I was doing my master's in analytic chemistry and mathematics at Morehouse. When I moved on to my first post at Monsanto Labs in St. Louis in 1958, she returned to Spelman for graduate school in social science. She was determined to work for civil rights and even more determined never to work as someone's servant again. Judah was raised by Grandma Mae; Leah saw him mostly on holidays. I was just a dear uncle, as far as he knew.

"After I moved to St. Louis, there was a long pause in my relationship with Leah. I had been away from your mother seven long years, and I returned to Vicenza with my master's degree and a job at Monsanto. I stayed a month—the most time my company would give me leave—and our love was rekindled. In fact, it had never been extinguished. I asked her to marry me. But when I told her about Leah and Judah, she refused, and I went through the grief of losing her a second time.

"I returned to the States more depressed than ever. I turned to Leah for consolation and she was there for me. She willingly accepted me, no questions asked. I continued to visit her at Spelman whenever she called. There were no strings attached, and she never wanted me to stay—or so she said. Besides, I had work to do. In between my visits to Georgia, I continued to study chemistry with a vengeance. While Leah was studying methods for social change and civil disobedience, I was getting my first patents for the new molecules I'd created.

"Leah's friends often had to pull her out of trouble for using white-only fountains and bathrooms. Leah wasn't afraid of anything, and those were dangerous days for black folks, Don. In the spring of 1960, James Lawson was expelled from Vanderbilt for participating in a sit-in, and Felton Turner was found beaten and hanging upside down in a tree in Houston, the signature 'KKK' carved in his chest. Many of us decided not to court trouble, but not Leah!

"She traveled to Raleigh to help Ella Baker organize the Student Nonviolent Coordinating Committee at Shaw University, and she helped establish a branch in Atlanta. She was so busy she barely passed her coursework for her master's. She went to work for the NAACP in Atlanta for almost nothing and lived with her grandmother and Judah. After the successful sit-in at the Woolworth lunch counter in Greensboro, North Carolina, she organized similar sit-ins in Atlanta department stores in and was one of fifty students arrested along with Dr. King. In 1961, she participated in the Freedom Rides and organized voter registration drives throughout the South. She marched in Selma, Montgomery, even Mississippi.

"I worried about her plenty but never went along. I had other dreams. I was too busy studying chemicals and equations. We saw each other less and less as time went on. In 1962, I took my first faculty job as an assistant professor at Loyola University here in Chicago. I still loved your mother and she still loved me. So in 1966, fourteen years after leaving Vicenza the first time, I returned again.

"By this time, we were both in our mid-thirties, unmarried, and her parents had given up hope of a more favorable marriage. This time they did not stand in our way. Your mother accepted me, but she laid down the law. I was to be faithful to her and was never to see, write, call, or even mention Leah or Judah ever again. I told her I loved her and gave her my promise. And I kept my word, Don. All those years with your mother, I kept my word."

DON WAS RELIEVED when Christmas break was over and he could get back to work, away from his father. When he entered the old anatomy theater, however, the familiar doubts returned. Hearing the laughter of Bruce and Frances pealing out of the seminar room upstairs, Don stopped a few steps from the projection room door, turned, and stared at the empty center of the theater. He imagined himself laid out on a dissection table, his innards exposed and probed as rows and rows of eager students craned their necks to watch.

Just then, Dr. Sampson arrived with a tall, thin woman. She had the slightly hunched back, glasses, and warm-yet-intellectual aspect that pegged her as a physician. She looked tired. Dark circles under her eyes matched her straight black hair.

The students found their places around the seminar table. Dr. Sampson and the woman sat beside each other on his side.

"We have a special guest today," Dr. Sampson said. "This is Dr. Sheila White, a longtime friend of the college. She is a family practice doctor and a lead physician in the Peabody Primary Care network in Boston. She advocates for primary care on the national level and serves as an adjunct faculty member for the health system science program here at the college."

Dr. White smiled and nodded.

"Before I turn it over to Dr. White, let me introduce today's subject. Physicians take an oath. You know it—the Hippocratic Oath. Every physician in the world takes some version of this ancient pledge, typically in a medical school ceremony where he or she first receives the emblematic white coat. The white coat symbolizes the purity of the physician's calling: *into whatever houses I enter, I will go for the benefit of the sick.*

"Every medical student is supposed to learn what benefits the sick and swear to provide that first and foremost. Primary care physicians provide most of these essential services, yet each year, fewer and fewer young physicians go into primary care because it's difficult work and poorly compensated compared to the procedural subspecialties.

"Who oversees this perverse payment system that pays the least for health services that matter the most? None other than our very own professional organization, the AMA. Dr. White will explain how this came to be and how the AMA works behind closed doors to perpetuate a broken system."

Dr. White smiled at Dr. Sampson and at each of the students in turn. Don was startled by the empathy her eyes transmitted when her gaze fixed on him. Could she see inside his head? Read his heart?

"Thank you for that dramatic introduction," she began. "Dr. Sampson's comments sound extreme, right? You might even be wondering if he's a wee bit crazy."

Everyone, including Dr. Sampson, laughed at this remark.

"Let me assure you, the situation in America is precisely as he says, and it's completely unknown to most Americans. My objective today is to describe the medical payment system in the United States and how it developed.

"There was a period of time in America many called the golden age of medicine—'golden' because medical services were so well paid. It started in 1965 with Lyndon Johnson's Great Society and the introduction of guaranteed payments from Medicare and Medicaid, and lasted until the early 1980s. Both public and private health insurers paid fixed prices for piecemeal visits and procedures, regardless of quality or patient need. Physicians developed wasteful habits and—for the first time in history—came to expect high income for practicing medicine. Physicians and patients disregarded the true cost and value of medical services.

"This fee-for-service payment system sucked us into a vicious cycle: to control escalating costs, insurers lowered what they would pay per unit of service. In turn, physicians struggled to provide more and more units of service per hour to replace the lost income. At the same time, more medical technology became available, further increasing costs of care. Because advanced technology, surgery, and procedures were once uncommon in medicine and expensive to provide, the prices for these things started out high, and new technologies took bigger and bigger chunks of the healthcare dollar.

"In the late 1980s, researchers worked with government to compare the relative work required to provide various medical services. Medicare, under the direction of Congress, changed the way it paid for physician services in 1992. They established the Resource-based Relative Value Scale, or RBRVS. The idea was for physicians to be paid for services based on the time involved. It was anticipated more emphasis and more payment would go to primary care, but something went wrong.

"Who among you has heard of the RUC?"

The students all looked at her with blank stares.

"No one? Well, you're not alone. The RUC is the Relative Value Scale Update Committee. It operates in the dark and may be the main reason primary care physicians and their patients are getting short-changed in America."

Dr. White had Don's full attention now.

"Needless to say, the specialists and proceduralists making millions off the Medicare payment system were not pleased to learn their payments might be cut relative to primary care, and these doctors with the most money control the AMA. They launched a preemptive strike through their lobbyists and got the government to put the AMA in charge of setting the relative value of various services under the new scale—basically, the government agreed to let the fox guard the chicken coop.

"Since 1992, the nation's largest insurer, Medicare, has entrusted the AMA to oversee the RUC and set physician payment rates. And how did the AMA make sure the specialists' and proceduralists' services continue to pay more? They stacked the committee. Every subspecialty has roughly equal representation on the RUC. I have served on the RUC for the past two years, representing the American Academy of Family Physicians. Primary care doctors—internal medicine, family practice, pediatrics, and general practice physicians—hold only a fifth of the seats, even though we account for well over fifty percent of patient visits in America and over forty percent of doctors. Eighty percent of RUC members are subspecialists who make their money from procedures.

"For primary care, each visit is coded and billed based on time spent, level of documentation, and decision-making complexity. Proceduralists, on the other hand, get paid flat fees for each procedure. In both cases, payment has nothing to do with quality of care or results. So, it's not whether you kill or cure, it's how you code the claim!

"At the RUC, we spend all our time debating the relative value of various codes. At our last meeting we compared the value of a physical therapist's and a primary care physician's time minute for minute. A radiologist at the meeting suggested the value of their time was equivalent. As he put it, 'work is work.'

"There is little respect on the RUC for the value of high-quality primary care. Primary care physicians routinely see patients with multiple complex needs. A patient may need evaluation for several acute complaints, ongoing management of serious chronic conditions, and essential preventive care, all in one visit. Good primary care involves work beyond the office visit as well: consulting with colleagues, nurses, and home health personnel to coordinate care, being available by telephone night and day, contacting patients to make sure they follow up and get the care they need. Primary care physicians don't get paid for any of that; they only get paid for office visits and minor office procedures. Meanwhile, the subspecialists, who typically deal with a single diagnosed condition, manage to get paid for almost everything they do, and at higher rates.

"To address these inequities, those of us representing primary care proposed the addition of one primary care seat to the RUC. Just one. This led to loud howls of protest by the subspecialists. Over one seat! In reality we need to add twenty primary care seats to the RUC and as many consumer seats. Primary care physicians provide the most valuable and lifesaving services to patients, like checking blood pressure to prevent strokes, treating coronary artery disease with aspirin and cholesterol medicine, and counseling patients to stop smoking. And patients want physicians who know them well. It is absurd the physician team leaders we need most should be paid the least, and that proceduralists should be put in charge of setting everyone's payment rates."

Don thought of the gilded priests in leaden cloaks his father had spotted in the front window of the Libreria Alighieri—in the old book his Momma later bequeathed to him. He imagined legions of radiologists covered in their lead aprons, marching one behind another in the dark, pretending to be the most important providers of health.

"So, what did the RUC decide at its last meeting? Primary care would not get more representation on the committee or any increase in Medicare reimbursement rates. However, they did increase pay for procedures once again. The private insurers, like always, will follow suit and will pay even bigger bucks for procedures at the expense of primary care. Surprised?

"Sure, payment rates have decreased slightly for some procedures, but the proceduralists make up for that by increasing volume and speed. They receive a fixed rate per procedure, even if it only takes ten minutes. Over the last decade their incomes have risen almost three hundred percent—and that's after inflation.

"In contrast, income for primary care over this period hasn't grown at all. Diagnosing and treating sick people takes time. Primary care doctors can only do so many visits in an hour. Every case is unique. You can't easily reduce the time you spend interviewing, examining, and counseling patients without lowering quality. Primary care physicians end up harried, stressed, and exhausted as they rush from one patient to the next, scrambling to increase volume without sacrificing good care. Have any of you seen examples of this?"

Don raised his hand. "I sure have. Talking with a patient is critical but it doesn't pay. A dermatologist working long hours in the hospital to diagnose mysterious rashes makes less than two hundred thousand a year, but one who specializes in taking off little brown bumps for cosmetic reasons can make half a million a year and take three months of vacation. One of my med school classmates is a plastic surgeon and makes a fortune on breast enhancements. I told him I was a general internist and he said, 'You mean…you take care of *sick* people?'—as if that was a crazy thing to do. In our current payment system, taking good care of sick people is economic suicide."

"Great examples," Dr. White said, "and sadly, they are typical. As a result of payment inequities, cynicism in primary care is growing. To get a job or make a good living, primary care docs have to churn—move people through as fast as possible—because the pay is all about throughput. Many doctors have given up trying to provide comprehensive coordinated care and preventive care, even though they know those services are most likely to save your life. It's all they can do just to respond to acute complaints, and most patients don't know the difference.

"As a result, there's a primary care crisis in America, and the legislators responsible for the trend-setting Medicare program don't seem to have the foggiest idea. With so many aging baby boomers, the day will come soon when it will be very hard to find a doctor to care for your elderly parent. Older physicians are leaving primary care practice in droves, and fewer than one in five young doctors choose primary care careers nowadays. Can you blame them? Why not double your income with only two more years of training?

"Of course, it's easy to find a doctor to operate, probe you with an instrument, or insert some new robotic device. Americans love gadgets. They believe gadgets and procedures offer the best lifesaving care, and the proceduralists perpetuate this illusion. But basic primary care is most likely to save lives with blood pressure control, pap smears, and counseling to quit smoking. Unfortunately, patients often don't get those things. Any questions?"

Out of the corner of his eye, Don saw Bruce slowly shaking his head.

"Thank you, Dr. White," Dr. Sampson said. "As you know, our topic today is hypocrisy in healthcare—groups or systems where the stated purposes of providers are contradicted by their actions. Dr. White explained how the group entrusted with determining the value of health care in America has done the most to undermine it. The AMA chooses to advocate for established monopolies rather than the care patients need most. Can you think of other examples of medical hypocrisy?"

"Sure," Don answered, "overlooking the malpractice of colleagues, like the blue wall that keeps policemen from reporting misconduct by other policemen. Or when doctors and hospitals let the lure of profit, rather than community need, dictate practice sites. Because of that, some communities have far too many doctors and others have none."

"Good examples, Dr. Newman," Dr. Sampson answered. "In our system, doctors commonly move away from the sickest and neediest. It's ironic, but physicians who have the best payer mix and greatest financial ability to do a good job typically provide less charity care. Doctors and hospitals provide less charity care every year. Hospitals that can't compete with hospitals whose first priority is profit. The public is left with health plans and providers with little inclination to provide care to people who cannot pay."

Don glanced over at Bruce. He was red-faced now, and tiny beads of sweat had formed on his temples. Why would Dr. Sampson delve into such a touchy subject again after calling Don out for the same blunder before Christmas?

"Do any other examples of medical hypocrisy come to mind?" Dr. Sampson asked.

"What about highfalutin' academics?" Bruce retorted, his words seething with sarcasm. "You've heard, 'those who can't do, teach?' Aren't teachers the biggest hypocrites of all, telling people how to do things they have never done themselves?"

Dr. Sampson was silent for a moment. Don, Frances, and Dr. White held their breath, stunned by Bruce's blatant disrespect.

"Yes, Dr. Markum," Dr. Sampson responded calmly. "You are right—teachers run a great risk of hypocrisy. All I can hope is that you will serve as my teacher in turn, and if my actions do not match my words, I hope you will correct me." Dr. Sampson smiled.

Bruce's preparation for battle was completely undone.

Dr. Sampson added, "Let's call it a day. Ms. Hunt, you are on next week, right?"

"Yes, Dr. Sampson."

Bruce darted out of the projection room and Frances followed.

Dr. Sampson asked Dr. White, "You look exhausted. When was the last time you got a good night's sleep?"

"Sleep? What's that?" she replied. "Every month the administration demands we see more patients in less time. They moved us to nearly one hundred percent productivity pay, and productivity is how many patients you see, not how many you help. They have invested nothing in the systems I need to do a good job. Our electronic health record is primeval. I can never find the records and test results I need. When patients call they have to wait forever on the phone. We have no system to handle abnormal labs or call patients with results. Sometimes an abnormal lab result comes back after hours, and no one even hears about it until I look it up on the computer the next day. Our system makes it impossible for me to provide good care for my patients!"

"What are you going to do?" Dr. Sampson asked. Don continued to methodically pack his books and waited for her answer.

"I've given up trying to get help from administration. They just took away the one decent nurse I had. The chief administrator says, 'You eat what you kill.' But it's not about me. It's about my patients. I finally gave all my patients my home number and cell phone. I can't live with myself otherwise. It's the only way I can be sure they get the help they need when they need it. It's not right, Virgil. In primary care we have to do the most to coordinate care, our overhead is highest, and we have the fewest resources."

"That must be hard," Sampson said.

"No wonder no one wants to go into primary care these days," she continued. "I'm sorry to rant. But it just isn't right! Virgil, this is the work I want to do. I'm just not sure how long I can take it."

Don pretended to look for something in his notes as Dr. Sampson and Dr. White left the classroom. He saw Dr. Sampson put a hand on her shoulder and heard his encouraging words as they disappeared down the hall.

Don turned off the lights to the projection room and paused at the top of the stairs. He stared absently at the center of the anatomy theater where the dissected cadaver would have lain, sacrificed for the greater good. At least the guy would be dead. If you're dead, maybe having your body sliced and scrutinized isn't much of a sacrifice.

But what about Dr. Sampson? Would President Lender scapegoat him for the greater good of the college, as he saw it? That was for real. If Dr. Sampson kept uncovering medicine's dark truths, what would happen to him?

Before Don left Chicago, he'd told his father about the bizarre summons he received from the president's office and the unsettling conversation with President Lender. Don's father snapped out of his gloom, his eyes bright and attentive, "Watch out, Don!" he warned, "sounds like they're out to get Dr. Sampson."

"It's probably not that big a deal," Don protested. "After all, I'm just one of hundreds of graduate students..."

"You don't know what you're getting into. Listen to me. You stay out of it, son! It's not your business."

That was so typical of his father. Don't make waves. Yes, the Newman men had a long history of staying out of other people's business. In New Orleans they'd hardened their hearts and pretended to be white. They didn't protest the lynchings of blacks, the bodies hung from trees. They were busy building business, and that would have been a dangerous distraction. The Newmans wouldn't have thought twice about owning slaves if they'd had the chance. Hell, maybe they did own slaves, back in the day.

It was all about money. That was how you made a difference, not by protests and marches. What was that he used to say to Momma? "Americans don't respect anything but money. I'll bring up blacks by doing better than anyone—white or black." Of course, whenever it was difficult or hard to be black, his father pretended he was Creole.

Don hated him for that. He was the worst kind of Oreo—a slave to the white man's idea of success. Achieving economic prosperity justified almost any means. He abandoned his father and his brother Ethan, from whom he was still alienated; he deceived his army buddies by denying he was black; he hid his blackness from Nonno Lábano and pretended to be a devout Catholic so he could marry Momma. Hell, he even let Momma believe he was pure when he was sleeping with Leah. What a hypocrite! Come to think of it, his father's hypocrisy was responsible for his own birth.

Don Newman, product of hypocrisy!

No sooner had he coined this epithet in his head, Don received a second, more painful insight like a punch to the gut. How could he not have realized it before?

My skin is so much lighter than his. It's easy for me to pass and I've taken full advantage of that. All my life, I've told people my bronze skin was from my Italian heritage, but Momma was a fair-skinned, northern Italian. Guess the apple doesn't fall far from the tree. I'm a hypocrite, all right—didn't defend Dr. Sampson in Lender's office—a hypocrite doctor, too—didn't notice my own mother was dying! I pretended to care, pretended to be a healer, but wasn't by her side when she needed my care and comfort. Oh, yes. My heart is as black as my father's. In my heart, there is only darkness.

24

The Image Makers

DON TRUDGED across the snow-covered quad on his way to seminar. His backpack felt heavy as lead as he dragged along, weak, sleepy, and cold. With each step, the white crystalline mantle collapsed, crunched, and seized his sinking feet in its cold embrace. Don's thin leather oxfords did little to protect his freezing toes. Why hadn't he worn his boots? He plodded along in slow motion past the thick trunks of the black oaks, oblivious to the menacing tangle of twisted limbs overhead and the invisible network of roots buried and forgotten beneath the covering of snow.

He stopped to rest at the fenced omphalos, purported center of the universe. Its gravity sucked him down and held him fast to the spot. His feet wouldn't move; his body was frozen from head to toe.

How tired he was! For weeks it had been too cold and icy to run. This time of year when the night outflanked the day was unnatural. Maybe he was depressed. But why? Seasonal affective disorder? Vitamin D deficiency from lack of sunlight? Maybe hypothyroid. Thyroid was the body's throttle and the thermostat. Don didn't seem to have either.

The previous night, Sarah had called him out of the blue. It was the first time they had talked since classes had started.

"Hey, Dante," said the sweet familiar voice when he answered the phone.

Don usually hated it when people used his given name, but with Sarah, he didn't mind. He wasn't sure why.

"Listen," she said, "I've got a little time off this weekend, and I was thinking maybe you could use a little time off as well."

"You bet I could," Don replied. "I'll tell you what. Let me check the emergency room schedule at New American, and if I'm not moonlighting, I'll come up to Boston on Saturday. We can kick around the harbor a little bit and then maybe go out to dinner somewhere around Faneuil Hall. Why don't I call you back as soon as I check out the schedule?"

Remembering Sarah's voice sent a trickle of warmth flowing into his body like rising spring tree sap. He stood motionless, rooted to the ground like the old black oaks, drawing sustenance from the frozen earth.

"Are you okay?"

Don snapped out of his daydream to find a uniformed guard facing him from the opposite side of the iron cage. A patch on the sleeve of the guard's green parka depicted the Florence College seal. The man's face was not visible behind the jacket's hood.

"I'm the night watchman, just going off shift. Are you okay?"

"Yes sir," Don mumbled through frozen lips.

Don continued his trek across the crusted snow, hunching his shoulders against the cold and lumbering along like a bear overdue to go underground to hibernate. He felt the watchman's eyes on his back. *He probably thinks I'm a nutcase.* Don had no idea how long he had been standing there, freezing to death and transfixed by the old omphalos. He reached Grafton Hall and stumbled inside, relieved to get out of the cold and away from the all-seeing eyes of the watchman. He descended into the bowels of the brick building and made his way to the old anatomy theater classroom.

Frances was already there, standing at a brand-new podium. It was outfitted with all the latest connections, including a built-in keyboard, trackball, and screen.

"Cool, isn't it?" she said. "President Lender wants to get these old facilities up to date and make this program first-rate. I hear he's pushing Sampson to boost enrollment tenfold. He wants to make our program a real centerpiece for the college."

"Great," Don replied half-heartedly.

He tried not to betray his sense of alarm. What would Dr. Sampson think? The disquieting conversation with Lender rushed back into his head. President Lender was serious. Maybe Dr. Sampson *was* out of date. Few people were crazy enough to enter his program—apparently it had always been that way. Well, it looked like things were changing, whether Dr. Sampson wanted them to or not.

Frances smiled and motioned with a graceful sweep of her arm to a sixty-inch flat-screen on the wall where the old projection screen had been. "Check it out! The anatomy classes are using it to show high-definition pictures of dissected cadavers from the web."

"Whoa, it's Vanna White!" said Bruce, who had just sauntered in. "Would you look at that—little Florence College has hit the big time." He plopped himself into one of the wooden seats in the front row of the amphitheater, his legs comfortably splayed apart and his eyes transfixed by the whirling images of the screen saver.

Don and Frances took seats on either side of Bruce. All three were soon mesmerized by the colorful photos of the radiological, lab, surgical, and other interventional suites of Florence Medical Center.

A rattling sound from above jarred them from their reverie, and they looked around to see Dr. Sampson struggling to open the door to the projection room.

How had he slipped past unnoticed? And what had happened to the projection room? The door was still there, but the window for Dr. Sampson's slide projector was gone.

Dr. Sampson struck the door hard with his fist, sending a thunderclap echoing throughout the silent hall. He turned on his heel and descended from the heights of the amphitheater like Moses coming down from the mountain after smashing the tablets. Fury etched his brow in a rare display of frustration and indignation.

When he had almost reached the bottom of the stairs he stopped, took a deep breath, exhaled it slowly, and spoke with measured calm. "It's locked. Looks like they've made it a storage room for tech support. We'll just have to make do."

He motioned for the students to join him and moved to the floor of the old anatomy theater. "We can sit together down here."

They pulled four chairs to face each other. Dr. Sampson sat with his back to the large screen, lost and insignificant beneath the massive display. He glanced back to follow Bruce's still-distracted eyes, which were trained on the high-tech podium. "Turn that damn thing off," he spat. He checked himself and nodded to Frances, adding, "Just for now—I know you want to use it later."

Dr. Sampson flipped open his notes and addressed the students from his seat. "People have always loved a spectacle. It's a part of our nature, a primal urge. From ancient times, people have been particularly interested in looking at, seeing, and knowing the insides of the body and the gruesome details of disease and death—the things doctors see.

"In Plato's *Republic*, Socrates tells a story about the human fascination with horrible things that are usually hidden away from the public eye:

> *Leontius, the son of Aglaion, was going up from the Piraeus under the outside of the North Wall when he noticed corpses lying by the public executioner. He desired to look, but at the same time he was disgusted and made himself turn away; and for a while he struggled and covered his face.*

> *But finally, overpowered by the desire, he opened his eyes wide, ran toward the corpses and said: 'Look, you damn wretches, take your fill of the fair sight.'*

"People have always loved the theater, the arena, the coliseum. Places where they can see the perverse, the diseased, the unnatural."

Don's mother used to tell him about the time she accompanied his father to the famous Olympic Theater in Vicenza, Italy. The theater was the pride of her hometown; its wood and stucco stage set was designed to reproduce the ancient city of Thebes. The slanted stage created an optical illusion of depth, giving spectators an omniscient perspective of the entire city, complete with walls, columns, and streets angling off into the distance. From their seats, Don's parents felt like gods looking down from Mount Olympus.

The play that night was *Oedipus Rex*, the very play for which the theater was built in the late 1500s. Don imagined his father sitting there on the bare board seats, surrounded by dozens of wood and plaster statues of the most famous kings and tyrants of all time. His mother had seen the play before, but what must his father have thought of *Oedipus Rex*? Oedipus' violation of natural laws—he killed his father and slept with his mother—destroyed an entire city. As king, Oedipus wanted to stand for the best of mankind, but came to realize that he represented the worst.

"Like Leontius," Dr. Sampson was saying, "people want to see. This old anatomical theater is a testament to our fascination with disease and death and the desire to see them up close. The oldest anatomical theater of all, the model for this one, is in Padua, Italy, at the oldest and most famous medical school of the Renaissance. Until the early 1900s, people came from all over Europe to witness the dissections there, which satisfied the desire to see but did little to help prevent and cure the diseases of the time.

"Goethe visited Padua in the late 1700s and wrote about the dissections. It was in the heat of the summer. The theater was packed with tourists and students and didn't have windows. No formaldehyde either. When they opened the abdominal cavity, Goethe nearly passed out from the stench.

"Today, a huge industry caters to this desire to see. General Electric and Siemens make billions selling imaging machines all over the world, and they design commercials to encourage and justify the craving to see. They promote the idea that images are of the utmost importance for health. But are they?

"You can get total-body MRI and CT scans at for-profit diagnostic imaging centers in almost any city in the country. Reputable imaging centers don't offer them, but less scrupulous centers advertise total-body scans in the paper as if they were the world's greatest preventive treatment.

"Here's what they don't tell you. One CT scan delivers more than a year's worth of solar radiation in less than one hour—radiation equal to the exposure of an atomic bomb survivor two miles from ground zero in Hiroshima. And Hiroshima bomb survivors, particularly those who were children at the time, have elevated lifetime rates of cancer.

"It isn't uncommon for a person to get as many as five or ten scans in a lifetime. CT scans likely cause more cancer than they detect and prevent."

Bruce interrupted, "What about MRIs? They don't use radiation."

"True, but MRIs can have serious unintended consequences as well. You read the Fisher paper. What is the big problem with using MRI scans to screen for unsuspected cancer?"

"Lead-time bias," Don answered. "Patients and doctors get fooled by it all the time. Finding something early doesn't necessarily improve your chance for a cure. People think early screening and treatment helps them live longer when in fact, they just started counting sooner. Also, scanners pick up all kinds of little spots that probably mean nothing, but doctors have to check them out with more testing, and sometimes the testing is pretty hazardous. For instance, most people have a few little spots in their lungs, but sometimes a biopsy causes lung collapse and death."

"That is a risk," Bruce conceded. "You wouldn't think people would die because of a scan, but we see it all the time. The scan can be the first step in a downward spiral for a little old lady. Sometimes you can even smell it before it happens. It's the sweet little old ladies that just want to make sure everything is okay, the ones that look like your grandmother. They're the ones most likely to spiral."

"MRIs have never been shown to detect unsuspected cancer early enough to improve the treatment of *any* kind of cancer," Dr. Sampson said, "but people don't want to hear this. The companies making scanners aren't about to tell them. Their advertisements imply computerized scanners offer the greatest hope for healing, and their salesmen show doctors how to get a fat return on investment by putting a scanner in the office. Pretty soon, everyone needs a scan.

"Radiologists love the beautiful images, and they believe the images help people. They think studies showing a lack of benefit must be wrong, or better technology will soon come along and revolutionize cancer treatment. Besides, if technology is available, patients demand it, so doctors figure the images protect them from getting sued. It never hurts to look, right? They will never admit the truth, that screening really exists for entertainment."

"Aren't MRIs good for anything?" Frances asked.

"Yes," Don answered, "for confirming a suspected diagnosis based on a thorough history and physical exam, and for following the progress of disease in many cases. But they are generally not good at screening for unsuspected disease."

"What other imaging technologies have dubious benefits?" Dr. Sampson asked.

"Fetal ultrasounds, for one," Frances said. "Doctors routinely order them on pregnant women even though ultrasounds do not contribute to the health of mothers or babies. We spend vast amounts of money on fetal images. Of course, it's fascinating and wonderful to see babies in utero, but it's ultimately like television—for entertainment.

"And then there's fetal heart monitoring. Almost every laboring woman in America has one of these useless monitors strapped to her belly as soon as she shows up at the hospital. It creates an electrical image—a tracing of the baby's heartbeat. The woman must lie still on her back so the tracing will look good. Research shows the tracings do nothing to improve outcomes, but doctors and patients still want them because they alleviate fear and provide the illusion of control."

"Are these entertaining medical images worth the cost?" Dr. Sampson asked.

"We read the paper," Bruce said. "We spend one hundred billion dollars on diagnostic testing—blood tests and imaging studies—in the United States each year. That's at least ten percent of our healthcare budget, yet a good deal less than ten percent of diagnoses come from these expensive tests."

"Where do you think most diagnosis comes from?" asked Dr. Sampson.

"History and physical—mostly history alone," Frances answered. "It's from nurses and doctors actually *listening* to their patients that most illnesses are diagnosed." She gave Bruce and Don a meaningful glance. "Maybe it would help if we paid doctors more to listen and less to test and cut."

"*That* will be the day," Don said. "A radiologist can earn more in one hour than a general internist in a day. General internists and family practice doctors have to move faster than one-armed paperhangers just to keep the clinic doors open. Radiologists, on the other hand, get paid bucket loads to sit in the dark watching screens and playing video games. They can get out on the golf course by one or two in the afternoon, take three months of vacation, and still clear half a million a year. I look forward to the day when all their scans, x-rays, and video are sent to India, where they can be read just as well at a tenth of the cost. And then their little game will be up."

"Do I detect a little jealousy, Don?" taunted Bruce. "Just because radiologists make a lot of money doesn't mean they can't do good. Look, most surgeons would rather operate blindfolded than do surgery without imaging studies to guide them. No doubt radiology is lucrative, but as long as the public's in the dark about what their work is really worth, I doubt the pay for taking a history and physical will match radiologist pay anytime soon."

"You are right, Dr. Markum," Sampson said. "People don't realize that listening and touch usually do more than x-rays to diagnose and heal."

Don said, "People say, 'seeing is believing,' or, 'I wouldn't have believed it if I hadn't seen if with my own eyes.' But seeing isn't always the best measure of truth. Perhaps Doubting Thomas had it right—he wanted to touch!"

Bruce snickered. "So I guess Doubting Thomas believed in the digital rectal exam, even though it's not as good as the PSA blood test for detecting prostate cancer?"

Dr. Sampson ignored the snide comment. "People who want to know the truth want to get behind the scenes," his eyes darted briefly toward the locked projection room, "to find out how things really are."

Don stole a glance at Frances's seemingly perfect breasts, remembering how stiff they felt and how disappointed he was to discover they were fake.

Dr. Sampson continued, "Our subject today is the business of images in medicine. Who profits from them and what is their real value? With that in mind, let's turn to Frances, who will present our case."

Frances walked up to the podium. Damn, she was drop-dead gorgeous! A tight pink sweater showed off her lithe torso, and tan corduroy slacks hugged her firm butt and thighs.

"It's ironic, considering our subject today," Frances laughed, "but I get to use the cool new TV!" She tapped a key on the console of the new podium—no whirr, no click, no clunk—and up came a picture of a gleaming silver and glass building with a graceful, curved front. "This is the Digital Hospital, and my case study is about the man and the company behind it.

"I first became interested in Richard Scrushy and HealthSouth Corporation when he and Larry Ellison, the CEO of Oracle, announced plans last spring for the Digital Hospital. They are putting millions into ideal healthcare, building the world's most high-tech hospital right in the middle of the seventy-acre HealthSouth corporate campus on some of the best real estate in Birmingham, Alabama.

"They broke ground on the Digital Hospital last month, and let me tell you, it is science fiction come to life. A completely wireless communication network with a centralized database will link everything: digital images from CT scans, MRIs, ultrasounds, angiograms, video from virtual colonoscopy, real time echocardiograms, nuclear medicine scans, and medical records. Physicians and nurses will have complete computer access in every work station and patient room simply by clicking a button on a lightweight handheld computer or touch pad."

Frances demonstrated. Her silent keystrokes brought up image after image of the latest MRI and CT scanners—an upright MRI to scan a patient standing up—pristine white and chrome surgical suites with video screens on swiveling arms to view from any angle—huge data banks of computers for medical records—a state-of-the-art patient room resembling an over-the-top luxury hotel penthouse.

"Oracle will handle the integrated clinical and administrative information systems and the relational database that forms the backbone of the hospital," Frances explained. "Every room will be connected to the hospital's central computers. Every bed will have a keyboard, a remote, and a widescreen TV. Patients can view their medical programs, favorite TV shows, even play video games."

Bruce was practically drooling over the lavish features of the imagined hospital.

"Ellison and Scrushy are kindred spirits. Both are ambitious, driven billionaires that never take no for an answer. Both came up from nothing. Ellison, the son of a nineteen-year-old unwed Jewish mother, became the head of the world's number-two software company and one of the richest men in the world. Scrushy started out as a gas station attendant and was a married father at seventeen. After two children, two divorces, a degree in respiratory therapy, and a third wife, he became founder, president, and CEO of HealthSouth, the largest operator of rehabilitation facilities, outpatient surgery centers, and diagnostic imaging centers in the country.

Last year, HealthSouth banked more than 4.3 billion dollars in revenue, employed over sixty thousand people, and treated over one hundred thousand patients a day. It operates over two thousand facilities in the United States and hundreds more in Australia, the United Kingdom, Puerto Rico, and Saudi Arabia."

Don relished this opportunity to study Frances from his seat in the theater. Her presentation was stunning, her delivery poised, confident, and smooth. He focused his imaginary opera glasses on her voluptuous curves, watching her breasts heave against the tight pink sweater with each breath. Turning on the glasses' x-ray vision, he penetrated the layers of her clothes—her sweater, then her slacks, then silk and lace—until they all fell away, leaving her naked on the stage, bare, flawless and beautiful. He zoomed in until he was standing right in front of her. The backs of his fingers grazed the soft skin near the crease where her left thigh met her body and traced a sinuous path across her taut belly to the cleavage between her firm breasts. Don couldn't see her scars, but as his thumbs circled her breasts, he felt the telltale, raised lines of tiny crescent scars that coiled delicately around the edges of her areolae. Her nipples magically crinkled in response. My God, her surgeon was good! The job was technically perfect; her nerves were intact. Don's hands wandered all over her body now, she his innocent Marguerite and he her possessed Doctor Faustus. He could hear the distant but growing strains of the orchestra and the deep bass of Mephistopheles singing Le veau d'or, the golden calf.

"Don!" An impatient voice snapped him back to reality. "I'll repeat the question. Do you know anything about Richard Scrushy?"

He turned to face Dr. Sampson, who was visibly irritated.

"Uh, yes, sir." Don answered numbly, desperately trying to reconnect with whatever was going on in the classroom.

"Right, Don. Glad you were listening." Frances's voice dripped with sarcasm, but she rescued him from the embarrassment of his inattention. "We were talking about what a generous philanthropist Mr. Scrushy is. He has given to almost every major university and charity in Alabama. He graduated from respiratory therapy school at the University of Alabama at Birmingham and donated money for a building there. Everybody in Birmingham knows about Richard Scrushy."

"Right, of course," Don blurted out. "When I interviewed for a residency spot at UAB, I saw where they had broken ground for what was supposed to be the fanciest building on campus."

Frances nodded. "That would be the Richard M. Scrushy Building for the School of Health Related Professions. Anyway, Dr. Sampson encouraged me to look deeper, so I called one of Bruce's friends who's a financial analyst on Wall Street,"—she gave Bruce a warm smile—"and he agreed to help with my research. We looked at growth trends in the industry. Turns out, Scrushy got into rehabilitation hospitals just at the point there was a lot of money to be made in rehab. Now that MRI units are driving profitability, he's into outpatient diagnostic imaging. HealthSouth's SEC filings for the last several years show a focus on diagnostic imaging and the outpatient surgery sector.

"Freestanding diagnostic imaging centers are the fastest growing segment of the U.S. imaging industry; the number doubled between 1993 and 2000. We will spend close to fifty billion dollars on images this year, about half of that in outpatient centers. Everyone wants to build them near neighborhoods where people with good insurance live, because the margin on radiological procedures is so high. Hospitals complain companies like HealthSouth steal their profit-making business and leave them the unprofitable job of taking care of the sick. But it's not illegal.

"HealthSouth was just one of many companies in the late 1990s buying up and building freestanding imaging centers, but it has completely outperformed all the others, gaining thirty percent or more in market value every year. Bruce's friend looked carefully to see just what they do differently. Know what he found? Nothing! I remember exactly what he said: 'It's almost like Scrushy has a magic ring to make him invisible so he can mint money without anyone seeing. I can't find anything technically wrong but something doesn't fit.' He couldn't find any reason they should perform so much better than the market. He even called HealthSouth's investor relations department for more details about their debts and assets but hit a blank wall.

"However, it's amazing what you can find online. Thanks to financial reporting requirements for CEOs, we were able to get a copy of Scrushy's 1998 contract. It's incredible. In that year alone he raked in over 106 million in salary and bonuses, making him one of the highest-paid CEOs in the country. He travels in style. When he got married for the third time, he chartered a Boeing 727 to fly Martha Stewart and one hundred and fifty of his closest friends to Jamaica."

Frances turned back to the screen and clicked to the next slide. It showed an unbelievable parade of riches.

"He has, like, two private jets, a Lamborghini Murciélago, a Rolls-Royce Corniche, plus thirty-two other cars and ten boats, including this ninety-two-foot yacht called the Chez Soiree. He owns a plantation in Alabama, a mansion in Palm Beach, Florida, and multimillion-dollar homes in Vestavia Hills, Lake Martin, and Orange Beach, Alabama. He has hundreds of valuable original paintings, including two Chagalls, a Picasso, and Miro's famous Le Visage s'invente, and his current wife's five favorite pieces of jewelry include over one hundred carats of diamonds. Scrushy even has his own band called Proxy, whose members include professional musicians from the Oak Ridge Boys. When they play a concert, his employees are pretty much expected to attend.

"The Florence College alumni office helped me find an alum, class of '93, who works at HealthSouth. I called her yesterday and it turns out she's an accountant at corporate headquarters. At first she said she couldn't help me, but when I told her I was studying economics and I just wanted to know what it was like to work there, she gave me the inside scoop.

"According to her, HealthSouth is a weird place to work. Scrushy likes to be seen and appreciated. People call him King Richard, and he runs HealthSouth like a king. Most employees who review financial statements only see income statements and asset listings, but not balance sheets. Only a few upper level employees seem to know the full details of the company finances. He demands loyalty from everyone and pays well for it.

"So, that's about it. In the business world, Mr. Scrushy is a success. But it's more about making money than promoting health. Scrushy is a marketing genius—he has built a beautiful façade of fancy technology that's about as good an investment for health as a Pinto is for car safety. And financial analysts wonder if something more devious is going on—whether he's cooking the books. He isn't called King Richard for nothing."

Her presentation completed, Frances sat down and settled back into her seat.

At that moment Don couldn't have cared less about Scrushy. He was too busy thinking about what a dimwit he had been. He had really blown it. Frances was beautiful and smart and he had blown his chance with her because he had been drunk and stupid. So what if she had a boob job? Tons of women have.

"I have a question," Dr. Sampson said, "what about patient outcomes? How many people regained ability to live independently as a result of HealthSouth rehabilitation centers? How many lives were saved in their surgery centers, or as a result of their imaging centers?"

"I...uh, I don't know," Frances replied. "There wasn't any data on that... saving lives isn't what they're about. They do knee scopes and hernia repairs."

"I see," Dr. Sampson's voice was quiet. "The case of Mr. Scrushy is an excellent one to study, but it is unfinished. We cannot judge him; time and history will do that. Naturally, people going into business are often attracted to the parts associated with wealth and power."

Bruce nodded his head in agreement at this last statement, but froze as Dr. Sampson spoke louder in his deep bass voice.

"But remember, publicly held companies put the benefit of their shareholders first. In most companies selling goods and services, this works out just fine. Customers shop around and the market is pretty effective at recognizing good value. But when a company sells healthcare to patients, something perverse happens. On the outside it may look like a healthcare provider," Sampson's voice boomed now, "but inside it is a moneymaker! Company shareholders want profit, remember? Each time corporate executives choose profit over health, it's easier to choose profit the next time. What is the result? Shameless promotion and escalated spending for tests offering little value. Prominent companies profit from total-body MRIs and coronary calcium heart scans by preying on people's fears and pretending these tests are good for health."

Dr. Sampson pointed an index finger at each of the students in turn. "Today it is easier than ever to become a screen watcher and detach yourself from the real world implications, but you must do more than watch! You must see the world as it is and know what goes on behind the scenes if you want to become effective agents for healthcare change. Good job today, Frances. Class dismissed."

After Dr. Sampson and Bruce left, Don made a pitiful last attempt to recover Frances's attention. "Hey, Frances, why don't we go over to the library after class? We can study our epidemiology."

Frances replied sweetly but took obvious satisfaction in rebuffing him. "Sorry, Don, I already promised to study with Bruce this afternoon. I'm helping him with his presentation for next week."

Of course. She liked guys in control, monarchs with wealth and power, men like Scrushy, Ellison, and Bruce. Who was he? Just some poor black kid from Chicago passing for white. He'd had a lucky moment, and it was history.

"Oh, but by the way, Don, what are you doing this weekend?"

"Oh, uh, nothing much. I don't think I'm on call until Sunday. What's up?"

"Well, Saturday night is like the big deal hockey game of the year: Florence College versus Yale. I've got tickets, but Bruce is headed out of town and can't go. Will you go with me?"

Her sparkling green eyes met Don's and entranced him all over again.

"Oh, come on, Don, it will be totally fun!"

Don knew she was only asking him because Bruce couldn't go. There was probably no way she would give him another chance. But still...

"Sure, Frances, that sounds like fun," he heard himself say.

Ice hockey. Football on skates. He had never seen it. It did sound interesting.

"Great!" She rewarded him with her perfect smile. "Pick me up at seven."

DON AND FRANCES had a great time at the game. They ate peanuts and hot dogs, drank way too much beer, and cheered on the Florence College Ravens as they put Yale to shame.

Everyone in the student section was dressed or painted in Florence College black and white. Three rows of shirtless fraternity brothers wore black body paint, their ribs painted white like skeletons. Everyone chanted in unison and waved black Raven banners, and the college band played wild party music non-stop throughout the game.

Florence scored its first goal. Fans in the student section pulled out packages of hot dogs from coats and bags and showered the ice with hundreds of the limpid pink missiles.

"What's going on?" Don asked a shirtless freshman with FC painted in white across the blackened skin of his chest.

"This is how we show the Yale Bulldogs they're pitiful little weenies. Hoo, hoo, hoo!" he chanted and pumped his fist.

"Gimme one of those weenies!" Frances called.

The guy laughed and handed her one immediately. "You got it, babe!"

"Take this, you Yalies!" Frances hurled the pink projectile with surprising force. It landed, bounced, and slid right through the feet of the Yale center lines-man, who was directing brooms in a vain effort to clear the ice.

The Florence College crowd roared with laughter. The tubas oompahed, the drums boomed, and the entire student section jumped up and down in rhythm as one. Don enjoyed watching Frances bounce up and down in her black sweater. All the guys around them were watching her as well. They figured Don was the luckiest guy in the world—little did they know.

Frances's company was familiar and their conversation comfortable enough, but he was no longer her soul man. She crossed her arms as they walked across campus to her apartment, and when they got to her door, she gave Don a quick peck on the cheek and disappeared inside.

His loins ached to see her go. He tried to put her out of his mind—even stopped at The Local to watch real football and have another beer—but he didn't have the heart to try to pick up one of the co-eds at the bar.

A SUNDAY MORNING hangover stretched into another sleepless call night at Florence New American Hospital. An endless stream of patients awaited him in the ER. For twelve hours he wrote admission orders and worked to "tuck them in."

It was a typical night. Diuretics for hypertensives with heart failure, to purge excess fluid in their lungs and legs. Breathing treatments, oxygen, and steroids for smokers with lung disease. Insulin and fluids for diabetics with out-of-control sugar levels.

Don got off work at seven on Monday morning. He was numb and heavy-eyed and almost fell asleep at three different red lights on the drive back to his apartment. The only good thing was he had just made twelve hundred dollars, enough to cover his loan payments for the month plus a little more besides.

Don had barely enough time to shower, make four shots of espresso for his travel mug, and head off for his statistics class at nine o'clock. At least he only had two classes, statistics and epidemiology. With any luck, the espresso would keep him awake through both.

25

The Sick Care Business

*...a serpent with six feet darted up in front of one and fastens on him
all over...Never was ivy so rooted to a tree as the horrid beast intertwined
the other's members with its own; then as if they had been of hot wax,
they stuck together and mixed their colours and neither the one nor the other
appeared now what it was before...Now the two heads had become one, when the two
shapes appeared to us blended in one face in which
the two were lost...*

DANTE ALIGHIERI, INFERNO, 25, 51–72

DON ENTERED the amphitheater two days later and was surprised to see the beaten-up old seminar table sitting center-stage where the old dissection table would have been. How many people must it have taken to wrestle the massive table out of the projection room and down the steps?

A single sturdy wooden chair faced each side. The three students and Dr. Sampson took their seats—Bruce opposite Don and Frances opposite Dr. Sampson—to begin their dissection of health plans.

"Last week we talked about the imaging business in healthcare," Dr. Sampson began. "I don't think any of us will forget the story of Mr. Scrushy, Frances. We'll all be interested to see what happens to him."

Frances smiled and nodded at Dr. Sampson.

"This week we continue the theme of business in healthcare, specifically health plans. Dr. Markum and Dr. Newman have both agreed to present today so we can compare two different viewpoints. Dr. Markum, you may start."

Bruce responded to his cue with the confidence of an experienced television news anchor. He leaned forward, rested his oxford cloth-covered forearms on the table, and interlaced his manicured fingers.

"It's about time we talked about how business in health care really works," he said. "I hate to say it, but you guys are naïve about the business world. Business is about entrepreneurial creativity. Figuring out what people will want in the future and making it easy for them to get it—that's what creates the capital that drives this country. Profit makes health systems better because competition for profit is one of the best drivers of innovation. Let me give you a few examples.

"Last week, you guys complained about the medical arms race and argued competition increases healthcare costs. Well, let me tell you, this so-called medical arms race has given Americans access to better CT scanners and MRI machines in every city and town than most countries have in their whole nation. Competition for the best scanners will eventually result in CT scans becoming a thing of the past. No one will have to worry about radiation from CT scans because every community will have plenty of MRI machines, driving down the cost, and everyone will be able to get scans that don't involve radiation exposure. That's what competition is all about. So you can complain about Americans getting too many scans, but blame government price-fixing, not competition.

"Likewise, you complained about independent surgery centers stealing business from hospitals, but think about it. Why are hospitals losing this business? High overhead—they can't do surgery as cheaply as independent centers. The independent surgery centers focus on one thing, so most of the time they do it better. They have revolutionized the industry. Almost everybody who can gets same-day surgery these days, and that's good, given how perilous the hospitals are. Getting people up on their feet sooner prevents all kinds of hospital complications. Now that hospitals have lost their monopoly and have competition, consumers benefit from safer, faster, and less expensive surgery.

"Look, competition isn't the problem. Competition is healthy. It's the way of the world. Providers compete for business, and we want them to. The real problem is a payment system that creates perverse incentives by encouraging delivery of expensive services regardless of need, when it should promote competition based on quality and service.

"Next, let's talk about not-for-profits. Let's face it; they're a lie. Everybody wants a profit. The only difference is not-for-profits make less profit because they are run so poorly. They're just an excuse for inefficiency. Management is soft and they waste money right and left. People never work their best unless there is real monetary incentive."

Don detested Bruce's mercenary philosophy. People work for all sorts of other reasons—to help others, contribute to society, for the joy of following one's chosen profession, because it's the right thing to do.

"Just look at some health plans that have undergone for-profit conversion. Back in the early 1990s, Health Net was a California not-for-profit health maintenance organization, or HMO, that wasn't growing. In 1992, the board converted it to the for-profit Health Systems International at a bargain price, and thirty-three board members bought into the new company. For just 1.5 million, the group got twenty percent ownership, and four years later, their shares were worth 315 million. Today, Health Net is publicly traded, which means it is accountable to its investors. It provides healthcare benefits to over five and a half million Americans through its PPO, Medicare+Choice, and veteran benefit plans, and six million more Americans through its mental health plans. It does about ten billion dollars in business annually. By pursuing an aggressive business model, Health Net is serving millions of people better than it ever could have before.

"Next, there's Wellpoint, the company that promises"—he glanced at his notes—"to *preserve people's right to choose, while keeping health care affordable,* and to *put individuals back in control of their health and financial future.* Truth is, they have done exactly that, by converting themselves from an underperforming Blues plan to one less encumbered by the Blue Cross Blue Shield bureaucracy. Here's how they got started. Blue Cross of California converted in 1991 by putting ninety percent of its assets into a new for-profit subsidiary, WellPoint Health Networks. Technically, the parent nonprofit company still existed, so they avoided the usual trap of having to set up a charitable foundation to oversee the profits generated by a sale. The rest is history. By 1995, the WellPoint subsidiary of Blue Cross was worth over 2.5 billion. Before the conversion, all that capital was tied up in an underperforming business and doing nothing. Now, WellPoint is one of the most innovative and successful healthcare businesses in the world."

"But the plan went from being a public benefit corporation for the people— for health—to being for profit," Don complained. "In a sense, the Blue Cross plan belonged to the people, and it was sold to Wellpoint investors at a substantially discounted value. Sounds more like stealing to me."

"Stealing candy from a baby," Bruce laughed. "The California corporations commissioner picked up on that technicality, and even though Blue Cross had made substantial charitable donations, he forced WellPoint to fund two new public foundations at a cost of 3.2 billion dollars. That slowed them down a bit, but they still have done far better than Blue Cross ever did at providing a good product. Like I said, *the people* hire lousy managers and give them inadequate oversight. Should they be surprised to lose important assets? It's better for everyone if they do. At least now the company's managed efficiently."

Bruce's tone betrayed surprise at his newfound ability to speak so openly. He had found his voice.

"So, should healthcare businesses act like kids at summer camp with everyone standing around and singing 'Kumbayah'? Of course not. They should operate like football teams. Competition keeps people sharp. If we want efficient organizations, only the fittest can survive. That way, consumers get the best in the end.

"Now the hospital industry, as you *all* know,"—Bruce cast a reproving glance at Don—"is something I know about. Let's look at the Hospital Corporation of America and Tenet Healthcare. Their cases illustrate how well for-profit hospital conversion works for America. Of course, they're not nearly as good as *we are*—they're a little clumsy—but they do know the basic business model. And yes, I did read our assigned article on HCA. Much of it was liberal claptrap, but Kuttner did recognize some of the key benefits of for-profit hospital systems.

Bruce flipped open his laptop, which he had connected to the big screen by cable. "I want to show you some pictures of HCA's newest hospitals."

Everyone turned to look. The first slide showcased a gleaming glass hospital tower with flanking wings, like some sort of new age spaceship.

"This is the brand-new Skyline Medical Center in Nashville, Tennessee, the city where HCA corporate headquarters is located. HCA targets areas with good payer mix, thriving local economies, and high population growth, and they are ready to meet the demands of aging baby boomers. And let me tell you, baby boomers want hospitals that look good. Here are a few of the hospitals they plan to open in the next couple of years—Tallahassee, Florida, one hundred eighty beds—Ocala, Florida, seventy beds—Sky Ridge, Colorado, one hundred four beds—and Smyrna, Tennessee, seventy-five beds. They've sold a lot of their unprofitable hospitals in major urban areas and focused their efforts in the suburbs, where people have money to pay their bills. And they are working hard to become the only choice in town."

Bruce showed slide after slide in quick succession. The modern buildings looked more like shopping malls than hospitals. The pretty façades of marble, stained concrete, and glass belied the sickness inside. Bruce finished the slideshow and closed his computer.

"This model has been enormously successful. HCA revenues were roughly eighteen billion dollars in 2001, with nearly twenty billion in assets, about one billion in net income, and almost one billion in working capital. Most years since 1990, the stock price has risen more than twice as much as the S&P 500.

"How have they done it? Basically like we have. For them, it started with Dr. Thomas Frist, Sr., and his businessman friend, Jack Massey. Dr. Frist had many well-to-do patients in Nashville. Everybody knew him and wanted to be his patient. He and Massey saw how healthcare was delivered in America and thought they could do it better. They knew if they made doctors shareholders in the hospitals, the doctors would help make sure the hospitals were financially successful."

Frances spoke up, "Didn't they run into trouble with the Stark law—the one that prevents physician self-referral because of potential conflicts of interest?"

Bruce smiled. "Good question, Frances. Congressman Pete Stark's initial provisions only took effect in 1992. In both the original law and the 1994 amendments, we made sure it said that if a public company owns a hospital or an integrated delivery system and is worth fifty million dollars or more, a doctor can be a shareholder. Under this provision, HCA gives doctors the chance to buy shares in their local ventures and become part of an exclusive integrated delivery network. The company provides convenient office space, sophisticated medical data systems linking the doctor's office to the hospital, and HCA ensures the doctor's own market share of well-paying patients through the system's exclusive contracts. This is how they build ironclad physician referral networks, driven and organized by the common desire for profit.

"So Richard Scott, the former CEO and architect of HCA, basically had it right when he said: *free market, competitive forces should be the driver* for real health system reform in America. Hospitals aren't charities. To run efficiently and effectively for customer benefit, they have to run like businesses. It works much the same as the deregulation and reenergizing of the steel, airline, and banking industries.

"HCA and Tenet have a simple strategy. They buy up underperforming hospitals at the lowest possible cost. Once they obtain dominant market share in a geographic area, they close duplicative and outmoded facilities, cut costs like unnecessary staff, and integrate inpatient and outpatient systems by taking advantage of economies of scale and group purchasing power. They have a huge advantage over community hospitals because they can pressure suppliers for the best deal by promising all their business to the vendor with the best offer. For example, HCA has a sole-source contract with GE to provide all their imaging equipment at a phenomenal rate for the one hundred fifty-plus hospitals in their system. Finally, they use aggressive marketing to sell their integrated care system. It links doctors and hospitals electronically and does more than the public market ever will to prevent medical errors. And you saw their beautiful hospitals. Who wouldn't want to go there?"

"I, for one," Don said. "These hospital corporations don't care about health. They're for profit, for God's sake, not health."

"Hang on, Don," Bruce said. "Who ever said it was about *health?* Like David Vanderwater, the former Chief Operating Officer of HCA said: *We are not in the health care business. We are in the sick care business.* As long as a hospital efficiently manages the sick, who cares if it's for profit or for health? Besides, for-profit healthcare companies give more back to the community. Let's face it. Not-for-profits are social parasites, like worms that suck on the communities they supposedly serve. Why should they get big tax breaks when they act like for-profits anyway? For profits contribute far more to local economies and the government. For a town whose local government is financially strapped, carrying a debt with a high interest rate on their old, money-losing community hospital, HCA or Tenet is a godsend. Not only does the town instantly shed these major financial liabilities, but it gains a huge increase in the tax base, and their hospital gets a five to ten million dollar makeover."

Bruce had it all wrong! The for-profit hospitals were the parasites, feeding on the communities they pledged to serve—like the Dracunculi, or Guinea worms, that Dr. Reese taught him about in medical school. One of the worst parasites ever to afflict humans. In ancient times, the Israelites drank water from stagnant desert pools. Dracunculus larvae hiding in the water grew into worms and mated in the Israelites' intestines. The blind Guinea worms burrowed through their guts, eating their way beneath the skin, oblivious to the burning pain they caused, oblivious to everything but their own need. The meter-long female fiery serpents would finally erupt into the light through the skin of the leg, showing their heads at the bases of angry ulcers. The only way to get them out was to slowly wind them on a stick, a process that would take days or weeks to complete. Dr. Reese believed the Dracunculi were the 'snakes' that plagued the Israelites and led to the story of Moses and the brazen serpent as well as the ancient medical symbol—a serpent wound around a staff.

Sure, for-profit hospital companies seem like the water of salvation when they arrive in a small town, spend fifty million dollars on bricks, and inject huge boluses of money into cash-strapped community governments. They rebuild an aging community hospital, cover it with marble, and make it look first-class. But the new marble hides a parasite—one that depends on proceduralists, funnelers, and rounders to feed it. The parasite begins to reproduce. More testing, more surgery, more hospital admissions, and more x-rays keep the larvae alive as they suck ever-increasing amounts of money from public and private insurance companies. The hospital drains more and more money from the community, from everyone who pays taxes or health insurance premiums. Ultimately, the small town that saw a for-profit hospital company as a godsend gets something it didn't anticipate: a hungry parasite, a hidden disease.

Maybe that was why Bruce couldn't see the problem. He and his father were the worms! Don imagined their faces on the bodies of slithering snakes, spying out the parts they wanted, pretending to care as they scouted out what they could take, what they could steal. *Like candy from a baby.* The steep-sided anatomical theater was a snakepit, where conquering kings threw the losers. Don hid in the shadows and soaked up Bruce's every word, plotting his rebuttal.

"…Tenet was in pretty pitiful shape before Jeffrey C. Barbakow," Bruce was saying, "but he's made Tenet a real competitor in the game. He was just a kid when he took over Tenet—didn't know much about hospitals, but he knew a lot about business and Wall Street. He got his early business experience in the entertainment industry as the CEO of MGM—he's the consummate dealmaker.

"Anyway, Barbakow bought up undervalued hospital chains and built Tenet's revenue up to 11.4 billion dollars in 2000. They have over a hundred thousand employees in well over a hundred hospitals throughout the country. His consultants from the auto industry are making hospitals efficient for the first time ever by introducing standard industry management practices like Total Quality Management and Six Sigma.

"Thanks to the companies like ours, HCA, and Tenet, who drive innovation in the hospital industry, hospitals are one of the biggest growth industries in America. For-profit conversions have soared, moving the percentage of hospitals that are for-profit from only five percent in 1965 to over thirty-five percent today.

"Here's a good example of why government has no business in healthcare. In 1993, Tennessee was going bankrupt because health care costs were out of control, so Governor McWherter, a Democrat, jumped on the managed care bandwagon. In just a few months, they launched TennCare, a statewide Medicaid managed care program. They contracted with for-profit and not-for-profit organizations to provide all health care services for the enrollees who signed up or were assigned to their plans.

"The cost was a fixed amount per head, what they call a capitated rate. Capitation was the latest thing in managed care, a guaranteed way to hold down costs. Coverage was expanded to most everyone who wanted it because the projected savings with managed care organizations holding down costs would pay for it. So, McWherter simultaneously turned over healthcare management to private companies and markedly increased the government's market share of the insurance business. On the surface all this sounded like a good idea. For once, the government would have a fixed budget for healthcare, and more people would get coverage. But Tennessee's bureaucrats were rank novices, and this was a complicated contract.

"One smart group of businessmen saw an opportunity too good to resist. They formed Access Med Plus, a managed care organization that contracted with Tennessee to provide care for people on Medicaid. Access Med Plus hired door-to-door salespeople in low-income neighborhoods where lots of people have Medicaid. They offered incentives, such as credit cards guaranteed by the plan, to attract healthy clients. With the fixed capitated rate for services, the key thing was to make sure nobody with serious illnesses signed up for their plan, and they signed up healthy people like no other plan in the state.

"They ran a slick marketing campaign and got their name out to every household. The name "Access Med Plus" implied access to the MED, the most trusted hospital in West Tennessee. Thing was, the MED was not in the network, so Access Med Plus wouldn't cover bills from there. The plan was genius, because as the major safety net hospital in West Tennessee, the MED was obligated to see all who showed up sick on its doorstep—at taxpayer expense. When their enrollees went to the MED, and they could deny payment because the MED was an out-of-network provider, they saved a ton of money.

"Man, did their strategy work! Access Med Plus had a low percentage of sick enrollees but got paid almost as much per person as the other managed care organizations. They made a fortune. The not-for-profit plans, particularly the academic ones sponsored by medical schools, got stuck with the costliest patients. The academic groups ended up with fourteen times as many AIDS patients, over six times as many people with expensive blood conditions like hemophilia, and over four times as many patients who got liver, kidney, or heart transplants.

"Access Med Plus understood the contract loopholes. For instance, every enrollee was to be assigned a primary care provider who would be paid to oversee their care, but the contract said nothing about the provider's qualifications or responsibilities. Rumor has it they assigned ten thousand patients to a single eye doctor as the primary care physician. The eye doctor was connected to the family that owned the company, and he was paid millions. This was one of the ways they were able to get around state restrictions and pay high fees to themselves. Unfortunately, they went bankrupt this past October, but not before their top officers had made their millions."

Don couldn't stand it any longer. "These people were transferring enormous funds intended for the care of sick people to their personal bank accounts!" he shouted. "How can you possibly justify that?"

"Everything they did was legal," said Bruce, "and so what if healthcare providers were left unpaid? It was their own fault—doctors aren't smart about contracts, either. That's why real businessmen need to run things. As you can see, the government didn't have any idea what they were doing. They were playing with professional business people. What fools!"

"But these professional business people deceived their customers!"

"Buyer beware!" Bruce spoke the words without a trace of shame. "Remember Don, the healthcare business is about making money. You know full well most of the care doctors provide really isn't very effective. You read the Bunker article. Business is what's critical to America's health. So what's good for business is the important thing."

"We're talking about people's lives, Bruce. It's not like buying cars, it's life and death!"

"Don. We're not talking about doing something wrong and getting caught. They followed the rules—nothing illegal about it. Remember those so-called wasteful regions in the Medicare Atlas? Those high-spending regions are actually where the business model is strong, where there's money to be made. Look, people waste money all the time on gambling, drugs, clothes—why not waste a little money on healthcare? It drives the economy and creates jobs so people can afford to buy televisions and watch football. The world is all about competition for resources. Let the market roll, I say."

"The medical profession is not a game, Bruce, it's…"

"It is a game, Don, and if you don't like how the game plays out, blame the referees or change the rules. Who makes the rules, anyway? The government, right? Don't blame the competitors for playing by government rules!

Government and employers could pay for quality and outcomes instead of volume and high-tech procedures if they wanted to. They could totally change the game. But people want their technology and lots of it.

"Look, a successful business defines the scope of business and cuts everything that doesn't serve the core goal. That's the path to efficiency. Whether it's carving out the right geography, or cutting out the sick and their high-cost utilization, healthcare businesses focus on the part that makes money. Why shouldn't they? Healthcare is valuable. Why should people get it for free? 'Healthcare is a right' is just a fancy way of saying I should pay your bill for you. You think that's fair? No. Everyone should pay his own way. America was founded on principles of independence and self-reliance. That's what America is all about.

"Face it. Free market competition works better and serves people better. Government-funded health care is a disaster. People in the government are finally beginning to see the light. The *Congressional Quarterly* recently said we should 'unleash free market forces' to attack the persistent problem of cost and accessibility in health care. All we need to do is give buyers of health care more information about cost, quality, and outcomes. Then the system can reward providers for innovation and excellence."

Bruce sat back in his chair and winked at Frances, and she positively beamed in return. He nodded at Don to indicate that the floor was his.

That cocky son of a bitch! Don cleared his throat and took a deep breath. He couldn't wait to wipe that self-assured smirk off Bruce's face.

"Thank you, Bruce, for showing us how healthcare looks from the great heights of your fancy business towers. Now let me tell you how it looks up close, from the patient's perspective. I will focus on actual data—you know, what the *evidence* shows—rather than self-serving ideology.

"First, let's talk about health plans. Is that really what they are? We used to just call them insurance companies, and they paid our bills if we got sick. In their quest to keep the money we gave them, they morphed into overgrown monsters with tentacles reaching everywhere. You delude yourself if you think these strange new creatures you call 'health plans' actually care for your health.

"Despite all your sugarcoating, the investor-owned Blue Cross for-profit conversions are the worst. They have the highest overhead of all insurers, some higher than twenty-five percent. Other commercial carriers aren't much better, at about twenty percent overhead, and the not-for-profit Blues plans are sixteen percent on average. By comparison, Medicare's bureaucracy has overhead of only 3.1 percent. Perhaps this would make them a lousy business investment, but you'll have a hard time convincing the people of America that making a handsome profit should be the primary role of health insurance plans."

Don looked over at Frances. She appeared as unimpressed as Bruce. Could neither of them see the obvious truth here?

"Bruce has one thing right; American health plans work hard to maximize profit. As he astutely pointed out, plans making the most money for shareholders do the best at denying care. They want their medical loss ratio—the percent of premiums spent on actual healthcare—as low as possible. Yes, they actually call money spent on healthcare *medical loss!* They trumpet the benefits of competition in lowering costs but have no interest in competing for the business of those who need the most healthcare. They increase profits by peddling unnecessary services to cherry-picked healthy people.

"Delays, denials, and billing errors are not simple mistakes. Bruce's presentation made it crystal clear; many insurance companies do these things on purpose to delay payments and maximize profits. Americans in for-profit plans are much more likely to have problems getting care and settling their bills. No wonder they're far less likely to rate their insurance or healthcare quality as 'excellent.' They pay a fourth of each healthcare dollar to someone secretly dedicated to keeping them from getting the care they need most.

"Don't assume their quality and outcomes are better. They're not. The data is clear. Medicare HMOs are the ultimate bait-and-switch. In general, if you enroll in a for-profit health plan, your children are less likely to get immunized, and you are less likely to get a pap smear or a mammogram or recommended diabetes care. You are even less likely to get lifesaving medication after a heart attack.

"Yes, let's look at healthcare up close, Bruce, not from the heights of some banker's tower. Read the papers in our syllabus, for God's sake! A number of studies clearly demonstrate the differences in quality and outcomes. For-profit HMOs use hospitals with higher death rates for heart surgery than do traditional insurers like Medicare. People who sign up with for-profit Medicare HMOs have a harder time getting basic services. Home care patients only get about half as many visiting nurse and physical therapy visits as people on traditional Medicare and are less likely to improve in their ability to care for themselves. People in for-profit Medicare HMOs are less likely to go to rehabilitation after strokes and more likely to end up languishing in nursing homes. Yeah, Medicare HMOs have great perks, so long as you don't get sick.

"No one wants to admit the truth. Put profiteers in charge of healthcare and you will get profit, yes, but health? Not so much. In a for-profit health plan you're more likely to die. It shouldn't be a surprise—the health insurance companies of America grew from companies that originated to provide death benefits—and they…"

"Wait just a minute, Dr. Newman," Dr. Sampson interrupted. "You're making several assumptions here. Federal payment rules govern private health plans. Aren't healthcare businesses just following government rules? Our current system maximizes profits for plans that play by those rules. You don't need to

attribute evil motives to explain the problems. They result from a poorly organized payment system."

Don's fervor was undeterred. "Maybe," he replied, "but what about those
insurance carve-out programs Dr. Markum loves?"

Don looked at Bruce, hoping to see him fuming, and was disappointed.
Bruce didn't even appear to be listening; he was staring down at the table, to all
appearances lost in a torpid daze, transfixed, as if he were staring into the eyes
of a snake in some holy-roller ceremony. Damn! Bruce had probably anticipated
an attack and resolved to remain unaffected.

"Carve-outs pay a middleman to manage a specific category of healthcare.
Behavioral health is particularly profitable for these bloodsucking carve-out
companies. Psychiatric patients make easy marks. Who's going to complain if
you steal from them? In their desperation to cut costs, many states have hired
for-profit companies to oversee behavioral health services for the mentally ill.
These companies typically slash expenditures for psychiatric patients and cut the
life out of the community mental health centers that struggle to keep mentally
ill people alive, functioning, and off the streets. The carve-out programs really
just pay mental health companies to say no. The more they say no, the more
they get paid. How can their administrators even stand to look at themselves in
the mirror?"

Don spoke louder and faster, trying to rouse Bruce from his stupor and
provoke a reaction, but Bruce seemed comfortably impervious to his attacks.

"These damn carve-outs discourage doctors from responding to people's
needs and coordinating their care. For example, most people get help for depression and anxiety from primary care providers. But guess what happens if a primary care doctor takes an hour to counsel a depressed person? The behavioral
health company pays zip for the visit, even if it prevents a suicide. Primary care
physicians only get paid to care for physical illness, as if the physical and mental
are not connected. Patients need care coordinated by one team in one place.
They can't just be carved up into pieces to be sent around to dozens of different
doctors!"

Frances gave Don a disgusted look, but he hardly noticed. He wasn't about
to back down this time. Don stared straight at Bruce and continued his tirade.

"For your next favorite, let's talk about the converted HMO, Health Net.
What does it do for its enrollees? Well for one thing, Health Net employees get
incentives to cancel insurance policies after people get sick. Yeah, that's right.
I have my sources, too. People like Patsy Bates, a hairdresser whose coverage
was cut by Health Net in the middle of her chemotherapy treatments for breast
cancer. Senior analysts at Health Net are paid extra to cut people like her, people
who have the misfortune to work for a small company whose business Health
Net can afford to lose. Of course, Health Net always manages to cook up some

technicality to make it look legitimate, like claiming there was an undisclosed pre-existing condition, but their business model is based on avoiding payment wherever they can.

"Your beloved WellPoint is no better. The subsidiary not-for-profit they converted, Blue Cross of California, has a special department that considers about fifteen hundred policies for cancellation every week. Here is an example of how they operate. Selah Shaeffer was only four years old when diagnosed with a potentially fatal tumor in her jawbone. When her medical bills hit twenty thousand dollars, her parents got a notice Blue Cross was denying coverage. Blue Cross retroactively refused to pay for Selah's treatment, even for surgery they had previously authorized! Selah's parents stand to end up with over sixty thousand dollars in medical bills and may lose their home. Why did they refuse to pay? Blue Cross accused the Shaeffers of hiding an undiagnosed bump on Selah's chin. Basically, they use flimsy excuses like this to dump all the sick policyholders they can."

Dr. Sampson tried again to slow Don down. "Dr. Newman, you make it sound like evil is everywhere in the healthcare industry. Is for-profit healthcare really so universally deceptive?"

Don shot back without thinking. "For-profit health plans aren't really health plans. They are more like undertakers, or snakes, eager to take their sick prey underground. They make the most money if their sick patients die quickly. This is not just about business, Bruce. It is about people's lives!"

Bruce smiled benignly at Don. His eyes were vacant, as if he'd been hypnotized not to take the bait.

Don was livid. Obviously, Bruce was comfortable with snakes; that was just business as usual in the Markum household. He had been transfixed by the snake at an early age. He probably thought being compared to a snake was a compliment!

Don gathered his wits for one last attack.

"I have two more cases showing the perversity of the sickness business in America. First, hemodialysis. High blood pressure and diabetes caused by overweight and inactivity have made kidney failure common, and people with kidney failure need blood-cleaning machines to stay alive. Thirty years ago, there were ten thousand people on dialysis. Now it's over three hundred thousand and growing by leaps and bounds. Huge dialysis centers pack them in—rows and rows of people, all of them stuck with needles and tethered to machines that suck out their blood and put it back in. Every person on dialysis has to do this three times a week for three or four hours each time.

"Think about the people in iron lungs during the polio epidemic of the 1940s and '50s. We worked hard to eradicate polio in this country and get rid of those iron lungs. But what are we doing to address the root causes of the plague of kidney failure? Hardly anything, even though we all know poor exercise and dietary habits are driving this plague! We don't invest in prevention. We invest in keeping the victims alive on dialysis machines. And guess what? There are vampire profiteers who live off this suffering.

"Hemodialysis is risky business. On average, one in four people dies in the first year of dialysis. The *New England Journal of Medicine* article shows dialysis patients at for-profit centers are twenty percent more likely to die than patients at non-profit centers. They're also twenty-six percent less likely to get referred for a transplant. And more than three quarters of our dialysis providers are for-profit.

"What makes for-profit dialysis centers so much deadlier? Turnover. The centers are paid a set fee per session, no matter how many hours the patient spends on the machine, so there's a strong incentive to get people off the machines quickly. So what if a few more people die? Who's going to know? So what if they have more complications? They get paid extra for complications."

"It may just be another example of getting exactly what we pay for," Dr. Sampson said. "Lots of ugly unintended consequences result from fixed payment schedules that have no regard for quality or outcomes."

"Another thing is for-profit nursing homes. We are filling them full of people who are essentially gone. They can't talk, can't walk, can't eat, can't think clearly. We call it compassionate when we stab sharp daggers through the walls of their inflated stomachs to place plastic tubes for long-term force-feeding. This would be fine if they had some hope of recovery, or if it was what they would have wanted. One can't help but think about the profit made from keeping the bodies of these poor people alive unnaturally. What else do they have to live for at this point? How can we justify putting them in such hell? Lying all day in bed, covered in feces and urine, unable to eat, drink, talk, or laugh, their only visitors the ones who come to jab them with another needle?"

Don paused to catch his breath. He had come to his grand finale. Don knew he couldn't talk about New American Healthcare Corporation. But hell, Bruce had brought up HCA and Tenet, just as Don thought he would. So here was his chance to present the other side of these companies. And New American Healthcare was just like them. He'd show Frances what a snake Bruce really was.

"Let's talk about the hospitals. Remember how National Medical Enterprises, the predecessor of Tenet, imprisoned depressed people in their Florida hospitals just to keep their beds full? And that's the tip of the iceberg. They bribed state officials, gave kickbacks for referrals, and had to pay the government a 379 million dollar fine for insurance fraud as well as some 200 million dollars in private settlements. These guys were crooks.

"As for HCA, the FBI raided their hospital in El Paso and found they had systematically overbilled Medicare for more than a decade. The FBI got fifty-one search warrants in seven different states and discovered these abuses were the norm throughout HCA's hospitals. Three HCA executives were charged with defrauding the government, and HCA's federal fines for fraud amounted to 745 million dollars.

"Fraud aside, we know for-profit hospitals cost consumers a lot more. So what do they get for all that extra money? More administrators, overseers, and bureaucrats, and fewer clinical personnel. This would be defensible if they got better care, but what does the data show? That people with common serious illnesses are more likely to die if they go to a for-profit medical center. At academic medical centers, where patient care is priority number one, patients fare the best. Go figure—an institution that prioritizes people over profits saves more lives.

"Sure, for-profit hospitals pay more in taxes, but they provide far less charity care and do little to support medical education. They avoid charity care by planting themselves on the best geography in town and attracting the healthiest patients and the rich, paying patients. Fancy waiting rooms and hotel-like hospitals delude people into thinking they are places of excellence, but the ugly truth is that if you go into their expensive marbled halls, you'll pay more and be more likely to die."

Bruce remained quiet, his expression one of bemusement.

Don was more determined than ever to wipe the infuriating smirk off Bruce's face. He pinched the knot on the bridge of his nose and clenched his teeth. "Where is all that money going—that capital Bruce claims is reinvested for the good of the American people? Where is that money *really* being invested for the good of America? In places like Jackson Hole, Wyoming, and Vail, Colorado.

"This year, your hero Barbakow at Tenet is probably the highest-paid executive in any publicly traded American company. Just last week, he made 111 million by cashing in some stock options. Add in his salary and he should clear well over 115 million total this year alone.

"Let's run the list of HMO executives: John Rowe and Ronald Williams at Aetna stand to make 8.9 million and 6.1 million dollars respectively in pay and stock options this year. Larry Glasscock at Anthem stands to make about 25 million, Edward Hanway at Cigna some 7.4 million, Jay Gellert at Health Net over 13 million, William McGuire and Stephen Hemsley at United Healthcare 79 million and 18 million respectively, and Leonard Schaefer at Wellpoint 19 million. Tenet's CEO Richard Earner was making around 10 million a year during the time Tenet was systematically defrauding Medicare, and he left in 1994 in the midst of the investigation with a pension of about a million a year, plus a lump sum of 2.6 million. Last but not least, Dr. Thomas Frist's total compensation was 127 million in 1992 as HCA chairman, making him the highest-paid hospital executive that year."

Finally. Don had gotten to Bruce, at least a little. Bruce's lips were pursed and his face red. After all, he knew these people. He had partied with them, been to their luxury vacation homes in Vail or wherever. Don decided to end it there. He really didn't want a fight; he just wanted to infect Bruce—and Frances—with a little doubt.

"So that's about it," he said. "In summary, you get what you pay for, or in the case of American health care, a lot less than you pay for."

Dr. Sampson stood up. "That is enough for today. We will reconvene next week in Washington."

Bruce grabbed his books and took off in a hurry.

Frances didn't wait for Dr. Sampson to leave before she turned on Don. "Oh my God, Don, that was totally slimy talking about Columbia HCA and Tenet like that," she hissed. "You know those people are friends of the Markum family. You were practically attacking Bruce! You are such a worm." She stormed out.

Don just stood there, too stunned to move. He hadn't seen that coming. He'd been sure Frances would see things his way. Maybe she was right; he was a worm, trying to weaken Bruce and insinuate himself back into her heart. Women were so impossible…

Oh, shit! Sarah! I forgot to call her back! I told her I might come to Boston and take her out to dinner, and then I totally forgot. Great. Just great. That makes two women who think I'm a complete jerk.

"Can I help you move that table now, Dr. Sampson?" The night watchman poked his head through the door from the hallway.

"Sure, Lucas."

The two men made it look almost effortless as they lifted the massive table and turned it on its side. The table was so big, it totally blocked Don's view of the watchman as he backed through the door. Don heard a small grunt from Dr. Sampson as they carried the table out through the tall doors of the amphitheater into a storage room across the hall.

Dr. Sampson returned alone. Noticing Don's quizzical stare as he moved the chairs to the sides of the room, he gave a rare smile. "We have to keep it looking nice and polished in here for President Lender," he said with mock reverence.

Don went back to his apartment to call Sarah and apologize. He called her pager, entered his number, hung up, and waited. She didn't return the page. After lunch he tried two more times and waited, even though he knew he'd be late to epidemiology. If he had a cell phone, he could go to class and not miss her call, but he wasn't about to spring for a cell phone on his budget. Still no answer. She was obviously furious with Don for blowing her off. Who could blame her? Don tried her apartment in Sommerville and got no answer there, either.

To hell with epidemiology! Don grabbed his keys, ran out the door, jumped into his rusting Ford Escort and headed for Boston. It was only an hour and a half away this time of day, and he got there just as dusk was approaching.

Don drove into the dark shadows beneath the towers of the University Hospital. He circled twenty minutes for a parking place, frustrated he no longer had a pass to the hospital parking deck. Someone finally vacated a spot on the street and he pulled in.

Don ran to the hospital's front entrance, passed under the gigantic pillars guarding the portico, pushed through the revolving door, and crossed the antechamber toward the familiar domed lobby with the swirling black floor.

"Mister," a voice called.

Don ignored the voice and continued walking to where the veined marble awaited his footstep.

"Mister, hold it right there," the voice commanded.

Don paused at the edge where gray marble gave way to a whirlpool of black. He looked around to locate the source of the echoing voice and traced it to the small reception window at the far end of the antechamber, near where he had entered.

"Mister, you can't go in there! Visiting hours are over."

"I'm a doctor," he called back.

"Then I'll have to see your ID badge."

Don turned around and approached the reception window. He no longer belonged here. Come to think of it, he never did. What if Dr. Desmond spotted him here? He should have considered that before. And Sarah was unlikely to be pleased to see him now. What would he say? Don thought about leaving, but it was too late now.

Don arrived at the window and looked inside. The same old guard was there, grizzled and haggard as ever. He stared at Don through the glass, his hand on the same damn nightstick dangling from his belt. He still didn't have any idea who Don was.

"I don't have a badge anymore," Don said, "but I used to work here."

"Visiting family here, are you?"

Don paused and swallowed. "No."

"Sorry, no one is allowed after hours without an ID badge or a special family visitor's pass."

"But I have a colleague who works here and I need to see her."

"What's her name?"

"Dr. Sarah Moore."

He glanced at his list. "Vacation."

"Excuse me?" Don replied, not sure he had heard correctly.

"She's on vacation. All this week. Doubt you'll get an answer. Want me to page her?"

"No...no, that's all right. I'll get with her later."

Don turned away, walked to the front entrance, and was hurled back into the cold by the old brass revolving door. No, he didn't belong here anymore. What a fool he had been to go back to visit, even to see Sarah. She probably didn't even miss him last weekend.

He got in his car and drove back to Florence. An endless line of oncoming headlights pierced the black night, lighting the path back to Boston. He resented the people in those cars; they probably all had friends or loved ones awaiting them, a hot dinner on the table.

Back in his cold apartment, he called and left a message on Sarah's phone. "Hey, Sarah, it's Don. Sorry about last weekend. I got caught up in some school stuff I couldn't get out of. Listen, I'm really sorry. Hear you're on vacation. Hope you are having a good time. Okay, well, see you later."

Don hung up. He assumed there was not much chance he'd be seeing Sarah again any time soon.

26

False Healthcare Counselors

Behold how great a matter a little fire kindles! And the tongue is a fire,
a world of iniquity, that it defiles the whole body, and sets on fire
the course of nature: and it is set on fire by hell. For every species of beast
and bird, of reptile and sea creature, can be tamed and has been tamed
by the human species, but no one can tame the tongue—
a restless evil, full of deadly poison.

EPISTLE OF JAMES 3, 5–9

FRANCES STUDIED in the back seat the entire way from New Hampshire down to Washington while Bruce and Don took turns driving the old college van. Thin patches of ice coated I-95, and refrozen slush lined both sides of the road.

Don's gloom deepened as they drew closer to the city. There was something else, too. Fear. Don had an overwhelming feeling they were approaching danger. He told himself it was irrational anxiety, but the uneasiness in his gut intensified into a knot as they entered the capital city through the northern ghettos.

He wasn't sure why this second trip to American University filled him with dread. On their first field trip to Washington the previous fall semester, he loved staying on the campus of the national university George Washington had dreamed of, in the city where big ideas and hard-fought decisions determined the country's future. Washington was the heart of democracy, a place that should pulse with life. But raw winds and bitter cold had emptied the streets. Corrugated black bark dominated the leafless trees, and the white marble monuments were cloaked in gray soot. The District of Columbia looked old, decayed, and dying…dead, really. Cold and dead.

Perhaps it was only the dreary weather of January getting to him more than usual. Or loneliness—he had blown it with Frances and there was no one else on the horizon, no one he could imagine warming his bed. Or maybe he was still feeling guilty about Sarah. She was a real friend, and he had blown it with her, too. He'd called her three more times but only got her answering machine. The third time, he left another pitiful apology and a series of excuses about how he had been on call, how dumb he was, how he really wanted to get together the next time they both had a break.

As soon as the students had put their suitcases in the bare dorm rooms, Don fled the confines of the concrete block bunker and took a brisk walk across campus. Glimpsing a building with a tall, green-domed rotunda, he went over to investigate.

The building was named McKinley Hall, after the twenty-fifth U.S. president. McKinley was assassinated by a disgruntled former factory worker who turned anarchist after getting fired and blacklisted for participating in a strike. Up until the moment he was electrocuted, the assassin claimed he was only trying to protect good working people from exploitation by wealthy industrialists.

Don climbed the limestone stairs and paused in front of a semi-circle of giant columns that framed the entrance to the building and supported the copper-roofed rotunda. Don paused to read the large bronze plaque next to the door.

BIRTHPLACE OF ARMY CHEMICAL CORPS

SOON AFTER THE UNITED STATES ENTERED THE FIRST WORLD WAR IN 1917, THE AMERICAN UNIVERSITY'S OFFER OF ITS CAMPUS AND BUILDINGS FOR WAR WORK WAS ACCEPTED.

THE PERMANENT BUILDINGS AND PART OF THE CAMPUS WERE TURNED OVER TO THE BUREAU OF MINES ON JULY 6, 1917, FOR USE AS CHEMICAL WARFARE LABORATORIES AND PROVING GROUNDS. MCKINLEY HALL SERVED AS ONE OF THE FIRST OF THESE LABORATORIES.

ON AUGUST 30, 1917, THE THIRTIETH ENGINEERS, LATER KNOWN AS THE FIRST GAS REGIMENT, WAS ORGANIZED HERE. COMPANIES A AND B AND FIRST BATTALION HEADQUARTERS MARCHED OUT OF THE AMERICAN UNIVERSITY ON CHRISTMAS DAY 1917, AND SAILED FOR FRANCE THE NEXT DAY...

DEDICATED IN 1960 BY VETERANS OF THE FIRST GAS REGIMENT

American University admitted its first class in 1914, and before they graduated, the military was making poison gas on campus? What would George Washington think of this legacy? Healthy young soldiers developed end-stage lung disease in a matter of minutes when poison chlorine gas seeped down into their muddy trenches in World War I. The smoke of the cigarettes they gave out like candy took years to do that kind of damage. During his medical school days in Chicago, Don had known a resident physician from Iran who had seen young survivors of Saddam Hussein's poison gas attacks. They were left gasping for breath for the ruined remnants of their lives.

Don pulled on the building's door, but it was locked. The cold wind whipped through the columns and pierced his old woolen coat. He beat a hasty retreat to his barracks for the night, where the cold deli sandwich he'd bought on the road for his supper and a fitful night's sleep did little to lighten his mood or lessen his foreboding. It didn't help that Bruce and Frances were dining out at a fancy restaurant. They had been courteous enough to invite him—an invitation he probably didn't deserve after his seminar performance the week before—but Bruce had made it clear it was very expensive, so Don had declined to join them.

Next morning at breakfast, Don picked up an abandoned copy of *The Washington Post* and sat alone in the cafeteria. Charles Krauthammer had written a chilling editorial on President Bush's State of the Union speech and the president's declaration that "Iraq with others forms an axis of evil." Krauthammer wrote: "The speech was just short of a declaration of war."

Well, Dr. Sampson's meager little battalion of four was here in the nation's capital to launch a war, also. A war on medical errors. Lives are at stake right here at home, in our medical centers and hospitals! Every day people are cut, medicated, and radiated unnecessarily in hospitals, nursing homes, and ambulatory surgery centers. Hundreds of thousands die each year from medical mistakes in the United States. No one sees the big picture. No one even seems to notice! It's up to us to call attention to it. Like Dr. Sampson said, we have to declare a war to get people to pay attention.

After breakfast, the students marched double-time to keep up with Dr. Sampson as he led them from the Capitol South Metro stop to the Russell Senate Building. They passed through the security x-ray machine and into a rotunda, where a statue of Senator Russell stood guard and a ring of pillars drew their eyes upward to the domed ceiling.

They took an elevator to the second floor and started down a seemingly endless corridor flanked on both sides by a long procession of dark doors. A plaque next to each door bore the name of the senator whose office it was. Every few hundred paces, the hall turned to the right and revealed another long passage with identical doors. Don swiveled his head from side to side to read the names as they passed, but Dr. Sampson stared straight ahead.

Dr. Sampson stopped at the last door on the left before the hall turned to the right a second time. He knocked and entered without waiting for a response, the students close on his heels.

A secretary looked up from her wooden desk in a corner of the cramped reception area. Her dark hair was streaked with gray, and a placard on her desk read *Janet Clifton*.

"Virgil Sampson, I presume?"

"Yes, we have an appointment," Dr. Sampson answered.

"Senator Josten will be right with you. Please take a seat." Ms. Clifton motioned for them to sit in the adjacent waiting area.

Frances, Don, and Bruce sank into an old, wine-colored leather couch next to a staffer's desk.

Dr. Sampson sat directly across from them and spoke in a low voice directed to their ears alone. "Your first trip to Washington was to study bureaucrats and how they implement laws. Now we study the political process and rulemaking. You're well prepared to present our proposed medical errors legislation, the Medicare Quality Improvement Act, and to answer Senator Josten's questions if you get the chance. Be concise and make sure he hears your best arguments. Remember, Senator Josten chairs the Senate Health, Education, Labor, and Pensions Committee, or HELP for short, so he's probably the most influential person on the hill when it comes to getting health care legislation through. He's a friend, so we can count on him to repeat our points later on."

Bruce leaned forward. "Dr. Sampson, you know my family has a lot of contacts here. Maybe I can get them to help, as well."

"Senator Josten will see you now," Ms. Clifton announced. She walked over to a tall, dark wooden door and swung it open, stepping aside to let them in.

The three students followed their general into the inner sanctum.

"Ah, Dr. Gil Sampson, my old friend. Thank you for coming," Senator Josten boomed. The tall senator stood erect behind his desk and extended a hand in greeting, forcing Dr. Sampson to lean across the massive desk to gain the senator's palm.

While shaking Dr. Sampson's hand, Josten sized up the students. "Dr. Markum," he said, raising his eyebrows, "it is very good to see you again."

Bruce stepped smoothly to the side of the burnished mahogany desk and took the offered hand halfway between them, meeting the eyes of Senator Josten with a steady gaze.

The senator turned and nodded unceremoniously at Frances and Don and motioned them all to take a seat.

Cool tendrils of warning danced up the back of Don's neck. He took a deep breath to calm his nerves and blew off his irrational preoccupation. The room was cold, that was all.

Dr. Sampson went right to the point. "Senator Josten, you know why we are here. We want your support for the proposed Medicare Quality Improvement Act..."

Don let his eyes wander around the room while Dr. Sampson explained the legislation. He was sitting in the office of one of the Senate's most prominent leaders! A large oil painting behind Senator Josten's desk caught his eye.

The painting was in the style of the old masters, but the paint looked fresh and clean. It was of an elderly, presidential man in partial profile, and the artist had depicted the subject in remarkable detail. The man's sideburns stretched to his jaw, and his graying hair was pulled back in the colonial style, revealing a very high forehead and a prominent V-shaped forelock that accentuated his bulging, wide-set eyes. The eyes appraised Don with a somber and calculating expression. One eyebrow was slightly higher than the other. He looked familiar.

"Gil, you know you have my full support. This medical errors legislation is certainly overdue. But my constituents are more interested in a Medicare drug benefit. Are you sure you can't think of some way we could link it to a Medicare drug bill? Then we could count on the full support of the pharmaceutical industry and the AARP." Senator Josten laughed heartily. "With those two together, why, we'd be unbeatable!"

"Senator, you know how little real value or health payoff that would have for the American public," Dr. Sampson replied calmly. "The only real winners would be the pharmaceutical companies."

"The cost of a Medicare pharmaceutical benefit would be extravagant, and passing it could take years," Frances added. "We think the Medicare Quality Improvement Act is too important to wait. It is much less expensive and provides important financial incentives for hospitals to adopt best practices, eliminate errors, and reduce costs."

"Yes, we think it needs to stand on its own," Dr. Sampson continued, "to let the American people know the vital importance of eliminating medical errors. This is your chance to launch a national war on medical errors that could ultimately save the lives of hundreds of thousands of citizens. As the sponsor of this legislation, you will be their savior."

Senator Josten laughed again. "Don't we already have the best healthcare system in the world? Really Gil, I've got to be ready to counter accusations that this whole endeavor is un-American. Besides, it's not clear to me anyone really wants to reduce healthcare costs. At least, the lobbyists I hear from don't."

Don could have sworn Senator Josten glanced at Bruce and gave him a barely perceptible wink. Did he imagine it?

"Just tell them you must do what's right for Americans," Dr. Sampson countered, "that we need affordable, high-quality healthcare, and with the right incentives, our doctors and hospitals can provide better care for less."

"Very good, Gil, very good," Senator Josten said as he swiveled and rose from his upholstered chair. He moved toward the door, clearly indicating the meeting was ending almost as soon as it had begun. As he passed Dr. Sampson, he clapped a hand on his shoulder, and Dr. Sampson stiffened under the patronizing gesture.

Don stole a final glance at the painting over the Senator's desk. Those eyes knew everything and missed nothing, like Dr. Desmond's cool, calculating eyes. They drilled into Don's brain, added up his attributes and deficits, and chilled him more than the room's cold temperature.

"So you noticed my painting," Senator Josten said. "Do you know who it is, Dr. Newman?"

"No, sir," he answered. Why did his voice sound so timid?

"Aaron Burr. Vice-President, champion of independence, and founder of the first great political machine in America, Tammany Hall. How quickly he has been forgotten. In his time he was much maligned, but no one could say he didn't know what was going on. A beautiful painting, isn't it?"

For a moment they were all transfixed by Burr's knowing stare.

"A good reminder, Dr. Newman, to keep your eyes open," the senator cautioned.

They had made their way back into the hallway when Senator Josten called out, "Oh, Bruce, before you go, I talked to your father the other day..." He motioned for Bruce to step back into his office and closed the door behind them, dismissing Dr. Sampson, Frances, and Don without another word.

Bruce was in Josten's office for twenty minutes. Frances and Don couldn't imagine what was taking him so long and could barely wait to hear his report. Dr. Sampson, on the other hand, did not seem surprised in the least. He occupied the time by strolling up and down the hallway and reading the signs marking the many office doors, as if he were trying to memorize them all.

"So?" Frances blurted out when Bruce reemerged. "Like, what did he say?"

Bruce shrugged, smiled his winsome smile, and said, "Oh, we just talked a little about the family business." He sauntered down the hall toward Dr. Sampson as if his little chat with the senator was an everyday thing to do.

"Come on, Bruce, out with it!" Frances implored him. "We know you're dying to tell."

"Oh, don't be so sure about that," he said with a sly grin. "It's more like you're dying to know."

Dr. Sampson interrupted. "Let's go find out where the committee meeting will be tomorrow and what time you need to be there to get in. I want you to see how these hearings are run. Follow me."

They walked back down the long hall and took the elevator to the basement tunnels connecting the Senate office buildings with the Capitol. They started off the elevator, but a uniformed guard stepped in front of them and barred their way. His badge read *United States Capitol Police*. He scanned the badges on their chests and scowled.

"Didn't you see the sign?" he demanded. "No one is allowed down here unless escorted by a staff member with proper identification, and you can't use the subway at all when the Senate is voting."

Dr. Sampson looked shocked but continued to hold the elevator door open. The alarm began to chime. "When did this happen?" he asked. "I've always taken the underground here before."

The guard was curt. "Ever since 9–11, of course. Please return upstairs immediately. This is a restricted area."

Frances pressed the button and the doors began to close, but Dr. Sampson pushed them open again and addressed the guard like a disobedient private. "We will return!" He let go and the elevator doors banged shut.

Without a word, they went back upstairs to Senator Josten's office, where Ms. Clifton was juggling callers on two phones. Fine wrinkles bracketed a tense smile that failed to mask her irritation at being interrupted again.

Twice Dr. Sampson tried to state his case, only to be drowned out by the ringing phones.

"Hold your horses for just a minute, would you?" She returned to her phone and called someone to accompany the four to the tunnels.

A legislative assistant wearing a charcoal pinstripe skirt suit appeared a few minutes later. "Hello," she chirped. "I'm an intern from Senator Josten's home state. Just follow me." She led them toward the door.

Ms. Clifton called her back and handed over a large manila envelope. "Take this, will you? Since you are going to the Dirksen Building anyway."

Senator Josten's staffer led them down the hall at a brisk pace. Don sensed she was eager to return to some important meeting, but she maintained the requisite hospitality, asking where they were from and what their top legislative concerns were. They stepped on the elevator again.

"How many people does Senator Josten have on his staff?" Dr. Sampson asked.

"It depends on who you include, since some work part time. About eighty work for the Senate HELP Committee, plus another forty or forty-five for his other work. That doesn't count campaign people, of course. Most are based in Hart and Dirksen. There's not nearly enough room for all of us here."

The elevator doors opened and the intern flashed her badge. Dr. Sampson set his jaw, held his head high, and stared straight ahead, making a point of ignoring the presence of the guard as they marched past him into a glossy underground tunnel, part of the labyrinth of subterranean tracks marking the connections of power in Washington.

Only a minute or so passed before a sleek miniature train glided to a stop before them. They boarded, and the train pulled out smoothly into a bright, tiled tunnel, whisking them beneath the Capitol complex buildings. They disembarked under the Dirksen Senate Building and took the elevator up. The doors opened onto another whitewashed hall with an endless succession of dark wooden doors.

"Here we are," the intern announced, "third floor Dirksen. You don't need to go back, do you?"

"No, thank you," Dr. Sampson answered, turning back to his students as the elevator doors closed. "This way."

They tagged along as he searched for the room where the committee hearing would be held the next day. Rounding a blind corner, they came upon a line at least a hundred people long. The queue was cordoned off along the side of the hall by a braided gold rope.

Don looked to Dr. Sampson, who seemed as puzzled as he was.

"What is everyone waiting for?" Dr. Sampson asked a young man near the middle of the line.

The man was wearing a sweatshirt, frayed blue jeans, and cowboy boots. The casual clothing was at odds with his air of authority. He flipped through his newspaper, taking his time before answering Dr. Sampson.

"Where are *you* from? We're waiting for the committee hearing, of course."

"But the hearing isn't until tomorrow," Bruce replied.

The guy sneered. "If you want to get in, you have to get here early."

"Who do you represent?" Frances asked.

Don guessed he was a hippie fanatic for some consumer advocacy group.

"Me?" he laughed. "Nobody. I'm just a placeholder."

They stared at him, not comprehending.

"I work for the Congressional Services Company. I get paid to stand in line and hold a place for someone who wants a seat in the meeting. I used to be a package runner. You know, one of those guys cruising the streets on bikes at high speed? But I got hit by a car and ended up blind in one eye. This was the best I could do. I'm not complaining; this is a great job. I get paid good money to stand around and do nothing. Like I said. I'm just a placeholder."

Frances tried to work her magic on him, like she did on every man when she wanted something. "Do you think we could, like, slip in somewhere?" she cooed.

"Oh, you want me to turn a blind eye?" He laughed at his own joke. "No way, sweetheart. You got to pay to be in this line."

"So who is paying you and all your friends?" Bruce asked.

"I don't know. I just stand where the company sends me. But it's a healthcare hearing. What do you expect? The usual crowd of people from K Street with money in the game—insurance folks, drug companies, hospital associations, AARP."

Dr. Sampson pulled them aside. "The meeting starts tomorrow at nine-thirty. I'm testifying at ten-thirty. I'll call Senator Josten's office and tell him we need spots in the hearing room for tomorrow." He didn't sound optimistic.

Don wondered whether they could watch it on closed circuit. He'd heard they do that sometimes. Or maybe they could use the internet. Frances kept talking about how you could get streaming video for anything really important.

Either way, it looked like Dr. Sampson would go to the HELP Committee hearing to give his testimony alone.

The three students and their teacher parted ways mid-afternoon in the Metro Center. Dr. Sampson headed back toward the Capitol for another meeting. Bruce said he was going downtown to meet some friends of his father, that it was his chance to get help for their cause. Frances and Don headed back to American University, but not before they cornered Bruce and demanded to know what Senator Josten had said.

"Okay, there is this little event coming up where I expect to see Senator Josten again. So, if you're a little more polite, maybe I'll let you in on the details later." Bruce flashed them an impish grin and vanished before they had a chance to learn anything more.

The next day, they all attended the HELP Committee meeting. Dr. Sampson had managed to get three staff passes. They heard his testimony, but it wasn't clear anyone else did. The entire experience was very frustrating. Everyone was whispering, rustling papers, waiting for something important to happen—and Dr. Sampson's testimony wasn't it. The remainder of the meeting was filled with meaningless motions, counter-motions, and introductions of documents into "consideration" by the committee.

Based on what he saw, Don couldn't fathom how any legislation ever got passed, but he was about to find out how decisions are really made on Capitol Hill.

27

The Lobbyists

*...my deeds were those, not of the lion, but of the fox; I knew all wiles
and covert ways and so practiced their arts that their sound went forth
to the end of the world.*

DANTE ALIGHIERI, INFERNO 27, 74–78

AS SOON AS the health policy lecture ended, the students blazed out of the
School of Public Affairs classroom and into the old tiled hall of the Ward Circle
Building. Bruce pulled Don and Frances into a huddle and glanced around
furtively.

"Look, Dr. Sampson is in over his head here," Bruce said. "When it comes to
lobbyists, you have to see how they operate from the inside. You know, first-hand
experience." He chuckled. "Yeah. First hand, then foot." His lips curved into a sly
smile. "I think it's time to take a little field trip."

"So what did you have in mind, Bruce?" Frances stood, hands on hips, and
tapped her foot.

"Yeah, Bruce, spit it out," added Don.

Bruce took his time, relishing their anticipation as he dragged it out. "You
want to see how healthcare policy is really made in Washington, right?"

"Of course we do," Don said. "That's why we're all here, isn't it?" His
patience with Bruce's dramatic performance was wearing thin.

"And you agree the lobbyists are the ones who really make policy in
Washington, right?"

"Sure, within limits," Don said.

"Come on, Bruce, tell us," Frances begged.

Bruce ignored Frances's plea. "No, Don, three nights from now lobbyists
will rule without limits. Say it, Don. No limits."

Don didn't want to play Bruce's little game, but Frances egged him on by
nodding her head quickly up and down, raising her eyebrows, and smiling in a
charming, expectant way that made it impossible for him to refuse.

"Okay, okay," he said. "No limits."

Bruce grinned. "Very good." His eyes narrowed and he leaned forward.
"Friday night, we are going to learn from the real lawmakers, and you, my

friends, are going to see firsthand how they work. You see, it just so happens there is going to be a gala…"

"Oh, so that's why you told me to bring my nicest formal dress!" Frances blurted out with childlike glee.

"Yes, Frances, that's why. Friday night at eight in the Willard Hotel. The biggest, most important gathering of healthcare leadership in the country, plus invited guests, including the most important senate and house leaders for health-care legislation. Hell, sometimes the president even comes. And I have invitations for the three of us."

Frances was spellbound. She gazed at Bruce, her eyes filled with deep admiration and anticipation.

"It's co-hosted each year by the hospitals and the insurance industry," Bruce continued. "The heads of every major hospital system, insurance company, and health plan will be there, along with their pet lawmakers. And *that* is where the nation's health policy for the year will be set. You'll see. So, I'll pick you up in front of the dorm at seven-thirty. Look sharp. The Willard is a classy place and this is a very elegant party."

Oh crap, Don thought. Did this mean he'd need a monkey suit?

"Don, you do have a tux, don't you?" Bruce asked, detecting the dismay on Don's face.

"Oh, yeah," he said. "Of course."

That son of a bitch. Bruce knew full well Don didn't travel with formal eve-ningwear. Obviously, he'd told Frances to bring the appropriate attire and hoped Don would decline to go. But there was no way he was going to be aced out. He'd just have to find a formalwear shop.

It was Friday afternoon before Don finagled the van keys from Bruce by tell-ing him he needed to run some errands. The weather was unseasonably warm for February, and the brown snow and slush lining the streets and sidewalks had disappeared. Don burned a quarter tank of gas at a standstill behind a rush hour wreck on Wisconsin Avenue. He fumed. *I could have run to the damn tux shop and back in half the time.*

Three hours later and a couple hundred dollars poorer, Don was back in his dorm room, unwrapping his packages and thinking how nice it would have been to have ditched the gala and gone for a long run instead. It had been no small feat to rent, last minute, a tuxedo and shoes that fit. Well, almost fit.

He glared at the shiny black shoes. They were vinyl instead of leather and pinched his pinky toes. The jacket was not tailored for a man with a muscular physique. Even unbuttoned, its broad lapels bulged out in front and the collar rolled at the back of his neck, and it was so tight across his shoulders he was afraid it would rip in half if he attempted to shake hands with any of the impor-tant dignitaries Bruce promised would be there.

Within forty-five minutes, Don had showered and dressed, except for the fake bowtie. He had vowed never to wear one, yet here he was, wrapping himself up like a birthday present for this dumb party. He looped the ribbon around his neck and had to let it out three times before he was able to hook the ends together. One look in the mirror revealed a ridiculous package no one would want. Well, at least it was warm enough he wouldn't need his moth-eaten overcoat. Don headed out the door and stood on the sidewalk where Bruce had told them to wait.

Frances came out a couple of minutes later and glided toward him. She carried her wrap over her arm, and her tanned, bare shoulders set off a glittering white strapless evening gown that hugged her every curve. Her golden hair cascaded in rivulets and splashed the shoreline where bosom dove beneath bodice. The gown flared out just below the hip, causing the airy chiffon to float up and flutter around her as she walked. Her bright blue-green eyes and sequined dress sparkled like stars under the streetlights. Frances was radiant, a goddess on a rare visit to earth.

Don was transported. "You're, you're beautiful," he stammered.

She smiled but gazed past him as if to say, "You had your chance."

He had, and he had blown it.

Don heard a shout and a loud engine zooming up behind him. Startled, he jumped away from the curb and spun around to see Bruce's head and upper body sticking through the sunroof of a huge black limousine.

"Get distracted there for a minute, Don?" Bruce teased.

The chauffeur pulled to a stop and walked around to open the passenger door. Bruce ducked back in and jumped out onto the sidewalk next to Frances. He was wearing an impeccably tailored, classic black tuxedo. With practiced grace, he gave a little bow and held out his hand for Frances.

Frances placed her hand in Bruce's outstretched one. Bruce placed his free hand on his heart and locked his eyes on hers. "Is this the face that launched a thousand ships, and burnt the topless towers of Ilium?"

Don couldn't believe it. Bruce quoting from *Doctor Faustus*?

"Sweet Helen, make me immortal with a kiss."

What a ridiculous line! Don knew Bruce had probably used it a hundred times. How could she fall for it?

But Frances did fall for it. Hard. Giggling with delight, she took a step toward Bruce, placed a beautiful manicured hand on each of his cheeks, and rewarded him with a lingering kiss.

Game over. Bruce wins. *I'm relegated to dorky chaperone at their fucking wedding party.*

As Frances got in the limo ahead of him, Bruce looked Don up and down and remarked, "Uh, nice suit you got there, bro."

It was going to be a long night.

Don tripped past them into the back of the limo and sank into the black leather seat. Bruce grabbed a bottle of champagne from the ice bucket in the bar as they pulled away from the curb. He ripped off the golden foil and shot the cork right through the open sunroof into the dark. Bubbles started to foam out of the bottle and Bruce deftly filled two crystal glasses in one hand. He passed them to Frances and Don before closing the roof and pouring a glass for himself. He lifted his glass. "Bottoms up! Remember, no limits."

"No limits!" Frances echoed.

They all clinked glasses and drank.

Twenty minutes later, the limo pulled up to the front entrance of the Willard Hotel on Pennsylvania Avenue. A doorman stepped forward to open the limousine door, and Bruce emerged with arm extended to assist his Helen.

"Welcome back to the Willard, Dr. Markum," the doorman greeted him.

Don clambered out of the limo and looked around. The white Capitol building glowed like a bright light in the night sky, dominating the night horizon at the end of the Mall and complementing the shining white of Frances's dress.

Bruce took Frances's arm and escorted her to the front door, basking in the admiring gazes they elicited. Not wanting to appear ungracious, Bruce brought Don along. "Come on, Don, I have something to show you."

The lobby was dazzling. The floor sparkled with thousands of gleaming white miniature tiles, like mother of pearl, all imbedded in a smooth mosaic of intricate patterns. There were massive faux marble columns and a hundred chandeliers gleaming with yellow-white electric light. From every nook, sculptured demigods and their earthly lovers looked down on dozens of couches covered with royal maroon damasks.

Bruce narrated. "Our family has been coming here a very long time. The Willard Hotel is a very important place. Pretty much every president has stayed here. Lincoln was smuggled into the hotel in 1861 by Pinkerton and hid out here until his inauguration to avoid assassination. At the same time, Northern industrialists and Southern landowners were here attending the Peace Convention of 1861, a last-ditch attempt by business leaders to broker differences and avoid a war that might lead to loss of profits."

Profits. Was that all Bruce thought about?

"My great-great grandfather attended the Peace convention, because at that time our family had the fastest boats going in and out of Charleston. He figured his fleet might help the South win. Of course, he hedged his bets by doing his banking in England." Bruce laughed.

My God, his family was here at the convention that could have averted the Civil War? Bruce made it sound like they hadn't really cared to avert it. They were just setting up to be a major supplier of the South's war effort.

Bruce noticed Don's disapproving look. "Don't feel bad, Don. Martin Luther King, Jr., wrote his *I Have a Dream* speech right here in the Willard. My family thought his integrated March on Washington was likely to be good for business in the long term, and by damn, I think we were right."

Bruce paused to admire the room. "Of course, the Willard is most famous for its lobby. Legend has it the term *lobbyist* was coined here after the war, because power brokers gathered in this lobby at the end of every work day to win over President Grant with his favorite brandy and fine cigars."

Bruce led the way—Frances on his left arm and Don alongside her—down the thickly carpeted steps to the level below ground. They stopped at the coat check to leave Frances's wrap. Bruce stuck the claim ticket in his breast pocket and offered Frances his arm again.

Tuxedoed doormen flanked the entrance to the Grand ballroom, and one gave a slight bow as the trio approached. "Good evening, Dr. Markum," he said.

Inside the ballroom was the most opulent spectacle Don had ever seen. In the center of the room and in each corner were tables sporting gargantuan displays of flowers of all types and colors. The towering bouquets presided over tiered platters of smoked salmon, fresh shrimp, oysters on the half shell, crab cakes, deviled eggs topped with caviar, dates filled with cream cheese and studded with almonds, and exotic fruits—fresh figs, star fruit, mango, blood oranges, kumquats, and a yellow prickly fruit Don had never seen. There were dozens of cheeses—yellow, white, even cheeses veined with blue and red. The dessert table included petit fours decorated with sugared orchids. On one wall was a huge silver fountain featuring mermaids spurting champagne from their lips into giant scallop shells. A string quartet next to the mermaids played chamber music, and on the walls were Italian frescoes of great American landholdings with green pastures, hills, and forests. Enormous crystal chandeliers illuminated the ballroom with soft light.

Frances and Bruce made their entrance. A hush fell over the room, followed by a low hum of approval, as a couple hundred of the best-dressed people Don had ever seen turned their heads to ogle Frances. She was clearly the belle of the ball. Bruce basked in the crowd's response and Frances positively glowed. No one seemed to notice Don, who slunk in ten paces behind the glamorous couple, and soon the guests turned back to their conversations.

Don was relieved to be ignored; in his mind he might as well have worn a neon sign flashing, *Rented Tuxedo! Rented Tuxedo!* He felt out of place in the tacky wide lapels and rented shoes, and his feet were killing him. He shifted his weight back and forth in a vain attempt to take pressure off his pinched toes.

Every other man in the place wore an exquisitely tailored tuxedo, and no hair was untrimmed or out of place. All of them radiated confidence. These were people accustomed to elegant dressing and fine dining. A waiter appeared and offered drinks from a silver tray—even his tuxedo was finer than Don's.

One voice boomed out above the sea of babbling voices. "Well, well, it's about time you showed up!" A large man with dignified bearing made his way over. "Hello there, son. Do introduce me to your friends," he said, shifting his gaze to Frances and grinning at her with what Don thought was a lascivious glint in his eye.

"Let me introduce you to my father, Bruce D. Markum," Bruce said. "We are both named for the same ancestor—he is the third and I am the fourth." Bruce turned to his father and pointed out that Don had gone to Sewanee and Frances was from California.

Bruce's father turned to Don and started chatting as if they were old fraternity brothers. "A fellow Southerner!" he exclaimed. "The South will rule again, won't we, my friend?"

Don started to explain he was from Chicago, but Mr. Markum was chuckling at his own comment and paid no attention. He cleared his throat. "So, Don, what are your career plans?"

"Well, sir, I'm not exactly sure how, but I want to work to help reform the healthcare system."

"You do?" he replied with mock incredulity. "When the system is doing so well?" He laughed heartily and turned his full attention back to Frances. "What about you, Frances? Are you out to reform healthcare, too?"

Frances took immediate advantage of his attention. "I'm looking for a leading management role in a major healthcare firm. I'm most interested in hospitals, outpatient surgery, and imaging facilities. My focus is the business side—buying and selling, mergers and acquisitions—to build profitable healthcare concerns."

Don regarded her with amazement. He had known Frances for months and had never heard of her business interests.

Mr. Markum's expression turned serious. "Very impressive," he said. "I can tell you're a woman who knows what she wants.

As opposed to your friend Don here, who doesn't have a clue.

"And what's your business background?"

"I trained as an advanced nurse practitioner at UCSF in health policy. Now I'm on the MBA track at Florence College, focusing on health economics."

"Very good, very good indeed. Call my office when you finish and we'll talk about your future."

"Thank you, Mr. Markum; I'd like that very much."

Mr. Markum glanced away and recognized a group of legislators standing nearby. One of them motioned him over. "It would be my pleasure," he said to Frances as he turned away.

"Well, you sure impressed him," Bruce said matter-of-factly.

"What else would you expect of your Helen of Troy?" she replied with a coy smile.

Mr. Markum's loud voice echoed from the huddle of legislators. "Yes, that's my son. Didn't you know? We're priming Bruce for a run in 2004."

A run in 2004? Had Don heard that right? Bruce hadn't said anything about it. Don decided to pretend he hadn't heard, but from then on, as they wandered from conversation to conversation, Don paid close attention and listened for clues. Was Bruce considering a political career?

Everyone they met welcomed Bruce as the heir apparent to his father's kingdom. He worked the room like a seasoned politician, either pointing out or introducing Frances and Don to all the key people on the House Ways and Means Committee, the Senate HELP Committee, and leaders from the executive branch, like the administrator for Health and Human Services. In other words, all the people that Bruce claimed "make the laws work for our business."

The CEOs and vice presidents of the biggest healthcare corporations in America seemed to know Bruce best. Just about every major healthcare concern was represented. They met CEOs from the top hospital corporations, like Tenet and Humana; insurance, including Aetna, Cigna, and United; imaging and testing centers, like HealthSouth; and all of the top ten major pharmaceutical companies.

"Big Pharma was a new addition about ten years ago," Bruce explained between introductions. "They'll be driving even more dollars in the years ahead."

"Did you see in our reading this week that the pharmaceutical industry currently employs over six hundred lobbyists in Washington?" Don pointed out. "That's more than one for every member in Congress. Why so many?"

"They're gearing up for something big, no doubt." Bruce's cryptic grin intimated that Don was an idiot not to know what was going on.

Obviously, Don was an outsider, not privy to the secrets of this underground hall that everyone else took for granted. He tried to make himself invisible so he could listen in, like a fly on the wall, but he lacked the cipher to interpret many of the comments he heard. One thing was clear: company representatives and lawmakers talked as if the interests of the public and their companies were synonymous. In this room, anything good for business was good for America.

Thanks to Dr. Sampson, Don was deeply skeptical of this attitude. And another observation nagged his mind as he tagged along behind Prince Bruce and Helen. Where were the doctors?

Bruce spotted Senator Josten, who was captivating a large circle of legislators and industry representatives with a story. Loud laughter erupted all around. Bruce made a beeline to join them, with Frances and Don following close behind. Bruce greeted the group and introduced his two colleagues.

A microsecond of irritation crossed Josten's face, but the senator recovered quickly and put on a big smile. "It's wonderful to see you students of healthcare systems here learning from the real experts. Well, gentlemen…Milady," he said, tipping his head toward Frances, "if you'll excuse me, I must be off," and he strode away toward the opposite end of the room.

A tall, wiry man with graying temples greeted Bruce warmly. The fine fabric of the man's tuxedo fit his lean frame like a glove. "Bruce, it's good to see you again…and your friends."

Where had Don seen this man before?

"Good to see you, Frank," Bruce replied.

Of course—it was Frank Pan, the drug company vice president who'd bought them martinis in the middle of their drug marketing research project.

"Bruce, I'd like you to meet someone. This is Representative Tauzin from Louisiana," Mr. Pan said. In a lower voice, he added, "I'm trying to convince Billy to leave the house and work for PhRMA, the Pharmaceutical Research and Manufacturers of America, in a year or two. He'd still get to work with Congress, but his work would be appreciated for a change, right, Representative?"

"If you say so, Mr. Pan. Nice to meet everyone."

"What's the big issue for the pharmaceutical industry this year?" Bruce asked them both with apparent genuine curiosity.

"Well, the Medicare pharmaceutical benefit, of course." Mr. Pan said. "Your dad may have told you I've been working with the PhRMA, and we're teaming up with the AARP here." He nodded to two colleagues who had not bolted from the circle when Senator Josten departed. "We think this is the most important issue for the health of older Americans."

"Wait a minute," said Frances, "I thought the pharmaceutical industry was against a drug benefit."

"Oh no, of course not," he laughed. "No, we just wanted to make sure older Americans get the Medicare benefit they need. Last year's proposal would have given them absolutely no choice and left most seniors unable to get their essential medications. This year we've come up with something better. Right, boys?" Obviously confident of their agreement, Frank Pan didn't even glance at the two representatives from AARP.

Don thought he spotted an old classmate from Sewanee standing alone by the buffet, so he excused himself and walked over to say hello. "Excuse me, but aren't you my old friend Fred from Sewanee?"

"Yes, I'm Fred." Fred's initial puzzlement changed to delight as he recognized Don. Don Newman? What in the world are you doing here?"

"Long story. How's it going? I thought I was the only physician here." Don knew Fred had gone to medical school after Sewanee; they had studied for the

MCATs together, but now he looked thirty pounds heavier and fifteen years older. " It's good to see a colleague."

"It's good to see you again Don."

The two filled each other in on their careers, and Fred told Don he was a physician executive for a large health plan.

"So tell me, Fred, what is the AARP doing here?"

"Come on, Don, everyone here is either lobbying for someone or they're here to be lobbied. The real question is, what is AARP lobbying for?" He sighed. "The general public thinks the AARP represents the interests of old folks. In fact, it is setting itself up to be the biggest reseller of private insurance in the world. The AARP stands to gain millions in business if the right Medicare drug benefit goes through."

"You're kidding, right?

Fred raised his eyebrows and gave a terse smile. He was deadly serious. That explained Mr. Pan's comment.

"So tell me, Don, what are you doing hanging out with Bruce Markum?"

"You know him?" he replied.

"Of course I know him; he was in my med school class at Vanderbilt."

Don explained about the program at Florence College and how he had come to be here at the Willard.

"Look, Don, watch out. That guy is cold. Let me tell you a little history on Bruce Markum. In med school, he was caught getting cats and dogs from the Humane Society under false pretenses and dissecting them in his house. Not just one or two animals, Don, lots of them. The school and his family did an excellent job of covering it up, but there you have it. Of course, they say he is, or was, a damn good surgeon."

Fred turned abruptly, scanning the room. "I've got to go," he said. "Careful, Don. These guys play hardball."

Don got a plate and helped himself to some food. He tried to think of the animal story from a surgeon's point of view. Was practicing on stray animals cold, or just a practical way to refine one's surgical skills? Surely Bruce wouldn't have let the animals suffer, would he?

Out of the corner of his eye, Don noticed Bruce was alternating between watching Don and flirting with Frances. Don acted nonchalant. He circled back by the champagne fountain, picked up a glass, and walked over to them.

"So, Bruce, how do they convince all these prominent politicians to come to a party to promote the healthcare industry?"

Bruce laughed. "Don. Who do you think pays for their political campaigns? The big healthcare money gets them elected. In return, the big donors get meetings and parties like this one where they can schmooze and make their cases. Hell, the AMA even has a representative here."

"But what about the American people?" Don said. "What do they get? When do they get a chance to present their views?"

Bruce laughed again, winked at Frances, and quipped, "Well, you're here, aren't you?"

Frances wrinkled her perfect nose in amusement and stared at Don's gaping lapels.

"No, really," Bruce added good-naturedly, "look around. The congress-men are completely surrounded by big donors. The little guys—consumers and agency bureaucrats alike—are hopelessly outgunned. Who's going to listen to them, when senators can get the inside scoop at a party like this? Besides, these big donors understand the big picture, how the system works. They're the ones who understand what's good for the people."

As Bruce spoke, Frances returned her gaze to him as if to its natural home. She was enthralled. As she stood by his side, at least five lobbyists or legislators approached Bruce, and each one told Bruce how his father's interests were faring on the hill. Frances beamed with pride.

As the night wore on, however, Bruce seemed to tire from the spotlight. He had been drinking a lot, but instead of mellowing he became increasingly agitated, as if preoccupied by some interior dialogue. At one point, Frances and Don were discussing Dr. Sampson and how his seminar had changed their per-spectives, and during a pause between suitors, Bruce jumped in.

"Damn Dr. Sampson!" Bruce cried out. "All he's done is show me a bunch of crap I would just as soon not see. Things that can never be changed!"

Before either of them could respond, Bruce grabbed Don by the arm and pulled him over to meet Representative Seymore, an obese, red-faced politician with a shock of white hair. He was a southern politician, and an old school one at that. He had been in Washington for thirty-five years. He knew how every-thing worked and was glad to let you know it. He got along with everyone and was hard not to like.

After the usual pleasantries, Bruce announced, "Don here thinks old Dr. Sampson at Florence College is going to be healthcare's great savior. He thinks Sampson will overthrow the bloated bureaucrats and turn our system around. Don't you, Don?"

Representative Seymour's smile evaporated. "You don't believe all the hog-wash that radical nut Sampson preaches, do you?" he bellowed.

"Uh, well, I ... no, of course not," Don stammered.

Bruce tilted his head back and crowed like a rooster. He punched Don in the arm. "Thataboy Don, you tell 'em!"

"Ha, ha, ha!" Representative Seymore guffawed, "listen to me, young man, don't get yourself upset over those silly bureaucrats." He broke out into a long and hearty belly laugh.

Don failed to see what was so funny, but was pretty sure he was the butt of the joke.

"Those bureaucrats? They're just our little toys. All us folks in congress—conservative, liberal, don't matter—we fight over who gets to play with 'em. Why, more than half these lobbyists here used to be senators, representatives, or high-level bureaucrats themselves. The ones that know how to get the job done? That's who the companies want. You best remember that, son." He winked and waddled off to join another group.

"Let's get out of here," Bruce said. "Come on."

Bruce led them out to the coat check and retrieved Frances's wrap, handing the attendant a five-dollar bill. The three headed back up the steps and out the front doors of the hotel. Bruce turned right and headed down Pennsylvania Avenue.

Frances struggled to keep up in her high heels. "Where are you taking us, Bruce?" she asked.

"We have more to see," he replied. "Don't worry, it's close by."

"I sure hope so," Don muttered under his breath as he limped along in his rented toe-crunchers. He spotted a pillared Greek temple building up ahead with a bronze statue in front. "What's that?"

"That's Alexander Hamilton and his Treasury," Bruce replied. "Thank God, he never was able to nationalize the banks. The government would have run them into the ground."

They turned right at the corner and walked alongside the Treasury building until they came to a covered entrance.

"The White House is just on the other side of the Treasury. But this is the real center of power in Washington. Where the money is!"

As if on cue, Frances and Don chimed in unison, "Follow the money!" They all laughed, but Don still felt uneasy.

Bruce pointed out the great stone banks surrounding the Treasury: PNC, Bank of America, SunTrust. When they arrived at a large limestone building inscribed NATIONAL METROPOLITAN BANK, Bruce motioned for them to follow and headed for its large corner bar. The name was written in gold letters over the door, THE OLD EBBITT BAR.

They passed through its revolving door and stepped into a crowded room lined with lustrous wood paneling and polished brass. Wooden bird decoys perched above the bar, in glass cases surrounding and dividing the room, on top of the partitions between the bar and the tables. There were ducks, coots, geese, and even sandpipers, all intricately crafted to deceive the natural creatures they imitated.

Bruce shouldered a path for them through the crowd of hunters dressed in suits and tuxes. A spot across the room opened up, and they snaked through the crowd toward it. Men stole discreet glances at Frances as she passed. When they finally reached a small space where they could stand, Bruce sidled up to the bar to get everyone drinks.

Don surveyed the room. The whole bar celebrated duck hunting and the Chesapeake. Right next to him was a glass gun case containing antique shotguns, an antique belt for shotgun shells, and a hunting vest. Through the crowd, Don caught glimpses of the many paintings that graced the walls: camouflaged men with guns walking in fields and alongside tidal ponds and estuaries; hunters with guns in blinds that camouflaged them from birds flying overhead; hunters playing poker in cabins by night, glorifying the power of the bluff. The scenes were all painted in the warm tones of the rising or setting sun or of firelight. This was a man's lair; there were few women present. Don only saw one painting of a woman. She was naked, of course, reclining and patiently waiting. Through the glass cases of the divider, Don observed men sitting at tables and having important conversations. These were Washington's elite, the movers and shakers.

Bruce maneuvered his way back from the bar holding high a gray green bottle of champagne in one hand and three glasses in the other. "I think you'll like this. It's 1990 Dom Pérignon Oenothèque," he said with a French accent. He poured them each a glass of the effervescent golden liquid. "The other room of this bar is filled with Teddy Roosevelt's trophies." He lifted his glass. "To hunting, Roosevelt's idea of what a national park is good for."

Frances and Bruce were soon talking and laughing. Don examined the decoys in the glass case separating them from the diners.

"You know there's going to be war," said a voice at the table on the other side of the case.

Through the case, Don could see two impeccably dressed men, one around fifty and the other about sixty-five, immersed in intense discussion. Don focused his eyes on the decoys and his ears on the conversation.

"Where?" the older man asked.

"Iraq. You know we've wanted control of that oil in the sand for a long time, and I think the War on Terror may give us the perfect opportunity to get it."

"C'mon, Paul...you guys are letting the progress under the current administration make you giddy."

"I don't think so, John. We have our sources within the administration. I can't really say more. But we are taking this seriously. We've even asked the Petroleum Institute to make fighting terror part of our mission. Hell, it's patriotic. And fighting terror is something our industry has to do for a stable gas and oil infrastructure."

"But everybody at CIA knows there is absolutely no connection between the terrorists that attacked the Pentagon and Saddam Hussein."

"Sure they do, but the thing is, nobody else does. Remember, John, the American public is gullible, and to them all Arabs are alike. I'm telling you, war is coming. There are too many powerful people that want it. And they want it bad. You'll see. It's a fait accompli."

"I'd watch out if I were you," said the older man. We certainly don't want another Teapot Dome."

"Teapot dome?"

"You know, the scandal that implicated the president the last time the oil industry got too involved in politics."

The self-assured younger man laughed, "Oh, you mean that little affair with President Harding? That was ages ago. Don't worry, John. This time the executive branch is taking the lead. We're just following along."

The distinguished older man shook his head. "Good God, I sure hope they know what they're doing."

Shit! Sampson's words echoed in his head. *Follow the money.* The war *was* about the oil, wasn't it? The oil companies had probably hoped for something like this for years. The perfect excuse to establish a real foothold in the Middle East: a war on terror. Don tried to hear more, but the two men moved their heads closer together and spoke in whispers he couldn't decipher.

By this time, Frances and Bruce were absorbed in their own little world. Don found their interminable babble inane and shallow compared to what he had just heard. Exasperated, he blurted out, "So Bruce, what is the Petroleum Institute?"

Bruce replied with the tired indulgence of a parent whose child is asking too many questions. "Only one of the biggest lobbying groups in the country. The main office is near here, right off K Street, and they have offices in most state capitols as well. Why do you ask?"

"I overheard someone over there—I think he was with the oil industry—talking about the Petroleum Institute, and…"

Bruce cut him off. "Yes sir, this would be where they would hang out. This is where the really big deals are made." Bruce shot a meaningful glance at Frances, and she leaned toward him and gave him a seductive smile.

"Our chariot awaits; let's go," Bruce said, still looking at Frances. "There is one last bar you simply must see."

Don had had enough. "Listen," he said, "I'll just be taking the Metro back to campus. I'm beat, and there's a stop right around the corner."

"Oh, stay with us, Don," Frances said dreamily. But her eyes never left Bruce; it was obvious she meant the opposite.

Out on the street the black limo was waiting. Bruce helped Frances into the back and climbed in next to her. Before the driver closed the limo door,

Don heard him spouting another corny phrase about "my fair Helen" and her giggling in reply.

The limo drove away with the night's laughter, and Don limped off to the Metro Center subway station, cursing his damn rented vinyl shoes.

28

Politicians Spreading Disease and Discord

See now how I split myself…all the others you see here were in life
sowers of scandal and schism, and therefore are thus cloven.
DANTE ALIGHIERI, INFERNO 28, 30–36

DR. SAMPSON AND THE STUDENTS arrived before seven the following Wednesday, excited to observe the next step for the medical errors legislation. They were all dressed for the occasion, Don in his old blue blazer from Sewanee days, Bruce and Frances in well-tailored charcoal gray suits, and Dr. Sampson in a white polyester dress shirt and an ill-fitting herringbone tweed jacket.

The students stamped their feet in the cold as they waited in a line that stretched across the parking lot. Dr. Sampson, despite lacking an overcoat, stood still, and watched the entrance with eagle eyes, oblivious to the cold. It took almost two hours for the four to inch across the parking lot, climb the stone stairs, enter the Capitol through two massive bronze doors, pass through the metal detectors, and wind their way to the Senate Chamber. They showed their gallery passes to the guards, climbed the long carpeted stairs, and at last took their seats in the balcony overlooking the old wooden desks of the Senate. They were barely settled in the red cushioned seats when the bell tolled three times to announce the commencement of the Senate session.

The Senate chamber roiled with the frenetic activity of a disturbed anthill. Senate pages blazed in and out from every direction. Senators sauntered in and took their places, though many seats remained unoccupied. One aged senator stood up and shuffled to the rostrum. A priest wearing a clerical collar joined him there and offered a short prayer. A few heads bowed, though most senators barely paused reading their newspapers or whispering to each other. The senators did stand and halfheartedly join in when the elderly senator recited the Pledge of Allegiance.

The stooped senator was the most senior member of the majority party; he served as the president pro tempore and led the proceedings. He rapped the gavel three times and called for the morning business.

A clerk called roll and began accepting resolutions, bills, and amendments from the senators, one by one. For the next hour the spectators could hear almost nothing as senators, along with their clerks and aides, took turns approaching his desk to discuss upcoming legislative and executive business. Other clerks sat at a long marble desk in front of the majority leader and dutifully recorded everything.

"See the two long wooden desks in front of the clerks?" Dr. Sampson whispered. "The secretaries and staffs for the two parties sit there, near their party leaders. The party leaders are like quarterbacks for their teams—Democrats sit on the right of the chamber and Republicans on the left—they keep party members in the loop about upcoming debates and legislation and tally the score on every vote. They keep tabs on which senators are loyal to the party line and which aren't. Look at how they keep the pages running."

Bruce leaned over to Don and whispered: "See the empty desk near the front?"

Don nodded.

"That's Jefferson Davis' old desk. He was the Mississippi senator who became president of the Confederacy. This gallery was packed to the gills in 1861 when he stood up and proclaimed Lincoln's election meant compromise on slavery was impossible. Davis called for the southern states to defend their sovereign rights and secede from the Union. He said Mississippi had no choice but to secede, and he hoped the federal government would let it leave in peace. He warned if they didn't leave the South alone, everyone would suffer. After that resignation speech, he and his fellow southern senators marched down the center aisle out of the Senate chamber and returned to their home states. People watching from the gallery wept. They knew it meant war."

Bruce seemed intent on telling Don everything he knew about the history of the Senate. Don was happy to listen, since nothing else was happening.

"A month later, Davis became President of the Confederate States of America. A month after that, Fort Sumter fell to the Confederates when Lincoln refused to let it go, and the war was on. Pretty soon, Washington was under siege. The Senate chamber became a barracks for Massachusetts soldiers, and the damn Yankees used that desk for bayonet practice. The assistant doorkeeper stopped them, saying the desk belonged to the government, not Jeff Davis. 'You were sent here to protect, not destroy,' he said. Still today you can see where the damage was repaired with two small inlaid squares of wood. That seat is reserved forever for the senior senator from Mississippi, in honor of Jefferson Davis.

"And see that door there in the back? That's the President's Room, where presidents used to sign all legislation into law. That's where Lincoln learned General Robert E. Lee had requested a meeting with General Grant to discuss peace terms. Lincoln didn't show any mercy. He ordered Grant not to talk to Lee unless it was to discuss unconditional surrender. Even after all the death and suffering, Lincoln wouldn't compromise a thing, wouldn't leave the South with even a shred of dignity."

"Well, that's the Charleston perspective," Dr. Sampson interrupted. "It's not the version we Pennsylvania boys learned in school."

Dr. Sampson pointed to the floor, where his Medicare Quality Improvement Act was supposed to be first up for debate. "Now look," he said, "the party leaders are negotiating how much time to allow for the debate. Time agreements require unanimous consent of all the senators. Leadership anticipates the concerns of senators interested in a particular issue and allots the time accordingly."

The bill was scheduled for two hours of debate. There was little chance they would take it to a vote with no further amendments. Senator Josten gave the opening statement and used some of the students' speaking points as reasons to support the legislation. Next up was the minority leader of the HELP Committee, who was generally supportive, as were the next two senators who spoke. However, no one seemed to be listening to any of it.

"How come half the senators are absent?" Don asked.

"No one really listens to this stuff," Bruce said. "Most senators show up minutes before scheduled votes on issues for which they have already made up their minds."

Don had expected real debate. Instead he witnessed a series of choreographed procedural maneuvers. The few senators present conspicuously ignored the presentations of the opposing party. For the most part he couldn't blame them. It was pretty boring. No reasoned discussion. Just "speechifying," as Don's father used to call it, designed to draw distinctions between *us* and *them* rather than clarify substantive issues. At least the legislation seemed to be moving forward; most of the speakers seemed to be claiming credit for it.

Then something strange happened. A senator from Josten's party offered an amendment that had not gone through Josten's Health Committee. He was allotted fifteen minutes but asked for additional time, insisting to the majority leader his amendment be read in its entirety.

The amendment added a new Medicare pharmaceutical benefit. In his preamble, the senator said that helping seniors pay for their drugs through a new, privately managed drug benefit program was the kind of healthcare reform Americans really needed.

Don watched Dr. Sampson out of the corner of his eye as this development unfolded. As Dr. Sampson absorbed the details of the amendment his jaw tightened, his lips thinned, and his face reddened. Although the senators hadn't applauded anything all morning, a standing ovation erupted on both sides of the aisle at the conclusion of the reading. Dr. Sampson stood up for a moment, his body tensed. Don thought he would shout out, but instead he sat back down and shook his head in disbelief.

The proposed amendment linked the legislation Dr. Sampson had worked on for much of his career to legislation he vigorously opposed—a fat pharmaceutical benefit managed by a whole new group of for-profit middlemen. Although support had been building for a Medicare pharmaceutical benefit, Senator Josten had told them it was premature—they had not debated the benefit in committee or worked out the details necessary to make a major new program succeed in passing through the Congress. Despite the popularity of the idea, if the amendment passed, Dr. Sampson's bill would certainly fail. Was this a deliberate tactic to prevent consideration of the merits of the medical errors legislation?

The senator demanded an immediate roll call vote on the amendment. To no one's surprise, the vote failed, and the Senate adjourned for lunch. Other matters were scheduled for the afternoon, so any debate on the Medicare Quality Improvement Act would have to wait for another day.

The four walked down the steps from the gallery without speaking a word.

At the door, a burly man in a navy blue suit stepped in front of Dr. Sampson. "Gil!" the man said. "How the hell are you? I've been waiting for you to leave the gallery."

Dr. Sampson hesitated, then broke into a wide smile. "Jack?"

"That's me. It's been a long time, old friend."

Dr. Sampson and Jack shook hands vigorously and clapped each other on the shoulders. Each was clearly delighted to see the other.

"What are you doing here?" asked Dr. Sampson. "I haven't seen you since Vietnam."

"Remember how I worked with the MPs after being transferred from your platoon? I've been in police work ever since. I moved up to chief and then was elected as the thirty-ninth Sergeant at Arms and Doorkeeper of the Senate. You know, the doorkeeper has served as the chief law enforcement officer of the Senate since 1789."

"We saw quite a number of your officers on the way in. It's like getting into Fort Knox!"

"We started building a new visitor's center and entrance to manage the crowds three years ago, after that crazy man Russell Weston shot his way in and killed two of our officers. Until that's done, security will continue to take a lot of manpower."

"Let me introduce my students," Dr. Sampson said. "Nurse Hunt, Dr. Markum, and Dr. Newman. This is Sergeant Jack Hatcher, only the finest noncom to ever guide a young officer through hell and back."

"No, you're the one that brought me back from the grave!" Jack protested. "Not a day goes by when I don't wake up remembering how you came after me when I drew the short straw, went down, and got captured in that damn tunnel complex south of Chu Lai. If you hadn't burst into that hellhole, swinging your jammed government issue like the jawbone of an ass, I wouldn't be here today." Jack looked at the students. "It's the truth. The Viet Cong were getting ready to slit my throat when Gil…"

"Enough war stories," a visibly embarrassed Dr. Sampson said. "How did you know we were here?"

"I noticed your name on the visitor manifest and saw you were scheduled to meet with the House of Representatives majority leader. I figured I would track you down at the end of the session before your meeting. You weren't too hard to spot."

"Your guys sure are keeping a tight rein here since 9–11."

"I'll say," Sergeant Hatcher replied. "You know, this was supposed to be ground zero for United Airlines Flight 93, before the passengers took it down in Pennsylvania. The Capitol was going to be the terrorists' grand finale. Congress was in session that day and everyone was here. We've had some sort of scare almost every day since then. You can see how it has turned my hair gray."

"I can only imagine."

"Let me tell you, Gil. Everyone is afraid, and you know how people turn fear into anger. The politicians are gearing up for war—it's all they think about. Do you know who Cofer Black is?"

"Isn't he over counterterrorism or something?" said Bruce.

"Right. He's been the head of the CIA's Counterterrorist Center since 1999. Right after 9–11, he told the president, and I quote: *When we're through with them they will have flies walking across their eyeballs…We're going to kill them. We're going to put their heads on sticks.* At first I couldn't believe anyone in intelligence would say such a thing, but I checked my sources. A lot of people heard him—it's true, word for word. His thirst for war has infected the entire executive branch, and now Congress can hardly think of anything else."

"If we go to the Mideast we'll be mired there for years, just like Vietnam," Dr. Sampson lamented. "Another generation of our boys maimed and killed. And it will cost billions. What a colossal waste! We could save millions of lives right here if we spent that money on preventing medical errors."

"Let me tell you, Gil, there's only one job I'd rather have than the one I have now. If the president put me in charge and gave me a thousand well-trained MPs and the support of our best police investigators and foreign intelligence in Pakistan and Saudi Arabia, I promise you we would bring bin Laden to justice. We cops know how to implement the law and we don't need a war to do it."

"I believe you," Dr. Sampson replied. He glimpsed at his watch. "Well, I hate to break this up, but we are supposed to meet with the House majority leader somewhere near here in ten minutes. Someone was supposed to meet us."

"That would be me," Sergeant Hatcher said. "I took the liberty of coming here myself instead of sending a page. I'm afraid I have bad news. The majority leader's chief of staff asked me to inform you—your session was cancelled."

Dr. Sampson's face clouded. "What? We've been planning this for weeks!"

"Something came up. That's all I was told. I did take the liberty of making a few calls on your behalf and was able to arrange for you and your students to meet with Representative Murdock, the House minority leader. Will that help your efforts on the medical errors legislation?"

"Absolutely. Sounds like you know exactly what we are up to," Dr. Sampson said.

"That's my job. And it's good to be able to help an old friend. Come on, I'll show you to Representative Murdock's office."

They followed Sergeant Hatcher through the halls of the Capitol. At a cordoned-off passageway near the rotunda, an alert Capitol guard nodded to him and unclipped the velvet rope, opening the passage before them so they barely had to slow down. Soon they were weaving through a labyrinth of halls between the new and old Senate chambers, whizzing by a stunning collection of oil paintings depicting the early days of the Republic.

By the time they arrived at Representative Murdock's office, Don was completely disoriented. The unmarked door was no different from dozens of other doors they had passed.

"I'll leave you here," Sergeant Hatcher said. "When you're finished, one of my officers will meet you and take you wherever you need to go. Here's my card. Let me know if I can ever assist you again in any way. I'll always be in your debt."

"And I in yours. Thank you, Jack. It's been good to see you."

"Good to see you, Gil."

They clasped hands and then arms before Sergeant Hatcher turned away and knocked on the door.

"Come in!" said a voice from inside.

Sergeant Hatcher opened the door, let them inside, and closed the door behind them. There was no secretary; the House minority leader came around from behind a glossy wooden desk to greet them.

Don noticed deep shade through the open windows and no sign of the Mall. This office was obviously on the backside of the Capitol.

Representative Murdock shook hands with each of them and the students introduced themselves. His warmth and youthful demeanor engaged them all instantly.

"Dr. Sampson, it is a particular honor to meet you," he said. "I have heard a great deal about you, and your proposal is clearly right on target for America."

"Thank you, sir," Dr. Sampson responded. "I appreciate you meeting with us on such short notice."

"You should know, even though your proposal was brought forward by the majority party, several of their representatives have labeled it *the liberal healthcare giveaway program from that way-out Florence College*."

"Wait a minute! Our group of health systems scientists who developed the proposal is completely non-partisan. And, as you probably know, I'm a Republican!"

The minority leader laughed. "That doesn't really matter, does it? Let me speak frankly, Dr. Sampson. I would sincerely like your bill to succeed. The bottom line is, all that really matters is how they make you appear, not what you are. They want to make you appear leftist, for some very simple business reasons. That's all I can tell you. Just think of the business interests your proposal could frustrate, and you'll find your opponents spreading the false perception."

Bruce nodded. He knew what the minority leader was talking about. In fact, he probably knew exactly who was opposing Dr. Sampson's proposal and why.

Dr. Sampson and Representative Murdock discussed upcoming healthcare legislation a few minutes longer before the minority leader thanked Dr. Sampson for his time and expertly directed them all to the door. In a flash, they found themselves standing in the hall.

Don felt beaten down and bewildered by the sudden turn of events, but Dr. Sampson stood ramrod straight, with muscles tensed and brow furrowed. He murmured something to the guard who had been sent to wait for them, and the guard turned briskly and led them back through the labyrinth of halls and doorways. They were about to enter the great rotunda when Dr. Sampson stopped cold in his tracks. Bruce nearly bumped into him.

"Hold it." He seemed struck by a sudden thought. "Officer!" he called.

The clean-cut policeman immediately returned to his side. "Yes, sir?"

"Take us to the crypt. My students will be better served by hearing what I have to say down there."

Did he say the crypt? The students exchanged quizzical glances, and Bruce rolled his eyes.

Without a word, the policeman turned and led them in the opposite direction, through the corridors and down a marble staircase that descended deep into the bowels of the Capitol. They ended up in a great circular room with a low, vaulted ceiling and no windows. The officer waited near the entrance as the students followed Dr. Sampson into the inner ring of two concentric circles of massive stone pillars.

Dr. Sampson pointed to a white circular stone at his feet. It was inlaid with a brass compass marking the dead center of the room. He motioned for everyone to gather around and spoke in a low, measured voice, as if they were on a mission and the enemy might overhear. He released his words one by one with the rhythmic oscillations of a pressure cooker letting off steam. "Who—is—in—charge—of the—health—care—system?"

No one said a word. Dr. Sampson waited, letting the pent-up pressure built in the silence.

Finally, Don timidly offered, "No one?"

"Right! No one!" he exploded.

The students flinched.

Sampson's words reverberated through the empty chamber. "In a democracy, the rule of law should prevail. We're supposed to be a government *of the people, by the people, for the people.* Laws governing healthcare should be crafted to serve the interests of the people. Instead, American healthcare is in a state of near anarchy!

"And why, you ask, do some politicians support anarchy? Because their pet interest groups want complete freedom from responsibility. They work to make sure the government's rules are not enforced. They use discord and division to pave the way for their favorite sons to riot and lord over others. They allow unscrupulous contributors to steal without consequence and take advantage of competitors who try to play by the rules. They justify it as competition.

"Fine, but healthy competition needs rules, like football. The rules of the game encourage strength, productivity, and safety of the participants. No competition is wasted. The weaker team gains experience to compete better in the next round. Fair ground rules ensure a good game. Would Super Bowl fans stand by with equal apathy if the referees never enforced the rules? Or rewarded the team willing to play the most viciously—the team that grabbed face masks and used late hits to wound and cripple?

"Don't misunderstand me. Overregulation is bad, too. It promotes listlessness and apathy. What if the referees blew their whistles so often the teams never got to play? Good rules are based on a common vision of the goals of the game. When properly implemented, they produce exactly what they are designed to produce. Good healthcare rules encourage competition on quality and price. They reward doctors, nurses, and hospitals that put patient interests first. They don't incentivize businesses to deceive, scam, and swindle people with fancy marketing schemes.

"Trouble is, most legislators have no idea what good healthcare looks like and no vision of how our system should work. They allow the most powerful coaches and players to manipulate them. As a result, unbridled competition for money and power controls the system, and that means no one is in control at all. What's best for patients is forgotten. When you look for good government and organization in American healthcare—founded on principles and designed to serve health—you find a complete void. Nothing good or fair is coming from Congress or the executive branch. Nothing!

He took a few deep breaths and looked around at the pillars holding up the nation's capitol, as if seeking something precious that had been lost.

"So, can anything here give us hope? Anything at all? Any tiny seed, kernel, or trace of DNA here in Washington from which we can find the order, law, or principle to build a better health system?"

No one answered. Dr. Sampson took another deep draft of the cool, still air of the crypt, gazed around the room, and shook his head. "Close to nothing. Only memories. Is a memory anything? Can a memory work any real good?

"This crypt at the center of the Capitol honors George Washington, one of our only presidents with enough wisdom and courage to assemble a cabinet of bitter rivals. Washington knew for a free nation to work, all views had to be represented and considered. He didn't want yes-men. He and his cabinet of adversaries could weigh the arguments of all sides and make the best decisions for our country as a whole.

"Did you know the first architect of this building, William Thornton, was a physician? He designed this space to remind the American people how George Washington brought us together: Federalist and anti-Federalist, moneyed elite and populist, North and South, slave and free. Although Dr. Thornton was born of Jamaican slave owners, he became a famous abolitionist and hoped for a day when all people would be free.

"He intended this crypt to be the entrance to Washington's tomb. The Capitol building would represent a nation borne of *his* root. Thornton was inspired by St. Peter's Basilica in Rome, where the altar is directly over the tomb and bones of St. Peter, and a dove representing the Holy Spirit descending is at the top of the dome directly above that. Thornton saw the Capitol as the center of the free world, just as Rome was once the center of the Christian world.

"Here we are, directly under the center of our Capitol's great dome, right in the center of the District of Columbia where all the state avenues meet, right in the center of our young country between North and South. And under our feet is Washington's tomb. Thorton wanted the centers of the rotunda and crypt floors to be glass so visitors could look down into Washington's tomb two floors below and up to see Washington glorified in heaven, as painted on the ceiling by a famous Italian fresco artist. At the crown of the dome is Freedom. She stands on a globe encircled by our nation's motto—a motto for which George Washington put his life on the line when he challenged the British. *E Pluribus Unum*: Out of Many, One.

"Unfortunately, Thornton's design for the Capitol was never fully executed. Round stone pavers in the floors of the rotunda and crypt replaced the glass portholes he envisioned. Although Martha Washington had agreed to have President Washington's body moved from Mount Vernon and entombed here, the War of 1812 set construction back several decades when the British burned the partially constructed Capitol to the ground. By the time the tomb was ready, Martha's great nephew was in control of Mount Vernon, and he was determined to honor Washington's wish to be interred at Mount Vernon. Washington never wanted to be deified. He refused to be appointed King of our new nation and believed the nation should be led by the people.

"Instead of Washington's body, the tomb holds Abraham Lincoln's funeral bier. Lincoln, another president known for his cabinet of rivals, was assassinated on Good Friday, April 14, 1865. Three days later, Easter Sunday, they placed his casket on this catafalque of rough pine boards covered with simple black drapery. This same bier held President McKinley after his assassination. John F. Kennedy's casket was laid out on Lincoln's catafalque in the rotunda above us on the third day after his assassination, and thousands upon thousands of American citizens passed by to honor him.

"Our country's greatest pain has been caused by people who demonized their political adversaries. John Wilkes Booth considered himself a noble Brutus killing a tyrant Caesar; he planned to cripple the government by killing Lincoln, Vice President Johnson, and Secretary of State Seward, all at one fell swoop. Leon Czolgosz called McKinley the *president of the money kings and trust magnates* and saw himself as a liberator. His last words before he died in the electric chair were, *I killed the President because he was the enemy of the good people—the good working people. I am not sorry for my crime.* Osama bin Laden attempted to destroy the World Trade Towers, the Capitol, and the Pentagon, all in one morning. Each of these murderers harbored a delusion he was performing a great service for society and killing was justified. Each killer was surprised not to be hailed as a hero.

"The healing of a nation requires understanding and compromise, not murder. In life, even Lincoln was unable to heal the bitter rift that led to the Civil War. But now, his catafalque lies hidden right under our feet, in the very place designed to be the artistic expression of our country's highest ideals, and it reminds us of the cost of the schism that rent our nation's heart. This cost—the pain of the rebirth of our Union—is still too bitter to bear. Yet here it is, almost hidden in the ground, at the foundation of our great nation.

"In Lincoln's time, when the money powers of America—both North and South—refused compromise, they conspired against our nation. They saw chaos as financial opportunity and denounced as unpatriotic anyone who questioned the need for war. Now we are living in a similar era of corruption in high places. The entrenched money powers in America prolong their reign by feeding the prejudices of the people, spreading disease and discord to increase their opportunity for easy profit. The powers will not be satisfied until all our wealth is held in the hands of the few and the Republic is destroyed.

Dr. Sampson raised his head. "Will we allow the Republic to be destroyed?" he thundered. "There are those in America who want to make us a nation under corporate kings, but let me tell you, change in American healthcare will come! And the Republic will survive." He took a deep breath and lowered his voice.

"The only question is, *how* will it come? Let us pray that it comes through common sacrifice, cooperation, and the triumph of common sense.

"This Crypt memorializes some of our greatest leaders: Washington, Lincoln, McKinley, Kennedy, and many others who chose to sacrifice and dedicate themselves to the common good. Their spirit undergirds our country and gives free people the courage to obligate themselves to one another through common government for the good of all. This same spirit is vital to American healthcare. Healing is an altruistic activity. In no endeavor is it more fitting to sacrifice for others as these great leaders did. Nowhere is it more important to have a common aim. *E Pluribus Unum*. Out of many, one."

Dr. Sampson pulled a thin paperback pamphlet from the inside pocket of his jacket. He opened its faded, light blue cover and gently turned to the second yellowed page. "Our founding fathers fashioned the Constitution with a healing purpose, to heal the divisions fracturing our new land. So it says:

> WE THE PEOPLE of the United States, in Order to form a more perfect Union, establish Justice, insure domestic Tranquility, provide for the common defense, promote the general Welfare, and secure the Blessings of Liberty to ourselves and our Posterity, do ordain and establish this Constitution for the United States of America.

"Will we continue to fashion laws to serve the special interests of a few? Will we allow corporate kings to hijack our healthcare system? Or will we foster the spirit of the commonwealth, to which our greatest leaders dedicated their lives? It all comes down to a simple choice. Will we be one nation, one people, indivisible, with true liberty and justice for all? Will we care for our neighbors as ourselves? You are the future leaders of our healthcare system. What will you choose?"

LONG AFTER Dr. Sampson left them for another meeting, Frances, Don, and Bruce wandered through the crypt and silently studied the chamber's artifacts, each of them lost in private thought. As they meandered past the gift shop and toward an exit swarming with Capitol guards, Bruce pointed out a door marked *Private*.

"That's the office suite of the majority whip of the House of Representatives, Tom Delay of Texas. There's a maze of offices in there—they call it the rabbit warren. Anyway, it's where that paranoid schizophrenic, Russell Weston, Jr., stormed through wearing a green fedora with a feather in it and with his

.38 Smith & Wesson blazing. Just think what might have happened if he'd had an automatic weapon. As it was, he killed two Capitol Police guards right here where we're standing. He shot the first guard point-blank in the back of the head at the exit there after he was asked to go through the metal detector. A stray bullet hit a tourist in the shop. Then he headed for Delay's offices.

"Weird thing was, fifty of Delay's staff members were in there, celebrating and drinking champagne. They had good cause to celebrate; they had defeated the Democrat's Patients' Bill of Rights, and their Patient Protection Act of 1998 had just passed the House.

"If the Democrat's bill had passed, mental patients like Weston could have sued HMOs and insurance companies willy-nilly whenever they were denied coverage. Frankly, I couldn't believe the AMA and the American Nurses Association were for the Patient's Bill of Rights. Of all people, they should know how important health insurance is for Americans. Anyway, the Patient Protection Act was a huge win for the HMOs and the American people. Delay and Representatives Mark Foley and Dennis Hastert had worked hard to get the bill through Congress. They drafted it behind closed doors in a special task force appointed by the majority leader."

"You mean it didn't go through the House Health Subcommittee?" Frances asked.

"Are you kidding?" Bruce scoffed. "Public hearings are deadly. No way. This bill needed people with real industry knowledge to draft it. Otherwise, the idealists and the trial lawyers would have had a heyday."

"But I read that the Patient Protection Bill limits the amount for which patients can sue HMOs to a quarter million dollars and requires sick people to pay for the independent reviews of coverage denials."

"Hell, Frances, I don't know all the details, but that sure sounds reasonable to me."

Don shook his head. "Bruce, if Russell Weston was mentally ill, he was probably dependent on for-profit HMOs for his care. Do you think Weston attacked Delay's offices because he was angry at the politicians in league with the HMOs?"

"What? Are you crazy too, Don? Anyway, blood was everywhere. Delay's personal guard wounded Weston after being mortally wounded himself. Senator Frist was one of the first people on the scene—you know he's a heart surgeon—and he worked to resuscitate the guard and the shooter. The guard died in surgery at George Washington University Hospital a little while later. Frist went in the ambulance with the shooter and helped resuscitate him. He survived."

Frances and Don were silent.

"Oh, yeah, and two days before the shooting, Weston killed fourteen cats with a single barrel shotgun and left them scattered in the yard around his house.

His elderly grandmother had insisted that he do something about the neighborhood cats that were becoming a nuisance. He did something, all right."

The students met Dr. Sampson outside the visitor's center at five o'clock. They all walked together across the hill by the House offices, overtaking a line of nearly sixty motorized wheelchairs. The wheelchairs snaked up the long sidewalk and around the corner of the building, casting long shadows in the late afternoon.

One wheelchair bore the name *Jungle Jake* across the back. The occupant's close-cropped gray hair barely peeked out from under the stars and stripes bandana tied at the back of his head. His starched shirt was open at the collar, and his black leather vest was covered with medals and emblems from the units he had served. As they walked past, Don looked over and took note of his polished brown shoes and dress slacks.

Jake caught Don's eye and sized him up. "What do you want to know?" he asked.

"What are you here for?"

"Same as you, I 'spect. We want to make a change. We're all members of ADAPT, American Disabled for Accessible Public Transportation, mostly Vietnam vets. We're lobbying for the needs of the disabled, particularly for better community based services for our comrades in arms." Jake seemed glad for an audience, and continued softly, as if sharing a secret. "It looks like our country is heading for another war, but we're not recovered from the old ones yet. Half of us can't get the health care we need to lead independent lives. The VA hospitals are crumbling. We're here to remind them about the cost of war; remind them of all the legless boys they'll have coming home."

Don felt sorry for him. How naïve these poor vets were to think they could make a difference. If they only knew how things really get done in Washington, how votes were bought and paid for. No money, no justice.

"So, did you get through?" Don asked. "Did anyone listen to you today?"

Jake burst out laughing. "Anyone besides you, you mean?"

"Yeah," Don smiled, "anyone besides me."

"No, just you…too bad you're not a senator. Good luck, kid."

They filed past the rest of the wheelchairs, followed the signs to the Capitol South Metro Station, and rode the station escalator down into the urban cave in the dark bowels of the earth.

29

The Alchemist

Know that I too have been in the wilderness, I too have lived on roots and locusts,
I too prized the freedom with which Thou hast blest men, and I too was striving
to stand among Thy elect, among the strong and powerful, thirsting
"to make up the number." But I awakened and would not serve madness.
I turned back and joined the ranks of those
who have corrected Thy work.

DOSTOYEVSKY, THE BROTHERS KARAMAZOV, PT. II, BOOK V, CH. V

DON WENT to the program office Monday morning to check his mailbox for the coming week's assignments. Dr. Sampson's secretary gave him a quizzical look as he passed her desk.

"There's a letter in there for you. Looks pretty important," she said.

On top of the stack of papers in his box was a linen paper envelope. The return was marked simply, OFFICE OF THE PRESIDENT. Don tore it open, unfolded the watermarked paper with trepidation, and read the typed message: *Report to President Lender's office on Tuesday afternoon at five o'clock.*

Don was alarmed. "Thanks, Bettye!" He tried to appear cheerful and nonchalant and hurried out before she could ask any questions.

The next day, Don got to President Lender's office five minutes early. He sat and fidgeted on the huge damask couch in the reception area, silently giving himself a pep talk and reviewing the points he wanted to make. He would speak up for the Health System Science Program and defend Dr. Sampson. His nervousness grew as he waited and watched the clock. Five o'clock passed, then five fifteen.

President Lender appeared at half past five. "You may go home now," he told his secretary, "I'll handle things from here."

In a matter of seconds, she grabbed her purse and disappeared through the doors of the outer office.

President Lender ushered Don into his office and indicated the same carved chair next to his own monumental one at the head of the long, venous blood-colored table.

Don sat down in the middle of the surreal scene. Intricate carvings of mythical creatures, griffins, and gargoyles decorated Lender's armchair. It was dark outside, and the dim office light left President Lender's face in shadows, but the whites of his eyes shone out from the deep sockets above his smooth and tan cheekbones. His flint gray eyes seemed illuminated by an interior fire.

"I have asked you here, Don, because you remind me of myself when I was your age."

How old was he? He struck Don as ageless, unbent by the worries that plagued Dr. Sampson.

I've seen your file. You have the fire and talent to serve as one of America's healthcare leaders, perhaps even to sit in this very chair someday." He patted the arms of his throne. "You and your colleagues in our Health System Science Program are among the very best graduate students in the country. It is no small feat to be admitted here."

"I'm honored to be here, sir."

"You should be. Did you know your colleague Frances Hunt had a perfect score on her GRE? Eight hundred on both verbal and quantitative reasoning. That's almost unheard of. No doubt, someone like you or Frances could lead this university someday. But first, you must see and accept the world as it is. It's time to grow up and take your place in the real world. Stop chasing after a fantasy world that will never be. I know you have lost your way, Don, and I am here to show you the right path."

Don was speechless. Of course it was true. He had lost his way. But how did President Lender know that about him? No one knew that about him. He barely admitted the depth of his disorientation to himself.

President Lender paused and assessed Don with fatherly concern. "I was at the University Hospital long before Dr. Sampson and Dr. Desmond, back when medicine really was a jealous mistress. We made real sacrifices back then. Medicine came first—before family and personal life. I had a mentor, one of the foremost leaders of American medicine, someone of whom you have certainly heard. I am going to tell you the truth he told me many years ago.

"In his last years he shared with me the secrets of a successful career in academic medicine, secrets that have made America the undisputed world leader in healthcare. Other countries look to us for direction, and we have been preeminent because we have, at the highest levels, remained true to the simple dictums my mentor taught me. And now, Don, I pass this sacred mantle to you.

"But first you must realize you've been led astray. To be successful and provide the healthcare people really need, you must recognize the basic principles Sampson is teaching you and your classmates are fundamentally wrong."

Don's mouth fell open. He knew President Lender wasn't happy with Dr. Sampson, but now he was discrediting the entire curriculum? His mind reeled as he tried in vain to recall his talking points.

President Lender leaned closer and spoke in a sympathetic tone. "Don, I know this is difficult for you to hear. But I know what I'm talking about. I, too, was once a student of the problems in American healthcare. Before I met my mentor, I followed the teaching of someone much like Sampson. Perhaps you have heard of him. Dr. Francis Peabody?"

Don nodded.

"Like Sampson, Peabody was an eccentric idealist. He looked askance at the conventional medical practices of his time. In a famous lecture he gave in Boston he said, *the secret of the care of the patient is in caring for the patient*. I believed him. I followed him through the wilderness of the healthcare wasteland, and—like you—I tasted the pure water of evidence-based medicine.

"Peabody directed a medical service and the Thorndike Memorial Lab at the City Hospital in Boston. I would have given my eyeteeth to work on that service. I was determined to champion evidence-based medicine, which was just coming on the scene. I wanted to help refocus the healthcare system on health. I saw myself as one of the harbingers of a bright healthcare future focused on prevention and health for all.

"But in the end, Peabody's science of prevention and caring failed to win the day. At first I was disillusioned, but eventually I realized his way was hopeless. I knew few people would benefit from his idealistic teachings or thank us for championing his cause. After all, Americans choose to be fat and sick and have little inclination to change. They don't strive for health; they live in denial until they get sick and then expect doctors to fix everything.

"I found a new mentor. He was a founding father of Florence College, and look at us now—one of the leading ivy-league medical schools in the world! My new mentor showed me the way, and I joined those who work for the good of humanity, for the good of academic medicine, and now for the good of Florence College. I belong to an ancient order representing the wisdom and wealth of many of America's founding families, and we will be the ones to lead America to a brighter future.

"You see, Dr. Peabody taught us to make three fundamental choices about how to practice medicine, but each time we made these choices for patients on his service I felt that something wasn't quite right. My new mentor explained the error of each of Peabody's three choices, how they were fundamentally misguided. Unfortunately, Sampson still teaches Peabody's same three mistakes."

Don started to protest, but Lender cut him off.

"No, Don. Listen. I have heard every defense of Sampson many times. I even audited his seminar a few years ago, so I know what he has to say. You cannot possibly add to his old argument now. It's time for you to understand where Sampson and his devotees fit in and where they have gone wrong. You must accept the world of consumption, disease, and death as it is. If you do that, you can be a real doctor in the real world of medicine, instead of ending up an impotent intellectual. I like you, Don. You have a lot of promise. That's why I'm sharing with you the wisdom my mentor taught me.

"Mistake number one. When Sampson encounters conspicuous consumption and profiteering, he prescribes discipline, fasting, and self-deprivation. But turning the American public away from self-indulgence—and American corporations away from chasing profit—is a fool's errand. Fasting and discipline? That's not what patients want! People want to enjoy life. They want to eat what they want to eat, when they want to eat it. They prefer to believe obesity is out of their control, that faulty genes cause high cholesterol. They want to indulge and take a pill to fix it.

"The truth is just too burdensome for average Americans to take, Don. People don't want to hear our moralizing lectures, and they won't change their ways anyway. We physicians have a sacred trust to protect our patients, shield them from unpleasant truths they can't handle, and reassure them that—with a pill or two and a doctor's supervision—they can indulge in rich food, profligate sex, and profiteering. Let them enjoy their fatty food and sugary drinks and cigarettes in peace. Ignorance is bliss. Why ruin their pleasure by telling them they are drinking, eating, and smoking poisons and their bad health is their own fault?

"Think about it this way. Only one in ten people is successful at losing weight. Why worry them with what they cannot and will not change? Why create fear and stress by telling them they are killing themselves with overconsumption, if they are going to die just the same? That would be cruel. As doctors, we have a responsibility to keep the unpleasant details to ourselves.

"This brings me to Sampson's second wrong choice. He has the power to heal but asks people to heal themselves! He refuses the physician's mantle—shirks his duty to heal those incapable of taking personal responsibility for their own health. He tells people the most important ingredients for human health are things they can do on their own. What nonsense! Why would people want that? Why would they need doctors if they could heal themselves? Why would doctors give away their sacred heritage for nothing?

"Besides, profit drives medical innovation. Sampson's way would mean disaster for any healthcare concern or medical school, since the profit is in the pills, potions, and gadgets that awe and mystify the public with the powers of medicine. Simple education never pays. And sometimes we come up with pills and procedures that do help people. If it weren't for profit, these breakthroughs would never happen.

"No, Sampson's way is impossible for most. How can you expect average Americans to analyze quality and value? They aren't healthcare experts like us. Given the suffering and ignorance of the American people, I choose to offer kindness to patients and give them what they want—an all-powerful doctor who cures disease and tells them what to do. They don't want to think for themselves.

"We *need* to be paternalistic, for our patients' sakes. That is, after all, what they pay us for—to speak with authority and assurance and make the difficult decisions. They're impressed by our mysterious scientific terms and jargon and powerful medicines. We are the modern priests of technology. Technology is what people want and technology is what they will pay for."

President Lender was completely caught up in his soliloquy, and Don found himself mesmerized. Maybe Lender was right. Maybe healthcare was too complex for average people to judge what they really needed. And yet...

"Sampson's third choice is his worst. When he has the chance to encourage faith in pharmaceutical and biotech marvels, he chooses instead to debunk the miraculous cures of modern medicine. He kills the hope for healing in a person's desperate final weeks, days, or hours. This is the ultimate cruelty. People want their doctors to be saviors, and we promise to play this role for them. We give them amazing cures through radical surgeries and powerful medicines and cloak everything in the language of science. Our patients are thankful because we give them hope. Even if we don't help them much, we assure them we have done everything possible.

"We are priests of the modern temple of science. Our PET scans, ventilators, chemotherapy, and gene cures are technologic wonders. We offer the sacred mystery and miraculous cures once found in the church. If one person in a hundred lives through our treatments for terminal illness, we claim credit for the miracle.

"Of course, hope comes at a price. I understand—same as you—that our huge investments in finding a cure for cancer and mapping the human genome have little likelihood of generating major cures. But these investments give people hope, and once in awhile we do discover something useful.

"Knowing all this, I choose the way of profit and hope. Remember, only Hope clung to the lid of Pandora's jar, and we are the keepers of the jar. Our medicine needs to be expensive to be good. If we give away our secrets for free and show people the hopes offered by the cures of modern medicine are false, people will only hate us for it.

"You do see, don't you Don, that's what happened to Sampson? His own family members distrust his cynical medical judgment. The doctors, the AMA, and all the leading healthcare corporations hate him for what he says and does. We doctors must assert the primacy of biological science, miracle, and authority offered by the medical profession throughout the ages. The naysayers like Sampson will be left behind or destroyed in the process."

Lender gazed at Don with an expression of benevolent compassion. "I would hate for that to happen to you, Don. You are destined for so much more."

Don's mind reeled. He didn't see how he could speak up and defend Dr. Sampson now, and he wasn't sure he wanted to. What if Dr. Sampson really was just a crazy idealist leading him down a ruinous career path?

President Lender took Don by the arm and escorted him to the door. His demeanor was grandfatherly and kind, like a trustworthy, old-time country doctor. Like Marcus Welby, M.D.

Who was Don to discard the rich old traditions of medicine—traditions passed down through generations and generations of physicians—traditions he was duty-bound to uphold? Maybe it *was* wrong to burden people with depressing truths they could never change.

At the door, President Lender embraced Don as a father would his son. "Good night, Don. I hope you'll consider what I have said."

DON'S ANSWERING MACHINE was blinking. He pressed play and heard a familiar voice.

"Dante, it's Sarah. I haven't been able to reach you, so I'm leaving a message. I knew you'd want to know. Sibyl Bellamy finally died. I know how much you cared about her…"

Did he? He barely knew her. Sarah was the one who really cared. She had bonded with Mrs. Bellamy's family. On the other hand, Sibyl Bellamy did have a habit of visiting him in hellish nightmares. Don shuddered with the thought. Maybe now her piercing stare would not accost him in his dreams. Maybe now she would leave him alone.

"…You know it took way too long for us to let her go. She was barely back in the nursing home before she came back to the hospital with pneumonia again. Thank goodness, this time I was on call, so I talked to her daughter and helped her understand the truth about what was going on. This time we finally did the right thing. We let her go, Dante. We made her comfortable. She died peacefully… I knew you would want to know. Listen, you take care now, okay? One of these days we must get together. Bye."

It pleased Don that Sarah had taken the time to call. Maybe she wasn't mad at him after all. Yes, they would have to get together soon.

30

Counterfeit Care

...the way to Hades is easy; night and day lie open the gates
of death's dark kingdom: but to retrace your steps, to find the way
back to daylight—that is the task...

VIRGIL, AENEID, 6, 175–180

SIBYL BELLAMY SAT bolt upright in her bed, fixed her piercing, white-eyed stare on Don, and opened her mouth. For a moment there was only the gaping hole and no sound, but soon came the unrelenting screams—demanding something of him—demanding his help.

AAAAAAAAAA! AAAAAAAAAA! AAAAAAAAAA!

Don awoke in a cold sweat but the shrieking didn't stop. It took him several seconds to remember he was in his call room at Florence New American Hospital.

He fumbled around on the bedside table for his beeper, shut it off, and read the number in the digital light. Strange—it was the emergency room number followed by the extension 911. Weren't the ER doctors supposed to cover codes at night?

Don called the ER desk, and a nurse with a vaguely familiar voice answered on the first ring. She was frantic.

"Don, it's Mary. Come quick! They're killing him! Run!"

Fully awake now, he shot from his bed, slid into his Nikes, and blasted through the door of his call room like it was the line of scrimmage. He raced down the stairs to the fluorescent-lit hall and ran on the painted blue stripe leading to the ER. Despite his speed, the scenery passed in slow motion. He strained to pass the sick wards, the laboratories, procedure rooms, and radiology suites. He dreaded what he might find in the ER. Why had they called him? There were two doctors on duty there every night.

Don charged through the swinging doors of the emergency department and spotted Mary Stuart standing in front of the nurse's desk wringing her hands, her cheeks streaked with tears.

She pointed him in the right direction. "You have to stop them, Don!" she begged as he ran past.

Don spotted a big commotion spilling out of exam room number four. He ran toward it and burst through the door, gasping for breath.

Two ER doctors stood over the bedside, one poised to stab a six-inch peri-cardiocentesis needle into the heart of a young man.

"Stop!" Don yelled just as the needle pricked the skin. "Wait just a second!" He grabbed the patient's wrist to feel for a pulse and touched cold flesh—really cold flesh. No pulse. Neck veins flat.

Don shoved the doctor with the needle to the side, forcing him to pull the needle out of the skin. A tiny red dot appeared on the deathly white skin of the boy's chest.

"What happened?" Don demanded.

"Hey!" the needle doctor shouted. "What in the hell do you think you're doing?"

"Resuming CPR." Don started doing chest compressions. "Now—tell me what happened."

"Who the hell are *you*?" the second doctor yelled.

The staff in the room—two nurses, an x-ray tech, and a respiratory therapist bagging the patient—inched away from the bedside.

Don knew he was way out on a limb. He'd just committed a serious breach of protocol, but at that moment he could only think of saving this young man's life, and he didn't have a minute to waste. He began deeper compressions of the boy's chest.

"Keep bagging," he ordered, with as much authority as he could muster. "I'm Dr. Newman." The tone of his voice implied the additional phrase, "and who the hell are you?" Don had often seen senior surgeons use this imperious technique effectively in the past. "Now tell me what happened to this boy."

The needle doctor silently fumed, but the second doctor bowed to Don's presumed greater authority. "Sudden death at a fraternity house," he said. "Apparently, there was alcohol involved. Some fraternity brothers brought him in. They were doing CPR in the back of a station wagon on the way, but when he got here he had no rhythm. We instigated the protocol for asystole."

The needle doctor barked, "And that protocol says we insert a needle into the heart because cardiac tamponade can cause this. It seems to me we're wast-ing precious time, Dr. Newman!"

Don glanced at the boy's neck once again to confirm his neck veins were not full. Tamponade was when blood leaked into the pericardial sac and pressed down on the heart so it couldn't pump, and the blood always backed up in the neck veins. No way this was tamponade.

"You're damn right time has been wasted here. No one is dead until they're warm and dead. Let's warm this boy up."

No one responded.

"And I mean *now,* dammit!"

That spurred the team into action.

"Get warm bags of normal saline and get them pouring in his veins in at least three large-bore IVs! And get more bags of warm saline to put over the large vessels of his groin and armpits! Do we have a bathtub here where we can immerse him?"

Mary Stuart stood in the doorway. She shook her head.

"Then get a warming blanket, and a stack of warm blankets too, lots of them." Don turned to the respiratory tech. "Put in an NG tube now! And let's get some hot water to lavage his stomach. We've got to warm this boy up. Someone get me a temperature."

The first rectal temperature was twenty-nine degrees Celsius. Less than eighty-five degrees Farenheit. Cold as death.

While shouting out his orders, Don hadn't missed a beat on the chest compressions. Sweat from his brow dripped on the ice blue flesh of the boy's lean, muscular body. When he was worn out, Mary took over the CPR, matching Don's thrusts for strength and depth. No one else offered to take a turn. The two ER docs just stood there and sulked while Mary and Don took turns spelling each other.

A nurse checked the body temperature again and it was just above thirty degrees. Within twenty-five minutes it was up to thirty-one, and soon after that there was a change on the monitor.

"Hold CPR," Don ordered. He searched the monitor for a line with some meaning. There was a rhythm! Sinus bradycardia. Just as he had thought. Once the hypothermic patient is warmed, the heart rhythm and pulse can spontaneously return.

"Is there a pulse?" Don reached for the artery in the groin.

The respiratory tech felt for a pulse in the carotid artery and called out, "Yes! There is a pulse! It's weak, but there is a pulse."

Pressing deeply in the cool flesh, Don found it. A weak, slow, but steady pulse. "We've got a pulse, let's hold CPR. And give him half an amp of epinephrine."

Within two minutes the pulse was up above eighty and gaining strength. Perhaps Don had made it in time. Cold drowning victims were some of the only ones that regularly survived CPR, if you got to them in time. Maybe this boy would be one of them.

He appeared to be about eighteen years old. He had close-cropped black hair, an athletic build, and a square jaw. So handsome. So young. Too young to die.

"Give me a temp," Don commanded.

Mary checked the rectal temperature probe. "Thirty-two point five! It's getting closer to normal, and he's in normal sinus rhythm with a good pulse."

For the time being, his body was out of the woods, but his mind was another matter. The boy hadn't woken up or made any spontaneous movements. Don pulled back the eyelids and shined his pocket light into the black pools. His heart sank. The light disappeared into black holes. Unmoving irises. Fixed and dilated. Very likely his brain was fried, and if so, Don had just resurrected an empty husk. They would wait and watch for two or three days to be sure, but it didn't look good. Don completed his neuro exam and found only the most primitive reflexes in the brainstem. No response from the higher brain.

"Hold the bagging," he called to the respiratory therapist. They waited thirty seconds and watched the oxygen saturation fall down below ninety percent. Nothing happened. No spontaneous respirations.

Mary saw the crestfallen expression on Don's face and her eyes welled again with tears.

"Let's get a head CT stat and check out his brain to make sure nothing else is going on," Don sighed.

The respiratory therapist resumed bagging and began to connect the ventilator.

"What's his name?" Don asked.

"He had a wallet," the second nurse said. "Here it is. Robert. Robert Webster."

"Have you called his parents?" Don asked the second doctor, who was still in the room.

The doctor shook his head. "Tell Dr. Mallock. It was his patient. Don't look at me."

Dr. Mallock was at the ER clerk's desk, writing in another patient's chart. He ignored Don at first, then looked up and glared at him with quiet fury. "So?" he said.

"Fixed and dilated. Want to call the parents?"

"I knew he didn't have a chance. You wasted your time—and mine. Given that you've taken over, *Doctor* Newman, *you* call them."

Don wanted to slug the supercilious son of a bitch. The smug, needle-pushing, so-called doctor could have saved the young man's life if he had started warming the ice-cold body up when the boy first came in. How could he have missed something so obvious?

He knew Mallock's type. Cowboy. Proud of his textbook ability to insert needles but oblivious whether doing so was warranted in a given situation. Mallock had all the accoutrements of a perfect doctor: starched shirt, white coat, good grooming, self-assurance, and amazing tools of technology at his fingertips. But the most essential ingredient—one no medical school test can measure—was missing. A heart.

Dr. Mallock didn't care about Robert Webster, except as it related to his own reputation. Don could see it in his eyes. He was preoccupied with himself now. How would he appear to his colleagues and the administrators? Don had made Dr. Mallock lose face, and Mallock hated him for it.

Don went to call Robert Webster's parents. Behind the secretary's desk, he located the chart and a copy of Robert Webster's Wisconsin driver's license. He found a phone number online for a Thomas Webster at the same address in La Crosse. He felt a familiar ache deep in his heart, drew a deep breath, and dialed the number.

After three rings a man answered. "Hello?" said the groggy voice.

"Is this Mr. Webster, Thomas Webster?"

"Yes, who's calling, please?"

"This is Dr. Don Newman at Florence New American Hospital. I'm the night duty physician for the ICU. Is Robert Webster your son?"

"Yes, Bobby Webster is my son."

"Bobby was brought to our hospital early this morning. His heart had stopped beating."

"Oh, my God," Mr. Webster was whispering now. "Is he ... is he dead?"

"When he was brought in, he was more dead than alive. We have managed to get his heart beating again, but right now things don't look very good."

"What happened?" he asked.

"We don't really know yet," Don answered. "Somehow he got deathly cold. There may have been alcohol involved, but I think his heart stopped because of hypothermia. We were able to get his heart beating again by warming him up." Don paused. "I think you'd better come right away. Your son's condition is very critical. It is possible he may not make it."

"We'll get the next flight out," Mr. Webster said.

Don could tell Mr. Webster was fighting to keep his voice under control. Mrs. Webster's panicked voice in the background kept repeating, "What is it, Tom?"

"We are moving Bobby to the ICU, where he will be cared for by one of the attending doctors. When you arrive, go straight to the ICU. If you want to check on his status, call the hospital and ask for his nurse in the ICU." Don gave him the hospital number and started to say goodbye.

"Dr. Newman, please, is Bobby going to make it?"

"I...uh, I don't know. But I promise you, we're doing everything we can."

Mr. Webster's voice was strong now. "We're on the way. Thank you for caring for my son, Dr. Newman. We'll pray for him, doctor, and we'll pray for you." And he hung up.

Don put down the receiver, leaned back, and took another deep breath. He opened the chart and went to work writing his note. In gathering the information he needed to complete the write-up, he checked the labs on the computer. The blood alcohol content was only 0.15, not nearly enough to kill or cause sudden death. And how did Bobby Webster get so cold?

The unit clerk appeared at the desk. "Dr. Newman, the young men who brought in Robert Webster are out front and want to talk to someone. The triage nurse told them to take a seat in the waiting area conference room."

"Thanks, I'm on my way."

Don entered the family conference room, and three anxious young men jumped to their feet.

"I'm Dr. Newman," Don announced in a grim voice.

The three faced him, frozen and wide-eyed. They didn't introduce themselves. Don waited.

Finally, a strapping blond-haired boy spoke. "We're Bobby's friends. How is he doing, doctor? Is he okay?"

"Is he all right?" a second one echoed.

They weren't immediate family, but Don figured they needed to know. Besides, he needed to find out how Bobby Webster got so cold.

"Well, his heart is beating now, but we're not sure if he's going to make it."

A tall, gangly boy with sandy brown hair was standing behind the others. He stifled a sob. "Jesus, I can't believe it!" His face was wet with streaks of tears. "Please, he's got to be all right!"

The blond group leader interrupted, "So, what happened, Doc?"

"That's what I'd like to know," Don replied. "What is your name?"

He hesitated. "Richard Townsend. The second."

The name sounded familiar. Where had he heard it before? Don stared straight into his blue eyes and waited, letting the quiet build.

Townsend blinked and looked at the floor. His confession, though casual, was calculated. "Well, I'm not going to lie to you. We were drinking. I know we're not supposed to, but our house is off campus, and, well, I guess some of the younger guys got a little carried away. Some of them were doing shooters. Anyway, I think Bobby was trying to show off or something. Before we knew it, we turned around and there was Bobby on the floor. And Jerry here, the Boy Scout in the group," he said with the slightest hint of sarcasm, "was doing CPR. Dr. Newman, do you think Bobby could have a heart defect or something?"

"It's possible," Don played along. "Why didn't you call the paramedics?"

"I thought it would be quicker to drive him ourselves. We had the station wagon right outside the door, the hospital was right around the corner, and Jerry here is an Eagle Scout and knows CPR. I made a snap decision. We wanted to do everything we could to save Bobby."

Richard Townsend's story didn't add up, and the other two seemed very nervous. Don had seen lots of scared friends and family members in his years as a doctor, and most were forthcoming with information. These two stayed quiet and kept glancing at each other behind Townsend's back.

"Listen boys," Don addressed the two behind the blond leader, "Bobby is fighting for his life. I need to know what happened. It's not the alcohol—he didn't drink that much. He did, however, nearly freeze to death. He was deathly cold when he got here. If we save his life it will only be because we warmed him up before it was too late. Don't waste my time. How did he get so cold?"

Two of the three faces feigned puzzlement, but the Eagle Scout broke down.

"Oh God, I never thought this would happen!" Jerry blurted out. "I knew we shouldn't have done it. We put him in an ice bathtub and made him stay even when he begged to get out. We—"

"Shut up, Jerry!" Townsend interrupted, his eyes flashing at Jerry with a millisecond of unbridled hate. He turned to Don. "He's completely freaked out. That was just a little joke. We would never do something to endanger one of our pledges."

"I've heard enough," Don said. "You had all better start praying Bobby survives."

He turned to go, but had a second thought and turned back. "Listen, I know you are all worried sick about Bobby. I can't let all of you back there, but I can let one of you visit for a few minutes. Jerry, come with me."

Jerry's eyes grew wide with fear, but he sheepishly followed as Don led him straight to Bobby's room and steered him to the foot of the bed.

The nurse and the respiratory therapist looked up from their paperwork in surprise, and Don silently mouthed, "it's okay."

Jerry stared with horror at the sight of his friend. He watched the rhythmic rise and fall of Bobby's chest with each gush of air from the mechanical ventilator, and listened to the rhythmic electronic beats of the monitors. He saw Bobby's waxen face, motionless and pale.

Don listened to Bobby's heart and lungs, checked the first blood gas results on the ventilator, and suggested some adjustments to the respiratory technologist, all in less than a minute.

He turned to Jerry. "Come with me," he ordered. "You've got some explaining to do."

Jerry hung his head. His face was pallid and his bloodless lips were trembling.

Don led him into an empty exam room, motioned for him to sit on a gurney, and closed the door. He sat on a rolling stool directly in front of Jerry, looked him square in the eye, and spoke softly but with authority. "Jerry, we need to make this quick. Tell me what really happened tonight."

"I don't know," he wailed, "it all happened so fast. I don't really know!"

"Just tell me what you saw."

"I can't," he pleaded, "they'll kill me!"

"If you don't tell, it'll kill you anyway. Look, Bobby is barely hanging on. I'm his doctor. I need to know what happened so I can help him."

Jerry's shoulders shuddered spasmodically.

"Tell me, Jerry, what fraternity are you in?"

"Well, it's not exactly a fraternity."

"What is it, then?"

"It's a secret society…oh, what the hell, everybody knows about it anyway."

Don could almost hear the key click when the lock to the dungeon of Jerry's dark secret opened.

Jerry took a deep breath and exhaled loudly. "We're called the Alchemists. There are a dozen or so societies on campus, but we're the best. We've got more pre-med and honor students than anybody."

"So what were you doing tonight? Having some sort of meeting?"

"Yes…um…no. Uh, you see, Bobby was tapped, like I was as a freshman last year. Oh, it all happens so fast. They come to your dorm room, and all they say is, 'The Alchemists have tapped you for membership. Accept or Reject?' Of course I accepted, and so did Bobby. It's a really big deal. If you're an Alchemist you've got it made. Members help each other out, and the alums are the most powerful graduates of Florence College."

Jerry paused, his chest heaving as he struggled to stifle his sobs.

"Bobby was in my dorm!" he blurted out. "I recommended him. Tonight was his freshman initiation. I don't know how it could go so wrong."

"What happened at the initiation?"

"I don't know much. I'm only a first level."

"Jerry, it's very important. Just tell me what you saw. I want the whole story."

Jerry clenched his jaw and took a deep breath. "We have this whole ceremony. It's in a really dark room, only candles for light. Twelve freshmen are surrounded by all of us elders in our hooded black robes. The freshmen stand before the master—Master Adam, we call him. Master Adam sits with the senior elders at a high table at one end of the room, and he shows the freshmen old relics, like skulls and bones that supposedly belonged to our earliest members. Master Adam says, 'You are nothing, freshmen! You hear me? You are shit! We will remake you. Make you more than the shit of which you are made. We will make you into something important, something gold. You'll always remember the night you became an Alchemist.' We all chant while the senior elders mix these smoking potions in beakers for the freshmen to drink, 'To prepare you for your baptism,' we all say. The potion is super cold from the dry ice, and I'm sure it has alcohol in it."

"And then what?"

Jerry shuddered again. "Then we walk in silence through a dark passageway and down to the basement. One by one, the freshmen have to take off all their clothes and get in the baptismal pools, which are just old bathtubs placed in a circle around the room. The tubs are smoking too, like the potion. The sophomores have to push the reluctant ones down lower, so that only their heads are above water. Most of the guys curse or yell because the water is so frigid."

Jerry stopped and put his head in his hands.

"It's okay, Jerry. You're helping Bobby. Keep talking."

"Bobby was...Bobby was diff-different. He was...quiet."

Jerry sat up straight and steeled himself for the next part of his story. "So, we were all chanting over and over again: 'For the good of all, the ends justify the means.' Each freshman has an elder dunk him all the way under—but only for a second—and tell him: 'Say it. For the good of all, the ends justify the means.' To get out of the tub, all you have to do is join in the chant. You just repeat the words and they pull you right out, give you a towel, and put a black robe on you."

"And Bobby wouldn't do it?"

Jerry shook his head. "I thought it was all over, but then everybody started chanting louder and crowding around one of the tubs. It was Bobby. He was shaking, and Richard Townsend was holding him by the shoulders and screaming, 'Say it! For the good of all, the ends justify the means!' But Bobby wouldn't say it. His lips were clenched. I don't think anyone one ever refused before. Richard wouldn't stop; he ducked Bobby under again and again. I didn't know what to do! They finally pulled him out when he went limp. I'll never forget what Townsend said: 'It's his own damn fault. Stupid freshman. All he had to do was say the stupid words.'"

Jerry started to cry again and Don handed him a tissue.

Shit—what am I supposed to do now? If Bobby dies, this has to be reported—right? But if I call the police, what will the other boys do to Jerry?

"Okay, Jerry. Here," he said, handing him a notepad and a pen, "give me your number and I'll call you later, once we see what happens to Bobby." *Once I figure out what to do.* "Now, listen to me. Keep what we talked about confidential. Don't tell them you told me anything. No matter what they ask, you just think of Bobby. Tell them you've been crying because of Bobby. Just describe what Bobby looked like in that hospital bed. Remember, you owe them nothing."

Jerry nodded.

"Now, you all should go home and get some sleep. There's nothing you can do for Bobby now. All anyone can do is wait. Are you ready?"

Don went to check on Bobby's lab values one more time and then went looking for Mary Stuart. The ER was quiet now, and he found her doing some charting on the computer. Her hands shook slightly as they hovered over the keys.

"Let's grab some coffee," Don said. "I want to hear what happened."

She peered in both directions, told the unit clerk she was going on break, and followed Don to the empty lounge. He poured two cups of coffee and gave her one. She sat down on the couch and started to cry. Don gave her a tissue and waited.

"I just felt so powerless," she finally said. "I didn't know what to do. Those two hotshot doctors like to pretend they're on the TV show ER. Worst part is, one of them is the Emergency Department director."

"What?"

"Didn't you know?" Dr. Mallock is my boss. I'm sure to get fired, but I didn't know what else to do."

"Mary, you did the right thing. My note will show that. They can't fire you for doing the right thing. So, what exactly happened?"

"From the moment they carried that boy in the door," she began, "I had this horrible feeling, like something bad was happening. Of course, we started immediately to resuscitate him. I felt for a pulse in the groin and then in the neck. Dr. Smith was giving lousy CPR—his wimpy chest compressions hardly generated a pulse at all. And the patient was so cold. I tried to say something at least three times, but Dr. Smith yelled at me. He said, 'I don't care what you feel! I'm doing good CPR.' But he was not. I persisted, as I was trained, and said there still was no pulse. Dr. Mallock screamed at me, 'Pipe up one more time and I'll have your job!' That horrible feeling—intuition I guess—just got stronger and stronger. I knew in my gut they were doing the wrong thing. The feeling became so overwhelming, I thought I would start screaming. And then I thought of you."

DON CALLED the hospital scheduling office the next day to find out which dates he would be working for the next few weekends.

"Uh, looks like they have taken you off the schedule," the secretary in the office replied.

"What do you mean, taken me off the schedule?"

"Apparently, there has been a complaint filed against you."

Don felt a surge of panic; he depended on moonlighting to make his rent. Before hanging up, he had the presence of mind to make an appointment for the next morning with the vice president for physician relations, the woman who scheduled moonlighting docs.

When Don arrived at the meeting, he was surprised to see one of the hospital's risk management attorneys. At that moment, it occurred to him that perhaps the best defense was a strong offense.

"I'm glad you are here," Don started. "You should know that when Bobby Webster arrived in the ER, he was cold as ice. He should have been warmed up first thing, for God's sake! Any person in New Hampshire ought to know that. His so-called friends put him in ice water in a cold basement on one of the coldest days of the year. He should have been warmed!"

"Now, Dr. Newman," the vice president for physician affairs said in a sickly sweet voice, "Dr. Mallock assures us there was nothing more anyone could have done. The young man had been without a heartbeat for too long."

"Bullshit!" Don shouted, "they brought him in fast, and an Eagle Scout gave him good CPR from the moment they pulled him out of the water, which is more than he got in our ER. He needed to be warmed up to have any chance to survive. He at least deserved a chance!"

"Now, Dr. Newman,"—she spoke in a vexed tone now—"watch yourself. Remember, you are an inexperienced moonlighting doctor just out of training. Doctor Mallock is the director of our emergency department. He is respected in this community and has practiced here nearly twenty years. Who do you expect me to believe?"

"But he's incompetent!" Don shouted. He knew he was getting himself into deeper trouble, but his anger—and Dr. Sampson's seminar—had emboldened him.

The administrator cut him off. "Dr. Newman, let me make this perfectly clear. We are not here to review the details of Mr. Webster's case. Our patient care committee will handle that. This little meeting is to inform you your moonlighting privileges here at New American are indefinitely suspended. A complaint has been filed citing your highly unorthodox and reckless behavior in the emergency department Sunday morning, February twenty-fourth. You are off the moonlighting schedule pending a detailed review of the case. Dr. Newman, these allegations against you are quite serious. You may want to consult an attorney."

Don could not believe it. Consult an attorney? The wind was totally gone from his sails. There was nothing he could do. The patient care committee cared nothing for him. It was certain to be filled with Mallock's friends, and Mallock would have ample opportunity to enlighten them with his warped version of events.

On his way out of the hospital, Don took a chance and walked through the ER, praying not to run into Dr. Mallock or Dr. Smith and banking on the fact that few in the hospital even knew who he was. He was in luck. The ER was buzzing with activity and a glance at the assignment board confirmed Mallock was not on.

Behind the secretary's desk he spied a familiar face. Laura, the daytime clerk, often greeted him with a smile and a joke when he arrived at the end of her shift.

This time, she glanced around furtively when he sat next to her. Seeing no one close by, she talked to Don through clenched teeth while pretending to work at her monitor. "I hear you got in some trouble the other night," she said. "I guess that is what happens when you try to save a life around here."

Don replied, "I'm glad you still think that is our business. How is Bobby Webster?"

"Still hanging on, but he hasn't woken up. Did you hear what happened to Mary?" she asked.

"No." Don shook his head.

"Mallock fired her for insubordination."

DON LEFT the hospital in a deep gloom. Twenty minutes later, he walked into Dr. Sampson's seminar.

"Don, you don't look like yourself," Dr. Sampson observed. "Is something wrong?"

Don shared the story of Bobby Webster. At least part of the story. He explained how a doctor with twenty years of experience at Florence New American had given a young Florence College freshman all of the form but none of the substance of care, and how he had breached standard hospital protocol. He didn't mention anything about the initiation ceremony.

"That is totally unfair, Don!" said Frances when Don told how he had been laid off.

Bruce just shrugged. "Upper-level corporate management at New American avoids involvement at the local level," he said. "Local administrators handle issues like yours."

"I'm sorry to hear about your difficulties, Dr. Newman, and hope everything works out well for you and the young man. It is not always easy to advocate for the best interest of our patients."

"Thanks, Dr. Sampson."

"Now, let's get started," Dr. Sampson said. "Competence has long been considered the most basic duty of health professionals. How ironic that our topic today is pretenders, those poorly trained practitioners who masquerade as competent providers for profit, pride, and personal gain. Dr. Markum, please begin."

"Frances and I focused on primary care. Don keeps insisting primary care is the most important for health, so we decided to see if it's true. Remember our lecture about the best clinics? Well, we focused on the worst clinics. We studied the Medicare atlas data to identify which region has the highest Medicare spending per person, figuring that would be where fraud in primary care would be greatest.

"Right away, we saw South Florida had higher Medicare spending than almost anywhere in the country. Frances found data from the Milliman accounting firm that showed private healthcare spending was highest in Miami-Dade

County as well—over ten thousand dollars a year for a family of four. So we focused our search for the worst clinic there. I'll let Frances tell you what we found."

"We called the Florida Board of Medical Examiners," Frances said, and requested information on the worst cases of fraud they'd uncovered in the past year. We hit like a treasure trove. Not only is South Florida the most expensive, but it has the highest rates of narcotic prescribing. Prescription narcotic abuse is now a bigger problem in Miami than cocaine.

"Many of the worst clinics in Miami masquerade as pain clinics. The docs in these pill mills are big narcotics prescribers; they cater to total addicts. Many patients who go there for legitimate pain turn into addicts because the doctors prescribe loads of highly addictive, short-acting narcotics.

"The clinics put all their addicts on an efficient monthly schedule. Addicts always show up for appointments, since that's how they get the drugs they desperately crave. Office visits in these worst clinics are quick. The addicts never complain, so long as they get narcotics. And what do the doctors get out of it?"

"Billing?" Don asked.

"You got it. Lots and lots of billing. Most pill mill docs see fifty to eighty patients a day. For comparison, the average adult doctor sees twenty to thirty at most. Every visit generates bills to Medicare, Medicaid, or a private insurer. And that's just the beginning. These worst clinics use every opportunity to generate a bill. And what types of services generate the largest bills?"

"Procedures. We all know that now," Don answered.

"Right, Don. These clinics love procedures. They inject steroids, narcotics, and anesthetics anywhere it hurts. They order blood and urine tests they can process in-house. They order on-site lung tests, exercise treadmills, heart echos, EKGs, and heart monitor testing on almost everyone. A patient often gets the same test several times a year. The clinics justify the testing to insurance companies by suggesting possible cardiac disease or other serious conditions.

"Patients bounce like balls in a pinball machine from test to test, ringing up charges as fast as possible, until all the money they can generate is jingled out of their pockets. These worst clinic doctors use any and every excuse to shoot the patient back to the triple-score bumpers. Patients are only allowed to escape past the pill pushers' paddles when they can no longer render income."

"Isn't that fraud?" Don asked.

"Sure, it's fraud," Bruce interrupted. "But when everybody does it, it becomes the legal standard of care, and then you have to do it to cover your butt. The actual quality of care in Miami-Dade and other high-cost areas—like New York, Chicago, and Los Angeles—is unbelievably low. The worst clinic doctors bill for lots of unnecessary procedures, and they're often incompetent to perform them.

"Take echocardiograms. At one end of the spectrum, you have internal medicine physicians who spend an additional two, three, even four years in a echocardiography fellowship at elite places like the University Hospital in Boston. At the other end, you have general practitioners who take a long weekend course in the Bahamas to learn how to do echos. Believe it or not, they're all paid the same. And remember, pill mill docs do lots of tests on nearly everyone. People get operations based on these worthless tests, even open heart operations."

Frances took over again. "It's not just doctors shamming patients in Miami-Dade County. Physical therapists in cities like Miami, Houston, and Baton Rouge have figured out their own insurance scam. One family practice doc in Miami, known as Rock Doc because of his spiked hair and movie star friends, has trained his 'office girls' in physical therapy. His version of PT includes heat packs, massage, and electrical stimulation for almost everyone, but none of the exercise components of PT proven most effective. His counterfeit PT practice clears almost a million a year from Medicare alone."

"Are you saying the whole healthcare system in places like Miami is fake?" asked Don.

"Well, not all fake," Frances said. "But let's face it. You doctors give fake care all the time. And it happens from coast to coast, in the big cities and even in little towns."

"Strange thing is, Medicare knows who these fake docs are," Dr. Sampson said. "Medicare pays the bills. All they have to do is see where the spikes in billing come from. Remember, to find the fraud all you have to do is…"

"Follow the money!" the three students said in unison.

"These South Florida pill mills take churning to a whole new level," Bruce added. "We estimate they often generate over twenty-five thousand dollars a year in outpatient charges per patient, almost all of it unnecessary. Most of their monthly visits, tests, and treatments are not proven to improve health. These fraud docs claim the tests and treatments help people and avoid malpractice, but it's really about the money."

"Exactly," Frances agreed. "Take breast exams, for example. Did you read the study in our syllabus? It shows medical students do better breast exams than upper-level doctors. Medical students take time to do a thorough job. Doctors often give superficial and hasty breast exams, if they do them at all."

"You're right, Frances," Bruce responded. "Most procedures can be done as well or better by technicians. Think about the other study we read. Nurse practitioners can do just as good a job as GI docs at colonoscopy and cost much less. So why aren't nurse practitioners doing all the colonoscopies? Money. The GI docs make it clear in the colon cancer screening guidelines they publish. First, they claim everyone needs a colonoscopy even though other screening tests work just as well, and second, they say only GI docs should perform them. These professional guidelines masquerade as science! They are all about protecting the turf of the guild."

Frances smiled at Bruce, and he smiled back. She listed more examples, he backed her up point by point, and she glowed with pleasure at his intellectual support. She proclaimed the ability of nurses to do any number of things doctors do, but Don noticed she did not mention surgery. Her eyes returned to Bruce after every few sentences, as if to assure herself of his approval.

Don was disgusted. Bruce was quite the operator, all right. 'Fair Helen, make me immortal with a kiss,' and all that shit. Frances seemed oblivious to Bruce's ulterior motives. He had her fooled into thinking he was an advocate for nurses! He was just flattering Frances in his quest to get in her pants, if he hadn't been there already...

Bruce's rising voice abruptly roused Don from his sleep-deprived daze. He looked up to see Bruce piercing Dr. Sampson with a challenging stare.

"Dr. Sampson, I'm a little tired of us putting our opinions out in front of the group and having you shoot us down with a smirk on your face. We're all looking for some answers here. Since you know so much, why don't you share some of your answers with us?"

Dr. Sampson let that soak in for a moment before answering. "Fair enough, Bruce. I'm not sure I can give you what you are looking for. I'm not sure I know the answers any more than you do. But I'll at least tell you how I see things from where I stand. Do your readings for next week carefully. I'll present. I guess it's my turn, after all."

Dr. Sampson picked up his papers and left the room.

Don sat in an exhausted stupor at the table and watched Frances and Bruce gather their books. Bruce was telling Frances how his family's company could give her a position, that she could make big money there empowering nurses. Her face lit up at the idea of an important job in the Markum Corporation, and he acted thrilled with the idea of giving her one. Bruce obviously cared little that just two hours earlier, Don had lost his job—the only means he had to pay rent, student loans, and his car payment.

"You know, Frances," Bruce was saying, "you need to talk to more people in the real world. That old weasel is full of secrets. I think for all his pretensions of being a conservative, he's really one of those closet liberals who want to give away free health care to everyone. Let's face it. Sampson isn't with it and he ignores industrial trends."

"Frances smiled up at Bruce. "Well, I guess we will find out for sure next week."

"Yeah," Bruce said, "He acts so smart about everything. Yet all we get from him are vague generalities—healthcare of the people, by the people, and for the people—a bunch of claptrap. No details. It's about damn time we learned more about what the old codger really thinks.

DON WENT BACK to his apartment to study but was too exhausted to think. Even so, he couldn't sleep, either. He needed that moonlighting job. Worse, he couldn't shake the image of Bobby Webster and his icy blue skin.

Don needed to clear his head and figure out what to do about the Eagle Scout's story. He was torn. On the one hand, he had a duty to maintain patient confidentiality, and he felt morally responsible to protect Jerry. On the other hand, he had an obligation to report the killing of Bobby Webster. He had tell someone. Others could be hurt by this secret society. It needed to be investigated, and the parents deserved to know what had happened to their son.

By the next morning Don knew what he had to do. He called President Lender's office to make an appointment.

"Oh, yes, Dr. Newman," Lender's secretary said in a pleasant voice. "May I tell him what it's regarding?"

"Just tell him it's urgent and I need to speak with him personally."

She put Don on hold for a few seconds, then came back on and said, "President Lender will see you this afternoon at three. Will that do?"

"That would be fine, thank you."

At three on the dot, President Lender greeted Don warmly at his office door and ushered him to the giant table. "I only have a few minutes but am eager to hear what you have to share with me today, Don." He leaned forward, his gray eyes glinting in eager anticipation.

Don had prepared his words carefully. He told him everything about Bobby Webster and the Alchemists—the details of the initiation and how it had gone wrong, and the names of the young men who brought Bobby to the hospital and what they said.

Lender nodded sagely as Don recounted the terrible story. His eagerness was replaced with steely, serious resolve.

Don was immensely relieved to pass on his burden to someone in authority. President Lender struck him as someone who would not tolerate such flagrant abuse on campus, and the president's response gave him confidence something would be done about it.

"Certainly, this needs to be investigated, and you can be sure I will deal with it personally," Lender said. "While I conduct my investigation, you are not to mention this to anyone else. For now, this must be kept quiet for the good of the college, for the good of all."

He jumped to his feet. "Well, thank you for sharing this with me, Don. I will be certain to get to the bottom of it. Oh, by the way, if you don't mind, before you leave I'd like you to talk with my assistant senior administrator in the office right next door. He is considering improvements to the curriculum and could use your input."

"Sure, I could do that." Don was so grateful to have passed the ball on the Alchemist's incident, he was happy to agree.

"Now, please excuse me," said Lender. "Ms. Ingram, please see Dr. Newman over to Mr. Hanley's office."

The assistant ushered Don through some glass doors to a small waiting room. Minutes later, a small man with dark hair came in and introduced himself as Mr. Hanley. He ushered Don into his office, which was much smaller than President Lender's but similarly appointed and paneled from floor to ceiling in mahogany.

"We hear Dr. Sampson is corrupting students and promoting pseudoscience," Mr. Hanley said. "I'd like to know what you have observed regarding the faults in Dr. Sampson's methods and leadership.

"Who told you that?" Don, caught completely off guard, couldn't think of anything else to say.

"I am not at liberty to share that information with you. I do need your perspective. After all, you are one of the premiere students in what we hope will become the best program of its kind in the country."

Could there be something to this after all? Some of the things Sampson said did seem pretty outrageous. The administration must be privy to information Don didn't have.

"I don't know," Don stammered. I really can't report anything good or bad."

"Does he refer to history a lot?" Mr. Hanley prompted.

"Well, yes."

"Then, doesn't he seem to you to be a little out of date?"

Don thought of Bruce. "Well, some people might say that…I mean, he is old-fashioned."

"Yes, tell me more." The eager administrator scribbled away on his pad. "Does he criticize the newer innovations in healthcare?"

"Well," Don heard himself saying, "I have to admit, he does criticize the big corporations in the healthcare industry quite a bit…and he doesn't go easy on doctors, either…but…"

31

Industrial Giants Whose Time is Past

*I had not long kept my head turned that way when I seemed to see
many lofty towers; I said therefore: 'Master, tell me, what city is this?'...
'know that these are not towers, but giants, and'...then more than ever
I was in fear of death...*

DANTE ALIGHIERI, INFERNO 31, 19–119

DON PLODDED across campus to class, fretting over his meetings with
President Lender and Mr. Hanley the week before. The more he thought about
it, the more uneasy he felt. He hadn't heard anything since. No word about
President Lender's investigation of the hazing. Worse yet, it was clear they were
out to get Dr. Sampson, and he had done nothing to defend him.

What a coward I was in that meeting! Sure, Dr. Sampson has his own way of
seeing things, but he hasn't done anything wrong. He's just trying to get us to
think critically. We interpret the articles ourselves, right? It's not like he spoon-
feeds us, though sometimes I wish he would. To top it off, I blew my moonlighting job and probably didn't do the Webster boy a damn bit of good. That asshole
Mallock will blackball me all over town—how will I be able to continue the fellowship? I sure don't want to ask my father for money.

Don had also met with the chief medical officer at Florence New American
to appeal his suspension. Dr. Dressler's office was appointed with fine antiques
and rich leather upholstered furniture and offered an excellent view of the new
physicians' office tower next to the hospital. The medical books on his lustrous
veneer shelves appeared pristine and unopened. A model of an artificial knee
joint—marked with the device maker's name and logo—sat on the desk to pro
claim Dressler's specialty in orthopedics.

Dr. Dressler wore a starched white coat, though he had not seen a patient all
day. He did mostly administrative work now. He was reputed to have performed
half the knee replacements in Grafton County, and he'd still do an occasional
artificial knee for a VIP.

Don told his whole story and insisted the ER physicians should be suspended, not him.

Dr. Dressler glared at Don. "Do you think I am going to suspend two of my
most senior physicians on the word of an inexperienced young moonlighter?"

"They were about to ..."

"Dr. Newman, you have already said quite enough. Now you listen." He appraised Don coldly. "I don't think you realize the fragility of your position. You are a trainee barely out of basic residency. Dr. Mallock and Dr. Smith are well respected and have been with us since the hospital's beginning. It is not easy to retain emergency physicians in a small town like Florence. You, on the other hand, are expendable. Moonlighters are a dime a dozen. You must wait on the decision of the patient care committee. I can do nothing to help you. Goodbye, Dr. Newman."

He turned his attention back to paperwork.

Don made one last appeal. "Dr. Dressler, what about Mary Stuart, the nurse that helped me care for the Webster boy? She's a good nurse. She was only doing what she thought was best for the patient."

"Nurse Stuart's situation is none of your business, but if you must know, she has been terminated. From what I understand, you are the one who cost her her job. Her personnel records demonstrate she is not a reliable team player, and we need team players here at Florence New American. Now goodbye, Dr. Newman."

Don wended his way through the anatomy department, rehashing these upsetting conversations in his mind. The moment he entered the old anatomy theater, Frances interrupted his painful rumination.

"Are you ready?" she asked.

"Ready for what?" Don replied.

"What do you mean, ready for what? Like, where have *you* been?"

"Don't you remember?" Bruce said. "The old weasel has promised to tell us what he really thinks about the major health care industries."

Don did remember. Dr. Sampson often held back his opinions and reflected questions back at them, as though he really cared what they thought. Of course, he'd had hundreds of students through the years and the three of them were unlikely to provide him with a new perspective. For weeks they'd been asking him how American healthcare could be reformed, and he always said they needed to understand its problems first. Except for his Senate HELP Committee testimony supporting the proposed Medicare Quality Improvement Act and his speech in the crypt, they knew little of what he thought about *the answers*.

Dr. Sampson entered the room appearing even more serious than usual and sat down with his three students at the old table that once again had appeared in time for seminar. He started to speak but stopped himself, stood up, and paced back and forth across the room. He walked up to the podium and examined the screen there, then returned to the table, placed his hands on it, and leaned forward, his hulking frame looming over them.

Don, Frances, and Bruce all shifted back in their seats.

"I haven't told you what I think should be done to fix the major health care industries in America because I don't really know. Oh sure, I have a few ideas. I'm convinced we must follow the money and examine who gets paid for what. But the truth is, I'm a professor in an ivory tower. I haven't worked for any of the major health care industries in America. I have little real-world experience. What knowledge I have is born of a distant view. I can only offer my perceptions of the swirls, currents, and eddies in American health care after they have already passed by.

"We health systems researchers study what has already happened. We analyze healthcare practices and their effects on a narrow set of predefined outcomes. As you know, there are thousands of health and economic outcomes we could study, but our research can only deal with a handful. We only have a small amount of information about the myriad effects of any single change in healthcare delivery. There are hundreds of changes every day, in millions of places, and what is true in one place or time may not be true in another.

"Dr. Markum has asked for my view of the general principles that govern the operations of the major American healthcare industries. I hope I do not disappoint. I would prefer to present clear scientific evidence to substantiate my perceptions, but there is no definitive body of scientific knowledge or textbook summarizing the subject. I can only offer the perceptions of one old observer of the healthcare industry, and I think the best way to depict the massive and complex healthcare industries in America is to tell a story. It's a fable, an allegory, but perhaps it will strike some chord of understanding within you. Will you allow me to do that?"

"Dr. Sampson," Bruce sighed in exasperation, "I've never heard anyone take so long to apologize for what they were about to say. Please get on with it, however you want to do it."

Frances and Don nodded in agreement.

"Very well, then. Many years ago, I visited Virgil's hometown of Mantua, Italy, and toured Palazzo Te, a great pleasure palace built in the early 1500s. The powerful Grand Duke Federico Gonzaga built the palace to entertain friends and escape court life. It was designed for leisure, dining, and sensual indulgence, and many of the architectural details and decorations are fanciful and humorous."

Bruce looked over at Don and raised his eyebrows.

Dr. Sampson stepped up to the podium and pulled up a website designed by students at Williams College. "This site allows us to go into the Palazzo Te on a virtual tour and look around, just as if we were there."

The stone and iron gates of Palazzo Te appeared on the flat screen. A click of the mouse advanced the students to the pale yellow stone walls of the palace, and another escorted them through a massive arched doorway into a large courtyard. Inside the palace, they advanced through a succession of rooms. The walls and ceilings were adorned with frolicking gods, animals, and satyrs.

Don was amazed at the technology. He'd never seen a virtual tour—it was almost like visiting this exotic foreign palace in person. Who would have thought Dr. Sampson would show them this?

But Dr. Sampson used the mouse to scan the rooms like a tech-savvy geek. Finally, he escorted them into the most wildly painted room of all.

"When you enter the Sala dei Giganti, or the Room of the Giants," he narrated, "you find yourself in the middle of a massive optical illusion. Just as Virgil's *Aeneid* describes the birth of Rome and the seeds it held for its own destruction, this room depicts a similar thing. To me, it is an apt image of the American healthcare system.

"The Room of the Giants is painted—walls, floor, and ceiling— with a huge panorama of war between heaven and earth. When you stand in the center of this room, the gods of Olympus tower over your head and the earthly giants surround you on the ground level. You are right there with the tribe of rebel giants in the midst of battle. Jove hurls thunderbolts from above. The giants have tried to conquer heaven, but Jove and the other gods throw them back down into the earthly depths. You are trapped with them in the destruction as the pillars, walls, and roofs of their ancient temples crash down upon you.

"To sixteenth century viewers, this room was like 3D or virtual reality. The trompe l'oeil painting is masterfully done; you can't see the corners of the room, and the whirling design of the river stones on the floor is disorienting. To look down is to spiral with the giants down into chaos; to look up is to face the angry gods. All around is nothing but destruction. One early visitor to the Room of the Giants said the following:

> So let no one think ever to see any work of the brush more horrible and frightening, or more realistic, than this; and whoever enters that room and sees the windows, doors and so forth all distorted and apparently hurtling down, and the mountains and buildings falling, cannot but fear that everything will crash down upon him...

"The Room of the Giants is American healthcare today. Our major healthcare industries are giants reaching for ever-greater power and control. These corporate titans have grown dumb, unaware of their own selfish motives and forgetful of their original purpose. They collect gold, grow without bounds, and build impressive temples. Those entering their realm become disoriented and bewildered. They search for guidance and cannot find it. They feel small and helpless. They sense something is wrong."

Dr. Sampson walked back over to the table and resumed his original position. He looked directly at Bruce and spoke with the calm but unwavering conviction of one who is unalterably certain.

"The day of reckoning is at hand. Americans will not tolerate much longer the hoarding of resources by giant, power-hungry industries that so obviously lack the ability or desire to promote health. The giants and their temples will fall. Not one stone will be left on another; all will be thrown down.

"The question is: will we all be destroyed along with the giants when it happens? The old era is passing and another age of better health care will come. The new order will see new gods led by Jove, the force of nature, of evolution, the force in the world that abhors waste and lack of productivity."

Bruce flashed Don a look that said, "Now do you see how crazy he is?"

Dr. Sampson's face was grim and serious as death. The corded muscles in his broad forearms bunched as he leaned on the table, arms and fingers spread wide.

Don could imagine him standing among the pillars of the University Hospital and pulling them to the ground. *Is that what he wants to do, to bring down the walls on himself and all of us as well?*

"Modern treachery brings money and power, just as treachery of old brought thirty pieces of silver. Corporations are not inherently bad, but they defend their power and market share and seek to earn money for shareholders. In the hospital towers there is plenty of money, but a large portion of it does not further health. Of course, those who profit so handsomely in the current system will resist, but in refusing to change or curb their ambitions, they sow the seeds of their own destruction. Unfortunately, many good people will perish along with them.

"Four giants dominate American healthcare today: Insurance, Pharmacy, Diagnostics, and Hospital. They are just dumb giants. But these four guard and support the greatest treacheries in healthcare. They are largely unaware of their betrayal when they put profit and power before healing. Like giants, they step all over the little people without realizing it.

"Let's name each of the giants. I'll call Insurance Nimrod, after the mythological giant who designed the city of Babel and caused the proliferation of languages so people no longer understood one another. Nimrod is a go-between. He's only necessary when people can't communicate directly, so he is determined to prevent the development of a common language. Nimrod loves chaos and thrives on lack of communication. He despises standardization: of benefits, claim forms, formularies, co-pays, or authorization procedures. He creates confusion and delays in billing, benefits, and coverage and takes a big cut for the service of sorting out the whole mess. Nimrod trumpets the benefits of competition in lowering health care costs but has no interest in competing for the business of sick people. He cherry-picks healthy people into profitable risk pools and banishes those who need care most.

"Pharmacy is Ephialtes, leader of the giants' revolt against Jove. Ephialtes piles mountaintop upon mountaintop and scales the heavens in his desire to be worshipped as a god. He fancies himself the source of all healing and promises the elixir of life, health, and eternal youth—if we are willing to pay enough. Ephialtes believes each new mountaintop is the best yet, and there is no limit to what we should spend for his explorations and magical potions.

"Diagnostics is Briareus, who has fifty heads and values knowledge above all. Briareus is more interested in diagnostic methods than healing or caring. Testing is everything—he pokes and prods with his one hundred arms and peers in every orifice with his one hundred eyes. He will spend any amount of money available collecting data, regardless of whether the knowledge gained will aid in healing. He's determined to discover sickness. If initial tests are negative he orders more; he believes everyone must be sick in some way. Any small abnormality is sufficient reason to get more tests, regardless of risks and side effects. Irradiation, perforation, allergic reaction, infection, and embolization give cause for more tests. Briareus especially loves it when disease sets in before the search for health begins.

"Hospital is Antaeus, the mythological Libyan giant who feeds on the blood of lions. Antaeus thrives on sickness. He beckons us to enter his marble and glass towers through sparkling lobbies, invites us to taste his gourmet meals and recline on cushioned beds. Once we accept, he drains away our physical strength and financial resources. He insists we lie in sickbeds to regain health. He commands us to lie still while he draws our blood again and again. He slips us drugs for sleep so he can do what he wants. We awake with muscles wasted, metals inserted, missing legs and feet. Antaeus claims this is good— if we will only pay him to build a higher tower he will bring a cure for cancer. 'Depend on me,' he says, 'for only I can bring the dead to life.'

"Nimrod, Ephialtes, Briareus, and Antaeus. The huge citadels and office buildings of the Insurance, Pharmacy, Diagnostics, and Hospital industries are fearsomely built, but not for the purpose of promoting health. Like medieval towers in the hilltop towns of old Europe, they are built to gather and defend wealth. That's their true purpose.

"The giants prevent you from controlling your own health. They micromanage every medical decision. It's in their interest to maximize consumer spending and minimize costs, because their real goal is profit. Doctors are their front men. Advertisers, artists, and filmmakers depict their products as irresistible and necessary, and lawyers, lobbyists, and legislators create complex legal structures to protect their thrones with the force of law.

"So, who's controlling the American healthcare system? Just these dumb giants! There is no brain behind it, no evil genius. Doctors, nurses, patients, pharmacists, administrators—most individuals try to do the right thing. But we all ceded power to trusted healthcare entities and allowed them to morph into selfish, corrupt giants. The giants developed systems to generate income and built towers to store wealth, and in the process forgot their original healing purpose. The system is the problem. It evolved and now exists to create wealth and power, not health.

"Everyone falls in line with the giants because the system requires it. Why should we be shocked when professionals and corporations follow the money? Why wouldn't they? That's human nature. Our Founding Fathers understood humans could be selfish and small-minded. That is why they created three separate branches of government, so one branch would not have unlimited power.

"The giant industries can no more be trusted to do the right thing than government can. These entities are not more trustworthy or smarter than we are. In summary, if Americans want better healthcare, they must overthrow the giants and take back responsibility for their own health."

Bruce rolled his eyes so only Frances could see, then wasted no time gathering up his books and leaving the room. Frances followed, giving Dr. Sampson only a quick nod as she walked past him.

Don sat there, towers crashing down all around him. Was he the only one who got it—who understood what Dr. Sampson was talking about? Or was he just getting carried away with the ramblings of an eccentric professor? If all this was true, what in the world was he going to do with his life and career?

"Don, are you all right?"

"Uh, yes sir," he replied, coming to his senses. Don had forgotten Dr. Sampson was still there. He decided to ask the question that had been burning in his brain ever since the night in the ER at Florence New American.

"Dr. Sampson, what do you know about the American Order of Alchemists?"

"Not much. I know they take themselves very seriously. They've been around a very long time, and even some faculty members at Florence College have been involved through the years. I have the sense they will employ just about any means to achieve their ends. And Don, their ends are probably not as noble as yours."

"Do you know anyone that could tell me more?"

"You could go back to see Dr. Chambers at the Preservation Society. Julia knows more about Florence College and its history than most anyone. In the meantime, don't go out of your way to make trouble for those boys unless you have a very good reason. Be careful, Don."

DON GATHERED his books and journal and went to the Sentinel after his classes finished for the day. He needed to get away. He needed to think.

Judith spotted him as soon as he walked through the door. "The back porch is all yours if you want it," she called out. "Want me to bring you a sandwich and a pot of coffee?"

"Yeah. That'd be great."

Don spread out his books on the back porch table. Why was everyone against Dr. Sampson? So what if he was eccentric? He was a good guide. He'd opened Don's eyes more than any teacher ever had, but when questioned by Lender and Hanley, he hadn't even acknowledged that.

Instead of standing up for Dr. Sampson, he had given fodder to those who were out to get him. Don had always been afraid of making waves, and probably with good reason. Look what happened when he jumped into the Bobby Webster case! In spite of that, Don felt he had to do something to defend Dr. Sampson. But what?

From the height of the Sentinel's back porch, Don stared at the massive New American Hospital complex on the far side of town. *I worked in the trenches for that giant!* How little good it had done.

Well, he was glad to be done with them. Hell, he might not work as a hospital test and drug pusher ever again. He had been naïve enough to think he worked for the patients. But hospitals made sure their payoff was first priority. Of course, the biggest take of all belonged to insurance companies, who could sign up healthy patients and reap a rich profit off the top. They'd have everyone working for them if they could. Damned if he was going to do it!

Don gazed out the window at the city far below. Florence was a medical town—he could see the entire medical-industrial complex laid out there in miniature. The insurance giant Anthem Blue Cross Blue Shield occupied the largest office building downtown. The Florence College campus at the base of the mountain was dominated by a brand new, ten-story, glass, chrome, and steel pharmacy school building financed by Big Pharma. Three more huge pharmaceutical buildings and a large LabCorp testing facility stood nearby in the College's new biotechnology research center on the edge of campus.

The titanic hospitals were the most impressive. Florence Medical Center next to the college and Florence New American Hospital near the outskirts dominated the skyline. Electric light in the early dusk illuminated them as if they were on the Las Vegas strip. Gleaming glass professional buildings, imaging centers, surgery centers, and other laboratory testing facilities surrounded each hospital, much like the cluster of neon- lit restaurants, entertainment complexes, and shopping malls in the orbit of a luxury casino resort.

Here were Dr. Sampson's four titans right before him—preying on the city of Florence! Don opened his journal to his diagram of healthcare hell and began to fill in the lower levels. The insurance, pharmacy, diagnostics, and hospital industries saved some lives. That couldn't be denied. But he had already accounted for that on the outpatient and hospital care levels. Now he wanted to consider the costs and benefits of their profit taking. Don poured through his health economics notes and totaled up the annual profits and payments to top corporate executives in each of these industries. He was astounded; the amounts were enormous.

How many lives were gained through the for-profit competition of these corporate giants? If there was real free market competition on quality and price, and corporations were rewarded for putting patients' interests first, then perhaps a few lives might be saved. But the corporate titans didn't compete on value, and they weren't rewarded for putting patients first. The health care market wasn't free and probably never could be. People who were sick couldn't comparison shop like people buying cars. So all that corporate profit and overhead benefitted no one! No one but the corporations.

Don carefully transcribed his final totals for each category into his version of Botticelli's map of hell, then sat back and scrutinized his work. Could it be? The more money that changed hands, the fewer lives were saved.

The U.S. spent nearly twice as much on hospital-based rescue care than on primary care, yet rescue care saved far fewer lives. Worst of all, huge portions of insurance, pharmacy, diagnostics, and hospital dollars were spent on nothing but hype. Maybe hospitals saved a few more lives than they lost. But that could never be said of the counterfeit care that generated the highest profits. Health plans that denied needed care, snake oil, and unnecessary tests, procedures, and surgeries all killed people and saved no one, and healthcare profiteers were raking in enormous sums for overseeing the whole sordid affair. Those who profited the most produced little health—instead, they profited from disease and death. The profits generated for CEOs and investors saved no lives. As things were, they cost lives, if anything. Fake care and profiteering killed thousands upon thousands of Americans year after year.

Don did some quick calculations. For the money spent on fraud and high profits in healthcare, Americans could hire ten million teachers! Which would do more good, maintaining exorbitant profits for powerful healthcare companies, or teaching our seventy million children to improve their own health? Sure, we want to drive innovation, but do we need corporate and federal kings to do the driving? Counting on greed to be the primary driver of good health care was obscene. Greed had its own end. He doodled a skull and crossbones in the bottom corner of his diagram.

Judith knocked on the door and brought in a pitcher of water. "By the way, Don, Bruce Markum was back about a week ago with his father and the president of Florence College. This time, Richard Townsend was with them! That son of a bitch hasn't been here since the clear-cutting started. After the way he pissed on our grandfathers' bargain, he has a lot of nerve to show his face here. Walked in like he owned the place. I'm not sure what they talked about, but I think it had something to do with Dr. Sampson. Oh, and I heard Townsend say something strange—he was joking about how his ancestors had grown vegetables, then timber, and now he was back to raising vegetables again. What do you think that was about, Don?"

"I don't know," Don replied. "But I'm going to find out."

32

Traitors to Family

Why do you mirror yourself in us for so long? If you would know
who are these two...they issued from one womb, and all Caina
thou may search and not find a shade more fit to be set in jelly.
DANTE ALIGHIERI, INFERNO 32, 54–60

THE TELEPHONE'S INCESSANT RING forced Don to abandon his books, which were spread all over the kitchen table. He welcomed the distraction. He'd been falling asleep anyway. He plopped down on the couch to answer the phone.

"Hello?"

"Don?" He recognized his father's voice, although it sounded unusually tentative.

"Yes, it's me." Don tried to conceal his surprise at hearing his father's voice. His mother had always been the one to call.

"Don, I need to tell you something important, something I've never told you before. Really, I've been meaning to tell you this for a long time, and like a lot of things, you know, well, I guess I just never got around to it..." His father's voice cracked.

Don couldn't believe it. This was uncharted territory. His father had never been one to reveal his feelings. Don tried to stop him, afraid of the welling emotion in his voice.

"Don't worry about it, Dad. There is nothing to tell."

"Yes there is, son! Yes, there is quite a bit to tell, and you need to know. So just shut up and listen. Damn, you are just like your mother! Give me a chance to say a few words."

He had Don's full attention now.

"I've been thinking about your professor—what's his name? Dr. Sampson? And I've got a bad feeling. A man like that makes some enemies, and no place can they be more heartless than a university. From what you told me, it sounds like you are getting into the thick of some vicious university politics. And you need to know how these things work. Fact is, I know. I may have been a pretty absent father..."

"But..."

"No, hear me out. I was an absent father, particularly in the early seventies in Boston, you know, when I was working on my Ph.D. Did your mother ever tell you why I left MIT without my degree?"

"She said you wanted to follow a new line of research back at Loyola in Chicago."

Don had never quite believed this. His parents had never seemed open to talk about it. He figured his father just couldn't make the grade at MIT.

"Well, as you may remember, I went to MIT in 1970 on a National Science Foundation faculty development grant to support my advanced training in molecular chemistry. It was the opportunity of a lifetime, to study in Cambridge at one of the best chemistry schools in the country. Loyola was glad to give me a prolonged sabbatical to work on my doctorate there—my tuition and salary were covered by the grant, and the program required me to return to Loyola for at least one year afterward. I was determined to make the most of it and threw myself into my studies with complete abandon. Nothing else mattered to me then.

"At MIT I worked harder than I had ever worked in my life. For my dissertation I wanted to develop an idea I'd been working on for years, a mathematical approach to predict the molecular structure of an enzyme or effector molecule based on simple characteristics of the enzyme receptor. The concept had broad applicability and the potential to drastically shorten the time to develop candidate drugs to target important biological receptors. At MIT I finally had time to develop my idea and take advanced organic chemistry and statistical modeling courses.

"I mostly kept the project to myself, because I wanted to refine it further before sharing it with my professors, but one of my project partners in the statistical modeling class became keenly interested in what I was doing. Ralph Braden was a chemistry and math major from Harvard and had graduated from Exeter Academy, one of the most prestigious prep schools in the Northeast. He was a Boston blue blood, but he went out of his way to be nice to me and praise my work.

"I was naïve, trusting, eager for friends in a new city, and thrilled to have someone to discuss my research with. We spent many days after class going over my equations in detail. We had long discussions about the key concepts, and I explained the difficult parts to him. In the process, I gained clarity and improved my organization.

"After the statistical modeling course that first year, I didn't see much more of Ralph. When I did, he was always in a hurry to get somewhere. I didn't make too much of it until I met with the head of the biochemical modeling group late in my second year. I wanted him to serve as the chair of my dissertation committee. I was confident about my equations by that time and eager for his endorsement.

"He spent a couple of minutes flipping through my figures and formulas, which were clearly laid out on fifty pages of graph and log scale paper. And then he said—and these were his exact words—'Mr. Newman, I am sure this is very fine work, but unfortunately I have seen this work before and will be unable to serve on your committee.'

"His words struck me like a physical blow to the gut. It was unbelievable! How could he have seen my work before? It was brand new. I had searched the scientific literature and I was sure no one had seen it before. No one except Ralph.

"It took me several months to ferret out the truth. Most people involved refused to talk to me, and only one of my former statistics professors would serve on my dissertation committee. All my professors and eventually most of the other students looked at me with suspicion and contempt.

"Ralph had played his cards well. Not only had he copied my work after each one of our sessions, he'd changed enough details to make it appear to be his original work. I think he convinced himself and rationalized in his own mind that it was. He made sure to engage all of the most knowledgeable professors for his dissertation committee early on, before I did.

"In my grievance hearing, Ralph admitted he got a couple of ideas from our conversations, but only rough and primitive ideas, not at all worked out scientifically. I distinctly remember he used the word 'primitive.' He thoroughly charmed them all with his sharp wit and erudition. Long before I even met any of them, he had them convinced he was a molecular organic chemistry prodigy.

"I think he was shocked I filed the grievance. He probably thought I wouldn't dare challenge him once I saw how well he had arranged things. It was obvious that with his powerful connections and careful cover-up of the crime, I could not possibly win. But people have a point past which you cannot push them, where they will sacrifice everything before they concede. And that was my point.

"One day before the hearing, I caught up with him jogging along a path by the Charles River. I grabbed him by the arm and said, 'How could you copy my work and claim it as your own?' And you know what he told me? He said, '*Your* work? What the hell are you talking about? Just because you happened upon a couple of good ideas means nothing. You had no idea what to do with them. What were you going to do? Go back to your precious little Loyola and share them with your pitiful students? Don't be ridiculous. Nothing good comes out of Chicago.'

"I knew everyone would see it his way at the hearing. And they did. He was calm and articulate, as were the many professors who spoke on his behalf. They all said what a shame it was things had come to this impasse and placed the blame squarely at my feet. I tried my best to make my case, brought two boxes of notes dating back five years showing the progress of my idea. But—as the chairman of the hearing pointed out—all those documents could have been copied and backdated.

"In his defense, Ralph told them he was embarrassed to admit it, but he had stupidly shared his detailed notes with me, out of charity. He said I had obviously plagiarized his work and backdated it to make it look like my own. He didn't give an inch. How else could an assistant professor from a minor Chicago university doing remedial education at MIT—how could a nigger, he implied—possibly come up with such a major contribution?"

Don cringed at his father's use of the N-word. He had never heard him say it before. He had never known him to lose his cool that way, but by this point in the story, his father was raging mad from reliving the memory of what had happened so many years ago, and Don wasn't about to interrupt him.

"My statistics professor knew my work and tried to defend me, but of course the rest of them believed Ralph. The verdict was fast. They ruled the physical evidence was equivocal, and since neither party could clearly establish prior claim to the research, they prohibited either of us from using it for a doctoral dissertation.

"Ralph pretended to be outraged, but I could tell he was also relieved. His reputation was preserved, and now he had a bevy of professors more eager than ever to assist him.

"I was devastated. This was my work night and day for five years— the foundation on which I planned to publish and establish my career. And just like that, the fruits of my hard work were stolen. I decided not to stay at MIT; we packed up and headed for home. At least at Loyola in Chicago the prejudice was not so bad. Nowhere before or since did I ever experience such terrible prejudice as I did in Boston, not even in the Deep South.

"They have a saying: in academic politics, the fights are so vicious because the stakes are so low. I don't know if that's true, because the stakes were high for me, but I do know academic politics can be harsh. A university should be like a family to its faculty, just as a corporation should be for its employees. But things aren't always the way they should be.

"Be careful, Don. Try not to get caught in the crossfire, but if you believe in your Dr. Sampson, then you stick by him. You're a man now. He may need your help."

Don tossed and turned all night, trying to process this new information. The very chapter of his father's life he thought demonstrated his weakness of character was actually the one where, against all odds, he had stood up against prejudice and risked everything for the truth. Like the MIT professors, Don had misjudged and underestimated him. His own father. Without knowing anything, Don had sided with the Brahmin traitor.

AT SIX Don drug himself out of bed, took a shower, and brewed a large pot of espresso like his mother used to make. He drank several cups of the concentrated black coffee and scanned the morning's *Florence Herald*.

There was still no news regarding Bobby Webster. He was sure the hospital and Lender's office must have reported it by now, and Florence was a pretty small town. Why wasn't it in the paper? No investigator had called him for information. It was as if it had never happened. The whole thing left Don with a queasy feeling in his stomach.

In seminar, Bruce appeared even more unsettled than Don was. Bruce was always groomed and immaculate, but on this day he looked like he had run to class. One side of his blue oxford shirt was untucked and the armpits were dark with sweat. Tiny beads glistened on his forehead, and a single drop leaked from his sideburn alongside his right ear. His brow was furrowed.

What could be on Bruce's mind? Don's own anxiety escalated. He pinched the knot on his nose and tried to shake the gut feeling that unseen actions were compounding and hurtling them all toward some predetermined catastrophe.

Frances flashed Don a smile, distracting him from his dark thoughts. "Don, did you hear? The Medicare Quality Improvement bill is up for a vote this afternoon. A petition for cloture was filed last Friday and yesterday they did the quorum call. Senator Josten presented the petition himself."

"What's cloture?" Don asked. He had no idea what she was talking about.

Frances was only too happy to fill him in. "Whenever senators want to push a bill to conclusion, they can petition for cloture. It's a French parliamentary device—sometimes called a closure or guillotine petition—used to cut off debate on a bill. Humphrey used it to end the longest continuous debate in Senate history, fifty-seven days of filibuster over the Civil Rights Act of 1964. Josten probably thinks he has enough votes to pass our bill and wants to move on with it. The vote on the cloture petition looked good. They got their three-fifths majority, and we figure"—she glanced at Dr. Sampson—"that's pretty much how the final vote will go tomorrow. Good news, huh?"

Dr. Sampson cleared his throat. "Very good," he said. "Now, let's begin. Remember our first seminar of the year, about how the first city was born of human need? Cities establish institutions to help meet the needs of their citizens. Each of the titan industries we discussed last week—Insurance, Pharmacy, Diagnostics, and Hospital—also began by answering real community needs. Those industries all began because people wanted their services and were willing to pay.

"The problem arises when industries begin to exist only for themselves. Can loyalty to a corporation induce its executives and employees to betray the people their business was established to serve? Dr. Newman?"

"Well, some CEOs would sell bad healthcare to their own mothers. Their identities get so wrapped up in the corporation they become cheerleaders for the product and blind to the downside. Drug reps sell their parents on dangerous new drugs for untested indications, hospital workers hospitalize family members for conditions treated more safely at home, and engineers recommend unnecessary high-radiation CT scans and expensive MRIs because they're proud of their machines. They don't even realize they're betraying their family members, but they are."

"Totally," Frances said. "One of the most common examples is when a family puts an elderly parent in a nursing home against his or her will. We see it all the time, where a corporate nursing home or hospital conspires against a helpless elderly person for profit."

"I can't count the number of people I've seen barely alive," said Don, "chained to breathing machines and feeding tubes they never wanted. But it's often because families insist we do everything possible. They demand ICU care for parents with terminal illnesses, even when a parent requested to never be put on life support."

"Dr. Sampson," said Bruce, "I know you like to pin the problems on evil corporations and bad doctors, but Frances and Don have a point. It's consumers demanding the products, not the other way around. Dr. Walter Freeman didn't go out to get Johnny Doe. It was the stepmother who begged, pleaded, and demanded a frontal lobotomy for Johnny because she couldn't handle him. It's easy to blame others, but don't people have to take some responsibility for themselves and their own families?"

"It does seem like corporations just sell what people want," Don said. "People want drugs for every illness, insurance against every ill, tests for every possible condition, and hospitals like resort hotels. They want to give birth in suburban hospitals with private deluxe birthing suites, room service, and marble lobbies, but they don't think to question the quality of care."

"And that," said Bruce, his agitation visibly increasing, "is exactly what New American Healthcare provides, the kind of hospital people want: clean, close to home, great room service. You can hardly blame us for giving people what they want."

Bobby Webster was in a New American hospital. Had his parents seen the elegant marble lobby and just assumed he had received the best possible care?

"What about the patient you tried to save at New American?" Dr. Sampson spoke as if reading Don's mind. "Was he treated the way he would have wanted?"

"Wait a minute!" Bruce cried. "Are you implying our hospital is responsible for what those two crappy doctors did?"

"You have to look to hospital leadership..." Don started to answer.

Dr. Sampson interrupted. "Over the last seven months, you've asked who the capo of the healthcare mafia is. Is there a big boss in a dark glass tower reigning over the health care system? Here's a better question: is there anyone to lead us in the right direction, or will everyone sacrifice health for power, wealth, and influence? Who can step up and lead effective healthcare change?"

No one spoke.

"You—know—the—answer!" Dr. Sampson's fist pounded the table with each word. "*You* are as close to a capo as there is. The leader of the future is *you*! *You* can decide the future of healthcare. *You* can be its conscience. *You* have the power you wanted. *You* have connections with the industries moving healthcare's future. It is up to *you*." Dr. Sampson looked directly at Bruce.

Bruce's reply was almost desperate. "What would you have me do Dr. Sampson—promote corporate regulation to my own family's financial detriment? That's not fair! I'm just trying to swim with the tide and keep my head above water. It's much bigger than me. I can't control it."

Dr. Sampson persisted, "Ah, but if you stand up, the tide will have to notice. Or will you just ride the waves?"

"Dammit, Sampson," Bruce exploded, "you want me to be a traitor to my own family!"

Sampson replied calmly, "No, Bruce. What you've got to decide is who your family really is."

"Oh, come on now. That's ridiculous! Listen, if there's a real traitor it's the American public. They want everything for nothing. They think they have a 'right' to this and a 'right' to that, even if they haven't earned it. They come to us all hours of the day and night and expect us to do unbelievable things. Here's an example for you. I told a woman her husband had died in surgery from a massive heart attack and she said, 'Couldn't you just transplant another heart?' As if we kept extra hearts in the storage closet! Is it any surprise we perform CPR on brain-dead people?

"And people have no concept of what things cost. Why should they care? They don't have to pay. All they have to do is show up in the ER, and they're entitled to whatever they want. Ask for payment and they get upset. Pay for healthcare? How? They have no savings! They've made no preparations for sickness or disability. They've given no consideration to what their family needs. No thought for family, only themselves. Just gimme, gimme, gimme, like babies without any discipline or concern for others. The government will take care of it, right?

"Just look at disability fraud. How come we haven't talked about that? A third or more of people on disability could work, but instead they spend their time and energy gaming the system, faking sickness and persuading doctors to prescribe narcotics they can resell on the street. Worst of all, they don't even appreciate the sustenance and support they get for free. Hell, honest workers are putting in fifty, sixty, or seventy hours a week, and paying nearly half what they make in taxes, so these bums can lay around, collect a check, and mooch off of people who work for a living. And the bums aren't just ungrateful—they downright hate the rich and castigate *them* for greed.

"Healthcare is only part of it. They buy the wrong things, eat the wrong things, believe the wrong things, admire and hate the wrong things. It's not like there are a bunch of medical bad guys. You want traitors? Look around! You don't have to look very far to find the real traitors to your family of man."

Bruce's eyes darted from Frances to Don, and last to Dr. Sampson, but he couldn't hold Dr. Sampson's steady gaze. "I think I'm done here," he mumbled. He grabbed up his books and stalked out.

Dr. Sampson looked from Don to Frances. "Well," he said sadly, "I guess we are done for today. Class dismissed. I hope you will check on your friend."

So they did. Frances went to Bruce's apartment while Don checked the library and The Down Under. They met back at Frances's apartment and decided to drive up to the Sentinel Bar and Grill. They took separate cars, but arrived at the same time and walked in together.

There was Bruce, sitting alone at the end of the bar, drinking his third Scotch on the rocks. He did not appear surprised to see them.

"Listen, sweetheart," he said to Frances, "you really should think about coming to work for us. Ditch this damn health system science program. With your background in nursing and business, you'd be able to write your own ticket. Hell, you could even work for us, too, Don. You know we're an integrated operation now."

Don shrugged and said nothing. Bruce's double meaning was not lost on him. He wondered if Frances had caught it.

"Really, between the three of us, we could drive the future of healthcare."

"You're going to come back to the seminar, aren't you?" Don asked.

"Are you fucking kidding me?" Bruce spat. "You want me to sit obediently in the Church of Sampson and listen to him pontificate? No way in hell. You can worship at his feet, but don't expect me to."

"No one's asking you to worship, or even to agree with him," said Frances. "We just want you to be there with us to the end of the semester." She tried to joke, "You know we can't face Dr. Sampson alone."

"Forget it. That pompous asshole doesn't have a clue about how the real world operates." Bruce leveled his gaze at Don. "You really like him, don't you?"

"Well, not especially," Don lied, "I mean, he can be a little pompous."

"Well, I don't know about you," Bruce continued, "but I'm not about to waste any more of my valuable time."

Frances firmly stated the obvious. "But Bruce, you'll get an incomplete for the seminar, and you need the seminar credit to finish the Health System Science Program."

"Damn the Health System Science Program!"

"Oh, you can't be thinking of quitting," Frances appealed.

"Well, I certainly can't imagine continuing to waste my time with such juvenile crap. I've got better things to do."

"Well, you know," Frances pointed out, "some people are saying Sampson's course and his leadership of the whole program are in trouble. I heard something about a high-level college review."

"I say it's about time. Sampson's focus is outmoded and he needs to work with industry more. Maybe it's time for the old dinosaur to be replaced." Bruce grinned. "Don't you think so too, Don?"

Bruce's question and smile caught Don off guard. He heard himself saying, "Well, maybe if we just had a combination of professors..."

Don stopped himself there but it was too late. He felt so ashamed. He just couldn't come up with the words to defend Dr. Sampson in the face of Bruce's smug derision. He felt sick inside and was suddenly desperate to leave.

"Listen, I've got to go," he said. "I'm going to the library to check up on the results of the legislative session for Dr. Sampson's Medicare proposal. Frances, do you want to come along to help out?"

"Sure," she smiled. "I have some research to do in the library as well. I'll follow you down in a little bit. Why don't you go ahead without me? I'll catch up."

"Don, I wouldn't worry too much about that legislation if I were you," Bruce said. "No way it could really change things, anyway."

Don drove back down into Florence and made his way to the glass room at the library. He was relieved to get away from Bruce's vitriol and eager to watch the launch of a new day in health care.

Dr. Sampson's Medicare Quality Improvement Act would attack medical errors nationwide for the first time— and save thousands of lives! It was the first step toward allowing Medicare to contract directly with provider groups and reward them for lowering costs by keeping people healthy and out of the hospital. Dr. Sampson was the prophet of a new age in health care and his work was about to pay off. Once his Medicare legislation passed, Dr. Sampson would finally be recognized for his genius in healthcare policy. No way did Don want to miss it.

He was able to find a live video feed from C-SPAN on the computer—the way Frances had shown him—and stayed at the library to watch the legislative sessions for the bill. The feed came directly from the Senate and a transcription of the proceedings rolled across the bottom of the screen in real time. The speaker called off the votes one by one, state by state.

Don couldn't stand the suspense; the session was taking far longer than he expected. As the roll call progressed he began to worry. The votes didn't seem quite right. Hadn't Dr. Sampson been promised support by some of those representatives? Hadn't Senator Josten reassured them Dr. Sampson's proposal would move forward, that it was clearly in the public interest and would demand bipartisan support?

By the time Senator Josten finally stood up to announce his vote, Don's unease had grown to a fever pitch. The vote was too close for comfort.

'Nay,' said Senator Josten.

Don looked at the streaming text on the bottom of screen. It matched the video. *Nay.*

Nay? How could this be? Don's heart sank. He thought of Dr. Sampson— was he watching this?

The president pro tempore announced the bill would be referred back to the Senate Health, Education, Labor, and Pensions Committee for further consideration. He advised the committee to take note of the common view of the senators and their constituents that a Medicare pharmaceutical benefit should be their first priority. Worst of all, he said the provision for expanded capability for Medicare to contract directly with provider groups for coordinated care should be dropped in favor of a simple expansion of the existing Medicare Choice plan, to encourage more private insurer participation in Medicare.

So that was it. All Dr. Sampson had shown them that was right and good was lost. Dr. Sampson was disgraced. Don's path forward was ruined, and he saw the hopeless waste would continue. Business as usual.

The library closed at midnight; Frances never came. Don walked out the front doors alone and gazed up through the skeletal branches of the old oaks lining his path from the library through the quadrangle. The sky was pitch black, a perfect reflection of the dark void he felt inside.

He wondered where Frances was. Sadly, he was pretty sure he knew.

33

Traitors to Country

'Oh,' I said to him, 'then art thou dead already?' And he to me:
'...know that as soon as a soul betrays as I did, its body is taken from it by a devil,
who controls it henceforth until its full time comes round.
The soul falls headlong into this tank here...
DANTE ALIGHIERI, INFERNO 33, 121–133

SPRING BREAK PROMISED to be bitter cold. A hyperborean wind had blown in and turned all the wet snow to solid ice, and the weather forecast predicted more of the same for the rest of the week. By Friday night, most students and faculty had abandoned Florence for warmer climes, but Don had stayed in town. Nowhere to go, at least not on his budget. On the off chance Frances might have stuck around as well, Don left her a message to call him during the break.

Don tossed and turned on the lumpy mattress in his cold apartment, lamenting the defeat of Dr. Sampson's bill but mostly fretting about Frances. He didn't really expect her to call. She was probably at Bruce's place—if she was in town at all. Don told himself he was over Frances, but he couldn't stop thinking about what the two of them might be up to.

I hate that bastard. The jerk's just using her. He's probably using her right now. *Damn that silver spoon-sucking son of a bitch.*

Venomous thoughts swirled in his mind, coursed through his veins, cooled his heart. Frances had almost been his. She was still his friend—she could've at least called to commiserate with him over the failure of Dr. Sampson's bill. Why did Senator Josten submarine it? How could Congress disregard hundreds of thousands of deaths caused by preventable medical errors? Why pass up an opportunity to save money and lives at the same time? Did they want to keep everyone in the dark?

Of course, Bruce, Frances, and Don all knew the answers to these questions now. Dr. Sampson had made sure of that. The industry lobbyists wining and dining in the lush Willard Hotel made a nice living influencing legislators, maintaining the status quo, and keeping the public ignorant. Of course they want people in the dark! Why would industry giants want to uncover their own scam?

Since the Institute of Medicine released *To Err Is Human* just two years ago, over six pieces of legislation had been introduced in Congress to address the horrendous problem of preventable medical errors, but none had passed. Not one single piece of legislation passed in either the 106th or 107th Congress to reduce errors or improve quality.

And now, the Medicare Quality Improvement Act—the country's best chance for improving the U.S. healthcare system—had been defeated. At the same time, the Medicare prescription drug benefit—a huge entitlement to the pharmaceutical giants but a boondoggle for the American taxpayers—was moving forward.

Don's wrath intensified as he considered the wastefulness, the unjustness of it all. Cold fury settled deep in his bones.

There was nothing he could do.

He turned the radio on in hopes it might lull him to sleep, but it was no use. He worried all night about one thing or another—the arrogance and greed of those in power, his failure to win Frances, his mounting student loans, his moonlighting debacle, the death of his mother, and the tragic death of Bobby Webster—and early Saturday morning just before light, Don was still awake and still troubled over his realization that in spite of his desire and his training, he was impotent in the face of all of it.

There was nothing he could do.

A song began on the radio with the rhythmic ring of an old-fashioned cash register bell, followed by clinking coins falling in the drawer, then a walking bass line rose and fell with the beat. A pulsing, driving guitar riff started on the offbeat.

Money!...Get a job.

Yeah, right. Well, he had certainly blown that one, hadn't he? He was on a path to nowhere. Who would ever pay him to be an "agent for healthcare change." What a joke!

There was nothing he could do.

Hell, he didn't even remember the lyrics to this song he had heard dozens and dozens of times. All he could hear through the booming bass was the screaming refrain, *Money!* Those making the money made the rules, and the last thing they wanted was change.

Wait a minute...money! That was it! Dr. Sampson always said to follow the money. Follow the money!

Don jumped out of bed, threw on his clothes, grabbed the internet phone and modem he had bought to make free long distance calls, and headed out the door. The Florence College library was hardwired into the backbone of the internet. That would speed his work, and he had a lot of work to do. He grabbed a large to-go coffee at The Down Under on his way and smuggled it into the library under his coat. Finding a cubicle with an internet connection in a secluded corner of the library's ground floor, he hooked up his laptop and began to search the web with maniacal intensity.

First, he downloaded the voting records for Dr. Sampson's Medicare legislation. Why had the senators supporting the proposal withdrawn their support at the last minute? The key senators of Josten's party had seemed supportive of it when they voted for cloture—the presumption was they voted to cut short the debate because they were ready to pass the bill. The news accounts confirmed it; everyone thought the Medicare Quality Improvement Act was a done deal. What had happened to change that? Don aimed to find out.

Don catalogued the results of the first vote. Sure enough, those who voted for cloture were pretty much the same ones the newspapers said were in favor of the act. Don reviewed the final roll call vote and charted how each senator voted on the bill. Seventeen senators had changed their votes. Most of them were from Josten's party or closely aligned with him.

Don figured he'd never find streaming video of the Senate proceedings but decided to search anyway. As luck would have it, a month earlier the majority leader had ordered that cameras in the Senate broadcast a wide-angle view. It was an effort to embarrass the minority party, whose senators were skipping most of the majority led sessions. For a brief moment in time, Senate proceedings were transparent and open, an unintended byproduct of a political squabble. It was a goldmine. Don was a fly on the wall of the Senate chamber. He could see everything!

Maybe the video would reveal who had defeated the good legislation. Don scrutinized the preparatory speeches and correlated them with simultaneous activity on the Senate floor. Using a seating chart he found online, he concentrated on those senators whose votes had changed and zoomed in on them until their images began to distort.

The work was painstaking. The hours ticked by and Don was so immersed in his quest he lost track of time. He took only a short break to get a bite to eat sometime mid-afternoon. Late that night, Don still hadn't found anything concrete, but he had a feeling he was missing something.

One moving head amidst the legion of listless senators caught Don's eye. Senator Josten. His profile was eerily similar to the painting he had seen in Josten's office a few weeks earlier. Of course, Senator Josten was the key. How could Don have missed what was right before his eyes all along? During his colleagues' speeches in support of Dr. Sampson's bill, Senator Josten's head swiveled from side-to-side like a bobble-head doll.

Don zoomed in and could plainly see Josten's face grimacing and contorting in open contempt. From Josten's seat on the second row, his smirks and sneers would have been obvious to the speakers and his Senate colleagues. The demeanor of one junior senator from Josten's party plummeted from confidence to confusion during his speech in support of Dr. Sampson's bill. It was obvious he realized midstream he was seriously off-message.

Don had to leave the library when it closed at two in the morning, but he was back when it opened the next morning at eight. He found more video of the Senate floor from the day of the bill's defeat and discovered that during breaks in the debate—sometimes during the debate itself—Senator Josten managed to pay visits to at least nine of the seventeen senators whose votes had changed. Josten was caught on camera whispering a word, giving a pat on the shoulder, leaning over a desk and pressing a point, or—in the case of the ill-advised junior senator after his speech in support of the Medicare Quality Improvement Act—shaking a finger right in the young senator's face.

On Monday, Don investigated the schedules of the other senators who had changed their votes. Something had to have happened between the first and second votes, and he wanted to know what it was. He started firing off emails to senators' offices, explaining he was a student doing research on the Senate lawmaking process and wanted to find out what a typical day was like for a senator. He asked to see their schedules for a two-day period, specifically Tuesday and Wednesday of the past week, including everyone with whom the senators met, the subject of the meeting, and how they spent their time.

Many staff members were remarkably forthcoming. Several responded the same day with everything he'd requested. If Don didn't get a response he telephoned, and if he got through to a staff person with access to the senator's calendar, he scribbled down whatever information they gave him. By the end of spring break week, Don was finally getting somewhere.

At least eight of the flip-floppers attended constituent breakfasts on the morning of the final vote, and Don obtained the attendee lists for three breakfasts. Representatives of AARP and drug company executives representing PhRMA attended all three. And who were the two biggest proponents of a Medicare pharmaceutical benefit? PhRMA and AARP.

In addition, at least half a dozen flip-floppers received AARP and PhRMA lobbyists in their offices that week. On the day of the vote, several met with top executives of AARP and America's Health Insurance Plans. And earlier that week, many of the mercurial senators conferred with the heads of the Federation of American Hospitals, the American Hospital Association, and the Pharmaceutical Care Management Association—the same players pushing to reframe the debate around a Medicare pharmaceutical benefit.

But that didn't tell the whole story. Something was missing. They didn't need to kill Dr. Sampson's quality legislation to build support for a Medicare pharmaceutical benefit. What else was going on? Don studied the data all weekend, searching for a pattern.

Monday morning he skipped class and tried one more time to get the remaining schedules for the vote-changing senators. Some staffers were still reluctant to give away much detail and a couple of offices gave him nothing at all, but he managed to gather enough information to cross-reference most of their calendars.

Don spread out his notes to look for patterns. Five leading senators in health-care had been visited by someone named John Baronoff in the two days leading up to the roll call. A quick web search showed Baronoff was one of the highest paid lobbyists in Washington. The Baronoff and Colleagues offices filled a whole building on the best block of K Street. It was rumored everyone in Washington owed him a favor. The question was, who hired him, and why?

"If you treat people nicely you will be amazed by what they will tell you." Don whispered this maxim of his mother's to bolster his courage, took a deep breath, and made his first call to Senator Josten's office. Don remembered the name of Josten's personal secretary from their visit, so when the staff person answered the phone, he asked for Sharon Clifton. He was put right through.

Don reminded Ms. Clifton who he was and explained he was still working on his healthcare legislation research. To his surprise, she seemed interested, pleasant, and unrushed, so he took his time before popping the big question.

After several minutes of general questions, Don went for it. "I'm trying to identify the most important voices in healthcare policy, the people who influence the workings of healthcare legislation. I know John Baronoff is important. Can you tell me when he last visited with Senator Josten?"

Don held his breath, but she didn't hesitate.

"Oh, he was just here, week before last."

Don could barely ask his follow-up question. "Can you tell me who he was representing?"

"No," she answered, "no, I can't really say. But you are right. He is one of the people who really influences healthcare policy."

Don thanked her, hung up the phone, and sat still for five minutes to calm his pounding heart. He pulled up the annual report for Baronoff and Colleagues on the web.

The report made it clear the firm was heavily involved in healthcare but didn't identify actual clients. A website called Sourcewatch indicated they worked with the Association for Health Insurance Plans, the Federation of American Hospitals, and the American Hospital Association Hospitals, but nothing more specific. There was one more call he needed to make.

Don took another deep breath, picked up the phone, and dialed Baronoff and Colleagues. The operator put him through to John Baronoff's assistant.

"Hello, I'm a graduate student at Florence College—working with Senator Josten's office on health policy issues? I'm researching the most influential people in healthcare policy, and they referred me to you. Could you tell me a bit about how your firm approaches health policy issues of concern to your clients?"

Baronoff's assistant gave her standard answer. She was brusque, but her voice was pleasant enough.

Don feigned interest and asked a couple of general follow-up questions about their various clients. He thanked her profusely and then, shifting gears, threw out his main question as if it were an afterthought.

"Oh, darn. I forgot my notes from Senator Josten's office. Could you remind me on whose behalf Mr. Baronoff visited the senator's office a week ago Thursday?"

"New American Healthcare, of course. Markum Industries, their parent company, is undoubtedly our most important healthcare client."

Don croaked a thank you as his heart filled his throat. His hand shook as he returned the phone's handset to its cradle. He was stunned, yet down deep he'd long suspected Bruce was somehow at the root of all this.

The bastard! So that was why Bruce stayed back to talk to Josten—he was giving him the Markum bottom line. Obviously, he and his father had been plotting the bill's defeat behind Dr. Sampson's back all along. What a backstabbing bastard! How could he do that to Dr. Sampson? How could he do that to all of them?

Don slammed his fist down on the table so hard his books and phone jumped into the air on the recoil. The sound reverberated off the glass walls of the study carrel. *Damn it!* He slammed his fist down on the table again. Dr. Sampson had been working for this bill—for this moment—for years, and now the moment was gone. The battle was over. Bruce and his father's cabal had won.

There was nothing to do. Defeated, Don sank back in his seat and covered his face in his hands. He rubbed the small bump on the bridge of his nose. Beaten! It wasn't right. Against these organized swindlers and their minions, Dr. Sampson never stood a chance.

The next day Don dragged himself out of bed and made one more trip to the library. He had one last link to investigate. Why had Richard Townsend been at the Sentinel Bar and Grill with Bruce's father and President Lender?

Don descended the staircase to the library basement, where the Florence College Historical Archive was housed. A tiny woman at a massive desk looked up, her bright, expectant eyes revealing surprise at the appearance of a visitor. The placard on the desk identified her as Mrs. Sutton.

He told Mrs. Sutton he was interested in the Townsend family and she led him into the stacks, slowly shuffling by shelves upon shelves of leather-bound books and yellowed documents. She seemed older than the bindings of the ancient books surrounding her. She was stooped, white-haired, and weighed no more than a hundred pounds. The skin of her face was soft, brown-spotted, and etched with deep wrinkles.

"Of course, the Townsend family is one of the most important and influential families in the history of New Hampshire, so the problem won't be finding too little information," she cackled, "it will be finding too much." She bent down near the back of the stacks, slid a large book off the lowest shelf, and handed it to Don. "Here is a good summary of the history of the Townsends in New Hampshire. Would you carry it?"

Don nodded and took the book. It was surprisingly heavy.

"Follow me." She led Don back through the stacks to a large oak table. "Sit here," she commanded.

Don sat there reading while Mrs. Sutton brought him one document after another. She had no one else to help and gave his project her complete attention for the rest of the morning.

The Townsends were an old New Hampshire family, one of the earliest white families in New Hampshire. The first Richard Townsend helped found Portsmouth in 1623 and the family played a leading role in the shipping industry there. They traded in everything most desirable in England and the New World at that time, including timber from New Hampshire, sugar from the West Indies, and very likely, slaves from Africa.

Through their connection with John Wentworth, the first magistrate of New Hampshire, they obtained some of the first and largest land grants in the colony. The largest land grant was in the area of Grafton County, where they cut and sold timber. When food prices rose during the time of the Revolutionary War, they put almost all the land under cultivation, growing wheat and corn in their fields and grinding it in their gristmills.

"This may interest you, Dr. Newman," Mrs. Sutton laid a large folio on the table and pulled out a stack of paper. She turned the pages gently, revealing sheets of old yellowed newspaper interlaced with acid-free sheets.

The first page was titled *Hampshire Gazette*, May 1, 1778. She turned to the next page. "Here is what I wanted to show you." She pointed to a yellowed ad in the far left column.

> *To be Sold at Public Vendue, At the House of Mr. Roger Townsend, Planter in Florence, on Wednesday the Seventh Day of May current, at Six of the Clock Afternoon, Three Negro Men and a Boy: The Conditions of Sale will be in Cash, or good Merchandisable Boards.*

Seeing those words made the hairs on the back of Don's neck stand up. Not only had the Townsends owned slaves, they had sold them, too. For the short period when wheat and corn prices were high, the Townsend farms must have been quite profitable.

Don thanked Mrs. Sutton and returned to his secluded cubicle on the ground floor. He pulled out his computer and went back online.

Townsend Timber Company popped right up, but there was little to learn there. On a lark he typed in *Canaan Manor Nursing Home*, since Townsend had been connected with the nursing home battle. From its website he navigated to the parent company, Elder Residence and Rehabilitation Services. According to its website, it owned almost a third of the nursing homes in New Hampshire and had facilities throughout the United States, making it the fourth largest nursing home operator in the country. Don downloaded their annual report and scanned through it, not expecting to find much. He was about to give up and go home when he saw the missing puzzle piece.

Near the end of the report, at the top of the list of the Board of Directors, was *Richard P. Townsend, Founder and Chairman*. Also on the list was *C. Hugh Lender, M.D.*

The president of Florence College was serving on the Board of Elder Residence and Rehabilitation, and likely for a pretty penny as well! That might explain why he was out to get Dr. Sampson. And no wonder Townsend had attended the town meeting where the big nursing homes defeated Dr. Sampson and put the care homes—like the one caring for Judith's grandfather—out of business in New Hampshire.

Don dug further. Dr. Sampson had mentioned that the president of the American Nursing Home Association had attended the town meeting, so he pulled up the ANHA website. ANHA was celebrating a tremendously successful year. In state after state, regulations were being put into place to benefit their members and supposedly their patients. Elder Residence and Rehabilitation Services was listed as a gold-level contributor. Don typed in the company's ticker symbol ERR.

Sure enough, their strategy was paying off. Since new regulations against care homes had passed in half the states, ERR's stock had soared, nearly doubling in three years. Townsend had returned to growing vegetables all right, only now the profit wasn't in corn, it was in nursing home patients like Sibyl Bellamy, kept alive in a vegetative state with feeding tubes and IVs.

In his mind's eye, Don saw Sibyl in vivid detail—strapped to her bed, the pool of liquid stool in her crotch, screaming and straining against the leather restraining straps, her wide, accusing eyes staring him down. He could smell the urine, blood, and feces she was helpless to control. Don shook his head and tried to erase the unwanted image from his mind.

He went to the Florence College website and clicked on *Giving*. Up popped an announcement about a two hundred million dollar fundraising campaign,

Investing in Healthcare Excellence. Don clicked on *Campaign Leadership.* They were all there.

Richard P. Townsend and Bruce D. Markum were co-chairs. Also listed was Frank A. Pan. Under *Governance,* Don found the board of trustees, consisting of the college president, the Governor of New Hampshire, and eight others, including Markum, Townsend, and The Honorable Senator Morris P. Josten.

My God—they're all in cahoots to remake the college to suit their business interests! But how are they all connected with Florence College? Why are they so interested in what goes on here? Could they all be members of the Alchemists?

Don shivered, remembering the feel of Bobby Webster's ice-cold body. What if they were all behind a cover-up? It made sense—it was a New American hospital. And Robert Townsend II was the evasive pack leader that brought Bobby to the hospital.

On a hunch, Don checked the Florence College alumni site. His student ID and password allowed him access to the alumni registry. He had to search it a year at a time, so he started with 1970 and worked backward. He hit the jackpot when he reached the 1960s.

One by one, year by year, Don found them all: Townsend in 1969, Pan in '64, Markum in '62, Josten in '59, and Lender in '52. They were all alums, and Don would bet his last dollar they were all Alchemists, too.

It all hit Don like a gut-punch to the stomach. Don had trusted President Lender to handle the whole Alchemist hazing incident! He'd dumped it on Lender—an Alchemist himself—and washed his hands of further responsibility.

Don went back down to the basement and found Mrs. Sutton hunched over her desk, examining an old letter with a magnifying glass.

She looked up and smiled. "Yes, Dr. Newman?"

"One more thing," he ventured, "do you know anything about the Alchemists?"

She gave him a curious look.

"I heard a strange rumor. I mean, is there some sort of secret group or something by that name?

"Ah, yes. The Alchemists. People have been wondering about them for a long time. To the best of my memory, the name first cropped up around 1614, when the *Fama Fraternitas* was published in Germany. Through the years a lot of people have asked me for that book."

"What is it about?"

"Well, according to the *Fama,* a secret brotherhood of alchemists called the Rosicrucians was poised to transform the world. Christian Rosenkreutz started the order and dedicated it to curing the sick, regardless of their ability to pay. According to the legend, after Rosenkreutz's death, his body was buried in a crypt hidden deep in the earth. His followers were instructed to *Visita Interiora*

Terrae Rectificando Invenies Occultum Lapidem. It means 'Visit the Inner Earth. Rectifying, You will Find the Hidden Stone.'"

Don was startled that Mrs. Sutton quoted from memory. Her eyes intensely locked on his, as if the old message were meant for him alone.

"They were searching for the philosophers' stone that could turn iron to gold and give the body eternal life. Critics say his followers became obsessed about finding the stone and forgot their ancient duty to the sick, but who knows? We have the book here if you want to see it."

Don shook his head.

"Oh, I see...you're interested in something a bit more contemporary and close to home. Well, I'm afraid I can't help you there."

The disappointment on Don's face must have been obvious.

"However...by any chance, do you know Dr. Julia Chambers, the curator of the historical society downtown?" she asked.

He nodded. "We met once."

"Well," she said, her eyes twinkling, "I seem to remember Dr. Chambers was doing some research on the Alchemists; I think she found some documents from around here. Something we probably need to get a copy of in the archives. You should talk to her."

At that moment, Mrs. Sutton winked. At least, Don thought she winked. It happened so fast—and he was so snow-blind from staring at the screen of his computer all day—he wasn't sure. He watched her closely and waited for her to say something more, but the old lady just sat there with a hint of a smile on her face.

THE REST OF THE WEEK Don dragged himself from class to class, try-ing to keep up appearances. He should have thought better of it, knowing how smitten Frances was with Bruce now, but he was dying to catch her alone and tell her what he'd discovered about Markum Industries and the leadership of the college. Thursday after class, he finally caught up with her outside The Down Under.

She was in a hurry and didn't look her usual best. The twisted tresses of her long hair looked dull, and her eyes had dark circles under them. Something was clearly weighing on her mind.

Don was desperate to share what he had learned, but Frances never gave him a chance. When he began to reveal what he knew about the real reasons for the failure of the Medicare legislation and who was behind it, she exploded. Her censure stung him to the quick.

"Don, when are you going to come out of your dream world? You are so unrealistic. Haven't you heard anything Sampson has said? There is not a conspiracy against good health care. It's about time you learned to work with industries, not against them. How do you ever expect to get a job?" She stormed off.

Don stood there for a moment, stunned, then recovered himself and ran to catch up with her.

Frances glanced back over her shoulder and turned to face him. "Haven't you heard?" she said. "Rumor is, the administration is about to remove your beloved hero from his little pedestal."

"Oh come on," Don said, "he's not exactly my hero."

"Oh, he's not?" her voice was laced with contempt.

"No, he's not!" he said, angry now. "Not really...I mean, he is an okay teacher and all that..."

She gave him a disgusted look, turned on her heel, and marched away.

If Frances had spit on him, he wouldn't have felt any more degraded. Her scowl stabbed him deep in the gut, condemned him for betraying Dr. Sampson once again by not speaking up for him. He had managed to fail Frances again, too. She'd wanted a fight and he hadn't obliged. Worst of all, he had failed himself by not standing up for what he believed in.

Don knew he had to do something. Regardless of what Frances or anybody else said, Don knew he was uncovering a far-flung conspiracy to manipulate Congress in order to generate huge profits for the healthcare industry at the people's expense. And he was more determined than ever to get to the heart of it.

Late that afternoon, he walked across town to see Julia Chambers. The moth-eaten black coat plus a scarf, hat, and gloves didn't begin to keep out the biting cold. The wind whipped through the icy streets and pierced every seam of his clothing. Gloom and dark foreshadowed more foul weather to come. Why hadn't he worn his parka and boots? He hurried down a deserted Main Street, buffeted by blasts of frigid air from between the buildings. How much more hopeful he had been when he'd walked this way with Dr. Sampson. Back when he foolishly believed things couldn't get any worse.

By the time Don reached the storefront of the Grafton County Preservation Society, his face, lips, nose, and ears were numb. Even his eyeballs felt like they would freeze open. He couldn't feel his fingers and toes and found it hard to grasp and turn the doorknob. Thank goodness the door was unlocked. The old brass bells clanged as he walked in.

Dr. Chambers stepped up to the counter from the back room and greeted him with a smile, as if she were expecting him. "Ah, Dr. Newman, you have returned. I wondered when I might see you again."

"Hello, Dr. Chambers. Mind if I come in out of the cold for a few minutes?"

"Certainly, you are always welcome here."

Don pulled off his gloves, stuffed them in his pockets, and rubbed his hands together.

She clasped his hands in hers. "You are cold as ice! Forgive me for saying it, but you don't appear well. Is something wrong?"

He shrugged. "I haven't been sleeping much lately, I guess."

"So you have not come for pleasantries. I see you have something on your mind. Come back here and sit with me. Can I get you some tea?"

Don shook his head. "No, thanks."

Dr. Chambers guided him into the room behind the counter and motioned for him to sit on a stool next to her at a large, wood frame table. The unfinished plywood tabletop was covered with old maps and blueprints, and shelves underneath were filled with books. All the walls were lined from floor to ceiling with unpainted lumber shelves, also crammed full of books.

"This reminds me of the Florence College Library basement," Don remarked.

"What were you doing there?"

"Just a little research on the famous families of Grafton County."

Dr. Chamber's warm brown eyes reminded him of his mother's. They twinkled with interest. "So you met my old friend, Mrs. Sutton?" she asked.

"Yes, Ma'am."

"She is definitely the one to see if you want to find original documents. Here, I'm afraid, we mostly have secondhand copies. Tell me, what is on your mind?"

"Both Dr. Sampson and Mrs. Sutton told me you might know something about the Alchemists," he began. "Can I, uh, speak with you confidentially?"

"Of course you may," she replied. "I'm good at keeping a secret, especially when it comes to the Alchemists."

Don spilled everything: the secret initiation, the evasiveness of the boys at the hospital, the lousy medical care Bobby Webster received, how he got himself fired from the moonlighting job, the rumor about Dr. Sampson's program closing, his own suspicion someone behind the scenes was working to keep everything under wraps.

"Perhaps there is something to that," Dr. Chambers clucked to herself. She got up, paced back and forth, then sat back down and appraised him quizzically. "It sounds as though you have gotten yourself tied up in something rather serious," she said in her lilting, Jamaican English. "I can understand why you've been losing sleep over them. Those boys take themselves very seriously."

She paused for a moment and looked through the glistening surface of his eyes, as if she were searching his thoughts. "You're black, aren't you?"

Don nodded.

"I thought so. I notice how people react to the slave graves here. Whatever the emotion—anger, denial, guilt, sadness—whites are distant, like it's just academic, like it has nothing to do with them. Not Virgil Sampson, though. He responded like a black man, with genuine sorrow. You were like that when you were here before. But let me tell you something, Don. If you want to find peace, you must gain understanding and sympathy for the master, not just the slave."

"There's something else," Don said. "I think the Alchemists are behind a conspiracy to profit from the disorder in American healthcare."

She laughed. "Oh my, everyone loves a conspiracy. The truth is almost always stranger than such fictions. Few who are sane conspire to rule the world. But there are many who, like you, just want to find someone to blame. Both paths are misguided."

"Please," Don said, "what can you tell me about the Alchemists?"

"Well, if you are looking for a conspiracy, I'm afraid you will be disappointed. Members of secret societies tend to focus too much on personal gain to do anything with common purpose very well."

She studied Don's eyes once again, took a deep breath and blew it out through pursed lips. "Well, I guess you need to know. I have learned quite a lot about the American Order of Alchemists over the last few years, something I didn't set out to do. I am an historian, but secret societies are not my area, and I've never published my findings. After all, why look for trouble?"

Don shivered involuntarily. Whether it was from cold or fear he wasn't sure. What trouble had he stumbled into?

"In fact," she proceeded, "I've never shared this with anyone; no one ever asked. I don't know why in the world I felt compelled to gather information about the Alchemists, much less what to do with it. Maybe I was meant to gather this information in order to give it to you."

Dr. Chambers walked to a bookcase at the end of the room, climbed a tall stepladder, and reached up to the top shelf. She retrieved a box marked *Florence College* and set it on the table.

"My interest began completely by accident about ten years ago, when I bought some old books from the estate of Dr. Tol Buchanan. He was president of Florence College from 1951 through 1977. Most of his books and papers went into the library's historical collection, but these were leftover paperbacks and battered hardbacks. Most of them were old translations of the works of existential philosophers like Hegel, Nietzsche, and Heidegger, and they had been read and underlined until their spines fell apart. I was going through them right here on this table when I came across this."

She opened the box. On top of the collection lay a clear archival envelope with an old, tattered paperback tract inside. Dr. Chambers wiped her hands on her pants, slid the antique document out of its envelope, and placed it on the table. The cover read, *Protocols of the Learned Elders of Zion, London, 1920.*

Don resisted the urge to pick it up. "What is it?" he asked.

"This is a rare first edition of a piece of hateful propaganda. It contains twenty-five protocols, or chapters, alleging a Jewish and Masonic plot to rule the world. The propaganda was quite influential in its time, and it certainly influenced Tol Buchanan's thinking."

"I don't see an author's name—who wrote it?"

"Who knows? The thing about the *Protocols* is it's a complete forgery—rather, a forgery of a forgery. Believe it or not, there have been dozens of versions of the *Protocols* through the years. All of them stem from a popular French novel in the 1860s entitled *The Mysteries of the People*, a fictional story about a Catholic Jesuit plot to rule the world. Over the years, that novel has been plagiarized, adapted, and presented as fact to accuse different racial, ethnic, or political groups of treason.

"In 1864, another French author adapted and renamed it *The Dialogue in Hell Between Machiavelli and Montesquieu*. It accused Emperor Napoleon III of leading a conspiracy to achieve world domination. A few years after that, a Russian journalist secretly copied *The Dialogue in Hell* almost word for word to convince Tsar Nicholas II of a Jewish plot to overthrow him. When the Russian Revolution began in 1905, the *Protocols* was used against the Bolsheviks. That was the version the *Philadelphia Ledger* translated and published under the headline "RED 'BIBLE' COUNSELS APPEAL TO VIOLENCE" on October 28th, 1919, the first time they were published in the United States."

She turned to the flyleaf, where someone had scribbled *The Red Bible! Bolsheviks and Jews—convenient scapegoats.*

"Tol Buchanan's reference to the Red Bible here indicates he must have seen the publication in the *Ledger*. Tol Buchanan grew up in Philadelphia, so that's certainly plausible. His comment indicates he knew it was useful as propaganda, but he probably didn't know the full history of it."

She slowly flipped the pages. The margins were filled with handwritten notes.

"In 1920, Henry Ford paid for the publication of half a million copies of this version in the United States. He was afraid of the Jews and the consequences of racial integration. Even more copies were sold in Nazi Germany, where Hitler made the *Protocols* required reading for German students in order to gain support for his eugenics program."

Dr. Chambers reached back into the folio box and pulled out another clear plastic envelope. "The first time I opened Dr. Buchanan's copy of the *Protocols* tract, this fell out." She passed Don the envelope without opening it.

Don gingerly pulled out a fragile piece of yellowed paper and unfolded it. It was handwritten in a beautiful, old-fashioned script and had a crease through the middle from having been folded for many years. The edges were stained and cryptic scribbles and notes covered both sides. Don studied the document with amazement, just as Dr. Chambers must have done the first time she saw it.

At the top left corner was a skull and crossbones. The title was *Revelations of the Overman, Black Tuesday*. Alongside the title in the right-hand margin, someone had scrawled the following:

> *The Protocols for the American Order of Alchemists: This will be our secret plan. This will be our protocol. We will use it against them before they can use it against us. Remember our three pillars: Bread, Miracle, and Power. The Tammany Society gave us fodder for the masses, the Templars, miracle, and Skull and Bones, the power of death. Bread rules all. Miracle is coincidence borne of chaos and will to power. Now is the time for power.*

The page's border was ringed by ancient and modern chemical symbols and formulas in different colors. The text proclaimed that secrets passed down from Alchemists of old were beyond the reach and understanding of the common man, that these secret teachings should only be passed down to worthy scholars in the laboratory sciences and business, that the secret teachings would be revealed in a progressive manner as ability and seniority dictated, and that Alchemist teachings led to hidden truths that would bring unimaginable personal benefits and power to the initiated. The document concluded:

> *Given these truths, we, the spiritual descendants of Burr, Philip IV, and Russell, hereby establish the American Order of Alchemists, Florence College, New Hampshire, this Twenty-ninth day of October, Nineteen hundred and twenty-nine.*
>
> *Signed, Tol Buchanan, Founding Master*
> *American Order of Alchemists*

"I have done quite a bit of investigation, out of curiosity," Dr. Chambers continued. "May I share Tol Buchanan's story with you? I've been able to piece it together with some material Mrs. Sutton helped me scavenge from the archives."

Don nodded, too busy processing this new information to speak.

"Ptolemy Buchanan was born in Philadelphia in 1907," she began. "His father was a prominent, Yale-educated physician who married a Greek immigrant, an unusual marriage for a man of Philadelphia's high society. Perhaps

Ptolemy was ashamed of his mixed heritage. He never used his given name on correspondence; he always signed his name 'Tol.'

"He was a brilliant young man and, like his father, attended Yale, where he majored in philosophy and economics. In 1928, at age twenty-one, he was refused admittance to the Yale School of Medicine, for reasons that are unclear. I suspect bitterness about this rejection followed him the rest of his life. He came to Florence College, entered the school of pharmacy, and continued his study of business and economics.

"His father lost everything in the stock market crash of 1929 and could no longer pay for his son's education, so Tol Buchanan took a job in the college laboratory. He worked there five years to finance his degree and prepare for his future work. In the crucible of that time, he founded the Alchemists, and from everything I can tell, he actively recruited physicians.

"After graduation, he used his network of college contacts to partner with physicians, helping them make money in the difficult economic times of the Depression. Working with the few surviving banks, he set up over twenty-five corporations in the 1930s, investing everything he made in insurance and pharmaceutical start-ups. His most successful start-ups made alcohol-based herbal elixirs with closely guarded secret formulas. As one of the early specialists in securitizing healthcare assets, he made millions.

"The rest is history. In the 1940s, Tol Buchanan was Florence College's largest donor. He joined the board of trustees and became president of the college in 1951. He served until 1977 and remained active in college affairs right up until his death in 1987."

Was Tol Buchanan the mentor President Lender talked about? The one who guided President Lender to his principles? Don turned Tol Buchanan's *Revelations* over and over in his hands.

"But why?" Don asked. "Why would he start an organization like the Alchemists?"

Dr. Chambers sighed. "Who can judge the heart, the inner intentions, of another person?"

Don's dissatisfaction with her answer must have been obvious.

"All right, then. Although I cannot speak to the heart of the man, he did leave a few clues. I've read his notes extensively. If you have time, I'll share my opinions regarding his motives, based on the things he appears to have admired."

"I have time," Don said. "That would be great."

"Very good then, but first you must let me make you a cup of tea. You look like you could use it."

This time he didn't refuse. She returned a few minutes later with two steaming cups of dark brown tea and insisted Don take a spoon of honey. He stirred in the honey and took a sip, relishing the sweet warm concoction trickling down his throat and thawing his bones. "Thank you for the tea, Dr. Chambers."

"Please, do call me Julia. Now, where were we? Oh yes, Tol Buchanan. You can tell a lot about someone by the organizations and individuals they admire. So, what and whom did Tol Buchanan admire? You've seen his *Revelations*. He seems to have been fascinated by secret societies and the power they could wield. The Tammany Society, the Templars, and Yale's Skull and Bones particularly fascinated him. Let's begin with the Tammany Society, founded by former Vice President Aaron Burr. What do you know of it?"

"Not much," Don admitted.

"Let me give you a little background. Burr's story begins around the time of the founding of our country. At that time, the bankers and merchants of America were politically powerful Loyalists, or Tories, profiting immensely from allegiance to England. The Burrs were one of these well-connected, aristocratic families. Maybe that's why George Washington never trusted Aaron Burr, or maybe it was because Burr served under Benedict Arnold early in the Revolutionary War.

"At any rate, Burr likely learned politics from his father, the second president of Princeton, but he recognized money was power and went to work on Wall Street. He was so sly, he tricked the savvy Alexander Hamilton into supporting a charter—supposedly to supply 'pure and wholesome' water to the people of New York after a yellow fever epidemic—that he used to establish a rival bank. He appointed himself and his cronies to the board. His Bank of the Manhattan Company became Chase Manhattan Bank, known today as JPMorgan Chase, one of the biggest issuers of credit cards in the world.

"Burr certainly despised Alexander Hamilton for his support of highly regulated national banks. He looked down on Hamilton for his questionable parentage–bastard child of a West Indies family–and was jealous of his self-made success and noted eloquence. When Hamilton dared to publicly denounce Burr as a traitor and a scoundrel, Burr had the excuse he needed. He challenged Hamilton to a duel and killed him outright. Aaron Burr murdered the man the French diplomat Talleyrand called the greatest mind America had ever produced—even though Hamilton had promised Burr he would not return fire. Hamilton was Burr's scapegoat.

"But Aaron Burr's most infamous legacy was the Tammany Society in New York. Through Tammany, Burr became the founding father of machine politics in America. He used political favors to deliver votes like candy. He demonstrated how easy it is to manipulate public opinion and convince poorly educated citizens to vote for whatever they're told—even for things contrary to their own interests. Tammany delivered to Jefferson and Burr the critical electoral votes they needed to win the presidential election of 1800. Without the Tammany Society, President John Adams would probably have won reelection.

"Even though Burr and Tammany won him the presidency, President Jefferson never trusted Vice President Burr. Jefferson knew Burr represented the banking interests of America, and despite Jefferson's opposition to Hamilton and the Federalists, the power of the banks worried him. Jefferson said: *I sincerely believe...that banking establishments are more dangerous to our liberties than standing armies.* In his second term, President Jefferson charged Burr with treason for attempting to start a war with Spain, in direct violation of the Neutrality Act.

"So, why did the young Tol Buchanan so admire Aaron Burr?" Don asked.

"I think it was because Burr knew how to manipulate others for wealth and power. He created the new world's first modern political machine and was a master of backroom deals. He used the Tammany Society to control men and deliver votes based on innuendo, propaganda, and favors. I think that's what Buchanan meant by 'bread' or 'fodder' in his *Revelations*.

"Next, the Templars. The order of the Knights Templar was founded by two French veterans of the First Crusade in 1119. The name Templar came from Solomon's Temple. The Poor Fellow-Soldiers of Christ and the Temple of Solomon were commonly known as the Knights Templar, the most famous Christian military order of all time.

"Their symbol, the skull and crossbones, referred to Golgotha— 'the place of the skull'—the hill where Jesus was crucified. According to legend, the blood of Christ trickled down the wood of the cross and into the earth to bathe the bones of Adam and redeem him from his original sin. This symbol reminded the soldiers of their mortality and prepared them to go into war without fear.

"The Templars established fortified hospitals on islands along the route from Europe to house and tend to Christian pilgrims. The skull and crossbones flag flown by the Templar ships was a banner for the crusades but also came to symbolize safety and health for pilgrim tourists on their way to the Holy Land. Unfortunately, Mediterranean pirates adopted the symbol in order to trick pilgrims into thinking that approaching pirate ships were Templars coming to help, and the skull and crossbones remains a symbol for piracy today.

"Holy war was a way of life for the Templars, but many of the top commanders of the Templars were bankers and financiers. They were more interested in controlling the major Mediterranean trade routes than in finding ancient Christian relics or persecuting infidels. Just as pirates used the Templar symbol to deceive, the bankers and financiers controlling the Templars used the order for personal profit and played the soldiers for fools.

"I think Tol Buchanan admired the Templar leaders for the way they manipulated religious sentiment to expand their power and wealth. They used religion as a front to win funding and support from popes and kings. They enjoyed freedom from taxation. The pilgrims and crusaders were guaranteed clients, and the Moslem people of the Middle East were convenient scapegoats to rally the Christian warriors and their backers. And he likely admired King Philip IV of France for the way he tricked the Templars in turn on Friday the 13th, in October of 1307. He accused their leaders of devil worship, extracted their confessions under torture, and burned them at the stake to avoid paying his debts.

"Now for Skull and Bones, the most famous and oldest of the Ivy League secret societies. Skull and Bones adopted the old Templar symbol. Like the Templars and the Tammany Society, it's connected to banking and big money in America.

"William Huntington Russell, the founder, came from an old New England Tory and Wall Street banking family. His cousin, Samuel Russell, started a small shipping company in 1823 to smuggle Turkish opium into China and used the skull and crossbones as the company logo. When Samuel and his Tory friends helped defeat China in the Opium War of 1839, it made Russell and Company the largest opium smuggling operation in the world.

"Meanwhile, William Huntington Russell took a year off from Yale to study existential philosophy in Berlin—some say so he could learn to use Hegel's 'historical dialectic' to manipulate economic markets. Russell's study paid off. He was valedictorian of his class at Yale in 1833. In that same year, he and thirteen other sons of powerful Wall Street families founded the Order of Skull and Bones at Yale. In 1856, he incorporated it as the Russell Trust Association.

"For Tol Buchanan, Skull and Bones represented power. It operated in secret, produced presidents, and influenced world events—all without getting tangled up in chaotic, messy democracy. He would have heard rumors about how the lifetime loyalty of members was secured by their induction ceremony in the tomb, their secret headquarters. Rumor is, Bonesmen have to lie naked in an open casket and recite the history of all their sexual exploits and greatest mistakes while their words are dutifully recorded.

"Who knows, perhaps Buchanan was a Bonesman himself while at Yale, but I think it likely he was not invited. And I suspect his father was a Bonesman who was disappointed his son did not follow in his footsteps. Regardless, when at Yale, Tol Buchanan would have heard about Skull and Bones and its influential members.

"Of course, this was before Adolf Hitler's secret society, the SS, used the skull and crossbones on their flags, equipment, and armbands to terrorize their victims. Tol Buchanan would not have known how the SS recruited Nazi Party elite to fill their senior ranks, nor how their secret initiation rites would involve confessions and oaths designed to impress initiates with the importance of secret brotherhood and allegiance. But I suspect he would have admired the effectiveness of their methods, too.

"Now let me be clear. The people who own the banks and the trading companies of America are well educated and interesting and contribute a great deal to society. They do a lot of good things, to be sure. But they occupy positions of great power and we need them to see beyond their own short-term business interests. We need them to do what is good for America, or at least refrain from harm. Organizations that meet in secret and demand strict loyalty to the group are narrowly focused on their own special interests and their members can easily act as traitors.

"So now we come to the Alchemists. The group formed in a time of great scientific progress in American medicine. Mr. Buchanan's writings make it clear the Alchemists are spiritual descendants of the Templars, the Tammany Society, and Skull and Bones. Each of these groups formed to represent a particular special interest. The special interest the Alchemists represent is that of the medical men.

"Tol Buchanan saw the future of scientific medicine and knew it would become big business. Nothing works like fear to encourage irrational spending or saving, and what could better generate fear than the sickness and death doctors confront every day? Buchanan was ready to help Wall Street financiers manipulate people's fear of death for profit. He recognized early on that insurance had the most potential to make money for nothing, so he worked hard to position himself as an intermediary in healthcare.

"There is no proof of a formal connection between Skull and Bones and the American Order of Alchemists, but there certainly was a connection in Tol Buchanan's mind. So that brings us back to your original question. Why did Tol Buchanan found the Alchemists?

"Consider the defining events of his life. He was shut out of Philadelphia high society because of his mixed parentage. His mother's heritage and even his own name must have embarrassed him. He was shut out of the Yale School of Medicine and perhaps Skull and Bones. On Black Tuesday in 1929 his father lost everything the family owned, requiring him to pay his own way through school. I think he conceived the Alchemists as his revenge and as a route to power and wealth."

"So what do you think of these secret societies like the Alchemists?" Don asked.

"After all this talk, isn't that obvious?" She laughed. "John Quincy Adams warned that those who take oaths to secret societies cannot be trusted to be loyal to a democratic republic. Secret societies like the Alchemists are dangerous precisely because they command loyalty. They are especially dangerous when they put personal or special interests first, as most do. They are all about exclusivity. Their initiations and oaths are designed to promote total allegiance to the group, the tribe, or the party.

"A secret society creates the dichotomy of 'us' and 'them.' It creates polarization between winners and losers, masters and slaves, good and evil. Non-members become villains, enemies, and convenient scapegoats. Secret societies lack the good purposes and professional standards that most guilds have; the purpose of most secret societies is private gain for its members.

"Now don't get me wrong. I am not against capitalism. But when people organize in secret to profit at the expense of others, that is bad. Why would a group need to be secret? When they are up to no good, that's when. As President John F. Kennedy said long ago:

> *The very word 'secrecy' is repugnant in a free and open society; and*
> *we are as a people inherently and historically opposed to secret societies, to*
> *secret oaths, and to secret proceedings."*

President Lender had to be an Alchemist. Don was certain of it now. His arguments, his examples, his ideals, were those of his dead mentor, Tol Buchanan. Don couldn't believe Florence College was so infiltrated with such bad chemistry.

"Do you know who belongs to the Alchemists?" Don asked.

"I don't have the roster, but I think you can assume President Lender is their friend."

"I know this stuff has happened in the past, in history. But do you think the Alchemists today   are they for real?"

"Don, if people believe something is real, they make it real."

"Do you think they are leading a conspiracy?

"Who knows? Maybe. But the Alchemists are a little boys club, a dangerous one, certainly, but one that is never likely to be very effective. They can only exist as a powerful force as long as they stay in the dark. As soon as sensible people know what they are up to, their power is gone. Their nefarious words and acts cannot stand the light. No matter what evil they wreak, they are childish, selfish, and laughable in the light."

THAT NIGHT Don still couldn't sleep. His head whirled as the disconnected events of the past year all came together. No doubt, President Lender was an Alchemist, but would he go so far as to hide the murder of Bobby Webster? Did Bruce betray Dr. Sampson? The words of Bruce's father at the gala echoed in his mind: "Didn't you know? We're priming Bruce for a run in 2004." Why would someone so cynical about government go into politics? Don didn't want to believe Bruce would betray Dr. Sampson and undermine the health of

America. But then, Bruce's father had gone to Florence College. He had to be an Alchemist too, along with Lender, Townsend, Pan, and Josten.

Everything in Don's life, on the other hand, was coming apart: friendships, career, Dr. Sampson's program, the whole country. Julia Chambers said the rich and powerful are too focused on their own personal interests to lead a national conspiracy, but they've been known to create polarization, spread sickness, even go to war for profit.

Frances is right. I have no place in this world. How can I contribute to a system that encourages sickness and preys on suffering? Traitors are everywhere. I've committed my life to a corrupt, foul-to-the-core healthcare system. There's no real hope of cure—a cure would be bad for business! The medical tower giants are no different than the selfish industrialists and plantation owners of the past who wagered young men's lives for the spoils of war rather than struggle down the difficult path to peace. Like the Markum men running guns in the Civil War, overcharging for basic supplies, and protecting money in Europe, doctors allow disease to take hold before stepping in to attempt a late rescue—for a price.

Thing is, I'm no different. *I'm just like them!* I didn't speak up for Dr. Sampson when I knew he was right. Instead I remained silent. No, it's worse—I said things that hurt him! I let my patients down. I knew where the system was corrupt but played along—didn't have enough spine to speak up for the poor, the sick, the people who entrusted their lives to me. What would Momma think of me now? I'm no doctor. I'm no healer. I'm worse than any traitor at Florence College. *I know better.*

Don started to fall asleep, but the sensation of falling jolted him awake. He gripped his blankets. He had a horrible sense of foreboding that wouldn't go away.

The system is on an unsustainable track; it's bound to collapse eventually. Should I jump before the towers crumble? Where else can I go? *Please, let it not happen.*

Late, late into the night Don finally fell into a fitful sleep. He dreamed he was in a tall tower, gazing out of a broken window into an abyss. Smoke obscured the ground below, or was there any ground?

What did I do to deserve this? I was just doing my job. Offices below in flames, mouth parched, eyes burning from smoke and heat. What do I do? Where's the helicopter? They always come in the movies, like in *Towering Inferno*. What would Steve McQueen do? He'd be a hero. I'm no hero. Nowhere to turn. Nothing to do. I hear the helicopter, invisible in the smoke. Where's the rope? Thick acrid smoke billows up from under the burning hot door to the stairs, swirls, pours around me, eyes burning, can't breathe. Wait, I can breathe if I hang out this narrow, broken window. Steam flowing from the floor, along the wall, turning to a layer of smoke carpeting the wall. Floor flames caressing their way up the wall. Curls of flame crawling closer and closer. Saint Lawrence lay down calmly on the grill. How could anyone do that? Flames all around. Others gone. Nothing to do but die. Hands dancing around hot metal window frame seeking less painful purchase. Singed arm hair. Can't breathe. Lean out farther. Farther! Blistered hands. Burning in agony. Sizzling smell of cooking skin. Can't breathe. No good choice. Abandon all hope of healing. Saint, or suicide going straight to hell? No matter. No one to witness. The wind is cool. *Choose the wind.* Jump.

I had to do it. It was the only control I had, the last choice I could make for myself.

I let go and fall through the whirling darkness head first, down from the towers. Falling, falling, falling. Hundreds of other jumpers around me—is there no one to help them? Is there no one to help me? Am I guilty?

Dr. Desmond's eyes watch me from the billboard. The billboard topples and the eyes change to the wide-open stare of Sibyl Bellamy. Staring at me in condemnation. The towers are all collapsing and soon there will be nothing other than steel skeletons, disease, death. Falling, falling, falling. Finally at the bottom, ground zero, nothing but blackness. Darkness. I am alone.

No...wait. In the midst of rubble, blood, and death, there is someone. Sampson is there with me.

34

The Betrayer Revealed

Back of everything is the great spectre of universal death,
the all-encompassing blackness
WILLIAM JAMES, THE VARIETIES OF RELIGIOUS EXPERIENCE,
THE SICK SOUL

HOW COULD he look so calm? Resigned, even. Here the world was falling down around them, and Dr. Sampson looked like all the fight had gone out of him. He sat directly across from Don at the old table in the amphitheater, his broad shoulders slumped as if bearing a great weight.

Everyone knew his program was falling apart, but he bore the shame in silence. Unbearable silence. The two said nothing, just sat there alone and waited. Don didn't dare ask whether they should go on with the seminar without Frances and Bruce.

Distant thunder cracked and rumbled through the floor. All else was silent. Dead silent.

After several minutes of awkward waiting, Don heard something—a faint tick, tick, tick. A clock? The ticking grew louder—not a clock. It was the distant clicking of heels approaching from far down the linoleum hallway. The clicking footsteps grew steadily louder and then stopped.

The door creaked open and Frances peered inside. She looked embarrassed at being late but glad to see them there. She took her place at the table, and they all sat in silence for a moment longer.

Dr. Sampson's voice rumbled in the vacuum. "Good, Frances. Now that you are here, we can begin." He looked from Frances to Don. "Let's move ahead with our lesson."

Don stole a glance at Frances. She looked like she had been through a hell of her own, with puffy eyelids and bloodshot eyes. He knew in his heart what had happened. He had seen it coming. He could just hear the cocky SOB.

I love you, Frances, you know I do. You've got something really special. But you know, we—our families—they're just too different. You know it would never work. Besides, with my career plans right now, I wouldn't be able to devote the time to a serious relationship that you deserve; it wouldn't be fair to you.

That was it, really, his hunger for power. Everything served that need. Bruce was addicted to power and influence, and for that he was willing to give up everything. Even love. Don knew that deep down, Bruce cared for Frances. They were a good match. Frances was savvy, beautiful, and possessed the empathy and compassion Bruce lacked. Bruce had thrown away something precious.

Yes, Frances had come out of loyalty to Dr. Sampson, and in doing so, she had left Bruce behind.

Dr. Sampson's deep, calm voice steadied them, "I appreciate your coming to this special Friday session. I apologize for the last-minute schedule change, but under the circumstances, I hope you understand."

Frances and Don glanced at each other and back at Dr. Sampson. They nodded in unison.

"I want to bring you up to date. I am sure you have heard rumors. I have been accused of engaging in propaganda rather than scholarship, participating in partisan political activities, and indoctrinating students rather than educating them. The board of trustees gave me a choice: agree to radical changes in the Health System Science Program or step down from my role as director. The president of the college and some influential alumni want to change the entire direction of the program, and only one board member cast a dissenting vote. Given the changes they insisted upon, it is impossible for me to continue as the director."

It was one thing for Don to hear the rumors, but to hear it from Dr. Sampson's own lips brought the enormity of it home.

Ridiculous! Partisanship? He's a professor, for God's sake doesn't the administration know anything about academic freedom? Of course he challenges conventional ideas about American healthcare, but we research and reach our own conclusions. Dr. Sampson doesn't push answers; he urges us to think for ourselves. And anyone can see we often come to different conclusions.

"I have initiated grievance proceedings. In the meantime, I will take a year's sabbatical. Frankly, I'm long overdue for one. I plan to develop a new program in Memphis, Tennessee. Any Florence College Health System Science student who wishes may transfer and continue our coursework there.

"Alternatively, you can continue your work here. You are discerning and have the tools now to learn what you need to know at either campus. Let me know if you would like more information about the Memphis program, or contact President Lender's office to learn about plans for the program here—it seems he has taken a personal interest and wants to be more involved in the coming year. I've asked Dr. White, the adjunct faculty member from Boston who lectured here earlier in the year, to assist in running the Health System Science Seminar in my absence. Depending on the disposition of my grievance, she may continue to play a major program leadership role."

Everything was happening too fast. Seeing Dr. Sampson brought down, disgraced, and beaten was almost more than Don could bear. If the Medicare bill had passed, Dr. Sampson would have been hailed as its champion. Everyone would have recognized his insight and wisdom. Instead, he was humiliated—packing up—heading off to a real backwater. Memphis? That was nowhere.

"This is our final seminar session. You have learned where health systems go wrong; now you must seek new ways to make them right. You are both excellent students. I am sure that whatever paths you choose, you will do much good for the health of our world. Take what you have learned and put it to use for those who need your help. I wish you the very best."

Dr. Sampson's eyes glistened, and Don thought he might shed a tear. But the instant passed and the inscrutable look in his steel gray eyes returned. Stoic to the end.

"What happened to Bruce?" Don asked quietly.

Frances stared at the floor. She knew.

"Bruce is dropping out of the program," Dr. Sampson said. "He will get credit for the year. I understand he'll work for the Markum family interests in Washington and may run for public office."

Of course. Bruce had been working for Markum interests all along! He was obviously Lender's informant—he and his father were chummy with President Lender and the board. Bruce had betrayed Dr. Sampson and undermined the legislation in Washington. His family and their henchmen knew all the congressmen in Washington and how to influence them. *That bastard! I will never forgive him.*

But it seemed like Dr. Sampson already had. Dr. Sampson showed no surprise, no anger, as if he had known all along that Bruce would betray him.

Did Bruce ever give a damn about health system science? Maybe he just wanted the training to justify a top executive salary at New American Healthcare, or maybe the Alchemists sent Bruce to Florence College to spy on Dr. Sampson and sabotage his efforts from the very beginning. Either way, he must have hated Dr. Sampson for challenging his ideas, positions, and family legacy, all at the same time. Dr. Sampson compelled Bruce to choose between power and truth, between might and right. Bruce couldn't have both…unless he discredited Dr. Sampson. Nothing less would do. Sampson had to go down.

"There are a few more things I need to share with you," Dr. Sampson continued. "Many of your mentors this semester have been reassigned to new positions. Mr. Fred Yeoman was demoted and moved out of management at CMS to the Office of the Actuary. Mrs. Beverly Thomas, Senior Program Officer in Behavioral and Social Sciences Research at the NIH, stands accused of releasing protected information and faces civil penalties for revealing NIH conflicts of interest to the newspapers. She was reassigned to the National Cancer Institute to implement a study designed to show improvements in quality of life for terminal cancer patients undergoing investigational chemotherapy. My friend David Graham at the FDA has been prohibited from releasing the results of two of his studies. He was moved out of the new drug review division because the drug company executives accused him, without any substantive evidence, of prejudice. Meanwhile, those experimental drug-eluting stents you heard about at CMS have made it through the FDA thanks to Director Thrash, who personally ordered the FDA to speed them through.

"These whistleblowers were punished in part because of their willingness to teach you. Of course, this is politics as usual. It has always been hard for whistleblowers. The government ought to protect its whistleblowers. The executive branch needs them desperately; our best leaders have always known that. Abraham Lincoln created the *qui tam* law to engage the citizenry in keeping government honest, and in the past the government often joined qui tam lawsuits brought by citizens against those who defrauded the government. But now, for the first time in recent history, executive branch bureaucrats are systematically working to ruin those who expose corruption.

"Despite this, you should know that Mr. Yeoman, Dr. Thomas, and Dr. Graham are undeterred. They have been your willing teachers and I'm sure will remain so. If you should need to contact them for further assistance, you can reach them through Bettye, the Program Coordinator. She is a stubborn old cuss and will not be leaving Florence College anytime soon. Even the current administration lacks the courage to reassign her. Should you decide to stay here, you can consider her a friend.

"Lastly, let me comment on the recent political events in Washington. Despite the undisputed fact that medical errors kill more Americans every two weeks than were killed on September 11th, the healthcare giants do not want this made public. They don't want to bring attention to their mistakes. They work hard to minimize government spending on healthcare quality. They profit from the status quo and don't want their income streams interrupted. They are afraid for Americans to look too closely—they might demand change!

"People want to blame others for their problems. That's true in healthcare just like everywhere else. Mark my words: when health care reform is brought forward again, those benefiting from the status quo will brand the reformers as villains. They will call them communists, socialists, and worse, no matter what party the reformers are in. And the branders and marketers will entice gullible people to follow right along, even against their own best interests.

"September 11th provided a perfect excuse for Americans to blame others. It encouraged us to look outward, away from ourselves, and justified huge new investments in homeland security and preparation for war. I have seen what killing machines do, and don't want to see them again. But I predict more cuts to domestic health programs and increasing neglect of domestic problems as we gear up to pay for war.

"America's health problems will not just go away. It is up to you to shine the light, to advocate for the victims of our dysfunctional system. Remember, to cure a disease you must acknowledge it, diagnose it, and bring it to light. The American health system is very sick; it cannot survive as it is. You must continue your work to diagnose and cure its ills so the things essential for healing are not lost when our outmoded healthcare system comes crashing down.

"Finally, I owe you an apology. When we looked out over the city from the Sentinel Bar and Grill that day, I realize now I told you something very wrong. I'm afraid I have not been a good teacher."

"That's not true, Dr. Sampson," Don called out.

"You've been a wonderful teacher!" Frances protested.

"Let me finish. At the Sentinel, I challenged you to stand up as intelligence agents and warriors for health system change. Deep down, I guess I wanted those outmoded towers of healthcare to fall. But I was wrong to call you to war, even a war against medical errors and waste of healthcare resources. The words we choose are important. Words call us forward in a spirit, a way of engaging ourselves with the world. As soon as we use the language of war, we've lost the path to healing.

"You have been schooled in the healing arts. If you shine a bright light on the problems in health care—if you serve as true diagnosticians—the waste and errors will go away, for no one will want them. Thank you for being my teachers."

Then he just sat there. Neither Don nor Frances knew what to say. Finally, Frances thanked him, managed an apologetic smile, and left the projection room. Dr. Sampson nodded to Frances as she left, then turned and looked directly at Don.

What was the message of those calm gray eyes? Was it hopelessness and despair?

No. Don saw it now. His eyes held determination.

Don said, "I need to tell you what I learned from Dr. Chambers about the Alchemists. I think it may bear on your grievance. I feel like I haven't done the right thing and now, well, I just want to do something to help." Don wanted to beg for forgiveness. He felt so ashamed.

"Don, it's too late. The die has been cast. You need to move forward; do not dwell in the past. I am leaving, but I'm not giving up on Florence College or the program. My grievance proceeding will allow me to share the truth, and my colleagues on the faculty know and trust me. The program will go forward in my absence, and the dialogue will continue whether I am here or not. Do not abandon hope."

"I just…"

"I am not without recourse, you know. I could go to war over what has been done with our program. Make it a freedom of speech issue. Threaten a civil suit asking Lender and his minions to step down. It might even lead to their ouster. But somehow," he concluded with a trace of warmth in his gray eyes and a wry smile, "I do not think that will be necessary." Before Don could say more he was gone.

Don slumped back in his seat. Despite Dr. Sampson's determination and talk of moving forward, Don saw nothing but darkness. No path forward. No hope. No future. For a long time he sat in the empty amphitheater. He put his face in his hands and fingered the knot at the bridge of his nose. Dr. Sampson's grievance proceeding with the university was a joke. It was over. Dr. Sampson had been beaten and President Lender was too powerful to stop.

As he mulled over the events that had led to this travesty, Don's simmering despair turned to a rolling boil. The object of his anger had a face—Bruce Markum. Bruce was the traitor responsible for all of this. And if Bruce hadn't left campus yet, he knew where to find him.

Don jumped up, ran for the exit, and burst through the double doors, slamming them into the brick walls of the building's exterior. He was surprised to find the sky nearly dark as night. Frigid blasts of wind scourged the icy snow's surface and stung his face as he shot across the frozen quad toward The Down Under. Lightning cracked the air and struck at buildings on either side, threatening to bring the high walls down upon him. He dashed down the stained brick steps into the room where Bruce typically held court.

Sure enough, Bruce was there. He didn't even have shame enough to hide. Bruce spotted Don and started to stand to greet him, but his curious smile changed—first to concern and then to fear—as Don barreled through The Down Under toward his table.

Don was thrilled to see Bruce's cool demeanor disrupted. He slammed his palms into the stiff press of Bruce's starched shirt and shoved him hard in the chest.

Bruce went flying back into his chair and toppled over backward, barely missing cracking his head on the wall behind him. He fell to the floor, stunned.

"You son of a bitch!" Don yelled. "How could you do it?"

"What the hell are you talking about?" Bruce's face displayed genuine confusion.

Don stood over him, fists clenched, ready to hit him again and again to rid himself of the wrath that was burning a hole in his gut.

"You know what I'm talking about! You and your father are the most despicable, low-down, dirty hustlers. You mow down anyone who gets in the way of your fucking business interests. I can't believe you would do that to Dr. Sampson!"

Recognition dawned on Bruce's face. He rose up like a lion remembering his majesty and roared in a fury all his own. "Get a grip on yourself, Don! You are way out of line. You have no idea what you are talking about."

"Like hell I don't! You betrayed Dr. Sampson. You helped your father and his friends defeat his legislation."

"If only I had that much influence! That Medicare legislation was worthless; it wouldn't have changed anything. What did you expect? Why would the hospitals want the government in their business any more than it already is? Markum Industries was following the lead of the industry as a whole. And do you really think I tell my father how to run his business?"

"Well, you're dropping out to go work for him."

"Hell, Don, if I finish the program, someone might mistake me for an academic. You know that wouldn't do. Besides, old man Sampson pissed me off one too many times. But that doesn't mean I don't respect the old doomsayer, or that he shouldn't be allowed to teach his course."

Bruce stood up, brushed himself off, and scanned the room—the coffee shop was nearly empty, and the few customers had returned to their own conversations.

"You told Lender and his henchmen his course was no good. Your father is on the board. You're the ones trying to run him off!"

"Sit down," Bruce ordered.

"I prefer to stand."

"Suit yourself, asshole." Bruce righted his chair, sat down, and glared at Don. "But either way, listen up. You know my father is on the board, but what you don't know is how he voted. Sure, he's a friend of Lender's, but that doesn't mean he does whatever Lender wants. You may have heard the vote was pretty much unanimous?"

Don nodded.

"That's not quite true. My father was the one that voted against. He said he wouldn't vote for suppressing the voice and spirit of inquiry fostered by one of Florence College's most notable tenured professors. Listen, Sampson may be an arrogant son of a bitch, but he knows his stuff."

"But what about those meetings at the Sentinel..."

Bruce looked Don squarely in the eye. "Development. Lender was hitting us up for money. You know, endowed professorships and that kind of thing. By the way, he did ask my opinion of the class, and I defended Sampson. What were you doing? Looking for conspiracy? It's high time you learned, Don—you can't judge a book by its cover."

DON LEFT The Down Under and wandered in the cold rain for hours, aimless and unsure where to go. When he finally climbed the back stairs of his apartment, he was chilled and bone-tired.

He sat in the dark kitchen alone, too exhausted to even turn on a light. Every ounce of strength gone, his mind blank, his heart stone. He stripped the wet winter clothes off his numb body and crawled into bed. He did not sleep, or if he did, he did not dream.

On Saturday the rain fell harder, yet not hard enough to liquefy the snow that still covered the earth. Don replayed the events of the previous week in his mind again and again, wondering how he would salvage his ruined hopes. He tried to study for his other classes but couldn't concentrate. Even strong espresso failed to clear his head. He didn't know what to do. In the late afternoon, he pulled out his map of healthcare hell and stared at it dully, searching for some secret key it might hold. But he was lost in a maze of despair and lacked compass or ball of thread to give him direction.

Turning in early, Don slept hard until the middle of the night, when he was awakened by a soft voice calling him from his bed. He felt rested and alert, and an inexplicable urge compelled him to go outside. He got up, pulled on his boots and parka, and walked out into the night air. The rain was gone, the temperature had warmed considerably, and heavy mist shrouded the campus. Florence was in the clouds.

He made his way down the glistening wet asphalt to the college and walked through the maze of brick and stone buildings toward the center of campus. Leaving the cobbled path, he stepped gently onto the white carpet beneath the great oaks and approached the middle of the quadrangle. The familiar black iron fence emerged from the mist and barred his way, but the stone omphalos pulled him like a magnet.

He stepped past the granite marker, grabbed the cold iron bars, gained purchase for one foot between the fleur-de-lis finials, pressed himself up, and jumped down upon the spongy snow next to the omphalos. The mist enshrouded him, obscuring the school buildings surrounding the quad and the dark limbs and black void above him. All he could see was the beehive stone in front of him, and it buzzed with hidden energy. He sank to his knees on the soft, snow-covered mud, fell forward, and dug his fingers into the boggy ground.

For the past year, he'd been trying to figure it out. Who was to blame for all the needless killing and torture? The businessmen like Bruce and his father? At least they were honest about their motives. The Alchemists? They were much less important than they thought they were. The gullible American people? Doctors used authority and fancy jargon to keep their errors hidden. How could you blame people who had never seen behind the curtain? What about the insurance companies, malpractice attorneys, the government? Who was hiding the mistakes in modern medicine?

Don felt the eyes of someone watching him. He raised his head.

There, enveloped in a shroud of fog, stood Sibyl Bellamy. Soft, white skin, pale as the snow. Wide-open eyes demanding his attention. Eyes not filled with fear or fury. Only sorrow. She held out her good arm, palm up, showing him the bruised and mottled skin. She pointed to the puncture wounds in her neck and chest where he had stuck IVs. Sad and silent, her eyes announced his verdict. She lifted her arm and pointed an accusing, skeletal finger. At him.

Guilty.

One by one, his victims rose up from the earth to take their places alongside Sybil Bellamy. One by one, they pointed at him. Their verdict was clear.

Guilty.

Mrs. Pinkney lifted her head from beneath a gossamer veil, revealing her gaunt face with its deathly pallor. She held out the plastic bag of bright yellow chemo he'd given her, still attached to her emaciated arm by plastic tubing. Her pleading eyes asked, *Why?* Blood oozed from the corners of her mouth and nose, trickled down her slender neck and body, and soaked the white snow at her feet in widening rounds of red.

Guilty.

Don's mother held her brunette wig in her hand. Every bit of her long, thick, dark brown hair was gone. Her pale, bald scalp contrasted with the undertaker's waxy orange makeup that masked her fine features. Her warm brown eyes met his. She nodded, reminding him she had died alone and afraid, looking for him, hoping for him.

Guilty.

I am the guilty one. I knew the difference between good and bad medicine and didn't speak up. I aided and abetted the pain and suffering. I failed Mrs. Bellamy, I failed Mrs. Pinckney, I failed to help my own mother! I looked everywhere for the monster—the one to blame for all the innocent killing.

I'm in the center of the labyrinth now, the heart of darkness…and I'm all alone. There's no one here but me, and the witnesses to—the victims of—the harm I've done. The victims! *I was supposed to be a healer, dammit!*

Sorrow swelled and stretched his aching heart. He clawed the ground, digging his fingers through the melting crystals and into the mud beneath. Don began to weep, watering the earth with his tears, and the spirits of his past patients confronted him through the swirling mist. There was Mr. Jacobs, his open chest stuffed with rolls of gauze, the ends trailing out behind him; Mr. Brady, his leather-strapped wrists and the translucent blue ventilator tubing hanging from the tracheostomy in his neck; Mr. Eldrich, holding up two

Vacutainer bottles of frothy yellow fluid collected from the dripping hole Don had made in his distended abdomen.

A cavalcade of spirits arose now from the dark earth to join them: Frances's friend Susie, her unworn support stockings dangling from her hand; the boys from Times Square, Tommy and Jared, carrying hot dogs and sugar-glazed donuts; eighteen-year-old Emily with her long, black hair, holding up her breathing tube; a serious Dana Carvey, pointing to the long scar down his chest from his botched bypass; silver-haired Andy Warhol, pale as death after his routine gallbladder operation; legless Willie King in his wheelchair, holding his surgeon's bone saw; Jesica Santillan, carrying the cooler marked *Blood Type A* that had held her mismatched liver; Solomon Salameh, arms bound by the belts that lashed him to the stretcher when they forced him from his home; and Johnny Doe, gripping the steel ice picks Dr. Freeman shoved deep into his brain.

Last of all, Bobby Webster. He stood apart from the others and— Don noticed right away—was no longer blue. Water dripped from his black hair onto his muscular shoulders. He cast aside the smoking potion in his hand, and the white fog whirling round him dispersed into the darkness. Then, with the faintest hint of a smile, Bobby shrugged and turned up his open palms.

Don looked up. The sick and suffering were not alone. One by one, the healers arrived and took their places alongside the others. Dr. Sampson appeared at the head of a tired corps of good physicians and nurses. Dr. Sheila White, her eyes underscored by dark circles; Dr. Terri Reese, her dark brown hair now streaked with gray; his old friend Jack Jordan, pale and haggard from lack of sleep; David, the burly head nurse from the bone marrow transplant unit, the good midwife, Nurse Tighe; Jim Kerner, the kind obstetrician; and his hero, Dr. Joe Gannon.

Young St. Roch appeared and stood before all the other healers. He pulled his rough, brown woolen tunic aside to reveal the draining wound in his thigh— the ruptured bubo from the plague. He pointed to the wound, looked into Don's eyes, and smiled in peace.

He is a wounded healer. And it's okay. They are all wounded healers. And I'm wounded too.

Don wept for St. Roch. He wept for all those who worked day and night to save their patients from impending disaster. He wept for Dr. Sampson. He wept for himself. His tears mixed with the melting snow and, along with the spirits, returned to the dark umber earth.

The swirling fog lifted with a gentle wind, and morning's first glow lightened the horizon behind the tall oaks and buildings. A flash of morning sun shot across the yard from the purple east.

Light! It seemed like years since he had seen it. He hugged the cool wet earth in gratitude and felt the mud accepting the warmth of his fingers, squishing between them the way it had when he made mud pies as a kid. On a gentle breath of air, he caught a faint but familiar scent emanating from the mud—an earthy, fertile, sweet hint of the long-awaited beginnings of spring.

Don rolled onto his back and beheld the tree limbs arching over him like a vast cathedral. A feeling of openness grew inside him, a sense of being extended far beyond his physical body until he encompassed everything around him. Until all that was without was within. The branches were his arms and fingers, reaching for the sky and connecting him to the heavens. The unseen dull roots, softened by spring rain, were his legs and feet, stretching down into the underworld. Water rushed through him, as if a channel coursed through his veins between the deep waters in the firmaments above and below, washing him clean and making everything clear.

He felt a deep connection to all life, reaching from the underworld, through the core of his being, into the sky. His boundaries were obliterated. Fingers of light extended far beyond him on all sides in a web joining him to all those he cared for and all those who cared for him: his patients, his family, Dr. Sampson, Frances, even Bruce. And Sarah. He felt an especially strong bond with Sarah. *How did I not see it before?*

The smell of earth, delicious and strong now in the first warmth of the morning sun, filled his senses, and a sparrow gave voice to the glad song of earth. He saw it all now. He had been through hell where people would least suspect it—in temples made for healing—and he could see what needed to change.

Don knew what he had to do. He rolled over and kissed the ground. *I will speak up! I will tell their stories. I will speak for them all.*

Don smeared the mud from his fingers across his face and started to laugh. He was filled with energy, determination, and a clarity of purpose he hadn't felt in years.

I will go with Dr. Sampson to Memphis. I will stand up for him—write a letter on his behalf—go speak to the board—testify at his grievance hearing. I will help him reform American healthcare!

He heard a voice. "Are you okay?" It was the night watchman.

"Yes, I'm fine," he laughed. "Just fine!" And he couldn't stop laughing as he imagined how he must appear to the night watchman: a crazy student smeared with mud, hugging the earth, laughing, and crying like a madman.

He eyed Don warily. "Well," he said in a gentle voice, "I guess you should probably get out of there now."

"Yes sir," Don whooped and leapt over the railing. "Thank you!" he hollered back as he ran full speed across the soggy, brown grass of the quad.

Great drafts of the cool woodland air filled his lungs as he ran. His mind was awake in a way it had not been in years. He was filled with new determination to tell the truth. In the clear morning light he knew exactly what to do. He would work to reform the system along with Dr. Sampson and maybe even Frances and Bruce.

Maybe even Bruce! He laughed with relief—his yoke of suspicion and jealousy was gone.

He would work with government, business, and healthcare leaders to make the changes needed. He would wake people up. He would tell the full story and show people how to choose real health care, how change was up to them, how to avoid wasting their lives and livelihood on a mirage. But there was one thing he needed to do right now.

He sprinted toward the Horn Gate at the front entrance of campus and bounded through the narrow passageway between the tall stones without even slowing, like an antelope at the first sign of spring. He ran right down the middle of Main Street into the early morning sun, veered onto the empty sidewalk, and slalomed through the center of town, weaving through parking meters, light posts, and street signs.

Only one building was open at this early hour—a white granite building with opaque glass globes on black light posts. Don stopped in front of it, took three deep breaths, and strode up the steps and through double doors emblazoned with the simple word, POLICE. He passed two men in blue uniforms near the front door and two dispatchers drinking coffee and answering phones. All of them turned, dumbfounded, and watched him go by. What a sight he was, unshaven, covered with mud, breathless, and filled with glee.

Don walked straight up to the main desk.

A gruff sergeant inspected him with unveiled skepticism. "Who are you?"

"I'm Doctor Dante Newman, and I'm here to report a crime."

Epilogue

JUST AS I WAS EXILED from my fair city of Florence seven hundred years ago, two good doctors, Dante Newman and his mentor, Virgil Sampson, have been driven out of their ivory tower into what appears to be an academic backwater.

Foresight is fallible. One can never be certain what the future holds or what will follow from one's actions. Heroes must face adversity and act without full foreknowledge. So it has been for Dr. Newman. He began his journey as an ill-equipped protagonist and unlikely hero. Yet in the hour of his greatest challenge, Dante Newman stood up to overweening authority, took charge of a desperate situation, and became the kind of doctor we all want—a courageous doctor willing to act against his own self-interest for the sake of his patient.

Dr. Newman had an inkling of the future. He sensed the tides of story and history moving through his life. A chorus of voices in his head demanded to be heard. Despite the pain of hearing, he listened. He heard. He acted. He did his job, even though he had no idea of the consequences for himself, his career, and the boy, Bobby Webster. His actions produced results far beyond his reckoning—sending ripples through time waxing into waves lapping distant shores.

The founders of Florence College had set a wheel in motion that reached an apparent terminus with the departure of Dr. Sampson and Dr. Newman. Yet, history is full of surprises. The leaders of Florence College did not foresee what would come of their plans to drive out Dr. Sampson. Dr. Newman's report of Bobby Webster's hazing, together with Dr. Sampson's grievance filing, led to President Lender's ouster, the resignation of three prominent board members, and the exposure and banishment of the Alchemists.

The most important consequence of Dr. Dante Newman's fateful year at Florence College is yet unknown to him. No one told him what happened to young Bobby Webster after his transfer to the New American Hospital intensive care unit. After three days in a coma, he awoke! Bobby Webster's eyelids flickered in response to his mother's voice, and shortly afterward he opened his eyes. He was transferred to a rehabilitation unit and is expected to make a full recovery. The young man will live, thanks to Dr. Newman. Dr. Newman was a good physician who served the true end of healing.

Dr. Sampson's prophecies about the future of American healthcare are proving true. Needless killing and senseless waste continue unabated. Now more than ever, Americans need healers who can blaze a path through the perils of modern medicine—physicians like Dante Newman, surgeons like Bruce Markum, nurse practitioners like Frances Hunt, physician assistants, nurses, pharmacists, administrators, corporate leaders, even patients—people willing to step forward to lead America's most important healthcare improvement initiatives.

Most aspiring young doctors have no inkling of the world they are preparing to enter. Most patients have no idea what lies behind the exam room curtain. But now you know the truth. You have seen behind the curtain. Everything necessary to find true health and healing is available. The rest is up to you.

So, what are you going to do?

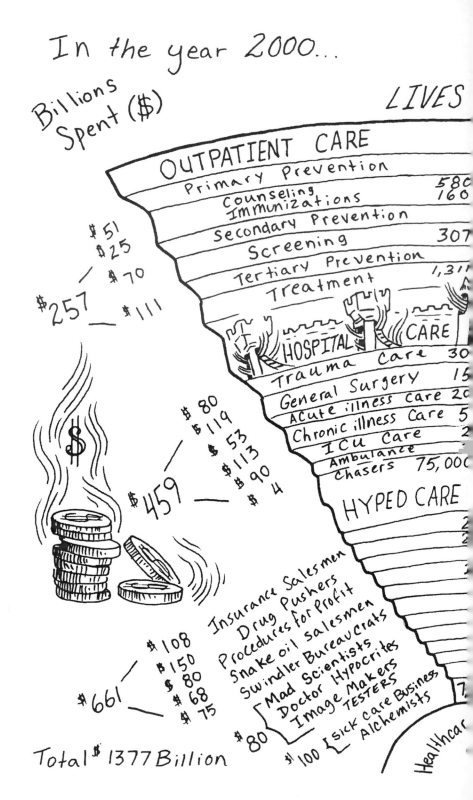

In the year 2000...

Billions Spent ($)

LIVES

OUTPATIENT CARE

Primary Prevention
Counseling   580
Immunizations   160

Secondary Prevention
Screening   307

Tertiary Prevention
Treatment   1,31

$51
$25
$70
$257 $111

HOSPITAL CARE

Trauma Care   30
General Surgery   15
Acute illness Care 2c
Chronic illness Care 5
ICU Care   2
Ambulance
Chasers   75,000

$80
$119
$53
$113
$90
$4
$459

HYPED CARE

Insurance Salesmen
Drug Pushers
Procedures for Profit
Snake oil Salesmen
Swindler Bureaucrats
Mad Scientists
Doctor Hypocrites
Image Makers
TESTERS
Sick Care Business
Alchemists

$108
$150
$80
$68
$75
$661

$80

$100

Healthcar

Total $ 1377 Billion

SAVED

LIVES LOST

Mutual Insurance

2,359,000 Total

Catastrophic Insurance

15,000 Drug reactions
5,000 Other medication errors
— 20,000 Lives Lost

7,000 Medication errors
20,000 Other errors
80,000 Hospital infections
— 107,000 Lives Lost

20,000 lack of Health insurance
106,000 Drug reactions & overdose
12,000 unnecessary surgery
— 138,000 Lives Lost

265,000 Total Lives Lost

ofiteers

Dr. Gil Sampson, Florence College

Health System Seminar Syllabus

Time: Each Wednesday 9:00–11:00 AM unless otherwise noted

Location: Florence College, Old Anatomy Theater, unless otherwise noted

Field Work: Two weeks in fall semester and three weeks in spring semester based at American University in Washington, D.C.

Expectations: Read assigned core readings carefully prior to each seminar. Each student will present at least two case studies

Syllabus Updates: Check www.endofhealing.com regularly for reading list updates, to recommend supplemental readings to your colleagues and to participate in online discussion board.

Office Hours: 2:00–5:00 PM weekdays by appointment in Health System Science Program Office.

- -

August 22, 2001—Seminar 1: Great Scientists Who Couldn't Cure

Core Readings:

Porter, Roy. *The Greatest Benefit to Mankind: A Medical History of Humanity from Antiquity to the Present.* Hammersmith, London: HarperCollins, 1997: 1–30.

Bunker JP, Frazier HS, Mosteller F. Improving health: measuring effects of medical care. *Milbank Q.* 1994;72(2):225–258.

Dubos, René J. *Mirage of Health; Utopias, Progress, and Biological Change.* First ed. New York,: Harper, 1959, Chapters 1–4.

Supplemental Readings:

Diamond, Jared M. *Guns, Germs, and Steel: The Fates of Human Societies.* New York: W.W. Norton and Company, 1997.

Sox HC Jr. Preventive health services in adults. *N Engl J Med.* 1994;330(22):1589–95.

August 29, 2001—Seminar 2: The Beauty Industry

Dubos, René J. *Mirage of Health; Utopias, Progress, and Biological Change.* First ed. New York,: Harper, 1959, Chapters 5–8.

Wolf, Naomi. *The Beauty Myth.* London: Chatto & Windus, 1990.

September 5, 2001—Seminar 3: Institutionalized Gluttony

Schlosser, Eric. *Fast Food Nation: The Dark Side of the All-American Meal.* Boston: Houghton Mifflin, 2001: Chapter 10.

Calle EE, Thun MJ, Petrelli JM, Rodriguez C, Heath CW, Jr. Body-mass index and mortality in a prospective cohort of U.S. adults. *N Engl J Med.* Oct 7 1999;341(15):1097–1105.

Allison DB, Fontaine KR, Manson JE, Stevens J, VanItallie TB. Annual deaths attributable to obesity in the United States. *Jama.* Oct 27 1999;282(16):1530–1538.

September 12, 2001—Seminar 4: The Healthcare Wasteland

Core Readings:

Winslow CM, Kosecoff JB, Chassin M, Kanouse DE, Brook RH. The appropriateness of performing coronary artery bypass surgery. *Jama.* Jul 22–29 1988;260(4):505–509.

Bernstein SJ, Hilborne LH, Leape LL, et al. The appropriateness of use of coronary angiography in New York State. *Jama.* Feb 10 1993;269(6):766–769.

Hilborne LH, Leape LL, Bernstein SJ, et al. The appropriateness of use of percutaneous transluminal coronary angioplasty in New York State. *Jama.* Feb 10 1993;269(6):761–765.

Leape LL, Hilborne LH, Park RE, et al. The appropriateness of use of coronary artery bypass graft surgery in New York State. *Jama.* Feb 10 1993;269(6):753–760.
Supplemental Readings:
Roos LL, Bond R, Naylor CD, Chassin MR, Morris AL. Coronary angiography and bypass surgery in Manitoba and the United States: a first comparison. *Can J Cardiol.* Jan-Feb 1994;10(1):49–56.
Chassin MR, Kosecoff J, Solomon DH, Brook RH. How coronary angiography is used. Clinical determinants of appropriateness. *Jama.* Nov 13 1987;258(18):2543–2547.
Chassin MR, Kosecoff J, Park RE, et al. Does inappropriate use explain geographic variations in the use of health care services? A study of three procedures. *Jama.* Nov 13 1987;258(18):2533–2537.
Bernstein SJ, McGlynn EA, Siu AL, et al. The appropriateness of hysterectomy. A comparison of care in seven health plans. Health Maintenance Organization Quality of Care Consortium. *Jama.* May 12 1993;269(18):2398–2402.
Nelemans PJ, de Bie RA, de Vet HC, Sturmans F. Injection therapy for subacute and chronic benign low back pain. *Cochrane Database Syst Rev.* 2000(2):CD001824.
Dugdale DC, Epstein R, Pantilat SZ. Time and the patient-physician relationship. *J Gen Intern Med.* 1999 Jan;14 Suppl 1:S34–40.
Streja DA, Rabkin SW. Factors associated with implementation of preventive care measures in patients with diabetes mellitus. *Arch Intern Med.* Feb 8, 1999;159(3):294–302.

September 19, 2001—Course Overview
No assigned readings.

September 26, 2001—Seminar 5: Medical Violence
Core Readings:
Kohn, Linda T., Janet Corrigan, and Molla S. Donaldson. *To Err Is Human: Building a Safer Health System.* Washington, D.C.: National Academy Press, 2000, Chapters 1–3.
Brennan TA, Leape LL, Laird NM, et al. Incidence of adverse events and negligence in hospitalized patients. Results of the Harvard Medical Practice Study I. *N Engl J Med.* Feb 7 1991;324(6):370–376.
Leape LL, Brennan TA, Laird N, et al. The nature of adverse events in hospitalized patients. Results of the Harvard Medical Practice Study II. *N Engl J Med.* Feb 7 1991;324(6):377–384.
Thomas EJ, Studdert DM, Burstin HR, et al. Incidence and types of adverse events and negligent care in Utah and Colorado. *Med Care.* Mar 2000;38(3):261–271.
Starfield B. Is US health really the best in the world? *Jama.* July 26, 2000;284(4):483–5
Supplemental Readings:
Gerlin, A. How Your Hospital Could Kill You. *Reader's Digest.* June 2000:174.
Institute of Medicine (U.S.). Committee on Quality of Health Care in America. *Crossing the Quality Chasm: A New Health System for the 21st Century.* Washington, D.C.: National Academy Press, 2001.
Leape LL. Error in medicine. *Jama.* Dec 21 1994;272(23):1851–1857.
Roemer MI, Schwartz JL. Doctor slowdown: effects on the population of Los Angeles County. *Soc Sci Med.* 1979 Dec;13C(4):213–8.

October 3, 2001—Seminar 6: High-Tech Suicide
Core Readings:

Bailar JC, 3rd, Gornik HL. Cancer undefeated. *N Engl J Med*. May 29 1997;336(22):1569–1574.

Bailar JC, 3rd, Smith EM. Progress against cancer? *N Engl J Med*. May 8 1986;314(19):1226–1232.

Saklayen M, Liss H, Markert R. In-hospital cardiopulmonary resuscitation. Survival in 1 hospital and literature review. *Medicine (Baltimore)*. Jul 1995;74(4):163–175.

Supplemental Readings:

Stadtmauer EA, O'Neill A, Goldstein LJ, et al. Conventional-dose chemotherapy compared with high-dose chemotherapy plus autologous hematopoietic stem-cell transplantation for metastatic breast cancer. Philadelphia Bone Marrow Transplant Group. *N Engl J Med*. Apr 13 2000;342(15):1069–1076.

October 10, 2001—Seminar 7: Health Care Assassins

Core Readings:

Starr, Paul. *The Social Transformation of American Medicine*. New York: Basic Books, 1982:199–232.

Porter, Roy. *The Greatest Benefit to Mankind: A Medical History of Humanity from Antiquity to the Present*. Hammersmith, London: HarperCollins, 1997:628–719.

Goodman, John C., and Gerald L. Musgrave. *Patient Power: Solving America's Health Care Crisis*. Washington, D.C.: Cato Institute, 1992.

Supplemental Readings:

Starr, Paul. *The Social Transformation of American Medicine*. New York: Basic Books, 1982:All of Book One–A Sovereign Profession: The Rise of Medical Authority and the Shaping of the Medical System.

October 17, 2001—Seminar 8: Ambulance Chasers

Core Readings:

Localio AR, Lawthers AG, Brennan TA, et al. Relation between malpractice claims and adverse events due to negligence. Results of the Harvard Medical Practice Study III. *N Engl J Med*. Jul 25 1991;325(4):245–251.

Brennan, T. A., C. M. Sox, and H. R. Burstin. Relation between Negligent Adverse Events and the Outcomes of Medical-Malpractice Litigation. *N Engl J Med* 335, no. 26 (1996): 1963–7.

Studdert DM, Thomas EJ, Burstin HR, Zbar BI, Orav EJ, Brennan TA. Negligent care and malpractice claiming behavior in Utah and Colorado. *Med Care*. Mar 2000;38(3):250–260.

Janowsky EC, Kupper LL, Hulka BS. Meta-Analyses of the Relation between Silicone Breast Implants and the Risk of Connective-Tissue Diseases. *N Engl J Med*. March 16, 2000;342:781,

Supplemental Readings:

Nelson, K. B., J. M. Dambrosia, T. Y. Ting, and J. K. Grether. Uncertain Value of Electronic Fetal Monitoring in Predicting Cerebral Palsy. *N Engl J Med* 334, no. 10 (1996): 613–8.

Kessler DP, McClellan MB, National Bureau of Economic Research. Do Doctors Practice Defensive Medicine. *Quarterly Journal of Economics* 111(2): 353–390, 1996.

Sloan FA, Mergenhagen PM, Burfield WB, Bovbjerg RR, Hassan M. Medical malpractice experience of physicians. Predictable or haphazard? *Jama*. Dec 15 1989;262(23):3291–3297.

Burstin HR, Johnson WG, Lipsitz SR, Brennan TA. Do the poor sue more? A case-control study of malpractice claims and socioeconomic status. *Jama.* Oct 13 1993;270(14):1697–1701.

October 24, 2001—Seminar 9: Unnatural Law Makers
Howard PK. *The Death of common sense: how the law is suffocating America.* First ed. New York: Random House; 1994.

October 31, 2001—Seminar 10: Insurance Salesmen
Core Readings:
Starr, Paul. *The Social Transformation of American Medicine.* New York: Basic Books, 1982: 235–334.
The World Health Report 2000–Health Systems: Improving Performance. The World Health Organization, Geneva, Switzerland, 2000.
Supplemental Readings:
Woolhandler S, Himmelstein DU. The deteriorating administrative efficiency of the U.S. health care system. *N Engl J Med.* May 2 1991;324(18):1253–1258.
Woolhandler S, Campbell T, Himmelstein DU. Costs of health care administration in the United States and Canada in 1999. [Prepublication analysis provided to Dr. Virgil Sampson for use in Health System Science Program only–confidential/not for citation.]
Blendon RJ, Donelan K, Leitman R, et al. Physicians' perspectives on caring for patients in the United States, Canada, and West Germany. *N Engl J Med.* Apr 8 1993;328(14):1011–1016.
Kassler, Jeanne. *Bitter Medicine: Greed and Chaos in American Health Care.* New York: Carol Pub. Group, 1994: Chapter 3.
Franks P, Clancy CM, Gold MR. Health Insurance and Mortality: Evidence from a National Cohort. *Jama.* 1993;270(6):737–41.

November 8, 2001—Seminar 11: The Drug Pushers
Core Readings:
Wazana A. Physicians and the pharmaceutical industry: is a gift ever just a gift? *Jama.* Jan 19 2000;283(3):373–380.
Supplemental Readings:
Wolfe SM. Why do American drug companies spend more than $12 billion a year pushing drugs? Is it education or promotion? Characteristics of materials distributed by drug companies: four points of view. *J Gen Intern Med.* Oct 1996;11(10):637–639.
Shorr RI, Greene WL. A food-borne outbreak of expensive antibiotic use in a community teaching hospital. *Jama.* 1995 Jun 28;273(24):1908.

November 21, 2001—Seminar 12: Procedures for Profit
Core Readings:
Porter, Roy. *The Greatest Benefit to Mankind: A Medical History of Humanity from Antiquity to the Present.* Hammersmith, London: HarperCollins, 1997: Chapter 19–Surgery.
United States. The Profits of Misery: How Inpatient Psychiatric Treatment Bilks the System and Betrays Our Trust: Hearing Before the Select Committee on Children, youth and families, House of Representatives: US Government Printing Office, Washington; 1992.

Woolhandler S, Himmelstein DU. When money is the mission—the high costs of investor-owned care. *N Engl J Med*. Aug 5 1999;341(6):444–446.

Supplemental Readings:

Valenstein, Elliot S. *Great and Desperate Cures: The Rise and Decline of Psychosurgery and Other Radical Treatments for Mental Illness*. New York: Basic Books, 1986.

Freeman W. Transorbital leucotomy. *Lancet*. Sept. 4, 1948:371–373.

Fogg-Waberski J, Waberski W. Electroconvulsive therapy: clinical science vs controversial perceptions. *Conn Med*. Jun 2000;64(6):335–337.

Stone G. Listening to electroshock. *New Yorker*. Nov. 14, 1994:54–59.

Glen T, Scott AI. Variation in rates of electroconvulsive therapy use among consultant teams in Edinburgh (1993-1996). *J Affect Disord*. Apr 2000;58(1):75–78.

Lindorff, Dave. *Marketplace Medicine: The Rise of the for-Profit Hospital Chains*. New York: Bantam Books, 1992.

Bogdanich, Walt. *The Great White Lie: How America's Hospitals Betray Our Trust and Endanger Our Lives*. New York: Simon & Schuster, 1991.

December 5, 2001—Seminar 13: Snake Oil Salesmen

Core Readings:

Beecher HK. The powerful placebo. *J Am Med Assoc*. Dec 24 1955;159(17):1602–1606.

Eisenberg DM, Kessler RC, Foster C, Norlock FE, Calkins DR, Delbanco TL. Unconventional medicine in the United States. Prevalence, costs, and patterns of use. *N Engl J Med*. Jan 28 1993;328(4):246–252.

Moertel CG, Fleming TR, Rubin J, et al. A clinical trial of amygdalin (Laetrile) in the treatment of human cancer. *N Engl J Med*. Jan 28 1982;306(4):201–206.

Cassileth BR, Lusk EJ, Guerry D, et al. Survival and quality of life among patients receiving unproven as compared with conventional cancer therapy. *N Engl J Med*. Apr 25 1991;324(17):1180–1185.

Angell M, Kassirer JP. Alternative medicine—the risks of untested and unregulated remedies. *N Engl J Med*. Sep 17 1998;339(12):839–841.

Echt DS, Liebson PR, Mitchell LB, et al. Mortality and morbidity in patients receiving encainide, flecainide, or placebo. The Cardiac Arrhythmia Suppression Trial. *N Engl J Med*. Mar 21 1991;324(12):781–788.

Supplemental Readings:

Moore, Thomas J. *Deadly Medicine: Why Tens of Thousands of Heart Patients Died in America's Worst Drug Disaster*. New York: Simon & Schuster, 1995.

Psaty BM, Heckbert SR, Koepsell TD, et al. The risk of myocardial infarction associated with antihypertensive drug therapies. *Jama*. Aug 23-30 1995;274(8):620–625.

Kunin RA. Snake oil. *West J Med*. Aug 1989;151(2):208.

Fowler, Gene. *Mystic Healers & Medicine Shows: Blazing Trails to Wellness in the Old West and Beyond*. Santa Fe, N.M.: Ancient City Press, 1997.

Holbrook, Stewart Hall. *The Golden Age of Quackery*. New York,: Macmillan, 1959.

Janssen WF. Cancer quackery: past and present. *FDA Consum*. Jul-Aug 1977;11(6):27–32.

Holland JF. The krebiozen story. Is cancer quackery dead? *Jama*. Apr 17 1967;200(3):213–218.

Marshall E. The politics of alternative medicine. *Science*. Sep 30 1994;265(5181):2000–2002.

Green S. A critique of the rationale for cancer treatment with coffee enemas and diet. *Jama*. Dec 9 1992;268(22):3224–3227.

Unproven methods of cancer management. Laetrile. *CA Cancer J Clin*. May-Jun 1991;41(3):187–192.

Herbert V. Laetrile: the cult of cyanide. Promoting poison for profit. *Am J Clin Nutr.* May 1979;32(5):1121–1158.

December 12, 2001—Field Trip, Washington, DC: Bureaucracy and Rulemaking in the Executive Branch

Core Readings:

Marwick C. Implementing the FDA Modernization Act. *Jama.* Mar 18 1998;279(11):815–816.

Berenson RA. Medicare+Choice: doubling or disappearing? *Health Aff (Millwood).* 2001;Suppl Web Exclusives:W65–82.

Greenwald LM, Levy JM, Ingber MJ. Favorable selection in the Medicare+Choice program: new evidence. *Health Care Financ Rev.* Spring 2000;21(3):127–134.

December 19, 2001—Field Trip: National Institutes of Health

Core Readings:

Alibek, Ken, and Stephen Handelman. *Biohazard: The Chilling True Story of the Largest Covert Biological Weapons Program in the World, Told from the inside by the Man Who Ran It.* First ed. New York: Random House, 1999.

Deyo RA, Psaty BM, Simon G, Wagner EH, Omenn GS. The messenger under attack — intimidation of researchers by special-interest groups. *N Engl J Med.* Apr 17 1997;336(16):1176–1180.

Supplemental Readings:

Ries LAG, Eisner M, Kosary CL, Hankey BF, Miller BA, Clegg L, Edwards BK ed. *SEER Cancer Statistics Review, 1973–1999.* Bethesda, MD: National Cancer Institute; 2002.

Blum, A.M., and E.J. Solberg. "The Tobacco Pandemic." In *Fundamentals of Clinical Practice: A Textbook on the Patient, Doctor, and Society,* edited by Mark B. Mengel and Warren Lee Holleman, xxiv, 515 p. New York: Plenum Medical Book Co., 1997.

Hasenfeld R, Shekelle PG. Is the methodological quality of guidelines declining in the US? Comparison of the quality of US Agency for Health Care Policy and Research (AHCPR) guidelines with those published subsequently. *Qual Saf Health Care.* Dec 2003;12(6):428–434.

January 9, 2001—Seminar 14: White Coat Hypocrites

Core Readings:

Zyzanski SJ, Stange KC, Langa D, Flocke SA. Trade-offs in high-volume primary care practice. *J Fam Pract.* May 1998;46(5):397–402.

Hsiao WC, Dunn DL, Verrilli DK. Assessing the implementation of physician-payment reform. *N Engl J Med.* Apr 1 1993;328(13):928–933.

Supplemental Readings:

Hsiao WC, Braun P, Dunn D, Becker ER, DeNicola M, Ketcham TR. Results and policy implications of the resource-based relative-value study. *N Engl J Med.* Sep 29 1988;319(13):881–888.

January 16, 2001—Seminar 15: The Image Makers

Core Readings:

Hampton JR, Harrison MJ, Mitchell JR, Prichard JS, Seymour C. Relative contributions of history-taking, physical examination, and laboratory investigation to diagnosis and management of medical outpatients. *Br Med J.* May 31 1975;2(5969):486–489.

Fowkes FG. Containing the use of diagnostic tests. *Br Med J (Clin Res Ed)*. Feb 16 1985;290(6467):488–490.

Sandler G. Costs of unnecessary tests. *Br Med J*. Jul 7 1979;2(6181):21–24.

Fisher ES, Welch HG. Avoiding the unintended consequences of growth in medical care: how might more be worse? *Jama*. Feb 3 1999;281(5):446–453.

Supplemental Readings:

Peterson MC, Holbrook JH, Von Hales D, Smith NL, Staker LV. Contributions of the history, physical examination, and laboratory investigation in making medical diagnoses. *West J Med*. Feb 1992;156(2):163–165.

Pellet J. HealthSouth's digital dream: CEO Richard Scrushy promises to build the world's most high tech hospital—with Lawrence J. Ellison's and Oracle's help he just may succeed—Technology and the CEO. *Chief Executive*. December 1, 2001:33–36.

Postman, Neil. *Amusing Ourselves to Death: Public Discourse in the Age of Show Business*. New York, N.Y., U.S.A.: Penguin Books, 1986.

January 23, 2001—Seminar 16: The Sick Care Business

Core Readings:

Hay JW, Ricardo-Campbell R. Rand Health Insurance study. *Lancet*. Jul 12 1986;2(8498):106.

Kuttner R. Columbia/HCA and the resurgence of the for-profit hospital business. (1). *N Engl J Med*. Aug 1 1996;335(5):362–367.

Kuttner R. Columbia/HCA and the resurgence of the for-profit hospital business. (2). *N Engl J Med*. Aug 8 1996;335(6):446–451.

Supplemental Readings:

The Rand Health Insurance Study: a spanner in the works? *Lancet*. May 3 1986;1(8488):1012–1013.

Himmelstein DU, Woolhandler S, Hellander I, Wolfe SM. Quality of care in investor-owned vs not-for-profit HMOs. *Jama*. Jul 14 1999;282(2):159–163.

Shaughnessy PW, Schlenker RE, Hittle DF. Home health care outcomes under capitated and fee-for-service payment. *Health Care Financ Rev*. Fall 1994;16(1):187–222.

Garg PP, Frick KD, Diener-West M, Powe NR. Effect of the ownership of dialysis facilities on patients' survival and referral for transplantation. *N Engl J Med*. Nov 25 1999;341(22):1653–1660.

Hornberger JC, Garber AM, Jeffery JR. Mortality, hospital admissions, and medical costs of end-stage renal disease in the United States and Manitoba, Canada. *Med Care*. Jul 1997;35(7):686–700.

Retchin SM, Brown RS, Yeh SC, Chu D, Moreno L. Outcomes of stroke patients in Medicare fee for service and managed care. *Jama*. Jul 9 1997;278(2):119–124.

Bailey JE, Van Brunt DL, Mirvis DM, et al. Academic managed care organizations and adverse selection under Medicaid managed care in Tennessee. *Jama*. Sep 15 1999;282(11):1067–1072.

Anders, George. *Health against Wealth: HMOs and the Breakdown of Medical Trust*. Boston: Houghton Mifflin, 1996.

Kassler, Jeanne. *Bitter Medicine: Greed and Chaos in American Health Care*. New York: Carol Pub. Group, 1994.

Kane NM. *Nonprofit hospital status: what is it worth?* Boston: Harvard School of Public Health; 1994.

Silverman EM, Skinner JS, Fisher ES. The association between for-profit hospital ownership and increased Medicare spending. *N Engl J Med.* Aug 5 1999;341(6):420–426.

Schramm CJ. *Blue Cross Conversion: Policy Considerations Arising from a Sale of the Maryland Plan.* Baltimore: Abel Foundation; November 2001.

Chang CF, Kiser LJ, Bailey JE, et al. Tennessee's failed managed care program for mental health and substance abuse services. *Jama.* Mar 18 1998;279(11):864–869.

Taylor DH, Jr., Whellan DJ, Sloan FA. Effects of admission to a teaching hospital on the cost and quality of care for Medicare beneficiaries. *N Engl J Med.* Jan 28 1999;340(4):293–299.

Gray, Bradford H., and Institute of Medicine (U.S.). *The New Health Care for Profit: Doctors and Hospitals in a Competitive Environment.* Washington, D.C.: National Academy Press, 1983.

Herbert ME. A for-profit health plan's experience and strategy. *Health Aff (Millwood).* Mar-Apr 1997;16(2):121–124.

January 30, 2002—Field Trip, Washington, DC: Senate Committee on Health, Education, Labor, and Pensions

U.S. Congress. *Patient Safety Act of 2001.* 107th H.R. 1804.

February 6, 2002—American University Lecture, Washington, DC: Healthcare Lobbyists

Young, B., Surrusco, M. "The Other Drug War: Big Pharma's 625 Washington Lobbyists." edited by F. Clemente, J. Knapp and C. Jervis. Washington, D.C.: Public Citizen, 2001.

February 13, 2002—Field Trip, Washington, DC: Politicians and Lawmakers

Dudley RA, Luft HS. Managed care in transition. *N Engl J Med.* April 5 2001;344(14):1087–92.

Drazen JM, Bush GW, Gore A. The Republican and Democratic candidates speak on health care. *N Engl J Med.* Oct 19 2000;343(16):1184–9.

February 20, 2002—Seminar 17: Alchemists

Core Readings:

Jonson, Ben. *The Alchemist: A Comedy. Acted in the Year 1610 by the King's Majesty's Servants,* 1870.

Supplemental Readings:

Porter, Roy. *Quacks: Fakers & Charlatans in English Medicine.* Stroud; Charleston, SC: Tempus, 2000.

Fowler, Gene. *Mystic Healers & Medicine Shows: Blazing Trails to Wellness in the Old West and Beyond.* Santa Fe, N.M.: Ancient City Press, 1997.

February 27, 2002—Seminar 18: Counterfeit Care

Macklin, Ruth. *Enemies of Patients.* New York: Oxford University Press, 1993.

Maule WF. Screening for colorectal cancer by nurse endoscopists. *N Engl J Med.* Jan 20, 1994;330(3):183–187.

Starfield B. Is primary care essential? *Lancet.* Oct 22 1994;344(8930):1129–1133.

March 6, 2002—Seminar 19: Industrial Giants Whose Time Has Past

Relman AS. The new medical-industrial complex. *N Engl J Med.* Oct 23 1980;303(17):963–970.

Illich, Ivan. *Medical Nemesis: The Expropriation of Health.* New York: Pantheon Books, A Division of Random House, Inc., 1976.

March 13, 2002—Seminar 20: Industrial Traitors to America

O'Brien LA, Grisso JA, Maislin G, et al. Nursing home residents' preferences for life-sustaining treatments. *Jama.* Dec 13 1995;274(22):1775–1779.

March 29, 2002—Seminar 21: Industries That Betray Their Architects

Hiatt HH. Protecting the medical commons: who is responsible? *N Engl J Med.* Jul 31 1975;293(5):235–241.

Harvey JB. The spin doctors: an invitation to health care professionals to reflect on the organizational dynamics of the Last Supper and why Judas was not the traitor. *Manag Care Q.* Winter 1997;5(1):76–82.

Acknowledgements

Countless discussions with friends, family, colleagues, and strangers furthered my insight into Dr. Newman's story and how to share it with the world. I extend my deepest thanks and gratitude to every person who shared an experience, gave advice, read a rough draft, or listened to me rattle on about *The End of Healing*.

Friends, fellow expatriates, and colleagues in Italy helped me in the book's early stages. Nita Tucker, author and founder of *The Florentine*, convinced me to embrace fiction and provided fundamental early direction and encouragement. I had many excellent advisors during that sabbatical year: John Skinner of Dartmouth College, Michal Tamuz of State University of New York, Sam Cohn of the University of Glasgow, Elaine Ruffolo of Syracuse University in Florence, Art Sutherland, Jim Iuliano, Piha Tovis, and Susi Bellamy.

Upon my return from a year abroad, Ernie Smith served me as nobly as Odysseus' good swineherd. Ernie's wife, Jill Smith, and my mother, Phyllis Bailey, served ably as the primary romance specialists for this work. If Don Newman's feeble attempts at romance—or Bruce's more assertive ones—bear any semblance to the attempts such men make in reality, I have them to thank.

My tutors from St. John's College in Annapolis, Maryland, especially Chaninah Maschler and Joe Sachs, offered frank criticism and expert correction. For their kindness to a former student and the willingness to read a very rough draft—despite their customary literary diet of the greatest books of the western world—I am forever in their debt. They remain among my greatest teachers. For the listening ears and good advice of many other tutors and alumni friends of St. John's, I am most appreciative. Mac Fleming, teacher of American history at Indian Springs School in Birmingham, Alabama since 1952, also reviewed an early version and attested to the accuracy of the many historical references to early American history in *The End of Healing*.

Notable medical historians Carlos Camargo of Stanford University and Jan Sherman of the University of Memphis helped ensure the accuracy of historical details. Chester Burns, former Director of the Institute for the Medical Humanities at the University of Texas, Galveston, was my primary mentor in the field of medical history. At a point when I despaired of ever completing this novel, Chester said if I worked early each morning for an hour, I'd finish.

Chester, wherever you are, thank you for making me laugh and for keeping me moving ahead.

Many good physicians offered guidance and encouragement. In particular, Dennis Schaberg and Hank Herrod staunchly supported my research into the history of medicine and comparative health system performance. My colleagues in the University of Tennessee Health Science Center Division of General Internal Medicine, especially Laura Sprabery, Robert Morrison, Bruce Steinhauer, and Jim Lewis, offered unflagging support and encouragement, and Bob Egerman and Amado Friere clarified issues related to obstetrics, maternal and fetal medicine, and pulmonary medicine. Christine and Tom Sinsky enlightened me regarding the mysterious operations of the Relative Value Scale Update Committee (RUC) and how it affects primary care. Geoffrey Smith's eloquent analogy between healthcare and pinball inspired Frances's speech about counterfeit healthcare. Michael Painter of the Robert Wood Johnson Foundation devoted long hours to the review and critique of an early manuscript and relentlessly insisted that the characters represent the best arguments of all sides in the healthcare reform debate.

Two of my best physician mentors exerted a tremendous influence on *The End of Healing* by providing the inspiration for Dr. Gil Sampson. Michael Copass of the University of Washington demonstrated to me that a physician must treat patients from all walks of life with the respect, compassion, and care one would want for one's own family. Dr. Copass models true aequanimitas, hard work, and decisiveness in a patient's hour of need. The pioneering work of Jack Wennberg of Dartmouth serves as a beacon of light for countless physicians and health services researchers trying to understand American healthcare. For more than forty years, Dr. Wennberg has documented the marked variations in health care delivery across the United States that Don Newman and his classmates study in their Health System Seminar. I cannot overstate the influence this body of work has had on *The End of Healing*. Anyone who hopes to improve American healthcare must begin by studying the classic papers and influential *Dartmouth Atlas of Health Care* reports of Jack Wennberg, Elliot Fisher, and their colleagues at the Dartmouth Institute for Health Policy and Clinical Practice.

For insights into the inner workings of federal and local government, I am indebted to Tom Hoyer, former Bureau Chief for the Center for Medicare and Medicaid Services. Tom first took me under his wing twenty-five years ago when I was lucky enough to intern for him at the Health Care Financing Administration. Tom was determined to teach me how the government works and where it goes astray. He remains a good mentor and guide through this often dark and difficult realm. For his guidance, careful review, and critique, I am deeply thankful.

Grady Garrison, Debra Whitt, Darryl Baker, Charles Key, and James Barton gave exceptional legal advice, critique, and counsel. Chuck Alston and Maia Kotlus-Gates at the global communications firm MS&L gave invaluable advice regarding marketing a very different sort of book. Bill Oates, of Oates Design, and Beth Sanders did exceptional work on the cover and website for *The End of Healing*. Mary Novotny, Andy Rodriquez, Phyllis Tickle, Paula Casey, Jean Middleton, and Ruth Bean were also all wonderful encouragers and excellent sources of marketing advice.

This book would never have seen the light of day without the generous readers who offered critiques, comments, and editing suggestions, including Bill Craddock, Hal Crenshaw, Courtney Cowart, Liz Griff, Andrea Johnson, Bill Kolb, Catherine Lewis, Cindy Martin, Sybil Macbeth, Celia Ridley, Novella Smith-Arnold, Charlotte Tomlinson, Miea Watson, John Hilgart, Shannon Brownlee, award winning author of *Overtreated*, Phyllis Tickle, founding editor of the Religion Department of *Publishers Weekly*, Ray Barfield, Eyleen Farmer, Tom Momberg, Ann Seiber, Khy Daniel, Gayle Spence, Raymond Spence, and Larry Pivnik. I especially thank Libby Broadwell-Gulde of Christian Brothers University, Bebe Gish Shaw of Athens State University, and Danielle Childers of BelleBooks for their detailed reviews. Libby's suggestions on point of view, Danielle's on the novel's beginning, and Bebe's on the novel's ending were critical to its final form. Many thanks to Jennifer Simpson and her eagle eye for copy-editing in the final stages.

Many medical students, residents, and faculty have participated with me in health system seminars, journal clubs, and research conferences at the University of Tennessee Health Science Center. Their stories, experiences, and passion have inspired me. I thank my research and clinical colleagues, especially David Mirvis, Professor Emeritus at the University of Tennessee Health Science Center, Cyril Chang at the University of Memphis, and Manoj Jain. Our long dialogues have been foundational and fun.

I learned much from my intrepid fellow travelers on seven Search for the Healthy City study tours in Italy. We explored first-hand the characteristics of best health systems and healthy cities and discussed them in seminar sessions. Our phenomenal trip organizers, Charly Lucas and Ann Freeman of Tuscan Affairs, made these travels both possible and delightful with their translation assistance, organizational abilities, and entertaining talents.

In my academic and research career I have received research grants, financial support, and/or consulting fees from the following: Agency for Health Research and Quality, American Cancer Society, American Heart Association, BlueCross BlueShield of Tennessee, Center for Medicare and Medicaid Services, Infectious Disease Society of America, Merck & Co., Inc., Novartis Pharmaceuticals, Novo Nordisk, Inc., Robert Wood Johnson Foundation, the State of Tennessee, and the Tennessee Department of Health. None of these pertain to this novel in any way or present any conflict of interest likely to substantially bias this work or distort the truth.

I wish to express my deep appreciation for the many corporate leaders who contributed insight to *The End of Healing*. This novel highlights the systemic problems within each of the major healthcare industries, and is not intended to indict individual corporations. In fact, some of the corporations featured in less than glowing terms are the very ones leading beneficial health system improvements in our country today.

Nanos gigantium humeris insidentes. We are like dwarfs standing on the shoulders of giants. Just as Dante was able to see further because Virgil held him up, this book was inspired and lifted up by many great works preceding it. Many scholars whose ideas contributed to *The End of Healing* have been suitably acknowledged by Dr. Sampson, the students, and in Dr. Sampson's Health System Syllabus at the back of this book, but several additional sources deserve recognition.

Many chapters benefited from extensive research and investigative journalism reported in the following nonfiction works: *Your Money or Your Life* by David Cutler (Chapters 4, 17, 19, 20, and 25), *Internal Bleeding* by Robert Wachter and Kaveh Shojania (Chapters 11, 12, 13, 15, and 22), *The Healing of America* by T.R. Reid and *Bitter Medicine* by Jerome Kassirer (Chapter 17), *Hope or Hype* by Richard Deyo and Donald Patrick, *On The Take* by Jerome Kassirer, *The $800 Million Pill* by Merrill Goozner, and *Overdosed America* by John Abramson (Chapters 18, 20, 21, 22, and 27), *Critical Condition* by Donald Bartlett and James Steele (Chapter 17, 19, 21, 25, 27, 30, and 31), and *Health Against Wealth* by George Anders and *Bitter Medicine* by Jerome Kassirer (Chapters 25 and 27).

Chapter 19 draws heavily on Jack El-Hai's remarkable book, *The Lobotomist*, and on the inspiring and courageous account on National Public Radio by Howard Dully, who told the story of his own lobotomy by Dr. Walter Freeman. Mr. Dully showed great courage by telling the full truth about the lobotomy that changed his life forever. I highly commend Howard Dully's book, *My Lobotomy*, to anyone interested in learning more about the history of lobotomy and the potential excesses of a procedure-focused healthcare system.

Chapter 20 draws on the works *McQueen*, by William F. Nolan, and *Steve McQueen: Portrait of an American Rebel*, by Marshall Terrill. Chapter 24 draws on Dr. William Cast's firsthand account of his partnership with Richard Scrushy and the activities and corporate environment at HealthSouth Corporation in his expose, *Going South*.

I am also indebted to the excellent journalists, investigative reporters, scientific writers, and researchers of America's best newspapers and universities. In particular, I acknowledge the excellent healthcare coverage of *The Wall Street*

Journal, *The New York Times*, *The Washington Post*, *The Boston Globe*, *Seattle PI*, *The Commercial Appeal* in Memphis, Tennessee, *Los Angeles Times*, and Italian newspapers *la Repubblica* and *Corriere della Sera*.

Numerous works of history provided historical context for this work. I am particularly thankful for Ron Chernow's *Alexander Hamilton* and Joseph J. Ellis' *His Excellency George Washington*.

Translations of Dante's *Inferno* are taken from John D. Sinclair. Translations of quotes from Plato, Pindar, and Virgil are from Loeb Classic Library editions of these works, except *The Republic*, Book 4 quote, which is the Allan Bloom translation, and the Book 7 quote, which is the Benjamin Jowett translation. Quotes from the New Testament are from *The New American Standard Bible*.

Above all others is Dante Alighieri, whose *Divina Commedia* inspired this novel and gave it the best bones any novel could want. Dante's stony glare pierced me to the core at least once a week the year I lived in Florence. Whenever I passed his statue in Piazza Santa Croce, he scowled down at me and demanded I finish my novel in all due haste. For his patiently waiting a decade and his service as narrator for *The End of Healing*, I thank him with all my heart.

My family's love, support, and understanding gave me the courage to write. My wife, Sharon, and my children, Claire and Spence, accompanied me on my quixotic journey into the world of fiction and maintained the patience and humor of Sancho Panza. Susie Spence, Phyllis Bailey, and Kathryn Mabry offered detailed edits and sharp commentary. Janet and John Holland shared valuable insight into the healthcare industry. Mike Mabry enlightened me on the perspectives of the business world. Susan Mattison gave brilliant advice on cover design, color, and marketing. Earl Bailey showed me how impossibly big projects can be undertaken and completed through vision, faith, good humor, and steady effort. He schooled me on the perilous world of academic politics, made sage editorial suggestions, and always pushed me to finish. Ranel Spence, who practiced internal medicine for sixty-one years, showed me what it means to be a physician and taught me the importance of story for diagnosis, and he could get a good story out of anyone. *The End of Healing* would not exist but for many long conversations in which we laughed, ranted, and raved over the ridiculous and wasteful mess of a healthcare system that has evolved in the United States.

Above all, this novel would not have been possible without Sharon Spence Bailey—my wife, best friend, and merciless editor. Her advice during hundreds of neighborhood walks helped me define the scope and structure of the story, and for her willingness to listen to my rambling I am eternally grateful. Sharon worked countless hours to edit and polish the manuscript and make it readable, and her encouragement and critical eye were essential. Much of the art, beauty, and craftsmanship you have found in *The End of Healing* I owe to her art, her beauty, and her craft.

CPSIA information can be obtained at www.ICGtesting.com
Printed in the USA
LVOW11*1522031114

411317LV00004BA/7/P